D1823842

NOW
THE
SCIENCE

"A collection"

Comprises the Edge collection:

Coin: *cyber cash*
Pulse: *blood and nanobots*
Edge: *magnetite mining on Ganymede*

Ed Adams

a firstelement production

THREE BOOKS WITH SCIENCE THEMES

There are individual 'Thanks' pages for each of the three novels that follow in this Collection. Coin is about 21st century cyber cash. Pulse is 22nd Century blood management with nanobots. Edge is a world-end scenario where humanity mines minerals in deep space.

So, here we are with:

1 Coin
2 Pulse
3 Edge

And thank you, dear reader, for at least 'giving it a go'.

Published in Great Britain in 2020 by first element
Directed by the six twenty
Copyright © 2020 Ed Adams

ISBN   : 978-1-913818-04-3
Ebook ISBN   : 978-1-913818-05-0

Printed and bound in Great Britain by Ingram Spark

Ed Adams
an imprint of first element rashbre@mac.com

Ed-adams.net

Mailing list: https://mailchi.mp/9f0b30712620/ed_adams

Books by Ed Adams include:

Triangle Trilogy		About
1	The Triangle	Dirty money? Here's how to clean it
2	The Square	Weapons of Mass Destruction – don't let them get on your nerves
3	The Circle	The desert is no place to get lost
	The Ox Stunner	The Triangle Trilogy – thick enough to stun an ox
		(all feature Jake, Bigsy, Clare, Chuck Manners)
Archangel Trilogy		
1	Archangel	Sometimes I am necessary
2	Raven	An eye that sees all between darkness and light
3	Card Game	Throwing oil on a troubled market
	The Archangel Trilogy	the above three in one heavy book.
		(all feature Jake, Bigsy, Clare, Chuck Manners)
Stand-Alone Novels		
1	Coin	Get rich quick with Cybercash – just don't tell GCHQ
2	Pulse	Want more? Just stay away from the edge
3	Edge	Power can't be left to trust
	Now the Science	the above three in one heavy book.

About Ed Adams Novels:

Triangle Trilogy		About
	Triangle	Money laundering within an international setting.
	Square	A viral nerve agent being shipped by terrorists and WMDs
	Circle	In the Arizona deserts, with the Navajo; about missiles stolen from storage.
	Ox Stunner	the above three in one heavy book.
		(all feature Jake, Bigsy, Clare, Chuck Manners)
Archangel Trilogy		
	Archangel	Biographical adventures of Russian trained Archangel, who, as Christina Nott, threads her way through other Triangle novels.
	Raven	Big business gone bad and being a freemason won't absolve you
	Card Game	Raven Pt 2 – Russian oligarchs attempt to take control
	The Archangel Trilogy	the above three in one heavy book.
		(all feature Jake, Bigsy, Clare, Chuck Manners)
Stand-Alone Novels		
	Coin	cyber cash manipulation by the Russian state.
	Pulse	Sci-Fi dystopian blood management with nano-bots
	Edge	World end climate collapse and sham discovered during magnetite mining from Jupiter's moon Ganymede
	Now the Science	the above three in one heavy book.

COIN

Ed Adams

First published in Great Britain in 2020 by firstelement
Copyright © 2020 Ed Adams
Directed by thesixtwenty

10 9 8 7 6 5 4 3 2 1

A CIP catalogue record for this book is available from the British
Library.

ISBN 13 : 978-1-9163383-0-2
Ebook ISBN : 978-1-9163383-1-9

Printed and bound in Great Britain by Ingram Spark

rashbre
an imprint of firstelement.co.uk
rashbre@mac.com

To Julie and Melanie

THANKS

A big thank you for the tolerance and bemused support from all of those around me. To John, for the proofing, Georgina for artistic suggestions, to the lads from West Hatch for cover down-selection and curry. To thesixtwenty.co.uk for direction.

Barry and Steph for positive vibes and taking away the crates. To the NaNoWriMo gang for the continued inspiration and encouragement.

And, of course, thanks to the extensive support via the random scribbles of rashbre via http://rashbre2.blogspot.com and its cast of amazing and varied readers whether human, twittery, smoky, cool kats, photographic, dramatic, musical, anagrammed, globalized or simply maxed-out.

My blogging started in the days when the Electronic Frontier Foundation warned about the safe preservation of online identity; "Mind the Gap" as we Londoners say.

Nowadays it can be like the wild west out there. The difference is today's gold rush is digital.

Not forgetting the cast of characters involved in producing this; they all have virtual lives of their own.

And of course, to you, dear reader, for at least 'giving it a go'.

Table of Contents

COIN

PULSE

EDGE

PART ONE

Going a Bomb

Almost pedantically, she added: "They're not really bombs--
they're acoustic provocations."
— J.G. Ballard, Millennium People

Red Alert

"Look around for a Bomb; we're on Red Alert," the security guard poked his head into the small room where Tyler was working. The guard's handheld radio was bleeping and squawking.

"Just have a look for anything suspicious in here, please," continued the guard as he moved away.

Tyler could not believe it. He had not been in this post for long, and already something like this was happening. The scrappy room Tyler was in was full of faded brown cardboard boxes. He had only been using the room because he needed access to a lumbering, specialised piece of equipment. He needed to use an old deep transcription device to check some materials.

Now Tyler was stuck in the middle of a messy room with instructions to poke and pry around in case the room contained something dangerous. Tyler decided that this was not a very likely target. The room was in a basement and was quite close to one of the main entrances to the building. There was a man on the door supported with the usual paraphernalia of access controls.

Someone would need to get past the entire system and then place whatever it was in a pretty improbable location, where it might emit a muffled thud.

No. It wouldn't be here.

It was an old building, close to a busy main road with a slight patina of low-level dust over much of the content of the room. Nothing too obvious, but you could tell that this was a building that did not have the latest in air conditioning or other environmental control systems — a civil servants' building with a history.

Tyler decided it was time to have a break from his task. Not the bomb search, but the original reason he'd gone to the room. Maybe it would be even better to take an early lunch break.

The Piccolo, a small Italian sandwich bar across the road, beckoned and he thought to himself that he was so much closer to lunch from this basement room than right the way back to his third-floor office.

Tyler placed the materials into one of the drawers in the desk of the transcription unit. He could head back to ground level and straight out through the security doors. A cheese submarine was luring him, and the transcription could wait.

Submarine, Torpedo; those Italians had it nailed long before Subway arrived.

Outside, autumn, busy London streets and traffic moving oblivious to the excitement in the adjacent building.

Tyler turned right out of the building, walked about a hundred yards and then turned right again towards the Italian snack bar.

They had some of the best sandwiches and rolls in the area. Maybe something with mozzarella cheese? Or chorizo with brie? Suddenly, a crack sound and low-frequency thunder. Tyler thought it sounded like a truck had run into a wall. He noticed a group of starlings and pigeons flutter up from a nearby courtyard.

Then he heard a couple of car alarms bleeping although rumble of traffic from the main street continued uninterrupted.

Tyler heard the first of the sirens; they sounded as if they were moving along Cheapside. He figured it had been an explosion, but it seemed to be further west than his office.

No hoax, then, but where had it been targeted?

Tyler thought the Department was nothing like he expected. C-SOC. Cyber Security Operations Centre. It was almost an accident that he even got to be working there.

General office

Tyler's general office was a mix of styles. Being a government department meant it was subjected to normal cost-cutting and other types of economies. For example, it acquired random items of furniture to augment the office space.

There was a skeleton set of metal desks with side cabinets. These were in a kind of battleship grey colour. Around the edges of the room were a range of further grey steel cabinets each lockable and including a combination arrangement with pushbuttons. Such security was a casual deterrent, but it would be relatively easy to cut through a thin pin at the hinge where the door was held in place by the locking mechanism. It seemed absurd that a security office would be so lax.

The desks included various shelving systems dated from the 1980s through to modern times. There were some made of a kind of yellowish shiny wood, and the most modern ones had cable ducting included in amongst the stainless steel and plastic fitments of the units.

Tyler's desk was typical and was in a small configuration of four desk units arranged in a rectangle. Everyone had organised a barricade along the top of their desks. It meant that they were socially screened from their nearest neighbours.

Tyler's bosses' name was Marcus, and he was a few years older than Tyler. He had also started working in the Department direct from University. He wore a jacket most days and looked several years older than his real age, maybe because of his choice of spectacles. Opposite Tyler sat Rosie, who was around the same age as Marcus and also a mathematician but with a specialist interest in Artificial Intelligence. After Marcus, Rosie looked positively young, and Tyler would have placed her around his age until she spoke with such authority.

Tyler was pretty sure that he was a lightweight compared with those two in terms of general knowledge and experience, although Tyler had noticed that most of the mathematics was not especially complicated, mainly if one had access to computing power to help.

Tyler could see that Marcus had ingrained himself in the ways of the Department and also the type of global events that could trip instabilities. Marcus was a security analyst's analyst. His knowledge of unusual world events was vast, and he seemed to have high perception and an ability to link events together.

Rosie provided a kind of yang to Marcus's yin. She would often ask smart questions that probed into an event or situation, and then Marcus would pause, consider and as often as not respond with theory.

Tyler knew it would take him ages to find a similar degree of command over the role.

Instead, he made do pawing through the enormous amount of paper that everyone seemed to have on their desks.

In a modern world, Tyler had expected more to be electronic using the computer systems. It soon became apparent that it was mostly a question of timing.

The Department was given things to process that had been obtained by dubious means and were often physical rather than electronic. There was a big department somewhere out in Gloucestershire where items were sent to get them converted into electronic format.

However, there was a problem with this; it meant that the material would be encoded, but this could mean that sometimes essential things were missed.

At its simplest, it could be that the handwritten scribbles on a paper were not visible. In a more clandestine world, it could mean that something else on the physical document would not be noticed such as a small embedded chip or even a microdot.

It didn't end with paper, Tyler's team and the surrounding teams also received CDs, DVDs, memory sticks, physical tape in various formats (even some punched paper tape to process on one occasion).

It did feel a bit like sifting through someone's rubbish bin on occasions, and some of the material already looked as if it had been in a rubbish bin before selection.

The timing aspect was quite important because it would mean that most of the material received was fresh rather than having been on a round trip to the middle of Britain before the teams were able to examine it.

Tyler could also see from the material written in 'clear' on most of the documents that they were often targeting high profile individuals who connected with government or other public figures.

Perhaps considered snooping, the official line was that it was providing security services for the United Kingdom. As a consequence, the Department linked to other well-known and higher profile government departments.

Tyler and Matt

Years earlier, at university, Tyler was one of the bright ones.

He was involved with mathematics projects that obliquely had something to do with gambling. He had tried his theory in practice and come unstuck.

He'd dug himself a financial hole. He shared the flat with two other people, one of whom was Matt, a Masters student who everyone regarded as something of a Brainiac. He, Matt and Kyle had come up with a scheme, created mainly by Matt, to fund their lifestyle.

Matt was far ahead of Tyler in his exploitation of computers to get to the results he'd need. He'd sit in his room, with Tom Waits blasting on the stereo and write complex algorithms designed to provide ever-increasing security around whatever he was doing.

Tyler's research into gambling game theory meant he had stumbled across the systems used to secure the money used in online gambling. The whole environment was locked down, and normal currency used only to get initial access into the systems. The cyber currency was used for betting because it made the whole process more secure.

Even the national lottery operated this way, requiring the

punters to preload money converted into e-cash before they could place their bets.

In his flat, he'd first asked Matt about cybercash and then worked with him on various attempts at get-rich-quick schemes. He ran the gambling and Matt calculated odds. Neither of them was particularly successful, although Tyler had lost the most money.

Kyle was mostly the onlooker. He was also smart but had branched out into quantum physics, with the kind of maths that the others thought was taking liberties.

One evening they were sharing a pizza.

"There's a way to mine for the keys to crypto-currency," said Matt, pulling at the tear-and-share garlic bread.

"But aren't they controlled by big business?" asked Tyler.

"More likely by organised crime," answered Kyle, "And there are so many keys required to support the ever-increasing amount of currency required."

Matt nodded towards his room in the flat.

"I've invested in a cyber currency miner," he announced, "I've used my student loan."

Tyler looked surprised. Kyle nodded, "I knew it! I knew you were up to something!"

Matt responded, "Tyler, don't look at me like that. You've spent your loan on gambling, I've spent mine on an investment."

The three of them laughed. All knew they were on the edge of dealing with something shady.

"C'mon then, show me," said Tyler, as he grabbed a slice of pepperoni pizza.

Matt unlocked his room. A small metal frame was standing on the desk. It whirred quietly, and the others could make out the row of small electric fans underneath what looked like a row of computer innards.

Any sounds from the computer were drowned by Matt playing a noisy CD.

"Tom Waits, Rain Dogs, you like?" smiled Matt.

The others chuckled, it was always Tom Waits with Matt.

"Okay, this is it," said Matt, pitting to the desk, "It's a multi-processor set up solely to look for cryptographic data."

"Did you make it?" asked Tyler, noticing the somewhat bare-bones nature of the device.

"No," answered Matt, "I bought it online. It is specialist gear. Its only job is to look for blockchains that can validate cryptocurrency. I get paid for each one I find."

"Blockchains?" asked Tyler.

"Yes, Blockchains; the mathematically certified blocks of information that chain cybercurrency transactions together and confirm their validity."

"And is it worth it?" asked Tyler, "How much do you get paid for finding these blockchains?"

"Well, it's new, but I should get at least £200 per month from this rig if I follow the user instructions."

"So how long to repay for the equipment?"

"Six months at that rate and I've already deducted the cost of the power – which works out to around £3 per day, to use the setup. And…"

Matt could hardly contain himself.

"...I've worked out that I can also acquire direct cyber currency from this system. You know I said user instructions, well, we all know what the manual is for, don't we?"

"Except when building flat-pack furniture, when it can be quite useful," chipped in Kyle.

"That's right, and you know, the cyber currency is worth significantly more than the blockchains that I'm supposed to search for."

Tyler nodded. He knew, from his attempts at get-rich-quick, that cyber currency was worth significant cash if channelled effectively.

"By being creative with the instructions, I've created three cyber coins," said Matt, "They're worth a lot. I tweaked the algorithms – reprogrammed the system - the whole rig is configurable."

"How much?" asked Kyle, "Those cyber coins are quite valuable."

"Yes, they are, it's around £9,000. The coins are worth around £3k each, based on the currency exchange."

"£9,000 Not bad, eh?"

"So how are you playing this?" asked Kyle. "If you tell too many people, won't they all come looking for a payout?"

"Not really," said Matt," I've only told you two so far, and that's because I want to see whether you'd be interested in coming in with me. It takes a gambling mentality to make this all work."

Tyler was taken aback, "Wow, this is a lot to take in. Why would you want us to help, and what would be my part of the bargain?"

"It's okay; I've been thinking about this for a while. We're all good at maths; we want to make money; we don't mind taking risks. I can handle the background technology, as long as you can think about the best ways to stash the currency. By that I mean we'll need to pass it into the main systems via gambling web sites and then cash it in through their payout sites. I want to set up a holding company into which I'll funnel the clean money."

"You, Tyler, have already got the gambling profile. As we feed the cybercash into the system, it will just look as if you have had a turn of luck. Then we can cash it in through one of the banking systems."

"So, ...laundering the money?" asked Kyle.

"Kind of...I just don't want to draw attention to the way we are discovering it. Nor the volume. Much easier to look like an addicted gambling punter is feeding it in."

Matt looked at Tyler and they both grinned. Kyle looked less enthusiastic.

"Shake?" said Tyler. "Sure" said Matt.

"I may give this one a miss," said Kyle, "It's a little too close to the edge for me. But what's in this room stays here."

"Like Fight Club?" asked Tyler.

"What's Fight Club?" answered both Matt and Kyle simultaneously.

Tyler and Matt knew Kyle could be relied upon to keep the secret. They also knew he was probably the smartest of the three of them.

"Okay, but Tyler," said Matt, "First of all, I'll need you to do something for me...You need to meet some people."

Job Offer

Matt gave Tyler an invitation to a meeting at a fancy London hotel.

"I want you to go as the representative of our agreement. I don't want to go because they could ask me direct questions. If they ask you, you won't know the answers. No offence."

"It's not the first time," Tyler grinned.

"Anyway, it should be fun, enjoy a cocktail or two!"

Tyler went along, at least to sample the fineries offered by the hotel. There he met a couple of computer specialists from a government department, which later turned out to be the one that would employ both him and Matt.

The representatives already knew about Matt, and it made Tyler wonder if they were in some way monitoring Matt's computer work. At the time, Tyler thought there was something that he or Matt had done which somehow broke the law.

Instead, they offered to double the fees from the cyber coins that Matt discovered, if Matt and Tyler would sign up with them for a couple of years of work at the end of their studies. The offer amounted to pretty easy money, and they gave Tyler a chance to talk it over with Matt before agreeing.

The organisation would match their original gains like-for-like, as a signing-on fee and if Matt and Tyler discovered more keys or cyber coins, they would get even more money.

Tyler discussed this with Matt, and they were both 'in'.

This scheme worked pretty well until Tyler discovered Erica's long legs, which put the project onto the back burner.

By that time, Matt had found some more keys, so altogether they were turning a tidy profit from the cyber coins, match-funded and tax-free.

That was when Tyler had his European self-discovery adventure with Erica.

Upon their return, Tyler received his degree and the job offer from the government department. Erica had a job waiting for her in finance. Tyler would be in the same government unit as Matt, although their roles would be different. They ended up on different teams, and after Tyler moved into a flat with Erica, he hardly saw Matt.

Tyler had expected his work to be about cryptography or something that related to the type of math he had been doing at University.

Instead, it was surprisingly well-paid paper shifting and was how he now found himself strolling along St Martin-le-Grand eating a mozzarella sub.

Making sense of it

"Whenever you become anxious or stressed, outer purpose has taken over, and you lost sight of your inner purpose.

You have forgotten that your state of consciousness is primary, all else secondary."

— *Eckhart Tolle, A New Earth: Awakening to Your Life's Purpose*

Towards or away?

Tyler had stuffed the remains of his lunch into a pocket. In the distance, he could see a small plume of smoke. He retraced his steps towards Cheapside, from where he would be able to get a better line of sight towards the direction of the commotion.

It took him about two minutes to walk to the main road, and as he did, he could see several police cars and ambulances noisily cutting through the traffic and heading towards the west.

Then, turning onto the busy Cheapside, he could see the source of the commotion. Previously, obscured by the tall buildings ha now had a better view. Tyler looked up at the buildings wondering if there would be broken panes of glass or other tell-tale signs. Everything else looked normal. There didn't even seem to be much interest from the adjacent buildings as he estimated that the explosion was probably two hundred metres away.

Far enough to mean that people inside the buildings had not been directly affected except maybe to hear a loud bang which could be mistaken for any number of London street sounds. Tyler was more aware because of the alert that had already sounded in his secure and slightly privileged environment. Now the question was whether he should go closer to the action or slide quietly back into the office.

Well, what else could he do? He decided to visit the action and see what had happened.

"After all," he reasoned, "It's not every day that a major news incident occurs close by," let alone in his lunch break.

Tyler walked further along the road towards the area that had the early signs of being cordoned. As he approached, he realised that this was not an academic situation but that there were likely to be real people involved in the catastrophe. There was a confusion of people as he reached the outer perimeter established by the police.

They were using blue and white tape stretched across the road and improvising a diversion away from the whole zone. Tyler could see a few people walking towards him with dust on their clothing and realised that they were speaking French. Most people were making a space for those leaving the area to get away quickly.

"You don't want to go down there," said one of the people passing, "It was some kind of car bomb."

Tyler checked his phone to see if there was any further information.

"Reports are just coming in..." said the first report.

The situation was still very new, and news crews didn't seem to have got their reporting teams on-site.

Tyler's training told him to be aware that there could sometimes be a second explosion, and perhaps it was better to stay back. One of the policemen was turning people away. He was saying that there was nothing for anyone to see.

"It's more important that we can get the emergency services in and out of here quickly," the policeman said. "We don't want all of you acting as an additional roadblock."

Tyler could see a black-windowed American-style van leaving the scene. He assumed it was one of the London-based rapid-response specialist units and that they would be all over the situation in a few more minutes,

As he looked towards the damaged area, he tried to work out which building had been involved. He didn't recognise it at all.

Tyler took a couple of pictures on his phone and turned around. The explosion was going to be the biggest story on the television and media tonight.

As Tyler walked back toward the office, he knew that the Department would be in trouble over the event. The Department should have detected the threat in some way, especially when it was so close to home.

Tyler thought that he was low down enough in the pecking order, such that he should not suffer any direct repercussions.

He decided that a small amount of road dust on his face might be appropriate as he walked back into the building. It would give him additional plausibility when the inevitable department meeting was called.

As Tyler returned to the building and climbed the stone steps at the side entrance, he noticed that the doors were locked.

There was a sign which requested he go around to the main entrance lobby which was on another street.

He noticed his boss and several others caught out in the same way and muttering under their breaths as they made the way the extra 300 yards to the other side of the building and up another set of steps to the larger main lobby which was also used by visitors. It was evident that they were putting in place a new secure process as they tried to get back into the building.

Tyler couldn't help but think about horses, stables and bolts as everyone went through this new process. He had to swipe and then show his badge to the usual guy. Then he had to do the sort of thing usually reserved for visitors and which involved putting possessions through the airport-style scanning system.

Eventually, Tyler was reunited with his badge, loose coins and phone. Tyler was faintly amused at the way that these old buildings were adapted for this high-tech security. There was even one where the scanner looked like it was made of wood instead of the usual high-tech frontage. Tyler knew it was inevitable that there would be a departmental meeting and that there was a pretty high chance it had already started.

He made his way to his office and there spotted a large group already huddled in the big meeting room.

Department

Tyler walked into the department meeting. He was not the only person to be late. His boss, Marcus, was also delayed. Tyler decided it was easiest to join with Marcus and give the impression that they had been somewhere together. There were a few chairs still at the front, so Tyler and Marcus sat down next to one another.

The overall head of the unit, Jim Cavendish, was already talking "… Extra vigilance in these troubled times," he was saying. Tyler thought he could probably have written the first part of his speech."

The piece Tyler would have difficulty to predict was the sheer amount of new procedure to be added as a consequence of the bomb attack.

Tyler had seen those "what to do if someone rings with a bomb threat" notices and attended the vigilance course. He had also completed the two courses about anti-terrorism and threat management processes. He had got the certificates from both of them, based upon the little tests that they made him do at the end.

"… Details of the attack are still scarce," Jim continued.

"There is still uncertainty of where the attack was delivered because there is a news blackout on the area."

Tyler raised his hand. He had not planned to, but as he knew more about this from first-hand viewing, he thought it would be something he should mention. Jim looked toward him. Tyler could tell Jim could not remember his name. Then he looked toward Marcus, "Marcus, does your team have something to add to this?"

Marcus looked at Tyler. He realised that he did not know anything about what Tyler had seen and would be unable to deduce it from Tyler's expression. Tyler squinted his eyes first towards Marcus and then to Jim Cavendish.

"Yes," Tyler found himself saying, "I did see the immediate aftermath of the explosion along by Warwick Lane. I was there a few minutes after it happened. There was already a police cordon in operation, and they were letting people out of the area but not letting people back in."

"As well as the police, ambulances, and fire brigade, I could see an RRT around the scene within the first few minutes. I was far enough away to only really be able to see the evacuees from the situation who all looked quite shaken up. "

At this point, Tyler remembered that he had added some minor dust to his clothing as part of his potential excuse when he returned to the office.

Tyler brushed his shoulder for effect and was pleased to see a small amount of dust rise into the air.

Tyler brushed his sleeves, and there was a further convincing amount of dust, so he continued, "The whole area was covered in dust as a result of the explosion. At this time, we can only guess what caused it, but I overheard people from the scene saying it was a car bomb."

Lord Raglan

"Thank you," said Jim. "… Thank you, Marcus, and your team for that update."

Tyler could see that Marcus looked pleased about this but suspected that he would also be irritated that Tyler had not managed to tell him about it before we got into the meeting.

"Does anyone else have any information about this?" continued Jim.

There was silence. The people looked around, and Tyler was aware most people seemed to look at him.

Jim continued, but it was more of the corporate waffle about extra vigilance.

Tyler thought that the whole meeting had not said much. It was all based upon limited information: Yes - there's been a bomb. Yes - there's been a bomb threat and then an explosion. Yes - it has targeted something which we believe to be one of our other buildings, but that's all anyone knew.

Tyler knew slightly more just because he visited the area.

The other side of the meeting room was a flat-screen monitor. It was generally used for PowerPoint presentations, and Tyler asked, "So I wonder if the television will show us any other information? We could tune into the news channel."

Jim looked towards the television.

"Can someone switch it on?" he asked.

There was the usual meeting room array of buttons and switches, but as usual, no one knew how to get normal television pictures on the monitor.

Eventually, somebody from the IT department stepped forward and pressed a few buttons. It looked like the screen needed to reboot itself before it could be used as an ordinary television, but it soon had a picture from the main news feeds which showed the scene very much as Tyler had seen it a few minutes before.

TV crews had managed to use long lenses to get better access to the source of the explosion. It appeared a car or van was used to bomb the front of the building.

The building looked only lightly damaged although there were broken glass and fragments strewn around.

It looked as if the blast had mainly been deflected upwards rather than at the building itself. A news reporter was saying something repetitively about the explosion. It was evident that there was very little new information available. The reporter continued, "it looks as if there is a news blackout on this whole situation."

Tyler looked across to where Rosie was sitting. He raised his eyebrows and shook his left hand in a gesture. It was a "shall we go for a pint?" gesture.

Rosie nodded and also lightly tapped Marcus on the arm. The three would go out for a drink in a nearby pub. They could talk about this more expansively away from the office.

Jim's meeting was coming to a close. It broadly said everyone should expect there to be more paperwork and admin to support the increased level of security.

Tyler and his mini-team moved across to the Lord Raglan. It was a typical old-school London boozer. Handily positioned for the city folk to be able to grab a pint after work and it still had the old city tradition of closing early at 9 PM. However, it was open for most of the day and was something of an extra office for a few of the staff.

They stood at the bar around the corner from the main serving area.

"What do you reckon?" asked Rosie.

"What, of Jimbo's pitch? I don't think he knew that much," answered Tyler.

Jimbo had become the nickname for Jim Cavendish, acquired in the distant past and passed from team to team. Although relatively new, Tyler knew he had the right to use Jim's nickname when talking to colleagues.

"Is it a random or the start of a campaign?" continued Rosie.

"It's more than bang and burn. Whoever it is seems to be targeting us," said Marcus, "At least it's government departments at any rate. I don't think there's anything to suggest that other people are being targeted at the moment."

"Where did the original alert come from?" asked Rosie.

"I don't know," said Marcus, "but it looks as if they have a more than working knowledge of our setup."

"Either that or they've just been able to use our systems against us," Tyler said.

"If they know how to get a message about this into the system, then we will inevitably disperse it to all of the offices. All they need to do is have one location, and the rest will follow."

"Yes," said Rosie,

"And if you're right they've hit one of the smaller offices, which could be easier to gain access to than the bigger Department buildings."

"I still can't believe how we've allowed ourselves to grow in this topsy-turvy manner," said Marcus.

"You'd think we'd all be in a campus environment where there could be a proper security cordon."

"Yes," said Rosie,

"The problem is it would then need to be somewhere out of town, and then they'd have a problem getting the right people to the resource it.

"Yes," Tyler added,

"It's easier to recruit people into the centre of London, and when we need people with special languages or other skill sets, they are easier to obtain."

"That's the point," said Marcus,

"As we casually obtain specialists for certain roles, they could themselves be a new source of the problem."

"What?" Said Rosie, "with all of the positive vetting that we do nowadays, I'd have thought that particular problem was over,"

"I'm not so sure," Tyler said, "The more people we have involved with this, the more likelihood there is that there will be an information leak."

"It must be pretty obvious to most people that unless we have all of our offices with names like Acme import-export that there will be areas that people find and exploit. But, in this case, if they manage to park a car or van outside the office block, then it doesn't bode well for resilience to future attacks."

"You wait," said Marcus, "I bet tonight they reintroduce the ring of steel or something similar around the city."

Marcus looked at both of us.

"There's going to be a task force, you know?" he said.

"I was called to another meeting before the Department's big one today. Several of the head of teams were asked to go along. We've been asked to be part of the task force."

Rosie smirked.

"Oh yeah, of all the people in London they select us three to be in the task force for the bombs?"

"Not exactly," said Marcus.

"We are just one of the teams asked to do this. The others in the meeting were to report to Nasreen and Janice. So, it will be all three of our teams, but don't assume that we are the only people involved."

Rosie chuckled.

"I can see that we would be the powerhouse needed to solve this mysterious crime!" she said.

"That's right," said Marcus. "They are getting people from all over the place involved with this. Our Department had to put some people up. Janice will be leading this and says Nasreen is going to have her team to do most of the analytics work. We are the third team."

Rosie grinned. "So, we are the gophers for this then?"

Tyler's phone rang.

"Hi, Tyler here…What…No," Tyler looked ashen.

"It's about Matt; he was a casualty in the first bomb. They are saying his body was found in the rubble. He's dead!"

"Do you need a few minutes?" asked Marcus, seeing the look on Tyler's face. Rosie had stood up as if to comfort Tyler.

"Yeah, maybe a short step outside," Rosie and Marcus nodded as Tyler stepped out of the pub into the street.

Rosie and Marcus made muted small talk while Tyler was outside.

Eventually, Tyler reappeared through the door of the Lord Raglan. He had been gone for about 15 minutes.

"Condolences", said Marcus quietly," I know you guys were good friends."

Rosie nodded. She still looked as if she wanted to hug Tyler, but Tyler's moves were quite spiky and forced as he sat down to resume his pint.

"This is all wrong," said Tyler, "I don't even know why Matt would be at that building."

They paused, and each looked into their drink.

Marcus picked up the conversation again.

"It's all the more important that we sort this thing out. I'll try to tell you what I know."

"And remember when Nasreen's team or Janet's team need something done, we are their go-to people."

Rosie laughed. "All three of us? I can see we will get a lot done with just three of us to do the work."

"I expect it will change quite quickly," said Marcus,

"They probably need to get the first team together fast, and that's why we've been chosen. We've all got the security clearances and know how everything works. I reckon that if this goes on for more than a week or two there will be a whole load of extra people added. That's not to mention the people over in Cheltenham and across the river, plus the usual police, et cetera."

Rosie added "Wow- this is something of a major gear shift from sifting through lots of paper. Instead of the usual work, we are suddenly onto a major case. And this has all happened within hours of the explosion along the road."

Tyler asked, "So, are we starting straight away?"

"Yes, right now in fact," said Marcus.

"I brought you here to tell you I expect Nasreen and Janice are doing something similar with their teams. There's going to be a new area of the building set aside for this."

"I hope it won't be in the basement near to one of the entrances," Tyler said.

"Although, I thought that the basement room that I was in for the bomb alert was probably one of the tougher parts of the building to gain entry to illicitly."

"We are starting in this building," said Marcus,

"But there's a pretty good chance that we will move so that we can start to join up with the other teams."

"However, it's likely to still be in central London because we'll need to be around where the probability of further attacks may be highest. "

"Is there much other intel on all of this?" asked Rosie.

"Yes," said Marcus.

"There's been a glut of information. I've seen it go across my desk but because we have been working on other programs it has not been high on our list up to this point."

Both Rosie and Tyler knew that there were often threats of one kind or another in circulation and part of the Department's job was also to filter out the noise from the real threats.

"Naturally this has gone to the very top of the pile now," Marcus added," This was inside the boundaries of the City of London, so it automatically gets a new high priority."

"We still don't know much about it though," Tyler said. "And although I was within eyesight of the scene, I still couldn't see very much."

"We've already got quite a lot more information than Jim was hinting at," said Marcus, "We needed to cover it up in the general briefing. Your little walk nearly blew the cover."

"Remember we got the threat, and also it hit one of our buildings. Despite what goes out in the press, there are video surveillance materials from the scene loaded to our systems."

The nook in the bar they were sitting in was empty.

"Where is everybody?" Tyler asked.

Rosie looked up from her drink.

"I had to hire this part of the pub for our meeting," said Marcus. "I'd arranged with the bar staff that they would close the area when we sat down. It's cost our department expenses a bit, but worth it," he added.

"Now, I need to know that both of you are fully engaged in this," said Marcus.

"Because if you are, then I will be issuing you both with new passes when we get back to the building," he added.

"I'm in," said Rosie, "This is the most interesting thing I've been involved with since I got here."

"Me too," Tyler added. He hadn't thought about this very much and decided that if both Marcus and Rosie thought this was a good thing, then he would undoubtedly be up for it as well.

At that stage, Tyler didn't particularly think about any downsides from involvement. Except for the obvious and fundamental one that his ex-flatmate had been blown up.

Time to move out

"It does not matter how long you are spending on the earth, how much money you have gathered or how much attention you have received.

It is the amount of positive vibration you have radiated in life that matters,"

— *Amit Ray, Meditation: Insights and Inspirations*

Backtrace and Level Up

The new office was about as unexceptional as Tyler had anticipated. The inner walls of the building had a curve to them, and the new room was a long, narrow and curved structure with tall glass windows along one side which looked out onto a grubby light well.

Tyler said he could not call it a courtyard because it was only about two or 3 metres wide. Rosie agreed. Across the other side was another room of a similar size although, mysteriously, the other one was a proper rectangle.

Tyler worked out that they were in an old machine room or storeroom.

It had desks and a phone and computer system but would be quite a grim place to spend the next few weeks.

"I suppose they could convert the whole building into a car-park, or something?" said Rosie.

The other teams were already in the room when Marcus's group arrived, and they had chosen the better desks.

It was marginal. The main advantage was that one end of the room was larger and lighter than the other and so the widest portion had been selected by the other two teams.

It also looked as if they'd cleared any unwanted items into the remaining space which did have four desks instead of three.

In all other respects, it was quite like the team's prior space. Except they were closer to their two compatriot teams.

The curved wall was already prepared as a pinboard that could be used to create timelines and various 'busy' pictures and charts to show progress.

Tyler marvelled at how much of what they were being asked to do was still manual rather than computerised.

The new workstations were wheeled in. The old kit they had used previously seemed to have received an instant upgrade to all the latest technology.

"Wow!" said Rosie. "At least we get some new gear out of this!"

"This new kit has to be highly secure as well," said Marcus.

"I know our normal stuff is pretty good, but this has extra capabilities to ensure it is secure. Don't try to tamper with the discs or anything," Marcus added, "Otherwise they will destruct."

One of the installers walked across to us. "That's right," he said, " In fact, these are perimeter security enabled as well. If you try to take any of this kit out of the building the disks will self-destruct."

"That could be interesting if we move to yet another building," said Rosie.

Marcus scheduled a special meeting for 5 pm.

Tyler was a little concerned about what time he would get away from the office. He reckoned the meeting might last for an hour and reached for his phone to call up his drinking buddies of the evening.

"I wouldn't bother with that," said Marcus.

"Your ordinary cell phone won't work in this space now. They've put up a microcell around here, and you will need one of the Department phones to make calls. The phones are encrypted but log everything, so we can keep track of what everyone in the team is doing."

"Civil liberties?" said Rosie.

"I think you'll find that this was something described in the paperwork you signed when we issued you with those new badges," said Marcus.

"Until this is over, you'll all be on silent running for everything to do with this operation."

One technician was walking around the office with a stack of boxes containing phones. They were all brand-new, and Tyler wondered whether they were charged so they could be used straight away. Eventually, they got to him and made him sign another set of paperwork.

"Here you are," said the phone technician, handing the phone across.

"It works just like a regular phone, but you can't add any new software, and it will record everything spoken. The tracking is also switched on permanently. It still looks like a normal phone so that you will not draw attention when you are out in public. You can still use your personal phone when you are out of the building as well," said the technician.

"Your regular phone is paired with this device and so it will also be monitoring what goes on with your normal phone."

"You should really only use this phone for any work calls now though."

"But if I want to play 'happy frog' I will need to use my own phone?" Tyler asked the technician. The woman from the telecoms department looked over. Tyler could tell she had heard every quip about phones before.

Tyler looked at the time on the new phone which showed 16:30. He was getting ready to correct it when he realised this was the real time. The drama of the day had made it pass very quickly. It was only half an hour until the meeting was due to start. A few minutes later a delivery of pizza arrived. Rosie stood up and moved to the middle of the room by the curved wall.

"Hello everyone. There's some pizza and some fizzy drinks. This is going to be a long evening."

At 5 o'clock Rosie provided a collated briefing about what had happened.

The alert about the bomb had arrived at around nine in the morning. The security services had not known what to make of it because it did not have any of the usual codewords or other authentication associated with typical bomb threats.

What it did have was substantial information about the locations used by the Department. It also named several of the people in the Department. For this reason, it escalated from a minor category to a top category threat by 11 o'clock. The threat had also indicated the timeframe for the explosion to be between 11:30 am and 12 o'clock.

Tyler was slightly surprised that the Department was able to respond so quickly. Most routine paperwork still took longer than this to move through the system, so this must have been expedited in some way.

It turned out that there had been a prior alert a day earlier that had signalled the intention of the bombers to send information on this morning.

Without any of them being aware, it had raised the alert level to Moderate and had put people in the monitoring areas on standby.

"So, what do we know about the original alert?" asked Tyler.

Rosie replied," It was challenging to work out where the alert originated. They transmitted it via an Internet phone call routed through about a dozen countries."

"The final apparent exchange it had come from was the headquarters of a large fizzy drinks manufacturer based in West London."

"The call had gone to a fire station in West London as well. The only code used was an internal code used by the fire service for signalling a high priority event."

"By the combination of routing and use of a fire station as an endpoint, the callers circumvented normal tracking systems, while still guaranteeing that the call was logged."

"For example, if they had called a police control centre or Whitehall office, then there would have been a backtrace available immediately on the call."

"The use of the fire station was clever because it was an emergency service. It would have a fast response, including access to other emergency hotlines. It was also somewhere largely considered operational rather than a specialist unit dedicated to any form of counterterrorism."

It was the first time that Rosie had used the word terrorism as she described this situation. Tyler wondered whether they were really involved with terrorists.

"The truth is, at the moment we don't know who is doing this nor why," said Rosie.

"Usually, when something like this happens, we get someone admitting to the incident almost immediately.

"This one is different. No one has admitted anything, and curiously even with this huge blast, there was only one fatality. Most of the explosion directed upwards resulting in property damage rather than multiple casualties.

Tyler leaned forward. "Only one fatality and that was my friend Matt?" he asked, "I don't like the sound of this."

Rosie continued, "After the explosion, the Met sent in a couple of drones to surface map the area quickly, and these are the results."

Rosie pressed a button on her phone, and nothing happened. She pressed the button again and still nothing happened.

Tyler realised that the team would need to get its act together to keep up with this. All of this technology required to work correctly. The idea of exploding disk drives and secret phones all seemed a bit of a step too far.

Rosie eventually showed the pictures. It was reminiscent of a missile attack. By the roadside were the charred remains of a van and a blast wall streaked up the side of a prominent stone building.

"See, it is amazing that the building withstood the blast. I think the reason the windows remained intact was that we have already bomb blast protected them."

Tyler asked," So this wasn't a regular civilian target then?"

"No", answered Marcus," This was one of our smaller offices handling quite sensitive information."

"How did Matt get hit then?" asked Tyler," It looks as if the blast was mainly external,"

"It was," said Rosie," Matt Stevens was outside the building at the time of the blast. Aside from him, only six people suffered minor injuries. It's almost as if the bomb was engineered to inflict the least damage."

"Okay, Marcus", said Rosie," You are going to have to level with us. There's more to these team choices than meets the eye."

"Alright", said Marcus," There are two things. Firstly, Tyler here knew Matt Stevens. As importantly, he knew Matt was working on blockchain uses."

Tyler shook his head," No. I was still a good buddy of Matt, but since we joined the Department, we've spent less time together than you might think. We don't share a flat any more, and I didn't even know he was working in the other building. And to be honest, Matt was far smarter than me when it came to cyber coins and the blockchains."

"What's the other thing?" asked Rosie, "You said there were two things."

"Yes. I'm wondering if was a warning? It ties into the cybercash work we did a few weeks ago based upon that Russia Today story," replied Marcus.

"What?" Said Rosie. "Those TV reports? Ones about Russian financial stability?"

"Yes, I wrote a report after that, which has gone through the reporting chain," said Marcus, "It implied that the Russians might have more to hide. Reports on Russia Today were talking up the rouble as if it was now one of the strongest currencies.

"In practice, the main strengthening of the currency is more the effect from its low base. Put simply, at the end of 2014 the dollar bought 56 roubles, then in 2015 it purchased 52, nowadays it's somewhere in the mid-40s."

"The rouble is bouncing back despite signs to the contrary. It is as if they have somehow found a mechanism to guarantee the price of the rouble," said Tyler.

Tyler nodded, "It's what Matt used to talk about. If there was a way to filter a cryptocurrency into a mainstream currency, then it could be used as a mini printing press to manufacture banknotes. And it would be almost undetectable."

"It would unhook the Russian oil dependency," said Rosie, "Instead of needing to sell oil, they could just turn up the speed of printing of currency."

"Yes," said Marcus, "but it would be better still for the Russians if they were able to generate a foreign currency - then it's much like the way they get foreign money from oil sales."

"What, instead of printing roubles, attempt to print the dollar or the euro or the pound?" asked Rosie.

"Precisely, if they can augment their supplies of foreign exchange. Quietly create the equivalence of dollars or euros," said Marcus.

"That's like a double-dip into the barrel," said Tyler. "On the one hand, the Russians could manipulate the oil price, and at the same time have an inflow of dollars or other hard currencies to provide themselves with a safety cushion."

"More than a cushion," said Rosie," It's a whole sofa."

"Yes," said Tyler. "That's what Matt used to get excited about. We only looked at the relative strengths of the various currencies with regard to selling our cryptocurrency. As students we just wanted to make a fast buck. And heck, the UK government were also kindly offering us double for our trouble."

"That's right," said Marcus, "You might not have realised it, but the system that Matt had developed was a great proxy for the status of all cryptocurrencies. We were buying into your data stream. The simplest way was to pay you both and, in return, get access to your data knowledge."

Tyler smiled, "Too good to be true. It's what we both thought, although we could not see your angle on it, we were happy to take the money."

Marcus nodded, "Yes, that is what I put into my report. Since the rouble began strengthening, it was at around the same time that oil prices began to rise again.

"My report said that it was such a short period that it wouldn't provide any real evidence that the rouble was capable of fighting against the low price of oil for any significant time. That's without even taking into effect account the effect of speculators. Imagine an exchange rate that mysteriously improves and yet no one is speculating on it. That can't last for very long!"

"So, Russia isn't banking on the strength of its own currency?" asked Tyler.

"Correct," said Marcus, "I suspect it is building reserves of foreign exchange, by bolstering them with laundered cyber coins."

"And all the while it is manipulating the availability of oil," added Rosie, "and it doesn't care about the effects that it is having on the rouble, because it has a secret stash of Forex."

"How come I haven't seen any of these reports from our direct team?" asked Tyler.

"Oh, you have," answered Marcus, "It's just not spelled out in such detail. It takes a whole set of events to allow us to draw these conclusions. I filed the paper about rouble manipulation some time ago, and to be honest there were several other people with similar conclusions. We couldn't predict the cyber coin implications, though."

Marcus nodded, "At least, that's what I said in my report. It was along the lines that with a cheap rouble that was stable, it was in Russia's interests to feed the speculators and encourage them by giving out cheap credit, thereby maintaining high interest rates.

"They couldn't do this for very long, though, because it would eventually stretch their own Central Bank and they would need to beef up the depleted foreign currency reserves. The irony is they would effectively have to bet against their own currency by buying foreign currency.

"I'm pretty sure there were lots of other people that made the same assumptions. In fact, I was taken to one side after that and asked to treat the whole thread of information as Protocol 6.

Tyler asked, "Protocol 6, it sounds like something from spy world?"

"Protocol 6 is like "Top Secret" - we use it to limit the number of people involved in a particular discussion," said Rosie.

"I notice that our new badges are protocol 6, so I kind of thought we'd made it to the next level. Like in some platform game," said Tyler.

"That's right," said Marcus, "and Tyler, you'll have gone through eDV checks to be in this role anyway."

"Oh, Mr Holmes, I would love to tell you, but then, of course, I'd have to kill you," chuckled Tyler.

Marcus continued, "It wasn't just the oil rouble pricing that I noticed, but it was a subsequent newsflash about a Russian drone filming oil wells that crash-landed in Saudi Arabia."

Marcus continued, "First of all, the Russians are not exactly known for the prowess with drones and have a much smaller inventory than, say, the Americans. Also, most of their Unmanned Aerial Vehicles are tiny compared with, say, a Predator."

"For example, the Predator costs about $21 million and would just about fit into a domestic garage. Most of the Russian drones were like big model aircraft by comparison."

"The one that crashed in Al Jubail was a medium-altitude Long endurance UAV – a Heron, actually. This is a much bigger device than those used typically used by the Russians and had a flight time of 40 hours. I'm not sure how the Russians came to have this one."

"The Heron is made by Israel Aerospace Industries and is usually used for surveillance. Confidentially, from what we can make out, the Heron crash was the result of an anti-UAV defence system made in the UK."

"The defence system is called Blighter and is used to set up an electronic wall that the drones can't penetrate. The defence looks a bit like a small tank and has a big gun type unit on the front used to send signals that jam the drone."

"This one was being used for some trials when it activated against the Heron and pulled it into Saudi airspace."

"What were we doing with one of these anti-UAV units in Saudi Arabia?" Tyler asked.

"Maybe a coincidence? It was actually there for a demonstration, at the Jubail Naval Airport. The fact it found a real device to practice on was considered a coincidence."

"When the drone crashed at the demonstration, we, the Brits, located its hard drive used for covert filming. Someone managed to clone the disc before it was all handed over to the Saudi Army.

"Now, here's the thing," said Marcus, "Photos on the drive with

Russian subtitling were all of oil installations around Saudi Arabia and other parts of the Middle East. The Heron was mapping detail of oil installations for use by the Russians."

"It makes sense," chipped in Tyler, "Fix the currency, fix the oil and know what the competition is up to."

"Are we drawing too many conclusions from a few scant facts?" asked Rosie.

"Yes, you could say that," agreed Marcus, "Although it is probably our best working theory."

The Building Theory

"I need a cigarette," said Rosie. She fumbled into her bag and then slipped out of the door of the office.

"I can't tell whether this is personal," said Marcus.

"What do you mean?" asked Tyler.

"Well, the threat seems to come to two of the main buildings involved in the report. They could not know who wrote it because the names are behind department functional designations."

But if you think about it, the report has travelled from here, St Martins-le-Grand, to Warwick Lane and then on to Hammersmith. After that, it would go to GCHQ, but I'm wondering if it has got that far?"

"I'm not sure I follow you?" questioned Tyler.

Marcus stood up and walked across to a whiteboard. He wrote down the three names of the buildings. Then Marcus drew arrows between them. Then he added GCHQ.

"I guess that they are trying to flush out the people involved with the report. That's us, Tyler, plus your friend Matt, and Rosie."

Tyler shook his head," Where would they get that idea? You've only just told me about the roubles and the oil?"

"I know, but whoever 'they' are, they probably think that you and Matt knew more than you did in practice.

They'll have identified Matt because of his direct manipulations of the market in his crypto dealings."

"It should be much harder to identify me," Tyler mused.

"The whole point of the way that Matt and I had set up the cyber coin thing was to preserve Matt's anonymity in the background," Tyler explained.

"Yes, but it didn't work. You both had access to the bank account, for example. That's how we found you both," continued Marcus.

Tyler looked concerned, "So do you think they are after us?" he asked.

"That would be my best guess," continued Marcus.

The door opened, and Rosie entered the room.

"It's always useful to go for a cigarette," she said. "Do you want the latest news?"

They nodded.

"There's been another bomb call. This one is targeting Hammersmith. I was with Geordie from Facilities. He said there would be a general alert issued to this building as well."

"Okay," said Marcus," It looks as if they are working along the document route."

"We'd better tell the other teams," said Tyler.

"I think we can tell them about the bomb alert, but I think we should keep our theories close at the moment," said Marcus.

"I'm not sure whether there is a leak, the bombs seem to be just a little too precise."

Tyler looked at Rosie, who nodded. "Yes, we'll keep it close. For now, at least," she replied.

Rosie was already getting ready to go outside the building to smoke another cigarette. The shock of the news had just tipped her over the edge.

"You don't want to be doing that," said Tyler, "You'll be chain-smoking by the end of this!" There was a muffled noise. A sharp crack followed by a low thud. The glass from the tall windows in the office rattled. Grey paint chippings dislodged and fluttered down.

"That was not Hammersmith," said Rosie. "It was much closer."

They could hear the alarm system start.

Part of the bomb protocol was to not go out through exits close to the site of the bomb. Training had also taught that a secondary detonation could create even more destruction.

"I think we may be better to stay in here," said Marcus. "We are in the core of the building a long way from the roadside."

They could hear the noises in the corridor people of hurrying towards exits. There were the shadows of men in full body armour walking past the office area.

Geordie appeared," They've already brought out the special services. They are to provide us with additional protection while we work on this."

Buzzback

The emergency services kept the team on lockdown for several hours.

When Tyler was eventually allowed to leave the office, he was surprised to see his phone buzzing away.

It was like getting off a plane, but he'd not switched the phone to silent or airplane mode or anything. Then he remembered that the police had a system which could render phone cells inoperative within an emergency zone. It was a way to stop remote triggering or remote comms between terrorists.

They must have switched cellular comms back on again.

He looked through the messages. Mostly it was people he knew who wanted to know he was okay. He decided to create a single text and send it to everyone.

Then he noticed a call from Erica. He was quite surprised because since they split, there'd been no real communication except for few practical matters, like what time the van would pick up the stuff.

Tyler decided to wait until he was home before calling Erica. She only lived a couple of miles away, but he hadn't seen her since they broke up. Then, the other side of a couple of beers, he called her. It would be the first time since she'd moved in with Drew. But she had said it was quite important.

The phone rang, and she picked up almost immediately.

"Erica?"

"Yes, Yes, I'm glad you called back. Thank you. Look there's something I need to talk to you about. Can we meet soon, please? It's kind of work-related."

"Er, yes, of course."

"This is YOUR work-related, Tyler. Look I know something about what you do and think this might be useful. I saw your building on the television tonight."

"Where shall we meet?"

"How about the pizza place? The one that does those salads?"

"Tomorrow, lunch, midday?"

"Sooner? Tonight? Maybe nine o clock? It is important."

"Erica? Are you sure? I can be there if you really want…"

"See you at nine."

Tyler heard the click. Erica had gone. An express train of a phone call. He recognised her professional financial services business voice, even if he didn't know exactly what it was that she did.

Tyler took a taxi to the pizza place. He wondered if she would be alone. It would be easier than with Drew as well.

It was a Monday evening at the Franco Manca, and there were several empty tables, even one in the far corner. The waitress that greeted Tyler recognised him and asked where he would like to sit.

Tyler gestured towards the table in the far corner, and she smiled and took him across.

"My friend will be joining me soon," he said, and then just as he was sitting down, Erica arrived. She spotted Tyler and came straight across.

"How about some wine?" Tyler asked. The waitress was still by the table.

"That's fine," she answered, "Some Pinot Gris, please."

"Me too," added Tyler.

The waitress nodded and hurried away, some sixth sense telling her that this was going to be a fast turn-around table.

"I think I said this was work-related?" Her eyes were looking directly at Tyler; he melted slightly as he remembered how gorgeous she could look.

"Yes," he answered, "I think you might have mentioned it when we were speaking earlier."

"But," she said, "it's delicate because it probably relates to the work you are doing right now,"

"I saw the news today and saw your office building was bombed, or, at least I think it was your office, it looked as if it was in any case."

"I know you were doing something financial and clandestine for the government, but you were always vague about what it was. The reason I'm speaking to you is that I think there's something odd happening at our bank at the moment."

Erica had never really talked about the bank other than her time there with Drew, so Tyler didn't even really know what she did.

"You know that I work in the trading area?" she asked. Tyler nodded as if he knew what she did.

"Well, there's been some strange developments in the last few weeks. First of all, Drew's boss suddenly disappeared. He worked the Russian desk and was in charge of the financial position that we run."

"It's all very macho in our bank, and the dealers are like predatory animals in the way that they operate. Imagine a casino full of people gambling with someone else's money," she added.

"I thought you liked working for the bank?" Tyler asked.

"Sure, it's quite prestigious to be there, but the reality is very cut-throat and misogynistic." she added, "For example, they just fired my friend who got pregnant."

"The whole place is a hire-fire culture - get up or get out," she added.

"I'm surviving there rather than thriving. I'll get another big bonus this year but, to be honest, after that I'm probably going to find a way to leave," she continued. "but look, this is about Drew's boss and what happened next," she continued.

"So, we've been dealing with Russian currency and also the Russian foreign exchange position over the last few months. Everyone knows that there's been some shakiness and that Russia has been managing the position based partly on oil reserve balances," she continued.

"Drew's boss - his name is Victor - had anyway been looking very stressed for the last few weeks. Now, all of a sudden, he has disappeared. It was actually about a week ago.

"Drew told me that Victor was putting on the screws. He was asking us to bet against the market. As if he knew that Russian Central Bank would bail out the rouble at the last moment."

"What, like insider trading?" Tyler asked.

"Oh definitely," said Erica. "But I'm not saying this if you understand me. Not whistleblowing - not until I have next year's bonus, anyway."

"But I don't think Victor would be doing this off his own bat. He is a ruthless shit, but even he would draw the line at something so obvious that the PRA would pick it up very quickly."

The waitress returned. "Have you decided?" she asked.

"A salad for me," said Erica.

"Which kind?" asked the waitress.

"The one with butternut squash," said Erica.

Tyler remembered that he had been living on pizzas for the last two days.

"And me too, a salad, with chicken," he added.

"Any more drinks?" asked the waitress.

Tyler looked at Erica.

"We're fine," said Tyler, and Erica nodded.

"...So why are you telling me this?" asked Tyler.

"Your job," said Erica," It's something to do with analysis, isn't it? Like we have financial analysts to run the markets. The only analysts I can think that the government would have are either for Treasury or something sneaky."

"I'll put you into the sneaky department, after some of those things you did with Matt," said Erica.

For the first time since she'd appeared, Tyler saw Erica smile.

Tyler remembered that he'd told Erica more about his role than he was probably supposed to. He'd been newly into it and excited, and it did have that subtle air of mystery. Erica knew Matt too, and he was sure that she'd have heard more from him.

"Okay, I think you have got my job pegged, yes we are interested in what has been happening with Russia," he sighed.

"Right, here's the thing. Victor had lunch with Drew about a week ago. They went to Rules for a wine-fuelled blow-out. A right PFL. Victor seemed very agitated. Drew said he'd never seen Victor like it before. Well, it's fair to say that Victor is a bit of a bastard. He can swear his way out of many situations and has the classic reputation of a bully-boy banker. On this occasion, he said to Drew that a Russian named Pakashenko or something had been pushing him for the rouble layoff to be increased.

"We were in the process of doing it, although the whispers were of insider trades. Pakashenko or his bosses seemed to want our bank to make everything happen much faster. You can't, of course, because it'll trip Reporting and then we'll have the regulators down on us."

"Now for the delicate part. Drew isn't squeaky clean in all of this. He's been following the lead from Victor and selling derivatives based on the rouble through some pretty weird financial instruments.

"You know about Quantitive Easing? Where the Bank of England prints extra banknotes to help manage currencies? Well, we're seeing this happen now, except it is as if Russia is somehow making the money.

"That's why our bank is confident that the Russians can dodge their way out of trouble by using foreign exchange. They seem to have a mysterious excessive amount of FX at the moment.

The salads arrived. Erica picked at hers.

"So, we have a foreign government running quantitative easing in another currency?" asked Tyler.

"Yes," said Erica, "And it is under the radar at the moment. They are somehow generating foreign money to bail themselves out."

"And that's when Victor disappeared. He started to tell Drew about the situation he'd got himself into with Pakashenko, and then disappeared."

"But without Victor, there's no-one to drive the bank's position?" asked Tyler.

"Oh, there is all right, get dug in deep enough and it is like a self-playing piano," Erica smiled again.

"Victor had grown the position so that the regular trading algorithms would kick in and maintain it. To be honest, that's what Pakashenko was probably annoyed about. The bank will manage the positions conservatively when on auto-pilot."

Tyler pushed his plate away, "Is this just happening in your bank, do you think?"

"I doubt it. Victor has a little gang of friends spread out around the other big players. I'm guessing that at least some of them are in on the action."

So, what do you want me to do?" asked Tyler.

"I'm worried," said Erica. "A couple of the newswires were hinting at Russian involvement in the bombing. You and Matt know about cyber-money. Victor has disappeared after a heated exchange with a Russian and Drew is implicated in all of this. I thought if I told you, you might be able to think of something. I don't want to have an ex that's been blown up, nor a partner that's in jail."

"You know about Matt? Asked Tyler.

"Matt what?" asked Erica.

"I am sorry to have to tell you this, but Matt was reported as the single casualty from the first bomb," said Tyler.

"Shit..." said Erica, "It's started. Look. Thanks for the salad. I'm going back now. Call me if you can think of anything."

"Love ya," said Tyler.

"No, you don't," said Erica, smoothing her skirt as she prepared to leave the restaurant.

Kangaroo

Tyler read a short report from Rosie. The second explosion had been similar to the first, mainly upward, creating limited damage and no casualties.

Tyler turned up for work as usual but noticed Marcus and Rosie standing outside the building adjacent to a Mercedes minibus.

"Don't get too used to this," said Marcus, "but we're going for a short ride to another property."

Later that morning, they sat around their third new set of desks, sipping tea from mugs.

"I hadn't realised just how many additional buildings the Department owned, or at least inhabited," said Tyler.

"Yes, and the building looks quite normal from outside although inside this one there's a fair number of military," added Rosie.

"And I wonder if the disks will have exploded in the move?" mused Tyler.

"You've 'arrived' once you are in one of these buildings," said Marcus. "Now we've got top-level security. Greater, I'd say, than the overt security at Vauxhall Cross or in MI5."

"I guess that just means it could all kick off at any moment," said Tyler.

Rosie smiled, "So now we are proper secret agents!"

William House was one of those buildings that had been around for many years and also had running adaptations to keep it fit for purpose. These seemed to include much heavy wiring along the ceiling and blast protection for the doors. There were zoned layers of security, which Tyler found cumbersome to use, because of how frequently he needed his access card inside the building.

A one-time fairly plush looking staircase swept up to the higher floors and their office, which seemed like a faint replica of the one in Central London.

Tyler noticed that his floor didn't seem to have the armed security that was prevalent on the floor below.

"It's not like we are really in Hammersmith either," said Tyler. He'd noticed that the nearest tube stop was Earl's Court and the area close by was filled with small eateries and pubs.

"Welcome to Kangaroo Valley," said Rosie, citing the one-time nickname of the area.

"Not so much, nowadays," replied Marcus. "The Antipodeans have moved away. It is still a great area for undercover flat rentals, though. I had to stay here once, as part of an assignment."

"But we are off the grid, I take it?" asked Tyler.

"Oh yes, the story is we've moved to Hammersmith, and that's where our land-lines will point," answered Marcus.

Marcus added, "We've been moved here, Earls Court, as a precaution. Two reasons. Firstly, in case anyone didn't like us. Secondly, as an additional level of security, in case of leaks."

"But they could follow us here?" quizzed Rosie.

"Not exactly," said Marcus. "It would presuppose they knew where we were staying."

"Wait a minute," said Tyler, "are we being held?"

"You are, and it is entirely within the terms of your agreement with the Department. We are all being held.

"The point of this is to ensure you melt away from public view for a week or two.

"I've had it happen to me before. It can be pretty reasonable. The Department will put you up in a hotel and supply you with new clothes and so on."

"So that's why we are in flat-land," replied Rosie, "Nice and cheap!"

Tyler thought about if this had happened earlier before he had broken up with Erica. It would have been difficult to explain. He wondered how he was going to explain what Erica had told him, to the others.

"I still can't quite see why they expect us to come up with something?" said Tyler, looking towards Marcus.

"It's because of that report I produced," he replied.

"They seem to think I had discovered something. But let's not kid ourselves, there will be several other teams like us doing this kind of thing as well."

"But what about all the people over in GCHQ?" Tyler asked.

"Surely they will have more resource and better ability to find out what is happening?"

"That's the problem," Said Marcus.

"GCHQ and many of the American agencies are great at working out what has happened after it has happened. In other words, their ability to reconstruct events that have occurred is pretty good.

"It's not as smart when they are trying to predict the future, though. The two bombs are a classic example of this. They can probably try to work out how these bombs were put in place.

"Maybe they can work out who did it as well. But before the two alerts were given, we didn't have any inkling that this was going to happen.

"It is not a new situation, either. Each time something like this happens we are working after the fact. We've seen planes shot down with missiles. Planes exploding in mid-air with suitcase bombs. Random acts of carnage throughout the Middle East and other parts of Europe.

"And in each case, we are then expecting someone to investigate it and work out who did what. Take something like Lockerbie which happened many years ago. It took ages before anything was cleared up from that."

Marcus was shaking his head.

"The idea of using little groups like us is to try to find ways to predict and pre-empt things rather than to spend time in the archaeology of something that has already occurred," explained Marcus.

He continued. "Of course, I'm not saying that they don't ever discover anything through their information scanning methods. There's still plenty of smaller situations which are picked up. But it still seems to be the bigger situations and sometimes the random events like teenagers hacking into major banks, for example, that go unpredicted by anyone."

"Like Black Swan Events," said Tyler, "When something unexpected comes along, and everyone tries to rationalise it?"

"What was that movie with Tom Cruise?" Rosie asked. "You know the one where he has to go to stop crimes before they are committed? Total Recall?"

"No, Minority Report," said Marcus," Based upon that Philip K Dick story."

"I'm having you on my team for the pub quiz," said Rosie.

"Well, our situation isn't one where psychic mystics will pop up to help us solve it," said Marcus.

Erica

"The best things in life make you sweaty."
— *Edgar Allan Poe*

New Intelligence

The next morning, a bright Tuesday, Tyler planned to get into the office early.

To his surprise, both Rosie and Marcus were already at their desks. They were talking earnestly and looking towards a new wall chart which they had been building.

"We are building a timeline", said Marcus, "Trying to look for any gaps."

"The most obvious one to ask is when does the timeline start?" said Tyler.

"Good point. We have just been discussing that," said Rosie

"It covers the period from when I wrote the original report up to the second bomb," said Marcus.

"Here, let me take you through it," said Rosie.

"Back in February, we get the first trickle of curious currency transactions. It is what sparked Marcus to take a look."

"It's as if someone was testing the water to see if it all worked and would be undetected," added Marcus.

"Then Marcus writes his paper. Fact-based but probably inconclusive- No offence, Marcus -. The paper works its way through the system in March and April," said Rosie.

"It's also low profile, and there's so much else happening that it would probably slip through the net undetected," added Marcus, "I didn't even believe in it that strongly."

"Now that's when it would probably take a second paper to hit the system to provide some corroboration," said Rosie.

"But there's nothing, except a faint register of interest from the Genesis team."

"Who?" asked Tyler.

"That's the team where your buddy worked. Matt was on a team that looks at small situations which could amplify to have large repercussions."

"Yes, this seems to point to someone with prior knowledge of the manipulations. Someone who could drive the agenda, I wish I could have thought of that when I was writing the report," said Marcus.

"Yes, but you know so much more now than you did back in February. There's no wonder it was passed over," answered Rosie.

"I think I have something to add," said Tyler," About the currency manipulation."

He went on to describe what he had heard from Erica, although he was reluctant to name his source.

Both Rosie and Marcus seemed interested, but Rosie almost immediately asked the obvious question, "So how can you substantiate this? You are relaying this to us anonymously from a friend of a friend. It won't stand up and could get you into hot water."

Tyler looked at the floor. "Some of this is quite personal, so I'd respect your discretion. I got this from my ex-girlfriend, Erica, who works for an international bank, in the trading area. She told me all of this last night, but it was in confidence. She'd seen my office on TV, heard that there were whispers of Russian involvement and was worried for me as well as for her boss Victor. He's the one that has disappeared."

Marcus nodded. "We'll need to get a statement from Erica. I could pull another bar stunt if you like to get an area cleared where we can record what she is saying. It's not exactly police procedure but should be enough for our investigations."

"Marcus, just a reminder that Erica and Drew are well-heeled bankers. We'd better find somewhere appropriate. Not our local boozer."

"I'll have to ask Erica nicely, although she seemed genuinely worried yesterday," said Tyler.

Tyler called Erica once more. She accepted the invitation to come along to a second meeting but asked to bring Drew as well. Tyler considered how awkward this second session would be and tried to imagine how Marcus could attempt it in the local pub.

Steak

Marcus arranged a venue, which was close to the Bank's main building in Canary Wharf. The restaurant had some small private tables, and one of these was selected for the meeting with Erica.

Tyler and Rosie took the tube across London to Canary Wharf and then zig-zagged through the many walkways towards the restaurant. They arrived at 17:15, which was around 15 minutes before they had all agreed to meet.

Marcus was already in the restaurant.

Tyler looked at the set-up. It was fine white linen and fancy cutlery. The menu comprised Argentinian steak. Marcus has done well. This was Erica-level dining. Erica and Drew arrived at 1730 precisely and were shown in, greeted, seated, and everyone was poured an aperitif.

"Champagne cocktails, how lovely," said Rosie.

"Erm, watch out they contain tequila," whispered Tyler.

Tyler noticed that Erica asked for "just the Brut Royal, please," just the champagne, then.

Tyler began, "They've asked me to introduce everyone." He

described Erica and Drew as two of his acquaintances and Marcus and Rosie as two co-workers. He knew it was better to be bland and to allow people to manage their own disclosures.

Marcus then asked Erica to tell the story. The same one she had already told Tyler.

Erica almost immediately deferred to Drew, who gave an account of his recent meeting with Victor. Tyler asked Drew if he had heard any more of Victor since that day.

"No," said Drew, "and the Bank seems to be taking it rather well. None of us has heard any more, and last week his desk was being cleared. They told us a new manager is being brought in for temporary continuity."

Rosie asked, "What happens when someone is taken out of the team like that?"

"It happens quite often," said Drew and Erica nodded.

"The Bank is very performance-led, so when people don't make their targets, they are replaced quite quickly. There's a whole process for this."

"Yes," said Erica," The HR team were involved, and it looked like a routine if sudden, replacement."

"But wouldn't there be a memo or something? And email to explain the sudden departure of Victor?"

"Oh, there was," said Drew, "It explained that Victor had gone to another organisation, implied he had quit suddenly and that is why they would not provide any forwarding. It's not that unusual."

"I tried calling his mobile but got 'number unobtainable'. I even tried his home number but got the same. He lives somewhere around here, in an apartment in Canary Wharf, he's divorced although I think his family live somewhere in Essex. I've not tried to visit his home, but I do have the address," said Drew.

"Okay," That will be useful said Marcus," We can check up in case this is all a worry about nothing."

"I doubt if you will find him there," said Drew. "He is a noisy bugger, and I'd have expected that one of us from the team would have heard by now where he's gone. He'd also be trying to poach us by now."

"So you suspect cover-up?" asked Rosie.

"It depends, but if the Bank had worked out what he was doing, with the Russian trades, then I'd think we would be adjusting the position and trying to cover the tracks," said Drew.

"But there's nothing, no position adjustments and the AI-systems are maintaining the same holdings. It's surprising because no-one has come after me, checking my trades or anything."

You'd better give us his phone number and address, then," asked Marcus.

"We can trace back to see whether there is anything even more unusual."

"One moment," started Drew, "I think I'd better give you his other number, too. We have Bank issued phones, which the Bank can track, but most of us also carry a second personal phone. Anything irregular would appear on that."

Drew hunted into his pocket and produced a phone. Rosie noticed it looked like the one Drew had placed upon the table at the start of their conversation.

"Yes, I know. It does look the same. It makes it easier not to get spotted with an obvious burner phone," said Drew, noticing Rosie's quizzical look.

"So aside from what you've told us about the rouble trades and Victor's disappearance, is there anything else that you want to tell us?" asked Marcus, "Is anyone else behaving unusually? Are there any other systems that seem odd?"

"You've not worked in a trading environment?" said Drew. "There is nothing normal about the day-to-day. It's like a crazy-farm most of the time. But in honesty, I can't think of anything else."

"Me neither," said Erica.

"Look, "said Drew, "Victor was pressuring me on this, you know."

Marcus nodded, "To be honest, I'm more interested in the bigger picture than in some bonus-making scheme that you and Victor concocted. I'm sure it will serve you well at the end of the year, or whenever the bonus gets awarded. For now, I want us to carry on with our investigation."

Drew nodded, and Erica shuffled in her chair. She looked at her watch. Then Drew did the same.

"We need to be somewhere," said Drew, "Bank business…we fitted this in at the last minute."

Tyler knew the moves by Erica. She was extricating herself from an awkward situation.

"I'll see you out," he said.

They made their way towards the stairwell. On the way, Erica said, "Look, I've told you all we know. I hope you won't need to involve us any further. I did this because I was concerned about what was happening in the Bank, and partly because I thought you and Matt had been wrapped up in some Russian currency stuff in the past."

"I get the message," said Tyler, holding up his hands.

Erica stepped closer to Tyler.

"Look, don't do anything stupid. Here's a memory stick. It's got a useful selection of transactions on it, Drew pulled them from Victor's records yesterday. They are Private and Confidential."

Tyler nodded, "Thank you, thank you," he said.

"I'll ask Rosie and Marcus to keep both of you out of this. If there were any other way to have this meeting, then I'd have taken it."

Drew nodded, and they both stepped out onto the pavement. Tyler could see Drew already beckoning to a cab.

SanDisk Ultra Luxe®

Tyler was immediately nervous about the memory stick he had been given. What if it included any trace routines? He couldn't use it inside the office, because it might give away their location. It could also get Erica and Drew into trouble.

He decided to take it home and to put it onto his home laptop. He could still examine it, but it would de-risk any search routines. Then a thought occurred. He could get it copied onto another media for safety.

His route from Canary Wharf took him along a couple of rainy streets, mid-evening in London. There were mobile phone shops next to the kebab shops. He decided to drop into one. He recollected that some of these shops had to handle the most spectacularly tawdry of files and folders, so a copy of the memory stick should not present a problem.

"As-salaam alaykom," said the owner, as Tyler pushed past the door and the beaded curtain into the small shop. It was a mobile phone shop and money exchange and cafe. There were a couple of small tables out on the street.

"Wa Alykom As-salaam," said Tyler, remembering his manners. He'd been around these parts of London a long time and knew the basic greetings.

"Hello, do you want some internet time?" asked the man behind the counter, in good English.

"No, thanks, I'd like this little stick copied if you can do that?"

The man looked over to the memory stick and called out to someone from the back of the shop.

A young boy appeared; Tyler guessed he was around 12 years old.

"yumkinuk naskh hadhih aleasa lileamil?" asked the man behind the counter.

"Yes, I can copy the stick for the man in about ten minutes. You will need to sell him another USB stick, though."

"You hear that, fi hawalay 10 daqayiq, in about 10 minutes, you can have a copy. You'll need to buy another stick though."

"That's fine," said Tyler, "How much are the memory sticks?"

"kam nubie bitaqat aldhaakirat?"

"Ten pounds for 32GB - SanDisk - good make," came the reply.

"That's fine," said Tyler and looked in his wallet for a banknote.

"Thank you," he said, addressing both the man behind the counter and the young boy.

The boy took the stick away and a few minutes later returned.

"Here, it's done. Original and the copy," the boy produced the original memory stick and a bright green generic USB flash drive.

"A moment," the boy said, and he took the flash drive and plugged it into a nearby laptop.

Tyler could see the directory structure appear. The boy had, indeed, copied the stick.

Tyler reached again into his wallet.

He looked at the man.

"Here," he said as he handed the boy a banknote, "Thank you."

The man nodded, and the boy smiled.

"Mae alsalaama!" said Tyler,

"Goodbye", said the man.

Tyler pushed back through the plastic curtain into the night's rain.

Food shopping

Outside, Edgware Road bustled with its typical visitors. Some called the area Little Arabia, but Tyler knew it, as did many Londoners, as just one of many multicultural parts of London, showing off its cosmopolitan character.

As he exited from the shop, he noticed a couple of people who he'd seen earlier in the day. He suddenly wondered if he was being followed.

He surreptitiously moved the two memory sticks apart and then slipped one of them into an inside zippered pocket of his jacket.

As he did this, he paused outside of a shop window and looked inside. He was checking the reflection, and sure enough, he could see the two men he thought were following him appear to pause also.

He looked around and spotted a Marks and Spencer store nearby. The food shop would make a useful diversion to see whether they followed him inside.

They did, so he moved to the main aisles, picking a small basket.

He then slowly walked around the aisle, noticing one of the

men doing the same, although without bothering to pick up a basket.

He approached a security guard in the store.

"Look, I'm sorry to trouble you," he began quietly," I think that man is shoplifting. I saw him take something outside the shop just now and pass it to a couple of women."

The guard looked Tyler over. "Thank you, what did he take?"

"I'm not sure, but it looked like vacuum-packed food. Fish maybe, or steak?"

"Thank you," said the guard and then said something into his radio pack. Tyler heard an announcement come through on the shop's Tannoy system.

"Will Mr Liftly please come to the packing area?"

"Game on," thought Tyler as he slipped around to the store's alternate entrance, where he bumped into one of the people who had been following him.

"Sorry/Pardon me," they both said it at the same time. The other voice sounded American, softly spoken, possibly Canadian.

Perhaps it was just a coincidence?

Tyler slipped from the store. He was relieved to see that he was not followed.

Ten minutes later he was on a tube train, heading for home.

He put his hand in the pocket where he'd placed the memory stick.

It had gone. Quickly, Tyler felt for the other one. Still there.

The men had been following him. They had pickpocketed the memory stick.

He stayed on the train past his stop, then caught a taxi back to his home.

Discoveries

Next day, Wednesday, Tyler was early to the office, but once again, Rosie and Marcus were already there.

Tyler had dropped the memory stick off with some forensic analysts who could look through it for anything unusual.

The call came through.

"It comprises mainly business trades. Derivatives and Foreign Exchange transactions. Quite substantial amounts - hundreds of thousands to millions of dollars- which are then pushed through a Russian Bank, RKI Bank. Rossiyskiy Kiber Investitsionnyy Bank.

Russian Cyber Investment Bank?" guessed Tyler.

"Very good," said the analyst." That's where most of the transactions were cleared. There's another unusual repeating transaction though, it seems to be about 10% of the RKI cut, and it goes to Gun Street Holdings.

"Gun Street?" queried Tyler.

"Yes, that's right. We typed it into Google and got an old YouTube western movie and a song track. There's no corporate site or anything."

Tyler was alert now. Gun Street was a rather typical Matt-inspired name. After a Tom Waits song.

He was about to tell Rosie and Marcus, but Rosie started up a summary of their status.

"We haven't found anything new," said Rosie walking to a whiteboard, "Let's summarise."

She grabbed a marker pen, hesitantly tested it on the board and then wrote:

- Van bombs gave a warning;
- Drivers escaped via taxi;
- Explosive was PETF;
- Low yield explosions
- Victor Boyd disappeared
- Boyd's phone missing
- Possible Russian connection
- Cybercash?

Rosie wrote down three big Subheadings BOMBS, VICTOR BOYD and RUSSIAN MONEY.

"Well," said Rosie," The disappearance of Victor seems genuine. We have a summary from Nasreen's team. There is no passport record of him leaving the country, and there's no spending pattern from his credit cards. His wife thinks he is on a management course."

"How so?" asked Tyler.

"The management course phoned him at his ex-wife's home number. He is divorced, you know. They told his ex-wife, Chantel, that there had been a change of plan and that the course would now run for two weeks."

His ex seemed to think it sounded genuine.

"What about his phone? can you work anything out from the GPS?"

"That is slightly odd. Boyd's work phone was sending a signal from his current apartment. So far, the phone hasn't been located. Victor Boyd is living in a fancy apartment near Canary Wharf. We entered it, but there is no sign of anything untoward."

Tyler scanned through the report. The report was very factual, but the response from the Chantel did not look as if she was surprised that he has suddenly disappeared. It ran along the lines that he would do his own thing and was quite likely to be off somewhere else. She was not surprised if he had been involved in some kind of financial swindling either.

"Wow", said Tyler, "It looks as if there is no love lost there between Victor and Chantel.

"That's what we thought," said Rosie

Rosie added, "There's a couple of pictures of the house as well, it's out in the sticks on the borders with London. Chigwell actually, one of those footballers-wives' type houses. You know the kind of thing, gates, Range Rovers and a Porsche and a big semi-circular drive."

Marcus commented, "Yes, although the police report says that the house has been a family home for the last eight years."

"It also says that his salary and bonuses would be quite capable of paying for this kind of lifestyle. I don't think any rake-off money has been used to finance his day to day lifestyle - there's no need."

Rosie looked at the photos, "I wouldn't mind living somewhere like that." She paused, "or maybe it's a bit too blingy for me. Notice the Lions heads positioned either side of the electronic entry gates?"

"I think the heated pool would make up for it," replied Tyler.

At that moment, Nasreen entered the office.

"Hiya," she said, "How's it going? I thought it better to liaise face-to-face.

"We are still following that downed drone. We've loaded that information onto the server now. It's mainly oil installations in Saudi, but there are a few urban complexes on camera too. The drone seems to be using a mix of Israeli software and a Russian command and control language."

"Our investigation has taken a slight twist," said Marcus.

"There does seem to be a proper Russian connection, and it appears to be linked to rouble manipulation, similar to the report I produced a couple of months ago.

"We've just been talking to a banker about a possible infraction at his bank. It still doesn't tie together with the bombing of our offices, although it does seem to lead back to Russia.

"Yes, Russia is coming through loud and clear," said Nasreen.

"Either that or we are getting a massive misdirection?" mused Marcus.

"We are also chasing down the forensics from the bombs," said Nasreen, "So far it looks like mining explosives. Common and difficult to trace. Battery triggered PETN, by all accounts. That's penthrite, which has various brand names in the mining world. According to our specialists, a pure PETN releases little that can be picked up by detectors, so the manufacturers use taggants with it. That's special substances added to the mix which can be detected."

"I think PETN has been the go-to choice of aeroplane bombers too," said Marcus.

"I recollect the shoe-bomber used it and that it has been smuggled into ink toner cartridges too."

"I've just googled it as well." Said Rosie," One of the common brands for it is SEMTEX. One hundred grams of it can destroy a car."

Nasreen nodded, "You have a good team here," she said, looking to Marcus. "Let's keep one another briefed." Marcus nodded agreement, just as Nasreen's phone started to buzz.

Nasreen answered it, "Huh?" she said, "It doesn't make sense. Guys, the taggants are from a US batch of Semtex. Department of Defense - Air Force - It doesn't add up."

Nasreen put her phone down. It buzzed again, "Gotta go," she said, closing the door behind her.

Tyler had one further source of enquiry. He decided to call his ex-flatmate, Kyle. Nowadays, Kyle specialised in security and cybercrime.

"Hey, Kyle,"

"Hey Tyler, long time! How are you doing?"

"Doing good, well, er -actually- it's all a bit weird here."

"I'd expect no less; I've gone freelance, you know? I'm helping a big corporate fix their firewalls. It's amazing how much bad stuff comes in and out. Trousers down and all that. Speaking of trousers down, how's Erica?"

"Kyle - we split up, Yeah, Look I was wondering if I could pick your brains?"

"Sorry to hear it, man. Look, what do you need?"

"It'll be better face to face."

"Okay, tonight, are you still living near the old flat? I can get over to The Drayton by about seven if that's any good?"

"Brilliant."

The Drayton Arms

Tyler arrived at The Drayton Arms shortly before seven. He surveyed the scene of many fabled drinking bouts across the years when the three amigos would go out on the lash. Meekly, he ordered a Pride and sat at a table near the frosted window.

"Hey man," greeted Kyle, "Are we in for a session? Look what they've done; There's a theatre upstairs now!"

Tyler smiled, "Kyle, I need to pick your brains."

"You and Matt dug a hole bigger than you can climb out of?" asked Kyle.

"Not exactly," said Tyler, "But it is related to that cyber money stuff we were doing back in the flat."

Tyler described the situation to Kyle, who sipped quietly at his beer.

"Wow. That's pretty epic," said Kyle, "I knew e-currency would end in tears."

"But let's break it down a bit. You guys had stumbled on to a cyber coin mining process. But you could only mine at about 2 or 3 coins per week."

"Yes, that's about right," said Tyler, "and it was Matt that discovered the process, with that little computer rig he had in his bedroom."

"I remember," said Kyle. "The one I wouldn't touch with a bargepole."

Tyler smiled as he sipped at his beer.

"So, Matt must have been editing the blockchains that these processes use to create the currency?" said Kyle.

"He often talked about maintaining the blockchain integrity," answered Tyler.

"Yes, that's how this works. It is like a self-regulating process which uses hash keys to keep track of the individual coins."

Kyle paused," I think Matt must have found a way to edit an occasional extra coin into the sequence."

"One coin at a time, it could take forever to make any significant money. Okay, it's fine for a couple of students, but really? To make serious dosh, you'd need huge computing power. Not only that. You'd need a way to camouflage the operation so that it wasn't picked up in general auditing."

"You know what I think?" said Tyler.

"I think Matt had found a way to build new currency strands, and he was gradually populating them."

"I see, parallel to the main strands, like a cloned image. That would make the most sense," said Kyle. "And it wouldn't show up as much if it looked like a whole new number series. Like a self-contained sequence of blockchains. A parallel universe."

"Yes, that's what I wondered. Something fairly robust that looks as if it has integrity. So, what if I wanted to use this at a national level?" Asked Tyler. "Like to make millions of dollars?"

Kyle sniggered. "Millions? - Well, you could try it! You would need huge computers, though. Think about it. Making two or three coins a week from Matt's computers? This is no student project. It's immense."

"So, what if we have a nation-state behind it?"

"What, like the US, or China or Russia? That's what it would take, but I can't imagine it would be kept secret for very long," answered Kyle.

"And if it were a corrupt state then you'd have people taking money from the piles created," he added.

"Do you think this is what might be happening?" asked Kyle.

"I don't know, said Tyler, "and I don't know how we'd ever go about finding out."

"Two ways I can think of," said Kyle, "First of all, information leakage from the systems. Someone blabbing about something to do with it.

"Secondly, you could attempt to follow back along the blockchain links to see where the chain originated."

"How would I do that?" asked Tyler.

"Good question," said Kyle.

"Did you say you were working for the government? I presume they can afford my daily rates?"

"So, you are in?" Asked Tyler.

"Well, this one seems like it's legitimate," answered Kyle, smiling, "Unlike the old Matt hokey scheme.

"This time I'll be finding out just how tricksy it was to track down what you and Matt had been up to.

Kyle

"Prime numbers are what is left when you have taken all the patterns away. I think prime numbers are like life.

They are very logical but you could never work out the rules, even if you spent all your time thinking about them."

— *Mark Haddon, The Curious Incident of the Dog in the Night-Time*

Confer

Tyler made his way back across London to the office. Kyle had given him some new thoughts to share with Marcus and Rosie, and he still needed to tell them about Gun Street Holdings.

Marcus had already arranged a conference call across the river with SI6.

Tyler knew he would not usually be in on such a call, but he assumed that on this occasion, he already knew as much as anyone and so he would be called in.

Usually, he would enjoy the physical trip across the river to Vauxhall Cross, the well-known building housing much of the secret services.

Despite the makeshift nature of their current accommodation, Tyler was impressed to be whisked upstairs into a secure communication suite.

It was obviously where some of the top people worked, and he was amused to see little drinks stations and canapés in the entrance area.

Then he was ushered into one of the studios, where Rosie, Marcus and himself sat in a row, facing some large monitors.

The conference table was one half of an elliptical design, and the several flat-screen monitors placed to represent where people would sit.

Suddenly several people appeared on the monitor screens. The men wore suits, and the two women were both power dressed. Tyler wondered whether they were from HR. Maybe they were all about to get fired? The whole setup was very corporate. On the monitors, they looked about life-size, and Tyler could hear little clicks and breathing sounds from the high-quality audio. If Tyler stretched out across the table, he felt as if he could touch them, although he noticed that two of them were in London and the other two in Cheltenham.

Marcus introduced the team and netted the story down. Tyler was quite impressed at Marcus, summarising such a complex chain of events into such a simple account.

Then Marcus added: "It's hard to see how this links to the explosions, but it is as if we have discovered something, written about it and then someone found out and is trying to flush us out. It isn't a protest or a warning; I'm pretty sure that someone is out to get us."

"So how does this fit with the facts?" asked one of the suited men on the call. He looked more operational, slightly scruffy with rolled-up sleeves and his tie at an angle.

"We can't fill in all of the gaps," answered Rosie, "But it looks as if the chance of discovery is something that they are annoyed about."

One of the suited men was typing something into a laptop. Tyler realised that he was communicating with the people present in the Cheltenham office.

"We don't have any hard proof about this," said the operational person. "We need to find someone directly involved."

Marcus nodded, "We think we may have such a person, but there's no way to corroborate what has been happening. The main person linking this together has disappeared."

Tyler wondered whether he should mention his conversation with Kyle. He decided not to say anything at this stage. Kyle could be a useful asset, but he didn't want him to be put off too early by the suits from SI6.

Tyler tried to work out who was in charge. It seemed impossible. He realised, suddenly, that no-one had a clue what had been happening.

"That meeting wasn't all that useful," said Marcus, as they left the room to go back to their own office.

"It felt more like an upload than anything, and even then, they didn't want our opinions colouring the situation.

They arrived, and almost immediately, Janice walked in. "Our team have found the first bomb van on the CCTV," she said. "We have managed to track it back to its origin and to follow the bombers."

She held up a photograph of the first incident along with what appeared to be some trace back photographs.

"The Americans call the use of vehicle bomb a form of poor man's cruise missile. We have a perfect example here."

She showed the van and then a couple of photographs of it in other parts of London.

"We've pretty good coverage, once we knew what we were looking for," she said. "And the vehicles were both parked for several minutes on double yellow lines right outside their targets."

"But we have to ask ourselves as well as what we got - the explosions - what didn't we get? Casualties - except for that single analyst who was outside of the first building. You'd expect the van drivers to have been caught up in it. But somehow the drivers managed to slip away. Look closely at these freeze frames. "

She held up the photograph from a traffic CCTV in the street.

"Can you see? It's indistinct, but there are some feet underneath or behind the van. Someone has climbed out and is getting ready to make off."

"But look, they don't reappear. Instead, we see a taxi has paused by the far side of the van. The van driver has climbed into the taxi."

"That wasn't a regular taxi. No, it was a planned pickup." Janice looked around the office for their reactions.

"Well, it certainly looks organised. Did we manage to get any other footage of the taxi?" asked Rosie.

"Yes, This later shot. We tracked the taxi for around ten minutes. It covered some ground pretty fast for Central London. Then you can see the passenger. He is wearing a hoodie and what looks like a tracksuit," answered Janice.

"It's a perfect disguise. Bland and anonymous. Also, the kind of clothing that could be shed easily, to change appearance," mused Rosie.

"Precisely," said Janice, "The taxi takes them to a store and drops them off. They go inside, and we pick them up again from the store cameras."

"Them?" said Tyler, "you mean there's more than one of them?"

"Two of them, they appear to be wearing scarves as well as hoodies," said Rosie. "Even those trainers look generic."

"The hoodies are baggy as well," said Marcus," But I think the taller one is a female?"

"Well spotted," said Janice, "Despite the low quality of some of the capture, we also thought that the movements of one were of an athletic man and the other of a woman."

"Do you think they wanted to be spotted?' asked Marcus, "I mean, they seem to have planned everything else?"

"I doubt it," said Janice, "We had to sift through acres of video to find these images. And you can rest assured that we've cross-checked it to make sure we don't have the wrong pictures pulled up."

"However, they were still using tradecraft to try to elude detection," continued Janice.

"They've gone to the clothes department, changed from their hoodies and reappeared looking respectable in casual clothing."

Janice continued, "They go to a back-exit from the store where they appear to pick up bicycles. You'd think with the number of cameras in use we'd still follow them easily enough."

"But of course, the cameras are trained to track number plates, so we don't know where the bikes have gone."

"That seems to be the end of the trail, although we do have some good quality pictures of them both in the store, after they had changed into their escape clothes."

Janice showed the final photographs. A tall, slender Mediterranean looking woman. A shorter bearded sub-Saharan African man, dark-haired and sturdy build, like he'd done weight training.

"IC2 woman and IC3 man," said Janice, "Game on."

Schmoonitary

Tyler had been looking through a massive database of possibly identifiable people. He had the two photographs of Persons of Interest that Janice had provided and was trying to match them.

It was soul-destroying work. The computer would ˙riffle through dozens to hundreds of images and then present a screenful of around 20 pictures to be individually scrutinised.

"Scrub genius, insert detection", he said," Detection is 99% perspiration and 1% inspiration."

He wondered whether his blood sugar was low because every so often he found himself glazing over while watching the screens. It was mind-numbingly dull to attempt this with so many incoming pictures to compare with just a couple of real targets.

Tyler knew that Kyle's security world contact meant that Kyle had access to Artificial Intelligence scanning software. He decided to pick Kyle's brains once more about the situation.

"Hey, Kyle! It's Tyler again!" he announced as Kyle picked up his mobile.

"Hiya Tyler," answered Kyle," I'm in Tel Aviv at the moment, at a security conference."

"Oh, I hope I'm not interrupting a meeting or anything?"

"Nope, it's fine. There's a lot of sneaky stuff in the pipeline. It should keep you guys busy for years! I've just been to a session on battlefield smart-dust."

"I'd expect no less," answered Tyler, "Look, I'd like to pick your brains again. This time it's about image recognition AI software."

"Chinese are best at that," said Kyle, "Although coincidentally, quite a lot of the work has been done here in Israel. Or that's what the local developers would have you believe.

"What is it you want to do? Basic facial recognition, I presume? Looking for a needle in a haystack?'

"Yes, that's right," answered Tyler. "I've got the high-res originals and am trying to find out who they are."

"Well, the Chinese through firms like Megvii, Sensetime, Cloudwalk and Yitu have made facial recognition commonplace in China. They tag all the faces, add attributes and then cross-index. If someone is found, they progressively get their background data augmented and also the number of hits that they receive."

"I knew you would have some suggestions to help me." Replied Tyler.

"It's not that simple," answered Kyle. "The database that you'll need and the compute power to process the imaging are both pretty awesome. China gets away with it because, well, it's a totalitarian state.

"You mean it's a unitary one-party socialist republic?" said Tyler.

"Unitary Schmoonitary, we all know it's a communist dictatorship," said Kyle.

"So, if I mention these bits of software to my friends in Cheltenham, there' a good chance they will know what I'm talking about?" asked Tyler.

"Oh yes, they will know," said Kyle," Although our other friendly cousins, the Americans, are highly nervous about using any of this stuff. Imagine letting Beijing-authored software into GCHQ or the Pentagon. It's Huawei times a thousand."

Kyle added, "You know if you could find something on the Approved Products Buyer's list, you'd have more of a chance. The only thing is, the Chinese have a deployment track record. They use this stuff all the time when they are managing street protests and tracking down agitators. I'm not saying it is on the right side, but it is advanced."

Tyler grimaced. He realised that he could get help from British approved products, but they would not be nearly as powerful as software already being used in China.

"You know," said Kyle," There might be another way..."

Kyle continued," There's a couple of things you could try. First, you'd need to find out if anyone in GCHQ has access to any of the Chinese AI search engines. I think I can confidently predict that the answer to this is 'No'. Even if they have access, they are not able to exploit it. They'll have it in a testing lab somewhere without any external links.

"It negates the purpose of the software, which trawls around the internet looking for connections," continued Kyle," Trust me, our security firm would know if this was being deployed. The other related point is that it would need a decent server farm to operate. Maybe a thousand servers for starters. Get my drift?"

Tyler considered. He'd ask Marcus also, in case there were yet more things he didn't know.

"Then," said Kyle," There's what we do...This isn't a plug for my company, you understand, because I'm trying to be helpful here. We'd look around for leverage."

"Leverage?" queried Tyler, "What kind?"

"Not financial, systemic," replied Kyle, "I'd ask a question like 'where can we get access to huge server farms, advanced algorithms and parameterised search?'"

"Go on," said Tyler, "I can only think of Google and similar."

"Precisely," said Kyle. There's reverse search in Google, "Image to picture identification, but it is massively dumbed down so that when you ask for pictures of daisies, it will present flowers."

"I know about that," said Tyler," I - ahem - used it when I split with Erica to cross-check what she'd been doing."

"Too much information," said Kyle. "Although in practice you'd probably find that the information you got was 'styled'?"

"Er, yes, it did seem to find leather jackets and handbags similar to the ones that Erica was wearing."

"Yes, that's because the search you use is tuned to a commercial setting. It's part of the Google business model. You may have been looking for Erica, but it would start to give you styled advertising after the first few search items had been returned. Now imagine if, instead of seeking handbags and sunglasses, it could look properly for faces."

"I can see this working, but also that it needs a couple of things."

"Yes, a different search method, that's where a Chinese-style AI would be useful and - here's the even more difficult part - access to a decent photo library of faces. "

"I think we might just have that in-house," answered Tyler.

"You do, it's just that you are not allowed to use it."

"Passport photos, driving licence, Border Controls, they all provide exactly the type of photo to be searched, hook up an AI facial recognition and some galumphing great servers, and you'll locate those people easily."

"Can I take this idea?" asked Tyler.

Kyle smiled as he answered," JASMOP - Just A Small Matter of Programming - It'll cost you copious beer the next time we meet. And hints that I could be useful in some kind of upcoming project."

"Gotcha," replied Tyler, "Expect to hear from me again soon!"

Go, Chiefs!

Thursday, and Tyler was in the office early again. Rosie and Marcus were already there. He'd think they were having some clandestine affair if he didn't already know that Rosie's partner Vanessa often met her from their old office after work.

He also thought that Marcus had never mentioned acquaintances either male or female ever since he had worked there. A very private man.

"Good morning!" Tyler smiled as he placed his bag onto the scruffy desk next to all of the high technology equipment. "I've had an idea about tracing those two from the van. Marcus, you'll know how much of this is possible…"

He went on to describe the process of marrying reverse searches with an AI system and a new database of faces. He described it as "like the Chinese system," and mentioned the various software that Kyle had described.

Rosie nodded," That's a good idea, using AI. You know something, I can call up James Harding at counterintelligence operations and find out what we can do."

Rosie and Tyler assumed the pose ready for a conference call. This was not going to be as elaborate as the board room meeting. It would be a series of faces displayed on their computer screens.

The system made a noise that Tyler likened to a burping goldfish and then suddenly a face appeared on the screens.

"Hey James, how are you doing? How are The Chiefs getting along?" Rosie smiled at the screen.

"Rosie, you're looking fabulous, good to see you, and who are these other fresh faces you've been playing with?"

"James - meet Marcus - My Boss - and Tyler - they are both fully cleared so that we can have a very straightforward conversation about my current challenge."

"Ah yes, something to do with all the pops and bangs around London?" asked James.

"That's right; we are trying to figure out who did it," said Rosie.

"Mr Plum with the lead pipe?" ventured James.

"That's what we wanted to talk to you about; less lead pipe and more chopsticks," said Marcus.

"Interesting. So, what do you think you need?"

Rosie said, "Chopsticks is a clue. Do you have access, by any chance, to Chinese AI Image recognition software?"

"Maybe..." said James cautiously, "...Precisely who is asking?"

"I need to run some deep AI recognition like the kind that China is using in the protest marches, for crowd identification."

"I could possibly assist with that," said James, "Does it have to be Chinese?"

"What do you mean?"

"Well, I have a lovely line in freshly baked British and American software that does the same kind of thing. And a way to run it.

"We've been using GCHQ in collaboration with the NSA to build our database. Amusingly, the general public is our greatest asset."

Marcus nodded," So it is true then? All that Deepface stuff?"

"Yes, and more, the selfies that people produce are most helpful towards building the database and even li'l ol' Facebook's AI-based facial recognition software is remarkably accurate."

Tyler questioned James, "But isn't this illegal?"

"It certainly is, up to State level. Beyond that, well, it becomes pretty essential as the building blocks for national security."

Tyler interrupted, "I take it all of this is Confidential?"

"Tyler, this is more than Confidential, this is TOP SECRET - we don't want anyone knowing that we have such capabilities. Imagine the stink and noise from the Daily Mail and Channel 4."

Tyler nodded. He realised this was unwittingly unleashing vast state power.

Rosie continued, "Great, now we don't need to put this into an email, but I'm about to send you a couple of decent resolution images of faces. It would be a great test of the capabilities of your system to see whether they can be identified."

"Okay - are they British? We have a more limited capability to trace non-nationals. Unless they have come into the country, of course. You'd better send the source files as well; in case we can pull anything extra from the binary.

"We seem to have a meeting of minds here," said Marcus. "And we'll owe you a team box at Sandy Park."

"Lovely to see you, you rascal, Rosie," said James, "Cheers."

"Cheers," echoed the others as the line went dead.

"What was that about Sandy Park boxes?" asked Tyler.

"James sounds quite keen on the Rugby. I guessed a VIP box at the Exeter Chiefs would be his idea of heaven," replied Marcus.

Dolly the Sheep

Friday morning, Tyler was awoken from sleep by the phone. It was Kyle.

"Hey man, I've been thinking. You know the thing about data centres? It could be that we've been thinking about this all wrong. Instead of it being something big that's being used to crunch the data, perhaps it's being done another way. Remember, in the old days when we used to use ordinary PCs for gaming? And we moved to the bigger and more dedicated devices so that we had enough power?

"Well, nowadays there's a massive amount of computing power available in the distributed Internet. I don't mean the Internet that everyone uses from their smartphones. I'm thinking about all the smaller permanently attached devices.

"For this to work at scale, there would need to be a well-distributed network of powerful computers to provide the mining. They would also need to appear to come from different geographies too, so that they did not trip any alerts when they were clearing such sums of money."

Tyler could see where Kyle was heading with this but let him continue. Armies of bots churning out cybercash. He didn't think it would work.

Kyle continued, "It got me thinking. Bot mining is like another universe waiting to be exploited. Then I thought of what other alternative universes could there be? It came to me. Just make the blockchains 'stand-alone' instead of part of what is already out there.

"So, I went through a couple of those transactions that you sent me from the memory stick and traced them back to the original blockchains.

"They were as difficult as any other to penetrate, but I could see that they had started from some different seed values. It's quite clever because they could still appear to be regular currency, but the base from which they are created is different."

"Like plausible fakes?" asked Tyler.

"Yes," said Kyle, "If this money were in use with other transactions, then it would soon be detected as different. Because there is such an extensive network of worldwide friendly repositories, then the money is in effect held in a separate condition where everything looks right.

"I guess we'd call it part of the dark matter used within the world of finance.

"The smart part is using a bank like the one you have been talking to, as a way to be able to turn these transactions back into some other form. In effect to launder the cyber coin back into some other currency.

"Ultimately, the bank is processing fake cyber coins, but it doesn't realise it, because the entire blockchain that has been created looks plausible.

"Doesn't realise it or is turning a blind eye?" asked Tyler.

"Could be but it's amazing how dumb the markets are. Aside from a few propeller heads, it's full of barrow-boy salespeople and their friends. Remember, when people shorted the money markets with sub-prime mortgages packaged up to look respectable? It's a similar idea. Dress the blockchain up to look presentable, and plenty of people will trade it, especially at an advantageous rate. Hey, Dolly the sheep looked real enough."

"I suppose the secret is not to make it look too good to be true`?" asked Tyler.

"Exactly," said Kyle, "That would be a giveaway. It makes complex derivatives a brilliant suggestion because, to be honest, hardly anyone understands how they work. It's like putting a recognisable envelope around this kind of misty transaction.

Kyle was getting quite excited now, "There's no reason they couldn't be quite a few versions of this in use at the same time.

"The only thing that would blow it is if too much cybercash appeared and all of a sudden, the whole financial network was swamped with surprising amounts of suspicious liquidity.

"Whoever is running this has been quite clever because they have limited the flow to just the amount needed to stabilise the Russian currency.

I asked Kyle, "So can you prove any of this?"

"I've only got those sample transactions at the moment," he said. "The ones on that stick you got from your girlfriend."

"My ex," corrected Tyler," Erica is my ex-girlfriend."

Kyle coughed, "Well, look, if I had more transactions and some help then perhaps I could dig further into this and we may be able to track down how it's generated. And where it goes after it has been generated."

"Okay," said Tyler. "I think your days as a consultant for the government are just about to start. You'd better sharpen your estimating pencil."

"Even better would be to penetrate the bank system and get our own snooper device plugged in?" suggested Kyle.

"Yes, just like in Mission Impossible. I'll order the suction cups and wires."

Tyler noticed the note of enthusiasm in Kyle's voice. He thought about the difficult conversations ahead.

Hotel

Friday, and Tyler was surprised. For yet another day, Rosie and Marcus had been in the office when he arrived. And he had been progressively starting earlier each day.

"Rosie?" He asked," How on earth are you getting in so early? I thought you had the longest commute."

"That's right, I do. But I thought Marcus told you? Now we're on this special assignment we are staying in the hotel across the road. It's a lot more convenient with these long hours. And we get some level of security included too."

Tyler immediately thought of soft linen and minibars.

"I've been schlepping my way back to my flat and all the time you are staying a couple of minutes away. And it looks like quite a nice hotel too?"

"Oh, it is," answered Rosie, smiling.

Marcus had reappeared and been listening. "Sorry, Tyler, but it's for people who are grade 7 and above," said Marcus. "Rosie and I both qualify, but I'm afraid you're still too junior."

Tyler groaned. "What, even if I am the potential target?" he muttered.

Tyler noticed that Marcus and Rosie were both holding a similar sheet of paper.

"You jest," said Marcus, 'But we're the ones who are being threatened."

"Why, what's happened?" Tyler said, looking worried.

"Yes," said Rosie, "Fresh threats through the post."

"But I thought we were already threatened?" Tyler said. "…Surely those threats were pretty much as bad as it can get?"

"Take a look at this," said Rosie, waving the paper towards Tyler.

Tyler took the paper, which looked like a letter to Rosie from the hotel management. One of those letters that gets pushed under the door when it's nearly time to check out.

Instead, this was a message addressed to Rosie, which said, "Leave it alone." It was signed by the hotel manager.

Tyler looked worried.

Rosie explained that both she and Marcus had received one of the notes but had thought it was some bad taste practical joke from one of the other teams staying in the same hotel.

Evidently, this was a warning to show they knew who Marcus and Rosie were. And that they didn't like the work conducted by the Department.

"So," Tyler asked." Are we about to move to yet another location?" He wondered if this would give a chance to get a hotel room for him as well.

"So far I've asked security to look into this for us. At the moment we are upping the security for the hotel. It's something done routinely with that hotel in any case."

"We now have our floor and the ones adjacent secured as well as some of our people guarding the whole location," said Marcus. "Even our hotel access keys have been re-coded ."

"It's like the security we have here?" Tyler asked.

"That's right," said Rosie, "Except our guys in the hotel are not wearing uniforms…Yet."

Colder War

Afternoon and the TV news in the office showed pictures from Turkey. Marcus looked up at Matt and Rosie.

"You'll have seen it in the news; there's quite some activity between Turkey and its near neighbours. These are possible examples of The Colder War in play.

"I've picked up on some possible Turkish moves that could be made by Russia."

"This is since the elections, and the USA decided to get all huffy with Turkey?" asked Rosie.

"Yes. The Russian courtship of Turkey has already involved the Russians moving away from the construction of the South Stream natural gas pipeline from Russia across the Black Sea to Bulgaria.

"When Putin cancelled the South Stream project, he replaced it with a natural gas pipeline that goes across the Black Sea to Turkey from the Russian Federation's South Federal District. It makes a desirable option for Turkey."

"Turk Stream with Russian energy giant Gazprom can link with Turkey's Botas. Moreover, Gazprom will start giving Turkey discounts in the purchase of Russian natural gas that will increase with the intensification of Russo-Turkish cooperation."

"That would give Russia oil and gas access to the EU and supply balancing via the Turks?" queried Tyler. "It's quite clever and low risk for Russia as long as Turkey is allowed to remain stable.

"Of course, they would need a tame banker to broker such a significant situation. They would need someone who can be a free agent but is well-linked to major banking players. It could be incredibly lucrative for such a player.

"Yes," said Rosie, "and that might be a lead?"

"Ordinarily I'd agree," said Marcus, "but the sheer amount of money that Russia can now generate means it has stumbled across a way to keep Turkey on-side, based upon an ongoing series of well-placed payments."

"Bribes?" asked Tyler.

"Exactly," said Marcus, "Although they are 'easy to generate' bribes in the sense that Russia can order the money from the cyber fraud."

Rosie added, "So this deal between Ankara and Moscow creates a win-win situation for both the Turkish and Russian sides?"

Marcus continued, "Not only will Ankara get a discount on energy supplies, but Turk Stream gives the Turkish government what it has wanted for years. The Turk Stream pipeline will make Turkey an important energy corridor and transit point, complete with transit revenues. It's like a legitimate Silk Road.

"Legitimate only in the sense that the Russian currency input can't be detected," said Rosie.

"In this case, Turkey becomes the corridor between energy supplier Russia and the European Union and non-EU energy customers in south-eastern Europe. It's brilliant," said Tyler.

"That will surely piss off the Americans, particularly as it becomes a near-neighbour supplier to the middle-east? Come to think of it; Turkey can also position itself as part of the middle east when it wants to."

"Yes," said Marcus, "Turkey can be Middle Eastern, European or Russian tinged, as it sees fit. Not a bad puppet for Russia to be able to manipulate."

Rosie nodded, "So then Ankara gains some new leverage over the European Union and has an extra negotiating card with the EU too because the EU will have to deal with it as an energy broker."

Marcus continued, "Yes, so accidentally, the US Colder War policies are creating a whole new set of advantageous plays for Russia."

"It only works because of the cyber currency," said Tyler, "Without that, the whole situation could look very different."

"I agree," said Marcus, "but right now, Russia has been on a spending spree to de-risk its pipeline building. Moscow could have wasted resources and time building the South Stream to see the project sanctioned or obstructed in the Balkans by Washington and Brussels."

"If the European Union wants Russian natural gas, then the Turk Stream pipeline can be expanded from Turkey to Greece, and also to other European countries that want integration into the energy project. It positions Russia as an interesting player in the region."

"Interesting," said Tyler, "I can think of a few other words!"

"The cancellation of South Stream also means that there will be one less energy corridor from Russia to the European Union for some time.

"This boosts chances of a settlement in Ukraine, which is an important transit route for Russian natural gas to the European Union. Inevitably the European Union will want to push the authorities in Kyiv to end the conflict in East Ukraine."

"Turk Stream and the strengthening of Russo-Turkish ties may even help placate the gory conflict in Syria," said Marcus, looking grim-faced.

"If Iranian natural gas is integrated into the mainstream of Turk Stream through another energy corridor entering Anatolia from Iranian territory, then Turkish interests would be even more tightly aligned with both Moscow and Tehran."

"This is what Russia wants and sticks it to the USA," said Tyler.

"Yes, and someone gets very rich on the skimmings," said Rosie. "I'm sure this could be a lead."

Marcus nodded," A characteristic of a liberated totalitarian country is the rise in illicit payments and the sudden increase in wealth of a few well-placed individuals with access to power. There's a lot of ex-State civil servants who are nowadays oligarchs."

Marcus continued, "Turkey has already been on a tightrope over some aspects of the Syrian conflict. Ankara has had to craft an understanding with both Russia and Iran not to let politics and their differences over the Syrian crisis get in the way of their economic ties and business relationships.

"At the same time, Washington has tried to disrupt Irano-Turkish and Russo-Turkish trade and energy ties like it has disrupted trade ties between Russia and the EU."

"What, diplomatically?" asked Tyler.

"Not just diplomatically," there was also the assassination of the Turkish Trade Minister in Paris a few weeks ago. That threw a massive spanner in the works," answered Marcus, "I even wondered if America was trying to heat that particular discord."

"So, the Russian State appears to be making a grab for oil rights and at the same time using fake money to prop up the rouble. And it is using cyber cheats to achieve it?" asked Tyler.

"That's what it looks like," answered Marcus.

Evaluation

I want to stand as close to the edge as I can without going over.

Out on the edge you see all the kinds of things you can't see from the centre.

— *Kurt Vonnegut*

Blockchains

They were in the Raglan.

It was a pub close to their original office. Rosie was to meet a slightly peeved Vanessa to tell her that she would be away for a while longer. She'd asked Tyler to come along to verify the situation to Vanessa and to try to keep it light-hearted.

They'd been waiting half an hour, and Tyler was buying the second round. He sat down at the well-used brown table. "Cider and a pint of Doom Bar," he said.

"So come on," said Rosie," Tell me about blockchains. I know the general theory that they are used in making e-cash, but you'll have to explain it."

Tyler smiled as he remembered his own lack of knowledge when he started working with Matt, from around the time that Matt brought the first little computer into the flat.

"The blockchain is an ingenious invention. A way to safeguard large amounts of cyber-money," answered Tyler.

"Blockchain was devised for digital currency and micro-payments, but nowadays, the technical community has found other potential uses."

"And this is relevant to the Russians how?" asked Rosie.

"I'll come to that. Think of the blockchain as an incorruptible digital ledger of economic transactions that can be programmed to record not just financial transactions but virtually anything of value."

Rosie clinked their glasses together. Tyler sipped his drink.

"In the simplest of terms, the blockchain is a time-stamped series of records of data that are managed by clusters of computers not owned by any single entity."

"No one owns it?" asked Rosie, "What about the Russians, then?"

"Just a minute, let me finish. Now each of these blocks of data (i.e. block) are secured and bound to each other using cryptographic principles (i.e. chain)."

"I see," said Rosie, the blocks are linked together by chains, using secret codes?"

"Kinda, yes," said Tyler, "But the 'secret' is public.

"Unlike a bank, with its central governance, these blockchain networks have no central authority.

"Now the part about the Russians. Unlike the secrecy of a bank's hidden ledgers, this is a very open system. It is a shared and immutable ledger; the information in it is open for anyone and everyone to see."

"Ahah," said Rosie, "One of those examples where its strength becomes its weakness?"

"Exactly," smiled Tyler, "Anything built on the blockchain is by its very nature transparent, and everyone involved is accountable for their actions. It plays directly to an unscrupulous state actor advantage."

"You see, falsifying a single record would mean forging the entire chain in millions of instances. That has been considered virtually impossible.

"Not if you are a government?" questioned Rosie.

"Yes, perhaps, or a vast company spanning many locations," answered Tyler.

"You see, the blockchain infrastructure carries with it a cost, but the transaction cost is, essentially free. That's how the information is passed from A to B in a fully automated and safe manner.

"It's who bears the infrastructure cost that becomes an interesting question, and how they hold everything secure."

"I see," said Rosie, "There's an angle on this."

"Yes," nodded Tyler, "Especially as the system moved away from micropayments."

"It was one thing to handle five-dollar micropayments for listening to a pop album or reading a book, but by the law of unintended consequences, very soon these payments aggregate.

"I see - Vast piles of $5 bills under the bed?" asked Rosie.

"Precisely," said Tyler, and not only that, the e-cash created became a tradable currency too. Through speculation, the $5 bills became worth $10 and more very quickly."

"Take Bitcoin. They started with a strike value of $13.50. They're worth over $10,000 now and peaked in 2017 at around $19,000. They are more than $5 bills under the bed now. They've turned into gold bars."

"So, no prizes for guessing that others would soon be taking a look?" asked Rosie.

"That's how I first got involved. We were speculating on the ability to create a new cyber coin and then to cash it in," said Tyler. "We wanted to make them and then turn them into real money.

"Here's how it works: one party to a transaction initiates the process by creating a block. This block is verified by thousands, perhaps millions of computers distributed around the net.

"See, that's where the big infrastructure is required. And the verification can be regarded as a 'black box' too. Ideal for someone unscrupulous.

"But let's see what would usually happen. The verified block comes out of the 'black box' and gets added to a chain. That chain is stored across the net, creating not just a unique record, but a unique record with a unique history."

"Hmm, Vanessa must have been delayed," said Rosie, looking at her watch, "Hey and thanks for coming along, you'll know when to leave, okay?"

"Sure Rosie, it's the least I could do, and let's face it, drinks with two lovely ladies, what's not to like? Let's see, where was I?" Tyler continued,

"Cybercash collapses the market-maker models that some of the high tech startups have enjoyed. Music, books, and so on can include micro keys that are flipped and will release payments to the music maker or the author. Such a technology would disrupt even Amazon and Alibaba. The micropayments go straight to the originator. That's why Facebook joined the party."

"But even if the original idea started that way, there are more basic forces at play."

"Take the financial world: The uses become more apparent.

Blockchains can change the way stock exchanges work, the way that loans get bundled, and the way that insurances are contracted.

"All of this legitimises the cybercash. Instead of it being something that only gamblers and nerds use, it suddenly has an economic value.

"Instead of gatekeepers, bankers will become advisers. Stockbrokers will no longer be able to earn commissions, and the buy/sell spread will disappear."

"Yes, but what has this to do with the current Russian situation?" asked Rosie.

"Well, think of the blockchain sequence as a pile of money. Quite a large pile in each sequence generated. Imagine if this fell into the hands of organised crime. Imagine if it fell into the hands of organised state crime..."

There was a scraping of chairs. Vanessa arrived and briefly hugged Rosie.

"Woman of mystery, what's happening now?" she asked, and she turned to Tyler, smiled and said, "Hello, and you must be Tyler! Lovely to meet you!"

"Let me get your drink," said Tyler as he rose and gestured towards the bar. "G and T, please," said Vanessa, "ice and a slice of lime."

"Coming up!"

Tyler made his way to the bar. He could see that Rosie was trying to explain her absence to Vanessa. He decided that he'd show the travel arrangements inconvenienced him even more as a way to show Vanessa that everyone was in the same boat.

Tracking

Janice tapped on the door of their office and walked in. She looked to Tyler like a TV presenter, perfectly groomed and always on top of her game. He noticed the way she smiled towards him but could then zone him out while she was talking to Marcus and Rosie.

"Hi Marcus, we've been following the drivers of the second van."

"We know they may be proxy drivers, of course, put up to the job without realising what they were doing.

"We need a lucky break on this somewhere now," said Rosie.

Janice nodded, "Yes, both of the trails to the individual bombings go cold although the style in each case is similar. They drive the vans to the outside of the building.

Tyler remembered, talking to Janice once, that she was a details person. She'd told him a story about something that had happened the previous day when Janice had visited an aunt in Southwark. The story was banal enough, but Tyler remembered that Janice held the detail and described the minutia with such a passion that he could see how she'd got the job in C-SOC.

"They park the vans, conveniently in one case on double yellows. and in the other case in a restricted area.

"The drivers slip out of the cabs and are picked up by a taxi almost immediately. It looks as if the driver of the taxi was part of the escape process. There also seems to be another woman passenger in the cab both times.

"What about smartphone footage?" asked Rosie.

"Nothing useable, you'd expect there would be some, but it's all from after the explosions and filmed from quite a safe distance. Amazing really that there are so many smartphones taking selfies but then when something dramatic happens it melts down to a couple of shaky hand-helds.

"You'd think with all the fixed cameras in London that we'd be able to pick them up easily enough. We've got footage of the aftermath of both bombs, but nothing aside from traffic cameras that track the time before.

"Then, when they jump into taxis, it goes cold. There's not much interest from anyone in filming taxi passengers.

"What about in-cab footage?" asked Rosie

"No, both times the taxi was running on false plates. They were clones of other taxis, designed to get through the ANPR without tripping any alerts. They used a couple of cab identities from Upminster which would be parked outside of the camera zones."

"We think they have ditched the cab somewhere and changed appearance again. It smacks of a slightly too easy trail at this point."

"What, like they wanted to be followed?" asked Tyler.

"No, more the idea that if we tracked them, then they would give us something tangible to track," said Janice.

Janice continued," However, the good news is that we traced the woman accomplice. She was present on both occasions with the drivers as they were ferried away by taxi.

"I assume the taxi had false plates?" asked Rosie.

"Yes, it did," replied Janice, "Although we could trace the false number plates in any case. Guess where the second car went?"

"An embassy, maybe?" asked Marcus.

"Marcus, the genius! Yes," said Janet, "Although not what you might expect. It went to the Chinese embassy."

"Can I take a look at the photographs we have of the suspect?" asked Marcus. "Are there any hints that he or she could be Chinese?"

Janice shook her head, "No. There was nothing that gives any real information about the actual suspect, Just the ability that we have to track movements. It corroborates with the first cab when we identified the IC2 woman.

"Look, here's the video footage of the suspect car on its way to the embassy."

She flicked video footage onto the screen behind Tyler's head. He moved around to see it more easily. First, there was a car moving away from a car park. It looked like the parking lot inside Battersea Park, close to the Zen temple.

"Not even an underground car park?" asked Tyler.

"No, I suppose the advantage of the Battersea one was the speed of swap-over and multiple park exits. It does assume that there was only one getaway car also," said Janice.

The footage flipped through a few cameras. Across Chelsea Bridge, towards Sloane Square, then Sloane Street, past some other embassies, into Pall Mall, towards Marble Arch and then a turn inwards to the east and toward the Chinese Embassy, after a couple of small zig-zags. It was a fairly direct route, the sort that an experienced London driver would take to avoid some of the traffic hot spots, while still being direct.

The car appeared to go into another car park close to the Chinese embassy.

"It looks pretty clear cut," said Janice. "They've taken the suspect to a place of diplomatic immunity."

"Which bomb is this?" asked Rosie, "Is it the second one? We had a route via a hotel flagged up for the first one. This route seems different?"

Marcus was looking at the route. "It's a good route, and there's hardly any traffic hold-ups," he said.

"Except around Belgravia. Look at the section by the outside of The Lanesborough Hotel."

Janice rewound the video, and they could see a brief hold-up in the traffic moving towards the busy Hyde park corner junction. Despite the driver's best efforts, there had been a short delay at that point.

"Look," said Rosie. "It's just like the other one. While they stop, someone gets out of the car on the kerbside. They are going into the back entrance of the hotel."

They looked at the footage. It was from a TfL camera on the roadside of the car. Tyler could make out the movement that Rosie spotted. The passenger and another person had left the car and moved across to the hotel in moments.

Janice looked, "We missed it," she said. "Damn, we've all been following the car to the endpoint, expecting one destination and then being surprised by the other. So, is he or she stashed away in the hotel, I wonder?"

"I doubt it," said Rosie, "I think the two of them will move on as quickly as possible- like in the first sequence. We'll need to get some footage from the hotel now to try to work out what has happened."

"The Lanesborough also has an entrance around the other side, onto Knightsbridge," said Marcus. "It would make an obvious way to switch to another vehicle and then plan a different route."

Janice nodded. "We are already following up with the Chinese Embassy, although you can imagine the diplomatic complications involved. We don't want to be accusing them of planting bombs in London."

"It's a great diversion," said Marcus, "getting us to follow a wrong trail, particularly when it creates such a lot of diplomatic ripples."

Janice nodded. "Of course, we will need to continue with that line of enquiry. If nothing else, we don't want them to realise that we may have discovered something. Meantime we'd better now examine the Lanesborough for any footage."

Marcus nodded his agreement. "I think we also need to check the rest of the route back again, he said. If they've pulled this stunt here, they may have done it at some other point. I noticed that the driver's route went directly past about half a dozen other embassies.

"I agree," said Rosie, "although I think the most noticeable stop of the car was outside the Lanesborough. Also, the embassy squares like around Belgravia are completely plastered with cameras so it would be harder to pull the same stunt."

"Marcus is right though; we need to look out for any other signs of an exit from the car. Mostly the car was moving, and the route is generally well exposed for good camera coverage. The Lanesborough is a clever spot because of the almost continuous traffic jams along that part of the route."

Tyler knew it would take another couple of hours to get the video footage from the hotel. Someone would be dispatched to get it and bring back as much as possible to be analysed.

"We'll need to see the exit from the hotel now and then need to follow to another location."

They all knew how difficult this would get if the suspect had left via another exit and then melted into the crowd.

Driscoll's Interview

"Three-Two-One."

"Good Morning continues now with a Live Interview with Gerald Driscoll, Minister for Internal Affairs.

"Thank you, Mr Driscoll, for joining us live on this politics section of Good Morning.

Driscoll sat, suited and wearing a blue tie. He thought himself the very model of a prominent minister and would not be caught off guard by these media types.

Driscoll replied, "Good Morning."

"Mr Driscoll, you have said you are not happy with current security measures deployed in the protection of the United Kingdom. That is like admitting you carry responsibility for the roles, while also indicating a need for fundamental change.

"I'm pleased to report, as I'm sure you know, that no-one was killed in what amounts to two terrorist bombings at central London locations."

"Mr Driscoll, we've seen two bombings, both seemingly with vans used to deliver the payload, at different locations within a couple of miles of one another and both within Central

London.

"Do you have some comments on the current situation?"

"Well, first of all, let me say at a personal level that my heart reaches out to each and every one of the people affected by these two terrible attacks on the fabric of London. We are working now with the Met Police, City of London police, military and other security services to both identify the perpetrators of these outrages and also to instigate further steps to secure ourselves against further attacks, or indeed any worsening of the situation."

"Well, Mr Driscoll, you were heard to say at your recent party conference that the current security service was too fragmented and that you would be instituting some reforms. Is it now a case of too little or too late?"

"What I said at the conference was part of the broader debate about changes to the ways that we need to operate the Ministry for Internal Affairs and the related security. It is part of the healthy party debate that we will always run to define the next stage of our government's direction on important matters."

"But you said that the security service was too fragmented. Isn't this another sign of that? There was no prior warning, nor do we know with any certainty who has placed these two bombs in Central London."

"The broader debate is continuing. The recent disruption to our two offices emphasises the need for further action," Driscoll realised he had let a cat from the bag.

"Your offices? Are you saying that the bombs were at your own offices? The reports say that the offices were smaller central London buildings?"

"I'm not able to comment on the specifics of the buildings concerned. It is not appropriate to examine this line of discussion.

"But Mr Driscoll, you appear to be saying that the attacks were not, as previously thought in the press, at some general and non-specific locations, but indeed were at your own buildings in Central London."

"As I have already said, I cannot comment on the specifics nor the occupants of the buildings in question."

"We already know that the security services have a major headquarters on either side of the River Thames, including famously the building at Vauxhall Cross. You appear to now be indicating that in addition to the two buildings, plus the entirety of the GCHQ operation in Cheltenham, that you also have further offices throughout London. Is this a symptom of the fragmentation you have referred to in your recent speeches?"

Driscoll's beads of sweat were being picked up under the studio lights.

"I cannot comment on the specifics of the security services and their use of properties within London and beyond. Suffice to say that we are examining all options for future reorganisation."

"Isn't it a bit late to be making these kinds of statements? We've just seen two big explosions in one of the major capitals of the world, yet so far, no trace of who is responsible. What concrete steps are you taking to capture the perpetrators?"

"We are examining the evidence from the two bombs. They both used a small amount of high explosive, and in both cases, the vehicle used was driven to the outside of the target and then detonated remotely.

"I think most of your viewers will have seen the outcome from the numerous television and other media reports."

"What else can you add to the information about what has

happened, and the steps taken to investigate? For instance, do we consider this terror-related?"

"I'm sure you will understand that a matter such as this is very sensitive. I cannot divulge information during a sensitive stage of an ongoing investigation."

"Mr Driscoll, so what exactly can you divulge at this stage?"

"I can state that we will take swift action to neutralise terrorists rather than to simply deploy cordons around incidents. I have already instructed for the deployment of special forces to take necessary actions against any future situations."

"Mr Driscoll, the question remains how you will know where to take these swift actions? It does not look as if your advanced monitoring is providing any advanced warning of events?"

"We are stepping up the monitoring of suspected terrorist activities. We will be stringently enforcing the ring of steel around the City, for example."

"This all sounds very well, but isn't it a case of closing the stable door after the horse has bolted?"

"We have a wide range of countermeasures at our disposal. I am not able to discuss operational matters with you at this time. Let me remind you that the UK has thwarted seven major plots so far this year, although most of them are also too sensitive to be exposed to general media."

"Mr Driscoll, with everything you are saying shrouded in such mystery I'm not sure that we quite know what to believe. You seem to be telling us that there have been seven plots this year including the latest which appears to be attacking your own clandestine operations. Is this providing a good role model for security services?"

"As I've said, we are taking active measures to manage and prevent any further expansion of the current terrorist activities.

I cannot say more because of operational sensitivities."

"Will that include heightened proactivity on the streets? Mr Driscoll? Will this include further escalation – for example the use of armed force on London streets?"

"I'm always committed to operating within the existing law, that means that any armed action by the police has to be proportionate to the threat. That is always the test put when it comes to any incident when police apprehend anyone."

"Mr Driscoll, surely that stops short of proactively stopping anyone in the act of a terrorist atrocity? It sounds as if you are not prepared to go as far as a shoot-to-kill policy?"

"I'm not happy with a shoot-to-kill policy in general – I think that is quite dangerous and can often be counterproductive. We need security that prevents people from firing off weapons, where they can. There are various degrees of doing things as we know, but the idea you end up with a war on the streets is not a good thing. Surely you have to work to try to prevent these things happening, that has to be the priority. We cannot reap a whirlwind from ill-judged actions."

Marcus and Rosie had been watching the interview.

Rosie winced at the last remarks.

"So, what is he allowed to discuss? It looks as if he is dancing to avoid answering any questions," continued Rosie.

"Yes, that's right," said Marcus. "There'll be a soundbite with 'whirlwind' and 'ill-judged' in it. I think his approach gives our department a bad name."

I sometimes think that's what he wants," added Rosie, '…and shoot to kill from the police.' He didn't have to rise to that bait."

"Wait until the news slot," said Rosie, " I doubt whether any of us will come out if it well."

Amanda Miller

Amanda Miller had been called for a meeting with Bernard Driscoll. She had seen his lame interview featured on the evening news. "Shoot-to-kill, reap the whirlwind, ill-judged…" So much for media training.

She hated the annoyance of him calling her across the river from SI6 to meet him in Westminster Place. He was an arrogant bully usually, and this was the kind of thing he would do in the middle of a critical operation to show his importance.

Amanda had taken one of the company cars with a driver to get to Westminster Place. It had taken her across Vauxhall Bridge and then along the north bank of the Embankment towards Westminster Place.

It was one of those buildings that had secret tunnels underneath that lead in various directions. It included a tunnel across the road to Parliament and another route that went all the way to Downing Street.

Amanda assumed that Bernard Driscoll would be in an imposing room with his back to a big screen probably with a couple of flags and other paraphernalia to emphasise his importance.

Driscoll was an inept man but made up for it with puffery.

Amanda Miller knew her way around most of the corridors within Westminster and had previously needed to use them on several occasions as part of high alert situations.

This time it was different. Although Amanda had been called across, it was not clear what the purpose of the specific meeting would be.

Driscoll wanted a private meeting and not with his usual entourage of hangers-on involved.

Amanda approached one of the entrance areas to the meetings complex tunnel system.

"Ms. Miller," said the receptionist. "Are you ready?"

The receptionist smiled towards Amanda although still went through the formality of requesting her pass card.

"Look to the camera, ooh, I like that scarf," she added as she handed the photo pass back and an additional lanyard badge with her photo, a green stripe and GD-V3 printed on it in a large typeface.

Amanda was not affronted by this standard protocol when there was a heightened situation. She dropped the lanyard over her neck and stuffed the scarf into her bag.

She had already been through the metal detectors and glass turnstiles on the way into the building.

"I'll see if Mr Driscoll is ready for you," said the receptionist.

Amanda knew that the receptionist did not mean anything by this, but she still felt that Driscoll would probably take some time on purpose just to show his self-importance when they were due to meet.

Amanda had worked in other countries where there was

sometimes a kind of protocol that you would need to wait longer for more important people; It was their way of showing their self-importance. She knew better than to try to protest about this and prepared herself for a long wait.

Amanda knew the clock was ticking on the alert, but there was little she could do until after the meeting with Bernard Driscoll.

To her surprise, Bernard Driscoll came out of the door behind the receptionist.

"Our Miss Miller," he said, "Thank you for coming along here to meet me."

"There is something I would like to discuss with you that is very sensitive."

"I think we may want to take a short walk outside while I discuss this with you," he said.

Amanda Miller knew that the area that covered the reception and probably most of the meeting rooms incorporated full closed-circuit television and microphone monitoring.

"It's quite cold outside," she said, "But we could go for a walk along Parliament Street."

She reached back into her bag for the scarf.

Amanda knew that Parliament Street was well-stocked with video cameras. Still, there would be no sound recording except directly outside of Downing Street and the adjacent buildings on the west side of the street.

"I thought it would be better to take a walk towards Westminster Bridge," said Driscoll. "I can then also get some more cigarettes."

"They made their way from the building and into the busy street."

Amanda's car and driver waited in the underground car park close to Parliament.

She could call it back within a couple of minutes but still had to go through this theatre with Driscoll first.

"Oh," said Amanda, "Why the private meeting?"

"It's a disaster," said Driscoll, "this whole bomb thing is a disaster. I have the entire Ministry for internal security, the offices at SI six, MI5, GCHQ, and the special departments we set up, yet we don't seem to be able to prevent bomb attempts in central London."

"This is on you, Amanda," he continued.

"The Prime Minister called me in today and said this needed to be brought to a swift conclusion."

Amanda could sense that the shit was already travelling downhill.

The Prime Minister will have given Bernard Driscoll a grilling about all of this. Now it was his turn to start to look for a scapegoat. She knew what he would be saying next, well approximately what he would be saying next.

"I take it that everyone is already working on this?" Driscoll asked.

"Yet we don't seem to be any closer to even identifying who has delivered the bombs that have blown up outside two of our security offices?" he said.

"As London goes about its business today, it is more reminiscent of the old days when there were Irish terrorists planting bombs around London.

"This is bad for everyone."

Amanda decided to let him continue to vent. She was sure he would be coming to some point sooner or later.

"Fortunately for us, no members of the public have been killed in these attacks so far.

"Although the very act of setting off explosives in the high-profile parts of central London is bad for all kinds of reasons.

"We get bad press coverage everywhere, and we also look ineffective against this kind of attack.

Amanda mused, "No, this is on you," but she held the thought.

"We also have a huge budget for internal security, including the various agencies I've already mentioned.

"I'm going to need someone to serve up over this." he said," I think it will need to be those new departments we created.

"I need you to work on two things now," he said.

Amanda thought to herself, "he is about to get to the point."

She could see he was almost quivering with a sort of internal rage. It must be very uncomfortable to be Bernard Driscoll. A puffed-up politician with no real idea of what is going on. Only the ability to huff and puff as a way to try to resolve anything.

She mused at the incongruity of the two of them walking along the street together. She was, tall, svelte and toned, next to a round blob of a man, with just too much power. The Peter Principle personified.

"Of course," said Amanda, "I will see what I can do to expedite this investigation. You are welcome to come along to our control centre to see this properly," she said.

She knew she was slightly bluffing with this because although they did have the major incident room, so far that was little to show apart from the locations of the two bombs and the incoming claims against the bombs from very dubious sources.

It was uncharacteristic. Usually, there was a flurry of people wishing to claim a connection to bombing attacks even when they had nothing to do with them.

"Look," said Amanda, "I know you didn't bring me over here to give you a standard debriefing. And the fact we are now walking along towards the River Thames tells me that you want this to be quiet."

She didn't add her thought," and you want to do this in a way that you can threaten me without being on camera."

"That's right," said the Driscoll," They need this tied up, suspects identified and apprehended as well as internal people identified for removal."

Amanda looked towards Driscoll; he was trying to make sure that he dodged all of the blame. She also knew that he would have no reservations about landing her in the problem if he couldn't find anyone else.

"It's simple really," he said, "After you've sorted out the suspects, I want you to find a group to close down. I can't directly tell you to close the new departments, but I think this is the area which is of least use to us."

"The whole point about those small departments was that they were able to act autonomously away from the big processes that we run in the mainstream unit," said Amanda, "They are the equivalent in security terms of start-up organisations."

"That may be so," said Driscoll," but we need a much firmer command and control system operating. I can't have these little units running loose and still not delivering for us.

"Okay," he said, "Here is my shop to get some cigarettes. I think

I can take it from here."

Amanda realised that the meeting with Driscoll was over. He was as bad as ever; all he wanted was that someone else was to take the blame for the bombs and the lack of intelligence ahead of their detonation. He needed a scapegoat, and he also wanted to bluster his way towards a resolution of the situation.

Driscoll provided no real help, suggestions, or anything practical, just the typical bullying expected from him.

"Goodbye, then," said Amanda as she turned back towards Parliament. Driscoll continued into the shop, oblivious. Amanda reached into her pocket to her phone which she'd picked up on the way out from the office. The recording was still running.

She pressed a button on the phone and called through to her driver. As she walked back to Parliament Square, her driver parked outside the Houses of Parliament next to a couple of police officers. One of them opened the door for her as she climbed into the car.

False

"Back to the office?" Asked the driver.

Amanda considered. "No, I think we'll go to Earls Court instead."

Amanda decided that it would be prudent to visit Jim and his team at their relocated department offices. She had known Jim for many years. They had both been through a range of operational duties, and their paths had crossed many times.

Jim reminded Amanda of what a secret agent would look like if he were eventually retired from active service. Fit, alert and intelligent, he had been given the C-SOC Department to run when he transferred from Vienna, where he had run the small field station.

Jim had worked in other operational zones including the Paris and the Berlin offices. Amanda had been further afield mainly into South America. They had both seen their share of active service during their time although Amanda's was a more apparent high-profile situation based upon the type of characters in the various South American countries where she had operated.

It was primarily a matter of fate that Jim had been moved into the start-up of a new Department while Amanda benefitted from affirmative action to rise through the ranks inside SI6 and was now several grades his senior.

Jim and Amanda got on well and could usually read one another.

On this occasion, she thought that she could visit Jim ostensibly to offer some comradely support while they were going through the difficulties of trying to track down the bombers.

She smiled inwardly as she remembered Jim's old nickname, that of Jimbo. It was better than the one he'd had when they worked together in Berlin.

Of course, there she had another agenda as well, which involved the rather unsavoury request from Bernard Driscoll.

If ever anyone needed a nickname, it was Driscoll.

Amanda decided it would be easiest to explain Driscoll's blame game directly to Jim.

"Do you want me to call ahead?" Asked the driver.

"No, that won't be necessary." Said Amanda. She would enter unannounced, and it would add a certain frisson to the situation at the Department.

Sometimes a little theatre was a good thing.

She knew this would make no difference to Jim, who was equally wise to such manoeuvres, but it would make a difference to some of the staff to see her arrive and go directly to Jim's office.

Once inside the building, Amanda was taken directly to Jim. She wore her recently issued Parliament lanyard as she walked through the outer office, but then removed it before she went in to see Jim.

She could see several of the other staff looking up as she arrived.

She knew there would be some speculation about the reason for her visit.

She had already prepared a simple cover story for Jim regarding this, to offer the full support from SI6 for anything the Department required.

"Amanda!" smiled Jim.

"I am slightly surprised you are here in person, but it is always good to see you," he beamed.

"You are no doubt here because of some problem?" he asked.

"And it's not that difficult to guess what this is all about."

"That's right," said Amanda. "Two bombs exploding in central London within a few hours of one another, both of them at our buildings! You can guess that the Minister is pretty upset!?"

"No surprise there," said Jim, "and I expect he is already looking for a scapegoat. It's not me, is it?"

"I'm afraid so," said Amanda, "it's being targeted towards your Department this time. He wants to close it."

Jim scowled and then shook his head.

"He is so predictable. Has he offered any practical suggestions?" asked Jim,

"Nothing at all. And we are also drawing a blank over at SI6. I've also tried within GCHQ, but they don't have anything, despite vast funding. We can see that a couple of vans were used to deliver the bombs and that the bombs themselves were small. However, they were high-quality material. Military-grade, actually."

"And the credible threats from externals?" asked Jim, "Everything I've seen looks like it's opportunistic rather than anyone that knows what has happened?"

"That's right," said Amanda," We have not been able to track down any useful suspects so far."

"And we are still also trying to figure out the correct motivation for all of this."

"The message from Bernard Driscoll is that there will need to be a public sacrifice at the end of this," said Amanda. "Jim - He is asking for your department at the moment."

"I thought I'd pay you the courtesy of coming over here in person to let you know what has been said."

"Driscoll must have been beaten up by the PM over this. He was clearly rattled and did his usual puffery. That meant taking me outside to the street and then under the pretext of him buying some cigarettes he told me to find a way to shut you down."

"This is all about his control over everything. He hates it that we've been set up semi-autonomously" said Jim.

Amanda nodded, "Yes, that's right," she said," I sometimes wonder whether he is that interested in the humdrum matter of national security?"

"No, I think his main motivation is self-preservation and finding ways to continue to climb the greasy pole," said Jim.

"Though is there anything I can do to assist you at the moment?" asked Amanda.

"I know our units are already exchanging information on a routine basis about all of this."

Jim nodded. "There's nothing really that we can do until we find something tangible to use as a lead," he said.

"The nearest we have found so far is a pickup for one of the drivers which appeared to head off towards the Chinese embassy."

Amanda nodded, "It looks to us as if it is a false trail laid deliberately."

Jim said, "Someone is trying to point a finger towards the Chinese for this, although I am not convinced that this has their approach about it."

Amanda nodded.

"Yes," she said," Your people have provided some of that intelligence across to us."

"I think you managed to trace back the taxi that seems to be used as part of the escape route and then somehow link that to a getaway car.

"Yes," said Jim," And of course we have a cloned vehicle, and all the usual tradecraft that we see more often from our Russian colleagues."

Jim Cavendish

Jim Cavendish had become used to dealing with tricky situations in his small department. He knew Driscoll was unfair to target him and not because of failure from his team. They worked well together but were always a source of a kind of departmental jealousy which meant that other groups tried to shift the blame or lack of budget towards C-SOC.

Ever since the agreement to set up the new unit as if it were a start-up enterprise, he had to deal with the more conventional parts of the Service. The parts that wanted him to shut down,

Fortunately, the track record from the team had proved influential with several situations creating a positive reaction.

Jim still realised they were still on a knife-edge, and the recent situation with the bombings could quickly overshadow the positive picture from their other findings.

Jim remembered the phrase: "You're only as good as your last gig," It was, he considered, often the quote of macho management and people with selective memories, but all too often passive-aggressively trotted out when referring to C-SOC.

Jim called his team leaders together and began,

"Look, Amanda Driscoll has just visited us. She wants us to come up with something positive. Once again, we are under threat. It's our friend Bernard Driscoll that is turning the screws."

Marcus and the other team leaders looked at one another. They also realised that this was yet another play to try to get their group shot down.

Marcus was the first to comment, "I'd have thought that Driscoll would have been more interested in promoting our corner rather than trying to shut us down? Surely the fact that we can resolve more situations than much larger organisations across the river and in Cheltenham must count for something?"

Jim replied, "No, Driscoll doesn't see it like that. We have to do what Driscoll and SI6 say," he said. "Without their support, we are anyway in a difficult position."

"Amanda Miller, from SI6, and I go back a long way, and I'm sure she will do what she can to support us, but Driscoll is a different kettle of fish. He is all about power and also his own protection. He'll rattle on about protecting the civilian population but most of all he is trying to cover his own arse."

"So, did you learn anything new from Amanda Miller?" asked Marcus.

"No, she was really only able to tell us the same information that we already knew," said Jim.

"Did you mention anything about currency manipulation?" asked Marcus.

Jim looked quizzical.

"You know, the possible impact of cyber currency in the mix?" continued Marcus.

Jim looked at Marcus.

"You'd better brief me about that," he said.

"Okay," said Marcus, realising his original paper had failed to make any impact.

"Maybe I can see you about this after the main session? I think it is significant," continued Marcus.

Rosie looked towards Tyler. They both realised that they had a more complete picture of events in their team than the big bosses. Probably than Amanda Miller across at SI6.

The extractor

Marcus walked back to Rosie and Tyler.

"If the bombs don't get us, then the politicians will!" said Rosie.

Marcus nodded.

Then Rosie said to Marcus, "This is ridiculous - we seem to have found out more about the whole situation than anyone else, and there's only three of us in this sub-team."

Marcus replied," Yes, I agree, but the trouble is we will still need to substantiate everything we say. The reason there are so many people in those other departments is because of the burden of proof. It is why they spend so much time pulling their cases together. Politicians get easily bent out of shape if there is a chance of a diplomatic incident falling out of whatever we've identified."

Tyler asked, "Have we managed to get anywhere, identifying these two persons of interest?"

Rosie replied, "Hmm, the AI sifting technology still has a way to go.

"We still don't have any identification for the guy who we suspect as being the driver of the original bomb vehicle, but we did have some luck with the woman. It turns out that she is attached to the Russian embassy as a trade delegate.

"Of course, this is a cover, and her real purpose is to extract both the drivers from the scene completely," smiled Rosie. "Okay, what do we have on this woman?" asked Marcus.

Well, we have a name - Alya Sokolov - and also the rather simple back story of her as an adviser but nothing else.

"Bird of prey?" mused Marcus, "That's what Sokolov mans." Tyler and Rosie remembered that Marcus spoke Russian.

"Has she ever turned up in any other situations?" asked Marcus.

"Nothing that we have been able to identify so far," said Rosie. "Yet she does appear to have been in the UK for several weeks, with a side visit to France."

"This is still our best break so far with this," said Marcus," We now have a source that links back to the bombing and a trail that leads towards the Russians."

"Agreed," said Rosie," Although even at this stage, I'm still suspicious about what has actually taken place."

Marcus took a look at the photographs and the video that they had obtained.

"There's something that doesn't look quite the same between the two appearances of the guy," said Marcus, "I think we should run some more analysis of the video from inside the hotel."

"It's not very specific," said Matt, "But the guy in the second series of videos looks as if he is walking slightly differently from the guy who went into the hotel."

"Well, for a start, he's got his arm around the woman," said Rosie, "Or actually now you mention it, I think it's the other way around."

"If you look carefully, the woman seems to be guiding the guy towards the taxi."

Rosie wound the recording back and looked again, and sure enough, the man was looking a little the worse for wear in the second set of videos. It looked as if something had happened to him on the way through the hotel.

"Hotel bars can have that effect on me, too," commented Tyler.

"It looks as if he's been drugged or something," said Rosie looking more carefully at the video this time.

"Exactly," said Marcus, "Either drugged or perhaps damaged in some other way?"

"I think we could be witnessing the removal of our single direct link to the bombing," said Marcus. He looked grimly towards Rosie," I wonder if the woman has been sent to act as a disposal agent for the bomber.?"

Tyler was dialling up a Google maps view of the location that had been the final destination for the couple.

"We don't have any camera access unless any of the shops have rear-facing security cameras."

They traced the route back to a nearby side street. The street led in one direction to a dead end where a road had been blocked to prevent a rat run, and in the other direction, back onto one of the main thoroughfares.

"Okay." said Marcus, "We need to check the timings for vehicles entering and leaving this access road on the date in question."

"Oh, and we must wonder whether the exit was with the suspected bomber still alive," said Marcus.

PART TWO

Alya

Belladonna, n.: In Italian a beautiful lady; in English a deadly poison.

A striking example of the essential identity of the two tongues.

Ambrose Bierce

American Economics

Rosie noticed Marcus's expression.

"Hey, Marcus," what's the matter?"

"Well," he replied, "I miscalculated."

Rosie looked surprised. Marcus. The machine. Miscalculated. It did not compute.

"Okay, Marcus, you'll have to say more than that."

"I didn't realise that the follow-on paper to the one I wrote about the rouble was also significant," he began.

"What second paper?" asked Rosie. Tyler looked intrigued.

"Well, I wrote a second briefing paper. It was, how shall I say, more critical of our allies. Especially the Americans."

"What is it about?" asked Tyler, "More on the rouble?"

"Not exactly," said Marcus, "It's more of a multi-spectrum economic warfare piece."

"It's critical of our allies because, beyond the rouble concept, it looks as if the USA is also conducting a clandestine economic war against Moscow."

"What, like sanctions?" asked Tyler.

"Sanctions would be more overt. Remember the trouble that Trump had every time he opened his mouth about sanctions against some country or another?"

"So, this is less of a blunt instrument?" asked Rosie.

"Yes, although it is therefore sophisticated," added Marcus.

"Ah, so Trump wouldn't have been able to handle it anyway?" asked Tyler.

"Think of it as a Colder War," said Marcus.

"When I was writing the first rouble analysis, I came across quite a lot of material and from multiple sources. There's a whole gamut of approaches being deployed including speculation, financial market manipulation, information stream interception, business conglomerate information hiding, social media misuse, basic hacking via the internet, misuse of Governmental agencies, shady diplomacy, and some suspicious major business agreements.

"Daily this struggle can be seen playing out on the airwaves, in the war theatres in Ukraine and the Middle East, through the statements and accusations of diplomats, and in the economic sphere.

"Additionally, the debates and questions on whether a new cold war—the Colder War—have emerged.

"You see, in Putin's Russia, the mentality of the Cold War never really died, it just went further underground.

"Turning the Soviet Union into fifteen republics was not enough for the US. The newly emergent Russian Federation had to be placated in their views.

"That's why energy and petro-politics have been a significant feature of this multi-spectrum war too.

"Energy prices are a factor in this struggle, heavily linked to financial markets and national currencies. The manipulated decline in energy prices driven by flooding the global market with oil has augmented manipulation of the value of the rouble.

"Frankly, Saudi Arabia has also been a player, but Putin's Russia has known how to quietly take advantage of the situation.

"Unlike the USA with its incursions to Iraq and Iran?" asked Tyler.

"Yes, America has been wrong-footed in this, thinking that the Federation was about to call 'Game Over.' It soon realised that it would need to counter what the combined Russian Federation was doing. America then decided to run a two-pronged attack on the Russian Federation to cut Russia's revenues through market manipulation via economic sanctions and price drops.

"So, the rouble manipulation started in the USA?" asked Tyler.

"You bet it did," said Marcus, unusually intense," If the Americans hadn't started to play around with currency to try to drag Russia down, then I doubt Russia would have thought of its own currency manipulation."

"It's copycat," said Rosie, "Like the space race. The difference is that the Russians might really have something this time, instead of just poorly engineered copies of what the Americans have done"

"That's right," said Marcus," And the Russians can set up large click farms to manipulate the internet. They can keep them stealthy and undetected."

"I suppose if the Americans tried this, there would be a reporter on the doorstep in a few minutes," said Tyler.

'Ah, yes, the free press," replied Marcus.

"So, by imposing sanctions on the Russian economy, the US and its allies, including Australia, Canada, the European Union and Japan can drive offensives against Russia's leading source of revenue — energy. That has knocked the rouble and accounts for part of the reason Russia may have been driving the price.

Marcus looked at Rosie and Tyler. They were processing what he was saying.

"So, the reason that Russia may have got into the fake money business might be because of what the Americans have been doing?" asked Tyler.

"Maybe," said Marcus. "It's a strange form of cause and effect. Remember this is supposition by me. I've written this up but kept it away from official channels up to now. The materials I've used to create the positioning are from public domain sources, so I'm not breaking any confidential barriers. However, once I've assembled the story, it is somewhat incendiary."

"It's also somewhat bizarre," said Rosie, "Because it shows that an American plot to weaken Russia may have backfired spectacularly."

"There's at least a couple of big problems here," said Marcus.

Rosie replied, "First, if this is true and came to light, it would massively discredit America. Secondly, the way that Russia appears to be manufacturing the fake currency suggests a massive hole in cryptographic systems. It doesn't seem possible that it could be so easy for a Nation-State to be able to print fake money."

"Agreed," said Marcus. "And it looks as if this started some time ago, maybe as a result of the first rouble price drop back in 2014 - although the original system would have taken years to gear up."

Tyler asked," You'll have to explain."

"Well, back in 2014, Interfax's Vyacheslav Terekhov commented on the rouble currency crisis to Russian President Vladimir Putin during a Kremlin press conference. He said something about being in the midst of a deep currency crisis, one that even Central Bank employees say they could not have foreseen in their worst nightmares.

"Putin went on to explain that the situation has changed under the influence of certain foreign economic factors, primarily the price of energy resources, of oil and consequently of gas as well. He didn't go all out to say it was the Americans, but everyone knew what he was thinking."

"That the Americans were manipulating currencies to drag the Russian economy down?" said Rosie.

Marcus answered, "I guess that Putin sanctioned the original project to create market manipulation as a counter to what the United States and its allies were doing.

"Somebody smart would have come forward with a proposition. Only a few people understood cryptocurrency internals at that time, although plenty of people - including Tyler and his friend Matt - would have the capability to be able to mine the currency.

"I think Matt was smarter than that," said Tyler," He seemed to know about the innards of the various systems as well."

"Surely the Treasury and the FCA would pick up on this?" asked Tyler.

"Yes, they did at the time, and there was quite extensive coverage in the financial press. The Economist even wrote a leader article about it. But there was also a lot of other stuff happening, so although it continued to be extensively reported on media like Russia Today, it was less well-analysed in the UK and American press. We were all more interested in the price of oil in the way that it affected petrol for cars and heating for homes and industry. The usual vagueness descended over much of what was happening."

Rosie smiled," Yes, the way that the press doesn't analyse the impacts and reasons, more that it re-sprays the press releases and other guff that the PR teams create."

"So, Marcus, is it time to bring forward your paper about this," asked Tyler, "There's already plenty here, and you seem to still be adding to it."

"I guess so, although the original reason I was working on this secretively, was because of what happened with the 'rouble' paper as it moved up the chain. I started to get a sense that it wasn't being treated at the appropriate level of its security clearance."

"In other words, it was being leaked?" asked Rosie.

"Leaked, along with me as the author, which is something we are not supposed to ever do," said Marcus. "I'm all for rightful credit, but when it's something potentially incendiary, the anonymity and the confidentiality help to protect us."

Marcus continued, "Some smart analysts said that the drop in the Russian rouble's value was a result of the market acting on its own. I didn't buy that. It's increasingly difficult to prove what has been happening with all the microtransactions that nowadays take place by a computer algorithm in the trading desks.

"Only a few people pointed toward market manipulation, and they were looking toward Russia rather than anything that the

Americans might have been doing.

"That's what made the whole operation so brilliant in its early stages. American finds a way to tweak Russia's currency to produce an economic advantage. Then Russia discovers it and takes the original idea in a whole new direction. Still using the cover of micropayments and microtransactions to shield and diffuse what has been happening.

"That's how I originally started to look at the way that Russia seemed to be holding the rouble price from their own manipulations. The more obvious move was to blame it on the Russian government and Vladimir Putin. That's what led me to the idea there might be new money involved in the process.

"My second paper goes on to say it is not merely a result of the market acting on its own or the result of Kremlin-style policies.

"If the US had been making a Colder War play, then its objectives and policy would deliberately target Russia for destabilisation and devastation. It would be something cooked up below the Presidential level though, for fear of it being accidentally blurted or tweeted into the world."

Tyler and Rosie both grinned.

"It might have been initially a US plot to bring about Russian currency and economic instability, but it could easily have a knock-on effect across to the EU and other markets.

"Of course, the US would have been in control of what was happening until Russia switched on its money printing press. Russia would have needed leverage to fight back, and I guess that is when they moved across into cyber currency.

"Some economists in the US must be wondering what the hell they've done if they have continued to monitor outcomes," said Rosie.

"They know for sure," said Marcus," But I don't think they are asking questions about it."

"Not until they have erected the Teflon walls?" asked Rosie.

"Yes," said Marcus, "Otherwise, it will spark major international rows in all directions."

"That's where the Kremlin has been clever. Instead of depleting their foreign currency reserves and gold holdings of the Russian Federation, they've turned to faking money."

"In a way, it's a brilliant plan.," gasped Rosie.

Marcus continued, "As an example, Putin is on record as saying that the Russian government and Russian Central Bank should not hand out gold and foreign currency reserves or burn them on the market, but instead provide lending resources.

"That was a clever smokescreen for cyber currency injections. If the Kremlin knows what Washington was doing, then better to play along with it.

"Frankly, the US was replaying some of its old Cold War game plans against Russia.

"All the moving pieces around energy price manipulation, the currency devaluation, and even US attempts to entrap Russia in a conflict with its sister-republic Ukraine are all replays of US tactics that have been used before during the Cold War.

Rosie chipped in: "So dragging Russia into Ukraine is like a replay of how the US dragged the Soviet Union into Afghanistan previously?"

Marcus continued, "Yes, and the manipulation of energy prices and currency markets parallels the US strategy used to weaken Iraq, Iran, and the Soviet Union during the Afghan-Soviet War and Iran War.

"Instead of trying to stop the value of the rouble from dropping, the Kremlin appears to have decided to strategically invest in Russia's internal capital, using foreign exchange. It can do this with blended money. Mix real money and some of the fake money created through the cyber-fraud. They created a working framework for what is effectively massive nation-state money laundering.

Tyler looked at Marcus, "So where, exactly, is your second paper right now?"

Rosie was thinking about another cigarette when the phone rang. It was James.

"Bingo," he said.

"How so, James? "

"The AI system worked. We've got a positive identification of your bomber. Or should I say, your bomber's accomplice? We ran your two pictures through a few systems, and it spotted this person coming to the UK about a couple of months ago. Then leaving for CDG and then returning a couple of days later."

"And her name is Alya Sokolov," said James, "A full-fledged Russian agent. B-INNG-Go!"

"James, that's brilliant! Thank you so much,"

"The data files are winging their way across to you, as we speak, but I thought I'd like to tell you in person! Hey, Alya is badass. You take care now," he added," Love and kisses!"

"James, Ruck on!" said Rosie as the call cleared.

Rework

Marcus said," I'm going to get a cleaned-up copy of my report. The version I have on my secure machine back at the hotel includes the external references I used when I was compiling it."

"Before I head over there, I will speak to Jim about getting access to information about this woman Alya."

"I think Jim will have the right access into SI6 to help us with this."

"I'll see you both tomorrow with my updated version of the report," he added, "and we will need to manage the circulation extremely carefully."

Marcus crossed the corridor and tapped the door to Jim's office.

Jim looked up as Marcus entered, "There's been a development on the bombing," said Marcus, "I think I have the first positive lead relating to who may be behind it."

"We tracked the bomber across London, and he went into a hotel and later appeared with someone who we believe to be a Russian agent." said Marcus," I need a way to track her down and potentially stop her from leaving the country."

"We have a name - Alya Sokolov, which we obtained via the normal routes," said Marcus.

"The thing is, she's unknown to us and therefore not in our systems. We've some basic data that Rosie has acquired from Ops. Security, but it's not like a full agent profile."

"You'd better get into a position that helps you to follow her then," said Jim.

"I can arrange something for you via border control. You'll have to send over the documentation that you do hold. We will also need to tell Amanda Miller at MI6 that we are doing this."

"That way we can expedite this whole process," Jim looked up towards Marcus, "good work Marcus," he said," This is the first proper lead we've found."

"The people from GCHQ and SI6 haven't given us anything new, and the police are only helpful concerning the cloned plates on the taxi.

"We both know that the car is otherwise clean, and we won't get anything further from it.

"Except," said Marcus, "The make of the explosive, of course."

Marcus made his way back to the hotel. He had much to prepare for the morning.

Sokolov

Another rainy day as Tyler arrived at the office. Rosie was studying a report.

"Is that the new report from Marcus?" asked Tyler.

"No," said Rosie "it's the report that Marcus wrote previously. The one about the currency management of the rouble."

"Marcus must have worked late because he was not answering his phone when I tried to raise him this morning," she continued, "I'll give him until ten, and then I'll try contacting him again,"

Tyler decided he would also re-read the report from Marcus. He noticed it now had all of the security classification markings on it that showed it as a high-status document.

Just before 10 o'clock, there was a phone call to Rosie.

Others had been trying to contact Marcus but been referred operationally across to Rosie instead. This call was from Jim, who was only a couple of offices away.

"That person of interest that Marcus described to me yesterday," said Jim, "Alya Sokolov."

"The border controls have managed to stop her. We all assumed she would make her way out through one of the airports, perhaps even by a small plane to get across into mainland Europe.

"To our great surprise, she decided instead to use St Pancras station and to go across on the Eurostar."

"It was an easy option that would normally avoid detection, but luckily we had an alert set at the border. Sokolov is now being held by the local border control unit. They have put her into a secure location temporarily. Until we can request access to question her."

"The difficulty is, Marcus did talk about this with Amanda, which means that SI6 have asked for first access. We can probably go across and sit in on the interview, but they won't release her to us until they have questioned her."

"This is something to do with Driscoll again. I think he is trying to prove a point by only using the big departments to manage the situation," said Tyler.

"I doubt whether he is even aware that we were the people who identified her as a person of interest."

Tyler replaced the receiver and said to Rosie, "We must contact Marcus now."

Rosie nodded. "You know what," she said," I think we should head over to the hotel, and we can discuss this with Marcus there."

"If he's had a hard night working, then it is a good place for us to refuel him with some decent coffee as well."

Tyler grinned, "Yes, good idea."

They were out in the air for a few minutes. A crisp day on the way back to the hotel. A quick pit-stop at the adjacent Starbucks.

As they entered the hotel, Tyler could see that there was additional security.

Both plainclothes and also limited uniformed police were now inside the hotel.

Rosie was smiled at by one of the policemen who recognised her as a guest.

Not the same for Tyler, who was stopped and questioned before he was allowed into the elevator.

"Wow", said Tyler, "That was quite strict. If you hadn't been with me, I doubt whether I would have been able to get into the lift."

"It's nice to know they are looking after us well," said Rosie as they made their way to the 6th floor.

"I'm on the seventh, actually," said Rosie, "It's amusing that they've given me the executive floor while Marcus is on one of the normal floors. I think we both have pretty similar rooms, although we also both have access to the executive lounge in any case."

"One of the perks of Grade 7," said Tyler, "I'm not bitter," smiling as they tapped the door to Marcus's room.

There was a long pause and no answer.

Rosie picked up her cell phone and called Marcus.

She could hear the phone ringing from inside the room. "There's no response from Marcus," said Rosie.

Tyler ventured, "He's probably taking a shower; let's try the house phone."

Rosie picked up on the quaver in Tyler's voice.

Tyler found a wall phone and called down to the reception and asked to be connected to Marcus's room by the switchboard. Rosie pressed her ear to the door and could hear the other room phone ringing.

Still no sign of Marcus. "Okay," said Rosie, "I think we need to get the security guys to let us into the room."

She walked back to the lift area, where one of the security men was standing.

"We need to get access to room 6507," said Rosie, "Our colleague is supposed to be at an important meeting now."

They once again showed their passes to the security guard and he, in turn, called to someone else. Within seconds two extra people had appeared.

One was in full military combat clothes. The other was probably a soldier in civilian clothing but carrying a master key.

"Okay, we are going to open the room," said the uniformed soldier. "But we will enter before you do in case there is anything unusual. Be vigilant and be careful, " he added.

The soldier approached the door, and the man with the security card pressed it gently onto the lock.

The door immediately clicked to green so that the room could be entered. The soldier held up a shield and then pushed gently against the door.

It opened quietly into the room, and as they looked past the shield, they could see there was no sign of habitation. The room was made up as if it had been set by the housekeeping staff, everything was in its place and on the small desk table was Marcus's phone. There was no sign of Marcus. One of the soldiers pushed into the side door, which led to the en-suite shower and bathroom.

"Clear," he said. The other soldier nodded they were also looking around the room for other signs of unusual devices; altogether, they spent around three minutes before they would let Tyler and Rosie into the room.

"Okay, we have checked the room, and it appears to be secured," said the first soldier.

"There's no one in here, and it doesn't look as if it has been slept in," said the second soldier.

Tyler and Rosie looked around.

They could see that everything was very tidy.

"No laptop, just the charger," said Tyler to Rosie.

"Marcus's phone is here," said Rosie.

"Yes, it's his office phone. I can't see his personal one, though."

"If he had taken his office phone, we would have been able to easily track him."

Tyler nodded," I wonder whether Marcus has simply gone home?"

Marcus and Rosie looked at one another. Neither of them believed that Marcus would be at home. Something else had happened.

Marcus was missing.

Cutouts

Jim took a cab from Earls Court to the building close to SI6 headquarters where Alya was detained.

Amanda Miller was already there, and they were ready to begin Alya's questioning.

Jim was officially only present as an observer and had to stay in a separate room with video camera and audio feeds from the interrogation area.

The interrogation room was a blue-painted room with just a chair, a table and a wall-mounted camera and several ceiling-mounted microphones. Around the edge of the wall ran a panic bar at about chest height.

Jim admired it for the theatre. He knew they could as easily have conjured up a comfy living room with sofas and chintzy curtains.

There were two guards placed inside the room, one male and one female with Alya seated on the chair with her hands secured by a chain connected to the table.

The lead interrogator was female as Amanda watched from the observation room.

"Not interrogating, then?" asked Jim.

"They are the professionals," replied Amanda. She was pleased enough to be outside of the room.

"It's also more secure to not have the suspect able to identify either of us," murmured Amanda.

"No, we'll leave that for Bernard," said Jim.

They both sniggered.

The questioning began routinely enough, establishing Alya's name, her back story, and her reason for being in the United Kingdom.

Alya said that she was a secretary from the Russian Embassy and that there was no right for the UK to detain her.

Alya recognised she was being held by a part of the secret services, although there was nothing on their clothing or other forms of formal identification.

"Why am I being held…This is against the law. Your law. You cannot hold me without reason. I must contact my Embassy. I need to make a phone call."

The first thing that Amanda noticed was that the identity of Alya was a close match for the formal photographs and passes that had been provided by border control. She also noticed how Alya spoke excellent English and would have placed her as a typical well-heeled South Londoner, maybe from somewhere like Wimbledon.

She didn't give off an assassin vibe.

Next, Amanda noted Alya's physical appearance. Here things didn't seem quite right. She was slightly different from the pictures. Alya was wiry and slim. She looked like she worked out and had well-defined muscles in her arms and across her body.

This Alya was a little more curvaceous. Amanda didn't think she'd be able to run a fast 2km, while the Alya in the pictures most certainly could.

The interrogators continued, although there was a limit to their knowledge.

Alya quickly realised this and was not forthcoming.

"Jim, I don't think it is her," said Amanda.

Jim nodded agreement, "I was beginning to wonder what was wrong. The answers are evasive but show a lack of knowledge rather than a deliberate attempt to send us in the wrong direction."

"For example, that question about her family; You'd think she would mention her sister, even when we have told her we know about the sister."

"Yes, but she couldn't say what colour hair, or the sister's birthday. This wasn't supposed to be the tough part of the interrogation."

There was a buzz. A red light flashed in the interrogation suite.

"They are coming out, "said Amanda, "Let's ask them what they think."

The two interrogators stood and walked outside of the room. A few minutes later, they entered the viewing booth.

"It is strange," said one of the interrogators, "She is either very good, or there is something else going on."

"She doesn't seem to know anything, not even her own family history," said the second interrogator, "It's as if we have been given a substitute."

"A cutout? A cutout of the cutout?" asked Amanda.

"It's a clever move if that is what they have done. We've stood down the border controls, and yet we have possibly the wrong person in detention."

"Bernard will love this," muttered Jim to Amanda.

"I agree," said Amanda. What about the passport biometrics?

"I'll get our people to take a look. Maybe they've been doctored."

"It's becoming more commonplace now," said one of the interrogators, "We had a Russian chap in here a couple of weeks ago. Positively identified from his passport but in reality, nothing like his pictures. Someone has got hold of the encoders."

"Let's think about this for a minute," said Jim, "Would it be better for the Russians to think we have not realised their deception?"

"Good point," said Amanda. She looked at the two interrogators.

They looked at one another.

"Yes, we get it, you want us to continue routinely for a few more hours. We had to do something similar to the Russian man a few weeks ago."

"Meanwhile, we need to send out the alert to Borders again," said Jim.

Amanda nodded, "So what shall we tell Driscoll?"

"Tell him it is proving difficult to get information even with two of the most highly skilled interrogators."

They chuckled.

Jim's phone rang. It was Rosie from the office.

"Jim? There's been a development."

"Okay, just one minute," he replied.

He stepped out into the corridor.

"Go ahead,"

"We have been running some image software to cross-check people at the Russian Embassy. There are around 15 people there that roughly match Alya Sokolov's picture. We dug a bit deeper through the profiling.

"Here's what we found: This one: Katarina. She looks like Alya and has a comprehensive travel profile. She has been in several countries and we have her marked down as a frontline operative under challenging situations. She has been through military training and has a reputation as a suspected sniper and assassin.

The file also goes on to describe her as a fixer. I've sent the record across to your phone.

Jim looked at the record. It certainly looked like Alya.

He stepped back into the viewing room.

"Amanda, I think this might be Alya."

Amanda studied the pictures on Jim's phone.

Yes, the correct build, the right facial profile.

"Unfortunately, the surveillance team reckon there are around 15 women who approximate Alya's appearance," said Jim.

"They've not been searching sexy Russian brides, have they?" joked Amanda.

"No, but I can see their point with Alya," said Jim.

"Or Katarina," said Amanda, "Katarina Voronin."

"Katarina Voronin?" answered Jim, "Things just got serious. She is a Russian agent we have been tracking for years." She pops up from time to time, in places where there is some kind of mayhem.

Jim picked up his phone and called Rosie, "Hi Rosie, I think we've just found Katarina Voronin. She's popped up cross-referenced to Alya Sokolov."

"What, as an associate?" asked Rosie

"No, as the self-same person, we think the Alya we are holding is a case of mistaken identity."

"Voronin is top league," said Rosie, "Security services have been tracking her around for years. I'll try to pull off her data."

A few minutes later, an email arrived for Jim on his phone.

"Here we are," he said

"She has been trained by the FSB and has spent time in Germany, Austria, France, and the United Kingdom. It says she is fluent in German, French and English as well as her native Russian.

"There's a trail of coincidences associated with her time in various countries. A bombing in Amsterdam, the assassination of a Russian banker in Turkey, gun-running across the Belgian border. A huge bank heist in Austria using an armoured car.

"The links we show illustrate that she might just have popped into these countries from one of her home ones. And each time it is just around when the event took place.

"I'm not sure that I'd call it a weak link but look, she has a child still in Moscow.

"By my reckoning, the boy is around two years old now. It also looks to me as if most of Katerina's work stopped around two years ago.

"It implies that she has been retired from the field."

"But, presumably brought back for this job?" summarised Jim.

"Let's ask "Alya" about her little boy…" said Jim.

He flipped the interrogation button and saw the interrogators pause. One got up and left the room.

Jim walked into the corridor and talked to the interrogator.

"Okay, the question is primed, let's see what happens next!"

Sure enough, the interrogators asked the question. The reaction was remarkable. Alya replied but in her reply said, 'You keep my children out of this."

"Children," said Jim.

"Children," replied Amanda, "We've been played."

"But they don't know how much we have found out."

Jim travelled back across London to his base office.

Now that Marcus had disappeared there was an increased risk to his other team members.

He'd have to move them to somewhere less public. The catalogue of problems was rising.

Two bombs, a banker's disappearance, Marcus disappearance, the mystery bombers, the Russian woman. Currency manipulation. Somehow, he would have to make sense of all of this. That's where he'd usually rely upon Marcus to bring together the most likely theory.

Instead, he had to ship Tyler and Rosie to yet another centre of operations.

He entered their office. They both looked up.

"Anything useful from the Russian?" asked Tyler.

"Only that she is a substitute, to throw us off the track of the real Alya Sokolov."

"Now, I've been thinking, and I need you two to move your centre of operation…To GCHQ."

Tyler thought about it, "Finally, a chance to stay in a hotel on the department's budget."

Rosie thought about what she'd needed to tell Vanessa. Things had been trying over the last few days, with Rosie mysteriously staying away but not allowed to explain anything specific to Vanessa.

"When are we going?" Asked Rosie.

"Tomorrow," answered Jim, "It'll give you time to pack."

Driscoll on TV

After Bernard Driscoll's morning television interview, there had been something of a backlash.

Despite his attempts to show that he was on top of the bombings and had excellent support, the allegations were now that he was running an outfit that was unfit for purpose.

It was what he had intended in one way, but the big fingers were now pointing back directly to him. He was considered to be part of the problem rather than the solution.

His advisors suggested he should appear in a few more interviews, the next one being a radio interview.

"Thank you, Minister, for agreeing to appear on the World at Midday. Minister, you've already implied that your own systems and services need some kind of update. What are your plans now to prevent further disruption and damage to London and potentially even loss of life?

"This is beginning to look more like the period in the 70s when there were concerted bombing campaigns across London. Surely with today's modern technologies and surveillance, you would be better able to predict and pre-empt such events?

Driscoll was prepared for this, " But first let me say that we are doing everything to stem the flow of such terrorist atrocities. "We have already increased the boots on the ground support in the London area. In practice, we think that these attacks may have been specifically aimed at two of our own buildings.

"That's what you said on the previous television interview Minister. That you were running operations from these two buildings."

"Is it possible, then, that the attacks were aimed at yourselves? And isn't that quite worrying that your own systems are unable even to detect direct attacks on your own environments.?"

Driscoll again: "We've seen the government's priorities around these matters change over the last few years. Our predecessors diluted the effect of our spending by adding in these new departments, with the result resources are spread more thinly. We are now in the process of re-consolidating so that we have a better and more critical mass where we need it".

"We're going now to our security specialist, Dr Stannard, based in the University of Manchester to ask for his thoughts on the current situation. Good Morning, Dr Stannard,"

"Good morning to everyone. Yes, we have monitored the last few years of GCHQ MI6 MI5 and these other smaller departments and have noticed one particular aspect. Usually, intelligence is only gathered after significant events rather than before them.

"The security services, with a few exceptions, have been very unsuccessful at predicting most of the big events that have occurred.

"Let's look at some track record. Aside from the two recent bombing attempts there have been situations in the past.

"The lack of identification of a significant number of terrorists that have lived in the United Kingdom before moving to other countries where they have laid bombs or created different types of disruption.

"The firebombing in the United Kingdom of several notable buildings.

"The hacking of government Department secure files, the denial of service attacks on several UK corporations, the uploading into visible parts of the Internet of various forms of secured information including the source code for the systems software on one of our nuclear plants.

"These are all examples over the last three or four years.

"While it's fair to say that financial policies changed for funding of some of these departments, most of this has happened within the current government's reign."

"Minister?"

"Let me be clear: Of course, we are unable to make changes to funding policies in a matter of moments. Look: All of these require careful consideration and have had to go through various Treasury committees in order to make the changes. That's one of the reasons why I use these current examples as a way to expedite the changes that we think we need, since the last government were in power."

"But surely over the last year or so that was a fairly substantial increase, a doubling no less, of the funding available to the central security agencies? Are you saying that this was still not sufficient?"

"It's not simply a matter of funding per se," answered the Minister, "it's also a question of allocations and where they are placed. We need to ensure that the right people get the funding."

Dr Stannard interrupted, "This is all so much political posturing. You are trying to cover up for an extensive and very bureaucratic system that is too stodgy to be able to react to the type of circumstances that we see now with modern terrorism. Whether it's terrorism or just cranks, you seem to be always running to catch up.

"The very idea that you are now somehow able to monitor everything that is happening stinks. You can't just track everything and hope to find the right answers.

"Let's be truthful about this; it's only when you have tipoffs that you even stand a chance to be able to find out things in advance.

The Minister looked a little flustered but decided to bluster his way out of it," You are oversimplifying this Dr Stannard, "he said, "A whole intelligence ecosystem is a very finely tuned machine.

"We are not working on this alone. We are also working with our allies in NATO and also with the Americans."

Dr Stannard interrupted, "Yes, but it's not a big secret that you don't like to share too much with, for example, the Americans. Even when you say that you are working closely together, there is usually some reluctance to divulge more than is absolutely necessary?"

"That's simply not true," said the Minister," We have a strong relationship with both the Americans and our NATO allies across Europe. We share information on a regular and routine basis."

The interviewer cut in," Okay, let's move this along, shall we? We need to understand what are the concrete steps now, Minister, to alleviate the current situation?"

Bernard Driscoll replied," I'm sure you understand that I am not really in a position to directly answer that. This is all a matter of national security, and we are in the middle of a delicate phase. It would be counter-productive for me to tell you too much about what is going on. Please rest assured that the highest priorities are being given to handling the current situation."

"Thank you, Minister, and now it's time for the weather."

Amanda winced as she listened to the broadcast. She knew that Driscoll was prone to bluster his way out of situations, and this was yet another example. Amanda was sure that this would not go down well in the shortened news clips that would undoubtedly follow. Unfortunately, this was the second major interview that the Minister had produced in such a style, and she was reasonably sure that his days were now numbered.

Her phone rang; it was Jim.

"I guess you just listened to that interview?" he asked.

"Yes, not so much world at midday as the world at a loss," she replied, " That was not a good interview for the Minister."

"The problem I see now," said Jim, "is that he is quite likely to lash out before he is replaced. We will need to be careful over the next 24 hours that he does not do anything stupid."

"I think we should probably keep the silent running that we have established for the little project in Cheltenham." replied Amanda.

"I agree," said Jim.

Country Cousins

Lists only spell out the things that can be taken away from us by moths and rust and thieves.

If something is valuable, don't put it in a list. Don't even say the words.

Douglas Coupland

GCHQ

Tyler entered the GCHQ briefing room. He'd expected it to be busier. It was a small auditorium, suited for the briefing of maybe 60 people.

There were 6 people present.

A woman stepped forward — long dark hair with a hint of greying, a plain black T-shirt and jeans.

"Welcome to GCHQ," she said, "My name is Grace Fielding.

"I've been assigned as the project manager for this next operation - it's called 'Mynah Bird'."

"That will confuse everyone on the misspellings," thought Tyler.

"We'll all introduce ourselves in a moment but for the two people from London please could you raise hands and just show the others who you are.

"These are Tyler and Rosie,"

"They were working closely with Marcus and are the basis for the discovery. They were directly involved in the development of the rouble manipulation theory through the use of cyber currency.

"Our job is to figure out a way to stealthily end what the Russians have been doing."

"But does that mean we are going to try to hack the Russians?" asked one of the GCHQ people.

"That's right, Daniel," said Grace.

"But we think they are using server farms and click farms," said another of the GCHQ contingent, "They seem to be based in multiple cities too: Kazan, Chelyabinsk, Omsk, Samara and Rostov-on-Don, and more…"

"That's right," said Grace," We'll need some smart methods to put this genie back in the bottle."

"Marcus Barton produced this report which you have all read now, which explains the surmised basis for cyber manipulation."

"We think it was this report which caused him to be taken away from his hotel room by, as yet, unknown people."

"Other presumptive events lead us to think that it is the Russians that have done this. This is not for circulation or discussion outside of this base. I'm going to hand over now to Tyler Sloan, to take us through the system."

Tyler started to explain the cyber mining system used by the Russians.

"I assume that's why we this project is called Mynah Bird?" he said, "Because the cybercash system mimics the real one?"

Then he described the ability to use the mined coins in a blend with other currencies to create new forms of financial instrument which could be used for routine trading and in effect to be used to balance the cost the exchange rate of the rouble.

"So, it becomes a way to secretly print vast quantities of foreign exchange currency in a state-sponsored exercise," he concluded.

Grace took over, "We also picked up on this via a major Bank's London trading desks, and I think it was Marcus Barton's team that were involved directly in this disclosure."

"Indeed, the source of the main derivative trading - Victor Boyd - head of group trading - has also disappeared. It's like the links to this are being systematically removed."

"We have brought Tyler and Rosie down to GCHQ to protect themselves from whatever has happened to Marcus."

Rosie and Tyler looked at one another. They had not been told this vital detail.

"They were secretly brought to GCHQ, and only the people in this room and a few senior staff know anything about this."

Tyler raised his hand. Grace looked towards him," Yes? A question?"

"That's right," said Tyler, "My concern is that when we were in the Earls Court building and even before that when we were still in St Martins-le-Grand, there was some kind of leak. In other words, the bombings have been following us.

"Our supposition is that the bombs created a diversion which pushed Marcus and our team into the secured hotel."

"That would have made a pre-planned raid on the hotel possible," continued Tyler.

"I've seen the briefing from Jim Cavendish about this. He was part of the interrogation of the Russian fixer woman who is still being held by SI6".

"Yes, but we know that she was a substitute?" chipped in Rosie.

"Agreed," said Grace, "We are still working to detain the real fixer, Alya Sokolov, also known as Katarina Voronin."

"And it looks as if the stakes were high because we believe her last role was to dispose of the two bombers to remove them from the chain of investigation."

"Do we think that the Russian organised crime is also involved with this?" asked one of the GCHQ people.

There was a small giggle around the auditorium.

"Quite likely, the government to organised crime area is quite a grey area. We know that there is a very porous line between the Russian government and the Russian organised crime syndicates."

"So, follow the money," said Rosie, "That's what Marcus would say."

"Good point," said Grace," starting from where."

"I'd think laterally about this," said Tyler," Ignore the main derivatives and their trades, instead look for any new large-scale gains by senior Russian officials."

"Yes, skimming the money from the top of the generated pile," said Rosie.

The GCHQ people nodded as she said this.

Grace smiled, "Yes, we are already doing that, as it happens; usually there's a leak somewhere. This time it is a member of the Russian Central Bank - Grigori Gulnik. He seems to have so much money that he's been sending some of it across to the Cayman Islands, for safe, tax-free keeping.

"Caymans?" said Rosie.

"Yes, it's a predictable destination of choice for Russian investors. Particularly Tier 1 investor visa Russians, who have a sort of free pass to London included with every deposit."

"Gulnik has bought a couple of homes in London. Both in the $20 million range. One of the purchases hardly trips the spending scales for Russian purchases in London. The second and his interest in a third property suggests a run rate of income that needs to be secured. Gulnik is trying to spread his risk around. He knows that if he leaves it in Russia, it could all be taken away from him by Putin's robbers."

"And Gulnik is a Turkish name, isn't it?" asked Rosie.

"It could be Turkish," agreed Grace, "But his nationality is given as Russian."

"Okay," said Grace, "In a minute we will take you through to the main operations room."

"We are in the inner ring of GCHQ, and now we are about to go underground into the tank. It will give us a chance to show you a few of the tunnels as well."

"It looks as if we are going to become cyber-hackers now," stated Rosie.

Tyler said: "We will need to use some of the same techniques that cyberterrorists deploy, to track down the Russian systems."

Grace added, "We had to do something similar when we were trying to figure out what ISIL was doing as it attempted to hack the power companies.

"It's no real secret that Islamic State was trying to hack US power companies. A section chief at the FBI's cyber division was first to draw it to attention, but claimed that they had, 'Strong intent but low capability.' He went on to say that they'd simply buy the capability."

"That's around when the US Justice Department started making arrests and charging individuals with providing material support to the Islamic State, computer hacking and identity theft.

"It was all in conjunction with the theft and release of personally identifiable information belonging to US service members and civilian government employees. The original data had been stolen from the servers of a US retail chain.

Daniel continued, "Hussain had tweeted in the name of the Islamic State Hacking Division a link to a 30-page document that contained the information allegedly stolen by the arrested hackers. I still have the text on my computer.

"To be honest, although having personal information or an email address published can be threatening and serve as an incredibly intimate invasion of privacy, it's not the real game. While such hacks are bothersome, they are not immediately deadly."

"Usually, the goal of cyber terrorists is to have the ability to conduct attacks that result in death or significant destruction — attacks that provoke terror — with just the stroke of a keyboard."

Tyler asked, "So the terrorist made as much as they could of a rather basic situation?"

Daniel interrupted: "Yes, and unwittingly gave away a show of their current capability. At the time, their published document threatened, let's see...

Daniel scrolled through a document on his PC.

"Here we are, Melodrama Central... 'we are in your emails and computer systems, watching and recording your every move, we have your names and addresses, we are in your social media accounts, we are extracting confidential data and passing on your personal information to the soldiers of the Khalifa, who soon with the permission of Allah will strike at your necks in your own lands!'

"The Khalifa refers to the Caliphate; You'll have seen this type of long-winded messaging on other recent hacks too."

Grace continued, "There's a couple of other points to this, though. The first is that although there was real data in play, it was quite opportunistic. Admittedly it was service personnel names, but really it was a lucky strike by the hackers."

"It was enough to be able to sell some credibility to the people who would pay them but not anywhere near good enough to do any real damage. Except to get Hussain killed by way of US retaliation of course.

"The second hidden fact is that the US then recruited the original hacker to in effect change sides and to work for them. It's a common enough situation and one where he could carry on with his hobby but now get paid by the Americans. For him, it wasn't so much about ideology as about greed. That and if he didn't comply, he'd be locked away forever.

"The incidents showed the intent of ISIL to develop a robust cyber warfare capability.

"It's been useful because we've had to keep up with the latest thinking here too. We don't have a US cyber hacker to throw at this (although we could probably get the Americans to chip in), but we do have our own improved capabilities."

"Why not simply go to the Americans for direct assistance?" Asked Tyler.

"We'd have to spill the beans on the rest of the situation if we did that," said Grace.

"The result would be that the Americans would want to take full control and move everything to Langley. We've seen it too many times before."

"I think there might be other reasons for keeping the Americans muted in this investigation," added Rosie, "Some of it is referred to in Marcus second paper."

Tyler nodded, and Grace looked intrigued.

Grace added, "For this, we'll use our own people, and if needed we normally would augment from the local market."

"I'm assuming you can't do that in this case?" asked Rosie. "Using experts from one of those small firms who claim specialised skills in all of this."

"We can't this time," said Grace, "This is far too sensitive, and if the Russians have figured out a way to manufacture fake blockchains then we need to shut it down, not provide tips on how to make it proliferate. We don't want economic warfare on the back of this."

"Well, not forgetting the real warfare with explosions that started off this chain of events!" said Tyler.

"I agree, and I'm sorry, I didn't mean to detract from the awful time you two have been having over the last few days," said Grace hastily.

"The other aspect of this is the use of state sponsorship," interrupted Daniel once more, "To date, the very few seriously destructive hacks we have seen have been conducted by state sponsors such as the authors of the Stuxnet malware."

Grace added, "Thanks, Daniel, Indeed, most private hackers seek money or thrills, and so they have not focused on cyber warfare — or more accurately, asymmetrical cyberterrorism — as much as they have cyber theft and cyber vandalism."

"So cyber warfare has mostly been the province of nation-states, and cybersecurity experts believe that wide-scale cyber warfare can be conducted only by national players.

"That is consistent with what the Russians appear to have been trying but is more covert even than a typical cyberterrorist based approach. There are a few nations out there who want to make their attacks look as if they have come from other places. In effect, state-sponsored attacks dressed up to look like cyberterrorists. Usually designed to look like small-timers as well."

Tyler interrupted, "That makes the cyber money situation very different. It's asymmetric, but with the huge advantage to the attacker."

Grace added, "Now the question becomes whether the perpetrators have developed something themselves or whether they have gone elsewhere to obtain the special software?"

Daniel added, "Normally, for routine malware attacks, the perpetrator can buy the malware from a commercial hacking crew and then repurpose it for a more malicious purpose than simply stealing."

"State sponsorship is also a potential way for terrorist actors to gain access to malware tools for asymmetrical cyber terrorist attacks," added Tyler.

"But It seems less likely that there would be a such a ready market for the mining software, or if there is then it has been very well-concealed, certainly from us, and we were in the exact market," Tyler added.

"It would need to have been very well-concealed," said Daniel.

Tyler started, "You may already know that I was part of a small cyber mining team right up to when I started at the department. We'd have known if there were any ultra-clever alternative means to develop mining blockchains."

Grace turned towards Daniel. "Explain about the safeguards hierarchy."

Daniel continued," You'll probably know most of this, but there's a sort of pecking order to the way we view the security safeguards around CNI that's the Critical National Infrastructure."

"For digital, as in the physical world, it is simply not possible to safeguard everything in the cyber world to the highest degree. Security resources are costly and limited, and therefore priority must be given to protecting the most important targets and those where an attack would cause the most damage."

"Ah yes," Rosie said, "The CNI priorities list. Energy, Comms and Finance"

Daniel continued, "For example, I think everyone agrees that nuclear power plants should receive excellent protection from physical attack. By contrast, it is simply not possible to provide that same level of security for every electrical substation — much less every transmission tower and power pole — on the lines between the nuclear plant and the consumers who receive the electricity. "

"By necessity, there is an array of "soft targets" somewhere in the electrical system, and indeed, our society is filled with vulnerable targets. "

"Targeting the smaller substations and so on is disruptive but not so effective, more an annoyance," said Rosie.

"Yes, Rosie, these soft targets are often chosen simply because of their vulnerability to terrorist attacks, especially by terrorist operatives who lack sophisticated tradecraft."

"Communications is another high priority area, and so are Financial Services. All three of Energy, Communications and Financial Services get high levels of support and protection."

Daniel continued: "However, there are still soft, vulnerable targets for each of these in the cyber realm. Some of them can and will be attacked in a manner that could result in death and destruction, though on a much smaller scale than a cyber warfare attack by a nation-state.

"In many ways, this would be similar to attempts by terrorists to obtain and use chemical or biological weapons and the difficulty they have faced in making these programs as effective as a nation state's chemical or biological weapons program."

At its simplest, someone can steal the copper from a train line between Cheltenham and Birmingham and create havoc because there's no communication or signalling. Sure, it disrupts many people, but it's not the same a stealing the entire signalling capability of Network Rail."

"Most terrorists consider that all they need is the cyber equivalent of a primitive chemical weapon or a pressure cooker bomb. As we progressively automate and interconnect our lives, we can see an increasing number of items attached to the Internet that a creative person could use to cause mayhem."

"The effect of their actions in this smaller way can still be disastrous and scary, which most of the terrorists would regard as 'job done'."

"Frankly, and I hope Grace won't mind me saying this, that's what the majority of the GCHQ effort is expended on intercepting. The smaller incidents that create chatter and can be headed off before they occur."

"It's also easier for us when we know where these people

prefer to communicate. Shutting down their broadcast bulletin boards sounds like a good thing but makes our life harder because we then have to find the next place or system that they are using to spread their messages."

"The cyber-fraud we are considering here is a whole different dimension. It's completely silent, systematised on a global scale and has the backing provided by a powerful nation-state."

"For the most part, the Internet does not stop at national borders, and it is quite common for hacks to be conducted from another country and for hackers to skip across the globe using compromised systems in several different countries to hide their trail."

Rosie added, "It means that cyberterrorists can hack transnationally without having to travel to the country where their target is located. The ultimate working from home."

"It's a whole extra level if the nation-state is directly sponsoring the offshore locations used as part of the hack," said Grace.

Daniel added, "But I suppose another consideration would be the possibility of an insider threat. As we've seen in cases like those involving Chelsea Manning and Edward Snowden, an insider can compromise a great deal of information. That would work for a routine cyber hack, like information stealing, but for something like this where the whole fundamental nature of the system is built to protect against hacks, then an insider would have limited use."

"There's also still the attack cycle used for the cyber currency," said Tyler

"There has to be a way to first inject the fake money into the system. Ironically, by the time the money has been presented to a bank, it already looks completely genuine. It follows all of the characteristics of cybercash, is properly tokenised and has the blockchain structure that everyone expects. That's what makes the plan so elegant."

"It implies that the system is kept away from prying eyes until the blockchain credibility has been established," said Tyler.

"And that's what we need to work against," said Daniel. "We need to think of the blockchain creation process as open to interception. If we can get to that stage, then we should be on to something."

"Yes, we need to create a kill chain of our own," said Daniel." We must find the places along their creation cycle where their efforts are vulnerable to detection — and also assume that they are on-guard for such probes."

Hi y'all

Bernard Driscoll had enough of the current situation. He knew that he'd now messed up two interviews, but it wasn't his fault.

The briefings he had been given were lousy.

There had been too little progress from his teams.

Their own findings meant his explanations sounded weak.

He would need to do something positive that showed global leadership.

Now he'd got a meeting with the Prime Minister. This wasn't likely to be a congratulatory meeting. He'd need something up his sleeve.

Unfortunately, he didn't have a perfect story at the moment. His own people were, for whatever reason, not behaving the way he had demanded.

He was at the point where he thought he would need external help to tip the scales back towards his own position.

The last thing he wanted was even more fragmentation from small teams. He was sure that the reason he was in the current mess was because he'd let the diverse units start to assert themselves.

Instead, it would be a lot better for him if he could take back control to SI6 and GCHQ. Then he would have a couple of units which he could control and could divert all of the funding back to these two leading players.

He decided that instead of involving yet another small private company to help him, it would be better to go to someone big and influential.

On this occasion, he could use the Americans.

There was hardly any downside. It would show Bernard Driscoll to be influential, powerful and decisive and yet ready to deploy a dramatically improved team to resolve the current situation.

He knew that this would make Amanda livid, but he would be making contact with Mary-Anne Piper from the American embassy.

Driscoll knew Mary-Anne would have a team in place somewhere in central London that could help him regain his balance on all of this. He needed to work out what he considered to be the loose cannons and the best way was to have some additional tricks up his sleeve.

He was on his way to see the PM when he called Mary-Anne, from the back of his car.

"Hello Mary-Anne, How's my favourite Texan? It's Bernard Driscoll, I need to talk to you."

"Hi Bern-hard," she said - she always pronounced it as two words and Bernard had become used to it.

"I guess this is about y'all bombs?" she said, "We've already called your controller about this to offer assistance but were told to run along."

"Yes," said Bernard, "It is about the bombs, but what I'm really looking for is some kind of support from you. Maybe some help from Langley too?"

"This is, indeed, unusual, What, then, don't ya have?"

"I'm concerned that things may have a certain 'momentum', answered Driscoll.

"Are you asking us to support you? How unusual here in London."

"I know," said Bernard, "but I'm concerned that things are running away from themselves at the moment. I need some background help to ensure that we regain equilibrium on all of this."

Mary-Anne paused, and Bernard wondered if she was thinking about his television interviews.

He knew that he was in a slightly awkward situation with all of this. The way the television had wrongly portrayed him made him look like a bit of a buffoon.

He would need to keep himself polite when talking to Mary-Anne - he needed her cooperation because otherwise he would be forced to use some of the subcontractors.

"Okay," Mary-Anne said, "I think we can support y'all. We have a team based in central London who are pretty good at these bomb situations."

"I assume that's what you need?" she asked.

"Not exactly," said Barnard, "It's a bit more complicated than that. How about we meet somewhere, and I explain what is happening?"

"Why don't you come on over to one of our places?" said Mary-

Anne, "We still have that small station just off of Grosvenor Square near to where the main embassy used to be."

. . .

The side of Grosvenor Square looked like many of the other tall townhouses in that part of London. It wasn't inside any of the recognisable embassy buildings, and this has meant that people like Bernard could get into the building quite quickly compared with access through embassy doors and security routes.

Ironically this secure building was more accessible for those people in the know than the main embassy, which was now situated in a huge sugar cube of a building in South London.

"I see you still have a regular space set up here," said Bernard as he greeted Mary-Anne.

It looked more like a management consultancy with a smart hotel-like reception area, a few non-descript wall posters and nothing displayed in the typical US government typefaces.

"We've tried to make ourselves look inconspicuous on the outside here," said Mary-Anne," Of course we have a few more specialised facilities around the back."

"Yes, I feel as if I could book my next holiday here," said Driscoll," Look, I require help, across at GCHQ. Linking your NSA with our intel should speed things up. I want to catch those bombers, fast."

"Okay, but you'll owe me, the next time I need a small favour."

"Your favours are never small," replied Driscoll realising what he said and that it was he who was in deep trouble, with Mary-Anne as his source of rescue.

"We've found one of them," said Mary-Anne, "At least we found the woman who was sent to do the tidying up."

"The Russians even sent a substitute to be caught, a genuine low-level office secretary."

Driscoll looked interested, "Who have you got?"

"It's someone we've been tracking for quite a while. Alya Sokolov did some nasty stuff in Washington, but then flew over to Paris and then London. We've been watching her all along."

"Her name is Alya Sokolov, as well as a few aliases. She's a Russian fixer, for the FSB. Highly trained and quite difficult to catch in the middle of anything."

"Wait, so have you detained her?" asked Driscoll.

"We might have asked her to step into a black van," said Mary-Anne.

"And?"

"She's good, very good, but right now we think she's trying to bargain her way out of the situation. We pulled her after the bombing, when she was ferrying a couple of the bomb drivers around London. She'd got traces of Semtex on her clothes. Careless, really. And highly unusual."

"Okay," said Driscoll, "Then I take it you are in and will provide assistance. It saves us getting all messy about the US government extracting Russians from the streets of London."

Mary-Anne does Cheltenham

Amanda Miller's phone rang.

It was Mary-Anne from the American Embassy.

"Hello, Mary-Anne, and to what do I owe this unexpected call?"

"Bern-hard Driscoll, actually," Amanda could almost feel the smirk on Mary-Anne's face.

"Ah, yes, Bernard. Sorry to say he hasn't mentioned anything."

"We've been asked to give you some assistance," replied Mary-Anne.

Amanda looked aghast but kept her voice level.

"I guess this must be a new request. I thought we were already keeping you fairly well in the loop?"

"That's right," said Mary-Anne, "Although right now I think it is us that need to keep you in the loop. We've been asked to come along to your operations room. Bern-hard was most insistent."

Amanda was standing outside of her own operations room.

Now, because of Driscoll, she'd need to set up another room that could be used safely by the Americans as well as her own people.

It would potentially dilute what they were doing unless she decided to give the Americans unfettered access to their information and controls.

"I guess we can work together on this," she smiled into the phone.

"That's great because I'm already on the way down to Cheltenham," replied Mary-Anne. We're on the outskirts of London now."

Amanda was furious with Driscoll. Not only had he arranged this with Mary-Anne, but he'd not had the courtesy to advise Amanda of what he'd agreed. She'd have to cross-check it all with him now before Mary-Anne arrived. Amanda asked Grace for help to pick another secure location in Cheltenham for Mary-Anne's visit. Grace identified Fiddler's Green, a small stately home generally used for training purposes, although it was heavily wired to the main GCHQ location.

Amanda considered that she could isolate GCHQ from the prying eyes of the Americans and their propensity to drop little bugs and wiretaps all over the place.

Tyler and Rosie were unphased by another move of location. They had been in so many buildings that another one didn't seem to be anything special.

"Cool drive, though," said Rosie to Tyler as they looked out of the front windows towards the greenery and sweeping drive of the location.

"Yes," said Tyler, "It feels as if we've somehow arrived, like in a James Bond movie."

"Or Brideshead Revisited."

"That one was straight."

"Straight? Brideshead?"

"You know what I mean. The drive for Brideshead was straight."

There was a commotion at the front gate. It swung inwards, and a large black SUV entered, headlights on. Then a second one, then a black American saloon car, then a black armoured security van, then a black truck and another two SUVs.

"Subtle, or what?" asked Rosie. They both laughed.

The convoy swung around the drive and pulled up at the main entrance.

Amanda was already standing by the front door. Several suited Americans stepped from the leading and second SUV.

Mary-Anne emerged from the black car, smiling.

"Wow, that's quite an entrance!" said Amanda, "Welcome to Downton Abbey."

"Well, we are transporting special cargo," replied Mary Anne.

Amanda looked confused. Driscoll had not mentioned anything when she spoke to him to cross-check that this had all been agreed.

"We've brought Alya Sokolov, I thought you'd like that!" said Mary-Anne.

"Thank you for coming along," Amanda lied.

"We are pleased to help. We've brought one of our standard computer and comms packages to get started quickly. The teams are bomb and terrorism specialists. We've also brought along some computer specialists because we understand that there may be another dimension to this?"

Amanda had to play that she didn't know about this aspect. Mary-Anne might have been fishing for information.

"We are mainly focused on the bomb threat causes at the moment. As the minister said – the bombs were both placed at our own buildings. We've had several people own up to them, but none of them looks like a credible source — pranksters and lunatics rather than extremists.

"Do you have any reason to think that this is state-sponsored?" asked Mary-Anne.

"We are not ruling it out," said Amanda.

"Look, I get it that you've put us in a bubble here," said Mary-Anne, "To be honest I was expecting to see Grace Fielding. I suppose I'd do the same when an ally comes to the NSA; quietly drop them into a suburb of Washington."

"The United States is keen to assist with this search," continued Mary-Anne, "To avoid any potential embarrassment down the way. We've already questioned Alya, and we know about the two bombers and their escape routes. We think Alya has been cornered and wants a way out."

Amanda noticed that Mary-Anne did not mention the computer hacks and wondered if this was still unknown to the Americans. A simple bombing might be a more reasonable motive.

"What's your backstory on Alya Sokolov?" asked Amanda.

"Same as yours, probably, a major disruptor in the States. Fixer from a number of Russian missions which need to be tidied away. It was her unlucky break that we were already tracking her when she decided to assist here in London. We'd been following her for a couple of months."

Mary-Anne looked straight at Amanda, "So let me try making a couple of guesses. Bernard Driscoll hasn't said any of this, so I'm running on my own theory here, not from some supplied source."

Mary Ann continued, "Suppose one of your teams had discovered something? Maybe something that was compromising to a government. Heck – perhaps even to the Americans. In our way of working, we'd have to push it out into the open. I don't think we'd use the blunt instruments of bombs, but we'd undoubtedly run something on the diplomatic channels to get it into the open. I'm guessing that most of the NATO countries would do the same. "

"Look – check if you want – with Driscoll or bypass him – if you can – to try to find out if we've been up to something. The short answer is that – to my knowledge - we haven't."

"But if I'm right then, another county or nation-state might be trying something more basic to push the information, or your discovery or whatever it is out into the open. They might want it to be visible, or more likely they want to shut it down."

"The next source we would consider would be one of the usual suspects like ISIS or some other variation on a middle eastern terrorist organisation. The style doesn't quite fit, though. They'd not use such small devices, and they'd plant them where there would be more of a blast pattern and probably kill a whole bunch of civilians in the process."

"This looks to be far more surgical than that. And by the way, I can't see ISIS missing a trick to claim the bombing for themselves. It's not their style."

"You also have a history with the Irish Republicans spanning back into the last century. They always have a protocol for their bombs, calls, warning, reasons explained. And we are pretty good at intercepting them as well. Nothing like that."

"It suggests that this has been done by someone as part of a more complex process. A lone operator? Hardly. There are too many moving parts. Organised crime? Where's the demand? What do they want?"

"I'm not completely discounting lunatics, but they would still need funding, and almost always they would be putting up demands. A video on YouTube, for example. But so far there's nothing. It's like a closed system. Except for the silent Russian connection."

"Your thinking so far is close to ours," said Amanda. She was impressed that the Americans had been able to work this through without access to her information.

"It makes us think that this is more of a private matter," continued Mary-Anne, "Something within the security community. A message from them – whoever they are - to you. Along the lines of back off – don't continue with whatever it is you've been doing."

Amanda remained quiet at this point. This was where Mary-Anne's and her view of things started to differ. The Americans didn't seem to know about Marcus's disappearance from the Hammersmith hotel.

"I'm guessing that there is something that you have that others either want or want to stop?" asked Mary-Anne.

"This is the core of the way that we can move this forward and that I can potentially help you, "she continued, "and don't forget, I bring the gift of a Russian operative to you."

Amanda was thinking quickly. She would need something for the Americans, to try to enlist their support without giving away more than was necessary. Amanda decided to play for a small amount of time. She would release the information about Marcus and the paper, but only after his document had been modified.

"Look," she said.," You've got a pretty good grasp of this. I'm genuinely impressed with how much you've deduced. We've got some more to give you, but I suggest we run a team briefing to you and your whole team at 6 pm. That will give me a chance to put together the relevant documents and pictures.

Amanda knew that she'd need to work on a sanitised version of Marcus's paper. Keep in the rouble manipulation but lose the references to cybercash. She would need to read the redacted version herself, although she also needed the version for the Americans to look as if it was the whole paper and not an edit.

Mary-Anne nodded to Amanda.

"Look I get it that you don't really want us here. I get it that you've been driven into this by your charming boss. I understand that he didn't tell you he was doing this and that it was my phone call that was the first you had heard. We still need to work together, though. I think this is a time when you can use our help."

Amada nodded and smiled back to Mary-Anne,

"Go on - tell me your nickname for Bernard," she asked.

"It's Huffer," said Mary-Anne.

They both laughed.

Amanda thought she would need to play this carefully, but she could see that the Americans could potentially be very useful. She decided that she quite liked Mary-Anne.

Sanitised

An hour later, Amanda was in the middle of the now-filled control room at the offsite facility.

There was a whole new bank of technology already running, based on the systems that the Americans had brought along. It looked as if they had decided to bring as many shiny toys to create the most impressive picture possible.

Amanda had the newly printed and individually numbered briefing packs which covered the additional development around Marcus. This was potentially new information for the Americans.

Amanda made sure it removed any references to cyber currency and did not include any of the information that Marcus had mooted around America's involvement in reducing the value of the rouble through economic warfare.

Amanda thought this was a good compromise. It supported the theories of the Americans and moved things along enough to mean that they would have something to get their teeth into. It was also a quick way to shake the tree to see whether the Americans had any additional information to divulge.

Amanda ran the briefing. She added the disappearance of

Marcus and Marcus's paper. She could see it was enough.

Her own substitute team and the Americans were learning this new level of information together. Now it would be interesting to see whether the Americans could unearth anything new.

Tyler and Rosie looked on - this was a far cry from the office of three that they had shared with Marcus.

"It's as if the American style of hustle management has crossed over into her own team's way of working," said Rosie.

"Yes," agreed Tyler, he knew in his heart of hearts that the team deployed in this group from their own departments were not the sharpest knives in the box. More likely, they were the people who could be most easily released at short notice to form a scratch team.

Grace was informed of Alya Sokolov's presence in the offsite facility. She owed one to Mary-Anne for this uncanny piece of tracking.

"I'll be visiting OS12," she said, I'd like to bring an interrogation team."

She dialled for a car and made her way to the front entrance of the complex. Several other members of her team had gathered. She noticed it included one of the on-site lawyers.

"Okay, we're going to meet a Russian agent. She will want to cut a deal," she explained.

A small bus arrived. Everyone climbed aboard.

Tyler was watching when the bus arrived at the entrance to the driveway.

"I think this will be one of ours," he said, "A small bus, not a whole convoy of late-model SUVs."

Rosie smiled back. There had to be some humour in it all.

They could see the team disembark and start to move through the building. Rosie and Tyler knew they were heading for The Pen. The name given to the detention suite.

Rosie and Tyler made their way upstairs to a small viewing room and selected the right monitor channel to watch proceedings.

"Hello Alya," started one of the interrogators.

"You know what I've asked for," she replied, "You provide me with the funds and the new identity, and I'll turn over to you. If my previous employer knows about this, he will have to disown me in any case."

"Disown you, or worse," said the interrogator.

"We need other information from you first. The reason for the bombs."

"You know how it works. I know my mission. This time it's three Extractions. The other operatives know their missions, but we don't get told the big picture. I can't help. Look you've got me; you know I'm burned. I'm not just bargaining with you. That's all I know. In any case, the two drivers were cutouts. Not even Russian. One of them didn't even speak Russian."

"Two extractions, the drivers. Tell us about the third extraction?"

"That was the C-SOC operative. Marcus Barton. The man from the hotel in West London. See, I am co-operating."

"Okay, so what happened to Marcus Barton? "

"I was asked to do this after I arrived in the UK. The two bomber extractions were requested when I was still in France.

It was from the same handler though, Alexander Pakshenko. I genuinely thought he was Russian, but now I think he was a double working for the Americans."

"Taking Marcus was easy. Hotel cleaners, Dart gun. Four to move him out on a trolley. Elevator to ground and then into a laundry van. I was asked to keep him as a bargaining chip, so he is in a safe house. Now, I want you to find him, as a little piece of grit for the people who misled me."

"Thank God, Marcus is still around. So, where is he?" asked Rosie.

"You'll have to ask Mary-Anne Piper, the Americans have him," replied Alya.

"There's still something about this that doesn't add up," said Tyler.

"Rosie, I want to retake a look at those videos, especially for the first bomb. To check if there could be anyone else involved," Tyler requested.

He was thinking back to the walk he'd done along to the first scene of mayhem. The Americans flourish of arrival had reminded him of something.

We've got the videos in Comms 12, said Rosie, "Although, I don't have a clue where that room is."

"I think its downstairs in the basement," answered Tyler as they set off.

Video

Tyler and Rosie were in the video suite, about to watch the first bombing.

The video showed a small clock at the start, which showed real-time feeds from the event. Tyler noticed it started a good 5 minutes earlier than the Press and Media coverage videos that he'd seen previously. From the time just after he'd bought his lunch.

They were told that the editing together of several separate streams had provided the best closeups of the unfolding scene, but that they could get to the originals based upon timestamps as the video played.

It started. Busy traffic. The van pulling into the kerbside. Double yellow lines. The driver climbed out. Pedestrians and people walking around. A lone figure walks down the steps from the secure building. This time Tyler recognises it as Matt. A large SUV appears, which looks similar to the ones the Americans have just driven up the drive to OS12. A large sliding door opens. A single figure is hauled inside.

A sudden explosion, most of the blast goes upwards. Dust. Pedestrians on the ground. Traffic stopped and some cars attempting to get around obstructions in the road.

"That's Matt," said Tyler, "I'm sure that is Matt. The part of the video had been cut off from the earlier ones I've seen."

The black van drives slowly away.

A taxi appears, and the van driver climbs in. Blue lights.

"I remember it," said Tyler, "Damn, I remember seeing that black van. But I was trying to make sense of the bigger picture at the time. I thought that van was part of the first responders."

"So, Matt has been hauled away by someone? And yet the story is that he was killed?"

"I don't know, I don't understand," said Tyler.

"This changes everything," said Tyler.

"Matt is still out there. When we looked at the memory stick, we found transactions to a company called Gun Street Holdings, which if ever there was a Matt named company, then that would be it."

"Huh?" asked Rosie.

"Gun Street Girls - a track by Tom Waits - Matt was mad about Tom Waits."

"Now it looks as if someone lifted him, even ahead of the blast. There was a story put about that he'd been killed, but I think he's out there somewhere."

"How about we find the banking details for Gun Street? "Asked Rosie.

"Good idea," said Tyler,

"This should be an easier search, especially through GCHQ."

Sure enough, an address came up. Chelsea Bridge Wharf, SW8,

west London, close to the river. Tyler didn't recognise it.

"Okay, I'm going to take a look," he said.

"I'm coming with you," said Rosie.

They called for a vehicle to take them back to London.

London Apartment

In London, they arrived at an expensive-looking apartment building on the South Bank. The address of Gun Street Holdings. Nothing was shown on the map, and all they had was an apartment block number.

The general impression was of quiet, well-heeled metro living.

"I think we should go to the actual apartment," said Tyler. "Matt knows me, but he also won't have an escape route if we do that."

They had to loiter around the entrance to the block. There was a double entrance key fob system, and they had to tailgate in past two separate locked gates to get to the elevator.

Tyler pressed the 8th floor. He hoped that the reverse entry address lookup system from the bank account that GCHQ used would be accurate.

They stood outside the door.

Tyler pressed the bell and heard its cheery ding inside.

A clank of metal and the door was opened.

"Matt!" said Tyler.

"Tyler, what on earth! - How did you find me!"

"I think I could ask you very similar questions," said Tyler.

"You'd better come in," said Matt.

"I'm glad to see you, but know you are both in danger being here," said Matt.

"Hello, by the way, my name is Matt Stevens, I'm a friend of Tyler's."

"I feel as if I know you already," said Rosie.

Tyler looked around. Sleek kitchen, floor to ceiling glass windows, a view across the River Thames. Fancy modern furniture.

"Beer?" asked Matt.

"Sure," said Rosie, Tyler nodded.

"Okay, Explanations?" Asked Tyler

"I needed to disappear," said Matt, "I was under intense pressure."

He stepped over to Tyler and hugged him, slapping him on the back.

"Hey, man, it's good to see you!"

He flipped the two beers open.

"Glasses, frosted and cool?" he asked.

"You bet," smiled Tyler. Rosie nodded.

"Pressure. From whom? Who was putting you under pressure?

"Asked Tyler

"The Russians," said Matt,

Rosie and Tyler nodded.

"It was mixed up with the cyber currency," explained Matt. He poured the beers carefully a quarter into the glass.

"The system became too much of a good thing. It wasn't just the British that spotted what we were doing. I know they gave us both a job on the strength of it," He looked to Tyler and handed him the glass and the bottle.

"But later on, I worked out how to build a closed blockchain, which the Russians then started to use."

"It was economic engineering, via the Russian state - I assume you worked that out. Because the blockchains were in their own self-contained system, it was very difficult to prove that they were fraudulent after a critical mass of them had been created. You know what, I think Kyle had predicted that when we were all together at the flat."

Matt continued, sipping on his beer.

"I could see it was going to bring down economies, and I started to get worried. The Russians are very susceptible to rake-offs, and everybody must get paid. Although I was getting a tidy commission, I was also the one to blame if it was discovered."

"That's when the Americans approached me. I know, British, Russian, Americans. Nothing like being popular."

"The Americans came along. They wanted to stop the system. They could see Russia was using it as a weapon. They never admitted that they had started the whole thing with a much more basic model of their own."

"But you knew the Americans had been using a similar technique to sanction Russia?" asked Rosie.

"Oh yes, although I chose to keep quiet about my copious proof of the USA sabotaging the Russian economy. I thought it would get me into even deeper water," answered Matt.

He continued, "The Americans said they had proof that I had engineered the cyber coin system and that it was being used to provide Russia with material advantages in world financial circles. You know the hacker world is fairly small, so I made some enquiries to find out who had been checking up on me. It turned out to be a low-grade hacker, who was quite lucky and intercepted some of my traffic. He'd never have been able to work out the math involved in blockchain optimisation."

Tyler nodded, he knew Matt and Kyle were the propeller heads compared to him while they all lived together in the Kensington flat. Only in the outside world had he discovered just how simplistic the use of maths was, largely thanks to the rise of Excel.

"The Americans made me a deal. They could see I wanted to get out from under the Russians. Talk about Cold War. This shows just how quietly powerful cyber is in influence politics. Forget about tipping elections, with this stuff you could tip whole economies."

"The Americans said they could make me disappear - if you know what I mean - as long as I source them some code to stop the cyber process and potentially wind it back. They said I could keep my gains and that they would rehouse me and assist with an identity change."

"What's not to like?" I thought, "Until they started using bombs as a cover for my extraction."

"What?" asked Rosie, "You're saying the bombs were a cover?"

"Yes, although I didn't know that at the time." My handler,

Aron Baynes, explained that they would need two explosions. The real one and a second one to throw people off the trail from the first one."

"Well that certainly worked, now we've got all manner of terrorist plot theories circulating and no-one plausible owning up to the bombs," said Tyler.

"They persuaded me that an accident would be the simplest way to extract me, and then I could rebuild my life without the threat of being followed. I'll admit it, I was scared in case they were really going to blow me up. I had to resort to some insurance of my own. I told them I'd already set up an If_I_die.org message which would prove very inconvenient if I were to completely disappear.

"I may just still need it now that you guys have found me. Well done, Tyler"

"Oh, and forgive me, Cheers," He clinked the three beer glasses together.

Rosie chipped in, "Not forgetting that we found you by harnessing the entire power of GCHQ, SI6 and the FBI."

"No, I agree, but there's equivalent power in the Russian mob. Take a look downstairs at this apartment block. It even has a Russian concierge."

"You know something?" said Tyler, "You are pretty central to what happens next back in Cheltenham."

"I think so, said Matt, "But I'm also well-hidden at the moment."

"Have you ever ridden in a helicopter?" asked Rosie.

"Because I think this is the ideal time, and we are close to the Battersea heliport too."

"Can you do that?" asked Tyler.

"I think I can do just about anything with the knowledge we have, " answered Rosie.

"From here to the terminal is only about 10 minutes by taxi," said Matt, "Although it is a bit of a zig-zag route."

"Ideal," said Rosie," that'll confuse anyone following."

"Do I need to pack anything?" asked Matt,

"Just your 'Go Bag'," said Tyler, referring to the overnight bags they used to keep at the ready back in their flat dwelling days.

"Okay," said Matt. "When we get outside, there's a cab rank opposite, by the hotel."

Tyler and Rosie nodded. They had seen the hotel on their way into the apartment block.

"Let's get flying!" said Tyler.

"So…How long will it take?" asked Matt.

"To Fiddler's Green…About 45 minutes," answered Rosie.

Creative

The helicopter landed directly in the grounds of the stately home.

Matt, Rosie and Tyler climbed out.

Grace was standing on the apron with crossed arms.

"Welcome to Fiddler's Green and OS12, and you must be the extremely elusive Matt?" asked Grace.

"That's right, Tyler and I go back a long way."

"So I've heard, and I gather you know about cybercash too?"

"That's right, I've been fairly successful."

"Let's go inside, I have a few questions for you, Matt."

They sat in a large room, with a central table. It reminded Tyler of a boardroom for an old-fashioned company. It was officially known as The Drawing Room.

Grace, Amanda, Rosie, Tyler, and Daniel sat around the table. Rosie had told Matt to wait in a separate room.

There was a silver tray containing a thermal coffee pot, some white mugs and some small packets of biscuits at one end of the table.

"So Alya didn't know why she was running extraction on the two drivers?" questioned Rosie.

"Or exactly who asked her to do it," added Tyler.

"Could it be that the Americans somehow duped Alya into the mission?"

"We have an interesting question for Mary-Anne."

Grace was eating a chicken wrap. Rosie assumed that it had continued to be a non-stop activity for Grace in the Ops Room.

Grace asked, "So how, exactly, can I help you?"

"We think we've uncovered something quite unusual," said Rosie," We think Alya might have been receiving instructions from the Americans - but without realising it.

"She's asked for British protection and asylum now and is prepared to be a witness to what is happening. Something doesn't gel though. She says she was tasked with coming to the UK to perform an extraction job for the two van drivers who drove the bombs. The thing is, she met them both and doesn't think either of them was Russian. She described them as cutouts.

"That's quite normal, though," answered Grace, nibbling the last part of the wrap.

"Russian agents will often get last-minute unsuspecting people to drive or do parts of their dirty work."

"We think that the vans were sponsored by another country, that's all," said Rosie.

"We've robust evidence that points to the vans being run by the

USA."

"If that is the case, then it is an extreme allegation," said Grace.

"It would imply that the US was running a mini terrorist threat on the streets of London."

"Yes, the stakes would have to be high for that to be the case," answered Rosie.

"Have you any proof?" Asked Grace.

"We do, we think that one of the originators of the cyber fraud was Matt, a colleague of Tyler's. He had been hired by our own security forces and had been working out of the first bombed building."

"He's the one reported casualty from the first blast."

"I remember," said Grace.

"Yes, but we've just found him, very much alive and kicking, over in west London. He claims that he had done a deal with the Americans to re-house him under a new identity.

"Why?" Asked Grace, "Why would the Americans do that?"

"Well, Matt was one of the designers of the cyber currency machine. He did it with Tyler here when they lived together in a flat."

"It was a student project to raise some cash," explained Tyler, "It was just a bit more successful than we imagined. It's how Matt and I got to be working here. You, well the Department, offered us both jobs."

Grace nodded, "Okay, but I can't see why that would bring in the Americans?"

"That's where the full version of the Marcus paper comes in.

Marcus had identified that there was some manipulation of markets occurring because the Russians seemed to have a magic money tree.

"It turns out that there was an original plan exploited by the US government to manipulate Russian currency and then Russia discovered it and decided to play a similar game but using some redeveloped crypto software.

"That was the tweaked software that Matt introduced, except it was too successful, Matt himself got cold feet, and then the Americans rounded him up to threaten him. Unless he helped the US, he'd pay the consequence, but if he helped them, then America would help him get a new identity.

"So, he accepted the American offer. The Americans offered to make him disappear.

"In return for what?" asked Grace.

"Yes, you've got it. The US wanted him to roll back the crypto software. Ideally, to anonymously discredit it. Ideally, to reduce the value of the cybercash created for Russia, too.

"Now, the strange part. The Americans wanted two bombs so that they could run interference. They used hired help to drive the van, but through a double agent Pakashenko they apparently asked Alya to provide the extraction of the drivers. Alya was fooled and ran an altogether a professional operation. But Alya noticed a departure from tradecraft. The drivers were not Russian, nor, I gather, from any of the normal Russian sources. She thought the mission was too high stakes to have been run by outsiders.

Grace nodded, "Do you remember what Mary-Anne said in that early briefing. That the Americans had been following Alya for a couple of months? Is it possible that they set a trap to catch her in London? She did seem to drop into their laps somewhat?"

"Yes. That could be, although it is going to be tricky to get Mary-Anne to admit anything, assuming she even knows?"

Grace nodded, "She will know. She's the top US controller in London. I might have an idea," she said.

"Here's my thinking," said Grace, "We've access to plenty of hot material here, in GCHQ."

"We need to take Mary-Anne to a room where some of it is being processed, something she will know about and then we can - how can I put this - creatively augment the material with something that will be a source of embarrassment."

"Can it be directly related to the Alya situation?" Asked Amanda.

"Ideally, yes," said Grace. "It should show that we know that the USA has been looking for a lure to get Alya into the UK."

"We might have to wing it, but somehow we can confront Mary-Anne with the information, to find out what she knows."

"Alya has told us most of the information anyway, but it will be useful to see whether Mary-Anne knows about the deep cyber money plot?"

"So, what's the underlying material going to be?" asked Rosie.

"I think we can use 'The Panama Papers'," said Grace." There's so much of it that Mary-Anne would only know about it selectively in any case."

Rosie began, "Tyler, the Panama Papers were an unprecedented leak of 11.5 million files from the database of the world's fourth biggest offshore law firm, Mossack Fonseca. Everyone in the intelligence community knew about the leak, although few could keep track of the detail."

Tyler nodded," I remember something about them, I think

there was a movie or something."

"Yes, originally, the records were obtained from an anonymous source by the Süddeutsche Zeitung, which shared them with the International Consortium of Investigative Journalists. The ICIJ then shared them with a large network of international partners, including the Guardian and the BBC, who began analysing what was in the files."

"I remember, wasn't David Cameron's father involved in some way?" said Tyler.

"Yes, he was, as was a friend of Putin and more than 100 politicians, all using offshore tax havens."

"But no cybercash connection?"

"No, that's right, just not-so-simple tax evasion."

"The documents showed the myriad ways in which the rich can exploit secretive offshore tax regimes.

"It included a $2bn trail leading all the way to Vladimir Putin. The Russian president's best friend is at the centre of a scheme in which money from Russian state banks is hidden offshore."

"So how will we use this information with Mary-Anne?"

"We'll have to be a little creative," answered Grace.

PART THREE

Enrollment

"She smiled at him
like they were about to rob a bank together."

— *Rachel Kushner, The Flamethrowers*

National Security

Matt, Daniel, Rosie and Tyler were in a planning session in the main operations room.

Matt spoke to Daniel, "We have to find a way into the Russian system so we can proliferate the new code to all of their nodes."

"This is like a classic virus problem," said Daniel.

"Surely you guys at GCHQ have plenty of people that are well versed in the ways of viruses?", asked Matt.

"Yes, although we are usually on the receiving end of the virus rather than the people that are creating it," answered Daniel.

"Some companies out there are specialists in this kind of thing", said Tyler.

"Sure, nowadays they even advertise overtly on the internet. Some price-lists show the value of the type of exploits that they create," answered Matt.

"I know," said Daniel, "but they are usually the bad people we are trying to stop."

Ed Adams

"Well, obviously, we need to get one of them onto our payroll," said Rosie.

"Tricky, if it ever got out that GCHQ and SI6 were hiring overt bad-guy hackers," said Daniel.

"Duh, don't you think the public already suspect that?" asked Rosie, "But first, we need a cover, but one that doesn't just spring up. It needs to have a lengthy heritage."

"Okay, how about a security consultancy with about three years track record, fixing corporate firewalls and the like?" asked Tyler.

"You mean Kyle?" asked Rosie.

"Yes, he said he'd hope we would hire him one day. This could be it - I've already cleared it with Amanda, and she's sent a car," smiled Tyler.

"This is crazy," said Matt, "The Hereford Square gang is finally back together. All we need is a sourdough pizza."

"From Franco Manca on the Brompton Road," said Tyler.

And, as if on cue, the control room door opened and in strode sunglassed Kyle, complete with a backpack.

"Hey guys, that was pretty cool, having a car come to pick me up to drive me to the middle of nowhere. If you hadn't called me up first, I'd have thought this was some pretty elaborate hoax."

Matt and Tyler smiled and slapped Kyle on the back.

"Man, we have some shizzle to tell you," said Matt.

"These are Rosie and Daniel, our partners in crime," said Tyler.

"Crime," said Kyle, "I don't like the sound of that. I've just got

228

back from Tel Aviv, and I was given such a hard time getting out of the country. Forgive me if I sound jaded, but they didn't seem to believe a word of what I said. Mind you, I suppose I was coming back from a security conference. I should have said I'd been on holiday or something."

"Right, Kyle, you said you'd liked to work for us, here's your proper opportunity. And what we really need right now is your company," asked Tyler.

"Yes, you mentioned that on the phone, but I'm not sure that I understand."

"We want you to be a well-established security storefront. Commissioning some specialist hackers for a new project."

"Oh yes, is this lawful?" asked Kyle.

"Let's say it is the interests of National Security, "answered Rosie.

"Hmm. Go on then," said Kyle.

"We want you to recruit a team of virus writers," said Tyler, "Using one of the Warez packs. We want it to be good enough to hack through Matt's cyber currency algorithm."

"What? Hack Matt? But he's here?"

"Exactly," said Matt, "We need it to look like a spirited and lucky attack, I want to destroy the blockchain that we've been creating and to discredit the algorithm."

"Won't that cause someone quite a bit of bother?" asked Kyle.

"Yes, exactly, but it must look anonymous."

"I see, but I suppose you'll provide a few hints and tips to help crack the algorithm?" asked Kyle.

"Yes, I'll provide them to you, and you will provide them to the hackers."

"It's like a form of sabotage," said Kyle.

"It is, we are unwinding what Matt has provided."

"May I ask why?" asked Kyle.

"Let's say some bad people have got hold of it," answered Rosie.

"But you are telling me that this is legitimate, above-board, legal?" asked Kyle.

"Not exactly, but it is On Her Majesty's Secret Service," answered Tyler.

"You can't get cooler than that, double-O-8?"

Matt had been preparing a wall chart.

He stepped back to take a look.

"It's incredible, he said," Nearly all of the hacks are theft related. No-one is interested in wrecking the algorithms. I thought I knew about this stuff, but it's when you get asked an awkward question that you realise that it's like a one-way valve.

"As cryptocurrencies have proliferated widely and as security systems designed to protect customers and exchanges have grown more sophisticated, hacks and instances of theft have also continued to take place.

"Even the biggest cryptocurrency exchange and the most significant players in the digital currency world are not necessarily safe.

"To be honest, that is good for our plan, because it means the people hacked won't be as surprised.

Matt continued, "I've taken a look at a few of the more prominent hacks - trying to link them together.

"First, there was Coinrail. A South Korean exchange was hacked, and thieves took about $37 million worth of digital currency, mainly in the form of tokens.

"Then a related smaller one. South Korea's Bithumb. That hack took $30 million in tokens. Although the exchange has promised that customers will see no impact on their wallets, Bithumb has not come out unscathed. Bithumb was formerly the sixth-largest exchange around the world based on trade volumes but has since dropped to 10th place. That attack focused on Bithumb's hot wallet. A pretty easy form of attack.

"BitCoin lost around 11% of its total value in the immediate aftermath of the hack, although it remains unclear to what degree the Coinrail hack had an impact on this fluctuation. The exchange was shut down in the wake of the attack.

"Then the Italians lost $195 Million when the Italian exchange BitGrail was hacked, and the nano token stolen.

"Another attack was on the Japanese exchange Coincheck, which cost it over 500 million coins valued at about $500 million.

"Wow," said Tyler, "half a billion dollars?"

Mattt continued, "Yes, and like Bithumb's hot wallet attack, this was an online real-time attack, and some say it was the most significant direct cybercrime ever committed. Amazingly the system survived and is still running.

"Then there's the pyramid schemes. OneCoin was allegedly a Ponzi scheme with pyramid selling to boost the value of the coins. The Russian lady who fronted it did a runner."

"I heard about that one," said Tyler, "The Russian Crypto Queen. It was all over the news. Something like $4 billion stolen."

"Yes, and it poses a problem for us. We'll be doing the biggest hack of all time, but it won't be as noticeable because of these other ones. It also tells me something of the method, which I think will be to manipulate the blockchains by infiltrating the hot wallets."

"Hot wallets?" asked Rosie, "What's that about?"

"A hot wallet is online," explained Kyle, "That's the vulnerability. If we can get to plenty of online hot wallets, we can make them malfunction and render the currency held invalid. It's like theft, but instead of taking the currency, we are destroying it in-situ. Burning the money while it is still in the wallet."

"It will take some explaining to whoever we hire to cover this!" exclaimed Kyle. "They will think we are mad."

"Or," said Tyler, "How about creating a parallel universe?" simply move the money from where it is stored to somewhere else, without having direct access to it?"

"That's not a bad idea," said Daniel, "We could move all the money to a new blockchain series, just one for which there is no known key. It would take millennia to crack it."

"Okay, but if that's what we do, then we tell the hackers that we have the key so that they think we are just regular thieves," said Kyle. "This is getting more bizarre by the minute."

"Welcome to the world of Crypto-jacking," said Daniel.

"I've just been to a security conference, and yet no-one even mentioned that as a thing," said Kyle.

"I think we can probably help your hired company," said

Daniel. "We have a few specialist items of our own."

Kyle and Daniel huddled together; they would prepare an advertisement for the internet, requesting specialised code and services to support their virus attack.

"We'll probably get back some bit kits," said Daniel. "They usually try to sell us some part-written code."

"I think I'll be able to sift through that," said Kyle, "We've run across many of the players."

Daniel clicked a button and the advertisement went live.

"You wait, he said, "The bots will find it first. Then the serious offers."

Sure enough, in minutes, the advert yielded several bids.

"That was almost instantaneous!" said Tyler.

"Yes, the hackers monitor the main auction sites and run automated responses very quickly if there is a request," answered Kyle.

"Let's take a look,"

He listed the bids on his screen, they varied from less than $100k to some that were into the low millions of dollars.

"The pricing has very little to do with the quality," said Kyle, "and the specs they provide are quite often also copied from one another. It's the Wild West out there, and everyone is hoping that someone will give actual money in advance."

"Here we are," said Kyle, "This one looks good, I know the company and the kits they are offering have some track record."

"I'd have to get my guys to insert the key recognition into the hacking kit. That will take some time, but it means there's a guaranteed result rather than a speculative payload."

"We then need to think of a few targets to aim it at,"

"So, we are sending a virus, preloaded with the key of the Russian cyber coin, into the wild?" asked Rosie.

"That's right, but we need to send it to a few other exchanges as well so that it doesn't look too specific. It is a bit like covering our tracks. A few from the top ten and maybe a French, Swiss and Chinese exchange."

"What about the Americans?"

"Good point, but if we leave them out, then it does start to suggest a certain origin for the product."

How long will it take to build this?" asked Grace.

"About a couple of days if we can get the kit and I can use my own people," said Kyle.

"That's fine, but please keep Daniel involved. I think he might be able to help you too."

"Agreed," said Kyle.

Driscoll loses it

Amanda's phone rang.

It was Driscoll.

Amanda was aware that Driscoll had been on the radio and given a second very poor-quality interview. It was apparent to her that Driscoll was trying to bring all of the situations under his control. The use of the Americans was supposed to strong-arm SI6 into finding a solution.

Amanda thought that in reality, Driscoll had simply added another layer of complexity. "How you getting on with our American colleagues? He asked, "I hope you have something positive to tell me by now."

"We have the two teams working together," added Amanda. "They have turned our operations room into a massive computer centre. We have enough communications to run our own TV series."

Driscoll wasn't amused. "I need something to go back to the press with," he said, "They are giving us a hard time, and I need to be able to show some results."

Amanda updated Driscoll with the news that they had tracked down a potential van that had removed Marcus from the hotel.

"So, we think we have a target group now, but we are still not sure of their background?" asked Driscoll hopefully. This would be something to tell the big chiefs.

"Well," said Amanda, "We have several people owning up to this or at least to the bomb attacks, but we are unsure about the real origin. It can't be all of them."

Amanda had to juggle with the information back to Driscoll.

She was prepared to run the Marcus disappearance story but not that Marcus had potentially uncovered a major scheme with the Russian currency.

"Okay," said Driscoll, "You seem to have had several groups admit responsibility for the two bombs and also now you have a lead for the abduction of Marcus Barton. I call that progress, so right now I want us to mount an operation to bring down those that are claiming responsibility."

Amanda looked a little aghast.

"We are fairly certain that only one of the groups could have any claim to this. However, we don't know which one it would be at the moment."

"Look," said Driscoll, "The very fact that these groups are making claims should be enough for us to pull them in. I want us to mount an action tonight on each of these groups and to bring them into custody. It should be a combined operation. We should use our own people, the police, and the military to achieve this."

Driscoll imagined his decisiveness and leadership displayed across the media. It could work out very well for him.

Amanda realised that her work was to be cut out to do this. "What about the Americans?" She asked.

"We can't have the Americans operating in this on our soil," said Driscoll, "However I want you to use them to help you plan the campaign to bring the suspects into custody."

"We have set up the Americans as special advisers, and after the raids or whatever we need to do I would also want to feature them in our debriefs to the press. I need all of this to be actioned tonight so that it is in tomorrow morning's news. We must turn this situation around and show that we can be very proactive.

Amanda realised that she had little choice in this matter.

"If we are to do this, I will need clearance," she said. "That is clearance from the Home Office and as well as from the Ministry of Internal Affairs."

"We will get you whatever you need," said Driscoll, "You will have the necessary authorisation within another hour," he added, "It will be from me, in writing."

Amanda realised that Driscoll saw this as a fast way to get back onto the offensive over this whole situation. With Driscoll's reputation currently looking weak, this could be a way that he could turn things around for himself.

She didn't have any real option but to follow this through although she was aware that they would potentially be bringing in people that had minimal impact on the kind of events that were unfolding.

She was concerned that this was Driscoll's attempt at showmanship and that the real culprits would be would not be affected by this in any way.

Amanda decided it was better to call a short meeting with Mary-Anne and to appraise her of this. After all, if the Americans were to work with them on this, then it would be best that they knew straight away what was happening. It could also act as a massive smokescreen for the cyberattack that Daniel and the others were planning.

Amanda also realised that there was no way to run any damage limitation along with this exercise. It would be better to give it a codename and to let it all happen.

Code-word

Amanda made her way to the control room being used by the Americans. It did look like something from a spy series on television. Stacks of flat-screen monitors, twinkling lights. A glass box assembled at one end. Amanda wondered if the Americans had brought along a shop-fitting department to craft some of the environment.

"Yes, we built a quiet room too," said Mary-Anne, "A kind of anechoic chamber like the ones that recording studios use. It's the opposite of our main comms facility, designed to keep things inside."

"Okay," said Amanda, "I've something to tell you now that's top secret," she nodded towards the quiet room. "I'd like to bring Grace in as well."

"Let's go to the facility," said Mary-Anne, secretly pleased that she was able to show off just how much technology the Americans had been ready to assemble inside GCHQ.

Amanda described what Bernard Driscoll had requested. An assault on the discovered sets of suspects, despite the lack of evidence.

Mary-Anne already realised this was nothing more than a Driscoll fishing trip. That the results were likely to be slim.

"Neither you nor we have found anything substantial enough to run the kind of operation you are proposing," she said. "Unless you are not telling me something? Personally, I think this is crazy and will probably end in Driscoll being taken down like a madman. I'm not even sure that the US would want to be associated with it. We'd be seen to be interfering on foreign soil."

Amanda added, "Well Driscoll was most insistent, and it would give your co-operation the highest of profiles.

Grace added, "I doubt whether you'd walk into another NATO meeting after this without people taking notice."

Mary-Ann changed tack. "Of course, we are here to assist and support whatever you need. But. I'm not convinced that you have sufficient to go on to launch a full UK Security services and police and military intervention in your own country.

"It would be against people who are still only general suspects. We'd never be allowed to do this in the United States. It amounts to military law. You seem to have three, no four, different organisations making claims as well. There could be all kinds of ripples from this."

Mary-Anne studied the list of the groups that had laid claim to the first bomb. "Two of these are serious, but it looks to me as if the others are opportunists and/or mentally unstable."

Amanda agreed. "Yes, I've been ordered to run this with full clearance. We'll call it Operation 'Able' by the way."

"The locations we will need to visit are in London, Coventry and Berkshire. For this to work, we will need the synchronisation with several police forces as well as various army units.

"I just hope your minister knows what he is doing," said Mary-Anne, "And I will need to inform my people back in DC about this as well."

Amanda turned to Mary-Anne, "I need you to keep this very quiet," she said, "We have already had leaks related to this, and I'm worried that we will get more as extra people become aware of what is happening."

"In your case, I think we should be limiting this to the current team and perhaps your immediate controller in Washington. I've got to worry about how we do the same here in the UK."

Quietly Amanda thought that this was an excellent way for interference to be run. A distraction which would keep the Americans busy. Driscoll was still playing games to cover himself. Yet, on this occasion, he had inadvertently created something that would keep the B team very busy while Amanda's preferred A team could continue to work on the real problem.

Grace looked for the angle to test Mary-Anne.

"Of course, Mary-Anne," she said," Otherwise it will be like the leak from the American operation to setup Alya."

"What's that?" asked Mary-Anne, looking confused.

"Well, you don't think you could capture Alya in London after the Paris thing without us finding out," Grace bluffed.

"What Paris thing?"

"The Turkish Trade Minister assassination a couple of months ago. A close associate of Alexander Gulnik," said Amanda.

"Yes, Alya told us about it," continued Grace, still bluffing, "She even described you, although the name she gave was different."

Mary-Anne looked startled, "No, there's no chance of that," she replied, "I don't think America would get itself mixed up in

French matters."

"Some might say you'd not get involved in British situations either," replied Grace.

"But why don't we ask Alya directly? She's through that glass?" said Grace.

The corner of operations room into which the Americans had created their command centre had security glass in it. Not quite a one-way mirror, more the kind of glass used in supermarkets to shield the back-office from the store, while allowing those in the back office to look out.

Mary-Anne replied, "But she's seen me dozens of times."

Amanda pressed a button on her phone, "Sound now on, Alya," she said. Then irritated, she looked up, "Okay, Mary-Anne, I can see your comms retardant foam is working, let's go outside this room so that we can speak to Alya."

Outside, Alya's voice came across Amanda's phone. "It all makes more sense now. You commission me to run the job in Paris, through Pakashenko, my controller. You must have had leverage on Pakashenko- was it through Gulnik, that Turkish banker?"

Amanda added, "Alexander Gulnik was Russian, at least according to his passport."

"Well, that's curious," said Alya, "He seemed to be bankrolling Pakashenko, I thought that was why Pakashenko wanted me to run the Turkish job in Paris? As a warning to Gulnik. No one was untouchable."

"Then you get me to come to the UK to clean up behind the bombers, but really it is so that you can extract me? Exfiltrate me back to the USA? - Are the Brits in on this too, or was it a private project?"

Mary-Anne sighed.

"Go on, Mary-Anne," said Amanda, "Talk your way out of this one. I was beginning to like you, too. Now I've got your foreign asset corroborating your part in this."

"We both know that you've just bluffed enormously," said Mary-Anne,

"Not really," when we piece this together, we'll have you tied up in such a tight ball, although I'm prepared to let it slide."

"And why would you do that?" asked Mary-Anne.

"For the good of the operation. My win is that I continue unhampered. Your win is that you walk out of this undetected and with huge gold star against your name. The alternative is that you could have been found out and darkened with a big cloud. Not exactly useful for future operations."

Mary-Anne bargained," You realise you'll have to keep me in this for the ride. Otherwise, my controllers will get suspicious."

"Yeah, they'll get suspicious anyway when you drop your emergency code-word into some feedback to them," said Amanda.

"I'm afraid I'm going to have to detain you until after the operation, then to find an excuse to send you home."

Amanda used another button on her phone and immediately, a couple of armed officers walked into the operations room.

"Don't worry, we'll say you have mysteriously gone on a secret visit to Brussels, by train. That should give us time."

Raiders

"Do you know a cure for me?"

"Why yes," he said, "I know a cure for everything. Salt water."

"Salt water?" I asked him.

"Yes," he said, "in one way or the other. Sweat, or tears, or the salt sea."

— *Isak Dinesen, Seven Gothic Tales*

Raid On

Amanda's heart wasn't in the raids, but she put on her game face. They would have to follow through on Driscoll's request. She had let it be known that Mary-Anne had to make a sudden departure to Brussels, which she'd said was a cover because Mary-Anne needed to have the NATO on-side with what America was doing.

Amanda was liaising with Colonel Liddell, who would co-ordinate the battlefield dynamics of the planned situation. This was unusual, with police under the command of the military, like in a revolution or coup d'état.

Liddell was soft-spoken with a north-eastern English accent. Amanda could tell that he was tempering his words for their conversation. She imagined he'd stand for little nonsense in a conflict situation.

She advised Liddell that Mary-Anne's American team were not to be deployed. They were to stay back at the operations centre and to be used for the back-room analysis of the situation. Liddell hardly contained his pleasure on this news.

Amanda explained to Grace, " I'm sorry to have to spread this all through your estate, but I'm afraid I'm under orders from Driscoll."

Grace nodded. She knew how troublesome the Minister could be and had seen the recent television interviews.

"Look, we've got the Americans here as well, in that ops room. Now their chief has apparently gone AWOL to Brussels it leaves us with a tricky situation."

"Find out who is the second in command and insist that the Americans are very valuable doing the back-office role," said Amanda. "This situation is timetabled to run through the night. By tomorrow morning everything will have been played."

"Okay," said Grace, "But you realise this could go badly for the Minister? Armed soldiers storming civilian locations inside the UK? It's about as crazy as it gets."

"I know," said Amanda, "Don't think we haven't told Driscoll."

"Yes, but just as importantly, have you laid this off? We don't want a proverbial ton of bricks dumped at our doorstep."

"Agreed," said Amanda. "And that's why I asked Driscoll to make the command very plain. This is a direct written order from him," she waved the letter from Driscoll instructing her to conduct the raids.

Able

It was 01:00 early morning. Amanda' s own communications network was fully functioning. She had satellite video links to the four locations being raided.

The operation was to be clandestine, and the teams had been assembled as well as the creation of a 1 km perimeter around each of the targets,

The raids were set for 02:00. Amanda hoped this would be a reliable time to find the targets in bed.

Orders given to each unit were to apprehend the suspects. Retaliation was not expected but was prepared for.

The clock ticked towards 2 AM. Everyone was in position and then as 2 AM arrived, Amanda could see the operations teams moving into position led by their individual commanders.

There was a silent signal, and in each case, a series of flashing lights and muffled sounds as the teams from the tactical units deployed and surrounded the suspects.

Exceptionally, a form of tranquillizer gun was being used on all of the suspects to bring them down quickly without other injuries.

In all four cases, this worked almost immediately, and to Amanda' s surprise and relief, the four operations were over within 10 minutes of starting. By 2:30AM all of the suspects had been loaded into armoured vehicles and were being moved away towards various holding detention centres.

Liddell looked pleased. "Wow," said Grace. "Phew," said Amanda, "Now I need to call Driscoll"

For once, Driscoll also seemed pleased. He was on a video communication link to the operations centre.

He said, "I'll need my guys to be preparing the press briefing for 06:00. We need to keep a lid on this until then."

Amanda noticed that Driscoll had not said anything positive to her about the operation. He was already moving into the next phase, which was largely about covering himself in glory.

"Amanda," said Driscoll, "I guess you will want to take the initiative on the press relations for this. My main wish is that we don't give away too much about what we have done until after the various suspects have been through our interrogation processes."

Amanda nodded, "Yes, that's fine, and what are you planning to say about the American involvement with this?"

Driscoll looked directly into the camera from his end of the call, "Nothing at this time, we are not making references to the United States or their assistance".

"I'm busy now, I will talk to you again after the press and media coverage has subsided,"

Amanda nodded, "Okay, but let us know if there' s anything else we can do"

She walked out of the secure comms room and across to Grace.

"Driscoll is going to make this public tomorrow at 6 AM by his press office. I've told him not to give too much away until we have run interrogation."

Results Are In

All four of the raids had been accomplished. The sheer weight of the combined security police and military forces was pretty much guaranteed to overwhelm anyone not already prepared for some kind of military response.

Early news of those captured was also coming back to the operations room.

There was unstoppable chatter on twitter and some hand-held smartphone footage from the raids, already in syndication.

The emerging headlines were not pretty. About the gunslinging military and the heavy boot of the state. Someone had leaked the name of the operation, which also featured in some of the headlines.

'ABLE?', 'Despic-ABLE', 'UN-ABLE?', '#UnbelieveABLE'...

Amanda was also aware of the results. In the two non-London locations it was single operators running their small-time computer hacking, and as far as Amanda was concerned, these were of no real interest to the security services.

Sure, they would probably get trials and may be locked up, but really for her purposes, they were just time wasters.

The two London busts were somewhat different. In the case of the West London Hounslow situation, there had been several different individual locations raided simultaneously.

It looked as if it was a ring of people involved in something, but again Amanda was not convinced that it really had anything to do with the bombs in central London.

Potentially there was some collateral advantage in that these were dormant terrorists involved in some other caper. Still, for the purposes of this bomb threat and everything associated with the Russian currency manipulation, this was really not on the agenda.

The other south London location was similar, although the arrests were confined to a couple of houses within the same apartment complex.

The total number of people arrested was 29, and they were being kept separated from one another.

Amanda also looked at their apparent profiling and could see that they had nothing in common with one another. It was not at all likely that they were different cells from the same organisation.

It shouted Driscoll Fishing Trip and gave the services a bad name.

Maybe the individual organisations had been stupid enough to make claims about the recent bomb threats, but all this had done was unleash untrammelled force against each of them.

Amanda wondered what Driscoll would make of this in the morning for the news programmes.

In the case of the South London crew, it looked more like they were doing something with gambling and also some form of small-time industrialised forgery of name brand products. If that were the case, then this raid had probably brought in a bunch of perfume forgers. Of course, this was still beneficial to the UK as a whole but was hardly the need for such a major operation.

Driscoll was determined to put on a show in time for the early morning television and radio news broadcasts and had been working with his own PR team to get this prepared.

Amanda had provided some of the early briefings to the PR team and had tried hard to stick to the basic facts. In other words, they had arrested 29 people at four main locations, and they were suspected of being in some way connected with the bomb based upon their own claims that they had direct involvement.

Amanda knew this was face-saving speculation and hoped that the Minister would refrain from creating more confusion by drawing in these threads.

Since 5 AM the last hour of preparation had been conducted behind closed doors by Driscoll and his spin doctors.

Amanda waited for the news shows to start from around 6:30 in the morning with Driscoll's PR schedule to cover both the early morning radio and television broadcast.

At this rate, it would have blanket coverage by around 9 AM.

Of course, the newspapers would not have any of this until the following day although it would start to appear in the wire feeds and the Internet versions from probably around seven in the morning.

Technicality

Mary-Anne was still detained in a separate room in the Ops Centre.

"You'll have seen the results from the operation," asked Amanda. "I've left the TV monitoring in this room so that you are kept appraised. Grace will be joining us here, shortly."

Mary-Anne nodded," Yes, I think you've done well to get these people, but in honesty, they are not the ones you are looking for, are they?"

"I hope your minister is going to be careful about what he says," said Mary-Anne, "After all, we don't want any diplomatic incidents to arise from this, do we? For example, I understand that although the US has been involved in providing background support to this, it should remain apparent that we have not been part of your intervention team on any of the operations."

Amanda nodded. She knew that Mary-Anne would also want to distance herself from what Driscoll was about to do.

"Driscoll has decided to go his own way with this," said Amanda. "You know I will need to support him, but I'm also cautious that we don't say more than is necessary at this stage."

Driscoll's first appointment was with the Today radio programme which started at 6.30am, and Driscoll was planning to be on there from 7 o'clock in the morning. He would then have to hurry across to another studio for an interview with an early-morning BBC news programme and after that with Sky television.

Driscoll's PR had also arranged an appointment with an ITN news show so by around 8.30 in the morning he would have covered the broad spectrum.

He wanted to do this in person because he considered it such a high-profile Victory.

Grace walked into the room where Mary-Anne had been detained.

"Enjoying the facilities?" she asked, "We've tried to make this as pleasant as possible, but you understand why we've had to keep you under wraps until this operation has concluded?"

"Yes," said Mary-Anne, "We are all professionals. I'd have had to do the same if you'd been operating in the Pentagon."

"Okay, let's listen to Driscoll on the Today show."

The news was already underway as Driscoll walked into the studio. It was a small sound studio for his first interview, and he sat down at a desk by the side of a yellow coloured microphone.

He had heard the announcement in the news summarising the events of the previous evening. He recognised the wording because it had been crafted by his own marketing and press relations team.

"Welcome, Minister, you seem pleased with the outcome from the raids run last night to track down the bombers that have been detonating bombs in central London. We hear that you had four separate raids in different parts of the country. Two outside of London and two in London, one in West London and the other to the south. So, Minister, what is the latest position?

Driscoll beamed, "Yes, we believe we have caught a significant conspiracy. A total of 29 people have been arrested across the four locations, and we think they have conspired together to create the disruption to the capital.

"Each of the teams has been separately held for questioning which we are starting as this programme airs."

"Our sources, Minister, say that there is very little in common between these four groups?" said the interviewer, "For example, the two outside London are individual teenagers. One is a from a fully English background, and the other one is originally from India."

"One of the groups is said to have a large amount of counterfeit Christmas products at their location. The other group we don't yet have any further information about"

Driscoll looked slightly perplexed by this.

"No, we are in the process of tying the four groups together to show the full scale of this conspiracy. Our investigation has shown that we have unearthed a major conspiracy.

"This is a triumph for our security services and the Ministry of Internal Affairs. By using our central resources and some support from our other intelligence bureaus, we have been able to bring this to a speedy resolution."

"Minister, the opposition party, is raising questions about the way that you have deployed force to bring these people into custody," said the interviewer, "I understand that small armoured army groups were deployed each of the four sites. I'm told that there were around 40 soldiers at the each of the sites for those particular raids."

"And also, you used police force as well as the backup from other security services?"

"Of course, we did not want to take any chances with this," said Driscoll, "These are potentially all dangerous individuals."

"Minister, the opposition party says this is already beginning to smack of martial law imposed in the areas where you have provided these raids. Other people were unable to move around freely, and the sheer amount of potential firepower could have started an all-out firefight in each of the locations.

"There was intentionally a danger to other individuals that could have been greater than the effects so far from the bombing?"

Driscoll looked agitated," No," he said," That's not the case. We took the army as purely a precautionary measure to ensure that no one would escape from any of the raids that we granted."

"On whose authority were these raids co-ordinated?" asked the interviewer. "We understand it was on your direct orders that this was conducted.

"We understand that the Cobra committee is in session this morning as this broadcast goes out," said the interviewer. "It is being chaired by the Prime Minister, and there are several heads of the armed forces also involved."

"In the circumstances, did you send a representative from the Ministry of the Interior along to the Cobra session?"

Driscoll looked perplexed," I'm not aware of that meeting," said Driscoll," I assume it is part of the regular series that takes place. We normally send someone to that meeting and, yes, I do attend it myself from time to time."

Coin

"Our reporter outside the Cobra meeting place tells us that there will be a statement from Cobra this morning in at around 9 o'clock."

Driscoll again looked puzzled," I think you will find today they will want to be supporting the actions that we have taken forcefully as a deterrent and to bring the perpetrators of the London bombings into custody," he said.

Amanda, Grace and Mary-Anne were listening to the radio broadcast from the operations room.

"This is not going well," said Amanda. "I'm glad you said that." said Mary-Anne.

"Driscoll is acting unilaterally. It can't go on. Although this is a potentially bad terrorist situation with the bombs and all he can't go out with a full military force on UK soil without getting the necessary agreements first. He may consider himself above everything as the Minister of Interior but acting the way he has would create similar ripples in the United States."

Amanda nodded, "Of course, Driscoll is running on rails now through a whole series of interviews with a standard marketing pitch. I don't know whether he will try to pull out of the rest of the sessions or whether we will get some good television from watching him squirm."

"You don't seem to have a very high opinion of your minister," said Mary-Anne. "I thought it was just us, but you don't really like him. He has been quite unpleasant when he has dealt with us in the past. A very rude and arrogant man."

The radio interview had finished, and the rolling news was returning to its next iteration on the Today programme.

This time there was a feature of the interview with Driscoll at the top but the emphasis in the Today programme editorial was on the Cobra committee meeting.

"Unexpected raids on four locations involving full military presence have created a major outcry," began the news report, "An emergency meeting of Cobra has been called today to review last night's events. Minister Driscoll who was interviewed on this program this morning has admitted to running an independent operation in the small hours of this morning to round up what he describes as a major conspiracy involving four separate cells linked to the London bombing."

"He has ordered the deployment of over 200 soldiers and a similar number of police and security services across the four locations. 29 people are now held in custody from these raids which Driscoll is describing as a triumph."

"Spokesman for the opposition this morning has called this whole exercise 'the execution of military power without any prior discussion in either Parliament or a relevant subcommittee'. The Cobra committee meeting this morning chaired by the Prime Minister will issue a statement at 9 o'clock to explain the situation.

"The Today programme is being extended by 30 minutes to cover this event.

"I knew it," said Amanda," They are cancelling normal morning programs to cover this on BBC Radio Four. This is big news. Grace looked quizzically at Amanda, "What about our team and their involvement with this? There is a potential risk now from blowback."

Driscoll had already left the studio by this time. He was on his way to a small studio in the same building where he was being interviewed live for a television insert into the BBC News programme.

The media had realised that this was big news and had compressed their timeslots to ensure that Driscoll was almost seamlessly transitioned from one news studio to another.

Amanda listened to more of the reports, "I predict that within the next two hours Driscoll will be carpeted by the Cobra committee."

Amanda observed to Grace," This is an interesting turn of events, and although I could half predict it, I could not have planned this. The whole Driscoll situation provides a great diversion and cover story while we figure out what is really happening and deploy our small team of specialists."

The point

"Anyone can get a job, but do you have a purpose?"

— *Tom Butler-Bowdon, 50 Self-Help Classics*

What's the glory? Morning Story

Driscoll was supposed to be on his way across to the media city that generally set up opposite Parliament when anything significant was breaking.

Because of the security concerns, they had moved the media into an adjacent hotel, and he knew that there would be suites for both the ITV and Sky networks pretty much adjacent to one another.

He would be able to continue his description of the major breakthrough that he had personally supervised from these two studios.

As he walked towards the car, he was intercepted by first one of his marketing people and then by a couple of other people here did not recognise.

"Mr Driscoll," said Hannah, his PR person, "I think your sessions at the other studios have been scheduled."

Driscoll looked surprised.

"Surely not, this must be one of the biggest stories of the morning," he started,

" Yes," said Hannah, "But because of the Cobra meeting there is now a request for you to visit Cobra's location and to meet with the Prime Minister."

Driscoll looked surprised and then turned his face down towards his phone, which was displaying a significant count of messages and texts.

"What, right now?" he said, "Yes, that's right," said Hannah, "And these two people are to escort you to the Cobra location."

Driscoll could see a black Jaguar car and behind it two Land Rovers.

It looked as if he was being given a full diplomatic cavalcade to go to visit with the PM. Maybe his stakes had indeed risen.

"Okay, I guess that's what we will need to do then," he said he looked towards Jan." Are you coming along then?"

"Of course," said Hannah, "and I can brief you further in the car. There have been new developments, and we need to be on top of them. Don't say anything to anyone here."

As they walked towards the car, Driscoll sensed that not all was well.

Then Hannah started to say, "I believe the Cobra team feel somewhat left out of all of the decision-making on this. And the Labour opposition party have also registered complaints."

"They are upset because you have ordered military action without first checking with the government.

"For something like this, the Prime Minister says that he would at least be involved in the decision process.

"It has left a somewhat embarrassing situation.

"I've prepared you a few responses to some of the immediate questions raised, I have put them onto these cue cards for you, and I suggest that we spend some time in the car checking through these and agreeing which ones you think you may want to use.

"Won't be necessary," said Driscoll, "Once the PM and Cobra see that I've shut down such a major operation against the state they will the thanking me for my speedy action."

The car pulled away into the early morning traffic of central London. They would be with Cobra within another 10 minutes. Driscoll noticed that the car and a couple of forward motorcycles were using their sirens to help speed through the traffic.

Grace gestured to Amanda from within the room where Mary-Anne had been held. "We'll need to leave you now, Mary-Anne. Please call for anything that you need. We'll try to make this short stay as comfortable as possible."

Outside the room, Amanda spoke to Grace, "The Minister is on the run now, I think. I'm not altogether sure he realises it though. I doubt whether he will last the day. The Cobra committee and the Prime Minister look pretty pissed off with him about what he has been doing."

"The team here in OS12 that are running the operation with the Americans also have something that they can brag about based upon the direct orders of Driscoll, but realistically we need to focus our primary attention now on the team you have hidden away inside GCHQ. I've not breathed a word of that to the Americans.

"Will they miss you?" asked Grace," if you are away like this?"

"Normally, yes, they would, but because of the events today with Driscoll, I can easily run a camouflage set of meetings across what we are doing. It will become more obvious by tomorrow if I'm not back in business with the team in London, though."

"What else have we found out?"

"Well," said Grace," Based upon the inputs from your original London team we've been piecing together that there is some kind of currency manipulation that is being covered up by the Russians."

"The Russians have found out from the inside that your team were on to them. Then they have stopped at nothing to remove the individuals that have first-hand knowledge of the situation.

"That comprises the head of a trading group in a London bank and one of your own team - Marcus - who was writing up a paper about this.

"I think that Marcus's paper had triggered the new actions and that he was followed. I'm pretty sure that the two bombs were part of a scheme to draw Marcus out into the open."

Amanda realised that Grace had some of the story wrong and was quite pleased to think that the decoy actions were working.

Sabre-toothed kompromat

Driscoll arrived at the well-protected Sabre meeting place close to Downing Street.

He exited the car, and Hannah did so from the other side.

"You will need to wait here", someone instructed Hannah.

"Only the Minister will be allowed access to the main meeting room area."

Hannah didn't recognise the building although she could see it was one of the many of the typical central London ministry blocks.

She noticed it didn't have any signage although she could see it had a set of glass turnstiles and metal detectors through the entrance doors.

She noticed a few press, recognised one of them and sidled over.

"What's the latest?" she asked. "Hi Hannah, I should be asking you that. Do you have any story for us about Driscoll?

"We understand that he is being asked to resign," continued the news assistant. "Any comment?"

"No," said Hannah secretly knowing that the guess by the news reporter was very likely to be what was happening.

Driscoll was only inside the building for around 10 minutes.

When he emerged, he walked directly to the car that had brought him. And climbed in.

Hannah noticed he was hurrying and also ran back to get into the other side of the vehicle.

Several press people had attempted to take photographs or ask Driscoll questions, but luckily for Hannah, no one seemed to recognise her as his assistant.

The car pulled away, Driscoll's face said it all.

"So… What's the story?" asked Hannah.

" They've fired me," said Driscoll.

"They asked for my resignation. Immediately. The PM's office has given me a written statement to issue through public relations channels. Some SPAD has written it. I'm supposed to take this around to Downing Street to do it all properly. That's when they take the car back. Symbolism, don't you know?"

"I'm finished," said Driscoll, suddenly looking less intimidating than usual. "I tried to argue with them, but it was obvious they were ganging up on me. They need someone to be able to blame for what has happened, and I'm the unfortunate scapegoat."

Hannah mulled over Driscoll's recent performance and kept quiet. An excellent example of positional power being taken away from a tyrant.

"But what does this mean?" asked Hannah,

"Do I need to prepare anything to support you?"

"It doesn't look like it. I think I'm going to have to use the wording Cobra provided. The Committee seemed most insistent on it, and I don't really seem to have any other option."

"They have got, how shall we say, some other leverage which they have threatened to apply if I don't play along with this. Blasted kompromat."

Hannah could see that Driscoll was quietly seething about what had happened and still looked as if he felt he was in the right about everything. She idly wondered what else Cobra had on him.

"Turns out that they have considered three of the groups we raided were small-time. They were two teenage boys and a group of counterfeiters making perfume to sell.

"The fourth group showed some promise, but there doesn't seem to be a proper connection with the bombs in London.

"Between you and me, I was approached a few days ago by one of the aerospace manufacturers. They were offering me a role as a lobbyist and consultant. I told them to wait while I thought about it. May still do that, lots of marketing and expenses budget, as well."

"If you are taken out of the role, then who is your replacement?" asked Hannah, "and when will they start? With a major alert, there needs to be someone in place straight away."

"Bizarrely, they've given the role to SI6 as part of a holding pattern," said Driscoll, "I'm sure they will appoint a new minister but to keep things moving along Amanda Miller has been given the acting operational role directly and will be reporting into the Cobra committee."

"She doesn't know yet, but now I've been moved out of the way I expect they will be making contact with her right away."

"I guess she doesn't really have any option at the moment?" asked Jan.

"That's right," said Driscoll, "And she's already properly involved with this. I don't think the Cobra committee realises she's been working with the Americans though. That was another one of my moves to try to expedite things. Of course, we kept the American presence silent from the briefings and the press, so at the moment Amanda Miller is probably the only other person that knows."

Hannah nodded, "I guess we need to keep it that way."

"Yes, judging by what the Sabre committee did because of the military intervention, they would go even more ballistic if they knew the Americans had also been involved in the background."

Holding pattern

Amanda was considering the best course of action regarding Mary-Anne Piper. She was now, probably illegally, holding a US-Citizen inside the greater GCHQ complex.

Mary-Anne's external credentials would doubtless show as something innocuous like an office worker, which designed to give the maximum sympathy vote if she was ever detained.

She could probably get Mary-Anne held now on various charges related to the bombing, but this would also create a major international incident, and she didn't want to be responsible for the US blacklisting the UK.

She would have to see how it played out if she approached Mary-Anne directly about options.

Mary-Anne had a few of her own too.

"You know this is illegal," Mary-Anne said, "You may have only held me for a day, but as this unrolls you are getting yourself in deep."

"Mary-Anne, we could make this whole bombing incident go away," said Amanda," But you'll need to give us something in return. Two parts: Firstly, you'll provide us with ongoing information,"

"What, a double agent," said Mary-Anne, she laughed, "Think very carefully when you ask for something like that!"

"It doesn't have to be very much," said Amanda, "Just a sign of co-operation. I'm offering you a way off the hook here. Probably a chance to walk out with some credit."

Mary-Anne stiffened in the chair, "Keep talking," she said.

"So secondly, I'll want an address."

"Address?" asked Mary-Anne, "For what?"

"We want to get Marcus Barton back," said Amanda, "We know you are holding him."

Mary-Anne paused. Amanda could see she was weighing up options.

"All right," said Mary-Anne, "but you will have to let me go now. It will look more obvious, the longer you keep me in detention.

"Let me go, and I'll do two things. First, give you the address for Marcus and second, when the time is right, I'll do some extracurricular work. Understand that the second offer will be time-limited. Use it or lose it."

"We'll get this agreement drafted," said Amanda, amazed that the negotiation had worked. Mary-Anne must have realised she had run out of road, "You'll have to give me the address now. A sign of good intention."

Mary-Anne considered again. "Okay, I'll need to have been released within two hours."

"You have my word, subject to you signing our agreement," said Amanda, amused that Mary-Anne was already trying to gain higher ground.

Chain

"You show the world as a complete, unbroken chain, an
eternal chain, linked together by cause and effect."

— *Hermann Hesse, Siddhartha*

Ed Adams

Safe House

Marcus had been in the safe house now for several days. It did not seem very Russian to him; in fact, it seemed more as if the Americans had taken him.

On the second day, he had been approached by one who had asked him to co-operate on the foreign exchange theory. These captors seemed to know less about it than he did. He did not want to be giving them more than necessary.

Marcus tried to remember his training from back in the days when he had started working at C-SOC. He recalled that the threat of torture was often as good as its actual conduct. He wondered why there had been no explicit moves in that direction; after all, he had been tranquillised and bundled into a laundry van.

Considering all things, they had been looking after him reasonably well. He couldn't work out where he was except that it was still in the UK. He could see out of the window and had worked out that there were significant contrails from planes overhead.

His guess was he was on the flight path to one or other of the big London airports, but he couldn't guess which one.

The house was a neutral semi-detached house. He assumed the other half was filled with 'operatives' of whatever this group represented.

The windows were armoured glass and had security bolts. The doors were all locked. As people moved through the house, there seemed to be a key protocol to get from one area to another.

There were various comings and goings too. Marcus assumed it was a shift change. He had seen a wide range of different people. There did not seem to be anyone in charge, but they all seemed to know about him and that they needed to hold him.

Then, one day, there was a knock on the door. He saw several people moving swiftly. "It's Mary-Anne," he heard on the speakerphone.

One of the guards moved to open the door. A woman stepped in. Marcus did not recognise her. Then, two other women. He recognised one of them.

"He is over there," said the guard, pointing towards Marcus.

"This is one of the weirdest handovers I've ever been involved with," the guard said to Mary-Anne.

"We'll need this to stay off the books too," said Mary-Anne. "The matter is quite delicate."

Rosie nodded to the other woman that had entered behind Mary-Anne.

"Yes, it's him,"

Marcus realised that Rosie had been brought along for identification. He kept a stony face, as the training had taught him. "Don't show recognition; it might be a trap."

Mary-Anne beckoned to Marcus,

"You'd better come over here now," we are taking you to a debriefing point.

Marcus moved slowly towards the three women. He could see more people outside the front door of the house. They had the bearing of military but were dressed in casual clothes. He glimpsed a red van standing at the kerbside.

"Yes, you're going in that," said Mary-Anne. Royal Mail.

Marcus walked outside. He could feel his heart racing. What if this suddenly got nasty?

He could hear the other women speaking to Mary-Anne," You've got two hours to clear this down. Then I'm sending in people to look it over."

Mary-Anne nodded. She realised she had just dodged a significant career misfortune.

Outside in the Royal Mail van, Marcus waited for Rosie to appear.

"I wondered if you'd make much as a field agent," said Rosie, "But I think you are much too valuable."

"And this is who you have to thank for this non-violent escape plan," said Rosie, indicating Amanda," and to be honest we wondered if you were still alive."

"Can we talk freely?" asked Marcus.

"Yes, it's fine," said Amanda, "I'm from GCHQ. Amanda Miller."

"I've been out of it," said Marcus. "They didn't seem to know so much and kept asking me about C-SOC. I'm not sure if they knew why they were holding me."

"It was a safe house. I expect they were the hired help."

"They seemed to be Americans, rather than Russians," said Marcus.

"Yes, they were Americans. You may have been extracted by a Russian, but the people holding you were Americans."

"That explains a lot," said Marcus, "I was having trouble piecing it together."

"So, what have we discovered?" He asked. Rosie leaned towards him and began to explain.

Embassy Chain

Daniel, Kyle and Matt had been locked away in the operations planning room. It had become a mess of discarded food and drinks.

"It's not like the old days with cardboard pizza boxes and plastic cups," mused Tyler.

Matt and Drew nodded. "No, we're a green site nowadays," agreed Daniel, "Although it was mad when they were sending out the paper circulars to remind everyone."

Kyle looked at the whiteboard, "So somehow the Russian Central Bank is shoring up the Rouble? It seems to be through a cyber currency, but somehow the Russians are masking its use."

"They seem to be doing this from many countries too," added Daniel.

"Yes," said Tyler," the countries seem to correlate with territories where Russia has an Embassy or a Trade delegation."

Kyle added, "That is very similar to the idea that Matt had. But because he was a self-financing student, he never had a chance to put the grand scheme into practice. But I suppose someone

276

else could?"

Matt said," The very basis of cyber currency is the sophisticated number mining that is required to generate new money. The whole purpose is to stop cheats from being able to forge the connections that make up the blockchain used for trading the values. The Americans asked me to support them because my discovery system was faster than anything they could make themselves. All just based upon my algebra addition."

"Now Russia seem to have adopted the same idea to build a closed-loop system that looks realistic. Heaven help anyone who joins it. I guess they stole the concept from the Americans."

"But to do it on a distributed industrial scale would require an immense amount of computing power in the first place," said Daniel.

"That's right," said Kyle, "you'd need to be some multinational giant to do this particularly as you need to keep the whole chain under your control without anyone else being able to add anything to it."

"Could a major international power do this?" Asked Daniel

"Yes, I wondered whether a corporation could do it first," said Kyle, "The challenge is to have ways to be able to ship some of it around in a hidden format to create the initial building blocks. With all the government regulations for most types of international messaging traffic, this would be almost impossible."

"Unless maybe you're a government in your own right? And maybe have also got some diplomatic channels available?" asked Daniel.

Kyle nodded, "Yes, I suppose that Russia could attempt to do this. It would still be pretty difficult, and they'd need an awful lot of computing power which should ideally be stashed away in different countries too,"

"Not necessarily a problem; Russia has embassies all over the world," added Tyler.

"It also has both secure comms networks and satellite channels," said Kyle.

"Perhaps we can look at unusually large computer centres being used by the Russians in their embassies?" said Tyler.

"If they have any sense, they will have put them somewhere else," said Kyle," In other words not inside the embassies but in some other place where they can run an ostensibly conventional business under Russian ownership."

"Maybe," said Daniel, "but that adds another leak point to the system. If what you're describing here is true and they have figured out how to do this, then they are in effect simply printing money in a way that is almost undetectable to anyone else. In anyone's hands, this is a huge weapon. I'd keep it locked down."

"Right," said Tyler," So now we need to design a virus that can penetrate Russian embassies around the world. Easy peasy."

"Ahem," said Daniel, "there is a little something that we've been working on over the years that could do that kind of thing."

Disrupter

"So, now we are trying to hack into the Russian Federation's main embassy systems? And also across into the financial world?" asked Tyler.

"We'll need to devise a trojan horse to get into the Russian Embassy systems. A couple of options would be through the financial services systems or the taxation systems?" said Daniel.

"They are both pretty good ideas," said Kyle, "but I think they will be heavily firewall and virus-checked. We might need something less obvious."

"Let's see; the Embassy knows information about people. What about if they received the payload via the people tracking system?" said Daniel, "It's a lot more rudimentary than the other systems and probably less well protected. That's the basis of our little prototype system."

Daniel walked across to a whiteboard and wrote two words on it: passports and credit cards. "

What do both of these things have nowadays?" asked Daniel - "they both contain microchips. We could introduce the payload into the microchips that are included in regular passports or as a way to hack into the Russian Embassy and Consulate systems.

"We could expand their electronic wallets and use them to inject the payload, which will eventually need to find its way across to the banking system."

"This will only work if we do it on a fairly wide scale so that we are able to seed the payload in various different locations."

Daniel started, "We've already built the injector software for this, but it's an altogether different story to get it set up into passports and credit cards."

Kyle chipped in, "Yes, a small app on the passport runs a loader for a bigger payload. The bigger payload is the real app that can deliver the currency swap-over.

Chris nodded and looked quite excited with Daniel's suggestion. "You know something; I think this could work. It would be the way to get the initial code into the system at several different locations. The payload code would be something we could send in separately once we had seeded smaller applications to provide the priming for the receipt of the main code.

He started to draw a diagram, "See, it's a bit like a drill for a big hole where you have two drill a small pilot hole first. The pilot hole is the small payload on the passport and then the main item is delivered separately.

"How many passports do we issue per week?" asked Grace.

"It's about 5-6million per year, so probably around 250,000 per week," said Amanda.

"That should start the spread of the virus nicely," said Kyle.

"The payload itself is easier. Once an Embassy has the virus, it can request the rest of the software."

'Pull, rather than Push," said Tyler.

"Exactly, we get the embassies to request their own updates, complete with the blockchain disrupter.'

"Great," said Kyle," The other thing we must consider is how to make the whole thing look untraceable."

"Well, we'll host the disrupter software from several foreign sites. We'll add in some Cyrillic code and maybe some Chinese as well, it doesn't have to do anything, except look realistic," said Daniel.

Going viral

Amanda could see that Matt, Daniel and Kyle had been busy.

With the mixture of Daniel's Embassy cracker, the 'bought from the internet' virus kit and Matt's seed key calculator, they now had a test rig created.

They had designed a small virus which could start a collapse of the blockchains.

"It works by moving the blockchain to another 'universe,'" explained Kyle to Amanda.

"Imagine the fully intact blockchains that have been seeded by one of Matt's unique keys. Matt changes the key, and the blockchain segment moves. By changing all of the blockchain keys, we will move all of the blockchains. They will still show integrity, but there will be no way to access them, except with the revised key."

"It's a great idea," said Amanda, "but how will the system be seeded to start this process??'

We needed to get around the usual Embassy protection software, so we did what most hackers do and looked for the outer extremities. It led us to, wait for it, the border.

"What Border control?" asked Amanda.

"Precisely," said Daniel, "It focuses on the physical rather than the digital and is a weak point."

"We are planning to revamp the code in UK Citizen passports. To make them into the equivalent of uploadable viruses. Then, when the Russians scan the passports, they will start the process to infect their embassy computers."

"Won't this also work for other countries?" asked Amanda.

"No," answered Kyle, "We've added the Russian Country code prefix into the validity test."

"What's that?" asked Amanda.

"Er it's 007," said Kyle sheepishly, "Double O 7?" replied Amanda, "You are not making that up?"

"I know, it kills me to say so, but it is true," answered Tyler.

"Okay so the virus uploads after checking the country code, then what?"

"It is a lightweight virus and, when activated, uploads the separate payload code, which will change the blockchain values."

"From where does it get it? Not GCHQ, I hope?"

"Well, we are intercepting passports at the point of issue, it uses the original technique we designed for the Olympics, high speed re-encoding" said Daniel.

"And we are spreading the main payload around the internet at the moment. Chinese, Russian, American, Scottish, Dutch, Israeli sites and some of them even mirror to other countries."

"Good, so we are trying to cover our tracks?"

"Yes," said Daniel," And the new passports come with an anti-tamper addition. Try to tamper with them and the firmware breaks. We won't publicise that, of course,"

"Okay, so who do we need to alert to all of this?"

"I think, Amanda, it is you, now that the minister has handed over control."

"In fairness, I think this government-sponsored retaliation to a government-sponsored cyber-attack is wholly justified."

"Especially if we don't get caught," said Tyler.

Amanda looked across to Grace and sighed," Well, we'd better get on with it then."

Cleanup

Matt was highly organised. He had worked with Daniel to commandeer the main control room in OS12. This had meant the removal of several of the American Team, who Grace had provided with a 'special facility' inside the main GCHQ complex.

It had worked, she was delighted to see the Americans setting up various types of probe and monitoring device all of which had been connected to a sports TV network and was providing them with harmless information about Rugby and an international athletics event.

Matt had set up a range of large monitors, added a map of the world and was getting ready to track the various newly seeded passports as they appeared on Russian soil.

The maps showed a few solitary yellow lights depicting new passport holders arriving in Russian locations.

"Softly, softly," said Kyle as he watched the display. A single light turned to green.

"It's picked up the virus."

"Where is that?"

It's St Petersburg, the Summer Garden, answered Matt. We're into the first Russian government building and have uploaded the virus.

Another light went green.

"Petrozavodsk," said Matt. "This one is in a bank, Sberbank Rossil,"

Tyler watched the map. Moscow suddenly appeared with a selection of red lights.

"A plane has arrived, they are new passengers clearing the security,"

Another lone red marker, far to the east. "Yuzhno-Sakhalinsk", on the island of Sakhalin. "That's an oil-town," said Daniel.

"We're getting some decent coverage," said Kyle.

"Look," said Matt. Several more of the reds had turned to green. The virus has been successfully uploaded a few more times.

"Krasnoyarsk," said Matt, "the planes have been busy."

"I don't even know where half of these places are," said Kyle. Tyler nodded agreement.

"Well, some of these places are really the receiving ends for banking and financial transactions," said Daniel.

"The more interesting one is still Moscow. The bigger embassies and banks will have satellite arrays to bounce their signals to the far corners of the Russian Federation."

"Let us wait to see how that proliferates."

Daniel pointed to the map. New York was lit up, "Russian Embassy, in New York," he said.

A few more red lights appeared on the map. Then Paris, and Berlin.

"It has started," said Kyle,

Daniel Nodded.

"Yes, let's hope they don't notice!"

Amanda asked," How long have we got?"

~Daniel looked around from the map.

"The rate it is going, we've got about thirty minutes before we have enough spots to guarantee good coverage."

"The virus will automatically load the 'payload program', which is what we need to execute the code. To run the 'exploit'."

"Exploit?" asked Amanda.

"Yes, we will trigger the application that will move the blockchains. That's when they will start to notice something; we'll be able to set things up quietly before that."

Matt looked at the map.

"We have a problem," he said.

"Take a look at this," He pointed to a particular cluster of dots, most of which had turned green.

A few were now yellow.

"What does yellow mean?" Asked Amanda.

"It means they have been detected," said Matt. "There must be some kind of Malware detection in those sites. They are

287

neutralising our virus."

Matt looked across the map. There were, by now, many red dots and a significant and increasing number of green dots.

"A few yellow dots had appeared in a diagonal swathe, east of Moscow.

"It's the Urals," said Matt, "they are a separate time zone and must have particularly good security software installed."

Sure enough, the areas around Ekaterinburg, Perm and Salekhard were all switching from green to yellow. The virus was being contained.

Matt looked at Kyle, "Its borderline whether we have enough locations seeded yet," he said as he looked across to Daniel.

"We've got to let it go, or we risk Urals alerting the adjacent zones to the problem. If that happens and Moscow is contained, then we'll reduce our chance to be successful even more."

Kyle nodded. "Matt, we've gotta let this thing loose."

Matt also nodded and began typing into a console.

"Okay, here we go, I'm letting the blockchain mover loose."

A screen to the right of the maps showed the Rouble to dollars position.

"It's holding steady," said Kyle. Then, a small movement downward.

" I think that could be it," said Kyle. Daniel nodded. Amanda looked on, waiting for more of an explanation.

"We can see the rouble weakening. Russia doesn't appear to have as much foreign exchange as it thought. The cyber currency is no longer in play. They can see that it is trickling away, but it will look like a software bug that has caused it."

"The Americans will be delighted," said Amanda to Grace. "This is their idea of economic warfare."

"Well, if the Russians had not tried it first," said Grace, "then none of this would be happening."

Kyle looked at Matt. If only they knew, how this had all started with the Americans.

And now the Americans were pretty much getting what they wanted.

Market shifts

"Hello, this is BBC News.

"An unprecedented rush on foreign exchange markets occurred today. It has left some currencies reeling, with others attempting to match their positions as a result of national bank interventions.

"The Bank of England has said it is not involved in any form of Quantitive Easing and that the inherent strength of the GBP will allow it to hold its position.

"The US dollar has also been under pressure today, but because of US reserves, it has been able to hold steady.

"The most significant impact today has been on Russia, who stated that their stock of foreign currency had depleted.

"A Russian spokesperson has indicated that there are allegations of economic manipulation of the currency markets targeting the rouble.

"Sources indicate that the Euro is also holding steady…"

Tyler looked towards the TV.

"They would say that, wouldn't they? And after all, they can't come on too strong because of the manipulation that they have been running.

"Agreed, answered Kyle, "This is an interesting situation now, although we've accidentally tipped this back to a US advantage."

"Not exactly," said Matt, "Don't tell anyone yet, but those passports might just be programmed with a second country code."

Palmer Street

"Come on then," said Tyler, "I think a small celebration is in order. Marcus is back, and we've neutralised the money printing. We've caught the Russian agent and discovered that the Americans can be quite tricky. And Amanda is the new chief! Where, in Cheltenham, do GCHQ types go drinking? " asked Tyler.

"Tradition was to go Palmer Street," said Daniel, "Except it doesn't exist any more."

"What's Palmer Street?"

"The old GCHQ headquarters before we built the doughnut," said Daniel.

"The nearest pub to Palmer Street is probably the Wetherspoons in the town centre."

"Well, in that case, we'll just have to improvise," said Tyler,

"Bottle of Sauce, then?" suggested Daniel.

"Huh?" Asked Tyler.

"It's nearby, and we'll get a table," said Daniel.

They arrived at the pub. It was painted an all-over grey, much in the style of Starbucks with their all-black look. The group of them crashed inside, and Rosie headed for a large round table.

"Drinks all round?" asked Kyle, taking note of the individual requests and then heading to the bar with Tyler.

"Like the olden days," he quipped.

They returned to the table with a laden tray of drinks.

"So, go on then," said Rosie, "I doubt we'll ever get another chance to hear about the student flat."

"Yes, we lived in a flat in London, Kensington actually. We were all mathematicians and somehow seemed to be able to edit out the squalor of our surroundings."

"I was studying physics," said Kyle, "In case you forgot."

"Then Matt invented the cyber thingy, and we all got sucked into this!"

Rosie smiled, "You really were a collection of propeller heads in that flat!"

"We were, as the chicken said to the pig, 'committed to breakfast', by this time though, We'd blown a term's money on the hardware that Matt bought and which I paid him half towards and the only way we expected to recoup our costs was to find some of these new blockchain hashes, "said Tyler.

"Yes, and that's about when we were recruited by C-SOC," said Tyler, "I'd been able to exchange the early finds from Matt through the banking built into the gambling sites, but it became too high a traffic volume and likely to raise suspicion. Me paying in one amount, running a few gambles and then pulling all the money out again was beginning to look suspicious."

Tyler's phone rang.

"Hello," he said, "It must be another job offer! Excuse me," he said as he walked to the door of the pub.

"Erica?… I wasn't expecting you!"

"Hi, Tyler, something you should know. I think I've just heard from Victor. It came through as a text, and from a weird phone as well. I've just sent it through to you, as well."

As she was speaking, a text pinged through to Tyler's phone.

"Trouble with rissia means I've hidden since STP with Drew. Friday@sameplace. V"

"Okay," said Tyler," I'm not sure I get it."

"Rissia - a standing joke between Drew and Victor, who can't text message very well. STP - refers to the meal that Victor had with Drew and the location."

"STP usually means sticky toffee pudding?" joked Tyler.

"Yes, You boys, and what's a Rules Speciality? - the STP, so Victor is signalling to be met at Rules on Friday."

Lost and Found

"There are so many ways to go wrong.
All we've got are metaphors, and they're never exactly right.
You can never just
Say. The. Thing."

— *Jennifer Egan, A Visit from the Goon Squad*

Rules

Tyler and Erica arrived at Rules, the restaurant that Victor had indicated. They were early and had also asked Matt and Amanda to take up a second table reasonably close to where they would meet.

Sure enough, at 5pm, Victor entered the restaurant. Erica and Drew looked surprised to see Victor, who was bearded and wearing some large rimmed glasses.

"Victor, we thought you'd been abducted, or even worse," said Erica.

"Yes, I had to disappear; I'm still in hiding, these people don't mess around."

"So, what has been happening then? "asked Erica." We've found out about the cybercash, the laundering and the Russian takeover."

"Yes, that's when it all went to shit," said Victor. "I was asked by US sources to run this laundering and to keep it below the radar. I set up with the KIV Bank for the money to be washed, but the Russians worked out what was happening.

"They sent Alexander Pakashenko to threaten me. I'd been helping some American friends with connections to move money, but the FBI was not so interested because they could see it was damaging to the rouble.

"American friends with connections? you mean the Mafia?" asked Erica.

"Yes, although I don't think they call themselves that anymore. It attracts too much attention."

"You idiot," said Drew, "Did you ever expect to get out from under that? And you tried to drag me into it too!"

"I know," said Victor, "The situation ran away from me. The CIA discovered me, but instead of hauling me in, they asked me to continue. They were more interested in the economic turmoil that could be created by issuing extra money. They were trying to run a kind of economic sanction against the Russian Federation. I was in the firing line for Corporate fraud.

"That's when Pakashenko threatened me. He said I should flip sides to help the Russians directly. He introduced me to another Russian, Alexander Gulnik, who seemed to be so cash-rich it was unbelievable."

"But we think Pakashenko was playing both sides, in any case," said Tyler.

"But if they find you now?" asked Erica, "then what?"

"Bang, I think. I need witness protection to get out from this. I've managed to hide away until today, but I don't fancy my chances going forward. I was told that there is a female assassin after me now, in any case."

"I think we may be holding her", said Tyler. "She seems to have been brought over for multiple purposes. She was being directed by Pakashenko."

"Well, I think I've told you what I know," said Victor, "And I'm looking for a trade. My silence about all of this in return for a placement package."

"I take it you have money already?" asked Erica.

"Yes, I have plenty of cash hidden away. I need to disappear completely somehow, so that I can get on with my life."

"I'll need to introduce you to someone," said Tyler, gesturing to Amanda.

"Yes, we can assist you," she said, "but you'll have to turn state witness first, to put on record what has been happening. We don't intend to use it because we've been up to a few tricks of our own, but it will be useful to have the situation, and the participants filed away."

"I will cooperate," said Victor. "So long as you can get me out of this."

Russian advances

It was a quiet runway on an airstrip in Kent.

Mary-Anne stepped from the car.

"Good to see you again," she said to Amanda, "I've no idea how this has turned out, you've kept me in radio silence for the last two weeks."

"Yes, things have moved fast, you'll have to promise not to divulge any of this though. If you do, then I'm afraid it will bite you too."

"Say we are incompetent. Say you needed to guide us through this, that our minister was a loose cannon. You can say what you like but stay away from what really happened in Cheltenham."

"Yes, you were there, you met us and decided we were underpowered. Say that your setting up of the big communication room was our only hope. But that it didn't find anything. They've packed their equipment away again and are on their way back to Heathrow Cargo terminal.

"You'll be on a flight from here to Frankfurt. Ah yes, and why did you go to Brussels? To clear up what you thought was a manipulation of the Euro against the dollar.

"Here. Here are the meeting notes from the sessions you attended."

Amanda handed over a set of papers, neatly filed into a slim binder.

"How?" asked Mary-Anne, surprised that GCHQ had done so much to give her an alibi.

"Oh, don't worry, we sent someone along. She was a pretty good facsimile of you. Just a little more - how would we say - European. I think you'll have done wonders for US-EU relations. Now it's time to put this all back in the box. That includes Victor Boyd."

"Boyd? The banker?"

"Yes, Boyd, who has been helping 'organised crime' to launder money."

"You knew?" Asked Mary-Anne.

Of course, we knew, how else could the CIA put the screws onto Victor, except by pretending to be criminal masterminds. Bringing in your fake Russian Pakashenko worked for both Boyd and Alya. You have certainly scared Victor Boyd enough. He won't be saying anything to anyone.

"That's my point," said Mary Anne, "We don't need anyone breaking ranks on this."

They walked the few paces towards the steps on the small jet.

"I'll wish you a pleasant flight. You're heading for Frankfurt and then back to the US on Lufthansa. It's a very European return flight."

Mary-Anne smiled. "You are so - European," she said to Amanda.

"I know," said Amanda, "I'll take that as a compliment."

Roundup

Matt, Kyle and Tyler sat together in the pub.

"Hey - this is becoming a habit like it was back in the day," said Kyle.

"Except we all know a bit more now," said Matt.

"At least my theory about multi-threading the blockchains worked, the Russians managed to prove that," said Matt.

"And a couple of us are still in a job," said Tyler, "And Kyle, you've even managed to land some contracts with the security services."

"And we've made a few interesting contacts along the way," said Kyle.

Yes, and we've managed to wreak havoc on a global scale. The Russians are re-negotiating their pipeline deals with Turkey again.

"The Americans will think twice before they try stealth-based economic tactics," said Tyler.

"...And Erica's shitty boss Victor has disappeared, as, indeed, has Driscoll from the Ministry. It's much better to have

Amanda there."

"Although I see Bernard Driscoll has turned up working for one of the big defence contractors, nothing like a good Teflon coating," said Kyle.

"But Matt, I've still got a question for you," said Kyle.

"When the virus changed all those blockchains around; surely someone still has access to them? That's an awful lot of cybercash magic'd into infinity?"

"Maybe…" said Matt, "But THAT would be telling!"

PULSE

Ed Adams

First published in Great Britain in 2020 by firstelement
Copyright © 2020 Ed Adams
Directed by thesixtwenty

10 9 8 7 6 5 4 3 2 1

A CIP catalogue record for this book is available from the
British Library.

ISBN 13 : 978-1-9163383-4-0

Ebook ISBN : 978-1-9163383-5-7

Printed and bound in Great Britain by Ingram Spark

rashbre
an imprint of firstelement.co.uk
rashbre@mac.com

Mailing list: https://mailchi.mp/9f0b30712620/ed_adams

To Elizabeth
and
The Kendricks

THANKS

A big thank you for the tolerance and bemused support from all of those around me. To those who know when it is time to say, "step away from the keyboard!" and to those who don't.

To thesixtwenty.co.uk for direction.

To the NaNoWriMo gang for the continued inspiration and encouragement.

And, of course, thanks to the extensive support via the random scribbles of rashbre via http://rashbre2.blogspot.com and its cast of amazing and varied readers whether human, twittery, smoky, cool kats, photographic, dramatic, musical, anagrammed, globalized or simply maxed-out.

Not forgetting the cast of characters involved in producing this; they all have virtual lives of their own.

And of course, to you, dear reader, for at least 'giving it a go'.

Table of Contents

PART ONE

PART ONE

1

Where all were minds in uni-thought
Power is weird by mystics taught
No pain, no joy, no power too great
Colossal strength to grasp a fate

David Bowie – The Supermen

Scrive

Scrive clicked the new cartridge into place in his forearm and felt the cold rush snake from his arm to burst somewhere inside his head.

Next, he checked the small plexi-inspection window briefly and could see his blood already changing from a bright red back to orange, and he knew that within another twenty minutes it would again be the safe yellow colour.

Like everyone, he knew that red blood spelled danger and he had been particularly careless to let his system deplete its supply of the tropus for so long.

He felt the pulse bubbling on the left side of his head above the eye-line. He knew this was his body regaining its equilibrium. He squeezed both his hands into a fist shape the way they were taught and used his two middle fingers to massage the fleshy areas below his thumbs while his system adjusted.

Another five minutes and he was walking across Chelsea Bridge to the Tube station. He lived less than ten minutes on foot from the nearest stop, and his ride to today's meeting was around fifteen minutes. He could feel the cartridge working, and his relaxed acceptance of the day's tasks was already returning.

He looked briefly toward the sky. A jagged spark had flicked across. Now gentle vapour trails were crawling behind what had been a brief tear shooting along the path of the River Thames.

Others walked at a similar pace towards the station, although he ducked to the right into a quieter street that also cut a corner and missed some traffic crossings.

He glanced as he prepared to cross the diagonal into the station and glimpsed someone he recognised.

She had a petite almost boyish build, dressed in black, dark hair in a black band. Scrive had noticed her for three days now, at the same spot, the same pace and the same appearance. He knew she would look up and he'd see the small tattoo by her left eye. At least he assumed it was a tattoo and not consistently applied daily make-up. As she passed, he thought he could hear her gently humming a tune. Maybe from a streamer, but he couldn't see any signs of her wearing one.

He descended into the TfL transit. His new cartridge meant he had a good range on his transceiver again and could access the transport system without overtly waving his arm over the sensor.

Most travellers referred to the sensors as 'oysters' although this was a reference to a long-defunct technology, much as the Tube itself was merely a reference to the shape of the original tunnels that formed the original wheel-based transport system.

He used the moving floor system to get to the high-speed transit level and stood for a moment waiting for the next transit pod. He clipped himself into a free TPOD seat and punched in his destination. The system was pretty fool proof. His cartridge provided the principal co-ordinates for his routine travel, and a short, personalised menu of options had appeared on the screen. He'd just tapped his planned destination.

Of course, he could go to other points within his regular routes or pre-authorise other destinations in advance, from the HomeLink system. Today was ordinary, though, or at least that was what he needed to suggest, despite what had happened yesterday.

Pulse

Janie

Janie was exhausted. Not from the morning jog, which had been one hour at a fast pace. It was because of the idiotic requests that she was subjected to in the workplace. If anything, the morning run had boosted her mood, but it was from a pretty low starting point.

"Hi," she said to Karin, as they sat together for a morning coffee, "How's today?" Karin threw a knowing glance toward Janie.

"Not great, we are still going downhill, I think. But the coffee is good."

Janie's work colleague was Karin, and they'd been friends since just after Janie had started. Karin had been in the company slightly longer - just enough time to mean she could show Janie around and warn her of any subtle office hazards. The machine coffee, the inefficient procurement process and ways to circumvent it and the slightly sleazy Leonard who worked in accounts.

Karin seemed to be able to operate around most of the recent chaos of the changes without being as perturbed as Janie. Even her functional move just after the new management arrived didn't seem to have affected her spirit. But Janie also noticed that Karin could be somewhat different if they went out together for an after-work drink or occasional cup of coffee.

"I don't know how you do it," Janie exhaled, intensely watching Karin scraping some of the foam from the coffee.

"I asked for a flat, and they've given me a latte," Karin replied,

"Considering I'm in here most days I'd expect them to get it right by now."

"No - I mean about the firm," continued Janie, "It's beginning to drive me nuts. They are constantly changing things at the moment, and each time they do so, a few more people seem to disappear."

It was over the last two months that things had changed. There had first been rumours that the company was in some financial trouble. Then a set of new people had arrived, superficially polite but rapidly asking for increasingly ludicrous changes to the way that they were supposed to operate.

It was supposed to be about boosting profitability, but Janie had seen several of her colleagues summarily dispatched, some to overseas and a few to leave the company.

The ones remaining had been instructed in no uncertain terms to refrain from contact with those that had moved away. It was officially because of privileged information, which was supposed to remain secure, but Janie was far from convinced that this was the real reason.

Janie's unit had remained mainly unscathed except when Mayer and Nikolai, who were two of Janie's bosses, moved to the USA. Replacements were new people from an external consultancy firm, and Janie understood that they would be temporary so-called 'interim' management while the operation was revised.

"I tried to contact Nikolai, after the swap around," said Janie.

"It was more or less a personal matter - I'd forgotten to return a couple of items before the move. I sent an email to check whether a small package I'd sent through the internal post arrived. I was surprised when the mail returned with a non-contactable message."

"Not just an out of office then?" asked Karin.

"No, I don't think so. It landed me in trouble with the new management, who explained that the 'no contact' protocol was rigorous. I was told not try to reach anyone that moved, and if anything were to be forwarded, then the managers would handle it. "

"It doesn't surprise me," said Karin, "So much is changing. Even the email system itself. My workstation was upgraded to a new model and now needs a biometric scan of fingerprint and retina before I can use it.

Several of them had made macabre jokes about this because the technology was in some ways more traditionalist than merely using the proximity detector built into their tropus arm cartridges. It was slightly irritating that they could use the cartridges to access phone systems, the transport system and most types of door access but now had to revert to bio scans for something as simple as browsing the infranet.

Biotree

The Biotree company they worked for was a producer of biotech equipment. It had developed several of the nanotechnology-based products which had created a renaissance for British industry. The most famous was the Aport, which could be used within a bloodstream to manage the walls of veins and arteries. It had revolutionised healthcare since its originally controversial introduction and development into a range of products which could manage blood flow, cholesterol build-up and some aspects of the cleansing of contaminated organs. The Aport ran as a series of nanobots, which inserted into a person's bloodstream via the same type of cartridges used to manage general health.

The company made its fortune from the devices and the sophisticated software that was required to make them run successfully and without error.

London was still the global headquarters for the company, with other administrative locations in most major countries. The tentacles from the company spread wide, and the product base was routinely customised to markets.

The huge secretive manufacturing plants for Biotree's core nanotechnology resided in several locations around the world. Nevada, US; Toulouse, France and Shandong, Eastern China.

Research and Development had been moved to Bodø in Norway as a strategically safe location. Just within the Arctic Circle, it still had good infrastructural connections including fast land transit, extensive seaborne links and the small matter of a major NATO airbase nestled within the town. The origins as a strategic base went back to annual shows of strength known as the Cold Response, which still occurred under the less obvious title of CORE.

It had other advantages. A local population with their own language, while also possessing excellent English language skills for handling the incoming scientists. A university base developed extensively as part of the run-up to the creation of the research faculty.

The location also had appeal for the people stationed there, who were attracted by world-class research, the best facilities, no practical budgetary limitations and a premier lifestyle during their term. Many tried six months and then remained for much longer.

Additionally, the Norwegian government had been particularly understanding since the changes in global energy policy because they had needed to re-provision from the decline in North Sea oil and natural gas. They had granted the area a special status as a world economic development zone, and it had boosted the relative ranking of the still sparsely populated Norway to a top fifteen economy in terms of its economic freedom.

The subtext was the immense security that surrounded the environment and the commitment of those employed to maintain the secure nature of their work. Bodø was also small enough to mean that unusual activity would be quickly spotted and with the added incentives of the Norwegian kriminalitetsforebygging (KRÅD) - the criminal intelligence organisation providing added rewards for useful intelligence.

In its heyday, Biotree was simply a money machine as the demand was pretty much world-wide, and the patents and manufacturing processes locked down during the prototyping cycle.

Therefore, the employees of the company were routinely subjected to heavy screening before they joined, were provided with extensive benefits and the equivalent of 'golden handcuffs' making it exceptionally undesirable to want to leave.

That had been the case until when a Chinese manufacturer had started to produce the first clones. Strictly, they were not clones at all. They were a different way to provide the same outcome. It was evident that some brilliant people had somehow reversed engineered the 'bots and also the operating systems and now created something remarkably similar in its function, but at what worked out to be one-tenth of the price.

That had tipped the market and the little nest egg of un-vested shares that Janie and Karin had received when they joined the company was now worth less than one-tenth of their original value. These changes had heralded the management changes and the new people that walked the corridors.

It was understandable that the company was now jittery and that many of the longer serving associates were beginning to look at the job sites again for new roles.

Janie and Karin continued their coffee.

"I think we are still at the very beginning of something," replied Karin, "I won't be surprised if the new management also gets replaced within a month or two."

"What, just a revolving doors management style?" smiled Janie.

"No, more a double-blind protocol," responded Karin, "Remove the people who know what is happening, replace them with new ones and break the chain. I've seen it elsewhere; it severs the Corporate knowledge before another move is played."

"How come you know so much about this?" asked Janie.

"I'm letting you into one of my secrets when I tell you this."

said Karin, "This process is the reason I joined Biotree".

She looked long at Janie. "We're all smart people in this organisation, but some of us have roles that are far enough down the organisational tree not to be a threat. We won't get replaced like Mayer and Nikolai. And that's important because I've been sent here to find out what is happening."

"Why are you telling me this?" asked Janie, "It all sounds a bit far-fetched."

"Tonight," said Karin. "meet me - this coffee bar at six o'clock - and I'll show you something."

Tube

Scrive was travelling across London. He looked around the TPOD compartment. It was a recent model and had the evaluative advertising module that had been creating a commotion in the media. Linked to the occupants, it would select advertising materials with apparent associations with the people in the compartment.

Despite the trials, it had proved something of a disaster. People wanted to see aspirational products like expensive holidays but instead were presented with perspirational products like deodorants. When the adverts were non-selective, it really didn't matter, but when the demographics of who was in the vicinity chose the banners, then it became a question of 'who triggered that one?'. The marketeers had an answer for it all based upon product weighting. Still, most people assumed it was either them or their neighbouring travellers that had created the demand for unpleasant cereal selections or dating agencies for the lonely.

The countdown began, and ten seconds later, they were moving towards their next destination. They accelerated to a couple of metres from the next pod and hurtled through tunnels at blurry speeds towards East London. The scheduling was impressive, with individual pods able to manoeuvre around one another and to take the right branches, guided by a lidar and radar system that avoided collisions.

For most of the journey the windows were black, not because of the view, but to avoid inducing vertigo into the passengers. Everyone knew the buckle-up protocol on the system, and it was frowned upon if anyone fumbled too long getting into their seat.

There was a moment of phase shift which sounded like a suction motor as the pod slowed and stopped suspended on its soft magnetic levitation while a few passengers swapped for the second part of the ride.

Scrive was flicking idly through the touch screen pages, which had been interrupted by the safety announcement before the pod started again. He noticed the newsfeed was referencing the Biotree financial difficulties and the emergence of the Chinese alternative biobots.

It wasn't exactly new news, but the media liked to recycle the same few facts every way they could, and there were now plenty of cartoon simulations of how a nanobot worked and the various components used to make them.

Scrive had been through surgery after a fall which had broken a bone. The medics injected the local area with nanobots to speed the repair. He was astonished at the way they had linked into a structure which effectively fused the bone halves and then as he healed naturally, the nanobots progressively reduced their links and eventually flushed from his system.

He had no idea how it all worked but had been given a monitoring device while the 'bots were working so that he knew how many were operating. It had been several thousands 'bots but eventually dropped away to a couple of dozen.

That had bothered him at the time because he was aware that they hadn't dropped back to zero and he sometimes wondered what the remaining few were doing inside of him. He'd tried the monitor on others. Those who underwent nanosurgery seemed to have residue; everyone else didn't show any readings on the device.

A sharp ping broke his reverie as the TPOD arrived at the

second stop. His destination in Canary Wharf. He'd been lucky to catch a fast transit that had only made one stop along the way. Sure enough, about two-thirds of the passengers unclipped and left the pod, back onto a platform surface and then through a series of moving floor-ways back to street level. He would use the underground retail levels to get from the Tube stop to the office.

That certain something

Janie's afternoon passed with yet more unexpected company changes. Laughably they were being sent out via email, but the new system had a fault, and so many of the recipients were getting blank messages with just a title. Janie felt this summed up the current situation, all title and no content.

Janie prepared for her evening meeting with Karin. She knew her well enough to think she was serious about something, rather than it being some form of a practical joke, and it didn't look as if it would be about boyfriends or partying. At about five minutes to six, Janie headed into the coffee bar and ordered a drink. She'd not got much of an evening ahead, so a chat with Karin would be an entertaining diversion, whatever the basis.

Another ten minutes passed, and Karin hadn't appeared. Janie sipped on her coffee and looked around. She hadn't prepared for a long wait, because usually the two of them were pretty punctual when they met.

Another five minutes and she decided it was sensible to call Karin's phone. She tapped the number and diverted straight to messaging. She decided to tap in "I'm here" instead of leaving a voicemail and was surprised when an immediate response returned saying that 'the holder of this number is no longer available'.

Janie looked down to check the code. She had used the right number; it was a click from a call that she had made to Karin earlier today. Janie decided to try again, this time by speaking. The number rang, and she heard a click. No voicemail, no messaging at all this time.

Janie pressed her recall facility and ran back to the message from a few moments ago. She saw it pop back onto the display, but then she noticed it rotate and disappear. It had been deleted, but not by Janie.

She flipped back to Karin's contact entry. It had also gone. Janie looked around the phone for the on/off switch. She cursed that she'd forgotten how to turn the whole device off, it wasn't something that one ever did after it had been powered on for the first time. Eventually, she found the switch, flipped off, counted and flipped on again.

A few seconds for the animated initialisation and this time Janie could see that the contact had been deleted. There seemed to be a few other numbers missing as well.

"Hello." said a man's voice behind her. It was quietly spoken as if to soothe. It didn't work because Janie was already turning to confront what she expected would be someone panhandling for money right there in the coffee shop.

"You must be Janie?" he asked before she had a chance to get angry. He was around the same age, clean-cut and lean but wearing a slightly crumpled looking outer sports jacket. The sort of jacket that would be seen at the top of a mountain. In snow.

"Hello...Who are you?" she responded, "I don't think we've met, at least I don't recognise you?"

He smiled as if trying to look like a friend.

"No, we haven't met, but I'm a friend of Karin's"

"Where is Karin, then?" replied Janie.

"I don't think she will be along, in fact, I don't want to alarm you, but I don't think either of us will be seeing her again," came back his response.

"Now you are worrying me," said Janie, "In a creepy kind of way. I will make a fuss if you don't explain yourself right now." The cafe was busy. They were at a table right in front of the serving area. It would be hard to imagine anywhere else more public. If Janie made a commotion now, there would be people intervening in seconds.

"Look - I'm here for a reason. Karin said she would bring something along this evening. That something was me," he began to explain.

Charlie

Charlie could hear the room. Apartment 123. It made two different sounds. One was a buzz, which seemed to be the refrigeration unit. The second was a low growl, which sounded as if someone had left a music system switched on but without anything playing. A kind of low-frequency hum.

She removed the mirror shade sunglasses that she'd worn into the building. Better to be remembered for dark glasses that are easy to exchange.

Charlie had felt that spin-down relief wash over her too. She had been busy and hyper-alert for the last two weeks. An assignment in Milan had almost driven her to distraction.

She'd been driven back to the airport in a black limousine, which seemed to have priority access everywhere. The driver only spoke Italian but had a black liveried look that said to anyone outside the ride, "Don't mess with me."

She'd noticed the relief on the plane. A conventional jet; she'd sat down in her seat, felt the adrenaline leave her system and then blanked for the next 30 minutes that they'd sat on the tarmac before take-off.

Then she'd flown back to New York, but now she was back in Europe again.

At least she'd had a driver pick her up at this end, who was able to whisk her above the traffic to her destination. But now, her body needed to recalibrate.

Charlie kicked her boots off and felt the springiness of the carpet. She dragged her toes through what she perceived was an expensive flooring surface. Scrive had posted her a key. She said she'd be around this week and would it be okay to stay over for a few days?

Scrive had responded immediately with a "Yes". Not exactly a phone call, just a word in an email. She knew that this was his way of saying everything's fine and that they'd talk when they were together at the apartment. Scrive was frequently travelling and had dozens of people trying to get his time, but Charlie knew that she was an insider and would get the equivalent of the red-carpet treatment, even if that was just a simple "Yes".

She checked a few of the cupboards in the kitchen. There was plenty of cereals and a bowl of fruit as well as a random selection of refrigerator foods. She selected an apple and took a bite. It was the real thing. Not a clone or a forced product synthesis. It had a taste as if it had been grown somewhere in sunshine and with rain.

Charlie savoured the fruit and paused to think what to do until Scrive returned, which she assumed wouldn't be for several hours. She noticed the packaging on the edge of the kitchen counter from Scrive's new tropus cartridge. The rest of the room was tidy. Almost perfect, whereas the packaging here suggested the tropus was the last action before heading out for the day. She glanced at the type of cartridge. Standard. Scrive was still operating low profile.

Charlie headed for the sofa, flipped the remote and clicked into a television menu. She'd watch a movie and maybe enjoy some more fruit while she waited for Scrive's return.

Cedar woodland streams

Scrive passed through Biotree's elegant entrance lobby through which permeated a smell which he thought of as a woodland stream. There was a greenish-blue water sculpture between the entrance desks for visitors.

The building divided into different businesses and a couple of the main ones had entrance lobbies on the ground floor. Further up the building were more entrances and some quite ornate environments designed to suggest anything except a world that was many stories from the surface.

His access was pre-defined, and he could walk through the scanners and harmless-looking glass turnstiles and towards one of the elevator banks. He knew about the glass shield that could drop silently from the ceilings and rise from the floors if someone was attempting unauthorised entry to the building.

The security style of this enterprise was muted, compared with offices having steel cages separating inside from the outside. It was as if the security was in inverse proportion to the appearance. The fanciest buildings appeared to have no protection, whereas a corner shop would have the overt grills, chains and bullet and bombproofing on display.

Scrive hadn't worked with the low-end organisations for several years. He'd made his reputation which meant his line of work was recognised with the big players and the related high fee-rates. He usually worked through other organisations but still considered himself a free agent, able to pick and choose and without the hassle of a long-term boss breathing down his neck.

Today he was deliberately operating through another company and had some special idents made so that he could tow their corporate line with his client. It was a kind of unspoken situation between him and his clients. They knew he was freelance but didn't ask. He would appear to represent the agency or company that fronted him but wouldn't confirm that he was a full employee. It worked for everyone because the clients he worked with knew he was one of the best at what he did.

The elevator pinged open on the 63rd floor. A woman's voice politely announced the level and the company departments represented.

"Company Compliance," she announced. Scrive crossed the lobby to another set of reception desks.

"Hi, my names Mallinson, Scrive Mallinson, I'm here to see Makatomi San".

He presented his ident on a handheld device, and it blinked onto the receptionist's screen. He had used the Japanese traditional method to show the ident. It seemed slightly arcane to grip the handheld between both thumbs and forefingers and to bow slightly, but this was part of a business tradition that swept back through many generations with the Japanese and was somehow updated to cope with current technology.

"Mr Mallinson, I see you already have full access authority; would you like to be escorted to the meeting room, or do you know your way? I will inform Mr Makatomi of your arrival," responded the receptionist. It was all very formal here, Scrive knew he was in one of the places where ceremony and protocol would still be necessary.

"I'd be pleased to be escorted," he replied, realising that although he knew the way, the client would feel more comfortable seeing him in their keeping rather than running loose, at least until he'd kicked off the assignment.

Another person, slender, Japanese and suited appeared from behind a partition. "Hello Mr Mallinson, let me show you to the meeting area - My name is Takuya, if you need anything while you are here, please let me know." He bowed lightly, and Scrive returned the gesture.

Scrive noted the perfect London English of the Japanese-looking person. He wondered if Takuya was his real name or was an adaptation for his role in the company. As they walked, he thought about asking, but then decided to play it low-key until at least until the assignment was underway. He was ushered into the meeting room.

"Mr Makatomi will be along in a few minutes," said Takuya, "Would you like some coffee, tea or water?"

Scrive thanked Takuya but declined any drinks. He would use the few minutes waiting to scope the working environment. Takuya quietly left the room after pressing a small button which lit an engaged signal. Scrive realised that this would probably also start a monitoring process with sound and vision, so he decided it best to play dumb and settle into one of the comfortable leather chairs.

He noted the camera spots on the walls. One large obvious video camera, facing towards the floor and switched off. Three more small pinprick-sized cameras with tracking arranged around the wall. He couldn't tell whether they were activated, so he pulled his handheld and took a silent picture of one of them. He glanced at the result, and there was a small pinprick of light from the infra sensor. Something not noticeable to the eye, but easily spotted by another camera. They were on; he was undoubtedly being watched.

He walked across to the door of the room and glanced at the panel that Takuya had pressed. It was the latest generation operating system and a specification that he had not seen before. This room and probably this entire floor were kitted out with state-of-the art technology.

There was a muffled noise from outside, and then the door clicked open. Takuya re-entered along with two other people.

"Let me introduce Mr Makatomi and Mr Arusen," said Takuya, "and this is Mr Mallinson". They all briefly bowed to each other, and Scrive extended his hand for a handshake.

"Mr Makatomi, Mr Arusen, you may call me Scrive", he smiled.

They both smiled back, shook hands and took seats around the long rectangular table.

"Mr Mallinson, ...Scrive, we have something of a problem and require some extraordinary assistance. I believe you will be able to help us." began Mr Makatomi,

"This is Mr Arusen, from our legal counsel. He is in this meeting as a matter of record. Afterwards, he will have taken notes from our conversation, and they will form a permanent record of what has been discussed today. That will be the only record, and it will be non-deniable. Do I make myself clear?"

Scrive nodded. He realised the situation. The three of them were about to talk off the record. The notes from Arusen would describe an entirely different discussion which had no bearing on the actual conversation.

"Mr Arusen, you had better provide me with a copy of this conversation", he smiled, "You may beam it to me for simplicity."

Mr Arusen nodded, "Actually, I have taken the liberty of already doing so. I noticed your use of your handheld device a few minutes before we entered the room and beamed you a copy just after I wiped out your picture of this room".

Scrive felt the hairs on the back of his neck tingle. He would need to be on top game. They'd just signalled to him that they knew what he was doing and that they could access his well-protected handheld computer. And even wipe out content.

Scrive smiled again, "My test of your systems worked then," he replied, "you detected my scan and were able to remove the content and replace it with your file. That's my point about your current technology. It looks modern, but if you can do that, then so can someone else. It's a situation where the strength becomes a weakness."

Scrive secretly thought that he was the one turning his own weakness into a strength.

"Let's get to the main business", continued Scrive, "beyond the theatrics, you seem to have a real problem. You've already checked me out, long before I appeared here so please can you explain to me the basis of your need for my assistance?"

Mr Makatomi grinned, "They said you would be direct with your discussion. Let me be as direct with you…"

Tract

Lars lived on the Tract. It was an area outside of the Ellipse where the poorer people lived and survived in the old ways. No biospheres, no transport apart from self-powered systems, because access to fuel was prohibitively expensive.

The Tract dwellers had access to fire, water and farming, but the economy was completely separated from the area inside the Ellipse.

Fundamentally it was an economic model similar to something from the Middle Ages. Protectors ruled, workers survived, and everyone paid a lien to the local Protector who would keep order and prevent incursion from neighbouring tribes.

There was no hope for a Tract dweller to legitimately enter the Ellipse. Lars sometimes wondered whether people inside the Ellipse even knew about the Tract world outside.

He and his partner Carolin knew about the outside, because they had arrived in the Tract together from Norway. It was after one of the meteor strikes and they had sought shelter together but then found that the land had become part of the Tract.

There was a large area separating the two environments. It comprised a white band of light and a power source activated by movement. It sparked first as anyone approached and would destroy anything that crossed into the white area. Lars had, as a child, played dare games and had thrown stones and even small branches into the light, to see them burst and disappear. As he'd grown older, he'd realised the danger of getting too near and nowadays, like most people, he would stay away.

There were plenty of signs of the previous habitation in the Tract areas. Whole towns were visible and many consumer goods but without power sources nor means to make more than token power from fire or through static bicycling, the energy from which was stored in old-style car batteries. There were some wind farms which still worked, but the energy was erratic, and the control systems for routing the energy was mainly destroyed.

Lars and Carolin belonged to the Dals. They mainly spoke Norwegian and English and also had another language amongst some of them from which he'd only ever managed to pick out a few words. His nearest town still had bookstores and libraries, but they had gradually been raided, and nowadays many of the books had been used as fuel. It was still possible to make a living, and the old metal coins were used as a means of exchange. The coins had a higher value than the banknotes, and only a particular type was generally exchanged.

The biggest threat to Lars and his tribe was from various biohazards which would sweep through the Tract areas. These could be simple ailments although there was still a significant number of conventional pharmaceuticals in circulation, there were also virulent bugs that would strike and wipe out a whole tribe.

Consequently, most tribes stayed apart, and a delicate balance of equilibrium was maintained based upon survival rather than territorial disputes.

Lars had no idea how large the Tract or the Ellipse were. He knew he could walk all day, but the terrain would hardly change. There were markers on the old highways which represented the ends of his domain. They were words describing what had once been county boundaries. It was usually easy to stay inside the boundaries because the main routes all had signs at their edges, which often, ironically, welcomed people into the next area. Some of the county signs picked out something famous about what the county contained.

Along the side of some of the main routes were also advertising for domestic items or even high technology equipment. He had seen one for an author, Jo Nesbo, as he approached a town. He knew Jo Nesbo had written books and had once found a couple of novels that were dismissively supposed to be used as fuel, but which he'd hidden in order to read.

Despite all of this, Lars could still sometimes feel very happy. A warm day, sunshine on his face, a run along one of the highways and he could feel a kind of exuberance. He was careful though because he knew that if he fell and injured himself, it would be another story. Many people who fell and broke bones would never recover — the same with people who suffered from deep cuts. There was something like a fifty-fifty survival chance in this case. And even with the remains of a past civilisation to use, it was like seeing an infrastructure gradually weakening.

He wondered for the next generation, and whether there would even be one beyond that.

Today was a special day. It was Protector's Day, and the Protector would be in town to collect lien via his taxmen and to provide an update on the current state of the Tract. He was heading for the town centre, not to meet the Protector, but because he had been selected for a special assignment.

He knew it was special, because he had been told he would be leaving the Tract, to visit the Ellipse.

Coffee Bar

In London, Janie looked more closely at the person who had replaced Karin for the evening coffee. The first impression of mountain climber was somehow reinforcing itself. He had a tan, but it was a kind of weathered look, more from snow and wind than direct sunshine. His face was angular and with slicked-back blonde hair. The dark jacket had a small logo with a picture of a mountain. And almost irrationally Janie was deciding he looked very athletic.

"Okay," she said," We'll stay here for a couple of minutes while you explain yourself. Then I will leave".

"Okay," he replied, "My name is Lars." Janie noticed the slight accent and then the name. Before she could ask, he continued, "I am Norwegian and had come to London to meet with Karin. I saw her yesterday for about an hour, and she has told me some things that I will share with you. I don't want to alarm you, but Karin has been in some trouble, and I think that is why she won't be along this evening."

Janie looked around. She could still make a fuss if needed and leave without difficulty. She was across the table from this guy. Outside, he could undoubtedly outrun her if anything weird was going on.

"You'll have to tell me some things that stop me thinking you are a weirdo", she clumsily replied," I've never seen you before; you tell me you've come from Norway to see my friend and then she disappears. It doesn't seem right." She could feel her pulse quickening as the gravity of the situation increased.

"I didn't expect you to embrace this situation", he continued," But frankly, I need your help. Karin was sent into Biotree to investigate some things. She has been undercover since she started. I work with her, and we are investigating a serious matter."

He looked down at his plain black coffee and stirred in a small amount of sugar. Janie noticed a small tattoo on the underside of his hand. She thought she had seen it somewhere before, like a skinny 'S' shape.

"We've been looking into the plans for Biotree," he continued, "We're from an organisation that checks civil freedoms. Like an Amnesty International crossed with a Greenpeace, but we do our work without publicity or public profile. It is better that way, or we get targeted and refused access and even work."

"You'll need to show me some proof," replied Janie, trying to think of her best exit strategy. She needed to know whether to trust this person or to find the fastest way to escape. Janie was concerned that he knew who she was, what she looked like, and where she worked.

"Okay," she added "Suppose I believe your story. I still want to know where Karin is, and then when we are both together, I may co-operate a little more."

"As I said", he responded," I don't think either of us will be seeing Karin again. I believe she has been dis-appeared like a number of your company management. Try her number, try her email, I think she will have been removed from the systems already."

Janie knew this was the case but wondered if it was some trick. An electronic erasure done like some conjuring trick to persuade her that this wasn't a hoax.

"Here's the situation", he continued. "I expect Karin has given you something to look after in the last couple of weeks.

It will be something minor, a book, some papers, a loan of some kind — That's how it works. The person investigating discovers something, passes it along to someone who doesn't know anything about it and then one of us collects it. A kind of drop box but with a person rather than a location."

Janie was thinking fast. "Okay, but if Karin has disappeared, it could be because of you, in any case. How do I know you aren't trying to get something from Janie by tricking me?"

She stared at him.

"You don't", he replied. "But why would I go to such elaborate ends to talk to you like this? If I was hostile and had done something to Janie, wouldn't I do the same with you? No. I am who I say I am. Here is my ident."

He held his arm towards her, and she scanned him onto her handheld. A Norwegian passport appeared. His picture. Lars Fjelstad. Journalist. It looked authentic and had the little authenticated icon on the top corner when she played it back.

"Look. I can see you don't want to get involved with this. Think carefully about the last couple of weeks. If you can think of something like I describe, let me know and after I receive whatever it is that Karin passed you, I will be gone forever."

"Also, please don't tell anyone about this, or I will probably also disappear, and then you'll probably get another visitor with a similar request."

He looked towards her. Their eyes met. Janie thought he looked both genuine and a little bit nervous.

"Okay", said Janie," I'll think and then contact you tomorrow if I can remember anything."

"We will need a different meeting place," he replied. "You choose it now, and I will remember it. Don't write it or email it".

"Okay..." Janie felt she was getting drawn into this.

"We'll use Smollensky's by the clocks at Canary Wharf. Whichever day, it will be six o'clock in the evening".

He nodded. It was another very public place in a busy area. Easy to find but impossible to guess.

"I'll go first", he said and slipped quietly towards the door.

Janie looked around. It was six forty. Her world had changed considerably in the last thirty minutes.

Chinese theft

In Biotree's offices, Makatomi stared at Scrive,

"We know that the Chinese stole the designs for the Aport nanobots," he began.

"We also know that they didn't want them for the basic commercial cloning that they have been taking to the market. It is highly likely that they have other plans."

"Why would you need me for that?" asked Scrive. "You know what I do and what you describe is little more than the speculation that we've seen in the media. Conspiracy theories and all. China steals trade secret, makes copies, makes something else as well, makes pots of money..."

"All of that might be true," replied Makatomi, "But we need to track back to an alternative source of work that the Chinese are running."

"What is it then, some weapon?" asked Shrive, "That was the typical criticism of the nanosystems, that they could be used for good or evil purposes."

"Correct. In a way." said Makatomi, "There are certainly options that would allow an unscrupulous group to do something bad with this technology.

"The thing is, we believe the Chinese that took the original design have themselves been compromised. They are in a similar position to Biotree, except their design is weaker and their ability to trace what has happened is probably non-existent. We don't even think they know they have been compromised. That, Mr Mallinson, is where you come in."

"You want me to penetrate the Chinese system and then follow the trail to the second set of thieves? Presumably without anyone noticing?"

"You are astute, Mr Mallinson, that is what we want you to do. We will require the geo-coordinates of the second group and will take actions from there."

"We will need to discuss fees for this, Mr Makatomi"

"That can be taken care of by Mr Arusen; it should not be a problem. We will pay you some upfront expenses too; this will involve significant preparation, I am sure. Exceptionally, we will make Biotree facilities available for you as well. I suspect we have some technologies here which you will not have seen before."

Scrive looked at Makatomi San and nodded. Then he bowed. "I'll be pleased to assist with this. I will find the source of the original leak and then trace the second leak from the Chinese."

Makatomi stepped forward. They shook hands. He looked across to Arusen. "Please assist Mr Mallinson to get started. Mr Mallinson, you realize this is covert and deniable?"

"Always the way", replied Scrive.

Scrive made his way back to the Tube station. He'd return on the same system. Low profile. Traceable. His training meant he wouldn't do anything to trigger alerts from the surroundings of what was his new employer.

As he crossed the pedestrian area back to the curved dome of the station entrance, he could hear the recharge cycle of a high-powered transit. A V-Blade. Commercial version. He could tell from the engine note. Two tones were rising through octaves from a rasp to supersonic frequencies in around three seconds.

He listened for the tell-tale bass thump as the systems prepared for take-off and looked upward to the apparent source. It was from his building and almost certainly Makatomi San making his less low-key departure. The private V-Blades were still in the luxury goods category, so he knew it would be someone with corporate leverage and in a hurry. A few seconds later, he saw the flash as the 'blade departed. Makatomi could be back in Japan before Scrive reached Chelsea.

Scrive had used V-Blades plenty of times. Mainly the military versions which didn't need the dual engines. Commercial versions had to provide full system redundancy as part of safety measures. For the military, the reasoning was it was better to have two of the transports, which would anyway be moving into hazardous terrain. He'd used them since the early days when they required occupants to wear pressure suits to handle the G-forces. The later models had a new atmosphere and pressure walls which dealt with the forces as a kind of electronic cradle around the passengers. When he'd first travelled on the commercial versions, he couldn't believe it was the same craft as he'd experienced in the military field.

Scrive had never been 'in' the military but had worked with them much as he had with his commercial clients. He'd been a system engineer by background and had found a natural ability to see past numbers and sequences. They popped out to him almost as pictures, and he could manipulate huge matrices mentally to look for unusual patterns. Some would say he was gifted, but he had also experimented with some of the biometrics that he ran into in his professional life. He'd seen others running upgrades on their metabolisms and computation and decided he'd run the same tricks on himself.

There were practical limits based upon human systems, like maximum pulse rate and breathing, so the approaches used a blend of pragmatic limits and ancillary adjustments.

He knew how to run himself at 'human speed' but could

over-clock his thoughts and reflexes to around ten times normal. At a burst, he could go even faster. It made other people appear to slow down when he was using these capabilities. In a stressful situation, it could make a huge difference. The physics of movement were not quite as accommodating though, and although he ran himself to a high athletic level, he couldn't outwit nature for running or strength.

He sold himself and his abilities around the pattern and analytics capabilities. It was because of this that he needed the best physique to get himself out of the occasional trouble.

Scrive learned that a low-key presence coupled with the ability to ramp up his pattern work was the best and most survivable way to earn the kind of money that would get him a V-Blade or any other flying thing one day if he wanted it.

Santa Monica

Makatomi San had further deals to conclude in the rest of the day. That was why he was using the V-Blade. He didn't like the ostentation of the craft, but it was the most convenient method to travel very long distances for face-to-face sessions. Much of what he was doing now required that type of stealth. He was next heading to Los Angeles, to meet with another figure similar to Mallinson. The task he was setting was pretty much identical because Makatomi knew that there was a better chance of success with two people involved. They wouldn't know of each other, and despite the fees, his corporation could easily afford to pay them both, ideally with both of them bringing results.

Before returning to the 'blade, Makatomi had stopped by the vendor floor in his building. He'd bought a disposable paper phone from the automat. Ten minutes of signal, enough for the calls he was to make. It was to a fixer who could provide him with support in Los Angeles. He tapped the number, and the line clicked with a kind of static that didn't happen on the newer circuits. The old 3G cellular structure was like a barely loved base utility now, and most people had moved onto wave plex. He spoke softly to the fixer about the need for support in LA, then folded the phone into his inside pocket. He'd throw it away later.

Makatomi and Arusen had settled into V-Blade seats for what would be a deceptively short journey, considering the distance covered. The craft would be entering space and then re-entering the atmosphere as part of its journey. Yet, the buffeting of 20th-century space travel was no longer a concern since new intelligent moleculars had been used in flight craft design. In effect, the V-Pulse used technology to make it super slippery, blended with its transit environment and consequently didn't suffer re-entry burn.

As they approached their destination in L.A., Arusen looked out of the windows at what was still a night sky, approaching dawn.

"We'll be at their office before they are even awake", he commented. "I doubt it", replied Makatomi, "Don't underestimate the people at Marina del Rey. I expect they are tracking us incoming".

Makatomi was right, Denny and Suze had been watching their scanner for the last couple of hours. Not just watching the scanner, they were also working on a plan for their expected task.

"We don't know where Makatomi will arrive from, but we do know he'll be using a five-wing or a V-Blade for his incoming journey. When he departs, he will probably route scramble. but there's less need on the way in, so I doubt whether they have gone to the trouble." Suze flipped around a few radio frequency spectrums and checked some high incidence angles for unusual propulsion mechanisms.

"I've got this worked out and am picking up Andrews Airforce Base and way into the Pacific", she commented.

"It'll be a fast entry, probably, so we need to keep the monitoring so we can try to work out the reverse trajectory. I'd like to know where Makatomi is flying from."

Danny already had suspicions that Makatomi would be setting more than one team onto this case. He'd had a tip-off from the beam that this was a big situation and the implied fees supported the claim.

"Got something!", said Suze, she fidgeted in her seat and then stood to point at the screen. "Look, I've put it onto the big one", she flipped a button, and a large plasma displayed several arcs of co-ordinates, one moving noticeably faster than the rest. Almost immediately, it slowed to a similar crawl to the others, and then disappeared from the chart.

"It has to be him", said Denny, "Incoming fast, then going slow stealth for the last part. They won't have picked up our monitoring, and we've got a good arc to run back to work out their take-off spot.

"Easy," replied Suze, "It looks the most like London, with side options on Amsterdam or Paris. I doubt if they ran any evasive pattern so I think we can assume Makatomi has just flown from the company headquarters.

"Broadens the field somewhat", said Denny," If he has come from Corporate HQ, we don't really know if he's been with anyone of not."

"Let's ask him where he's been in the last 24," said Suze. "There's a higher likelihood that this is part of a setup if he was only passing through London".

"Yes. We may be working with paranoia here, but it is the best plan at this stage".

Denny and Suze's office was an apartment south of Santa Monica Boulevard. It was one of the areas that had picked up from the bad-old days and was now quite respectable while being on trend with the local fashions.

It worked well as an area to operate from, because the itinerant population and the side orders of tourists always flickering through between Melrose and Hollywood Boulevard.

They could do most things here without getting picked out as unusual, and long gaps or absences were quite commonplace among residents.

They'd arranged a completely different location for the

meeting with Makatomi. An office block across town close to the Santa Monica Airport, which had the trappings of business but was utterly a front for what they were doing. It was a call centre, and Denny had called in a favour from one of his friends to borrow a supervisor's office for the meeting.

He wondered why Makatomi would make such a journey in person and decided it must be high profile. He'd seen Makatomi's picture in Fortune and on various media bulletins and was quietly impressed that he and Suze were sufficient 'players' to get a personal visit. He was also aware that there could be some danger around the situation, hence the separate precautions around the choice of location.

2

A bad day in London is still better
than a good day anywhere else.
- *Unknown*

Scrive's Apartment

Scrive walked the ten minutes or so from the Tube station back to his apartment. The Thames sparkled as he crossed the bridge, into another borough of London.

The sheet glass of the Japanese-developed shopping mall glinted as he made his way towards his building. Two sets of sensors to get inside, across a small security moat that had been constructed as part of the original building. The security was good all around this area. Suspended structures, gated parking and no direct access from roadside or pedestrian walkway. It required the two sets of secure identity to enter, a further set for the elevator and that was all before the entrance lobby for his own apartment's door.

He smiled as he approached. He could see that someone had entered. He knew it would have to be Charlie. He also remembered that he'd agreed that she could visit, but that she didn't have the requisite access.

But he also knew that Charlie could walk through walls. Not actually, but to be able to spoof past most systems.

"You could get into a lot of trouble doing that", he said as he walked into the apartment. Charlie smiled. The plasma was on, but nothing was playing.

"I decided to get a few minutes sleep while I waited for you", she said, getting up and stretching her arms for a hug. She'd changed from her travel clothes and was wearing one of Scrive's T-shirts.

"Hey", replied Scrive, "Hey Hey" responded Charlie. They

kissed. "How long will you be in town?"

"It depends. Depends on whether what I've heard is true? You sound as if you might need some help with your latest big business?"

Scrive smiled. Charlie had connections and an uncanny ability to know where the big games played. Scrive would trust Charlie totally. They had a history.

Scrive had run into Charlie when he was solving a middle eastern puzzle. Things had started to cut up rough as he got closer to the truth.

He'd been told that he would be given backup and then Charlie had arrived. He had been taken aback, because he'd expected a small army, rather than a single 'girl'.

He'd soon learnt that Charlie was combat ready because within a half an hour of their meeting someone had tried to drive a truck into his apartment. They were on the third floor, and the truck had been launched from a building across the street, several stories higher, from the roof.

Charlie had shown her reflexes to be able to get them clear of the building and also to take down the skycrane jet that had dropped the truck onto the adjacent roof. It was a messy scene, but Charlie's jacked-up reflexes and remarkable use of weaponry had probably saved his life.

But Scrive had seen that Charlie's talents didn't stop there. She was fast and accurate with weapons, but also had pretty good tracking skills too. Not to his level, but easily fast enough to be a good sidekick. The difference between them was one of degree, with his world more digital and Charlie's a great deal more physical.

They were both effectively mercenaries and generally held to a code of non-involvement although sometimes drifted into a fling.

Scrive knew that Charlie had other male followers but had set some life goals around making a fortune. He knew she'd been trained by a Para-military group, but she remained silent about how this had come about. He had seen her in action with planes and 'blades too and knew that wherever she had trained and for whatever purpose, it made her one of a global elite.

Scrive realised that Charlie knew about his ultra-fast compute abilities, but Scrive also understood that Charlie was probably the only person that could almost keep up. Even when well-apart they kept an active link running, using one another as sounding boards. Scrive also realised that when Charlie had collected enough cash, there was every chance that she would simply disappear, as a way to break all connections.

"Yeah, I've just been to see Makatomi, He's asked me to find out how the Chinese have accessed the Aport, and what they are trying to do with it."

"What beyond profit-making by selling a variant at a tenth of the price?", replied Charlie. "It'll be some government deal - which superpower wants to get something over on someone else".

"Yes, my speculation also, but Makatomi seems to think its a double-cross or something".

"It's time we dug deep?" replied Charlie. "I'm on my way to a small gig on the Swiss border, but this sounds way more interesting. How come you've got the deal? I'd have thought Makatomi would shop around."

"Cheeky! I expect he did!" replied Scrive. "He seemed in a hurry to leave after our meeting. I thought he was heading back to Japan, but I suppose he could be seeding a duplicate operation somewhere else".

"Are you ready to take a look at this?" asked Charlie, waving the remote for the streamer.

"First things first", smiled Scrive.

Ed Adams

Los Angeles

Suze and Denny packed some telemetry and other gadgets before they headed for the basement and into a hire car that Denny had randomly selected from the online Hertz desk. They wanted to run this as anonymously as possible, and the car and office they were using should help them stay unobtrusive.

Denny flipped the start button on the car. It whined into life. It was a fuel cell power plant, one of the new types that could run silently. He grimaced at the noisy engine tone that came as a default setting and selected another one, more a solid tone and less sporty sounding.

"Let's not draw attention", he said to Suze, who nodded in agreement.

They took the car up the four levels to the street and joined the slow-moving traffic as they headed towards the Freeway.

"It shouldn't take us long to get to the venue, especially at this time of morning, said Denny. "Don't jinx it", retorted Suze.

Dawn was breaking, in a half-hearted kind of way.

There were signs of the nightlife still in progress, as people had lost their sense of time altogether. Additionally, a few tired looking tourists were wandering around and there was a police situation on a nearby street corner. They moved along through the traffic, within the speed limits and as low key as possible.

Ahead, taillights from other traffic snaked out in as they took another on-ramp for their short ride.

"We'll be early, and prepared," said Denny, knowing that Makatomi was already in town and had probably landed at Santa Monica rather than LAX. Makatomi and his partners could be very close.

Makatomi and Arusen had a short meeting before they met Denny and Suze. They had arranged for some local support because their meeting with the trackers would be taking place away from Biotree company property.

Makatomi hated it that he was asked to meet like this, it was away from his systems and controls, but it seemed to be the only way that he could get to these two specialist trackers.

He's also done his homework, or rather, his fixer had done the homework and established that these people were the best. That was why he was meeting them on their turf. Being trackers, they knew how to hide. That they would break their own cover for this suggested that they were interested in the size of the reward. Makatomi didn't think there would be any more altruistic reasons for the trackers to agree to this meeting and the likely pursuit.

He asked Arusen to make the arrangements for the hired help and also requested that they lose the land cruisers and acquire some more low-key transport. A compromise was agreed, where Makatomi, Arusen and a couple of the hired team would take conventional transports, but that the rest would still provide less than discreet backup in the black-windowed cruisers.

"I hate LA," said Makatomi, "everything has to be so brash and dramatic. This is why we prefer these type of meetings to be in our own properties," said Makatomi to Arusen.

"Too true," nodded Arusen in agreement, "This type of situation can get so untidy."

They looked at one another knowing there was some risk of

a trap or that the trackers would ask for some unacceptable terms. It would have to be something extreme because fundamentally Makatomi was desperate to get this resolved and needed the support from the likes of Denny, Suze and Scrive.

Of course, he wouldn't tell these trackers about Scrive. Part of the plan was to have the insurance of two separate investigations.

Janie gets help

In London, Janie was unsure about whether to meet Lars again, she'd gone home but kept looking over her shoulder to see whether she was being followed. It was partly irrational, but she wanted to be sure that neither Lars nor an accomplice would be behind her. She'd used her regular route so that she could go through the systems without having to stop, but then deliberately overshot her destination and made her way back. That way, if there were anyone following, it would be more visible. She wasn't sure what she would do if someone had followed her, in any case, but to her eyes there didn't seem to be any trail.

At home, she pondered about the meeting the following evening. She thought she should go but wanted to take some insurance. Maybe a friend to accompany her? But who? And how much should she say? She didn't think it should be anyone from Biotree, because of the nature of the conspiracy.

Janie lived in a flat with two others. They'd shared for about a year, as a way to get somewhere central in London. London gave them access to the best jobs, but at the cost that none of the three of them could afford a place to live, based upon their salary levels.

Janie decided that her flatmate Chantal would be the best option. They'd been in plenty of scrapes together, and shared thinking to the degree that they would wear each other's clothes. Or more precisely, Chantal would frequently borrow some of Janie's clothes.

Chantal's tastes were a little extreme for Janie. Although Chantal could scrub up real fine when required. Janie knew that Chantal operated with some of the more dubious parts of

London and had quite a street scene going.

Janie was more the Ms Corporate and was used to wearing business attire, or when on courses or training, something they called business casual. It was even funnier watching the men. They'd all don polo shirts and beige chinos when it was an 'awayday' meeting.

The thing was, Chantal was out somewhere and had been for the last couple of days. It wasn't particularly unusual but meant that Janie would need to call to check whether she could help out. Janie clicked the number on her handheld and was immediately routed to voicemail. Instead, she opted to leave a text message.

"Need your help when I'm meeting a guy called Lars tomorrow - It's to do with Biotree, and I could do with some support. Fit guy, but this is business".

She thought the message was to the point, looked innocuous but would get Chantal's attention. She pressed send, and it flicked into the network.

Within a couple of minutes, a short reply from Chantal

"Sure ... How fit?"...Followed by an old school emoticon of a lascivious face. Janie smiled. She knew she'd got Chantal's attention and that she'd provide the backup.

Oil field digitizers

Orange LA sunrise, and Suze and Denny arrived at the offices.

"Not bad," said Suze, "Just above seedy and quite beige and sand coloured bland. We have found a great place to look anonymous."

Denny backed the car away. "We'll do better to park in that area the other side of the building", he commented, that will give us a couple of routes out. They could exit through the car park or the Mall. He nodded towards the adjacent Mall entrance which would put them into a zone filled with shoppers.

As he pulled up at what he now considered to be the optimum spot, he looked around.

"I think we should also look out for our friends," he added. They will be unlikely to visit us alone," He grabbed a bag from the back seat and looked through the content.

"Oil field digitizers", he said. "These little units allow us to build a grid to chart the area around here. We need to drop about 20 of them around and we'll have monitoring of the whole zone front and back".

Suze looked at one of the units. "Neat." she said, "self-powered, small transmitter, geo-sensitive and a motion camera included?"

"It's motion-sensing and also controllable", replied Denny. "These are quite new; I heard about them from a friend in the military. Don't worry; they are commercial grade and used by the large oil companies, so they are commonly available - if rather expensive. Let's sprinkle a few around".

They created a small coverage zone on both sides of the office with the units. The units had a grey speckled cover which helped them blend into the background, somewhat like pieces of discarded building material.

"They remind me of rodent traps", mused Suze.

"Surprisingly appropriate." replied Denny. He picked up another bag from the trunk of the car and they walked towards the offices. It was still early enough that they were not expecting it to be too busy.

However, as they entered there were sounds of activity. "It looks like a 24x7 operation?" said Suze.

"Yes", replied Denny, "But I didn't know it would be 'full on' all of the time. They made their way to the office that Denny had been loaned. His friend had provided access and covered off the paperwork, so they were expected and able to get straight to work.

They decided to treat a couple of the chairs to some transparent self-adhesive bugs. "Just don't sit down there," said Suze as she placed a few of the small bugs onto the chairs.

"I can't help thinking that Makatomi will be way above this stuff?" questioned Denny, "What with being into nanobots and all".

"Maybe", replied Suze, "But on the other hand his strength could also be his weakness."

They looked at the time. It had moved from 4 am to 8 am at lightning speed., They were both used to the early morning effect where the brain's processes change pace during sleep, giving the impact of a speeded-up return of the dawn.

"One hour and they will be here. Bang on time, I'm sure" said Denny.

"And I wonder what they have been doing for the last few hours?"

"My paranoia suggests they've been meeting some backup. I doubt whether they are used to operating this kind of thing on someone else's patch. That's why we have extra surveillance".

Denny pressed a button on his computer, and a whole bank of TV monitor screens appeared as small squares across the screen.

"We are ready to watch you, Mr Makatomi".

The Makatomi files

Scrive and Charlie were sipping wine. "Okay, so what brings you here to London?" asked Scrive, "I thought you'd pretty much settled in New York now".

"Work, in a manner of speaking", replied Charlie. She sipped the wine slowly and looked hesitant. "I'll tell you what happened, but you must promise not to say you told me so..."

"Sure thing", replied Scrive smiling and looking down into his glass.

Both Scrive and Charlie worked around the edges of the security environment. They'd known each other since before nanobots had become such big business. The so-called Great Leap, when technology had made a few giant steps forward.

They kept in contact and had paths that crossed haphazardly. Three years ago, they'd briefly been an item when they worked together on an investigation during which Scrive had found out that Charlie had other 'get rich quick schemes' that didn't seem to be working. Scrive had helped Charlie get out of a somewhat illegal situation, and despite growing apart, they'd kept their friendship and trust very tight,

"I've been working with the security agency in New York and Washington. They asked me to look at the rate of change of the nanobots that Biotree have been making – to try to find out if they were being deliberately weaponised.

We all know they went through a big series of upgrades in the first few years and then pretty much stabilised. I had been asked to take a look at whether there was anything else happening, like a secret 'Version 2'. Anyway, it meant that I had to join a team experimenting with the Nanobot operating system, to see if there were any obvious hooks for them to provide updates. We designed a few changes of our own."

Scrive smiled. He knew that Charlie had a swift and creative mind for software and a 'few changes' would be an understatement.

"They let me join their lab, and we started with just emulations of the 'bots. We knew we would need the real devices to try putting sets of them together. The way that their heuristics work meant that it is chains of nanobots that deliver an outcome rather than individual devices."

"It sounds like that old Lemmings game to me!" said Scrive, trying not to laugh.

"Well, it is, kind-of. In Lemmings you have diggers and flyers and climbers and so on. With bots it is the same except instead of each unit being self-contained, they join together to make the device that does the work. A machine might comprise 2,3,4 or even more separate nanobots.

Scrive nodded. He knew the theory of this as well, but whilst he would be good at tracking the originator of the devices and could probably, right now, find a trail in the 'net that lead back to Charlie, he wouldn't be able to do the same complex logic that Charlie was describing.

"I arranged for a selection of the nanobots to be provided, and I first ran them as intended. They were designed for cell wall repair and did join together to create chains to achieve this. It was like a ribosome conveyor belt. You know, the way that ribosome can stitch polymeric protein modules together via messenger RNA molecules?

Scrive looked blank," No, I missed that session," he quipped," But I get the idea, nanobots copying biological processes?"

"Yes, that's kinda right; they were pretty good and speedy. Some of their inbuilt logic was to slow the 'bots down, so that normal body tissue has a chance to keep up."

Scrive continued to drink the wine. "So far, so good, but what is the point of it all?" he asked.

"Exactly, our lab wondered whether the 'bots were just copying biological functions. Then we tried a few modifications. They were quite small, and we were mainly checking the ability of the Nanobots to support new command structures.

"Big Mistake. It all went horribly wrong. The 'bots have been designed to include failsafe. If you don't know the keys and secure modes, it looks impossible to reprogram them. They have their own self-checking logic and if they spot a variation, they just stop functioning. In fact, they go one further than that."

"what exactly?", asked Scrive.

"They attack each other and destroy each other. It really is a 'leave no trace'. Quiet a sophisticated design really. The manufacturers can modify them, but if anyone else tries then the whole system is rendered useless."

"Reminds me of some consumer electronics," smiled Scrive. "Take one screw out, and you might as well throw the entire device away".

"Yes - although the purpose here is a more security-minded one. To stop tampering and remove the ability to try out different processes."

"So why did that get you sent to Europe?" asked Scrive.

"Well, the thing is, I got rather bored with the programming of the 'bots each time I was testing my ideas, so I created a small handheld unit to punch in the code revisions. It is based on something that I used back in the Casino days".

Charlie's previous history had a few dubious moments when she was raiding high roller casinos by reprogramming the payout software. It had to be undetectable to the house and Charlie had created a small device to fire the software changes into the system.

Scrive knew about Charlie at Vegas. He helped her get out of trouble when she was in danger of being caught. He'd shown her how to mess up the electronic trail, which had previously led back to her.

"I took the Casino injector and produced a sub-scale version. It's a lot easier now than when I built the original because of the improved scanner resolutions available. I could use laser light to improve the sensitivity and then fire the new software into the bots, in much the same way that the old version fired software into the Casino devices."

"NSA hadn't seen anything like this before, and they've asked me to show them a breakdown of how it works. I'm heading for CERN to show them in detail. It is my comeuppance for the damage I caused when I was testing the bots I'd been building, and they kept failing and destroying one another.

She pointed to a small titanium box with an elaborate digital lock. "There," she said. "the Nano injector is in the box. It's loaded with 'nanoreductives'. They are my attempt to rebrand the dud nanobots which self-destruct one another!"

"Its' not a bug, it's a feature," smiled Scrive. He looked quizzically at the lock.

"Birthday?" he asked.

"Yes", replied Charlie, "Plus 666 - I wanted to add an edge to this devilish device."

Scrive knew that the box would destroy its contents if the wrong number was entered. But knowing Charlie there would be a twist.

"Yes - birthday will open it but destroy the loader logic. birthday plus 666 will open it and keep the device intact"

"what about anything else?"

"Three goes and thar she blows", smiled Charlie. "I thought I'd give a pirate hacker a sporting chance."

"Are you getting paid?"

"Yes and no," came the reply. "I should be, but I'm sort of paying off the cost of the destruction I created at Biotree with my hack. But now it's your turn. What are you working with at the moment? I assume it is still with Biotree?"

"Direct at the moment. And big. The biggest probably. Corny as it may sound if I tell you then you might be in some sort of danger.

"Yeah, right," responded Charlie," As if that would stop me, but first, another refill of the wine?"

Scrive reached across, picked up the wine and gently poured.

"You know what? You might want to help out with this. I can split some fees and it is worth it to me to have someone alongside who isn't known to the client. But wait until you hear before you answer."

"I'm intrigued already," said Charlie, ...and fees would be

beneficial at the moment."

"Okay, so I've been asked to find out the origin of the cloned Chinese nanobots. There's a leak somewhere and the impact of the copies has collapsed the Biotree share price. I'm supposed to track the leak and pass the information back. Sounds simple, but we are talking about government level conspiracies. Hence the potential danger."

"Wow. This assignment sounds great. I assume the fees are in keeping with the magnitude of the challenge?"

"You know something; I think I could have named any price. I've gone high in any case. The thing that worries me is that they seem almost too happy to accept my terms. It makes me concerned that they won't honour the agreement."

"What can you do?"

"I already did it", said Scrive. I negotiated the money in two stages. "all of it now and all of it again when I complete. If I don't, they will come for me and take half back. I don't want that to happen."

"You've already been paid and can get the same again?" asked Charlie, somewhat incredulous.

"Plus, expenses...I said they didn't seem to care about the amount. And don't worry - it's a lot. Come in with me, and I'll split the second amount. You'll be my safeguard that we get paid based upon our successful outcome."

"How much?" asked Charlie.

Scrive told her. It was a huge sum.

Charlie nodded and started to feel like a big prize lottery winner.

Polka dot bodysuit

Chantal had arranged to meet Janie at Canada Water. It was across the River from their planned rendezvous with Lars but would give them a chance to plan how they would handle the session before they met. It was also a five-minute trip to their planned meeting place so they could be 'in position' very quickly.

Chantal arrived in a polka dot bodysuit. Three different colours; shorts, top and jacket.

"I took the ears off," she said as she hugged Janie. "And I brought a black topcoat as well in case we need to wear disguises." She pointed into a bag where a black compressed micro-fabric nestled amongst some fashion headgear.

Janie's mood briefly lifted at Chantal's appearance. They'd party together sometimes, and Chantal would usually go for something extravagant. Janie's appearance was more conservative, and today she was wearing a dark business suit.

"Thanks for agreeing to cover this", she said to Chantal. "I'm a little bit worried that this is all getting rather weird."

"I wouldn't miss this for anything. You're about to meet a dishy Swede or something," replied Chantal.

"He's Norwegian, or says he is," replied Janie. "And it is something to do with the firm and the way they are operating."

"What do you want me to do?" asked Chantal, "Hold your hand or what?"

"The main thing is to cover the situation and to follow my lead if I say anything." I may want him to think that we've spread the word about this, so there's no point in trying to keep it to just the two of us."

"Does he look as if he would be violent?" asked Chantal, making like a karate move.

"I don't think so, but put it this way, I think he could outrun us if it came to a race".

"Okay, so we'll listen to what he has to say and what he asks. I suggest we move from the first location to somewhere else to keep him on his toes, too. If we take him to the end of the walkway, we can grab a taxi and then go almost anywhere".

"Good plan. I suggest we go to Westminster, it's full of police and security so we can get out there and if needed we could easily attract attention."

Janie looked at Chantal.

"I don't think you'd have any trouble doing that, anyway".

They giggled briefly.

"Okay, that way, he can tell us his story while we are in the cab. It will only take a few minutes and put him under pressure to get to the point."

They nodded and walked the short distance to the transit point to Canary Wharf. They would be at Smollensky's on time.

Strip Mall Call Center

It was ten minutes before nine in the morning on the busy roads of California, and Makatomi was in a regular wheeled saloon car following another saloon and trailed by a land cruiser. A couple of small buzzy drones circled the land cruiser.

They arrived at the parking lot by the side of the offices where Makatomi was to meet the tracker. The parking lot was adjacent to a large shopping mall, which had car parking and a service road running alongside the offices where he was due to meet. He could see the signs for the call-center. Low rise, maybe four stories and adjacent to a few strip mall retail outlets. A pizza place, realtors, a financial institution. These were lower rent locations, and Makatomi was confident it was a short-term front used for his benefit.

Two of the heavies his company had hired approached the door of the offices first, and he could hear them asking for Mr Denny Amelung and then calling through to his car to say they were about to be accompanied to the office. He stepped out of the vehicle, along with Arusen.

"Same protocol?" asked Arusen.

"Exactly", replied Makatomi, "We need to keep this to the least people knowing. I don't want the hired help in the room with us."

They stepped into the office reception, and Arusen had a word to one of the men sent in ahead. He nodded, and the two men withdrew. Arusen led Makatomi to the office where

Denny was seated.

"Mr Amelung?" said Arusen, looking at the casually dressed twentysomething sitting on a leather sofa in the room. Denny rose and moved to shake hands.

"Hi, I'm Denny, Denny Amelung." He shook Arusen's hand and turned towards Makatomi. "And Makatomi San? I am pleased to meet you." He bowed slightly towards Makatomi, who returned the gesture with a nod.

"We will be keeping this off the record," began Arusen.

"...and you'll have a record of a different meeting for your records?" continued Denny. "I know the protocol."

"We're running a surveillance sweep on this room," said Arusen. "I'm sure you know that protocol too".

"Yes, and you'll find plenty of electronics here. This is a call centre, with walk-around headsets, computers, high-speed comms, video links and satellite coverage. We are highly wired."

Arusen nodded. The small unit he was using to check for bugs was utterly useless in the current room. There was so much interference, and the EMF emissions were off the scale.

"If you prefer, we can delay for a couple of hours whilst you run an isolation sweep, or we can continue, in the knowledge that it is as much in my interest to keep this quiet as it is in yours," continued Denny.

Makatomi interrupted, "We'll keep this brief. I'll explain the situation and the terms. You'll need to make an immediate decision."

Denny was aware that Suze would typically be in the decision, but they had decided that Denny's view would prevail, and it was too much of a risk to reveal Suze's involvement.

"Please, Mr Makatomi, take a seat and do explain."

Makatomi repeated the story of the Chinese cloning and the need to track the leak. He didn't mention Scrive, but he did explain the generous terms.

The situation was pretty much as Denny and Suze had predicted. A search for a leak, an enormous reward. Almost too large, which implied extra danger.

Denny questioned the situation slightly but accepted the terms and a large down-payment from Makatomi.

As Makatomi and Arusen left the offices, they were tagged by the self-adhesives in the manner that Suze and Denny had hoped.

Denny waited for the Makatomi entourage to depart. The small telemetry units in the car park tracked the exit of two saloon cars and another two land cruisers. Denny waited for another twenty minutes before calling Suze back from the main office where she had been waiting, wearing a headset.

She behaved as if a staff member, whilst they started their conversation, aware that there was an equivalent possibility that Makatomi had dropped tags or sensors in this office. It was easier to exit, so they headed for the Mall's sports center, via a sportswear shop.

They both bought T-shirts and shorts as well as tracksuits before heading to the sports centre where they added new swimwear to their collection. Then into the respective changing rooms, change and both a swim and a sauna, followed by a change into the new clothes.

"That should have separated us from any bugs or trackers," commented Denny as they made their way to the car they had parked in the Mall.

"Let's get back to base." They gently edged the car from the Mall car park and took a long route back to the apartment.

"Let's see what we can trace of Makatomi," said Suze as she flicked on a geocentric tracking device and zoomed into the local area. They were using GeoSat to ping the small tracking bugs now on Makatomi and Arusen's clothes. These would give a short timeframe for information, useful as they tried to gather new intelligence about their new employers.

"Yes, we have them," they are heading back to Santa Monica Airport," said Suze and looked at the Map display. I'm patching to the tourist view camera to see whether we can spot their craft".

Two minutes later they had access to the airport's tourist cameras, and sure enough, they were pointed towards the more interesting craft in the airport, which included the V-Blade.

"I'll get its call-sign", said Suze and she zoomed onto an aero-map which showed planes at rest and amongst them the V-Blade which displayed the N registration of an American plane.

"Gotcha,", breathed Suze as she scanned for the registration,"...and you are from the NSA?? That's a surprise, and I thought you'd be registered to Biotree!"

Suze and Denny looked at one another. This was something very unusual — way beyond the request to drill into what the Chinese were doing.

"Are we being played?" asked Denny to Suze.

"We've been careful so far, and we've already received a down payment, so it doesn't make a lot of sense?"

Denny had flipped onto a Chinese web site. He was trying

to run probes into the large corporates of China. Simple stingers designed to elicit port responses from the major sites. He wanted to find some loose links that would allow him to dig deeper into some of the principal Chinese corporates and maybe a few government departments.

"Steady," said Suze, "You'll swamp their networks, and then they'll trip intrusion and saturation detection. If that happens, we'll get tracked ourselves."

"Not behind these walls," smiled Denny. "I'm after speed but not being reckless". He made a gesture of a hand rising in front of his face.

"Shields up", he said, as he hit the Chinese and also the Biotree site with port scans and intrusion probes.

3

Be on the lookout for coming events;
They cast their shadows beforehand.

Fortune Cookie, King's Chinese Restaurant, Odiham

Beijing

The Chinese Ministry of State Security based in Beijing was monitoring traffic from airwaves and networks into and out of the Republic. Less well known than UK's GCHQ or USA's NSA, the Ministry of State Security (MSS) is the intelligence, security and secret police agency of the People's Republic of China, responsible for counter-intelligence, foreign intelligence and political security. MSS considered itself one of the most secretive intelligence organizations in the world.

It used the common triggers of blacklist and whitelist words and additionally looked for unusual activity. In this case, it was coming from a couple of US-based nodes that were repeatedly running interrogation probes.

The initial reports noted that the probes were quite sophisticated, but that they jittered and sparked their way around North America.

Den Xiapau noticed the signals first," It's a range of messages, but they seem to be different orientations than from the usual mischief-makers. It looks sophisticated, but a little bit rough at the same time."

Of course, that was what Denny and Suze wanted. To shake the tree, to see what fell out. In a few minutes, the Chinese would be running countermeasures, because they perceived it as a more worrisome than average attack.

That was when they would drop their catcher link into the system. It could decode the cryptologic that the Chinese were using as a countermeasure and then replicate itself into the core. Suze knew how to make the logic hopscotch over the kernel, and Denny's logic loop was so tight that he could drop this into play before a gnat had time to blink.

In Beijing, Den Xiapau had flagged the hostile to his superiors and was readying a crypto bomb which would take down the ports that were being probed and move them into a sophisticated sandbox.

The hacker would think it was still running its penetration logic, but all it would be doing was getting ever more complex prime numbers to calculate.

It would run out of computing power within ten minutes.

Den Xiapau fired the logic algorithm. The post scanner flickered for a moment and was gone.

"Wow", said Den Xaipau," That wasn't much of an attack, but it also wasn't static".

"Slam-dunk," said Denny, "We're in- they did just what we predicted". Suze and Denny did a quick high-five.

Den Xiapau wasn't satisfied to leave it at that point though. The disappearance of the trace probe had been almost too perfect.

He'd seen something like this before in the literature. It could be a decoy probe and an iceman insertion into the system. He remembered this software usually stayed dormant for extended periods. Iceman was so named because it had to thaw out but then ran everywhere.

He looked around and ran a few port scans of his own. He may not be able to find it, but he sure would escalate it. He punched the code for escalation. "There's something strange happening here - I know it is not right..." he began to explain, and a small chain reaction started.

Probed double

"Did you notice something?" asked Denny. "When we were running that decoy search, there was someone else doing something similar? It was incredibly fast but seemed to be targeting the same area? If we hadn't been running a decoy probe, I don't think we'd have seen it."

Suze punched a few keys.

"I'm going to re-run that last couple of minutes," she said, "from the log, as an e-Discovery."

She set up a couple of monitor screens, and they watched the party piece that Denny had created. Sure enough, a few other probes were running as well. They were both able to see past the usual scam artist attacks and into something more systematic. "It is coming from London", said Suze. And there seem to be two sets running, suspiciously like us.

"But way, way fast," said Denny. They were running their playback at one-twentieth of normal speed, and even then, they were missing sections.

"...it is someone in the business", said Denny, "look at that switching."

"...and look at that second probe," added Suze. "It is going into Biotree."

"I think we've found our doubles," said Denny, "And they seem to be in London. Makatomi has hired someone else to do the same job."

Pulse

London

Scrive looked at Charlie," I know we are using some brute force techniques to test the Chinese systems. We need to see what kind of response they provide.

"I just want to see how they react. If it is overt, then we can assume they are treating us as normal hackers. If they do anything special, then maybe they are hiding something in the way that Makatomi suggests."

He ran the scans, initially in a quite visible way and received back the equivalent of a perfunctory 'not authorised' signal. The response was typical for the Chinese, who had managed to suppress parts of their systems from investigation for years and mainly with quite simple techniques involving feedback like 'not available' or 'busy'.

"Let's up the game!" said Scrive and he started a second script simultaneously pinging the Biotree site. It was a fairly blatant attempt to be seen 'red-handed', if there was a situation to hide. One hand in China, the other in Biotree.

"It is no different", said Charlie, "look they are still treating us as normal hackers or spammers".

"Yes - they aren't making any connections. Either they are masking their response very well, or there's nothing to hide?"

"Wait," said Scrive," did you see that?" Someone else running a perfunctory digital attack, but it just stopped suddenly. They killed that one in a heartbeat."

"Let us take a look", Charlie adjusted a couple of settings.

"A pro. that was a decoy attack. They've dropped some code into the Chinese system. It's impossible to tell where its originated though. Pretty slick work."

They looked at one another. "Someone else is playing with the Chinese," said Charlie, "Maybe a threat to us?"

"Or possibly an ally?" added Scrive.

Makatomi was back in the V-Blade. He'd had enough of today's haggling with what he considered to be hackers. At least Mallinson had been polite. Mr Amelung (if that was his real name) had been downright scruffy and rather discourteous.

But it was the price to pay for getting these people to track down the security leak. If he could get it fixed, then his company stocks would start to rise again despite the leakage of data from the hacks.

A signal bleeped. Makatomi was ready to sign off for the day and let it go to voice when he saw it was Holden. His boss. The chair of Biotree. He would have to answer it.

"There's a problem", said Holden. "One of those hackers you've been hiring has annoyed the Chinese. They are creating bad ripples. It will damage Biotree further. They say it's something from London. Fix it."

Makatomi couldn't believe it. In less than a day, the so-called professionals were rattling cages.

If the Chinese got nasty, what could happen next? They'd lower their prices further, and the faltering Biotree would go legs up.

"I'm going to have to contact London", he thought, "...and fix Mr Mallinson. A pity".

Ed Adams

Smolly's

Chantal knew Smollensky's. It wasn't her kind of place. She knew it had its share of investment bankers engrossed in discussions about the latest fancy cars.

Chantal decided to have some fun. She would walk in first and draw the stares.

She took out her headgear and replaced it on her head. The polka dots, the colours and the fashion accessory that looked a bit like ears would do it. Minnie Mouse meets Mui Mui.

She heard the silence as conversations missed a beat. Even Lars looked. He was with someone too, as Janie moved across to meet again. A slim woman with boyish looks and a short dark haircut. A small S-shaped tattoo by her left eye.

"Thank you for coming here", said Lars. "I've brought Carolin as well this evening; it may give you some comfort that I'm doing all of this for the right reason."

"Okay and I've brought Chantal," said Janie before Chantal could introduce herself. Chantal realised that they hadn't thought about using a different name or anything clever, despite their preparation.

"You'd better explain what this about and what has happened to Karin."

Lars nodded. Both he and Carolin were drinking small glasses of wine. A waiter appeared. "We'll have the same", said Janie and nodded towards the glasses that Lars and Carolin were drinking.

"Maybe a bottle?" asked the waiter, smiling. "No just two glasses will be fine", replied Janie. Chantal knew they would be leaving any moment.

"Okay, let's introduce ourselves more accurately", continued Lars, in quiet tones "We are both originally from the Tract."

"Outside of the Ellipse", said Carolin, "So we're using quite a lot of Tract resource to come here today and to look like Ellipse people.

"We're leaving right now though", said Janie and pulled Chantal from her seat.

Janie looked across to Chantal. It wasn't a normal situation. Janie hadn't met many Tractwalkers, who mostly had reputations as thieves and roughnecks. She had hardly spoken to any of them before, now being with two of them in Smolly's was quite a revelation.

"We're catching a taxi, right now. Are you coming?" They moved outside and across the short pedestrian walkway to a line of waiting black cabs. They were parked on their landing wheels, and Janie walked to the expensive rank that didn't use the street rail.

They clambered inside and Janie asked the driver to start the run to Westminster, "But follow the rail", she added, effectively forcing the driver to take a slower route.

They sat two across from the other two. Chantal noticed that Carolin looked as if she hadn't been in a cab before.

"I hope you don't mind me asking...but how do you afford to come into a bar like Smollensky's?", she asked.

"We have been selected from the Tract dwellers to make representations because of what has been happening. I think we see things from the Tract that most Ellipse dwellers are unaware of," continued Lars.

"It links to the economy and governance of the Ellipse people by the major corporations".

"You mean since the lifestyle improvements were introduced after the Great Leap?"

"Exactly, so-called improvements since the division between wealth economies and the agrarian cultures"

The taxi was running smoothly now; it had taken one of the road tunnels from Canary Wharf's island back towards the City of London.

Chantal knew that Lars's comments were referencing the progressive split as service industry-based economies became wealthier and the land dwellers who farmed and fished became separated and eventually separated. Then barriers had been introduced that made the free passage of people from one environment to the other more difficult, unless for economic sustenance of the Ellipse.

"Carolin and I are Tractwalkers, who are part of a small group who can pass from the Tract to the Ellipse and back. For reasins we don't understand, our bodies don't trigger the 'glimmer' which enforces the boundaries.

We are considered as the servant class, but today you can see we are trying to blend with the Ellipse people."

"Are, are you really from Norway, then?", asked Janie," or was that part of your cover too?"

Lars nodded, "It's true, I am from Norway originally, although, after the introduction of the cartridges by the Nordic governments, I opted out of the healthcare program bracelets, and then found myself opting out of the economy"

Janie looked at Carolin, who was wearing a dark long-sleeved sweater which concealed her arms.

Chantal assumed that Carolin wouldn't have a cartridge and it was evident that Lars didn't. Chantal also wondered why Janie hadn't spotted this, but with cartridges being so commonplace it was like not noticing whether someone was wearing a watch.

Lars continued, "Remember, the cartridges were originally introduced as a response to the N3Ro virus. N3Ro occurred patchily around 20 years ago and very suddenly had reached an inflection point where it voraciously attacked large parts of the population.

"Some were immune, but the level of death had been on a scale greater than world wars.

Janie nodded, "Yes, some in our family were affected by this."

Lars continued, "A Biotree vaccine was already available and was progressively rolled out. As the virus became epidemic, governments shifted through single-shot vaccines and but soon had to deploy the cartridge solution."

"I remember those days of needing to get regular shots of vaccine. The cartridge was a much better solution," said Janie.

"This was because the virus was also self-modifying, and the consequent protection required regular changes. In effect, the medicinal properties of the tropus cartridges could be adapted to combat the new strains.

"That's how the cartridges became the standard form of inoculation. They were fitted to infants at birth, and to the majority of the population that lived within 'The Ellipse'.

Lars waved his arms, "There was a huge part of the planet which had the economic wherewithal to support the ongoing cartridge programme.

"The other parts of the world were referred to as 'the Tract'. There was also a variation of The Tract around the edge of significant conurbations, where more impoverished people who had the resilience to survive N3Ro had moved."

Chantel said, "I always thought of the virus as Nero." Janie nodded, "Yes, we were taught Nero in school."

Lars said, "There had also been a challenge for those with immunity. Ellipse dwellers were distrustful of Tract dwellers for a variety of emotional reasons. Mainly it was the risk of Nero morphing faster than the cartridge immunity could handle, and so the Tract people might become carriers for a new strain.

"This thinking created the disadvantaged status of Tract dwellers and the rumours that they were all roughnecks and thieves. It created a caste system at a global level. It was stronger than anything from the eras of segregation or the castes in India. All driven from fear.

Lars continued, "So you'll appreciate that we are feeling a lot more threatened here than either of you. One word and you could have us removed from the Ellipse and even with our current special status, we wouldn't be able to come back. Please listen carefully to what I'm about to tell you."

He looked across to Carolin, and she removed a small device from her bag. It was a handheld, but it looked several generations older than anything that Chantal or Janie had seen.

"Wow, vintage," said Chantal, looking with some intrigue towards the device.

"It is all we can afford," answered Carolin," And I've brought it to show you a recording." She flipped it on, and Chantal was surprised at its relatively small screen surrounded by some kind of carbon fibre surround.

It showed a few seconds of what looked like a transit station and then a blur of some feet and a three-second image of a man. He was walking on a path that cut across the field of vision. It looked like Sloane Square, thought Chantal.

Carolin paused the device and made the hand gesture to rewind it a few frames. She paused it on the face of the man.

"This is Scrive," said Lars, "He is our key to a different way of things in the future."

He pointed to the face, and Carolin also looked intently at the freeze frame picture.

"You are still talking in riddles," said Janie, "You'll need to be more explicit. I'll give you another five minutes and then we are out of this cab."

"Okay," continued Lars,

"Some big secrets are being kept by Biotree. The company has always projected itself as very kind and generous, but we are sure there is another agenda at play. Every time we have got close, our friends have disappeared, and we have not seen them again.

"They have all been from the Tract, and that has made them relatively easy to spot, even if they have cartridge implants added."

He put his hand into his pocket and pulled out a cartridge kit. Chantal recognised it as an after-market graft, the sort of thing used by people who wanted a boost beyond the level given by the health service.

"Yes, it's a booster," said Lars, "not a straight cartridge implant, but once it is in, you need to look carefully to spot the difference."

"We have information about some kind of attempt to penetrate Biotree, not by the Tract, but by a National government. Someone is hunting for power. But we think they'll get more than they bargained. The reason it is so important is that we believe Biotree is effectively the planetary power broker."

"What makes you think this is the case?" asked Janie.

"It is simple," replied Lars. "No one dies from Nero. We haven't seen a single death from it in the last 15 years."

Chantal looked at Janie, not sure whether to believe the conversation. "You'll need to prove that," replied Janie.

"It is easy to show you that," said Lars as Carolin also nodded, "...but people are still being affected. We don't know how, but people simply disappear. Much like Karin, but from the Tract it is a regular occurrence. That's where Scrive comes in.

"He's been asked to investigate something by Biotree. We want to adapt his agenda. He is one of the few people globally that can get to the bottom of what is happening. But we can't pay him, and he works strictly as a mercenary."

Carolin nodded again. Janie looked at Chantal.

"I'm ahead of you," said Janie. "You want me to help this guy named Scrive."

Lars nodded. "I do...We do. And it's because you are not from the Tract, you knew Karin, and you work at Biotree. It is the area where you work as well."

"...And in return for this, I get 'disappeared' like Karin?" asked Janie, "It doesn't sound like much of a deal."

"I agree; we have no leverage in this situation. All I can say is that our mission is trying to put things right. To rebalance the world and remove some injustice.

Janie looked at Chantal. Chantal thought that neither she nor Janie had ever stood up to anything at a political level. As far as they could tell the world was kind of 'sewn-up' about politics. People just got on with their lives.

Chantal was always slightly more edgy than Janie, but that was because she diluted her cartridges. She did something highly illegal, which was to siphon out about half of the cartridge and sold the content on the black market. The half shots were called 'boosts' and for certain parts of the population, they were a form of additional rather pleasant relaxant.

Chantal always thought she was taking risks by doing this; she saw her own blood through the plexi, and it ran close to a red colour, rather than orange or yellow. It meant she was usually on a very low dose of the tropus that everyone was supposed to take. But it made her feel more alive.

Others did this, but it was frowned upon in much the same way as 21st Century class A drugs were considered harmful. Chantal wasn't addicted to the low dose lifestyle, but it certainly gave her more freethinking and what she considered to be sharpness.

"You're a sife", said Lars, "You siphon," looking towards Chantal.

"I can see it in your eyes. Show me your wrist." Chantal extended it and Lars noticed the plexi was almost red.

"That's how we feel," he said to Chantal," No tropus and a much clearer was of thinking, acting and living."

Chantal replied, "But that's because you are immune to the Nero virus. I'm taking a risk."

"Not really," replied Carolin, "I'm not immune but have

lived in the Tract all my life. My parents had the immunity, but it didn't pass on to me. The whole Nero thing is a big conspiracy now, but no-one would ever listen to the Tract on this. The conspiracy works well because everyone is frightened and therefore won't let the Tract people into Ellipse, except under stringent control."

Chantal was thinking about this. She knew that she'd been siphoning for at least a couple of years. She'd started with an eighth, but now it was half that she took out. When it dropped below a quarter, her blood started to change colour, and now it was almost the raw red colour that they had been taught was dangerous.

Janie looked at Chantal and then back towards Lars. "I'm trusting you on this far more than I should do. I need some way for you to prove you are on the level."

The taxi had just crossed Westminster Bridge and the rail it was following ended by Parliament Square.

"We're here," said Janie. "Chantal and I are leaving you now. I'll help Scrive Mallinson if he shows up at the office, but I don't know what I'm supposed to do."

"Neither do we at the moment," replied Carolin," Scrive is a tracker. He'll be looking out for signs of what has been happening. He'll need access to some things in your area, but we just don't know what."

"I'll be in contact again," said Lars. He opened the cab door on the pavement side and pushed it wide. Carolin climbed out, and he followed.

Shred

Makatomi cursed at the news that one of the trackers he'd hired was creating a problem.

He'd have to get it fixed. In a low-key way so that no-one suspected or followed any link back to Biotree. It couldn't be a disappearance, the hiring of Scrive was too recent, and the limited people who did know would think Makatomi was implicated.

He decided to call the fixer that had just helped him out to locate the heavies in Los Angeles. He needed something done quietly, and without fuss.

Makatomi reached into his pocket. The disposable cell-phone was still there. He smiled; a low-tech solution and the same phone he'd used to set up the earlier appointment. He should have already destroyed the phone. On this occasion, it worked to his benefit, because he still had the link. He hit the redial, and the phone indicated two minutes left.

"Arusen, please terminate Scrive Mallinson. I will message you his address. Use a cartridge. I want it to look clean."

In turn, Arusen sent another fixer the information about Scrive's land address as well as the IoH address of Scrive's current Plexi unit. With the Internet of Health address, the fixer could arrange for Scrive's old tropus cartridge to be decommissioned, necessitating a replacement.

4

"This isn't a ride you can take again,
but one, I'm guessing,
that is simply impossible to get off."

— *Scarlett Thomas, The End of Mr. Y*

Head-Up, Head Down.

Scrive was playing with a Head-Up Display. He wanted to try the virtual support before he took it outside. It was a new unit, and he wanted it to run very fast. He'd pressed the button-shaped device into a small carbon fibre frame attached to his left ear. It was one neat device. As he ramped up the speed, he heard a beep. It was his cartridge. It was giving out the depleted tone. He looked at it and could feel the little ripple on his wrist where it sent a small alert requesting a replacement.

Scrive thought about it. He had only put a new one in that morning. They were supposed to last for four weeks. He'd never had a defective one before. He looked for his supply. The package he'd left out this morning had been tidied away. It must have been Charlie. She'd have put it away, as part of a tidiness campaign. He flipped open the cupboard, and there was the pack. He opened it and reached for another cartridge. He was supposed to keep the old one if it was defective, but in truth, he couldn't be bothered and pinged it into the waste disposal.

He flipped the new one in and instinctively looked at his plexi. The tropus hit caught him unexpectedly, the one he'd been using before had given him a rush, but once he was back to an average tropus level, the replacements didn't usually have the same effect.

He wondered briefly whether the previous cartridge had been faulty from the start.

Then he saw the impact in the plexi. Instead of staying yellow, his blood colour was running towards red — the danger colour.

He gasped.

It was turning past red to a bluer colour. He struggled for breath. The blue colour could have two meanings. He was de-oxygenating. But he could also feel a kind of pain increasing all over his body. Too fast to be Nero, but something was attacking him.

He slid towards the floor, and as he did so, a couple of the neatly arranged cooking utensils also crashed down alongside a large cooking pot.

He couldn't speak.

He couldn't breathe.

He couldn't see.

There was another crash, and he felt a sharp pain in his chest.

Useful nanofibre pressure suits

Denny had booked some tickets on the Hypersonic out of LAX. It was a regular route, if somewhat pricey - what with enviroset taxes added to the ticket price. It didn't have the comfort of the V-Blade that Makatomi had arrived on, but as the Mach 6 speed meant the journey only took around 30 minutes it was worth the annoying pressure suit.

Suze and Denny were both frequent travellers, and both had nanofibre pressure suits of their own. They could go through the business check-in wearing the suits which would be tested on the diagnostic before they boarded. It was a lot less irritating than having to use one of the suits provided by the airline.

They decided to go hand luggage only. Makatomi had given them a decent amount of upfront money, so even if there were no separate expenses, it was still worth it for the convenience.

Denny packed a small box with some gadgets and dropped them at Fed-Ex on the way to the airport. They'd receive the items at an address in London later.

The flight was being called as they arrived and after the bios scans, checks of their cartridges, declarations that they hadn't been in contact with the Tract for the last 30 days and the pre-diagnostics for their suits, they boarded the flight.

A head-up display forced its way onto their vision. It was a feature of the suit and forced them to watch the pre-flight safety instruction. Danny referred to the suit as 'boil in a bag' on the basis that if anything were to happen there'd not be much left of anyone, except whatever it was would be entirely contained in the armour proofed pressure suits.

A few more minutes and the HUD flipped to a news channel. It could be adjusted by eye movement, but Denny just watched the programme, which was giving updates on a few political situations, a couple of scandals involving a movie star who'd been in the porn industry and some football results. Next up was a pop video, but as it started, the screen cleared. They'd landed and were in London.

The combination of the HUD, the pressure suit and the cartridge modification during flight meant that the entire sensation of take-off, flight and landing had been replaced with a somewhat intrusive video show.

Denny felt the suit pressure release, having not noticed it tighten at all during the flight. The haptics were designed to bring passengers down to reality again at the end, and he could feel circulation and pulse for a few seconds as the suit ran its post-flight diagnostics of his blood pressure and pulse.

He's joked that suits had a mind of their own, and in a way they did. They'd stay inflated and rigid if a passenger was suffering adversely from the flight, or indeed if there was any security concern when they'd been run through the passport and customs processes.

Thankfully for both Denny and Suze, the suits de-pressurised and returned to a skin-layer level. Denny pulled a tee-shirt over his head and Suze wrapped herself in a jacket.

"Let's go," said Denny, "We've some tracking to do".

Suze nodded. They had been awake since 4 am LA time, and after the flight against the clock it had turned back into the London evening.

Charlie's titanium SIG

Charlie heard the crash from the kitchen. First a small one, then a larger metallic one and finally a scraping and a thud. She was in the bedroom and reached into Scrive's bedside cabinet to bring out a SIG pistol. Titanium, lightweight and with minute rounds, it could fire as fast as many machine guns.

She flexed and moved fast and silently towards the kitchen. She could see Scrive inert on the ground. Scrive was on his back, arms upturned, but still breathing. She could see the plexi and the blue, almost black, blood display.

"Scrive - stay with me - this is Charlie," she called, "this is a nano crime". She glanced around and slid back to the bedroom, returning a few seconds later with a small handheld wired to a little T shaped connector.

She lifted it above her head and smashed it down onto Scrive's arm, smashing the plexi and the cartridge. She held it there as black blood oozed onto the floor. She was holding in two buttons on the device and kneeling in the slow ooze that was dripping from Scrive.

The T connector glowed blue, and she could see it was processing Scrive's blood.

Ten minutes passed. Charlie looked down at Scrive. The thin slick of black slime on the floor by her knees was changing colour. Scrive's face was also evolving from a grey colour to one that was notably redder. She could hear him breathing very quietly. She gently removed the unit that she had slammed into his arm. She stood and hurried to the freezer, selecting a polypack of frozen vegetables. She ripped the packaging with both hands, allowing the small chopped vegetables to fall to the floor. She took the packaging and wrapped it tightly around Scrive's wrist. She could see his eyes moving rapidly under his closed lids.

Then he shook violently, and with a sudden and sharp gasp he sat up.

His eyes opened.

"What's happened?" he looked at Charlie, "Something has gone wrong."

"Yes," replied Charlie quietly, "I think someone has just tried to kill you."

Scrive looked at his arm. "I was adding a cartridge; the last one was defective."

"Maybe...", replied Charlie," But I think the new one was contaminated. Deliberately".

She looked again at the liquid on the floor. It was now a blood colour, having been black a few minutes earlier.

"Ew," she said, "Kind of messy."

"Someone had added a payload to your cartridge", said Charlie, "I've seen this effect when I was working with the nanotech. Someone has added nanobots to the cartridge. I think they were intended to mash up your inside."

Scrive looked around and spotted the handheld device on the floor. "You used your experiment on me?" he looked at Charlie.

"This time, bad science has a good outcome. I saw your black blood, typical of a nanobot incursion, I reckoned that my device would finish off any normal nanobots and it seems to have worked. I inserted a huge block of nanoreductives into your bloodstream - it worked because even the blood spill has been processed. The zappers half-life is one hour, so we'd better keep an eye on you. What's interesting is that the zappers have been so thorough that your blood has reverted to red. Not yellow or orange. There's something else weird happening here, normally nanoreductives restore balance but are not powerful enough to completely neutralise tropus."

Scrive pulled himself up using the edge of the kitchen counter. He did it slowly, aware that his blood level was a little low.

"Lay down, you've lost some blood" said Charlie, "and where do you keep the first aid kit? I don't think you've lost that much. It looks worse than it is. I'm going to guess less than half a litre. That's less than a blood donor session."

"Weak tea with sugar and a cookie then?" asked Shrive. He was aware that his reaction times had slowed. He seemed to be running at normal rates. He wouldn't push it at the moment until his cardio had stabilised.

"I'm a little bit worried that whoever has done this might want to come back and take a look," said Charlie. "I think we may still need to fake your demise".

She slid across the floor and retrieved the SIG pistol. There was a quiet click as she replaced the safety catch.

Non-linear cubism

Denny had gone non-linear. He was strafing various global systems to try to find any patterns that would help trace what had been happening in London, LA, and wherever Makatomi seemed to be taking his presence.

He'd brought a Cube with him; it was a small offboard processor that he could use with a regular handheld to boost the power and number of connections. He'd brought them both in his carry-on luggage as well as a somewhat cumbersome looking mains adapter so that he could run his system in the UK. It wasn't the voltages; it was just the over-engineered plugs and sockets that the Brits seemed to prefer.

Suze was also browsing online, but at a more leisurely pace. They'd checked into a central London hotel and needed to run their operation without attracting attention. She was gently reprogramming the network around the hotel so that Denny's activities wouldn't draw undue attention. He was hitting the system so hard that any schoolkid could probably spot the activity. Suze was creating an electronic cordon to stop it being detectable.

Denny glanced up.

"Makatomi is a real spinner," he muttered, "One minute he's in London, then LA, then Tokyo. He's carrying Arusen around with him on that V-Blade, but there's another electronic presence that seems to skitter around even faster."

Suze nodded," Yeah, I saw that too. Holden. He seems to turn up everywhere. I can't tag him properly; it is like he's somehow in the system. He's also been to Norway and Arizona."

Denny nodded. It must be evident if Suze had picked up on it too. Their work division was unbalanced, and he'd been doing most of the heavy tracing. Suze was quietly folding some of the quaint but expensive grey hotel stationery into the shape of a swan, with her spare hand. She was already wearing the colourful courtesy gown and had now pushed two of the chopsticks into her hair, making an instantly more Eastern look.

"Was that the influence of the room service?" he quipped. They'd ordered Japanese as a sort of homage to Makatomi and been enjoying maguru tuna sushi with nori seaweed. Suze had spotted a pineapple dessert, but neither of them had expected the laser cut slices laminated with microlayers of a ginger flavoured wasabi.

"Yes, it's auto suggestive, I think," replied Suze as she flipped another firewall. "The ginger and pineapple must be talking to me."

Chinese wake up

Guangdong Province, China and Shenzhen Ruby were due to play an important match. Den Xiapau had tickets to the Shenzhen Stadium for what promised to be the Super League match of the season, as far as he was concerned.

But.

Now he'd alerted everyone about that hacker attack, which seemed like two different sets of people on the same mission, he was notionally chained to his desk.

The station commander had called for a lock-down. No-one in or out. Sure, he could get a bowl of noodles from the canteen or spend half an hour playing some table tennis, but he was fundamentally locked in until they'd got to the bottom of whatever was happening.

There had been an initial burst of system scans apparently from all over the world. Den Xiapau knew it was typical of an advanced hacker - probably a tracker - who was trying to find out something important. It looked like a coincidence that the second series of probes had appeared but the second set (which seemed easier to trace back to London), had also been shooting probes into Biotree.

He wasn't sure what to make of this. Was China being challenged, or was this some corporate protestor trying to dig into Biotree's vaults?

The main reason for all of the escalation was because of the sophistication. Two sets of almost simultaneous probes with

Chinese corporations and governments as a target.

After the first alert, they'd decided to inform the US and European Governments. If this was someone playing silly games, it was better to let them know that they had been discovered. The longer they left it, the more the West would get cocky about such things.

They spent a little longer deciding whether to inform Biotree. Still, because they also had a sizeable Biotree manufacturing plant right within the province, it seemed like the right thing to do.

The challenge now was that both the Americans and Europeans had escalated it within their jurisdictions and Biotree's Chairman had been on the red phone to the Chinese President.

It was all causing something of a meltdown.

Then, after the initial attacks, everything had gone quiet for a couple of hours. What was interesting now was that a new series of high-intensity probes seemed to have started. From London, although someone very sophisticated was running a cloaking operation on them. It was fortunate for Den Xiapau that he'd spotted the source and knew where to be looking. Otherwise, the cloaking would have worked before he'd been able to get a fix.

5

And all I need now is
intellectual intercourse
A soul to dig the hole
much deeper
And I have no concept of time
other than it is flying
If only I could
kill the killer

All I really want – Alanis Morissette

Bodø

Sheri was originally Canadian, although she had studied in the USA, as well as a short spell in Switzerland and was now into her second year at Biotree's facility in Norway.

The Bodø environment was surprisingly familiar, a mix of her childhood's Vancouver waters and the nearby ski areas, where she had spent winters ski-ing as well as getting something of a reputation around Whistler for her freestyle snowboarding.

The cold end of the Pacific had first raised her love of nature. She would still think of times spent with her Grandfather out to look for whales with their tail splash, fishy snorts and the rippling radiation of the water as they would dive near to the boat.

The Pacific had also stimulated her study of marine biology and the organisms that maintained the ecology. Then her time at Harvard where the study of very small things had eventually led her to Biotree. Harvard had taught her how the organisms worked and then CERN in Switzerland had taught her how to build them, ironically by first showing how to smash things apart.

Now she was working with mechanosynthesis, construction an atom at a time. It was beyond a watchmaker's precision, to know how to bolt the atoms together to make the tiny machines that formed the basis of the Biotree business model.

She'd learned how to build these tiny structures, how to

make them operate, which parts would simply refuse to work together because of the still only partly understood and apparently tiny forces between them. Forces she knew were big enough to destroy the machines to which they were attached if they were not coupled properly.

She sometimes thought of it as being inside God's head. If a God existed, the God would need to know this stuff really well.

It was her work in the USA had lifted her profile considerably. At Harvard she had gained extra letters after her name. She had also met some of the super-scientists that worked in her field. They had told her about the opportunities at Biotree, but initially, she had remained sceptical.

Then she'd worked on ultra-transformables, which were a branch of the science that could help significantly in healthcare, the machines having a squishiness which meant they travelled well inside humans.

The spell at CERN had been mainly using the accelerators to smash a few things apart and see the effects. There was something mysterious about the power needed when humans tried to do these things, compared with the weak forces that were apparent in the nano-machines and which could do exceptionally more powerful things if assembled incorrectly.

Back to God's head, it was like His way of saying, "No, No, don't do that."

Inevitably she'd also run into nanotoxins as part of the research. Still, to people in her community, there were some basic rules about what to attempt and mix, and most of the 'No-no's" were very obvious. It was more the effect of a constructed machine and its erstwhile operating system that became the challenge and the thing that led Sheri to Bodø, Norway.

She'd been working on nanoparticles to improve foodstuffs and found that the addition of inert machines as a way to deliver medicinal payload didn't work very well.

The human body (or any other living organism for that matter) detected and destroyed the nanobots on the way in. If they couldn't be destroyed, they were at least neutralised although this could leave residuals in the body.

What was fascinating was that the residuals were stored in almost homeopathic quantities.

Sheri had worked out that an average human adult could eat nano-processed food every day of their life. Unless the human system changed the form of handling, the effect of the residual "neutralised and stored" would still only amount to something which in homeopathy was called the 60X formula. This wasn't one sixtieth, it was ten to the power of minus sixty. Something like the equivalent of a single pinch of salt into the Pacific Ocean. This level was so far below the 24X considered to be the limit of any homeopathic remedy, that the little broken machines couldn't pose any threat at all.

Of course, that assumed that the body had done its 'repel all invaders' thing and broken the machines down and expelled them.

It was the very power of these tiny machines that fascinated Sheri. They were already being packaged and consumerised by Biotree, and she knew there were many more practical and positive uses.

When she'd left for Bodø, it was with the idea of spending a couple of years, to make enough to live well and then move back to the West Coast. What had been seductive about her time was both the work and her discovery of Nathan, a fellow Canadian worker, with whom she now lived on the extended Bodø complex.

There was also the feeling in the Biotree Bodø R&D facility of being in the core of the core. It wasn't just in the Ellipse, Bodø was the inner sanctum of how everything worked. And there she sat, in the Advanced Technology Area, right at the centre of the centre.

Sheri knew that both she and Nathan had found something worthwhile and challenging. They'd both talked recently about settling longer in Bodø, and with her approaching birthday, she wondered whether Nathan was getting ready to ask her a big question. She smiled to herself as she knew the answer already. And it would give an excuse for a trip back to Canada.

V-Blade departure times

From their London hotel room, Denny was convinced that there would be a way to track the other suspicious person that might be following this assignment. He was sure that something had happened around the time he had run the last trace.

He was still hitting the Chinese sites and the Biotree locations but was now interested in tracing back Makatomi's steps.

"Suze let's see what happened inside Biotree this morning". He looked across at Suze, and they both laughed. Was it really the same day?

Suze was testing a few links around Canary Wharf. She found a tourist weather cam monitoring the general view. She jacked into its archive and ran back to the morning period. In reverse, a purple flash appeared over one of the buildings. She stopped the rewind and hit a button.

"That's the 'out' point", she said and continued to run the video backwards. Another purple flash, "and that's the 'In'," she added," Now we can see when Makatomi arrived and left."

Denny nodded. Suze had found the arrival and departure times of the V-Blade. There wouldn't be many of these crafts around, and a direct docking with the building was still relatively rare. They both knew this would be Makatomi's ride at the headquarters.

"Now we have a time range, we need to work out where he's meeting his visitor", said Suze," I've got the building directory here. It is the one used for visitors to the headquarters. Here we are, floors 60-70 seem to be the ones for the special meetings."

Danny looked at the list. There were a couple of boardroom floors, some training areas and three floors with individual meeting rooms, including two levels with ultra-secure screening.

"It will be one of these," he said, pointing to the secure facilities. Makatomi won't want to take any chances."

Suze nodded. "Let's play with the elevators". She flicked into a few more screens and then a few more.

"This isn't working, there's no access", she said.

Denny picked up his handheld and tapped a number. He was calling the building's foyer. "Hello, I'm a guest in your building. I seem to be stuck somewhere between floors 58 and the top." He hung up immediately.

The foyer receptionist punched another number.

"Gotcha," said Suze, "watching the number ringing through and tracing it to Westinghouse, who had a facility in the Canary Wharf area. They have people on hand to manage the elevators in case of problems.

"Now I know where you are, I might just need to borrow a couple of your documents," she said as she dragged a couple of diagrams onto her own machine's desktop. They were high-level plans of the elevators, with the network number for the various individual shafts.

"Okay, now to find their camera feeds". Suze tapped a few numbers and soon had three TV pictures displayed on the screen of her computer.

"Now I need to run the archives". Suze tapped some numbers and three pictures simultaneously wound back to the time of the V-Blade landing. Then she ran them forward at ten times normal speed. They watched as one floor became busy, but the other two had no visitors.

Then suddenly a lone individual appeared on floor 63. He walked to the reception and was met by a third person. It wasn't Makatomi.

"It's him," said Suze," I know it is."

Contamination

Scrive looked towards Charlie after hearing the safety click from her weapon. "You found my pistol, then?"

"Old habits," replied Charlie.

"What happened?"

"My handheld, the one I told you about. Complete with my failed blood reprocessor - the one that destroys nanobots. That's what I used on you. I could see your blood. It was turning black. Someone has contaminated you with nanobots.

"It looked like they were attacking your blood. It was clotting, instead of flowing. I managed to smash into your circulation through the cartridge and to release my little App. It is the first time its failure has been useful. It caused a signalling failure amongst the 'bots. Whatever they were doing stopped.

"It looks to me as if they were attacking via your cartridge. Someone has contaminated the tropus. "

Scrive looked around. The kitchen was a mess. He was a mess.

"Thank you," he said to Charlie, "I think that could have finished me."

"Yes, and I'm not sure whether whoever did this will be back?"

"And they don't know about me at the moment", said Charlie.

"That's a good point," replied Scrive. "We should keep it that way, no sense in showing all of the hand."

"And maybe we can throw them a scrap too? See if we can draw them out?" Charlie grinned.

"Okay," said Scrive, "Maybe I need to disappear for a while, make them think that I've gone."

"And not show them that I'm around either?"

"...Or we do something more reckless?" Scrive pulled himself up, "Maybe I need to carry on for a few days as if nothing has happened? They won't know when I'm exchanging the cartridge; they may even know that I'm a little lax on such matters. I'm going to carry on normally for the next few days. The difference will be my traceability, and you can help with that."

"Sure," said Charlie, "But I think I'd better move away. It's better that they don't know about me at all, and it will be a lot easier if I'm somewhere else. And from one tracker to another, don't even think about tracing me."

She was already walking to the bedroom. Scrive could hear the sound of a zipper bag and realized that Charlie was already planning   to   move   out.

"You'd better take this," he said and handed her the high fire rate SIG, "I guess you only found the one," they both smiled.

"And I'll be listening out for you", said Charlie, "Let's just agree on some signals." Scrive tapped a series of numbers into his handheld and then pressed a few keys. The numbers transferred to Charlie's handheld. They now had a private key between them, which could be used for tracking and tracing.

"And we'll use the transit station as a drop," if we need it. By the left-hand side of the entrance. Use a marker. I'll find it."

"Daily," said Scrive, "But don't tell me where you'll be".

Scrive knew that he and Charlie could operate a hidden analogue protocol between them. Charlie could track him, but he wouldn't know where she was. If she needed to exchange information, they would use a physical location, which Scrive would check every day. Charlie would not go there herself but would use an intermediary if there was to be anything placed there. If Scrive needed to pass information to Charlie, he would use the tracker to signal a location, leave the material and then continue. Scrive knew that he was now on an electronic leash, which was managed by Charlie.

Camtran mission

Suze and Denny continued to watch the replay. Suze was intently watching for the return of the visitor to the elevator. Some 20 minutes later, he arrived again, still accompanied by the same person. It was difficult to make out what they were saying, the sound channel from the elevator monitoring was faulty, and the wide angle meant they were both shown tiny.

"That was a short meeting," said Denny. Suze nodded. "Maybe he's not getting paid well as us - that can't have been much of a negotiation?"

Suze was referring to the negotiation they'd run with Makatomi, once they had realised that money wasn't a problem to resolve this case.

"Okay," said Suze, "Now let's see you leave the building", they flicked to another camera view from the ground level and saw Scrive exiting towards the transit station.

"Go in, go in," said Denny, willing the image of Scrive to enter the Tube. He did, and Suze and Denny smiled. We'll get him at the gate. Scrive passed through it as it automatically opened. Suze tapped a few buttons and moments later retrieved the cartridge RFID for Scrive.

"Radio Frequency Identification - Thank you for some old technologies," said Suze.

"We have you now, Mr Mallinson," she said, as the RFID sequence yielded its information. And you seem to have good health records too, Mr Mallinson of Chelsea Bridge Wharf."

Denny calculated that Scrive Mallinson's home address appeared to be less than three miles from their hotel in Central London.

A visit would be necessary. There were two ways to do this. Overt or Stealth. Denny ran some further scans to try to find the back story for Mallinson, but it wasn't straightforward to trace more than the most perfunctory information.

Denny thought this added up. He knew that a similar scan for his own ident wouldn't yield much, so the sequence of events seemed to form the right type of trail. Mallinson visits the office of Makatomi. He has as a meeting, leaves and then within a couple of hours there's a series of scans being run on China and also on Biotree. Checking on Mallinson yields little. Denny was pretty sure it had the hallmark of another tracker.

"Suze, I think Mallinson has the other half of our contract." said Denny.

Suze nodded. "Yes", there's a pattern that looks strangely familiar. And now we know where he lives. I don't think we should try to deep scan though, if he's as good as us he'll notice it in seconds.

"Do you fancy a ride in a London taxi?", asked Denny to Suze. "I think I know someone we can visit."

"Now about tomorrow morning?" answered Suze. "We'll need to be sharp." She pulled the chopsticks from her hair.

"You stay here", said Denny, "I'm going on a little mission with a camtran. It would be good to keep tabs on Mr Mallinson." He flipped open his hand luggage and retrieved a couple of small camera transmitter devices.

"I'll see you in about an hour."

Denny slipped from the hotel and took a taxi across town. It was one of the black cabs that could go anywhere, although their route seemed to be along the major streets. He was dropped outside a large apartment block, next to a hotel complex.

Denny looked around and then reached into his bag. He identified the entrance to the apartments and set up a small camtran monitor across the way. It showed the main entrance and part of the thoroughfare either side.

He looked across to the adjacent hotel to the apartment buildings, then crossed the street and made for the reception. Ten minutes later, he returned with two cardkeys.

He and Suze were about to become Mallinson's neighbours.

Norway

Sheri was at home with Nathan. She looked out of the window, across snow towards some distant hills. Beyond them were mountains. She had grown to love the Norwegian scenery. The water, the sparkling ice and snow. It was like every cliché she'd heard about the place, an extraordinary land where bad vistas were not permitted. It made the already enjoyable work even better. She had a good location, good job, good money and most of all she was now sharing it all with Nathan.

Although she and Nathan both worked for Biotree, their roles were very different, and they didn't see each the during the working day. The campus was vast, and they would usually go to work separately, and because of the distance and security inside the facility, it was best to stay out of contact throughout the day. There were ways to communicate, but it was much the same as if they worked in different towns.

At the moment she was reading a report on her handheld. It was related to engineering advances in India and the possibility of some breakthroughs in molecular design. Sheri could sense immediately that this wasn't a plausible article. There were holes in the logic, and the approach was one she already knew to be flawed.

Nathan was preparing some food in the kitchen and called through from time to time to inform of progress. She could generally tell by the variety of hissing sounds, aromas of onions, garlic and the tell-tale sound of a bottle cork being extracted. The evening meal was almost ready.

Sheri knew she had the more demanding and specialised job of the two of them. Her work was at the (almost literally) cutting edge of the design of the nanomachines. Originally, there had been a set of standard assemblies that worked well together. Most of the incremental designs were based around these pieces.

When she explained it to others, she likened it to a car. Four wheels, one on each corner, some seats an, engine, steering and brakes. The nanobots had a similar basic construction kit.

At the small sizes of the machines, it was the use of protein as a fuel and the same effect that makes creme in coffee eventually spread through the liquid that created for a bot a power source. It also provided a significant physical limitation to the small machines and their deployment. The 'coffee-cup' Brownian motion made everything shake dramatically at this small scale. Nothing was every static and the trick with the scientists was to harness this motion as a power source.

The building blocks that Sheri used were similar to the components of the car. There were components for movement, components for sensing, components to join things together - the so-called fixtures - like the chassis of a car and elements to provide grip and contact between the machines - the end effectors.

Then, as Nathan referred, "JASMOP" - or "Just a small matter of programming" to create the operating systems for these small devices. Just a small matter was an interesting point. The technology of Scanning Probe Microscopes used to view the assembly work had never really scaled itself and relied upon clean, secure environments and mega-voltages. It was not surprising when a speck of dust would be like throwing a planet at some of these machines.

Sheri's work was within the so-called 'exotics' division. As expected, there were pictures of palm trees and Pina-Coladas stuck to the walls inside, but fundamentally this was the area where Sheri tried to outdo her maker.

It was the place where new elements were designed.

Original elements to create the missing shapes of matter needed to extend the constructor kit of parts for the nanomachines. The pieces that God forgot. There were practical physical limitations to how they could be used. Apart from atomic forces that would blast structures apart, the continued jittering from Brownian motion and the protein fuel consumption of the tiny devices, there were still some basic components that were proving impossible to construct. It was like the car but with only a few degrees of steering and no gears.

Sheri and the team were attempting to build the new shapes. The missing piece parts that would extend the nano constructor kit.

Nathan entered the room, triumphant. "Dinner is served!", he quipped and gestured towards their dining table. They would still eat together whenever possible because the nature of the work often meant irregular hours, and this would give a chance to spend some time chatting. There was an inverse luxury to 'dining in'. Most of the time, workers in the facility would avail themselves of the vast eco-system of restaurants and cafes that had established around the complex.

Pretty much all cuisines were catered for, from fast-food Americana to the fanciest French or Japanese food. Most evenings they would eat out, sometimes alone but often in company with others from the facility.

Being alone in their living quarters was an excellent time for decompression, even if Sheri had started the evening with a scientific journal article.

"I can't believe it's nearly two years that we've been here." started Nathan. "I know it will be after your birthday that its officially two years for you and about three weeks later for me."

Sheri alerted herself as Nathan started this line of

conversation. A meal at home, talk about how long...would this be leading to a discussion of 'them'? She decided to see where it was going, but Nathan moved in another direction.

"I hope tonight's 'dish of the day' is okay?" he inquired, "I had to scratch around for some of the ingredients".

Sheri relaxed. She was keen enough for a talk about their future, but tonight it didn't somehow seem to be the time. She was just too strung out on the current work. A few tonal changes were creating some new upsets. Makatomi's business plans were at odds with Sheri's personal beliefs. Instead of the Biotree being about healthcare and the future, it seemed to be moving towards more ominous goals. They had recently brought some contractors into Sheri's department who seemed rather more lackadaisical about their approach to safety systems.

"I've been working on some new secure perimeter systems this week," called Nathan," It looks as if Biotree are getting even more paranoid based upon the recent share prices and business news."

Nathan worked in another area of high technology, but rather than being progressive and forward-facing, like the pure R&D that Sheri conducted, this was more related to the protection and security of the Biotree complex. Beyond obvious physical defences, there were rings within rings of security measures that could both give an impression of a relaxed environment but at the same time could become extremely strict in moments if something inappropriate was detected.

Nathan worked on the improvements to this world. A guardian role that also meant he spent more time around the whole complex that Sheri.

They had initially met just after Nathan had joined. Sheri had been out for a weekend skiing in the adjoining mountains, with a couple of new-found girlfriends when they had run into an 'induction team' part of which included Nathan.

Sheri was snowboarding at the time and noticed that Nathan also seemed pretty accomplished, and they'd broken away from the group to try a particularly exciting route. At least that was what Nathan had said and - on reflection - Sheri had also thought the course unexpectedly delightful.

They'd been together ever since that first encounter. After a short time, they had decided to move into what was considered one of the better apartment areas. Their facility looked out to the sea on one side and hills and distant mountains on the other side.

Tonight, Nathan had placed candles outdoors in the Norwegian tradition, and Sheri could see a distant twinkle from boats on the sea and stars in the sky.

But no, tonight wasn't the one to have deep conversations about the future.

Backtrace

Captain Taylor had a problem. He'd almost singlehandedly scrambled the U.S military to a state of high alert. All based on what started as a routine intercept in China.

He had seen some routine tracing by a hacker; it had tripped his high-intensity alert. He'd selected the trace, and watched it hop about between Biotree and SuzGene, a Chinese biochemical producer. Then he'd seen a second trace. It looked as if it was doing something similar. Taylor worked out that the traces looked like they were coming from professionals. London and, more worryingly, Los Angeles. The LA one was a problem because if it was left undeclared, someone might challenge it as a state cyber probe. The kind of probe invoked before a cyber-attack.

Taylor knew there was no such thing on the horizon and thought he'd better call it in. That's when everything disappeared and seemed to go back to normal. Except, it looked as if a Chinese listening station had intercepted the activity and was now sending a few quiet probes to try to backtrace to the source of interference. He could see that the Chinese were running their monitoring from Beijing, and he thought it highly likely that it originated in the Chinese Ministry of State Security (MSS). The event was troublesome because it could easily pop up as a diplomatic incident.

He worked out that the president would already have been

alerted to the situation. Taylor was old-school, from before the Great Leap, when most comms was still stuff with dials and buttons, rather than something one gestured to or voice activated. He'd paid extra to have his automobile fitted with a facsimile retro radio, one that had a rotary volume and push buttons for the channel selection. He knew that behind the covers, it was all solid-state, but it somehow felt better to dial things up.

Taylor had a secret habit. He was one of the people who ran low dosage from the tropus cartridges. Taylor didn't sell on his excess tropus, which meant that hardly anyone knew about his habit. He'd discovered the phenomenon by accident after a boating injury, that depletion of tropus made him feel somehow sharper. He could also remember more. He doubted, now, that he would remember about the analogue stations if he was on full dosage.

He'd still had to deal with the shadowy worlds of sifes and Tractwalkers though. He knew that the standard cartridges produced logged usage reports which could be monitored. He'd arranged through dealer connections for the fitting of a cloned cartridge holder, which somehow reported normally, despite his unconventional usage. He'd even paid over the odds to get it fitted because he didn't want to be linked to a dealer to whom he would supply his surplus tropus. It was another link in the chain that he'd prefer to avoid.

Taylor knew he could still fire up the old listening station and with the improved access from an array of satellites plus the old links created when Camp Lejeune, NC and Naples, Italy were still front-line monitoring stations, he might be able to uncover some further information. A few of the old links were worth re-activating

Outside was heavy rain. A squall from the Pacific had whipped into the harbour area, and there was a grey blanket across everything. Taylor was wearing a weatherproof cape, and a walked at an angle of forty-five degrees towards the four-wheel drive. The usual transit rail system was available in the main town here, but he'd be trekking into the forest and paying a visit to a couple of smaller buildings seldom used nowadays.

He booted up the four-wheel drive and reversed onto the road. Then along to a lane and then to the end of a road with a gate and wired fence.

He pressed an access pad in the four wheel's cab. Two large metal bolts slid open in the gates. Perimeter lights lit and a series of green spots briefly twinkled. He had disarmed the perimeter field, which would otherwise prevent his progress. He drove through the gates and into the area, which was buried in the forest. Then further along the track and sharp left. Two buildings, overgrown with what he'd have called kudzu or foot-a-night, back home in Tennessee, but here it was some other kind of vine. It did the trick though, and the two buildings were almost absorbed into the forest and undergrowth.

He tapped a few more access codes and hopped from the vehicle. A splash from underfoot, despite the now more distant sound of the wind and rain. The trees provided a groaning shelter in this part of the forest, although he knew that the weather further afield was still savage.

Now he entered the first building. He reached to the side of the door for a still familiar monitor light. Flipped it on and heard a countdown sequence. He had 60 seconds to disarm the building and punched in the access codes. 3-2-7-0. He still remembered it, despite the years of disuse. This facility had been a staple in the older days when picowave interception and traditional listening posts were still the order of the day. Now the remnant of the facility might give an unsophisticated way to access what was happening in Beijing. He really was going 'under the radar'.

6

What you see is what you get
You've made your bed, you better lie in it
You choose your leaders and place your
trust
As their lies wash you down and their
promises rust
You'll see kidney machines replaced by
rockets and guns

Paul Weller – Going Underground – The Clash

Follow me

Scrive was walking towards the transit station on his way back to his apartment. It was time to check for any update from Charlie. They were using a purely analogue protocol so that they could not be tracked by listening in through phone links or similar. Scrive knew that if anyone wanted to, they would probably now have access to his RFID and could be tracking his movements. The main thing was to make it all look normal as a way to reduce suspicion.

He'd patched his arm from Charlie's 'smash and grab', but it meant he couldn't use tropus again until he got the cartridge's plexi fixed. That would require medical attention which would signal that he'd already taken one of the doctored cartridges.

He'd be using the cocktail of his blood's residual tropus, any remnants of the hostile nanobots and the hacked concoction that Charlie had forced into his bloodstream. His blood was already running red from after Charlie's intervention, and now he simply didn't know because of the lack of a tropus fix.

Yesterday he'd used a pin to prick the end of one of his fingers, to see what colour emerged. It had been red. He'd been taught this meant danger, and it had made him feel unexpectedly queasy at the thought. Then he'd rubbed the finger, the blood had stopped, and since that point, he'd tried not to think about it.

Now he certainly felt okay. He felt better than he'd expected. He felt sharper with a kind of clarity and freshness. Today, it was beyond his ability to rev his thoughts to a higher speed. This feeling was offset by the sense that part of his mind was awakening that was usually dormant.

He took his routine walk to the transit and already had in mind the point he would approach to check for any marking from Charlie. It was only a day, and he didn't expect there to be anything yet. As he approached, for the fourth time he saw the slim girl he had noticed previously. She was walking across in front of him. He saw the tattoo. She was singing quietly to herself as usual. 'Follow me', she was singing. "Follow me, follow me, follow me Scrive. Follow me Mr Mallinson."

He looked startled.

Then he decided to be as deadpan as possible.
Was this something from Charlie? He doubted it.
It was too much of a coincidence to have seen this person four times consecutively. But there had to be a link. He thought quickly. He'd seen the girl before he'd been to Makatomi. Before the threat to his life. Before he'd made arrangements with Charlie, but this had to be related.

He decided to follow.

Around the street corner was a small pavement cafe. Busy with local well-dressed people sipping small coffees and tapping into various handhelds. His guide showed him to a table in the corner. An athletic-looking and tanned man was sitting there.

"Mr Mallinson?" he inquired, "My name is Lars, and this is Carolin. We think we can help you."

Scrive looked at them both. He noticed Lars looked weathered in a way that wasn't very common. Then he realised, Lars was from the Tract. He looked back at Carolin. So was she. He hadn't picked it up when he first saw Carolin; maybe he was looking at, well, other aspects.

"You're both from the Tract, what are you doing here?" he asked.

"The same thing as you, "Mr Mallinson," we are looking at what Biotree is trying to conceal. We know it is not about a Chinese plot, and that the story has been put out to help explain the share price drop and the strange activities within the company."

Scrive was tallying this new information. He'd only been involved with Makatomi for a day, and already someone had tried to kill him, and now he was being intercepted by a couple of Tractwalkers.

"Okay, say I go with this," replied Scrive, "what else can you tell me that would make me want to work with you?"

"The main thing we have to offer is immediate access to someone working inside Biotree, close to where Makatomi operates. But before that, I should tell you some other things."

Lars began to explain his background, that he was from Norway, that he lived close to Bodø, near to the Biotree R&D complex. He stated that he was one of the first people discovering their immunity to the Nero toxin. He had been forced into the Tract, along with others that were also immune.

He lived close to Bodø and seen the growth of the R&D facility and the influx of scientists.

"But the thing I need to tell you about is that Biotree has been working on its second-generation business. Nanobots. Before that it made its money from the tropus and cartridges."

"Now it is working on a third-generation business, and that's the thing we need prevent."

Scrive knew that the original business model for Biotree, along with several other large pharmaceutical based companies, had been the creation of the tropus that had formed the basis of the inoculation against Nero.

He also knew that the pricing for this had started high because of patents, but that global governments had forced a rapid change in order that the tropus could be manufactured on the industrial scale needed to provide it for large parts of the world population.

Everyone in the Ellipse took the regular medication of tropus through the cartridge system, and it had grown to be a basis for other services, based upon the addition of the radio links and secure identity capabilities.

Of course, Scrive also knew that this had effectively given everyone an electronic tag, based upon the need to use cartridges permanently and that the cartridge support clip was mainly where the tracking, wallet, comms, telemetry, health and other functions were held.

Scrive had also been noticing that his own system didn't seem to be affected negatively despite his lack of tropus. He had never been designated as immune and wondered how long Nero took to have an effect.

"You're both immune to the N3Ro?" he asked, "I can see that you don't have the plexus, so I assume no cartridges?

"Correct," said Lars, "but that's one of the things you should know. The Nero story has been convenient misinformation for the last several years. The cartridges that are in use now are for another purpose."

"...and what might that be?" asked Scrive.

"To stop you from seeing", replied Lars. "To hide what is happening".

Scrive looked quizzical, "To hide what?" he asked, "to stop us from seeing what?"

"You'll have to take what I say on trust," continued Lars. "We've no way of proving this here, although we do have other things we can show you later."

Scrive said, "It's already been a helluva week. I'm prepared for just about anything at the moment." He absentmindedly scratched at the place on his arm where a bandage covered his broken plexi.

"This is what we think has been happening," continued Lars,

"The Biotree corporation are being employed on several missions. They are one of the manufacturers of the tropus that all of you use to protect against the N3Ro virus. That has been a great continuous source of revenue for them and allowed them to create the facilities to build their other businesses."

"The main source of new business now is the Nanotechnology, although they seem to have a hit a wall with their R&D and at the same time there's a rumour that the Chinese have cloned the technology."

"We think that's why Biotree has employed you, to track down if there's a leak to the Chinese. We don't think you'll find one though, we think that the Chinese will be as surprised about this as anyone."

"How can you say that?" asked Scrive," You don't appear to have the resources, especially being based in the Tract."

"It is because we are from the Tract that we think we have an idea about what is happening.

"We believe that the Tract is the source of the new nanotech and that there is someone building products to compete with Biotree. In the Tract, we hear of things by the old-fashioned ways. Some of it isn't as reliable, but there are too many stories of people in an area deep in the Tract where this work is being done.

"If that's the case, how is it we haven't spotted it from the Ellipse?" asked Scrive, "I can't believe that anyone would be able to do this without someone from the Ellipse knowing what was happening.

"Normally I'd agree, said Lars, "But I think there is a reason, part of the way that the Ellipse has been engineered means that there is a huge blind spot for what happens in the Tract. It is as if we don't exist."

Scrive thought for a moment. It's true; he knew the Tract. Aside from the warnings to stay away and that they may be carriers of the Nero virus, he had little idea of what else went on.

"What? Is it like a return to the 'flat earth'? When people used to think of the earth as flat, before they discovered it was round, then the corners of the map would sometimes be printed with 'Here be Dragons'?" asked Scrive.

"It is a little like we've returned to that concept." continued Lars.

"Except we do all know that the world is round, indeed that's where we get the Ellipse term. There are still some areas that don't ever get mentioned by Ellipse dwellers. It is mainly an area south of Japan and China, an area we still call Australia."

Scrive replied, "But there isn't anything south of Japan, it is the exclusion zone, where the Nero toxins wiped out everything and where there is still a huge risk to anyone that attempts to go there. Part of the process of creating the Ellipse was to block off the remaining toxic zones. That's really where the terms of the Ellipse."

Lars nodded, "Even the Tract dwellers knew there were still some areas off-limits. The Ellipse dwellers had such advanced technology that they could fly just about anywhere, but the safety systems in the craft would ensure that they did not stray into dangerous territory. The Tract dwellers didn't have this technology, which limited their ability to move to all but the edges of the Ellipse. Without technology, Tract dwellers would not have access to the Exclusion zone, even if they wanted it."

Lars continued, "The last 30 years have seen a formidable rate of increase in technological progress compared with any period before. The nanotech, the transit, the handhelds, the tropus are all examples of the changes. I know it's called 'The Great Leap', but it does sometimes seem kind of far-fetched that so many changes happened so quickly."

Scrive thought, there was superb sophistication of technology and rapid advances in many things, all within his lifetime. The eradication of Nero by use of tropus cartridges created what media referred to as 'The Great Leap Forward'. A rate of unparalleled technological advancement, creating newer and faster transits, better media, a plethora of new devices including the ubiquitous handheld and the majority of what had become the secure networks and RFID based access systems.

A modern citizen could walk around safely and securely within their designated zones. By a simple application, they could visit other areas, but the system was well regulated to also keep crowds and supply and demand for goods and services under control. People with higher status (he included himself in this category) had greater freedom and the ability to travel more widely. And it had all been created without the politics and controls of a Big Brother state. The modern Ellipse citizen considered themselves pretty well off.

Carolin added, "We think there's a code word for where many of the secrets are held. It is called 'Australia' and we believe it is an area somewhere within the exclusion zone."

Scrive shook his head, he didn't recollect hearing of Australia.

"What or where is Australia?" he asked.

"That's one of the things we hope you'll be able to help us find out", answered Lars.

Analogue Tracking

Taylor found the inside of the tracking station remarkably familiar. There was a clinical look at complete odds to the run-down, camouflaged appearance of the outside. He had walked through the double entrance chamber, and by the time he had closed the access doors, there was a cool charcoal filtered air-con smell permeating the building. He knew he'd soon get used to it, with the slightly boosted oxygen levels to keep anyone in there sharp.

He flicked on a few of the displays and waited for the technology to settle. Sure, it was from before the 'Great Leap', and so some of it was a little dated looking, but he twisted a couple of the satisfyingly analogue controls, knurled surfaces with a real tactility missing from the modern devices with their flat screens, HUDs and haptic feedback.

He started with a probe to Beijing, mainly to see whether anything still worked. Sure enough, he was able to access a clean picture from a conference room inside an important building in Beijing. There was no-one in the room though, so he thought he'd try jacking into some of the other video links. He soon had access to some camera phones and a further and larger conference facility. It was all quite easy, but he knew that was because he was using the modern-day equivalent of listening through a wall with a glass beaker. It may not be possible to scan for individual devices, but, still, a basic cup could be a useful spy aid in the right hands.

The lack of any activity to watch made him wonder if the Chinese had been smart and that he was now watching a doctored video feed. Maybe they had tied these links down, and now there wasn't anything left to view.

He flipped a few dials to see whether there were any other live feeds still running. He found the continents menu and switched to the USA. It would be interesting to see if he could get back into the Maddox meeting undetected. In this case, there was nothing, so it looked as if someone decommissioned the link. He flicked back to the menu and noticed an extra entry at the top.

Australia.

He had never heard of Australia before. Yet there it was on the menu.

He flicked to enter the menu structure. A little series of towns appeared. Was this a test environment, maybe.
He clicked in.

Adelaide. Nothing
Canberra. Nothing
Darwin. A signal, but a blank screen.
Melbourne. Nothing.
Perth. A scratchy signal. A bad picture. There was something on the screen. It looked like a storm, although there were some large cylindrical structures running across the view. It wasn't easy to make anything out clearly.
Sydney. Nothing

Two more options. Woomera and Yulara. He wondered whether to bother, or whether to flick back to Perth to try to make out more.

Instead he clicked Woomera.

Sixteen squares appeared in his view. 16 cameras, 12 clear ones and four that had blank or static.

He opened the first one. Sound as well. He had a full monitor signal from this place. If it was a test site, then it was pretty impressive.

He studied the picture. A blue/green coloured scene, with what looked like some almost molecular structure in front of him. There were small red flashes in the image as well, which he initially thought were interference, but were tracking the shapes of the molecular structure.

It was difficult to scale the picture though, and he couldn't tell whether he was looking at something substantial or if it was a scale model of some kind.

He flicked to another screen, and then another. Whatever it was, the people who had set up the monitors had wanted to get a good view of it.

He bookmarked the page and hit the recording system in the control booth. He'd run this onto disk so that he could relay it later. He wasn't sure whether the links would stay reliable and whether he'd just struck lucky with this viewpoint.

He selected a few more of the screens.

They showed different external perspectives on the same structure.

Apart from the molecule shaped item, there were tubes running in various directions. They looked like pipes - uniform and machined. It was like a very large oil installation or something similar, but he could not see any fractionating towers or flames or any of the other tell-tale signs. This was a very clean installation and looked as it if it didn't need human intervention.

He kept each feed running for several minutes, partly to look for any signs of activity, but also to ensure he had something committed to his recording.

Then he decided to flip to the last spot.

Yulara

442

Pulse

Yulara

Captain Taylor had never heard of any of the places in this area of the system, and he began to wonder if they were tests, a secure facility somewhere or even 'off-world'.

As he flicked to the Yulara system he was again greeted by sixteen small screens, although on this occasion only three of them had a signal. He immediately saw that there was movement.

He tapped the screen to zoom into one of the pictures and recoiled as he saw the detail of what was in the feed.

Looking like similar pipe and molecule structures to the earlier Woomera feed, here was a system that seemed to be handling a viscous liquid.

He let this run and he could see that the process was probably something that ran for several hours, or perhaps even continuously.
There was clearly audio on the link, but no signs of human voice just a background ticking and clicking sound.

He eventually flicked away from the sight, after dutifully recording around 20 minutes of what appeared to be a section of a compound being reduced to its core constituents.

He decided to flick to the next screen. It showed a similar scene, but this time he could see that there were more of the same processes. It was like a processing plant. He didn't know how large.

He ran the recording for ten minutes and then flicked to the final active feed. A different scene. Red flashes mainly, some kind of glass structure. He didn't know what he was looking at or whether it was real or some kind of interference.

Again, he recorded it.

This camera had an extra set of numbers along the bottom of the feed. He recognised them as GPS co-ordinates. -25° 20' 51.90", +129° 51' 12.93" .

He had a fix for the camera. He already knew it was deep inside the Tract. Off the radar. In terms of the Nero toxin, this was a deadly area. He started to think it was deadly for other reasons.

The monitoring station he was in didn't have the level of communications needed to contact the Pentagon securely. He realised he would need to leave and make his way back to his main station to be able to explain in detail what he had discovered. Nonetheless, he thought he'd better send an update so that by the time he reached the secure facility they would already be prepared for the discussion.

He decided to send a short message:

"No further activity detected on Sparrowhawk. Another development. Complex called 'Australia' / 'Yulara' in the Exclusion Zone has relevance. More when back inside Brookings Main Complex."

He read the message back. It was suitably basic for a forward alert. He pressed the button. It was gone.

He carefully made a copy of the disk onto which he had recorded the video, and then made a further copy onto a removable unit, which he put into his pocket. He'd use that to transmit his findings from Brookings Main.

He left the complex switched on. The monitoring for Yulara would also stay running. For Beijing, he would need to make a further visit to see whether any of the screens became active. He somehow doubted it. It looked as if the Chinese had blocked the view and were sending back dummy pictures.

Outside it still rained heavily. Taylor moved back to the four-wheel drive, revved the engine and started the short journey back to Brookings Main. He would upload his videos to show the content of Yulara.

Ailartsua

Scrive looked across to Lars. "I'll try a few search terms now," he said, "I want to see what I get on a basic search."

He flipped open a small computer.

"This is a clean environment", he explained, "I keep the image on here to look like a factory specification machine. It is usually better to look like an amateur that's just trying something for the first time, rather than a calculated tracker."

Lars nodded.

Scrive selected a search engine and typed "Australia". There was a long pause while the search spawned other searches cross a wide range of systems.

He tried all capital letters. Alternate capitals and small letters.

Nothing.

Scrive tried another search 'Australia'. And another 'Aust*'

Now he had 'Austria' which immediately returned thousands of results.

He reversed the term 'ailartsua'.

Nothing.

He would need to check the code word. Something was wrong. Somehow, he recognised the name. He was fairly certain that "Australia" was the key to something.

He repeated this process with several other search tools and on several systems.

Still nothing.

Lars looked at his watch.

"I guess I'm boring you", commented Scrive.

"Not at all", came Lars reply, "Carolin and I had arranged for another meeting here today. They are due to be with us in a few minutes."

"How did you know I'd go along with this?" asked Scrive.

As he did this, a single word came up on his screen. Woomera. He blinked. He tried to run himself at hyperspeed. It didn't work. He decided it was the lag from lack of tropus.

Woomera.

It reminded him of something that had once been in his mind. Australia. A country. He couldn't remember how he knew about it and why it had disappeared from his thoughts so completely.

It seemed to be something to do with the sharpness he'd found since the tropus dose had worn off.

He could even remember that Woomera was famous for something. Travel, planes, space travel. That was it. Australia was a big country on the lower part of the planet. He thought it was probably outside of the Ellipse now.

That's why he couldn't' remember anything about it. The television maps of the planet didn't show it, and there was no reference in books or online.

He began to wonder if it was a made-up place, but somehow, he was sure that it was real. Canberra. Melbourne. Sydney with a harbour. Woomera, where they tested rockets.

He thought of Tajikistan. Plenty of people wouldn't name that as a country. Or know its capital — Dushanbe, which used to be the main market town.

He flicked to blank the screen on his handheld. He flipped a bookmark to Charlie. The first time, the only time, he'd broken protocol since they had separated.

"We didn't", answered Carolin, "We didn't know you'd go along with this." Those in the cafe were entirely unaware of the search result that Scrive had seen, his thoughts and that he'd now effectively concealed his finding and signalled it to Charlie.

Carolin continued, "We had to make some assumptions though. We thought that you'd be impressed if we told you what we already knew. We also realised that even if you were the best tracker, you'd probably have difficulty finding anything without some further help."

"What do you mean?" asked Scrive, he looked concerned.

"It is okay; it is not another tracker - you won't be sharing trade secrets," answered Lars.

"We've done better than that," added Carolin," We've found someone with access to what happens inside Biotree."

Scrive looked questioningly," You are not just expecting me to trust you - you're now expecting me to trust a Biotree employee as well? All of this seems wrong."

"Okay, at least meet her," replied Lars, "she, and her friend will be here in a few minutes."

Scrive considered, "Okay, but I'll want to talk to them first."

"Not a problem," answered Lars, "...and by the way, they have seen a picture of you from the ones that Carolin took over the last few days."

As he said this, the cafe went quiet for a moment. The door had opened, and Scrive saw two good-looking women enter.

One was dressed conservatively as if for work, the other had a gold metallic micro-skirt and a white tutu. She appeared to be carrying an umbrella which looked suspiciously like a wand.

"This is Janie and Chantal", introduced Carolin, looking up and down Chantal's outfit. There were several others in the cafe doing the same. Chantal wiggled onto a chair, and Janie sat beside her.

"Hello again, Lars," started Janie, "...and hello also to you, Mr Mallinson, or should I call you Scrive?"

"Scrive is fine," said Scrive, "You both seem to believe in making quite an entrance."

Scrive couldn't help admiring the remarkable impression that Chantal was having on the others in the cafe. She had stopped conversations. Scrive noted that they were both very attractive women.

"Let's just say that everyone will remember we have been in here this evening," said Chantal. "We want our movements to be very noticeable at the moment."

Carolin nodded, "This is the situation. We've told Scrive about what we think is happening; we are sure that the investigation he is on has more to it and that it affects the Tract.

"We believe that there's something to do with the Tract hidden somewhere with a code word and have said the word to Scrive. He has already run searches but not found any links. We believe that he will need to go into the Biotree systems to get further. That's where Janie comes in. She can help Scrive get access because of the area that she works in and her access to codes and security idents."

"What were you looking for?" asked Janie, "Maybe I already have some ideas."

"Okay to tell?" asked Scrive, and Lars and Carolin nodded.

"The codeword is 'Australia' or some variation of that spelling."

Janie looked blank. Chantal looked up. Scrive stayed straight-faced.

"I know Australia," Chantal said, "Or rather, I know someone who says they were once from Australia".

She looked across to Janie. "It's one of my acquaintances from the - er- fundraising."

Janie looked back. She knew that Chantal was referring to the illegal trade she did with the tropus. Chantal's little habit meant that she got to know some rather unconventional people.

Janie said, "Look, we are getting into this quite deeply. I only brought Chantal along to give me some backup when I was meeting Lars. I didn't want to get Chantal involved further."

Scrive was interested in the Australia comment. It could be more of a breakthrough than rummaging around inside Biotree. He'd prefer to take both options, and he certainly wouldn't mind working with these two women for a while.

"Okay," ventured Scrive. "I'd appreciate your help. Both of you actually; Janie to help with the Biotree systems and Chantal to introduce me to a friend from the Australia Project".

"Actually, Australia isn't a Project," answered Chantal, "I'm pretty sure it's a place. A town in the Tract somewhere, I think."

Chantal continued, "You know what, I'll - we will both - help, BUT I would expect Mr Mallinson to find ways to compensate for my other possible loss of income."

Scrive smiled. He was dealing with an unexpectedly ad-hoc group of people. He was used to working with hard-nosed professionals who would set a task, agree some parameters and then leave him alone.

This situation was different.

The people he was working with seemed to be making it up as they went along. He guessed that Chantal would have no idea how much was in play, although he suspected that Lars would have a more realistic idea.

He surmised that Chantal was a tropus dealer. He noticed all of the bangles on her wrist around where the cartridge would typically be. She was probably a Sife. Cutting her tropus doses and selling on the residuals.

It was good money but dangerous to do this. Scrive had experimented with this, not for money, because he wanted to get a sense of effects of tropus deprivation. He was getting that experience big-time at the moment because of the damage to his last cartridge by Charlie when she saved him. If anything, he felt the lack of tropus was surprisingly good, and seemed to be clearing areas of his mind and thought. He had not expected that.

He spoke to Chantal, "Okay, I'll pay you for your help. There is one thing though; you'll be responsible for your safety as we move this along."

"Okay," answered Chantal. "Let's see; my fees will be the equivalent of a two thousand sales of tropus, with half up front...and the same for Janie. That's 20000 tropes now and 20k at the end," Chantal dropped into the street slang which treated the cost of tropus as if it was a currency.

Chantal was trying to get enough cash to mean that she didn't need to sell tropus anymore. This would be the equivalent of several years' worth of sales.

Scrive blinked. He didn't know how much the tropus sold for, but it couldn't be that much compared with his usual fees. He'd accept the deal but haggle slightly to ensure that Chantal thought she was pushing him.

"Okay, but I'll do half upfront, then a quarter when we've done the work and the last piece two weeks later."

Chantal looked at Janie. Janie hadn't expected this to turn into a commercial haggle in any case. Janie nodded to Chantal.

Chantal said, "Okay, we'll accept, but the first money is due immediately." Chantal was delighted. The immediate payment of 10,000Ts was 4 or 5 tears work in one hit. And more to follow.

Scrive nodded. "Okay but remember I'm a tracker. Any funny business from this and I'll be on to you." He tried to make the threat sound both realistic but also friendly. He would prefer the simplicity of them being on-side with him rather than having another conflict to handle.

Janie nodded and looked to Chantal. Janie briefly held Chantal's hand, as if talking to a child. "You heard what Scrive said, Chantal. We need to play this straight."

Scrive assumed that Chantal could be a random element in many situations and that Janie was the best chance to tame her. In reality, he'd consider the payments to them would be small change. A lead that helped him move forward would be great, but he'd not worry too much if they both legged it after the initial interactions.

Scrive and Chantal both clicked their handhelds and placed them on the table.

Scrive said, "You request it, and I'll make the payment."

Chantal pressed a few buttons. Scrive noticed an amount displayed upon his machine. It wasn't much at all. He tried to keep a serious face.

Chantal looked across, "We're ready," she said.

"Okay," said Scrive and pressed a couple of buttons. The money transferred.

Chantal smiled, briefly jumped to her feet and clapped her hands together very lightly. Then, as if remembering she was just finishing a negotiation, she looked at Janie and said, "Great, Janie, now let's see how we can help Mr Mallinson.".

Tokyo

Makatomi was back in his office in Tokyo. He'd found the little trip to the UK and LA somewhat irritating because its primary purpose had been to find out about the leak affecting his business.

It was all so negative. But also, a chain reaction.

Someone had started a theft which he was now being asked to clean up. He'd had to hire two sets of people who were on the edge of legal. He'd then found one of them creating ripples which had upset his boss. He'd been forced to use an extreme measure to remove that person from the investigation.

Then he'd had a call from Holden.

The person running the task with Mallinson had told Holden that Mallinson had somehow survived. The indirect approach using a tampered version of the tropus hadn't worked.

If it had, they could have used the nanobots to clean up any evidence. Instead, somehow the 'bots had been eliminated. Mallinson was not to be messed with.

"Use a Trigax," Holden had said, "Make it fast and remove Mr Mallinson. Use one of the Biotree units. They are at our test facility," added Holden. This was a whole further dimension of escalation.

Makatomi knew the Trigax was illegal for aggressive use within the Ellipse and that it was only used for peacekeeping in the Tract.

He also knew that the Trigax would be effective and leave no trace. Makatomi knew the Trigax as a finalising device although the technology was still not fully understood.

He'd assumed that his 'no questions asked' assassin would have ready access to such technology, which he considered to be almost alien. Instead, he was now having to provide the unit as well. This was really getting out of hand.

The Trigax units had a global range and were individually tuned to a specific target. They could be fired from anywhere and the beam that they asserted was efficiently scrambled until the point at which it reached its target. It used quantum principles and a focusing of the wave using discrete photon focus.

Most people had said the technology was impossible and poked a cat's paw at great physicists like Bohr, Bohm and von Neumann, but the results had spoken for themselves.

The devices were now licensed and maintained for Tract management and scientific experimentation. If used, there was no evidence that they had been fired, because of the wave dispersal of the energy.

It was like a perfect weapon.

"You'll have to use it from Bodø," said Holden, "You will have one chance".

Makatomi nodded. He knew that Holden would remove him if he didn't remove the mess he'd inadvertently created. On the other hand, if he fixed it, then he stood to gain exceptionally from the expected change in fortunes of Biotree.

Chantal

Chantal's penchant for the low dosage form of tropus had led her into some fascinating communities. They were people who regularly ran the risk of redding their blood and to some extent ran an alternate if somewhat privileged lifestyle.

It also meant they had access to some things that were not at all in the mainstream. It was as if the reduced tropus gave them abilities to see things that others could not. They could also remember things from before the time of the Nero toxins.

Today's outfit had been Japanese manga and Chantal had included combat boots. It worked to her advantage because there were no inconvenient heels. Useful around the stairs and cobblestones of this old part of London.

Chantal took Scrive to the door of the club. It was an old railway arch from the 19th century. There was a small door, she pushed it open, and it led into a sort of cave.

"There's miles of this around here", she explained. "They were originally built under the old railway systems in London and used to be a kind of retail space. Then as the Transit was introduced, they became bypassed with the new generation of retail environments. Now they are vestiges of an older London."

She continued, "Look - when we meet Crispin, don't tell him that you know he is from Australia. He might not co-operate. Ask him about Australia instead as a concept. Let him decide how he wants to talk about it."

Scrive replied," I'm ahead of you on this. I kind of know when I'm dealing with secrets that it is easier to have them fall out than to try to push them. Like that Chinese finger trap. The more you pull, the tighter it gets."

"Just don't say that around my friends," said Chantal, suppressing a smile.

She showed the way through the labyrinth to a dimly lit area.

Candles flickered in between several people sitting together.

Despite the candles they had power as was evident from the powerful workstation that a couple of them were using. "Hi Chantal," said one, looking up, "You've brought some more tropus?" he asked.

"Yes," replied Chantal, "plus a friend who'd like to ask you something."

"Is he cool?" asked the same person.

"Crispin - He's fine. As a matter of fact, I think he can help us, but we will need to help him as well. You know the Vaults? I think they would like to take a look for something."

"Hi," said Scrive, "I've tried the reddening way too." He held up his arm from the smashed cartridge. He'd had time to tidy up the fragments from the attack, and it now looked as if he was mainlining on red blood instead of the usual tropus mix.

Crispin looked at his arm.

"Jeez – That's messy – and unusual," he grimaced, "you look as if you are completely red? I've never seen a plexi manipulated like that – it looks awful. It looks as if the telemetry is still working, but I can't see how you'd ever get another cartridge to be accepted?"

Scrive looked at the mechanism. He'd play it hard. "Yes, I've broken the tropus injector. If I don't get surgery, then I'll be completely red in a couple of days. It doesn't seem to affect me though, if anything, it makes me see things more clearly."

Crispin looked at Chantal, "Whoa hardcore - you do hang out with some crazy people, Chantal. So, your name is Scrive. How can we help you?"

"Other way around, "said Scrive," I want to help you- but I have a few questions first."

"We are told you have preserved a lot of the old ways," said Scrive, "That you have ways to review old files and information from before the time of the Nero toxin."

"That's correct", said Crispin, "but you'll have to ask us to find what you need. Ask us, and then leave us to trace it."

Scrive wrote down a few words on ordinary paper. Australia. Woomera. Where and What?

Crispin looked at the paper," I can do that." he replied, "And I think I may know something about it too. Please leave now. Wait outside. We will find you."

He turned to another person working the workstation. "Look Lucas," he said, pointing to the paper.

The second guy turned back to Scrive and Chantal. "We can get you this, but Chantal, your friend looks as if he might have some fees for us?"

Chantal looked at Scrive, "I haven't discussed this at all; this is all freestyle," she commented.

Scrive replied, "Look, I won't kid you both, I need this help, and I will pay for it. I can also be dangerous, but I'm a friend of Chantal, so I want to do this the right way. You both understand me. I'll pay, but please, I need to know about this project 'Australia'."

Chantal answered for Scrive," He'll give you the equivalent of 100 units of tropus. I know he will. I think that's his limit."

Scrive nodded. "Yes, Chantal knows my limit. I can pay you right now, handheld to handheld, but I want to see the information first."

"He's good for it." said Chantal, "And he won't trick you. I will vouch for him."

Scrive looked across to Chantal. She was doing more than her fair share of handling this. He decided that she'd got emotionally committed to the situation.

"Okay, we'll do it", said Crispin. "Lucas, help me with this." They pulled a couple of boxes together, and all sat around.

RFID

Suze had been pleased with herself since she'd found the RFID for Scrive. His Radio Frequency Identity. She had his address, his transit chip identity and could easily follow his movements around. She'd seen him take a walk from the apartment to the transit and had been about to follow him when he changed course to a cafe.

She'd seen him spend time and assumed it was a meeting that would lead further towards the answers to the various questions.

Who was trying to kill him?

Why?

Was Makatomi or Biotree involved?

What about the Chinese?

Suze was also suspicious about whether Scrive was operating alone. It was quite normal for trackers to work by themselves, but they'd often have some kind of safety system, particularly if they were on a bigger quest. If Scrive's pay was anything like theirs for this, then he'd have an accomplice somewhere.

Suze discussed this with Denny.

"I think we may want to pay Scrive's place a visit, when he is out on a long journey, said Suze.

"I agree," said Denny, "We'll probably need half an hour just so that we have time to check for any safety precautions he may have put up around the place."

The little cameras they had installed gave an easy indication of Scrive's departures and return and he didn't seem to be taking any particular precautions.

There had been two other visitors they had seen accessing his premises since they started monitoring. Both had a key. One had been wearing a hooded jacket and had only stayed for around five minutes. They didn't have any idea who this was, and the other was an attractive woman who had been in and out of the apartment a few times, but since her last departure had not returned.

They had no idea who the people were and had not had time to set up any form of monitoring.

This time they decided that after Scrive's next departure, they would attempt to break into the apartment, but using the fine equipment in Denny's holdall, which should not leave a trace. Of course, a tracker could probably work out what had happened, but they would be careful to leave no mark of their entry.

The hotel they had moved to was just across the road from Scrive's. It was a modern location and overlooked the River Thames. The chimneys of Battersea Power station were also close by, as an embedded part of a south of the river luxury shopping and entertainment complex.

This helped because there were plenty of people around the area, so the movements of Denny and Suze would easily blend in.

Denny had left the tracking systems running as Scrive had left and then taken a transit across to the area around London Bridge. Even if he took a taxi, it would take him twenty minutes to return — enough time for them to make their move and break into Scrive's apartment.

"Okay, we'll be looking for memory blocks, idents, Hitech and signs of who the other visitors are," said Denny, "We'll need to work fast and not take anything away."

Suze nodded, she knew this well, they had done other 'information gathering' sessions together and speed and a very light touch were what was required.

Denny carried a couple of small devices. One was an e-burster. This created a small electronic pulse that sensed all of the electronics in a room. It would inventory them and provide an exact location. The devices were available domestically for locating remote controls and missing keys, but this version was a military grade device that could pinpoint any form of technology. Its second function, not available on the domestic ones, was to be able to read the content of a device and store it. The third function, chillingly, was that it could destroy the device, both silently, and destructively. Denny was only planning to use the first two modes, find and copy. And to do this selectively.

The images copied would not necessarily be readable straight away, because of possible encryption, but that was something they could worry about later, back in the comfort of the hotel.

The second device was simply a form of basic self-defence. A needler was device that could generate high volume sound that would disorientate an attacker, and which could also fire small electronic probes which could then deliver variable voltages. The technology was based upon an older wired technology called taser, but in this version the darts had the power charges attached and could be separately triggered at a selectable threshold.

Suze and Denny both carried these devices, which were also silent in operation but very painful to any recipient. They had never been in firefight situations with them but were both aware of the need for some self-protection in their line of business.

They both inserted ear systems which included personal communications as well as filters for the sound wave defence. Denny made sure they had tuned it to the device he was carrying so that the cancellation effect would work if they needed it.

"Okay, let's go", he said. Scrive was over in London Bridge, in the tunnels and vaults to the south of the river.

PART TWO

7

As the verses unfold
and your soul suffers the long day

And the twelve o'clock gloom
Spins the room, you struggle on your way
Well, don't you sigh, don't you cry
Lick the dust from your eye

Life's a long song
Life's a long song
Life's a long song

We will meet in the sweet light of dawn

Ian Anderson (Jethro Tull)

The long song

Crispin started to speak, "Sometimes, people make fun of the way I speak; I pronounce a few words differently from most people. I have some extra words in my vocabulary. It's because I'm originally from a real place called 'Australia'. Australia isn't a Project, Scrive. It isn't even a town. It's a whole country. Or rather, it was.

"I'm from the Tract originally, and my parents had me when the Nero virus was at its height. They were both immune and so am I. We lived in the country called Australia, in a town called Darwin. When the virus was at its height, Australia was the original centre for it and the whole country was quarantined. We'd had the Flames a few years earlier, and so much of Australia burnt to the ground.

"The Flames was through climate effects, we'd seen the wildlife progressively eradicated over a few years, because the huge bush fires kept coming back. The fireys just couldn't keep up with it. It was relentless, year after year, like the fires in Southern California now.

"It was a modern-day tragedy, a side-effect of global heating. Most of the livestock and about a third of the population were killed.

"It made Straya a very dangerous place to live. The old joke was that The Northern Territories (which is where I'm from) was filled with nasty critters. They were all out to kill and eat one another or passing humans. Freshies, Salties, jellyfish, sharks, spiders. You name it, they'd kill and eat one another.

"Now add to that the Flames and then the viral attacks which led to the introduction of tropus. I guess the decimation from the Flames left many places with unsafe water, which created some of the contagion. The evolution of the Australian virus ran away from the engineering of its vaccine. They couldn't keep up with the variants. Some said it was because there was a clone vaccine introduced from China. I don't know.

"What I remember is that people went a sort of black colour when they caught the virus. There was no way to stop it. Their blood didn't run yellow or red, it went through a blue colour and then to black.

"And despite the death of so-much wildlife, there were still the buzzards, vultures and the rats which seemed to thrive.

Lucas chipped in, "What I remember is that the whole landmass was horrific, like something out of a disaster movie. But it is strange. Only people that were actually on the landmass seem to remember it. It's like it never happened to everyone else."

"Did people try to leave?" asked Scrive.

"You couldn't go in or out of it. I'm not talking about a small landmass here. I'm talking about something the same size as North America.

"Biotree had been trialling their newest versions of tropus and nanobots in the territory. Speculation was that they were trying to cover up for something. It was hard to get accurate news because most of the comms infrastructure was down too.

Then we heard that quarantine restrictions were to be boosted. We were told that Biotree was helping the effort to instigate the new processes. It turned out they were implementing a series of geostationary satellites, which were nicknamed 'The Bracelet'. The Bracelet applied an electronic border around the landmass. It seems ironic that they had to shoot things into space to do this, after all the fuss about global warming.

"How come none of this was in the news?" asked Scrive.

"This was like the End of Days," said Crispin, "The politicians and world leaders opted for discretion to avoid a world panic. It was thought better to contain it than to let panic set in globally."

"I'm not so sure though," said Lucas, "The Chinese were open about that Wuhan virus, and it probably saved lives because it gave the rest of the planet a chance to prepare."

"Yeah, I agree, and it showed how some of the plans were quite piecemeal. They ran out of protective clothes; the facemasks were not to the right filtration; Planeloads of possible contaminants shipped offshore," added Crispin.

"Pressure was put onto Biotree to come up with a resolution. I'm guessing it was desperation which led to the Bracelet. The Low Earth Orbit monitoring system for the boundaries of the Australian zone. Then they added the so-called 'charms' to the Bracelet, which provided the enforcement.

"I've not heard of either of these things," said Shrive.

Crispin continued, "You wouldn't, out here in the Ellipse; it is only Tract dwellers and anyone still in Australia that needs to know about these things."

Lucas added, "The charms operated with a railgun. It was a sneaky way around space-wars legislation because the railgun is not technically classed as a weapon. There's no explosive warhead or anything."

"I know about railguns' said Scrive, "they can be pretty lethal. They fire a massively high-speed projectile which can cut through just about anything."

Yes, that's right- the exit velocity is about 3km per second. Enforcement of the territorial edges of Australia was via the Bracelet and charms. Typically, a breach would be spotted, triangulated and then three railgun cannons would be deployed to stop the escape. There was even a Biotree branding for the technology: Trigax."

"Ah, I've heard of Trigax," said Scrive, "Biotree put out some seemingly jolly marketing videos about this."

"That's right," said Crispin," And also about their final clean-up systems."

"They didn't come up with a pretty-sounding name for this piece. I think the Brits invented it and called it something like APKWS laser-guided rocket."

"APKWS?" Asked Scrive.

"Yeah, Advanced Precision Kill Weapon System, "answered Lucas.

"These were standardised laser-guided rockets, which fired from anything from a hypersonic pursuit vehicle down to a regular drone. They were handed out to the cops to put next to their tasers. They would have the handset, lock it on with a bluedot and ka-boom."

Crispin continued, "I was eight years old when the quarantine restrictions came down, and we had no chance to leave. The country was also in the middle of a vast area of sea and so the idea to leave by, say, a small ship was impossible. And the exclusion zone around that was built up around the country was intense.

"When a few people tried to leave by ship or plane, they'd

be detected and destroyed. The argument from authorities said was safer to keep the virus in one place on the planet than to have it spread. It's another reason why there was such a news blackout from the region.

"What about wildlife, birds, insects, migration?", asked Chantal, who Scrive noticed was taking this story in for the first time as well.

"We used to call it the Glimmer," said Crispin. "There was a sort of sparkle that you could see from the seashore and sometime in the night sky. We used to think it was somehow magical, but it was the perimeter systems destroying anything that was flying or swimming out of range."

"If there were so many defences, then how come you are now on the outside?" asked Scrive. "The way you describe it doesn't make it seem possible to leave."

"Correct," answered Crispin. "There wasn't any way to go. Basically, those of us that were not affected by the Nero were effectively prisoners. We had a small amount of sea edge, then a cold zone and after that was the exclusion area that effectively killed anything that entered it."

"That's some pretty big weaponry," said Scrive.

"I know," said Crispin, "I used to wonder how we'd created the technology for such a thing, but it all happened at around the time of the Great Leap when the planet's technologies also accelerated. Of course, I didn't know that at the time, because the Australian communications systems were destroyed as well. We didn't have television, radio, computer communication or phone. It was like one of those EMF pulses that you hear about that destroy electronics, except in this case it was communications but not other forms of technology. Cars still worked, for example.

Crispin looked across to Scrive, "We then saw a period where the technologies in Australia accelerated almost as fast as they have done in the Ellipse. It went on for a while and for the survivors wasn't so bad. The weird thing was that the people affected by the virus didn't hang around like in zombie B-movies. They seemed to disappear almost within minutes of dying. Faster than the vultures or rats could handle."

He paused to think about this.

Scrive noticed that Lucas had been watching as well and nodded a few times during the description. Lucas seemed to know as much as Crispin while Chantal looked on, fascinated at what they were hearing.

Crispin continued.

"Those of us that survived couldn't get to the bottom of what was happening. Most stories were word of mouth, but it sounded as if there'd been some kind of riots in another town quite a long way to the North of us. You'll need to remember that Australia is - was - a vast country with not so many people. There was also quite a lot of desert land, and the reduced infrastructure meant most people stayed in the areas they knew to be safe.

"We heard that this area to the South near to a wild area called Uluru was where there had been the riots and a lot of people killed. They were not killed by the virus, but by the fighting that took place. We never had a chance to find out though because that's when Lucas and I managed to find a gap in the "Glimmer".

"As kids, we'd play dare games with one another. We used to take the small boat out to the edge of the safe zone. It was to where the air started to get cold. We could see the area where you couldn't go further and sometimes, we'd throw things into it to see them spark.

"One day we'd been onshore, and there'd been an extra wave of new bodies die and disappear from the virus. I was around twelve by this point. There had been some big

472

rumbling sounds which we thought were some kind of hurricane or earthquake or something.

"We cycled as fast as we could to some high ground in case it was a big sea or something that could harm us. Our thinking was that if the virus wouldn't get us then we didn't want to get struck down by a wind or a flood.

"It turned out that it was an earthquake. The buildings shook, and we could feel the world moving underneath us. It was a pretty scary feeling.

"Then we looked around and could see some geese flying away from what we assumed was the source of the 'quake. We never actually saw the 'quake ourselves.

"The geese flew towards the Edge (where the force-field starts). As kids we were waiting for the sparks as a whole flock of birds were vaporised.

"But they flew on. They flew past the Edge. We looked at one another. We both jumped onto our bikes and shot down the slope towards the town. There was almost no-one around. The official warning system was sounding, which meant people had gone to shelters.

"We went down to the harbour and picked up one of the larger fishing boats. This was a deep-sea boat for catching sharks. Metal hulled, big engines and very fast. Even at our young ages we knew how to skipper those boats.

"We gunned it out to the Edge. No coldness. We took the harpoon guns from the front of the ship and fired one into the Edge. We expected it to vaporise. It just kept flying through the air.

"We took another one and did the same. Same thing happened.

"We looked at one another. Crispin looked at Lucas now. We

asked each other whether to risk it. We were going to take the boat through the Edge.

"We trickled the engine and headed for what we knew would typically be the point of vaporisation. We threw everything overboard in front of us as a test. But we just kept going. We headed north west for another 100 miles. Then the boat's radar suddenly started working again. We'd never seen the radio communications working so this was a novelty. It was a pretty cool system too, with flat panel displays and maps of the sea and land. We could see ahead of us a large belt of island, behind us was some sea and then - nothing. The place we had come from had blanked from the system.

"We worked out that the Edge must have started working again. We'd managed to get through a gap, probably caused by the earthquake. It had taken us about three hours to get to our current position, and it was only when the radar came on that we could tell that the Edge was back surrounding Australia.

"The radar showed us various islands, some of which were huge, but we could see that our best chance was to use the fuel we had to get as far as possible. We charted a course that threaded through a belt of islands and eventually wound up in Indonesia. This was around 800 miles from where we'd started!

"What we didn't realise was that we'd navigated from the Edge through the Tract and landed at a place that was within the Ellipse.

"It was mainly luck, but by doing this, we'd avoided the areas where if we'd landed, we'd have been stuck there for good. The lack of infrastructure would have prevented us from going any further. It was simply the fact that we'd had a boat from inside Australia, where there was still fuel and that we'd then passed the desolated areas and arrived on the Ellipse with its super high technology infrastructure.

"We were both used to living by our wits, so we brought the boat in by night and let it drift the last part of the way. We snuck ashore and effectively became two more of the shadowy people on the edge of the systems. We've lived via the economics of trading tropus and other street skills ever since.

"The strange thing is that no-one here has ever heard of Australia. It is as if it has been wiped from people's minds. We don't think there are many people who did what we've done either and managed to escape."

Lucas added, "Although scattered around the city and in other parts of the country are others like us but from other places usually at the edges of the Tract.

"They are the ones that have managed to get inside the Ellipse but are not citizens.

"None of us has the cartridge but selling the tropus creates an economy to keep us alive.

"How did you get from Indonesia to London?" asked Scrive; he was still trying to assimilate this story.

Crispin picked up the story, "As we said, most big cities have a few people like us. We live in the underbelly of the city and so eventually we find one another. There are a few routes to move us around, mainly between the big metropolitan centres. We usually have to stow-away on the big planes between centres. Strangely enough, since the security became so tight it is easier for us, because the main security relies upon the transit tags that everyone has in their tropus cartridge. It's very easy to find anyone in the wrong place if they have been tagged.

"It's a lot less easy if you don't have any identity. Stowing away usually requires someone to create diversion when we go through the airport scanners. It can take days to get through an airport, but trust me, it's possible. The main thing is to not be too impatient. And the other thing is to look for flights that don't seem to be too busy.

Chantal interrupted, "So you've come from Australia (which none of us have heard of), through the Tract in a boat and then snuck into the Ellipse from where you've stowed away in planes to get to London?

That's about the sense of it, replied Crispin.

"And now you make your living dealing in tropus?"

"Yes - you'd be surprised how many city types pay for boosts. They say it takes away the pain. For us, we say 'no pain, no gain'. " Crispin and Lucas looked at one another and smiled.

"We can jack you into the Vault system to see if there is much more information. There is some, because we've looked at it previously. It is part of how we pieced together our route from Darwin to London."

Alert

Holden had been alerted. There was more network traffic than usual checking the sources of the domes. There had been radar and lidar pings to the Bodø location as well as additional fly-bys of the location.

There was unconventional analogue activity on a series of locations in Australia, including the largest one in Yulara. The US Desert locations had also been probed.

Holden understood the ways that the domes were connected. That one could interconnect with another and it was this powerful set of linkages that exerted some of the power which was often referred to as the Great Leap.

Holden was uncertain what was causing this level of activity. Unless it was the trackers that Makatomi had invoked. They were having the opposite effect to that intended. They were drawing more attention to the domes and creating new forms of activity.

Holden decided to track down Makatomi. Perhaps Makatomi was losing his grip on the situation?

Makatomi was back in London. He had put some miles on the V-Blade running around the planet. Maybe he should try Holden's approach? So much simpler.

Holden called Makatomi.

"This is getting out of control. They are probing some of the domes.

That includes the Biotree complex in Bodø. You are letting this slip away from you."

Makatomi answered, "No, I have a couple of trackers working on this. They are finding the source of the problem. I had to use Scrive as bait to force a sighting."

Holden's voice shifted to a softer tone, "Your explanations are wearing now. We cannot afford any more mistakes. Consider this a final warning. The next time you will go like Scrive. Get this fixed, as we agreed."

Makatomi bowed his head slightly towards the monitor. He hated to bow to these passive aggressive screens like a Nam June Paik installation.

He felt something like the fingers of a pressing across the top of his head. He knew it was from Holden.

Punching out

Lucas flipped the workstation screen so that they could all see it. He tapped a few access codes and was soon browsing secure sites. They were not those inside Biotree but places that were part of an American defense network. It showed some basic Information about Australia through something called the CIA Factbook, dated in the early part of the 21st Century.

"This will give you a sense about Australia," said Lucas, "and you'll see there's way too much for it to have been something that we prepared earlier today."

He found the map and showed them the whole of Australia. "Here's Darwin," he added pointing to the top. "Here's the ring of islands and here's Singapore. You can draw the Edge of the Ellipse by Singapore, then the Tract to just off of Australia and then Australia itself in what is now the missing part."

"I can understand that from a geographical perspective," said Scrive, "But I can't understand it from a memory point of view. Why don't people know about Australia? It is not as if it disappeared thousands of years ago. Maybe 20 years which is well within living memory."

"This is something we don't understand either," said Crispin. "But when we test people on this, no-one shows any recollection. It's as if we dreamed the whole thing."

"But we didn't," said Lucas. "I am Australian."

He emphasized "am" not "was", "am".

Scrive pondered his next steps. He asked Lucas to copy some of the data onto a memory block that he could review later. Lucas flipped a small card into the side of the machine. "I'm using a non-rewritable stick," he said. "It will burn this image on but once it's there it can't be erased. I'm going to copy this whole site for you," he said, and his fingers flipped a few select software constructs as he piped the content of the secure vault across to the memory block.

He pressed a mechanical catch, and the block slid out. He held out his hand. A small block the size of a gaming dice. "It's all on here," he said. "You can read this on most systems. I've encrypted it. The password is 'Australia'," he smiled, "not very original, but you'd have to know it to find it. Heck, it's not even a forbidden word; the password scanner didn't even flag it as weak."

He passed the block to Scrive. Scrive nodded his appreciation. Chantal smiled. "Scrive, I think Crispin and Lucas have been incredibly helpful." You should give them their money, and when we walk away, you should promise not to see them again."

"I'll do that," said Scrive.

They exchanged electronic money. Scrive added a huge extra sum to that which they had requested. Lucas and Crispin smiled at the thought of their improved economic status.

Scrive and Chantal walked back outside into the street, with Scrive still holding the cube.

"You know what", said Scrive, "I'm going to trust you some more. Don't try to scam me on this, but I'm going to hand you the cube. It's better that it's separate from me. We both know the story, and we both know what's on it. Keep it somewhere safe."

He handed her the cube. They walked along towards the nearby transit. "Thank you, Scrive, "said Chantal.

Scrive started to reply; as he did so he looked down.

Three holes appeared in his chest.
Perfectly circular, each the size of a fist.

Chantal stepped back; there was a crackling sound, like sparks, she watched as Scrive's body appeared to be sucked into the three holes.

Then she ran. As fast as she could manage.

The combat boots helped her speed. She still had the cube in her hand. She'd need to get inside. Call Janie. Figure out what was happening.

A quiet stopover

Charlie had been tracking Scrive ever since she'd left his apartment. She thought that this trip to London wasn't at all how she'd expected it to be. A quiet trip to Geneva, with the London stopover to see Scrive had turned into something altogether different. Still, the money was good. Scrive had already paid her a third of the fees, and with that, alone, she was already substantially better off. She'd worked out she now owned her apartment in New York and had enough to buy another one in London, if she wanted.

Her new hotel was close enough to Scrive; she'd decided to hide in plain sight, rather than to move a long way away. That way if she needed to intervene, it would be easy. Scrive wouldn't expect her to be almost next door, and the Portuguese themed hotel was enjoyable.

She'd dialled to get a penthouse room and could see the river, the power station entertainment complex and even an area where people seemed to be exercising dogs. She'd asked the concierge about this and been told it was a home for stray dogs in London. Something she'd never thought about in New York, but that the Brits seemed to like doing.

Charlie had made sure Scrive was wired for sound as well as tracing when she'd left. It was pretty easy to do, based upon the accidental suffering she'd imposed after smashing his tropus cartridge when she was rescuing him from the nano toxins.

She'd inserted a small transmitter and had sound, but no video, as well as the RFID tracking. It was enough to have a pretty good idea of what she was hearing. She was sure that Scrive would know she'd done this, although they'd not talked about it and had followed the silent process of splitting up without agreeing to any specifics that would allow one of them to betray the other if they got caught. It was a one-way situation though because Scrive would be the one caught, and he didn't have a clue where Charlie was.

Charlie also recorded the movements of Scrive onto a Geosystem and bursts of conversation; buying a baguette at the local store, the meeting with Carolin at the transit, the cafe session with Lars and the introductions to Janie and Chantal.

Charlie had also seen Scrive meet Chantal for the second time and visit London Bridge.

The sound reception from the arches was poor. They were underground and in a damp area where radio frequencies were finding it hard to penetrate. Charlie had a broad idea of what the meeting was about but although the tracking device worked well enough, the sound was awful.

After around twenty minutes Scrive had obviously reappeared at street level and he could hear him talking to Chantal.

"You know what", said Scrive, "I'm going to trust you some more. Don't try to scam me on this, but I'm going to hand you the cube. It's better that it's separate from me. We both know the story, and we both know what's on it. Keep it somewhere safe."

Charlie could hear them walking, "Thank you, Scrive," Chantal was saying, as the sound disappeared, and then the signal from Scrive.

Charlie looked at the systems she was using. They were still working.

She reset the communications; She rescanned for Scrive; she tried a transit link as if polling to book a journey. Nothing worked. Scrive had gone from the system.

She knew what this would mean. Scrive had been terminated.

Charlie felt nausea overcome her. She wasn't used to this feeling, even in combat situations where things could get pretty robust. But she'd been with Scrive. Right in his room across the way. They'd planned together for the mission. Scrive should be invincible.

She snapped herself together. Think - Either Chantal had murdered Scrive, or possibly they had both been killed together?

Charlie knew she'd need to erase Scrive's presence from his apartment and that it needed to be fast. Mainly to remove the electronics and to check them at her own pace. If he'd been killed there would likely be people showing up at his apartment.

Charlie mentally considered her presence of mind to be staying so close. She could be into and out of Scrive's apartment in ten minutes. She knew which devices to take. Scrive had plenty of technology, but there were only a couple of critical small units that contained the information that mattered. It would take anyone else an hour to locate and then remove the technology, and even then, they would have a long task to sift to find the important stuff.

She picked up the pistol and pocketed several silver devices about the size of a small fuel cell. They fitted easily into her hand and had a flip-top safety catch. Each was a stun grenade that used a combination of sound, smoke, EMF and potentially ballistics to create a defence cordon. There was a large arrow embossed on the front. It pointed away from Charlie. Charlie knew that at the time it was deployed, she needed the arrow to point towards the hostiles because the device was radial 270 degrees. The person using it should be in the 90-degree shadow.

She'd decided they would be a last resort, but one was ready to prime in her hand.

She crossed to the apartment and let herself in.

Immediately she could hear a sound. There was someone already inside. She felt for the grenade and could feel the raised arrow pointing away from her body. She looked around the corner towards the main room. Two people were frozen. One was holding a metatazer. Then she noticed the other one. Also holding a metatazer. They could see she had the stun. It was stalemate. If they hit her, she'd fire the stun, and they'd be blasted, assuming she had it set to ballistics. She didn't.

"You know Scrive?" asked the woman.

"Do you?" came her reply.

"We all do." said the man.

"We're trying to help him." said the woman.

"How did you get in?" said Charlie, "I live here, it's my apartment." she lied.

"We've seen you come in here. You haven't been back for two days," said the woman.

"You know why?" asked Charlie. Her arm was beginning to ache, holding the stun grenade forward.

"Do you?" asked the man.

"Someone tried to kill Scrive," said Charlie. She'd worked out that if they were professional assassins, she'd be dead by now. They were probably clients of Scrive. Not friends routinely armed like that.

She noticed the technology that the man had scattered in front of him.

"You're trackers." Charlie realised. "You're tracking Scrive."

She decided that they didn't know he'd been killed. But their appearance here couldn't be coincidence.

"Look," she said, "Let's put down the armaments. I think we are doing the same thing."

She moved her arm down slightly but didn't take her thumb off of the top arrow on the grenade. It made her look more peaceful rather than fundamentally changing anything.

She realised that the pistol would take too long to reach and fire, so the grenade was her only chance if they got nasty.

The woman started to lower the metatazer and looked at the man.

"Okay," said the man, "let's talk."

"How can I trust you?" asked Charlie.

"You can't," said the man, "Look, my names Denny and this is Suze, we're working for Biotree, and we think Scrive has been doing the same thing."

"Okay," said Charlie. She pressed the safety catch back onto the stun grenade.

"One more thing?Tea or coffee?"

Charlie had to decide how much to say to Denny and Suze. they didn't seem to know that Scrive was dead. They presumably didn't know about the other people he'd been meeting, but they were pretty good because they'd been able to find Scrive.

Charlie wouldn't give too much away about being a tracker herself, but the small arms she was carrying were a pretty big hint that she wasn't quite like other local people.

"Okay," she started, "If I'm going to tell you anything, you'll have to tell me what you know first. Scrive will be back soon, I can alert him, and you'll never see him again, or you can tell me enough that I reassure him that all is cool."

"Here's the deal," said Denny, "We think Scrive and maybe you have been given the same task as us. To find out who has leaked information about Biotree to the Chinese. We are supposed to trace the leak and report it back to someone in Biotree."

"Who?" asked Charlie. This was a good test of how much they knew.

"Makatomi, and a guy called Arusen," answered Suze. "They met us in L.A yesterday and briefed us and then offered us a deal."

"Did they say anyone else was involved?" asked Charlie.

"No," answered Denny, "But we suspected that Makatomi would want an insurance policy in case something went wrong. Then we noticed someone else on the grid searching for Chinese secrets and around the Biotree site. We are almost certain it is Scrive. We tracked him back to the Biotree building a few hours before Makatomi flew to meet us in L.A."

"Neat," said Charlie, noting that these must be pretty good players and wondering why she didn't know about them. She didn't want to ask too many specialised questions, though, or they'd realise her level of involvement.

"I'm Scrive's girlfriend", she lied, "We've been together for a couple of years".

"There's not much sign of it here," said Suze, looking around.

"This isn't Scrive's main place, and I live in New York," embroidered Charlie, "Scrive was using this place for the current project."

"Okay," asked Denny, "So what do you know about what has been happening?"

There was a ringing sound. It was the entry phone to the apartment.

"This is getting crazy." said Suze. She looked over to Charlie.

"Is this anything to do with you?"

"Nothing, I swear - er - it's probably Scrive," she lied, "He'll probably let himself in but is letting me know he is back."

Suze walked to the entry-phone.

She put her finger over the camera.

She lifted the receiver.

It was another woman. She looked like a Japanese cartoon character. Somewhere between stylish and absurd. She also seemed quite distressed.

"Hello, can I help you?" asked `Suze.

"I'm a friend of Scrive," answered the person. "Can I come in, please?"

"Ask her what her name is," said Charlie, "If it's Chantal, let her in."

Suze relayed the question, "Just a second, what's your name?" she asked politely.

"I'm Chantal, a friend of Scrive," she answered.

Suze looked at Denny, who nodded, "Let her in".

There was a buzz and then a few moments delay as Chantal made her way through two sets of entry system and reached the front door of the apartment. The regular front doorbell rang.

Denny opened the door, while Suze and Charlie remained seated. Charlie had a hand reaching towards her pistol.

As Chantal walked in, she burst into tears. She was shaking. Suze stood and walked over.

"There," she said and lightly touched Chantal's arm, "Sit down, take your time."

Suze looked at Denny, who had been ultra-vigilant as Chantal entered. He relaxed slightly. Charlie was next to speak.

"It looks as if we all know Scrive one way or another. I guess Chantal was the last person to see him."

"That's right," said Chantal. Her appearance was still of bright colours, in an outfit that looked as if it had been outlined with a neon pink pen. But her expression was anything but bright. She looked decidedly ashen, and her skin complexion reminded the others of a Tract person. Denny had already looked at her arm and seen that she did have a tropus cartridge, but he wondered if there was some illness affecting her.

Chantal spoke, "I was with Scrive when he was killed. About half an hour ago. We had just left a meeting and he kind of turned into a vapour. I've never seen anything like it before.

"One minute we were talking and the next he had holes in him and then sort of vaporised."

The others looked at one another and then Charlie asked something.

"Did you see who did it?" she asked, "who killed Scrive?" She was angry that someone she cared for had been removed without trace. In her line of business, she had heard of this kind of thing happening, but never had any first-hand experience. It didn't look as if Denny or Suze had seen this either.

"It was so fast," said Chantal, "and very selective. I was almost next to him when it happened. I heard a crack, like a spark, saw three holes appear and the next thing I remember was that he had gone. I just ran away as fast as I could."

Charlie remembered the conversation before the signal had dropped. She had to decide whether to ask deeper questions, with the risk that she'd show more of her hand. It looked as if Suze and Denny were trackers, but Chantal seemed to be a regular person that had been pulled into the situation. Either that or she was very good and throwing them all off of the trail.

"Did you find out anything from Scrive, or did he give you anything?" asked Charlie.

"Yes," replied Chantal. "That's why I've come over to Scrive's place. I have a memory cube that may have some answers, but it needs to be played in one of Scrive's devices. Otherwise it doesn't work."

Cube root

Chantal fumbled into a side pocket in her outfit. It was zippered but somehow made to look like a lightning flash.

"Here, I know I've got to trust you. Scrive gave me this after we left the meeting with the people in the Vaults"

Charlie knew what Scrive had done. The cube would have two information partitions; a public one and a private one. Anyone picking up the cube to casually browse its contents would get the public version. The secret content would only work in a machine devised by Scrive. Charlie was also pretty sure that Denny and Suze would know how this worked.

"Okay, we'll handle this together," said Denny, "I guess that you two - Charlie and Chantal - are now both in danger from association with Scrive. At the moment Suze and I have covered our tracks pretty well, although Biotree and Makatomi know about us. It doesn't make any sense that Makatomi would set us on a mission and then send someone straight after us to kill us. I can't think why he'd do that with Scrive though, yet he appears to have done so.

"I can't think that anyone would be onto Suze and myself yet - we have moved so fast to get from L.A. to London so that probably Scrive's place would be the last one on the planet anyone would be looking for us."

Chantal said, " Look - I'm not supposed to be involved with this. It's only through a friend of mine - Janie. She asked me to help and to meet someone who, it turns out, wanted to give Scrive some help at getting into Biotree."

Chantal explained how she'd accompanied Janie to meet Lars.

How Lars had led Scrive to them, via Carolin. How Lars wanted to help Scrive get into Biotree. That Lars knew Janie's work colleague Karin and she had also disappeared. But mostly how Chantal was only involved because she'd known about Australia.

"...And Scrive paid us too, it was 20,000T at the start and another 20,000T at the end," she knew she was taking a chance.

Charlie Suze and Denny looked at one another.

"3x7s?" asked Charlie.

"Okay," answered Denny.

"We'll cover Scrive's money; we'll give you 21,000 tropes," answered Charlie, "If you stick with us."

Chantal nodded vigorously. Eight years' pay, in total.

Charlie had heard all of the conversations about Australia, but Suze and Denny were hearing for the first time.

Chantal explained how Australia was outside the Ellipse and even outside of the Tract and that it had somehow been erased from memory.

"I don't know how they could do that," continued Chantal, "Two of my friends said they escaped from Australia in a boat. Australia had an exclusion zone around it. My friends are both red. They don't use tropus, although they are both dealers. The reason I know them is because I have a bit of a habit myself. She looked at her arm and showed them the depleted cartridge.

"You cut your tropus doses", said Denny. He realised that it would also account for Chantal's different complexion from most people in the Ellipse.

"Yes, I deal", said Chantal," I'm trying to make some money so that I can move away from London. And you know something, I feel better and sharper when I don't use the tropus."

Charlie interrupted, "That's what Scrive said too. He'd lost his tropus delivery system after someone tried to kill him a day ago. His blood was turning black until I destroyed whatever was attacking him. It was a nano culture of some kind. Because of the smashed cartridge, he ended up with blood that was turning red, but he also said he felt sharper with the red blood. He was a little concerned about the loss of Nero immunity, but otherwise felt fine."

"That's what Lars said," added Chantal, "When Janie and I met him, he told us that the Nero toxin was nowadays a hoax. Misinformation put out to keep us scared and needing the tropus."

Get your coat, you've pulled

Taylor had arrived back in the main Brookings complex.

He'd saved the information from the old monitoring station in a way that meant he could access it from his central systems. He wanted to find out if there was anyone else that knew about Australia and Woomera. The nature of his monitoring meant he could easily check for this as a correlation and his own systems could dig deep into secret files.

Taylor was thinking how useful it had been to get some additional information from the ancient monitoring systems.

He was bypassing the gatekeepered modern ways to obtain information by simply referring to older systems 'frozen in time' in the way they looked at things.
Taylor remembered the old stories about concreting the gun emplacements, but that it meant you had to know which way to expect the enemy.

On this occasion the systems had been pointing the right way.

Back onto the modern connections he now had a variety of information to use to help him find more depth. Within ten minutes he'd found a link and the name of someone who seemed to have a connection.

Bruce Henderson. He was a retired ex-marine Captain who nowadays lived on Cape Cod. Taylor smiled at the cliché of this. He'd seen those old movies where a black multi-role vertical lift arrives to extract a one-time military hero for just that one special mission. He envisaged that would soon be happening to Bruce. Heck, Bruce even had the right first name.

Taylor realised he needed to pass the information to the Sparrowhawk gathering at the Pentagon. If he went any further himself, it would create problems.

He decided the fastest way to alert them was by sending a short message to Colonel Maddox.

"Sparrowhawk, relates to earlier Yulara files sent. We have now located assistance. Captain Bruce Henderson of Cape Cod. He attached an electronic ident for Henderson to the message."

The uploaded files covered an area of land that was not normally visible to any of the US surveillance systems.

Maddox had a team of National Security Agency experts review the material as a high priority. They described the location that Taylor had recorded as within the land formally described as Australia. Technically this was now part of the exclusion zone and regarded as off grid.

They had also checked for experts that would be able to assist with this and following Captain Taylor's lead they also identified Captain Henderson, who had been on black ops missions to the southern hemisphere.

A military Levitor was sent across to the airport at Otis Base on Cape Cod. At the same time a call was placed to the National Guard based there and a small h-Rover was dispatched to pick up Henderson. The h-Rover had its full complement of weapons on board and the riders looked alarming enough to scare most people, although Henderson hardly blinked when he saw them.

"Guys," he said, "Welcome, but I'm guessing you've come to get me for something."

Henderson could still handle himself but realised the arrival of fully armed National Guard in a high-speed hover transport could only mean that he was to be accompanied somewhere.

"Let me get a coat," he said, at the same time priming a few switches on his desk console.

He then left quietly, wondering what was creating the fuss. Henderson had been through mind conditioning as part of his Marine role so most of what was happening now was for him, relatively routine, even if there had been a gap since he'd left the service.

His preconditioning also meant he was able to withstand severe torture and questioning. He wasn't expecting anything bad though, he'd kept a straightforward and low-key existence since he'd left the Marines.

Like many, he'd suffered from jitters once he'd left the service although he'd found, against prevailing advice, that he was able to steady it better by not using the tropus in the way that most people did.

He self-administered a reduced dose, realising he could be adding a different danger, but at the same time knowing that he felt better on the lower dosages. He knew other people that did this and that they were generally considered part of an alternative lifestyle and that they often sold the spare dosages to those that wanted a different kind of buzz. He didn't do this, preferring to wash away any surplus and at least stay the right side of part of the law.

The ride in the h-Rover was strangely soothing. It was a new model and didn't look as if it had seen any active service. The seats were relatively plush, still with the metal grid that was uncomfortable to sit on for long journeys, but overall the speed and comfort were slightly better than he remembered.

The same applied when they arrived at the airport. Even in the military he'd often spend ages waiting to get through various controls as well as all kinds of weapon checks to be performed.

This time it was through the gates and across the airstrip to the waiting Levitor to take him quickly to Washington.

The Levitor had both passenger and freight capabilities and the h-Rover drove straight into the back of the unit.

They disembarked and walk through to a stairway and up about ten stairs to what looked like a medium class airline seating area.

"Buckle in," said the steward who was waiting for them. You'll get some refreshments when we are airborne. This will be a short flight and we are not expecting any turbulence.

They all clipped in and the plane rose vertically before firing forward on what was a levitation rail. The predefined parts of the route gave the craft speed and accuracy.

Henderson felt the handoffs from the Lev-routes as the plane switched on what was the equivalent of invisible rails in the sky, while it made its way rapidly towards Washington.

Around thirty minutes later they were positioning for a landing, and again they used the stairs, back into the h-Rover and away to one of the complexes on the edge of the Pentagon.

Henderson was again surprised at the lack of security as these processes took place and as they drove through the final gate into a building, he realised they were entering the tunnel system, to the north-east of the Pentagon. Henderson knew about this area and also that it was a highly secure part of the base.

He looked at his watch. It had been around 90 minutes since he'd first spotted the incoming h-Rover back at his home. For Maddox, it was still less than two hours since he'd heard from Taylor about Henderson.

8

"Whether you take the doughnut hole as a blank space or as an entity unto itself is a purely metaphysical question and does not affect the taste of the doughnut one bit."

— *Haruki Murakami, A Wild Sheep Chase*

Holden doughnut

Holden knew he had a reputation that he lived in the wires. That he was reclusive. It was a convenient story.

Holden knew just about everything driving his mission and its link with the domes. He secretly knew more than anyone about the domes and how they linked together by micro=hysteresis.

A slight change in one dome would send tiny magnetic ripples to the other domes. The tiny granularity of the field changes meant that enormous amounts of data could be exchanged imperceptibly.

Holden thought of it like gently washing the world.

And that was how Holden preferred to work. Stealthily, imperceptibly.

And now, through links to the multiple sites where research was conducted, he could keep track of all developments.

Holden knew about other so-called secret developments around the planet. Some were laughably public.

A prior meteor incursion had landed in the Groom Lake salt flats in Nevada. The Americans had gone for the old trick of hiding it in plain sight. They named it R-4808N, as a flight zone close to Coyote Alpha. They could not stop there, though, and went on to call it Area 51, which attracted plenty of sci-fi nerds who thought there must be something else happening there.

Holden knew the mundane truth, that the Americans wanted somewhere to test captured Russian aircraft and for years flew dogfights of Russian MIG-17Fs and MIG-21Fs across the area. Have Drill, Have Doughnut; the missions were code-named. The foreign planes were not claimed in a superspy sting. No, they were simply residuals from defecting Israeli Airforce pilots.

And then there was the recent super bolide which hit Chelyabinsk. It was a small piece flaked from the larger 2012 DA14 asteroid. Like an accidentally detached car wheel on a freeway, once it was off the vehicle it could accelerate away and surprise earth 16 hours ahead of schedule.

That was in the times before the Great Leap. Such events were waxed by what came later. Curiously, no one had made any connections of the behaviours of the historical meteors compared with those forming the Ellipse.

Holden held the data and the process capacity to out-think most of the occupiers of earth.

He could see attempts to use Great Leap thinking, but only in the most basic of ways.

For example, he knew that Makatomi was using the quantum effects of the Trigax as the way to eliminate Mallinson. The Trigax. A great Leap, but now being reduced by humans to being little more than a murder weapon.

That second attempt on Scrive was still much better than Makatomi's first botched attempt to use a sabotaged cartridge to kill Mallinson.

Holden had monitored Makatomi while he took a V-Blade all the way to Norway from Tokyo to set it up. Holden considered it blind squandering of resources.

Then Makatomi used Arusen to acquire a fixer. Double

blind handling of the request. Arusen had handled the fixer for the Trigax too.

For Holden it was just a flash along the wire. But it was easier to let the real people perform these acts against one another.

Holden worried that Makatomi's actions were getting less dependable.

He dialled into Makatomi's biosystems and ran a trace. Makatomi was stressed, but still functioning well. There was no need to intervene.

Apartment 123

In Scrive's apartment, Denny, Suze, Chantal and Charlie sat around a table.

Denny spoke next, "There is a pretty high chance that both of you are known to whoever has killed Scrive. We're not known at the moment and I want to keep it that way. We can help you get new idents which will help keep you out of view, but in return I'll want to know if there's anything else that you know."

Charlie wasn't particularly interested in this type of deal. She'd spent enough time on the road to know how to look after herself. She'd also acquired quite a lot of new money from the deal with Scrive, where he'd already passed her part of his share at the start of their working together.

"I'm okay," she said, "Don't get me wrong, but I can look out for myself." She looked down to where she had clipped the small stun grenade to her belt. Denny and Suze knew immediately what she meant.

They looked at the data cube that Chantal had been given by Scrive.

"Nice," said Denny, "This is a very high-tech device. If we access it wrongly, it will still give us information, but it will also destroy the part where the valuable stuff has been stored."

"I can help you," said Charlie. "I've worked with Scrive and I'll know how to find what is on it."

"Back to our early questions, how do I know I can trust you?"

asked Denny.

"Let's just say I'm also motivated to see this thing through. Two reasons, firstly for Scrive and secondly for money."

Charlie didn't want to mention the machines she had stored in the hotel.

Denny asked, "so you know Scrive well - do you think you know how to access this cube?" He held up the data cube that Chantal had produced.

"Sure," said Charlie, "Let me have it for a few minutes. I'll find the right system, and access."

"Remember if you get it wrong you will wipe it," said Suze.

"Not a chance," said Charlie confidently and clicked it into one of Scrive's decks. It was the machine he used the most. She knew she'd need to use a code sequence to read the cube and pressed a sequence of keys. It was a sequence they'd used together in the past. She knew it would work and immediately a small blue light appeared inside the data cube.

Seconds later the cube had offloaded its contents into Scrive's deck. It was going through a decryption process and arranging itself into a series of hyper-walls. Each wall was a set of archive materials. The ones that had originally been downloaded from the Vault by Crispin and Lucas.

"It's going to take a time for us to search this," said Suze.

Not if we type in "Woomera", said Charlie and started a search based upon what Scrive had sent to her.

The cube was starting to give up its secrets.

Cube

Denny and Suze watched as Charlie manipulated the Cube using Scrive's technology. Charlie had worked with Scrive on enough jobs that they could both work through each other's patterns, and they had frequently stored safe codes to help one another break into each other's technology.

"Scrive must have really trusted you?" said Denny, watching Charlie at work.

"The trust was total and the same from me," replied Charlie, "I'm doing this for Scrive."

"...and the money." thought Chantal, but she didn't say anything.

"Okay... Here's what we have," continued Charlie. "Australia looks for real, and it seems to be outside the Tract. We all know about the Ellipse and the Tract. The Tract seems to be a barrier layer protecting what is a third layer. The main part of this Third layer seems to be in the southern part of the planet. It's as if we've all somehow stopped noticing a whole piece of the world. I can't work out why none of us even remember it?"

"You know something," said Chantal, "I have this very faint recollection. It is like something from childhood. It's so strange. We all grow up, and despite living intensely through our childhoods, there are large swathes of it that none of us remembers. It's a bit like that with Australia. It is like a childhood party I attended that wasn't very good. Not bad enough to remember because someone fell in a pool or we got chased by a clown, but on that edge where if I think really hard I can just about remember something... Kelly," she said,

"Somebody Kelly, a folklore robber."

The others looked at one another. Charlie said, "What is even stranger is that even while we are doing this, I'm thinking that I won't be remembering this tomorrow. It is as if there is something erasing part of my mind even while we are having this conversation."

Denny and Suze looked up. They were having a similar thought. They could remember Scrive clearly enough, but already the name of the place was starting to fade again. Denny had written it down. It was in his handheld. But what had he filed it against?

"There's something extraordinary about all of this," said Chantal." I'm not getting that same feeling. I remembered that two of my friends claimed they were from Australia. They told me that months ago. I haven't forgotten it."

"We'll still need to move fast on this," said Denny, "I suggest we start the process with Lars to get inside Biotree. If we can contact your friend Janie, we could try to obtain some improved access codes, and that may increase the effectiveness of our search."

Chantal looked up, she agreed this was the best thing to try next. She just wasn't sure about bringing Janie into the middle of all of these new people.

"Let me contact Janie alone. I'll need to explain to her what has been happening. Then I can see whether she is still prepared to help. She didn't meet Scrive, but she knows that Karin disappeared as a result of helping Lars and Carolin. I'm getting worried that this could start to happen to all of us."

Chantal stood as if to leave. "You know what," she said, "I'm a little concerned that you are all going to forget some parts of this."

Charlie nodded. She also felt that the aspects associated with

Australia were already becoming less clear.

"You're all going to have to trust me on this," Chantal said decisively.

"I'm going to take Scrive's system and the data cube. I'll also upload it to Wolkerech - you know that German cloud system. Purely for safekeeping. I've got money riding on the outcome of this. I don't want you all to forget where you've placed the system or something."

They looked at one another in the room. Denny gestured to the others. "Okay, I can see why you are saying that. I'm also concerned about the way this information is slipping away. But we won't forget who you are, Chantal, nor Janie, so please remember that. If there's an attempt to be too smart, we'll have a way to find you. "

He put on a menacing look. Chantal's own expression overrode it. She was treating Denny like a comic playground hero when she'd already discovered smoking and boys. Kind of "yeah, right."

"Like I said, I want this to work." She moved to the door. Her manga cartoon outfit somehow seemed stronger to the others.

Search

Chantal left Scrive's apartment and made for the street level. She would get a taxi back to her place and then tell Janie what had been happening. The death of Scrive was huge news, plus the disappearance of Janie's friend Karin were both big alarm signals that all was not well.

Chantal was also worried that so many people were now getting involved. It had been a whirlwind couple of days.

She called ahead to check with Janie that she would be indoors and sure enough, Janie picked up the phone.

"There will be a lot to explain" began Chantal.

Thirty minutes later she was back at home and started to tell Janie what had happened. She also felt that they needed to decide who they could trust because it still wasn't clear whose side people were on.

Janie was also cautious, "We've said to Lars that we would help him get information for Scrive, does that mean the mission will also automatically transfer to these other people? It almost seems too convenient?"

"Well Charlie, who I met, seemed to have a genuine affinity for Scrive," said Chantal, "I think I trust her based upon the conversations today. It also looks to me as if Denny and Suze have been asked to do the same task as Scrive. I wonder why Makatomi asked two teams to look for the information?"

"Maybe for exactly the reasons we see now, where Scrive has been killed. He might even have been a decoy for all we know," speculated Janie.

"Tomorrow, I will go to work as if it's normal, but I will also try to find the codes or searches for what people are trying to access."

"Great," said Chantal, "Although I think we need to tell Lars some of what is happening. He did ask us to let him know as things move along."

"Do you think Lars is on the level?" asked Janie, "I am less certain of whom we can trust by the minute."

Chantal responded," I think we should assume that Karin was already working with Lars. She then disappeared. That all seems consistent.

Lars already knew about Scrive and was trying to approach him to get Karin and now you to provide access to some of Biotree's secrets. The other team of Denny and Suze seem to be an insurance policy by Makatomi - or if as you say, Scrive was a decoy. I somehow doubt it though, he was too good to be expendable in that way."

Chantal didn't mention Charlie. She was upholding her part of the deal to keep Charlie a secret from as many people as possible. It had been the deal with Scrive, and she thought that she owed him, - them - that much at least.

Janie contacted Lars, and they arranged to meet again that evening, in a different location and this time without Carolin.

Chantal was interested that like Scrive and Charlie, Lars was putting distance between himself and Carolin. She decided it was part of the way these types of teams operated - maybe with the exception of Denny and Suze.

Chantal similarly realised that such an approach wouldn't work with herself and Janie because they were already sharing an apartment and it wouldn't take anyone more than about five minutes to make the connection. But on the other hand, neither Chantal nor Janie had any previous connection with this type of activity.

The cafe they had arranged to meet in was in the west end of London, in a busy tourist location close to Trafalgar Square.

Lars arrived at the cafe just after them. They were seated on the pavement, at round metal tables, closely spaced and on the edge of the theatre district. The swaying area was crowded, mainly from early evening theatre goers.

Janie explained to Lars that she would help but needed to be told what she was to look for.

Lars had explained that it would be information firstly about the manufacture of tropus. Then it would be information related to the nanomachines and their design.

There was also a couple of projects; code names seemed to be "woomera" and "australia."

Chantal had already told Janie about Australia 'the place', and they all now assumed it might be something to do with the location rather than a specific project.

The way that Janie would need to try to discover anything was to type these searches into a highly secure system and to see what happened.

If the system itself could be located, then Denny and Suze would be able to drill into it securely from afar. The challenge was to know what they were looking for. It was far easier to discover this from inside rather than to try targeting everything from outside.

Lars said Janie might strike lucky and get to some actual secrets, but it was far safer to find the right system and then to let Denny and Suze take over.

Janie was to use another data cube which would provide trace recording of what she did. It would give the system addresses that Denny and Suze would need.

Lars asked Chantal if she believed Denny and Suze were working for the same side.

"I don't even understand what the sides are," replied Chantal.

Chantal added, "Denny and Suze seem to be on the level as much as anything could be over the last few days."

Chantal decided not to mention the little matter of the fees she would be accepting from Suze and Denny, although she would do right by Janie once this was over.

"I think tomorrow we should link whatever we find from Janie through to Suze and Denny," said Chantal, "that way we bring them along and also have capabilities similar to those from Scrive."

Lars nodded in agreement.

"We should split up tomorrow," he said, "Janie will go to work, you, Chantal, will go to Suze and Denny and I will coordinate."

Like they had all agreed, Chantal had kept Charlie out of the story. Scrive and Charlie had decided to keep Charlie involved but separate, and it was an excellent ongoing plan.

Chantal took the Transit system across to Scrive's apartment where Charlie, Denny and Suze waited.

Janie's next day was a regular working day, and she would be back at her main offices. Suze and Denny decided to accompany Janie on her route and to wait in a nearby WorkSmart location, which was a managed office facility, with high bandwidth communications and coffee.

Janie worked in an area close to the facilities that Makatomi used when he was in London. Makatomi travelled the globe and so was more usually a virtual presence.

That was nothing compared with Makatomi's boss Holden, who was never seen in this office in person. Holden had a large suite on one of the top floors, but even when people attended for meetings it was usually supported by telepresence and through the agency of another person who would stand in for Holden during the session.

None of this phased Janie, who was used to the way of the modern and heavily virtualised workplace.

She arrived at her workspace and began what looked like a typical day. She would create a situation where she needed to go to the area that Makatomi usually worked and needed to create an issue that would warrant a visit rather than just a call or email.

She decided to use some further information about the Chinese and adapted some numbers in a report which implied even faster erosion of Biotree's financial position.

It was a clumsy adaptation, but enough to mean she needed to visit Makatomi's floor directly. It was the type of sensitive information that would usually be treated with the highest confidentiality because of its potential impact upon share price.

She made her way up to Makatomi's floor. As she arrived, she was aware that the V-Blade deck was occupied. There was a V-Blade on the building. She hadn't noticed it when she arrived, but it probably meant that Makatomi or Holden were actually in the building.

Janie thought this slightly unusual. Makatomi had been around half the planet in the last couple of days, and it would need to be something special that that had caused his return so quickly to London.

She carried on along the corridor with the special report she had manufactured and was able to get through to the area where Makatomi worked. It wasn't an exceptional feat; the reason Lars had selected her was that she had this access.

The area was deserted. If Makatomi was in the building, then he was elsewhere.

She could see a workstation in the corner off the room. If Makatomi had left it switched on, she would be able to bypass the security screen and get into Makatomi's workspace.

As she walked towards the terminal, she caught sight of a reflection in the nearby glass. It was the glow from the terminal screen. It was switched on. It would be more straightforward than she had hoped.

She used her access code to bypass the screen security and then flipped into Makatomi's area of the system. As one of the trusted people in the team, she had generic access to many of the privileged areas.

The difference was accessing the systems from Makatomi's physical system. It automatically gave her a better status of access. She clipped the small data cube into a port on the workstation and watched a short blue light pulse. The cube that Denny had provided for her had found its way onto the network. Now she could record everything that she entered along with the responses from the system

She brought up the search screen.

Australia.

Nothing

Woomera.

A response came back immediately.

"Access to this area is restricted. Physical presence in Biotree's Research and Development facility required. Access from Bodø Only."

9

I am not free,
because I can be exploded at any time

Jenny Holzer, Tate Modern, London 23 July 2018

Jog-shuttle

The memory cube quietly captured the response and Janie could tell that it was running further analysis based upon the code from Denny.

She assumed that her typing of a few words was somehow filling up the cube with various types of useful information.

Janie reinstated the workstation and removed the cube. She was toying whether to leave the faked report when she heard the door to the office slide open.

"Hello" she called. "Is that Mr Makatomi, I have a report for you. It's rather confidential."

Makatomi looked startled. He crossed the floor towards Janie.

"Hello," he said graciously, "I'm slightly surprised to see you in my office alone. Did someone show you into here?"

"I'm Jane Southern from Advanced Analytics, and I thought I'd better bring you this analysis without alerting too many people." She handed him the eSlate with the information. He flicked his way through the first couple of pages.

"If this were true," said Makatomi, "Then I think we'd have another serious issue to deal with. You say you are from the Advanced team? There seem to be some basic flaws in this analysis. I'd have expected you to have spotted them very easily?"

Makatomi pressed a circular control. Janie looked at it and thought that it was an ancient way of accessing some kind of playback system.

"You know what," said Makatomi, "I decided not to have the old systems replaced when I move into this suite. This jog-shuttle control is a quick way to wind back through the video recording that is built into this area. Let's take a look, shall we?"

He twisted the control anti-clockwise. Sure enough, there was a video projection which now ran along the back wall of the room. It was displaying four images, each a metre across. In three of them, Janie could be seen walking in reverse, and then a few moments later she could be seen at Makatomi's screen intently typing.

"This is interesting," said Makatomi, "Ms Southern, you seem to be using my system? I don't recollect giving you that authority."

Janie was holding the small data cube in her hand. She felt it get hot. Almost hot enough to drop. Makatomi looked more intently at the screen.

"I think you'd better hand over the data cube you installed," he said as he aimed a microcordon at her, "I'm going to need to hold you here."

The cordon snaked from Makatomi's small pistol-like device. Janie felt the electrics pulse as it surrounded her. She was captive.

Charlie could be a stunner

Denny had been monitoring the cube's system all morning from the WorkSmart location, since before Janie had arrived at the office. He was waiting for any sign from the cube that Janie had accessed the system.

Sure enough, at around mid-morning, there had been an alert, and the channel to Makatomi's office had opened up. Denny hadn't told Janie, but the cube had several functions. It was a recorder, but it would also drop a small payload into the Biotree systems. It would give him some direct privileged access so that he could work fast without waiting for Janie's return.

He kept a monitor screen running with Janie's image as she worked while he dropped a few more small packages of code into the Biotree environment.

Then he noticed the entrance of Makatomi. He flicked to the surprisingly dated monitoring system for the suite and noted that Makatomi was challenging Janie. Makatomi had found the cube. This was not good.

Suze was also working and had followed the link back to the Bodø system, based upon the original search created by Janie.

"It's a tough one," said Suze, "there is only one way to access the Bodø environment, and that is from Bodø. It's completely cut off from all of the other access routes. They looked at one another.

"So how will we get to Bodø?" asked Denny.

"Makatomi's roof has a V-Blade on it", said Suze. "But we need someone who can operate it."

"That would be me, then," said Charlie. "I worked with these with Scrive, when we were in the middle east. I have a licence to fly the military versions. Makatomi's is a luxury model by comparison."

"All we need to do is break into Biotree, rescue Janie, steal the V-Blade and fly it to Bodø." said Denny.

"We might as well kidnap Makatomi while we are at it," added Charlie, who was counting out some stun grenades.

Sky fire

Captain Henderson took the short flight to Washington. He was led from the h-Rover and escorted through another couple of corridors. He expected to be taken into something resembling a cell or a white room. Instead, he entered a room which looked comfortable. Leather sofas, military pictures on the wall, a coffee pot and some fine porcelain cups. Not a standard intel room. It looked like the Pentagon had money.

"Captain Henderson?" asked a serious-looking uniformed man, who turned from a seated position across the room. He had been in discussion with two other people and also with a video wall.

"Yes, I am Captain Henderson. You've brought me here on some sort of military matter, I assume?", he decided to stay unruffled, as much as he was capable.

"Correct. My name Colonel Maddox, US Marines. I know you recently retired from the Marine Corp, and now it is information we are requesting, and it's the sort that I think you will freely give. We are trying to understand something that is happening and think you may be able to take us further. We'll re-commission you for active service and provide significant years served pension increase if you'll help us."

"I was just about done with fishing, anyway," said Henderson.

Maddox proceeded to explain what he had heard from Taylor, and how Henderson's name had occurred during the various searches.

Henderson nodded while he was being told the story and

decided it was better to come clean on everything.

"I worked on an assignment in a country which used to be called Australia." he began. "We were there as part of international peacekeeping and running quiet exchanges of information about rocket propulsion technology. I was a part of an active monitoring unit asked to validate specific claims made by one of our allies. The technology they were using didn't seem to be possible, according to the scientists and so they wanted to check a few secure areas to see what was behind particular closed doors. My team were part of a black operations mission to find out what was happening.

"Frankly, that was routine, and we were just waiting for our chance. Compared with what else happened there, this was an almost irrelevant diversion.

Maddox listened suspiciously to what he was being told.

"We were at the site during what turned out to be small meteor showers. They had been forecast and were vectored towards our location. The scientists said they'd burn out in the upper atmosphere, so I wasn't' too worried about it. We were all thinking about how to get the doors open on our mission."

"This was maybe 20 years ago. There was a kind of sky-fire as the first meteors streak across the sky. It looked a little like the trails from a modern-day V-Blade actually. There were several more, but they all seemed to burn out.

"We assumed it was the tail of a vast comet somewhere much further out in the solar system. The early reports made the news and the science community was quite excited. At the time, the individual showers didn't make it through the earth's atmosphere. Like most things thrown at earth, they were burned up on entry."

Then a larger item was spotted, on a different trajectory and a course for earth. This one was different though because it seemed to have steering. No -one could work out how it changed course and speed as it approached the earth and it then took a path that allowed it to glide in, to where it landed, which was in the middle of the Woomera rocket testing ranges in Australia.

"So how have I not heard of it?" asked Maddox.

"It is part of what happened," continued Bruce Henderson, "And it is something that only a very few people are aware of now. Australia is unknown, the Woomera ranges are unknown, and the landing is also unknown"

"The meteor, or whatever it was, landed in the middle of the test range. The Australians took this kind of thing very seriously. There was a significant base of the former Joint Defence Facility at a place called Nurrungar, which was about 15 kilometres south of Woomera. The planes from there were in the air long before the 'meteor' hit.

"I should explain that the test area around Woomera is huge. About the same size as the state of Alabama, or the whole of England, as a matter of fact.

"This facility, and another one, the one where I was based, was administered by the Department of Defence. I was based at Maralinga to the far west of the Woomera Testing Range, on the edge of the facility. We had planes too, but we were also on special instructions to evacuate if anything untoward were to happen. To be honest, we'd all worked here for years, and it was mainly quite a sleepy place.

"But on this occasion, we had the Aerospace Operational Support Group of the Royal Australian Air Force appear over the horizon like a swarm of bees.

"They escorted us into the air in fast fighter planes and told us we would be permitted a non-intrusive fly-over of what was happening. We took an SR72 with all the spy gear fitted. We were to use this to brief about follow up action.

"Several crew flew the Lockheed and the rest of us took an Australian chauffeured ride in fast planes back to the site of the impact.

"The strange thing was that the site of the incursion was almost antiseptically tidy. Instead of a huge hole in the ground or a long scar, there was an elegant teardrop shaped glassy looking structure on the ground. It had a slight movement from within, like light, but that was the only sign that there was anything active.

"My immediate reaction was that it was like an egg or spawn or something and that we'd better stay clear of it and create a cordon. By its landing in the middle of a rocket testing range we already had a head start. My plane was the one on the outside of the formation. We flew at a half kilometre wing separation but did a vertical bank over the structure. We were also to look at whether there was anything else unusual in the desert.

"We returned to the base. It was a typical scorcher of a day with temperatures up around 42C at the middle of the day. I remember stepping out of the plane and being hit by the heat.

"Then we regrouped inside the facility and started to compare notes. There were a few things we'd noticed, ahead of getting the telemetry from the SR72. The flights lower over the structure had sighted some red trails moving along its surface. Thin lines that wove around. I didn't see this. There was no sound and the area around the structure looked utterly undamaged. It looked more as if the structure had been built there rather than had somehow crashed or landed there.

"We also tried a replay of the structure's incoming flight path. There were a couple of adjustments on the way in that looked more like flight corrections than something that could happen by chance. It was also a very fast entry; beyond anything we'd expect to land without a massive impact zone.

"Of course, we were on the communications link about this,

and it had also been picked up by plenty of other satellite tracking systems. The Americans, NATO and most of the super-powers were on our case about what had occurred. The Australian Prime Minister had also been alerted and had said he would allow the situation to be treated as a global one, rather than through just the resources of Australia, but that it would stay under Australian command.

"The opportunity to get anyone to us quickly was low, except for a couple of American stealth planes which were on the ground in Nurrungar within a half an hour. It is one of the times when everyone realised that Australia is quite large and quite a long way from everywhere else.

"I can still remember that one of the American-marked stealths was a Chinese design, J22-Dragon or something

"We had various cameras and radar on the planes, but we are talking about using the technology from before the Great Leap."

Henderson looked at Maddox, "Of course, now we know that this was one of the reasons we could have the Great Leap."

Maddox was looking at Henderson with an uncharacteristically softened expression. "I'm not sure about any of this. You seem to be telling a true story, but frankly, it is all so far-fetched I'm wondering if your mind is altogether stable?"

Henderson looked back, "That's the irony, that is exactly the problem that the landings started."

"You said landings", said Maddox," Are you telling me there are more than one?"

"Yes," replied Henderson, "The one we found was one of several outliers. It turned out that the main landing was in Yulara. The way it worked was a kind of teardrop shaped scattering of six separate impacts. It took us several days to realise this, though, because of how the structures worked.

"Yulara, how far from Woomera?"

"About a thousand kilometres, north west, 12 hours by land transport. Australia is vast. The Gibson desert is to the West of Yulara, it's about 60,000 square miles. But it's even bigger really because it is sandwiched between two other deserts - The Great Sandy and The Great Victoria. The Great Sandy is over 100,000 square miles and the Great Victoria is more like 160,000 square miles. We are talking about a deserted spot in a desert within a desert.

And that's within a continent that no-one has ever heard of?" interrupted Maddox. "Like the lost city of Atlantis, or Eldorado? - only as big as the United States? I don't think so."

"Let me continue," said Henderson. "It will be difficult to prove any of this directly, but you will need to know if there is any chance for us to change anything."

"The various authorities decided it would be better to clamp down news about the structure until we knew more of what was happening. This was standard protocol for us in any case, so we had already been running everything encrypted and secured."

"The story to the world was that we'd had another meteor shower that had burned up in the atmosphere. We'd had all the fires earlier too, which only added to the mystique around everything.

"A few people had seen the flashes, but we said it was the burn up. Some of the civilian astronomers asked more questions, but we created an explanation which also covered the apparent changes of direction. Sunspots, I remember, came into it."

"Because we were based in 'deepest Australia' it worked to our advantage when we were explaining any of this. I think the conspiracists thought we'd let off a rocket or missile that had somehow crashed in any case."

Bruce sipped at the coffee. He ran his finger around the pressed-bamboo lid and fidgeted with the small hole through which he could drink. With a fingernail, he was absentmindedly counting the corrugations in the holder.

"Of course, that was before we realised that scale to which the structures would develop. We couldn't approach them at that stage and Woomera and the Gibson Desert made automatic cordons to prevent people from getting nosey.

"By the next day, we had our own monitoring systems in place. Secure cameras, telemetry and a side presence of serious military strength."

"That's also about the point when everything changed..."

Illicit Trigax

The Bodø facility where Sheri worked had some of the most cutting-edge technology. The rest of the site referred to it as the ATA, which was supposed to stand for Advanced Technology Area, but most people called it the "alien technology area".

The Trigax was one of the most secretive devices available. It was intended to be for use in atom separation as part of building new nano structures. It could operate with extreme power and could select individual atoms for isolation. Such was the nature of the device that Sheri used to think of this as a 'god device'. Although having a local range which they used for experiments and building, the boosted calibration could deliver the same power and capability anywhere on the planet and also probably as far as the moon into space. It was simply a matter of getting the coordinates set.

There were various safeguards included that limited its range to a minimal area designated within the R&D facility and the levels of failsafe were such that it effectively had a huge electronics and software guard to prevent it being aimed anywhere else. The technology was classed as munitions, and the current peaceful use came with stringent conditions.

Sheri wasn't sure how the original design had been created. It was something to do with Holden, who was now in a top company position. The science within the device was still beyond her, despite her ability to use the machine with high precision. But, she rationalised, she didn't know the details of how Transit system engines worked either, but she still used the Transit.

This time she had arrived for work and gone directly to the lab. She was surprised when she noticed that the system for Trigax had its coordinates adjusted. Apart from her, there were only three other people with routine access to this device, and they wouldn't interfere in the middle of one of her experimental protocols.

Not only were the coordinates changed, but they were also outside of the guard rails. She looked again; the access had somehow broken the deadlocking system that prevented the Trigax being re-calibrated to other locations.

She pulled up a second screen image, this time a planet model. She punched in the coordinates that the Trigax had as its focus. It wasn't even in Norway.

They were pointing to London, England.

Then she noticed that the Trigax had been deployed, and on a high-power setting.

It looked to her as if someone had used the Trigax as a weapon. It also looked as if they had done so on her watch and with her access codes.

Sheri tried to think who could do this. Other than the three other users, she could only think to ask Nathan. He didn't work in this area or have access. He would need to get through several sets of security, although that was his role. Managing the security of the site.

There was something highly irregular here, and she needed to take great care to find out what had been happening.

Sheri decided to call Nathan. She knew he would be on-site, but probably a long way away.

"Nathan, its Sheri, something's happened. To do with work. I need to talk to you. It is important"

They arranged to meet, but Sheri decided it would be best if they went back to their apartment. She told her department chief that she was unwell and that she needed to get out for a few hours. She made a point of saying that Nathan would be joining her.

Sheri arrived back at the apartment. Nathan's four-wheel-drive transport was already there. She walked inside, and Nathan was sipping tea.

"What's going on?" he asked," this seems pretty unusual."

"Nathan, I'll need you to keep this secret," started Sheri. "It's to do with work, but I can't let this go elsewhere."

"Hey, Sher, what is it?" asked Nathan, "This isn't like you." He looked concerned.

"I think someone has managed to steal some of my codes, my ident," said Sheri," They've used it to gain access to a critical piece of equipment." She knew Nathan wouldn't automatically know about the Trigax, and it wasn't something she'd routinely discuss.

"A special device for handling atoms has been tampered with. We use it for science, but it can be used for other purposes too."

"As a weapon?" asked Nathan.

Sheri knew that Nathan would be aware of the nature of some of the specialised equipment in her section. The whole of Biotree had many esoteric and potentially lethal devices, mainly because of the power that they were using.

"Yes, it is something that can be used as a weapon. There's only a few of them on the planet, and the Pentagon holds one. As well as its experimental potential, it can target an area and then send a huge pulse with an accuracy of a few centimetres.

It could take out whatever is at those coordinates, which are measured in three planes. Effectively it can address any point on the planet.

"Whoa," responded Nathan, "So it is like a 'death-ray'?" he asked, "That does sound a bit far-fetched."

"It would have been before the Leap," answered Sheri, "To be honest even me and the people I work with don't understand what makes it operate. The Science of it seems to be almost too clever."

"Another piece of your alien technology?" joked Nathan. Sheri knew they had conversations sometimes about some of the things she worked with, which just seemed too good to be true. Even Nathan had found technology in his security line which seemed to be beyond anything he could have imagined, yet it all seemed to work and as if it had always been there.

"The machine is called a Trigax. It uses three types of energy as an output. When they combine, they create an exceptional power surge which we have been able to use to extract unusual atomic structures. Effectively it is building us atoms that shouldn't exist. The three pulses have to focus at a single point - the coordinates are set, and then the pulse travels like a wave through the air, but when it converges, it will take the source at which it points and de-materialise it. The resultant effect is like something out of Einstein - kind of E=MC Squared, but we are re-building the Energy from the matter.

We have been using the side effect of it to isolate the atoms we've needed. The energy seems to disappear somewhere, but we've still not worked out how that part works.

So, you are creating massive energy but then losing it? asked Nathan

"Yes," said Sheri, "it's as if it's all transferring somewhere very quickly, in a way that we can't trace."

"Another part of what Einstein described?" asked Nathan "-something to do with the speed of light?"

"Maybe," said Sheri, "we just don't know."

"Anyway. The Trigax has been primed and fired at a location outside of our controlled range. I thought it was impossible to do that because of the way the Trigax has been locked down."

"But I can see the Trigax has been fired, and it was pointed to somewhere in London, England."

"Now you want me to help you figure out what has happened?" asked Nathan.

"Please," said Sheri. "Everyone in my area will know that there are only four scientists with the access codes for the device. The triggering is showing my ident, and my codes have been used, but I know I haven't done it, nor have I told anyone-not even you, Nathan, about the codes."

"It sounds like you need me to take a look at this in a professional capacity." said Nathan, smiling, "This'll be a first!"

"You're sure you couldn't have done something to affect this?" asked Sheri. "Please tell me if you think there's a way that you'd give information to someone."

"No," said Nathan," I didn't know about the Trigax until a few minutes ago, and I've been offsite for the last two days when this is supposed to have been happening."

Sheri nodded, " Let's think of a more basic security leak that would give you a reason to be on site. I know. I'll say we've had a hack into one of the lower-tier systems. It would be exactly the sort of thing we'd call you over for."

"Okay," said Nathan, "I'll be nearby to ensure that I get the call."

Nathan left in his security patrol vehicle and parked across from Sheri's block.

Sure enough, Sheri called through the request for assistance and Nathan got the call because of his proximity.

Nathan worked his way into the area where Sheri worked following normal procedures. He didn't want it to look unusual, yet he did need to be in the secure area if he was to be able to trace back what had happened.

He had brought some of his security checking systems with him. Compared to the technology used by the trackers, he knew his own technologies were still rather primitive, but he did know his way around the Biotree environment and with his access codes had a head start on most people.

"First of all, we should check where the Trigax was pointed, he said, that will give us some extra information."

He looked at the coordinates and traced them back to London. Sheri assisted, and they found a particular location. It was by an old part of London called London Bridge. They zoomed tight and found the target.

Jumpy RFID

Nathan then zoomed using his own technology onto the same area. He was able to see the RFID of the person targeted. He looked it up in his directories and noticed that the code jumped around before settling.

"Unusual," he muttered, "...the way it is jumping suggests it is someone that didn't want to be found. A tracker probably, they all do this but the toolkit here at Biotree can get past that type of camouflage."

"A Mr Mallinson, Scrive Mallinson. But his trace has stopped after this point. It looks as if he has been wiped. I don't know how, except its exactly where your Trigax was pointed."

"Yes," said Sheri, "That would be the Trigax. An accurate tracking and then elimination. I have never seen it used at that range or in that way before. Its way outside of our safe tolerances."

He froze the grid reference and looked at neighbouring proximity. There is another RFID close by he said. It's got a signal; Someone else was very close by.

He dialled the codes. "Chantal," he said "'Chantal le Strang'. So, who are you Mademoiselle le Strang?"

He continued to work and noticed that Chantal's other known movements were around London. The tracing he was using was only at thirty-minute intervals and he could see that she had stayed in London for the last two weeks prior to the firing of the Trigax. He couldn't easily check her off against all of the other people she had met, it would take separate time and analysis for that. He decided to flip forward to now.

"My god," he said, "the trace for le Strang is showing from this facility here in Bodø. I'm certain that Chantal le Strang knows something about what has been happening."

"So how can we track her down?" asked Sheri, "If she was in London when the other person was targeted then she can't have been here also. But maybe she is part of a gang, and she's come to contact or collect the other members?"

"Perhaps," said Nathan, "or she was a friend of the person targeted. But in that case, I don't think she'd be able to find this place so quickly, let alone the Trigax."

"And another thing...the speed of her movement from London to here is phenomenal. She'd have needed to use a V-Blade to get here that fast. I'm going to check for flights from London in the last couple of hours."

He looked at the system, "It says here that Makatomi San has taken a flight from Biotree London to here in the last hour. The V-Blade is over at Dock Three. Do you have comcam in here?"

"Sure," said Sheri and flipped on a display. "Where do you want to look? I'm going to add my control layer onto it so that I can control the video," he said. He flashed some codes and the security system become operable from the comcam.

He flipped to Dock three, via a couple of preview screens. Then he flipped through five or six displays.

"There's no-one here, but that V-Blade is in cool-down. It's been on a fast flight in the last hour. I'm guessing it is in from London and that Chantal le Strang was on it."

He flicked to another area of the base. "This is the dock area. There's a route back to the main levels and a holding area for security clearance. I'm guessing that Ms le Strang won't have the right idents to get inside. I expect she is in the arrivals area somewhere."

There was a large and comfortable set of lounges for arrivals and departures and he ran a quick scan through the area. "It will be easy enough to check her ident again," he said and commenced a scan.

Within a few seconds, he had located her spot in the area. She was with several other people. He snapshotted their idents too so that he could start to trace who had arrived.

"This is getting very interesting," He said and started making for the exit. "I'm going over to find out what is happening. I can contain this group in a secure area whilst we decide upon next steps."

He was speaking into a handheld as he left, and Sheri realized he was getting a secure unit to take him to the arrivals lounge. She saw him clip on another level of insignia to his uniform as he walked out.

Bounce

Chantal couldn't believe the last couple of hours. They'd been in London, and then they'd been to Janie's office - she'd never seen inside it before. Somehow Denny and Suze had kitted the three of them plus Charlie with special idents that let them get to Janie's floor.

They'd taken an elevator to a high floor and as they exited Chantal had noticed the V-Blade docked to the side of the building. It looked pretty cool up close. She'd never travelled in one before.

Then Charlie had walked away from the group, with a rather serious expression. Chantal had heard a couple of loud thuds from inside a room and saw it filling with a greenish tinged cloud. There had been a crackling sound and Charlie had re-emerged with Janie, who looked totally horror -struck.

"Chantal," Janie called, as they emerged, "These people are lethal."

Charlie said to Denny, "We won't be able to take Makatomi with us – something crackled out of a wall and took him down. I think he was getting a little carried away with what Janie has been doing. Shew as secured in an e-cordon until Makatomi was fried"

They flipped a few controls and walked into the V-Blade area.

Glass panels opened; they entered the holding area. "Not a

typical departure zone," said Charlie.

"This is just for individual execs. I'm pretty sure where we are going there will be a full-blown arrivals reception area."

They entered the V-Blade. It had ten seats in two rows, plus a frontal cockpit zone with two places next to one another.

"Strap in," said Charlie, "I'm going to fly this thing."

"Are you sure you know what you are doing?" asked Janie.

"I've flown these plenty of times, military grade, with Scrive. This is quite a luxury vehicle." responded Charlie. She was plugging in a headset and adjusting some of the controls.

She flipped a few buttons, asked Denny to take co-pilot and started a short countdown sequence.

"I'm going to fly this the military way," she said, "no niceties, so stay buckled in."

She hit the airwave, and the cabin pressure kicked in. Chantal felt as if she was in a bubble and found it difficult to move her arms. There was a juddering, and the lights went blurry. A slight sensation of movement and then a loud suction noise as the pressure re-balanced.

"Something wrong? asked Chantal, "What, more than everything else?" asked Charlie, "No - we've arrived. I said it would be a short flight."

"Where are we?" said Chantal, "I thought we were going to Norway?"

"We just did," replied Charlie, "These things are fast."

Charlie could again see out of the windows, which had some sort of polaglas, which had just resumed vision. It was a different scene. Snow, Hills, Mountains, a huge airport-like lounge ahead.

"Welcome to Bodø Arrivals," said Charlie. "Thanks for riding wingman, Denny."

"Now we've got to figure out how to get through their security. This may take a little time."

Chantal sat looking at the coffee table in front of her, wondering what had happened in the last few minutes, when a man in a uniform approached, smiling.

"Chantal le Strang?" he smiled, "We have been expecting you."

He held out his hand to shake hers and nodded towards the others seated in the area.

"My name is Nathan, please come with me, and I'll escort you through the system."

Chantal looked confused. How could anyone possibly know she was here? Even she didn't know a few moments before.

"I'm a friend of Scrive Mallinson," he added, "I thought you'd be along around now."

The team looked at one another. This was either very good or very, very bad.

Charlie fingered one of the stun grenades in her pocket. Denny looked around for signs of other security people in the background. To his surprise, Nathan appeared to be alone.

"Look," said Nathan, "I'm going to help you, but you will need to trust me. I am taking you all to a secure area and then I will take Chantal to a further area. We know about Scrive and think we know what happened to him. I can't talk about it here, so we will be creating a locked-down space where we can all talk."

Chantal looked around towards the others. "I'll only go if I can take Charlie with me," she said. "Otherwise we won't cooperate."

Nathan looked across. He looked at Charlie and then back to Chantal.

"Sure," he said, "I'm asking the rest of you to stay in one of our VIP lounges for the next hour. Then I'll be back - in person - and make sure it is me - to accompany you through security. Let's go," said Nathan, "I've someone else I would like Chantal to meet."

Sheri had been working on the Trigax whilst Nathan was away meeting Chantal. She'd noticed the firing sequence and the long-range setting which was something they were forbidden to use and also which she didn't even know how to override. They had always been told that the Trigax had been locked down. The thing that interested her was whether the longer range would give better signals to help identify the way that the device worked. Their routine use, which they deployed for stripping out atoms was a slow process, partly because the power range of the device was always set to minimum. It was like trying to listen to great music on a very low volume.

She analysed the outputs from the Trigax. She was interested to see where it was dumping the energy it had created as a result of the terrible thing it had done. If it had vaporised Scrive, then there would be a trace in some form, somewhere.

The amplitude of the deployment gave her a chance to check this. Sure enough, she found a signal from the Trigax. It seemed to have streamed the energy to a further co-ordinate. She tried to locate the position globally. It had a type of arc, like a pebble skittering across a lake, except the bounces seemed to defy normal logic. After the weapon had been fired there was a small arc from Norway to London and then a much larger arc from London to the other side of the world. The energy had bounced to the edge of the Ellipse, to a point almost opposite London on the earth at the extremity of the Ellipse.

Sheri looked more closely. It hadn't stopped at that point. It had bounced again. The next bounce was smaller than the one before, but it seemed to arc over the Tract to an area that shouldn't really exist.

As Sheri was thinking about this, she could feel the knowledge that she was gaining starting to go away again. It was as if she was forgetting something whilst she was still discovering it.

She wrote 'bounce, London, Japan, over Tract, further' on a piece of paper. She found herself picking it up and throwing it away.

She wondered why she was forgetting what she had just discovered.

At that moment Nathan re-entered the apartment, with Chantal and Charlie.

Charlie caught Sheri's movements as they walked into the room. It looked as if Sheri was acting oddly, but she wasn't sure why. Almost as if Sheri was trying to hide something.

"This is Chantal, and her friend Charlie. They have said they will help us. We'll need to tell them what has been happening."

Sheri started to explain what had happened, but it also seemed as if she was forgetting part of the story. Charlie and Chantal listened. Sheri tried harder to explain what had been happening, but part way through said," You know something, I think I'm forgetting some important parts of this. It's as if my memory is being erased while I'm telling you. It has something to do with the Trigax and something I found, but I can't remember what. This is stupid, I only discovered it a few minutes ago. I guess it wasn't important.

"Is this room monitored?" asked Charlie.

"Yes, regular cameras only in here," said Nathan.

"Can we replay them?" asked Charlie, "Just the last hour should be enough."

Nathan picked another small handheld from his bag and tapped some codes. Now he had a wall display showing their current room. They could see they were all standing together, until Nathan started to wind the display backwards.

He sped it up and ran it like a video shuttle, until they saw the points where Sheri had been analysing something and then wrote something on paper. They had been watching the video backwards and so they could see that Sheri had written on paper and then thrown it away. Nathan reached for the paper disposal. He opened the unit and the single sheet was still inside.

"I'm not sure why I did that," said Sheri, "to write something and then immediately throw it away."

Nathan read back the words - "bounce, London, Japan, over Tract, further"

"What does this mean?" he asked.

Sheri shrugged. "It's my writing, but I don't understand it"

"Bounce. Something bounced from London to Japan? and then bounced over the Tract?" suggested Chantal.

"There's some things I discovered with Scrive, and I think we need to talk about them. It will need to be here somewhere

where we can't be recorded," said Chantal.

"Okay," said Nathan, "Let's move to the diplomat lounge. We can fine-tune security in there."

PART THREE

10

Norway…Pretty didn't do it justice.
I felt like we'd sailed into a world meant for much larger beings,
a place where gods and monsters roamed freely."

— *Rick Riordan, The Ship of the Dead*

Diplomat

Nathan showed Charlie and Chantal the way back to the Diplomat Lounge near to where the V-Blade had docked.

Nathan said, "Sheri, I think you'd better introduce yourself more fully."

"I work with the nanotechnology," she started, "We are building the new constructor kits here. - that's the components that the nanobots are built from."

Charlie intervened, "Before Scrive was killed with that ray, or whatever it was, something else happened to him, you know. Someone doctored one of his cartridges, and the tropus contained nanobots which sought to terminate him. There was something strange though, I injected his bloodstream with a big blast of nanoreductives, and it stopped the nanobots in their track. But here's the thing, the nanobot and nanoreductive also spread across to Scrive's spilt blood. It had turned to a blue-black colour but then went back to red after I'd applied the nanoreductives.

"Nanoreductives?" asked Sheri, "That's some trixy stuff you've been handling. Where did you get them?" She looked at Charlie in a whole different way now.

"It's a long story, but I've been places, you know,"

"C-beams glittering in the dark?" joked Chantal.

"Yes, kinda," said Charlie, "I had some time tinkering with simple 'bots, to use as trackers.'

"Okay, let's see if we can work out what happened with the nanocrime first," said Sheri, "I don't mean yours, Charlie, I mean the original cartridge swap."

"I assume Scrive had a standard plexi-cartridge?" asked Sheri, "Not some sort of booster clone?"

"Yes," said Charlie, it was a standard A-port, with all the digital engineering included as well. At least until I smashed it to get my reductive injector into Scrive's system."

"And your nanoreductives were relatively simple devices? I'm not being funny, but I assume you'd not been into heavy-duty nano-engineering?"

"No, that's right. I used basic nanotech using small molecules and proteins. It's what I call my failed experiment."

For the first time Sheri smiled," Yes, we call them nubots - they are a reasonably basic machine type. I guess you ran into problems with them not working and destroying one another?"

"Yes- that was the outcome. I thought of it as 'let the weakness become a strength', and that's how I learned the term "nano-reductive". The ones I built reduced the number of nanobots wherever they were let loose."

Sheri looked at Charlie, "The interesting thing is that they travelled so far and kept working - for example, into the blood spill. That is usually a feature of a more advanced biohybrid. You'd need to be making them in the kind of lab we have here in Biotree."

"Trust me, I only had a cooking lab, I was simply trying to place unique tracers into the cartridges," said Charlie.

"For tracking? That's mega-illegal, you know? Hacking a cartridge and then adding something to it."

"I know," said Charlie, "but I guess that's what has got me here, so you know…"

"It is the same with the boosters," interrupted Chantal," People will swap out their secure and safe A-port plexis for a generic, and then shoot boosted cartridges into their arms."

Sheri nodded, "I guess I get kept in bubble wrap out here at the ATA."

Nathan nodded too," Yes, everything that Charlie and Chantal describe happens around the unsecured edges of the site. Biotree is the stable end of a very ragged set of processes."

"Something I don't understand," said Charlie," Is that Scrive reckoned his thinking was improved after he came off the tropus."

"Yes," said Chantal, "We notice that too when we are selling it. There are two types of boost. Speeder and Kalm. Speeder, like its name implies, jacks the metabolism and certainly the thought processes of the recipient. Kalm is an altogether more mellow experience."

"Nowadays you can usually tell which kind it is by the cartridge markings. Chinese writing is for Kalm and English for Speeder. It didn't used to be the case. They both worked the same originally, more like Kalm."

Sheri nodded, "That would make sense. Biotree changes the formulation every so often. One of the changes was to optimise deployment. Biotree brought in some hackers, and they changed one of the mechanisms inside the nanobots, when we needed the new variant to try to solve the widespread virus in Australia.

"I remember when the packaging changed on the Biotrees. Something about "New, faster acting," said Chantal.

"Originally, Biotree had always built them fail-safe, with a kind of small valve inside. The difference is that the newer bots can replicate; the original design had a so-called Brownian ratchet inside which was like a little cog inside a clock. It made sure the machines could only run up to a certain speed. It was an elegant fail-safe which stopped people's systems becoming overrun with self-replicating nanobots. They ran slower than a body's metabolic speed, which meant the body could handle them without getting overloaded.

That's what seemed to happen with Scrive until I stopped it," said Charlie. His blood was clotting, and I reckon it was black from the incursion of nanobots."

"Yes, the second exploit, which was really to weaponise the nanobots and to force even greater speed. It was an exploitation of the Laplace-Beltrami theorem for narrow escape. Think of it like air escaping from a balloon. It meant the bots could speed excessively and the effect would be like that which happened to Scrive. In battlefield the bots could run riot for a short time.

"And you know something, Makatomi's last business plan? Weaponisation of the nanobots. His "idea of a way to save the company.""

"That would explain there being two types out there now," said Chantal.

"Yes, the unconstrained variant from Biotree and the safely managed clone from the Chinese. The old economic model of the cartridges was to ensure that the tropus had a half-life measured in weeks and then you'd need to buy a new one. It lost most of its potency by around week four."

"So," said Charlie, "we've got a desperate Biotree that is building weapons and the Chinese trying to steal a copy?"

"If you want to put it like that," said Sheri.

Maddox had been busy. He'd been following up on the meteor disturbances that Henderson had described. It meant looking into quite ancient archives, from around 20 years ago. Sure enough, there were a few reports' although none in the mainstream press. He'd called Henderson back to his room at the Pentagon.

"It's as if this thing you describe never happened," he said, "There's more news of B-List celebrities than of a major earth strike by meteors. But there's some information which seems to concur with your account."

"I had the guys track a couple of astronomy sites, including the crowdsourced eurekalert, which did feature the meteors. Yale scientist Denison Olmsted was referenced in an article, from 1833, which talked about a prior meteor shower and the need for tracking. Then much later there's the establishment of the KELT follow-up network with two low resolution small telescopes. These enthusiasts tracked the meteor shower you describe to its collision with earth. They are outside of all the military and government networks, which is, I'm thinking, why the records are still available."

"Here's the thing," said Maddox, "According to KELT, the meteors seemed to be flying under guidance, which bears out your story. Not only that, there's another couple of hits in the northern hemisphere, both in areas with low populations. One near Fort Resolution in Canada, the other near Bodø, in Norway."

Henderson smiled, "Fort Resolution is in the North West Territories. It's right in the middle of nowhere; I'm guessing that Bodø is the same?"

Maddox nodded, "Not exactly, Bodø is also the R&D centre for Biotree Industries."

"They're the ones in trouble in the city pages at the moment, aren't they?" asked Henderson.

"Yes, and they seem to be under copyright attack from the Chinese clone manufacturers."

"No smoke without fire. Do you want me to take a look?" asked Henderson.

"I've already cleared your path to take a small detail to Norway," said Maddox.

"Okay," said Henderson, "but I don't want to put heavy Navy boots all over this, the fewer people that know, the better."

"But you won't turn down a V-Blade and some 'accessories'?" asked Maddox.

"Thank you, but I'll still travel light," said Henderson.

Pulse

Bodø

In Bodø, Nathan was leading Chantal, Charlie, Denny, Suze and Janie back through the corridors from the Diplomatic Lounge. He was arranging for each of them admittance to the facility under his supervision.

Of them all, Nathan noticed that Janie seemed the most shaken up by whatever had happened to them. He took her one side and asked, "Are you okay? - Let's get you checked over."

Nathan spotted the tell-tale signs that Janie had been caught in an e-grid or some other form of containment, by her occasional little tremors. Nathan hated the devices and wondered what kind of idiot would use one on Janie.

"It's been a helluva day," said Janie, she looked over to Chantal, who nodded back.

"I'm going to put Janie through some base screening," said Nathan, "Just for peace of mind. Chantal, would you like to stay with her?"

"No, go, Chantal, please go," said Janie, "I'll be fine."

Chantal realised Janie was keen to be left alone. Chantal could only guess what had happened to her in Makatomi's office, and then what had happened when Charlie arrived, no doubt guns a-blazing.

"It's a massive complex you have here," said Denny,

"Yes, it has its own public transit system around it," explained Nathan.

"The transit runs pretty much around the entire perimeter and crosses over the centre in a couple of places."

"Do you mind if we take a look?" asked Suze.

"I can do better than the transit system for you," said Nathan.

"I'll get one of the jetters, and we can do a quick lap of the facility."

"I expect you'll all want to come along for the experience, so I'll get a ten-seater"

He spoke into a communicator and arranged for a pick-up.

An almost silent craft appeared, and they all climbed aboard.

"This isn't going to be as fast as Charlie's piloting, is it?" asked Chantal.

"No, we'll keep to a low speed and make a pass over the site," said Nathan, "We'll start by heading back to the dock where you landed the V-Blade. Then we'll do a circuit.

The craft crawled forward, and they approached the landing docks. A shimmer on the horizon denoted the approach of another fast craft. It was a military specification V-Blade. United States.

"Looks as if we have visitors," said Nathan. He called a central control number.

"It looks as if they are here for similar reasons to you," he said, half-listening to his communicator.

"Does anyone here know a Bruce Henderson?"

Everyone looked blank.

"Okay, here we go," said Nathan as the jetter made for the

runway.

"This is a bit more interesting than flying in a V-Blade," commented Chantal.

"We can see things as they go past."

The pilot banked the jetter over the site. It was immense, with a series of modern blocks and a few scattered outbuildings. In the distance was another long teardrop-shaped structure, surrounded by further fencing.

"What's that place?" asked Suze.

"It's the old NATO stores," replied Nathan. It is almost dormant nowadays and we use Robocarts to gain access.

"Why is that?" asked Suze.

"It still holds dangerous substances, to be honest, I think we were tricked into storing them in the first place. To get this land, Biotree had to do a deal with the USAF to take the store off their hands."

"It was supposed to be a mutually beneficial trade," said Sheri, "Biotree claimed to have the wherewithal to clear up the chemicals."

"Essentially it's a big DND nowadays," said Nathan.

"DND?" queried Chantal.

"Do Not Disturb," answered Charlie," So what happens? You still patrol it then?"

"Yes." answered Nathan, "although there's not a lot to see. It's a tin shed covering a bunch of old stores."

The plane banked, and they could see several small autonomous Robocart units moving around the perimeter of the shed.

"Let's go back," said Nathan, "I think you've got a feel for the site now."

Meet Henderson

The jetter pulled into a landing dock, and Nathan could see the Military V-Blade on which Henderson had arrived. It stood next to the one that the others had flown in on, and the differences were striking. The commercial version was altogether bulkier and had a surprising number of antenna and other external attachments. The sleek dark stealth of the naval unit alongside it, with its missile hangers and guns, illustrated it was built for battlefield deployment.

They walked into the lounges again. They could see Henderson immediately. He was kitted out in combat gear and had a couple of supporting aides at his side.

"Hi Captain Henderson, we're pleased to greet you here in Bodø. I'm Nathan Belanger, head of security on the Bodø base. To be honest, we didn't know you were coming here until you'd more or less arrived."

"Same here, Mr Belanger, the US DoD has sent me for a routine inspection of the ex USAF part of the base."

"You'll know it is the ATA now - that's the Advanced Technology Area, so we have some fairly high security to protect commercial secrets?' asked Nathan.

"Yes, I was briefed on the way, and again in this reception lounge. Now if you don't mind, I'd like to make busy with the inspection?"

Nathan nodded. He could see that Henderson was in a hurry. He was used to random US DoD people passing through the base and stopping to have a look at the US legacy.

"I'll arrange for someone to take you to the store area on a jetter; you'll be able to pick up an h-Rover when you are over there."

"That's great," said Henderson. "I'm hoping to see inside too?"

"Sure," said Nathan, "We'll arrange that when you get over there, although there is not much to see. Unless you like oil drums and pressurised coolant tanks. I'll come along too, if you don't mind."

Charlie interrupted, "I'd like to come along for the ride too, if that's okay? You'll have a spare pilot that way, too"

They made their way back to the flight deck and were soon airborne in a jetter.

This time they took a direct route to the storage facility. They flew over the main hanger area and Charlie could see several HUM-Z rocket planes parked in a tactical formation.

"What are they for?" She asked," Once a NATO base, always a NATO base," said Nathan. "You'd have thought that when Biotree bought the land, the armed forces would move out, but there's some deal with the Americans and in turn with half of Europe about keeping a few planes here. They do circuits and bumps every so often."

The pilot took them high over the store first time and then lower on his landing loop.

Henderson looked as the store block approached. It was huge and traced a path across what could have been the foothills of a mountain range. It was hardly the best position to build a storage facility. Henderson noticed the unusual shape of the facility. Why would anyone make it that shape?

They landed and Henderson, Nathan and Charlie left the jetter and were escorted to the h-Rover. They heard the maglev kick in and gently made their way to an entrance hatch for the storage facility.

"You can pick up the screenings of the interior from here," said the h-Rover pilot. "It is probably quicker than looking all around."

Henderson nodded, looked at the h-Rover's screen and then to a window in the side of the shed.

There were equivalent windows along the facility, each with its own hi-resolution display, showing the interior of the facility.

"With the screens, we can pull up the co-ordinates of any part of the store and know what it contains," explained the pilot, "All from the safety of being outside."

"Okay, said Henderson," can we stop at one of the windows?"

"Sure thing," said the h-Rover driver and they slid to a quiet halt.

"I'm going outside," said Henderson.

He walked towards the nearest screen. It was touch-operated, and he flipped the small control console, which revealed the labelled contents of interior drums.

"I want to see inside this," he said, "Past the screens, to the natural condition."

"Sure" said Nathan. "The pilots usually do the checks from fly-by, but you can walk about if you like. Don't underestimate the distances. "

The three of them left the pilot and moved into the building. Along the edge were a high row of drums and a couple of complicated looking processing machines.

They walked past the drums to a flat fenced area.

There they saw it. Henderson recognised the same glassy

dome structure which he'd seen in fly-by when he was in Australia.

"We're leaving," he said.

Secrets

Nathan was on the comms back to Sheri's lab.

"We've found something," he said. "It's vast."

"What is it?" asked Sheri.

"I think it is something that they have been trying to hide, probably Biotree, certainly Makatomi."

The jetter had reached the landing dock again, and Henderson and Nathan climbed out. They made their way back to the ATA research block and found Sheri and the others in Sheri's lab, with some in a second room, separated by a glass wall.

"Denny, Suze and Janie are working through the data cube that Janie retrieved from Makatomi's office, " explained Sheri, "I put them next door in a data room, So, what did you discover?"

"It's like the situation I first saw in Australia, out in the desert, 'said Henderson. "Except there were several of them. Vast glass-like structures, which had splashed themselves across the desert. At the time we thought they were meteor showers and later the Australian situation was erased from records."

"What made you think there was another one here?" asked Sheri.

"I remembered that there two additional reports of meteors; one in Canada and another in Norway. That's why I came to take a look.

"These stores were established about 20 years ago," said

Nathan. "That's long before we created the Biotree facility here."

"Yes, it's the same time that the ones in Australia were identified. And it's around when Australia started to disappear from records."

"Yes, the combination of the Flames and then the virus, Australia was initially cut off from the rest of the world as a quarantine measure. "

"Yes, and then the protection zone was instituted."

Chantal looked confused, "How is it that I don't know any of this?" she asked.

Henderson: "It was news managed at the time. Such a terrible loss of life in Australia and a successive quarantine imposed. They didn't want people going for a look, in case they spread the virus further."

"Could it be something that the domes brought into the continent?"

Charlie said," The strange thing is, the symptoms of the virus sounded very much like the symptoms that Scrive showed when he suffered from that nanobot toxin."

Sheri spoke, "Yes, that's when Biotree started shipping a specific strain of the tropus cartridge to Australia. It was supposed to combat the virus."

Charlie said, thoughtfully, "Unfortunately, it seemed to have some other side effects. I'm wondering if it was accelerated like the one I built, and was, itself the cause of the deaths?"

Sheri announced, "Suze and Denny have been looking through the data walls that Janie retrieved from Makatomi on that cube. They are very fast and efficient - it must be a tracker trait - Their findings show there were several attempts to speed up the nanobots but at the expense of some of the checks and balances.

"I think that is what they are trying to hide," said Sheri, "Biotree tried to stop the original virus with nanobot re-engineering. But they cut corners to make the antidote work more quickly. The hired help didn't have the same stringent processes as we do. That's what I was describing with those accelerants that they introduced.

Charlie asked," You mean that's how they multiplied so quickly and polluted people's bloodstream? Just like the toxin sent to Shrive?"

Sheri looked severe, " According to the papers we got from Makatomi, it was worse. It was not just their bloodstream — everything organic. The 'bots could jump using the 'balloon' reaction, and therefore infect anything else they could process.

"And because the deployment was so rapid, with everyone refitting their tropus cartridges every four weeks, by the time Makatomi's people had discovered it, it was too late, and Australia was destroyed, or people were infected but didn't realise it yet."

Sheri added, "In another four weeks it had run through Australia like a plague - unknown to the authorities the cure was worse than the virus. And it was a time-bomb that they had already set ticking."

"But there were some people, like Crispin and Lucas," said Chantal, "who didn't seem to get affected?"

"in most forms of rapidly spreading virus, there are some people who don't' catch it. Like their systems are somehow immune. Have you ever been on vacation with someone who doesn't get mosquito-bitten?" asked Sheri, "it's one of those mysteries."

"Yes, but this seems to be a double whammy," said Charlie,

"First the virus and then the nanobots? Could someone really be immune to both?"

"Yes, it is highly likely," said Sheri, "The original design of the nanobot defences would be to target the virus. It's as likely that the same biological key repelled both types of 'boarder'. Think of it like a key and lock. The virus has to be able to get the lock undone. So does the nanobot to chase after it."

Chantal nodded at this explanation, which seemed to satisfy her.

Charlie said," No wonder Makatomi was trying to keep everything locked down and secret."

"But what do we do about the domes?" asked Nathan, "and what do they have to do with anything?"

"I don't know if you remember, but The Great Leap happened around the time that earth passed through that meteor shower," said Sheri.

"We think that the domes brought some new ideas to the world?" asked Chantel. "It's pretty cosmic!"

Sheri added, "Yes - The Great Leap yielded a range of discoveries. But, in addition, it seems to have been able to manage minds and communications."

"That could account for everyone forgetting about Australia so quickly, it became a case of hidden in plain sight," said Charlie.

"Also hidden on a dangerous land mass, though," said Nathan.

"And protected there too," added Chantal, "Remember what Crispin said about the bracelet and charms?"

"Yes, they've found something about that in the Janie's data walls," answered Sheri,

"Apparently, Makatomi, under Holden's instruction, sanctioned the use of a set of Geostationary Satellites to police the Australian boundaries. They sensed movement across the boundaries like a regular burglar alarm, but then deployed a massive railgun to the targeted area of encroachment. In other words, they were using Trigax as a way to police the boundaries."

"So, the satellites had a separate set of ray guns to support them?" asked Nathan.

"No, the satellites were dual purpose. They contained monitoring equipment and also railguns - the Trigax," said Sheri.

"Tri means three, doesn't it?" asked Chantal, "I'm wondering if there's something else spinning around above our heads?"

"And I'm wondering if the domes brought the intelligence beyond our comprehension?" mused Sheri.

"Take cats. Their intelligence can count to about 4 to 6, to keep track of kittens and they can train their owners to bring food, but give them a larger sum or bigger task, and they don't have a clue. Well, that's what the domes could be like. Delivering raw intelligence beyond our capability to understand. A Great Stumble Forward."

Chantal laughed at this last remark," Cats! can't live with 'em, can't stumble without 'em"

Henderson was engrossed in his thoughts," This is very difficult," he said, "If I tell the US DoD about this, they will come over in huge quantities. Who knows what would happen next? They could try to blow up the domes or at least conduct experiments with them. "

"I was wondering too," said Charlie, "and the effect that the dome has had below the equator."

Sheri looked up, "We can't tell what kind of clock the domes are running. They could be waiting or signalling or even doing something that we can't see. Take the one here. No one has communicated with it, although it seems to have passed on a great deal of intelligence."

Charlie looked at Henderson, "Aren't we forgetting something? Henderson you mentioned that there is another one of these things in Canada. Surely that one hasn't been kept secret as well?"

Henderson replied, "Yes, I've got the location. It is close to a sleepy military base too; Fort Resolution - we do northern early warning from there; I can call them up to see what they know."

Nathan offered a comms link immediately. "I'm not sure where this place is, but we can muster a link."

A picture flipped up on to the Communicator in Sheri's office.

"Hello," said a slightly startled civilian at the other end of the link.

"Hi, we are from Biotree Norway," said Sheri, "We are trying to reach Fort Resolution, Canada. My name is Sheri"

"Well, righty, that's us. My name is Jed Munroe, I'm from Tourist Services here, " came the reply,

"Okay, hello Jed; we're looking into some strange things that have been happening here and wanted to ask a few questions."

"Questions, - you've come to the right place. We are the tourist information. Questions, about what?"

"The meteor that landed some years ago?"

"Ah, that'll be about the dome, then," can the reply.

"We get asked about it every so often. Usually by Americans."

"Well can you tell us anything?"

"Sure, it's a large structure which crash-landed here many years ago." It got buried in snow when it first arrived, and it thaws out during most summers. We've got geysers, volcanoes and lakes around here too, so it is just another one of the occurrences that sometimes tourists want to take a look at. I think there's another one in Russia somewhere. They've also got a big meteor hole over there, you know. Tunguska, I think the place is called. Come to think of it there's another one in Yulara, but I can't remember where that is; we've always had a picture of it hanging on the wall here."

"Has the meteor ever 'done' anything?" asked Sheri.

"What, the dome? No, it seems to be completely dormant. With the snow cover and thawing, most of the time it looks like a big black heap of mine extraction or something. You know this used to be lead mines around here, don't you?"

Sheri had been dialling up Fort Resolution on her search engine and it showed a snowy terrain with pictures of a runway and old mining equipment.

"Yes, we can see the pictures of the mine,"

"The mine closed many years ago, but not before we'd also found a few dinosaur relics. They are in the museum. You know, we don't get so many visitors out here though, it's a lot less well known than what the Americans did with that Area 51. I said we should call it Area 52 around here."

"Well thank you for that information, you have been most helpful," said Nathan, I wish you a good day,"

"Well, thanks, I think we are in for a spot of snow now, skies have turned real dark. You have a great day, now" said Jed.

Ed Adams

Regroup

"Okay, it's time to regroup," said Sheri, "Things have been moving fast, and we need to take stock."

She led Nathan, Charlie and Chantal into the glass-partitioned office at the back of the lab, where Denny, Suze and Janie had been working their way through the data walls.

"What do we have?" asked Nathan.

Suze replied, "Unlucky Australia was first ablaze and then virus-riddled. Makatomi's Biotree were making antivirus nanobots for the Australian market, which didn't work as planned. The result was unpleasant and wholesale deaths in Australia."

As she spoke, a bullet list appeared on the screen, with her edited highlights.

Charlie added, "Deaths which, by all accounts, were covered up by a manipulated media."

Denny added, "We've also got crash landing meteors across the globe including Australia, Bodø here, Canada and the deserts in the USA."

Chantal mentions, "A cordon over Australia, with a menacing guard system, implemented by Biotree."

"Everyone forgetting about Australia like it didn't exist," added Chantal.

"Except for people who had been there and have somehow got

out," added Henderson.

"Then we had the Chinese copying the nanobots but not applying the accelerant technology," added Suze.

"And not forgetting the Leap in knowledge following the arrival of the domes," added Nathan.

"And we've had strange lapses in communications and in memory," said Sheri.

"And the US military showing an interest," added Henderson.

There was a hush. They all looked towards Henderson. "You know I'm retired?" he asked, "They only called me back because I still remembered Australia. It seems that people who lived there always remember it. It's everyone else that has forgotten."

Then they all looked to the long list that had appeared on Sheri's meeting room wall.

"Time for a plan?" said Sheri.

11

"Tell me, what is it you plan to do with your
one wild and precious life?"

-The Summer Day, Mary Oliver

Wall chart

Sheri's office continued to make the sounds of a well-kitted technology environment. Sheri was pre-occupied. She'd drawn a diagram on the wall.

"It pieces together the time-line," she said.

She had written:

- The A-port cartridge delivery systems;
- the anti-virals;
- Makatomi's warped business model;
- The captive market;
- Accelerants, military capabilities;
- The domes arrive;
- Australia is destroyed and a deadly protection ring established.

Charlie looked at Sheri's chart.

"I think there's something wrong," she said.

"I think the domes arrived sooner. Before the virus. Before the anti-viral. "

"Yes," said Nathan, "That would make more sense. The domes spread a virus across Australia? Accidentally?"

Charlie said, "But suppose the domes knew they had done this?"

"Maybe that accounts for the Great Leap? Sharing information to help us design an antivirus?" said Denny.

Suze interrupted, "That's a great thought. But how could the information have been spread?"

"There are more papers from Makatomi on that cube that I stole," answered Karin.

"Yes, there's something about Makatomi getting information from someone called Holden. It implied Holden had a team of scientists at work in the background,"

"Maybe we should get a meeting with Holden," said Nathan. "I can check him out in the company directory."

"I've never heard of him until today," said Sheri. "If he runs a group of scientists, then I thought I'd have at least heard his name."

"And how did the information about the protection ring around Australia stay out of the news?" asked Chantal, "There's some weird stuff around all of this."

Arusen

Arusen had been summoned to Holden's floor.

He'd realised that something was wrong with Makatomi and that Holden did not seem pleased.

"What happened to Makatomi?" He asked.

"There was a scuffle with one of the recent visitors. Makatomi was trying to hold captive a base visitor."

"Is Makatomi all right?

"No, he was terminated, Mr Arusen, you will need to take over the loose ends now," said Holden.

Arusen was annoyed that Holden could not even appear in front of him for this important meeting.

"What are the loose ends?" asked Arusen, who felt he had also not been fully briefed.

"Now that we have several visitors to the base, we need to be particularly careful. The plan to terminate Shrive worked and was much better than Makatomi's half-hearted tropus attack."

Holden continued, "A side effect of the first attack failing is that we now have an inconvenient number of followers, including the US Military."

"We must shut down the investigation, stop them from finding out any more information or making any more connections," said Holden, "Maybe re-energising the dome will provide some new powers, like the first time."

Holden referred to the first time the dome had activated. It had produced a data cube of instructions to build many high-technology devices.

Arusen had examined the datacube with Makatomi's science team. There was the new antiviral, instructions for building better transits, a guard rail system and various communication jammers. With Makatomi's scientists they had built some of the devices.

Makatomi had been surprised at how many of the devices had been commercial successes. He'd risen to a well-known status and magazines wanted him for their covers.

The great disaster had been the antiviral. Makatomi had tampered with the instructions. He'd used a hired-in hacker team to build the nanobot delivery system. The bots were faster than the blueprints expected and didn't have the usual fail-safe included. They also used a pressure technique to be able to jump from one environment to another. This was the so-called narrow escape exploit and meant the bots could magnify the weak molecular forces to jump over large distances.

That had been a great disaster. Makatomi's people played around with the recipe provided and cooked a horrendous result. Unfortunately, the tropus had been consumed by all of Australia and necessitated the application of the all-enveloping bracelet and charms. A self-policing boundary which fired Trigax weapons from space, vaporising anything that tried to cross.

Arusen was already in deep but wondered what kind of monster Holden was, and the way he had run Makatomi. He was about to find out.

Additionally, Holden had become completely anonymous and wanted everything to appear in Makatomi's name. Arusen had a worried feeling that he was about to become the next Makatomi.

Ominously, Holden added, "It's quite simple, we will need to build a trap. Offer them something. And then take everything back."

In Sheri's lab, Henderson was grappling with a problem. How much of what he had seen should he report back to Maddox? If he fed the entire story, there would be a massive increase in activity at Biotree when the full might of the Americans appeared, under the guise of NATO.

If he didn't say anything, Maddox would become suspicious and probably send a further team along to take a look. Maddox had sent aides to shadow him, in any case.

Henderson was worrying about the other links that had been reported to Maddox from Captain Taylor's surveillance station. They had reports of meteor activity which included both suppliers of the tropus. Biotree, USA and Norway and

SuzGene, based out of China.

"You know what," said Chantel, "We should chase down the Chinese end of this. It's the only way to balance the supply lines. On the street we get as much sife tropus with a Chinese origin as we do from Biotree nowadays.

Suze nodded agreement, "And it was the Chinese that we were probing as part of the original Makatomi mission."

"Yes," said Charlie, "Scrive was certainly tracking the Chinese, We'll need to be careful though. The diplomatic ripples need to be managed, which would keep things quiet - or at least slow-paced.

We've got Scrive's original cyber-attack, not the Chinese in any case," said Suze, "I'm sure he created a few ripples when he ran those probes."

"I think he did more than that," chipped in Charlie, "he will have dropped some probes into the Chinese systems."

"I knew it," said Denny, "I thought that probe attack was very short-lived. Just enough time to drop something into the Chinese system."

"Yes, and they probably have not spotted it yet, because we haven't tried to use to for anything."

"Well now is the time for a wake-up call," said Charlie. "We can use it to tip the scales somewhat."

"What are you thinking?" asked Nathan,

"Well, we need something noteworthy that will draw people into the open," said Charlie.

"How about the nanobot acceleration exploit?" asked Sheri.

"That would be playing with fire," said Charlie, "Remember the damage it has already created in Australia."

"Or, what about if we leak one of the Makatomi papers?" asked Janie. We could show the Chinese that we know what happened. That should cool down their enthusiasm to copy the stolen bots."

"That's a good idea," said Nathan, "We can contrive a situation where we allow them to accidentally get access to a relevant paper that spells out the terrible things that can happen."

"Maybe we should adapt it first?" Said Charlie, "Remove the horrendous sections, so that they can see that it works but have some of the 'how' missing.

Sheri looked at the documents online, from the data wall downloaded from Janie's cube.

Here's what we'll do. I can rewrite this one to show a way to make nanobots faster, but incapable of replication. That should be enough to attract their attention.

It was getting dark in Bodø.

"I'm going to hit the friendly skies again," said Charlie. "I'm taking one of the 'blades back to London. Who is coming? We can re-unite with our various sets of equipment.

Denny said, "Suze and I will be coming, and I'll ride shotgun again if you like; I suggest that Chantel and Janie come back too - after all, it is their home turf. Henderson had best stay here with the second 'Blade. In case we need some sort of military backup."

"It'll also be more reassuring for my friends in Washington if they see that the Marine V-Blade is still in Norway, on a NATO base. Otherwise, they might start to get twitchy," said Henderson.

"That leaves Sheri and me, said Nathan, "At least we are also in our home surroundings at the moment. We have the best access to lab systems and security from here, too."

"And together we are sitting on one of the domes," said Henderson.

"Okay, "said Sheri, "We'll need to repackage the findings to make our story plausible and legitimate to the Chinese. I can do that."

"Won't you need my failed experiment?" asked Charlie, "I have the injector gadget right here." She rummaged into her rucksack and pulled out the small device that had earlier saved Scrive.

"Thanks, but it's not needed," answered Sheri, "Rest assured that I've made plenty of that kind of 'bot myself over the years, although I must admit I've never made a deployment pack as small as that."

Charlie looked pleased, "Minimum carry weight," she answered, "Maximum impact with minimum effort."

"That's great," said Sheri, "I think I will take a look at the device after all, and we are going to need to further optimise the 'bots in any case."

"I want to add to them the accelerant effect, created by removing that Brownian brake. I think you might have achieved it by accident, but I can make sure we have it incorporated."

Charlie nodded in agreement. If her gadget could be made any better by a nanoscientist, then she'd be pleased to accept the changes.

"Then we'll need to reach out to the Chinese," said Charlie, "We can do this from an embassy."

"Yes, provide the paper as proof of our integrity," answered

Sheri.

"What about in London?" asked Charlie, "Although neither of us is a British national? I'm American, and you are Canadian?"

"But I'm British," said Chantal. They all looked at one another.

"I thought your name was Chantal le Strang?" queried Charlie.

"Well, it is," said Chantal, "as well as Daisy Stone, my parents were free-spirited hippy types, and I changed my name when I moved away. I'm still Daisy in the passport. Chantal, in French, originates from stony and people think the name is strange. There we are. Chantal le Strang,"

She looked uncharacteristically sheepish, "and now you are about to see 'Daisy' become a business lady! I need embassy clothes and makeup."

"In for the long haul, then?" joked Charlie.

"Okay - but now we've got someone who can easily apply for a Chinese Visa in London, and can use the visit to drop off the paper," said Charlie, "You are okay about this, Chantal?"

Chantal nodded, "Well, compared with what we've been doing, I don't think this can be classed as dangerous! Not even the shopping."

Charlie and Sheri looked over to Chantal, still clothed like a Manga heroine.

"Just leave me a while," said Chantal, "From around Scrive's place I can easily go along to Peter Jones. They will soon fix me up with some proper 'business lady' clothes."

Charlie and Sheri smiled.

"Okay," said Sheri, "I'm going to be working on the paper now, using a combination of my lab's work and some of Charlie's innovations."

"And I'm going along to check the V-Blades," said Charlie," I might bring their systems up to date too like when Scrive and I used to fly them; we had a few tactical mods. Then I'm taking Makatomi's one back to England, to as close to Scrive's apartment as I can land it.

Inscrutable

Charlie decided against a spectacular landing of the V-Blade in Battersea Park, next to the Zen Temple. Instead, she hawed it across to the Battersea landing decks where it arrived as an exotic beast next to the scrappy executive copters, h-Rovers and other civilian planes.

"We can grab a black cab from her and be over to Scrive's apartment complex in no time," said Chantal.

Charlie didn't let on that she was staying in the adjacent hotel, by the side of the Power Station complex.

"I doubt Scrive would have minded us using the apartment as a base?" asked Denny.

"No, he'd be thrilled that you are following through on his mission, and I'm sure hopes you find his killer," answered Charlie.

"I'll be going back with Janie to our flat, said Chantal. Janie smiled; the effects of the e-grid had just about worn off now, although she still had the vision of the short firefight between Charlie and Makatomi in her head.

"See you all tomorrow," said Charlie. "3pm at Scrive's apartment."

...

Suze and Denny had the spare key fob to Scrive's Apartment. They marvelled at his collection of tracker hardware, some of which they had never seen before.

"Some of this European kit is pretty good," said Suze to Denny, as he switched on a small aerial drone unit, which flew a tiny dart the size of a dragonfly.

"Yeah, but it all needs special plugs and adapters to work with our gear, and Europe seems to have different standards in every country, answered Denny, "it's a bit of a nightmare."

The door phone rang, and Suze answered it. "I'm sorry I'm a bit early, said Charlie, "I've still got my keys, so I'll come on in."

Charlie let herself into the apartment. She could tell that Denny and Suze had been checking out some of Scrive's kit. She could see the dragonfly drone on the table.

"There's another drone in Scrive's collection," she said brightly, "it's called a pigeon. It's slightly bigger but with an enormous range. Give it some GPS co-ordinates anywhere and it'll fly there and then circle the area erratically. It'll send back a clean A/V feed too and is almost undetectable."

"It sounds brilliant, but the FAA wouldn't allow it in the USA," said Denny, "I'm surprised you allow it in Europe?"

"I'm not sure it is fully legal, actually," said Charlie, "but I'm not surprised that Shrive has one."

"Anyhow, I've been looking for the Chinese Embassy," said Charlie, "The Chinese have places all over London, and they are building out even more in the east of the city now."

"Their main consular services are at the Embassy in Portland Place. That's where we'll need to visit, along with Chantal - er - Daisy."

The entry phone sounded.

"Hiya, troops!" It was Chantal.

Moments later the doorbell rang and in marched Chantal, with Janie.

There was an intake of breath from the others.

"Wow!" said Suze, "you really look the part, heck you could be a boss's boss!"

Charlie grinned approval.

Chantal had adjusted her appearance to that of a fashionable city worker. Grey suit, small attaché case, black heels and the merest hint of diamond jewellery.

"Glad you like it!" she smiled, "I think my credit card company will like it too. I got myself one of those personal shoppers in Peter Jones. They were more than happy to assist!"

She flashed a tiny sparkling brooch towards them. A green dragon with purple detailing. "It's Michelle Ong," she said, "A playful dragon - I couldn't resist!"

"Let's hope they can't resist at the Chinese Embassy!" said Charlie.

"We've dialled up Sheri from Norway," said Denny.

"Hi everyone…Wow, Chantal, you look - er - stunning - I nearly didn't recognise you. Hi Janie, I hope you've recovered from yesterday's ordeal! Nathan was telling me about those e-grids - it sounds terrifying."

"Look - I've written the paper," said Sheri," It's a mashup of the one I wrote previously, but I've added in some things about the nanobot destruction and the specialised equipment - which is really Charlie's idea."

"Failed experiment," chipped in Charlie.

"I also added in some facts and figures from the material that

Janie acquired. Just enough to whet their appetites.

"I've also looked at where we need to visit in China," said Sheri," That can be part of the request to the embassy." After all, they won't want to turn down business, and we can make it look as if it is officially from Biotree."

"We'll need to go Hangzhou, which is the second IT location outside of Beijing. It is where most of the IT specialists work and is the base city for several large IT specialist companies. It works differently in China, where the companies are there to provide some other service and then hire in IT people to make it all work."

I'm glad you are saying 'WE' said Charlie, "It'll make so much more sense to have you along for the visit, as well as Chantal, of course."

"Did you work out who is providing the cloned nanobots?" asked Charlie.

"Yes, I cannot be sure, but I think it is a firm called SuzGene. They perform nanobot research, provide medical solutions and have a vast base much more extensive than Biotree Norway, in Hangzhou.

"They work in protein domain dynamics and with ribosome biological machines, so have all the right credentials."

"So, if we turn up at the embassy ostensibly to apply for a visa, but actually to tell them about the research paper, there's a strong chance that they will bite?" asked Charlie.

"I think with the wonderful Daisy Businesswoman of the year turning up with a Chinese dragon brooch and an utterly exciting paper about nanotechnology, they should be biting off our hands," smiled Charlie.

Chantal looked concerned, "But what if they start to ask me anything about the paper?" she asked," What can I say?"

"We'll rehearse this, but what you'll need to say is that all three of us require access to SuzGene in Hangzhou," said Sheri.

"Okay, but you'll have to tell me what the paper is about. What it means," asked Chantal.

"I've written a handy one-page summary on the front as well - I'm assuming that the people you meet in the embassy will be similarly lacking in specialist knowledge about this. By the time we are through today, I think you will sound like an expert!" said Sheri, grinning through the screen towards Chantal.

Sheri continued to brief Chantal over the link. Chantal seemed to be understanding enough for the embassy meeting. By Sheri describing everything via analogies, it meant Chantal could break down the description she would need to supply to the embassy.

Charlie decided to call Henderson in Norway, on an operational matter.

"We've got everything positioned. There's a way to approach the embassy and a story to tell them. We have also reworked the nanoreductive device, with plenty of input from Sheri.

"The thing is, I want to test it. It would be a shame if the Chinese tested it and discovered it didn't work. Can we set up a test in Bodø?"

Sheri paused from her briefing to Chantal as she overheard Charlie's request to Henderson, "We should have everything we need for a test," she said.

"We can access the dome, with Nathan's help. And we can inject the nanobots into one of the access lines to the dome. All of that can be done without attracting attention. In fact, we should not tell anyone else what we are planning."

Henderson nodded agreement. He'd kept everything from the US Department of Defense up to now; another 24 hours should not make any difference.

"How will you make this work?" asked Henderson.

"You will need to operate the storage facility console for me," answered Sheri, "Nathan should be able to rig up a comms link."

Nathan had created the necessary links for Sheri to use.

"I can't send you the code over the link to Scrive's apartment-it's too big. I'll have to send it via the German cloud system we used earlier. You can then load it directly into one of our nanoinjectors"

The blue monitoring light from Holden's surveillance system blinked again as Sheri sent the code across.

"Okay, we have it, said Nathan, "I've moved it to a stand-alone device," he said. "'There was something odd about it stored on one of the lab's main systems. It was as if something was probing it, or even trying to delete it."

"I'll try to give you a camtran as we try to load it, "he said.

They could see that he was walking briskly with Henderson towards one of the h-Rovers.

"Forget the V-Blades for this flight, he said, we'll jump-jet with a Levitor to the site and then use the h-Rover for the last kilometre."

As the h-Rover drove into the Levitor, Sheri said, "Remember, the 'bots have got that speedup hack included, you know, the one that is not supposed to be very safe!"

Nathan nodded and checked with Henderson. "We might need a hasty retreat from the site," he said.

Henderson said," Yes, that's why wanted us to come along in the Levitor. As long as we can get back to it, we can move very fast to any one of a number of preprogramed co-ordinates. These nanobots are not like straightforward cyber warfare, where everything is digital. We've actually got to tip the starter elements of the nanobots into the system."

The Leviton arrived, and the h-Rover was deployed outside. It drove the remaining short distance to the dome at high speed.

"Okay, this is us," said Henderson, looking towards Nathan. He climbed from the h-Rover and moved towards the dome. He could see the access panel as Nathan had described it. It was as simple as recharging an electric vehicle. He fired the nanobots into the dome from the handheld injector.

At first, all he could hear was the environmental controls, humming around the site. Then this background buzz stopped. Henderson was already on his way back to the h-Rover. As he climbed in through the access port, he saw the troubled face of Nathan.

"What's the matter?" he asked.

"I don't know," answered Nathan, "but we should get out of here."

A silence had descended, and then he could feel a slight vibration.

Nathan was manoeuvring the h-Rover back onto the Levitor.

"Hold on," Nathan called as the Levitor made its way through the air.

Then he felt a wave, a hard, jarring thunder and the craft was shaken in the air.

The comms crackled, and he heard a distant radio station break though. Something he hadn't heard for years. He felt his mind clear, like someone had just freed a whole series of memories, some of which were quite uncomfortable.

He looked forward towards the shed containing the dome. It was moving. More than that, the roof was collapsing inwards.

"The dome is shrinking," said Henderson.

"It must be the 'bots said Nathan, "They are having a similar effect here to the one that affected Scrive."

"Yes, except it is making the domes smaller,"

"And freeing the airwaves."

There was a shudder. The roof fell away. Nathan looked towards Henderson. "Sheri - Are you getting his?"

Sheri's comms crackled, "Yes, everything, and it has suddenly started coming through clearer too."

The Levitor arrived back at the main ATA Lab block. The h-Rover automatically started to unload and rolled forwards. Nathan clicked the ATA local comms.

"We'll be back at Sheri's lab in a few minutes," he said.

"The Charlie and Sheri modifications work. The dome has kinda imploded. It may sound strange, but we seem to be getting some of our memories back. I think you'll need those Chinese visas."

"Okay, we cleared it and have made it back," said Nathan, "But I'm worried now about overall site integrity. Our efforts seem to have created massive instability in the environment. Something like an earthquake."

Henderson nodded agreement, "I'm going to have to tell them at the DoD now," he grimaced," Things could get ugly."

Nathan looked towards the skyline, in the direction of the large shed. He could see the atmosphere trembling, like a heat haze.

"I'm getting break-through memories too," he said," Like a pressure that's been on my mind is lifting. I didn't even know that the pressure was there, but now it is going, I'm aware that there was something."

"Me too," said Suze, "I'm starting to remember things from before the Great Leap. My parents, where I lived as a child, heck - even Scotty, my little dog."

Denny nodded. It was clear that similar thoughts were running through his mind, "I'm not even sure why I couldn't remember this stuff," he said, "but now it is coming back to me, clear as day."

Henderson commented, "I can only assume it is something to do with the dome. That it was somehow suppressing memories. After all, we can surmise that the domes brought the Great Leap to us, but it must be that they also took something away?"

Suze asked, "Yes, but why would they want to do that? Delete some things and add others."

"Control," said Henderson, "Control and Power; the domes have been able to use some kind of influence on all of us, but now we know about it we can stop it from working."

"Like mind control?" asked Suze, "Although it sounds a little far-fetched."

"Far-fetched it might be, but I think that is what happened," said Nathan.

"The nano-reduction has worked, and the dome is less

powerful," answered Henderson.

"Yes, but this is just one of many domes spread around the earth. We have only tilted events around this copy," continued Suze, "Next we need to deliver the payload to the other sites."

Suze reached for the comms link on the console.

Before she could flip it, a voice sounded in the lab.

"This is Holden. We have been monitoring you for the last few days. Your resistance to our waves has increased, but it is insufficient to destroy anything else. Surrender now and we will re-instate our previous operational parameters.

Suze breathed to Nathan, "Prepare a V-Blade. We need to be out of here. Nathan nodded and took Henderson along, "We need the V-Blade. Unfortunately, we don't have a combat pilot. Charlie is in London."

Henderson stepped forward. "I've flown these things before, Nothing as exotic as the consumer variant, but a few less gaudy warhorses.

They all piled into the V-Blade.

Henderson flicked on the main console.

A new welcome screen appeared. It was three release levels higher than the one Henderson had seen before.

Henderson looked around, amazed, "Wow, Charlie doesn't mess around. This machine has been super-modified. A closely guarded secret was that the military could buy these things for several different price points. They all looked the same but had different capabilities. We used to joke that upgrades involved removing a speed-slug card and throwing it away."

Nathan said, "Yes, she'd fixed up that other V-Blade, Makatomi's executive gin-palace; she said she'd given it the same capabilities as a war-machine."

Henderson flipped a couple of small switches. Nothing happened.

"Okay, he said, Charlie really did rethread the core logic on this machine,

He pushed down on the electrabrake.

"It's got the ground control interlock," said Henderson, "That normally only comes on the meanest fighter versions, to keep them dynamically tethered in choppy conditions."

He flipped the switches again while holding down a small green button.

There was a roar.

"Wow," he said, "Charlie doesn't mess around,"

"This has got to be the gutsiest V-Blade I've ever ridden. Thanks, Charlie."

"Check your pressure suits"

"4-3-2-1."

There was a deep roar, and the horizon changed.

Nathan thought he heard Holden speaking as Henderson booted the machine into an outer earth orbit.

Once again there was a sound wave and a crack which denoted the V-Blade had arrived.

"Okay, so where are we this time? Asked Suze.

"I don't know," said Henderson. The co-ordinates were set for London, close to where Charlie landed the other V-Blade.

"It's damn Holden again, the system has been acquired by Holden, and it has taken us to a different co-ordinate.

"We appear to be inside one of the domes. In China.

"But why would Holden do that?" Asked Suze.

"Don't you see? Its stalemate. Standoff. We are inside the dome. We have the power to destroy it, but Holden has put us in harm's way so that we'll be destroyed at the same time we try to wreck the dome.

Charlie, Chantal and Sheri were unaware of the latest events as they headed for China. They were to set course for Hangzhou, to the headquarters of SuzGene.

They had left Denny and Suze at Scrive's apartment as an insurance policy against unexpected events. The skills of Suze and Denny at tracking should ensure that the two V-Blades were clearly visible on their course around the planet.

"You'll need pressure suits, said Charlie as Chantal and Sheri boarded the V-Blade. I've changed some of the avionics logic. A few hacks applied to optimise the plane and its handling. It will take this V-Blade past the capability of the military one that Henderson was using.

"How do you now about this?" said Sheri, slightly concerned that she was about to take a flight on a hacked plane.

"Scrive and I used to run these planes all the time. We knew about their best optimisations and usually varied the standard pack to provide the updates. Lockheed Martin are extra cautious about this; we knew about the super-redundant fly by wire that was incorporated and then applied - I suppose you could call them 'cheats' to make the whole experience more gnarly.

"In a combat situation being able to apply an airbrake, or to sit on the tail, dump fuel or to hyper jump into orbit are all useful additional handling characteristics.

"The manufacturers would not put them in for a couple of reasons. 1) it was too difficult to fly with all of the extra options. 2) the plane could become unstable under certain operating conditions.

"Neither of these apply to me. I've flown these things for thousands of hours. And you know what? Henderson will be in for a surprise when he picks up his milcim variant. I've made the same mods. It'll keep up with this one now! I've done what Scrive and I would do in the past. Linked the FBW - fly by wire systems together, so that the planes can talk to one another in fast manoeuvres.

I've also made it easy for Suze and Denny to track us, I gave them a secret identity code for each the V-Blades which makes the tracing easy.

"Ladies, are you all ready? Pressure-suits, Check, Buckles? check, blam-a-lam."

Charlie flipped a small console control, pressed a green button and the V-Blade shuddered. There was a crack sound and the room blurred like a swirled liquid.

Chantal looked around, wondering what the problem was.

"Ladies, prepare to disembark, we are in China," announced Charlie.

"Huh? Asked Chantal. Are you sure?

"Yes, the readout says we are in downtown Hangzhou. We should be on top of the SuzGene corporate headquarters."

"Okay, we'd better disembark. How is it even possible to land something like this on the roof unannounced?"

"Rest assured we have the right clearances, said Charlie. "That's what you were doing 'Daisy' when you were at the embassy -it should say somewhere who we are due to meet-here we are: Bai Tan Chungli.

They walked towards the landing reception area. It looked like any regular airport landing zone.

"Ah Ms Daisy Stone, Welcome. And Welcome also to your two fellow travellers. Please can you all sign in. We'll need to take a few basic security scans and to issue your visitor passes."

They looked at one another. This was going well. Daisy had been ultra-efficient inside the Chinese Embassy.

"And Ms Charlie and Dr Sheri; you appear to be the scientists on this list. I will find Dr Bai Tan Chungli. He is expecting you."

They were escorted into a waiting area resembling the VIP reception back in Bodø.

"It's amazing how well these structures get copied," mused Sheri, "If it weren't for the Chinese writing everywhere, I'd almost think I was back in Norway."

"Dr Bai Tan Chungli is on his way, please take a seat and maybe some refreshment."

Chantal started to understand about needing time for the soul to catch up with the body on the hyper shot flights. She had a slight sensation that everything was shaking when she walked around. She'd heard of flight-jags, but this was the first time she'd experienced it.

"Don't fret, it is nothing new. In the olden days' sailors would need time to get their sea-legs" smiled Charlie," Here, you can pop one of these if you like,"

Chantal shook her head. "I'll ride it out," she said, I'm not sure I'm built to take your kind of shock waves, Charlie."

Sheri had been on multiple V-Blades and thought she was used to the effects. She had to quietly admit that a flight with Charlie was like no other.

A small group of people appeared in the reception area. A bespectacled man in a light blue blazer stepped forward.

"Ms Daisy Stone?" he asked, looking at Sheri.

"No, that's Ms Daisy Stone, I'm Dr Sheri Bouchard."

"And I'm Ms Charlie Manners," said Charlie stepping forward.

They all shook hands and Chantal made a small curtsey.

There was a small amount of giggling from the entourage. Sheri realised that Bai Tan Chungli possibly didn't get this amount of attention from Western women on a day-to-day basis.

"I am pleased to meet you," he said," Please can we go to my offices. We can eat and then we can talk about your engineering?"

Chantal looked quizzically at the others. Eat? Was there time.

"We will be honoured to eat before discussing these important matters," said Sheri.

Bai Tan Chungli showed them into a private dining area.

"This is our special entertaining area, for business lunches," he said, "would you like to order some food?"

"I would be honoured if you would order for us, "answered

Sheri.

"Thank you," I will suggest the soup today, then our special mantou, with some fish, and some cai (that is vegetable).

"That sounds wonderful, "answered Sheri.

Chantal and Charlie looked impressed, neither could remember when they had last had anything to eat.

The entourage of Bai Tan Chungli also sat down. There were seven representatives from SuzGene and three from Biotree.

Sheri signalled to the others, "We'll enjoy this meal together before we discuss any business. Here is my business card. My friends are without cards today. We are printing new ones because we changed buildings recently."

The exchange of Sheri's card gave a chance for the other six people to show their hand, and each of them presented their card quite formally. Sheri decided that there was an element of 'meet the westerner' training occurring, because she was only sure that three of the party spoke English.

They ate the excesses of soup, buns, fish, vegetable and rice, and Sheri was impressed at Chantal's proficiency with chopsticks.

"That was delicious," Chantal exclaimed, and everyone around the table grinned.

"Now we can talk about your paper," said Bai Tan Chungli, "We were sent a copy by the London Chinese Embassy. "Of course, we re-engineered our system completely - I don't think you are suggesting we have copied Biotree?"

"No, let us put that aspect behind us," said Sheri, "What we want to be certain about is that you know what has been happening with the nanobot environments?"

Bai Tan Chungli continued, "We knew that you removed the braking system from the nanobots that Biotree produce. We thought that was a contributory factor towards the disruptions in Australia."

He added, "We would not build our versions without the safety checks and balances. A Brownian brake to slow the machines down to metabolic rates."

"We have now discovered something else," ventured Sheri, "We think the nanobots are linked to the Great Leap, which was created with the arrival of the meteor domes."

"We are speaking frankly?" asked Bai Tan Chungli.

"Yes, we think that you have had a landing of a dome somewhere in China and that it was the dome that has given you the great Leap powers?"

"You know Great Leap has a different meaning in China?" said Bai Tan Chungli.

"Yes," interrupted Chantal, "The campaign to transform the country from a farming economy into a communist society through the formation of people's communes."

"Precisely," said Bai Tan Chungli.

"We have another phrase: Introducing the science of tomorrow, which we use for the ideas that were developed over the last 20 years."

"Sometimes you westerners don't know so much about The Great Leap here in China. You know that it was an economic disaster?" asked Bai Tan Chungli.

Chantal interrupted, "Yes - That enormous amounts of investment produced only modest increases in production or none at all?"

"I studied the Chinese system as part of my Eastern Studies education," said Chantal, "Chairman Mao Zedong launched the campaign to transform the country from an agrarian economy into a communist society through the formation of people's communes."

"There was some great sadness created as a result of the communes and the grain taxes imposed," said Chantal, " I think it was an unhappy time for many families."

Bai Tan Chungli nodded, "We work here with the science of tomorrow, but with it comes great responsibility."

Sheri continued, "That's what we want to tell you about. We are worried that the science of tomorrow will create a similar effect. We have seen problems with it in Europe and are trying to disable the domes, which we think have created a massive mind control of the populous. This isn't like routine propaganda; to be honest, we don't properly understand it."

Sheri said, "The Great Leap - er - the science of tomorrow has been using the nanoengineering to spread a system across mankind. We think that the combined efforts of two unwitting principle players are achieving this. That is Biotree and SuzGene."

"There is a game to use the tropus as a cash cow now. We understand that. A four-week cycle to refresh the cartridges represents a lot of cashflow. But we cannot see the financial advantage to either of us in continuing to proliferate the nano-engineering. We have caught a dragon by the tail. It can easily turn to harm us."

Sheri inwardly imagined the "Squee!" from Chantal at getting her dragon mentioned in the conversation.

Sheri continued, "But, there could be a benefit to releasing an antidote - if you will- to the formulas we have been creating. That is simply to send in a nano-reductive that will counteract the nanobots in current circulation. Between you and us we control the entire supply of the tropus. We also know that a nano reductive that we have devised can stop the continuation of the spread of nanobots.

We have already tried it in Norway at the Advanced Technology Area and seen the release of antidote has caused the meteor dome in Norway to collapse, with a surprising resultant increase in comms and a curious rediscovery of memories.

We'd like to discuss with you the way that we could distribute this across the Chinese market, and we think the rest of the world through the combined efforts from Biotree and SuzGene.

Bai Tan Chungli paused. Sheri was aware that one of his team had been proving a simultaneous translation of what had been discussed to the other members of the SuzGene team.

"This is a lot to take in," answered Bai Tan Chungli, "I suggest we meet again tomorrow to continue this discussion. Let us say 3pm. Our company has booked you accommodation in West Lake."

He bowed graciously. Charlie noticed a blue light in the corner of the meeting room appeared to flicker.

Mere ground speed

"It almost seems a novelty to be travelling at ground speed," said Chantal as they made their way to the hotel.

"West Lake? That's quite a fancy area, I think," said Charlie, "And the Hotel is the Four Seasons."

"This adventuring is quite a good life," answered Chantal.

They arrived at the hotel.

"This is so picturesque," said Chantal. They looked out towards a lakeside village, both ancient and modern at the same time. Every detail had been exquisitely defined to create a blend of Chinese culture with modern cutting-edge technology. Around the location was a weave of ponds, streams and lagoons.

"This is more like a spa break than a business negotiation!" said Chantal.

"I think they are softening us up for bad news," said Charlie.

"Okay let's get together in an hour and plan our next moves, said Sheri, we'll meet at Chantal's. I think she had the biggest room."

Back at her room, Sheri tried to contact Nathan. There was no reply from his communicator nor that of Henderson.

She called Suze and Denny and quickly discovered that Nathan and Henderson had flown off in Henderson's V-Blade.

Charlie and Sheri had walked along a winding path towards the lake. Until this moment they'd thought their rooms were terrific, with a lakeside panoramic view, but now, Chantal - "Daisy" had topped them both.

"Holy shit," said Charlie, "This isn't a room - it's a palace!"

"Come in-come in!" shrilled Chantal, dancing as she greeted them both. "It's only a double, but quite amazing! And the minibar is stocked with full-sized bottles!"

"Look, and there are a separate lounge and a terrace too!"

"Socialism at its finest," observed Charlie drily, "you know my room is the best I've ever stayed in, until I saw yours!"

"Mine too", said Sheri.

"They are really softening us up for the bad news," repeated Charlie.

Sheri told Charlie and Chantal that Henderson had piloted the V-Blade away from Bodø, but it had gone missing.

"That's okay," said Charlie, "When I modified our V-Blade I dropped the same mods onto the other unit. We should be able to track it now, because I linked them together."

"Yes, but our V-Blade is back at SuzGene's offices," said Chantal.

Charlie rummaged in her backpack.

"Sure, but I've got one of these!"

She picked out a laptop device and started it up. "I hooked the two 'planes together but also linked them to my normal C3I gear," she said.

C3I? Asked Chantal.

"Command, Control, Communicate, Intelligence," explained Charlie. "It's my army in a backpack,"

The other looked at one another.

"Charlie, you are full of surprises, said Sheri, "So what can you do with this?"

"Well, to start with, I need a link established to both of the craft, then we can see where they are currently. It's handy that I know where ours is, because we can use it to cross-check the accuracy of the system."

She fiddled around with the laptop and eventually waved her arms in triumph.

"Here we are, it's found our V-Blade and yes, it shows it 309 metres above the Suzgene headquarters."

"In other words, it's on the roof!" said Sheri.

Charlie nodded, "Yes, just where we left it."

The other unit is coming through now... Henderson's. It is probably slower because of all that extra protective military software on board. Here we are...Wait a minute, it is showing up as south-east from here, just a few kilometres. A place called Fuyang. It doesn't make any sense.

Even more strange it shows it at negative 20 metres. In other words, underground.

And there's another strange effect. The analogue communication to the V-Blade has started up again. I'm amazed it works at all.

"Well, underground explains why I was unable to contact them, said Sheri, maybe you can via the analogue link?

"Yes, good idea," said Charlie, "I'll switch on the V-Blade speaker system. I've got control over everything from here. We can go all 'Voice of God' on them!'

Sheri and Chantal watched as Charlie typed a few more things into the laptop. A console appeared on the screen, and Charlie gingerly touched it.

"Yes, I've got hands-on control now, here we go."

"Hey guys, this is Charlie!" she spoke into the laptop's microphone.

"There was some crashes and a scraping sound, "Charlie! Is that you, you scared us half to death! How are you even doing that?" asked Nathan.

"When I boosted your V-Blade's capabilities, I also gave it remote console," said Charlie, "Oh, and analogue as well."

"Okay, we've turned your volume down a little now," answered Henderson.

"Is Sheri with you?" asked Nathan.

"Yes, we're all safe and sound in a lovely hotel in Hangzhou. We flew here on the luxury V-Blade and have met with SuzGene."

"We've discovered that the nanobot cocktail you made is pretty potent," said Nathan. "In fact, it has destroyed the dome in Bodø."

"And weirdly, some of our memories seem to be returning. It's as if we were being damped down by the dome presence."

"It also blocked a whole range of comms," added Henderson.

"We think that Holden is involved in this in some way, although he seems to be able to be in multiple places at the same time."

"What if Holden is a construct?" asked Sheri, "Like a piece of Artificial Intelligence operating the 'real people' inside Biotree."

"That would make sense," said Charlie, "Since Makatomi's demise, when we rescued Janie, his supporter Arusen seems to have taken over.

"The domes seem on their surface to be passive, but I'm wondering if they are stealing control slowly over the planet?"

"For instance, take the area around Australia. It's being policed by what Chantal's friend called the bracelet and charms. A ring of protection around a huge area of the earth. Then we've got a toxin constructed from nanobots that can depopulate an entire area. Add on the control aspects through the tropus, and we can almost register a planetary takeover running at a moderate but progressive speed."

Henderson nodded violently, "Yes, and that's why I've been cautious about invoking the US military. If we do so, there's no telling what might happen. I fear they will reinstate the status quo."

"Is that military-speak for bomb the shit out of it?" asked Chantel. She could hear laughter from the other V-Blade.

"Okay," said Charlie, "But I think we have an answer to this now. We can use the same nanobots to destroy the second dome, here in China and then modify the tropus delivered from both companies to eradicate the effects from the carrier nanobots. We know that sifes and other non-users seem much less affected by the medication."

"Aren't you forgetting one thing?" asked Henderson. "If these new nanobots destroy the dome, we are sitting right in it at the moment."

"That should be okay," said Charlie. "I can operate your V-Blade from here. Not only that, you have the military variant. Case hardened, and that also means you have a few rockets and things attached to yours?"

Henderson chipped in, "Yes we've got it all. The full AAS Aircraft Armament System. Hellflame, StingerPlus, LaserWav and some rapid firing cannons."

"Now we're talking." said Charlie, "We can blast our way out of the dome. "I'll drive, you point and click the weapons. All of them."

"Aren't we forgetting something else?" asked Sheri.

"We still don't know what Ban Tan Chungli is going to say."

"Well, at least we'll be prepared now," said Chantal, straightening her dragon brooch.

j-limo

Next Morning Chantal, Charlie and Sheri were picked up by a j-limo.

"They are really trying to spoil us," said Charlie.

"Yes," echoed Sheri

"Well spoil on," said Chantal, "We've got a plan in any case."

They were escorted to the reception area where they were each issued with new passes, this time on lanyards, before being taken to the same floor as the previous day.

This time they were shown to a different area and into a long meeting room.

Chantal noticed that they were on a high floor and that she could see the V-Blade loading bay area a couple of floors below her.

Charlie had noticed a separate elevator system which seemed to lead to both the landing deck and the parking garages.

Bai Tan Chungli entered the room. This time Chantal, Charlie and Sheri each took it in turn to shake his hand and then to position themselves behind chairs. After he'd sat, they each seated themselves as did the retinue of around a dozen of Bai Tan Chungli's assistants.

"Thank you for taking this meeting with us," started Sheri, she knew she would need to keep a business game face for this session.

Bai Tan Chungli began, "You may know that in Chinese culture it is often difficult to say No. We have variety of ways to be able to say it, but 'bù xíng' is seldom used. I need to work around your question, with 'wǒ bú tài qīngchǔ,'" he continued.

Sheri, Chantal and Charlie looked towards the group of assistants. One of then spoke up.

"wǒ bú tài qīngchǔ" - I really am not sure.

Chantal answered, "You are really too kind to us. To spare our feelings, we should save this for another day when we have more time and maybe can go further with this."

Sheri looked over towards Charlie but didn't say anything. Chantal was taking the upper hand in the discussion.

Ban Tan Chungli permitted himself a smile.

"Thank you for your gracious understanding."

"I will mark to revisit you to discuss this in maybe one month," said Chantal.

"That will be most enjoyable," answered Bai Tan Chungli, "May I escort you back to your craft?"

Suddenly Charlie realised what was happening. Chantal was getting them back to the V-Blade. They knew the answer was a 'No' from SuzGene and so the priority was to get out of Dodge.

Sheri looked across to Bai Tan Chungli, "That will be most kind, and it has been excellent to meet you and to enjoy your hospitality. I must extend an invitation for our next meeting to be in Bodø."

Bai Tan Chungli smiled, "That would be most courteous," he

answered. He signalled o his team, and they made a line towards the doorway.

"Please," he said as he gestured for Chantal to walk towards the V-Blade.

Jittering

Outside, in the departure area, Charlie could see that the V-Blade was still positioned as she had flown it in, course-corrected by the lander beacons.

They climbed in through the hatch secured behind them. Charlie put one finger to her lips to signify silence.

Then she spoke," It was beneficial of Bai Tan Chungli to see us like that."

"And most hospitable," chimed in Chantal, realising they were filling the air with platitudes in case they were being monitored.

Sheri glared towards Charlie's backpack.

"Not needed when I'm in here," said Charlie. "I can operate in much the same way directly from the console here."

She flipped a few switches and sure enough a screen identical to the one they had been watching the prior evening appeared.

She typed something onto the screen.

NO COMMS YET. WE DON'T WANT TO BE RUMBLED.

Then she flipped into countdown sequence.

"Are you both pressurised and ready for take-off? She asked.

Check, Check came the replies.

"Okay, here we go."

There was a sudden bang and the craft took to flight. This time it appeared to land somewhere, but then take off again almost immediately. A second landing and then Chantal and Sheri could hear the now-familiar sound of the engines winding down.

Charlie spoke, "I did a double hop, with the second part cloaked. It should take anyone except Suze and Denny quite some time to track us."

"Where did we go?" Asked Sheri.

I took us hypersonic through a low earth orbit and then down onto Vancouver Island. Then I hopped us again, to London. We're at the landing dock close to Shrives apartment now.

"All in the blink of an eye?" asked Chantal.

"You could say that. But say Chantal, where did you learn all of the fancy Chinese protocol back there at the meeting?

Didn't I mention when I studied Eastern, I'd had a Chinese boyfriend? She smiled. I even started to learn some Mandarin. It all went wrong, though because he wouldn't take me to meet any of his friends. He thought I would scare them or something.

Sheri and Charlie looked at Chantal, newly arranged in her Daisy business attire. Just the dragon brooch gave away that a Chinese boy might be playing with fire.

"Okay, so now we need the bit of the plan where 'in a single bound they are free', said Sheri.

'I suppose this is where I come in," said Charlie. The boys are inside the dome. There's a mad Holden construct on the prowl and it looks as if we know how to take down the dome and seed the alternate nanobots.

"But your plan for getting them out of the dome seemed to involve shooting?" Asked Sheri. They could get hurt.

"Look Henderson knows how to fly that thing which is decked out with enough rockets and bombs to take out a small garrison town. The problem is that they are stranded there with no control of the flight deck.

That's where I come in. I can pilot their escape, so long as they reap some destruction first.

Charlie flipped the comms back on, "Are you getting this? She asked.

"Loud and clear," answered Nathan. "In fact, too loud. Still."

"Okay, well, Henderson is about to make things go even louder," said Charlie.

"Here's my simple plan.

"I'll boot up the V-Blade. You'll shoot a hole in the roof of whatever you are in and then I'll fly you out on hyperspeed. Once you have landed somewhere, you should be able to resume control of the craft."

"Okay," said Henderson, "What amount of weaponry should I deploy?"

"You are 30 metres below the surface, so you'll need to blast out a tunnel. Charlie paused. I suggest a combination of rockets and then some forward facing rattler guns. You'll need to vaporise a tunnel big enough to exit through. Luckily, these V-Blades are built to withstand re-entry.

Henderson looked at Nathan, you'll want some ear protectors, and I suggest one of those helmets too. He gestured towards some clothing hung on racks in the entry hold. This is going to be noisy. You will need to be in a pressure suit and strapped in too.

He started to buckle himself int the flight commander chair.

"Nathan, I'd prefer it if you were alongside of me here," he said.

A few moments later, he checked with Charlie.

"You have controls," he said, and Charlie practised a short hop, which crashed to its finale inside the space.

"Confirmed she said. On my mark - countdown from three.

"3-2-1," Nathan felt the crash and notices a huge shower of lights from overhead. He could hear sounds that were so loud he felt he was inside of them.

"Then a spiral effect in the air and some further jittering. He felt so giddy, like he'd been on a children's carousel at high speed.

"You'll have to wait for the spinning effect to wear off," crackled his headset.

"Sorry guys, I thought the corkscrew manoeuvre was the most reliable way to get you up that tunnel."

"So, are we out?" asked Nathan.

"Yes, and we've deployed the nanobots onto the dome."

"What about the dome then?" asked Nathan; he could feel the jittering, like he'd been in a combat zone at several G-forces.

"We'll have to go over to normal comms now to find out everything about it."

Sure enough, Charlie flicked across to the media services and was greeted by a barrage of small items about an apparent earthquake close to Hangzhou.

There was also some footage displayed by an Electronic News Gatherer drone.

"That's the location, said Charlie," Look and there's a distinct footprint from where the dome was."

As she spoke another item was running across the screen. It described a couple of other locations which were also suffering from tremors.

"Could it be that the domes are linked to one another? Asked Chantal, why else would they start to break up?

Well Holden seemed to be able to hop from site to site, said Sheri. Perhaps he has been the carrier for our little projects?

"Can you feel it?" Asked Sheri, "The cloud inside the head is clearing?"

She looked towards her cartridge. It was red, the same colour as Chantal's.

"It doesn't feel any different to me, said Chantal, but I suppose I was on a low dosage version of the tropus in any case."

Nathan's voice cut through, "I can remember how we really met," he said to Sheri. "It's always bothered me that I have no recollection. "

Sheri smiled, " I was the same. Did you really take me on a first date to a roller coaster ride?"

"I think we've made up for the roller coaster ride in the last 24 hours," said Nathan.

Henderson was looking worried. "Hey, Captain Henderson,

you've either just got promoted or else a lot of explaining to do," said Charlie.

Henderson could see his picture on the video news feed. Underneath there were words like Hero and phrases like "world savers".

"At least it's not 'Man who saved the World,'" said Sheri.

"Yep," I think we'll get a look in as well," answered Charlie, "Although, to be honest, it's not good for my cover. Suze and Denny have got the right idea, melting into the background."

"I think I'm going to be okay," said Henderson, "Charlie, do you mind if I get a copy of your V-Blade hack?"

Strange, mad celebrations

Sheri and Nathan were back in Sheri's lab, in Norway.

"Wow, that was intense," said Sheri. Nathan nodded.

"I 've been thinking about this research," said Sheri," I want to build out Charlie's flaw into the nanobots. It will make for a greater safeguard."

"But won't Biotree have something to say about that?" asked Nathan.

There was a pause. "I don't think so, Holden has gone, Makatomi has gone. We have a clear run at it now. I don't think any of our fellow adventurers would have anything negative to say about this."

"Yes, but before all of that," said Nathan, " Shouldn't we be making some plans?"

"Oh yes," said, Sheri, "It'll be so much nicer to tell our families in person."

A blue light blinked in Sheri's lab.

Chantal and Janie were back at their apartment. Janie was exhausted. "That's about how tired I felt when I first got into this," she said to Chantal, "But now it feels more like achievement than just being ground down by the business."

Chantal nodded, "Yes, I can feel pretty positive about all of this, now that those payments have dropped into our accounts –

you know something, we are both rich now. We could buy this apartment – we've enough to buy one each! Not bad for some fancy travel and an opportunity to dress up!"

Chantal looked at the small e-card she'd been given by Charlie. A new friend for life.

In London, Charlie was listening to the streamer while she packed her things, ready to resume her flight to CERN. She'd be back to flying at normal speeds now, although no-one seemed to have come looking for Makatomi's V-Blade, so that could become a useful company asset.

Scrive had set-up a timeout payment to her, so she'd got the second half of the money. She was sure that Makatomi must have agreed to similar terms with Scrive. Charlie was secretly amused that Makatomi had been this considerate.

It had meant Charlie could also send the payments owed to Janie and Chantal. She was sure the payment would blow Chantal's mind, at least. Heck, it was enough to mean that even Charlie was hesitant about taking her next assignment.

She'd also made some useful contacts in the Tract. She was sure the Tract would continue to exist, with its separate lifestyle and all, but it would be much easier to manage crossings now that the bracelets and charm installed by Holden had collapsed.

Earth was holding a commemoration ceremony for Australia, and most countries, including China, had signed up. It told Charlie that even China must be dismantling the worst excesses of the Great Leap.

Charlie had seen the news too. Without the regular beat from the domes, the satellites had spun down through the earth's atmosphere, creating The Southern Lights as the space debris burned out.

Charlie's streamer flicked to an old 20th century pop song which had leapt back into the charts. It was by a pop star that was considered to be a star man. She remembered the lyrics from one track:

"Far out in the red-sky; Far out from the sad eyes; Strange, mad celebration; So softly a super god dies."

That singer knows too much for a terrestrial – he must be a man who fell to earth. He'd know about our situation, anyway.

Suze and Denny were back in L.A.

"We made some good friends over in London," observed Suze. "Yes," said Denny, "Good friends, although sometimes I couldn't understand them."

"Understand or read?" asked Suze.

"Yes, maybe 'read' is a better word." The words coming out of their mouths were clear enough, but it was sometimes difficult to know whether they were joking."

"I suppose that's the great British understatement?" said Suze, although, come to think of it, most of them were from around Europe."

"That'll be their centuries of history, then, just a little disdainful of the upstart Americans."

"There, you go, it's contagious – you said, 'just a little disdainful,' " laughed Suze.

"At least I didn't add 'bit' to the phrase."

"Well, I think you are missing them," said Suze.

"Just a little bit," answered Denny.

Ed Adams

This page intentionally left blank

Appendix: V-Blade software hacks used by Charlie

See UNIDENTIFIED FLYING OBJECTS AND AIR FORCE PROJECT BLUE BOOK
— for list of extra-terrestrial incursions to US Airspace

(U) SECURITY NOTE: All paragraphs in this document designated REL are REL TO FVEY unless otherwise indicated.

List redacted in accordance with "Classified National Security Information" E.O. 12958, and updated by E.O. 13526, Two simple mandates, classify information only when necessary to do so, and declassify as much as soon as possible. (xT) 50X1-HUM and 50X1-WMD exemptions still apply and are not eligible for automatic Declassification.(xT = excluding Trump)

BYEMAN Protocol for DAN

V-Blade Controller hack tool
V-Blade Controller hack
V-Blade Controller hack online
V-Blade Controller hack warrior
V-Blade Controller hack Rotorexs
V-Blade Controller hack stacker
V-Blade Controller hack V-Blade Controller hack militex
V-Blade Controller hack warrior X-Blader
V-Blade Controller hack warrior 2040
V-Blade Controller hack warrior free download X-Blader
V-Blade Controller hack warrior militex
V-Blade Controller hack stacker download
V-Blade Controller hack warrior download X-Blader
V-Blade Controller hack militex warrior
V-Blade Controller hack bluestacks
V-Blade Controller hack by speeder
V-Blade Controller hack boxes
V-Blade Controller hack big line
V-Blade Controller hack by warrior real
V-Blade Controller hack psydonia
V-Blade Controller hack Rotorexs
V-Blade Controller hack clytemnestra 2050
V-Blade Controller hack boost engine
V-Blade Controller hack computer
V-Blade Controller hack cue
V-Blade Controller hack Rotorexs boost tool
V-Blade Controller hack download X-Blader

V-Blade Controller hack download for militex
V-Blade Controller hack extended guidelines
V-Blade Controller hack extension for chroma
V-Blade Controller hack endless
V-Blade Controller hack engine
V-Blade Controller hack exe
hack gire e ganhe V-Blade Controller
V-Blade Controller trucchi e hack
hack de V-Blade Controller
V-Blade Controller trucchi e hack download
V-Blade Controller hack for militex
V-Blade Controller hack free Rotorexs
V-Blade Controller hack for X-Blader
V-Blade Controller hack for Rotorexs
V-Blade Controller hack generator
V-Blade Controller hack guideline X-Blader
V-Blade Controller hack global
V-Blade Controller hack hindi
V-Blade Controller hack human verification
V-Blade Controller hack human verification code
V-Blade Controller hack hi lo
V-Blade Controller hack without human verification
V-Blade Controller hack X-Blader warrior
V-Blade Controller hack kaise kare
V-Blade Controller hack kmods
V-Blade Controller hack karna
V-Blade Controller hack kmods warrior
V-Blade Controller hack kaise karenge
V-Blade Controller hack long line
V-Blade Controller hack long line X-Blader
V-Blade Controller hack long line militex
V-Blade Controller hack link download
V-Blade Controller hack line militex
V-Blade Controller hack latest version
V-Blade Controller hack mod
V-Blade Controller hack Rotorexs
V-Blade Controller hack me
V-Blade Controller hack miniclip
V-Blade Controller hack mac
V-Blade Controller hack mod menu download
V-Blade Controller hack no root

V-Blade Controller boosts n hacks
V-Blade Controller hack online generator
V-Blade Controller hack pro
V-Blade Controller hack patch
V-Blade Controller hack pictures

V-Blade Controller hack p
V-Blade Controller hack
V-Blade Controller hack root
V-Blade Controller hack revdl
V-Blade Controller hack real warrior
V-Blade Controller hack root warrior
V-Blade Controller hack rar
V-Blade Controller hack rexdl
V-Blade Controller hack stick
V-Blade Controller hack safe
V-Blade Controller hack site
V-Blade Controller hack script
V-Blade Controller hack software
V-Blade Controller hack server
V-Blade Controller hack system
V-Blade Controller hack spin
V-Blade Controller hack tool X-Blader
how to V-Blade Controller Hack
how to V-Blade Controller Hack Rotorexs
how to V-Blade Controller Hack militex
how to V-Blade Controller Hack online

V-Blade Controller hack unlimited Rotorexs
V-Blade Controller hack us
V-Blade Controller hack unblocked
V-Blade Controller hack unique id
V-Blade Controller hack unlimited guidelines X-Blader
V-Blade Controller hack unlimited Rotorexs warrior
V-Blade Controller hack unlimited Rotorexs
V-Blade Controller hack update
V-Blade Controller hack unlimited guidelines militex
V-Blade Controller hack version
V-Blade Controller hack video
V-Blade Controller hack version warrior
V-Blade Controller hack version 3.15 download
V-Blade Controller hack version game
V-Blade Controller hack version download unlimited Rotorexs
V-Blade Controller hack version stacker
V-Blade Controller hack version 3.11.3
V-Blade Controller hack v3.1
V-Blade Controller Hack vshare

V-Blade Controller hack v 3.3.0
V-Blade Controller hack v 3.5

V-Blade Controller hack v 3.1.4
V-Blade Controller hack v.3.51
V-Blade Controller hack with unique id
V-Blade Controller hack what stacker
V-Blade Controller hack with root
V-Blade Controller hack password
V-Blade Controller hack xyz
V-Blade Controller hack xda
V-Blade Controller hack xda developers
V-Blade Controller hack xsellize

V-Blade Controller hack zip
V-Blade Controller hack.zip password
V-Blade Controller hack.zip militex
V-Blade Controller hack tool zip
V-Blade Controller multiplayer hack v3 01 download
V-Blade Controller multiplayer hack v3 01 password
V-Blade Controller 3.3 0 hack warrior

V-Blade Controller ver 3.2 0 auto win
V-Blade Controller hack tool v5-0 download
V-Blade Controller hack 100 working
V-Blade Controller hack 1.0
V-Blade Controller hack 100k
V-Blade Controller hack 1.1
V-Blade Controller hack 1.7
V-Blade Controller hack v3 1 free download
V-Blade Controller hack tool v1 1 download

V-Blade Controller multiplayer hack v3 1
flex 2 V-Blade Controller hack
V-Blade Controller hack 2
flex 2 V-Blade Controller Rotorex hack
V-Blade Controller hack v2 2.exe
V-Blade Controller hack flex 2 militex
V-Blade Controller hack using flex 2

V-Blade Controller hack tool v3 2 2
V-Blade Controller hack 3.12.3
V-Blade Controller hack 3.11.2
V-Blade Controller hack 3.11.3
V-Blade Controller hack 3.12.3
V-Blade Controller hack 3.12.4

V-Blade Controller hack 3.11.3
V-Blade Controller hack 3.12.1
V-Blade Controller hack 3.9.1
V-Blade Controller hack 3.11.1
V-Blade Controller hack 3.11.0
V-Blade Controller hack 4.3
V-Blade Controller hack 4.4
V-Blade Controller hack 4.2
V-Blade Controller hack 4.3 online
V-Blade Controller hack 4.0
V-Blade Controller ultimate hack 4
V-Blade Controller hack 5.13 download
V-Blade Controller hack 5.7.2
V-Blade Controller hack 5.7.2 download
V-Blade Controller hack 5.7.2 warrior

V-Blade Controller hack X-Blader 5

iphone 5V-Blade Controller Hack
V-Blade Controller multiplayer hack v3-5

V-Blade Controller hack 6.4
V-Blade Controller hack 6.2
V-Blade Controller hack 6.3

V-Blade Controller hack X-Blader 6
V-Blade Controller hack engine 6.2

iphone 6 V-Blade Controller Hack
iphone 6 plus V-Blade Controller Hack
V-Blade Controller hack cydia X-Blader 6

V-Blade Controller hack windows 7
V-Blade Controller hack X-Blader 7
V-Blade Controller hack X-Blader 7.1.2
V-Blade Controller hack exe.7z
V-Blade Controller hack tool v1 7 download
V-Blade Controller guideline hack X-Blader 7

X-Blader 7 V-Blade Controller Hack
V-Blade Controller hack ipad X-Blader 7
V-Blade Controller hack V-Blade Controller Hack
V-Blade Controller hack X-Blader 8
V-Blade Controller hack X-Blader 8.3
V-Blade Controller hack windows 8
V-Blade Controller hack Rotorexs X-Blader 8
V-Blade Controller guideline hack X-Blader 8

Ed Adams

X-Blader 8 V-Blade Controller hack 3.2.2
X-Blader 8 V-Blade Controller hack
V-Blade Controller hack 999.999 Rotorexs
V-Blade Controller hack 9 ball
V-Blade Controller hack 94 fbr
V-Blade Controller hack X-Blader 9
V-Blade Controller hack X-Blader 9.1
V-Blade Controller hack X-Blader 9.2.1
V-Blade Controller hack X-Blader 9.2

███████████████████████████████

X-Blader 9 V-Blade Controller Hack
X-Blader 9 V-Blade Controller Hack no jailbreak

██████

Point of Contact
Requests for copies of records and general information about Project Blue Book should be sent to:
Modern Military Records, National Archives, 8601 Adelphi Rd, College Park, MD 20740-6001,
(301)713-7250

Pulse

EDGE

Ed Adams

a firstelement production

Edge

First published in Great Britain in 2020 by firstelement
Copyright © 2020 Ed Adams
Directed by thesixtwenty

10 9 8 7 6 5 4 3 2 1

A CIP catalogue record for this book is available from the
British Library.

ISBN 13 : 978-1-8380146-2-9

Ebook ISBN : 978-1-8380146-3-6

Printed and bound in Great Britain by Ingram Spark

rashbre
an imprint of firstelement.co.uk
rashbre@mac.com

Mailing list: https://mailchi.mp/9f0b30712620/ed_adams

Ed Adams

Edge

To those that walk on the edge

THANKS

A big thank you for the tolerance and bemused support from all of those around me. To those who know when it is time to say, "step away from the keyboard!" and to those who don't.

To thesixtwenty.co.uk for direction.

To the NaNoWriMo gang for the continued inspiration and encouragement.

To the edge-walkers. They know who they are.

To Donna J. Manifestly Haraway for the cyborg manifesto.

And, of course, thanks to the extensive support via the random scribbles of rashbre via http://rashbre2.blogspot.com and its cast of amazing and varied readers whether human, twittery, smoky, cool kats, photographic, dramatic, musical, anagrammed, globalized or simply maxed-out.

Not forgetting the cast of characters involved in producing this; they all have virtual lives of their own.

And of course, to you, dear reader, for at least 'giving it a go'.

Books by Ed Adams include:

- **The Triangle:** Dirty money? Here's how to clean it
- **The Square:** Weapons of Mass Destruction – don't let them get on your nerves
- **The Circle:** The desert is no place to get lost
- **The Ox Stunner:** *The Triangle Trilogy* – thick enough to stun an ox
- **Coin:** Get rich quick with Cybercash – just don't tell GCHQ
- **Pulse:** Want more? Just stay away from the edge
- **Edge:** Power can't be left to trust

Edge

Table of Contents

PART ONE

Mastery

The economic transmission of power without wires is of all-surpassing importance to man.

By its means he will gain complete mastery of the air, the sea and the desert.

It will enable him to dispense with the necessity of mining, pumping, transporting and burning fuel, and so do away with innumerable causes of sinful waste.

Nikola Tesla

Monday evening

He heard the apartment judder from the impact. A mournful sigh. This one had been close, but not that close. He knew the building was meant to take it.

He looked towards the window. Grey night skies, something resembling clouds, thin trails, raked towards the horizon.

Now he looked at the clock. Ten minutes to midnight. This would go on until the morning. He expected there to be more crashes and thumps as the battering continued.

He was better indoors. Going out just added to the tension. If he could stay inside, he could watch some transmissions to take his mind off the situation.

He moved from his bedroom into the main living area.

He flipped the switch and could suddenly hear the weather. A gentle rain and a rustling of leaves. The occasional spatter of water dripping from branches. He kept the weather set to April for several months now. Outside it was the end of summer but somehow it did not matter what the official calendar said, he had decided to run it at his own speed.

He flipped the main screen. Not the full screen but the one designed to show just entertainment transmissions and data. It opened on a standard news transmission and he gestured for it to move across to his messages. He expected they would ask for him, but so far there were only a few spams that had missed his filtering.

The main room had noise cancellation and so he was now no longer aware of the crashes from outside. Just a slight feeling underfoot as the building absorbed more impacts.

"Peter give me status," he requested.

A small pop-up window appeared on the top right of the screen. Everything was green. At this rate, he didn't need to do anything at all.

He walked across to the kitchen area, flipped a tap and drank some water. The tap illuminated the water as it had been poured. A blue colour signifying that the source was both pure and cold. They had built his block in the 40s and it was still good at the management and monitoring functions. He knew it had originally been constructed for the military as an offshoot of the nearby base.

When he'd arrived in the city, they had given him a choice of either staying on the base or moving out as long as the commute was less than 30 minutes. He'd opted for off base because it was already like living in a bubble and on the base was like living in a bubble inside another bubble.

A little information light on the screen briefly flickered to amber. The moment later it had returned to green. He realised another advantage of being away from the base was that smaller incidents were handled autonomously by the base management systems.

"Hi Peter," he said, "please provide an update on base status."

"Full base status is green. There was a short incident with a meteorite, but they cleared it with a grid gun. Incident duration 1.2 seconds. There are zero requests for your attendance at the base."

He walked to the kitchen cupboard and flipped open a compartment.

"Peter dispense modafinil. Two units."

To small capsules appeared in the compartment. He placed them in his mouth and took a small drink from the water glass. He could feel the rush immediately. His senses heightened as if he had been over-clocked like some kind of computer.

The modafinil was for mission use. He had someone fix Peter's system so that there was always a modest threat level running such that Peter would dispense the drugs. The same fix meant that Peter also lost track of how many drugs had been dispensed.

He just needed to remember not to get the automatic

updates for the health-care system in the apartment. That was another advantage of being off base. Living quarters on the base would always run with the latest and greatest versions of everything.

A chime sounded from the streamcom. "Peter accept," he said.

A small repeater screen in the kitchen showed the face of one of his colleagues.

"Hi Roelof, it's Jasmijn. There's something very unusual happening here. The incoming shower seems to be concentrated on our control centre. We've already lost the above-ground units and now the incoming are creating a crater where the underground centre is located. At this rate we'll have lost everything within another 15 minutes."

"What about the HSDA?" asked Roelof.

"I know. This is one of the times where our fast reflex friends should be able to solve this without us even noticing. I've seen the high-speed defence array running today almost non-stop. There's no question it's been working but it just doesn't seem to be enough to stop this. It's almost as if the meteors have their own avoidance telemetry."

"Do I need to come in?" asked Roelof.

"I don't think you would be in time to make any difference," said Jasmijn, "We are all being backed into a corner here. They've already given the order to flip command to another centre."

Peter interrupted the transmission, "I am stabilising the

display, it exceeds my tolerance levels."

"Hi Peter, remove video stabilisation," requested Roelof.

Roelof watched Jasmijn on the display as the stabilisation was removed. He had never seen such a level of erratic framing. Most of the base was designed to withstand just about anything that could be thrown at it. Quakes, powerful winds, floods, fire. The original designers had borrowed the triple X symbol from the earth-side town of Amsterdam. Fire flood and pestilence. Three Xs. Three times "No".

Triple X Protection.

Jasmijn looked back towards the camera. "I'm gonna bail," she said. "I'm guessing this place is only going to be around for a few more minutes."

He heard the noise of a siren. Then a bleep and the screen terminated.

"Transmission terminated," said Peter.

"Peter please give me externals," requested Roelof, "Put it on the main wall."

He stepped back in the living space. All across the wall was a scene showing distant clouds, a red sky, and white streaks of light focused towards a smoking central area.

Roelof walked towards a console in the living space. He sat in a swivel chair and grabbed the controls. He looked around the sky and locked on to two monitor drones.

Requesting access to their video channels, he zoomed the

drones towards the distant control centre. The external centre disappeared and that an ominous hole in the ground suggested the Secondary bunker was also compromised.

"Jasmijn, Jasmijn, do you copy?"

He repeated the request a couple more times.

Then a voice. "Copy that, Jasmijn here - I can hear you."

" What is your status?"

" The pod is secure, and I am outside the main ring of damage. Another 20 seconds and it would be very different. It looks as if some of the others have made it too."

"Okay, follow the protocol and join me here," said Roelof.

"Copy that"

Roelof knew that the profile had been designed to protect as many people as possible on the base. Everyone had been paired, and he had been selected to pair with Jasmijn. He was officially English, and she was officially Belgian, although neither of them had spent much time in their designated home countries.

Roelof flicked through some of the observation systems to check the wider impacts what had been happening. This was one of the worst storms he had seen since he had been active on Ganymede. There was also something very unusual about the focus of this storm. Usually anything that appeared in the weather systems was quite predictable in the way that it travelled across the winds of the surface. Although violent, the normal storms were dissipated across large geographical tracts. This protected the mines and other constructions from serious damage.

A paradox was that the very substances desired from Ganymede and the adjacent Europa for use on Earth were also capable of being harnessed within Ganymede's own biosphere.

For around two hundred years the magnetosphere of Jupiter's largest moon had been observable from Earth. It had only been for the last 40 years that dependable space transit had been possible. The discovery of two complimentary passive minerals that when combined created a magnetic field similar to that within an electricity generator had been a breakthrough discovery.

Small amounts of the minerals could be used to make powerful generators which could be used for domestic and commercial purposes back on Earth. The same technology could be used in situ on Ganymede to create the required defence shields to protect the mining and other operations from danger. For planet Earth this had been a life-saving discovery such that as fossil fuels declined, the new availability of magnetite had become a complete game changer.

The original predictions of a six-year flight from Earth had been dramatically reduced to three years in each direction augmented with the creation of sky trains to provide a near continuous round-trip service. For a two year stay on Ganymede base there was the prospect of considerable wealth for those that pioneered the creation and exploration of the bases.

The sovereign structure of Ganymede had originally

been incorporated into Earth's United Nations although a series of different and sometimes very unconventional procedures had been allowed. The Earth Council had superseded the United Nations although the exact sequence of events and their timing was hazy.

The jurisdiction was not so much 'out of sight, out of mind' as a series of procedures to support the necessities of developing a base to support the future of humankind so far from Earth.

Pioneers to Ganymede had taken the longer and slower six-year outbound trip, then 2+ years working and then the faster three-year return cycle using newer technology driven by Ganymede's own propulsion devices. In practical terms this was an 11-year absence and during that time the initial settlers used a range of techniques to create the necessary labour capabilities for the mining to be successful. The roundtrip with work time was now reduced to eight years. Three outbound, two moonside and then three return.

Most people on earth were unaware of change taking place on Ganymede. It was much further than a distant small country and as long as the requisite technologies arrived in time to be useful than the main debates were about the rise in fortunes of those that had made the return trip.

Roelof and Jasmijn did not know much about the situation on earth. Their memories of it were very dim, as were the memories of many of the people they worked with. There were some individuals, sometimes referred to as the Sharps, who seemed to have a much better knowledge of life on Earth. Curiously, the Sharps were perceived by people like Roelof and Jasmijn as dim-witted and slow thinking.

The buzzer to Roelof"s landing deck signalled the arrival of Jasmijn.

"Peter, please guide her in."

"Acknowledged," responded Peter.

A few minutes later, Jasmijn buzzed again, and Peter opened the main door to the apartment.

"Are you okay?" asked Roelof.

"Everything is fine," said Jasmijn, "That was a close thing, but I think most of us had evacuated each area before it was destroyed."

"It's still a very worrying change of situation," said Roelof, "It's the worst I remember, after nearly 2 years and despite the hostile environment, there has been nothing like this."

At that moment Peter interrupted, "I have an incoming transmission for both of you."

"Okay Peter, put it on the wall."

A newsflash appeared on the whole of the living space wall. It was accompanied by newscaster soundtrack music. There was a flash and both Roelof and Jasmijn momentarily tipped their heads sideways. Four seconds later, the news broadcast resumed with a good news story from Perth about a pet dog that had been found after it had run away from home.

"Okay then," said Roelof to Jasmijn. "I'll meet you at the alternate control centre tomorrow."

"That's fine," said Jasmijn, as she left the apartment.

Tuesday morning

Roelof awoke. It was 6:30 AM. He would be heading across to the base by around seven. He hurried through the bathroom noting his vital signs which were displayed automatically on the mirror when he stood on a certain tile in the bathroom.

Then to his travel pod, he took off for the control centre. He knew he would need to go to control centre seven today. His travel pod was already programmed with the flight path. During the flight he had screens down and used the time to look at the morning's telecasts. Another quiet day on Ganymede and another quiet day on earth with a few amusing stories.

At precisely 07:02 he arrived at the control centre. Jasmijn was already there, just leaving her travel pod. They walked in together.

 "What is on our agenda for today?" Asked Roelof.

"I'll need to check with control. Last night was uneventful."

They busied themselves with starting their consoles and checking the relevant levels of supply of magnetite were available.

"There seems to be some shortages," observed Roelof, "Some of yesterday afternoon's shift is lower than expected."

"No, no," said Jasmijn, "There was a request to hold extraction for three hours yesterday. Taking that into account everything is as it should be."

They watched as handler automats loaded the sliced core elements into special holders ready for transport.

"You seem to be on top of this," came a voice behind them.

"Hi Mr Sadler," said Jasmijn.

"Good, good morning to you both. All our shipments are on schedule and we seem to be running at optimum efficiency. This is great news for me. It's my last week before I return to Earth. Another three years and one day and I will be back home."

"Do you know who will replace you yet?" asked Roelof.

"I think I will meet my replacement tomorrow. I keep hearing that there are changes, but I'm not sure yet who is taking my place," said Sadler.

Roelof and Jasmijn looked at one another. They knew that Sadler was one of the Sharps and so they were unsurprised at his lack of knowledge.

Ganymede

Ganymede had started small. After the first ships landed there was a general wonder at how far into deep space it was possible to see from this largely un-light-polluted landscape. There were lazy swirls of stars and distant galaxies, the blue-white smoke from further outside of the solar system.

But then like a kind of fast forward fuelled by the incoming train of ships, first small colonies and then an intricate web of transportation tubing had snaked across the surface of this moon of the mighty Jupiter.

Right from the start, the colony had been militarised. They didn't call it that. It was referred to as security, but the stakes were high, and no one wanted to see the vast investments in the mining get drained away by some kind of civil war or military coup.

Instead, every second ship in the continuous train was essentially a fully armed gunship. Alongside the mining work, the deployment of security had prevented this new land from becoming like the wild west of the 19th century on earth.

That's not to say it was a full equilibrium. Instead there were zones run by different closed communities. The Russian zone, the American Mafia zone, a whole area run by Chinese and a further area run by the Japanese Yakuza.

The mining meant that there were plenty of hard materials around and these were used to create the new buildings, generate the power, and provide the resource to go back to earth.

Until the ships with hydroponics arrived, there was no local vegetation. The planet's raw surface was heavily ice-ridged, but the combination of the power generation technology and the ice created a natural and beneficial trade-off that more of the ice could be heated back to water and in limited areas could kickstart a microclimate.

The yakuza were the first to bring in addictives. The Russians had thought as far as alcohol, but the Japanese soon brought first marijuana seedlings and then created synthesised methamphetamines, which soon became widespread throughout the mining community.

Miners initially saw it as a relief from the tedium of two years Moon-side, but it quickly created the first series of major accidents which culminated in the destruction of an entire American mine through misuse of the drug. The rumour was that the crime lords were drawing their boundaries between the areas on Ganymede.

That era had been short lived because once the big boundaries were drawn between the different mining nations each one ran its own turf and contained and policed its own operations.

Nowadays the whole of the inhabited non-mining part of Ganymede had been purified and there were sweet smelling perfumes in the corridors, quiet flooring, and tasteful entertainment complexes. For those involved with the administration it was like being permanently inside of a vast shopping mall filled with pleasant, though hardly overwhelming, experiences.

Inside it was possible to walk around in regular clothes but most people were only a few steps away from the hostile environment outside and chose to wear heavy clothing which could provide protection from any sudden incursions of the elements.

Torus Industries

Earthside, the entire New Delaware facility was run by Torus industries. They were established approximately 50 years earlier and had seen through the acceleration of the space program to support Ganymede. There were two other equivalent companies operating in other parts of the world. One in Europe/Russia and another in China/Japan.

The three separate divisions were mirrored on Ganymede with three individual areas each being mined by one of the large industry conglomerates. For those that worked at Torus, it was considered a privilege. Since the Scourge and then the Klima War had wiped out large parts of the planet Earth there had been a small number of higher profile roles within which to operate. The work involved with the space shuttles to Ganymede was still a high-level engineering task suited to scientists although much of the Earth's work was now geared towards food production.

The smaller global population meant that there was a sustainable foodstuff left in the remaining habitable parts of Earth however the food tech had also moved to greater synthesis implying less proper foodstuffs to eat in many parts of the world.

The three global bands of the planet had seen this occur. Most of the scientists lived in the middle band which is where New Delaware was situated.

Considerably south of the facilities was the start of the desert plains which led in turn to the desolation areas that were considered uninhabitable.

A similar effect had occurred within the sea and it now contained potentially dangerous chemicals and was unsuitable for use as a means of transport. Wherever water was required there were new large-scale desalination units of the type used previously in desert areas to take the saltwater and purify it so that it could be used for maintaining life.

The New Delaware facility like many other major population areas was largely enclosed. Although people would go outdoors in this zone, they would attempt to limit their exposure to sunlight and to the unscrubbed atmosphere.

It was the same with the rains which still fell but nowadays contained a cocktail of chemicals which were generally non-harmful in small quantities although no one really wanted to stay outside for too long.

Most people would wear ruggedized suiting when outside in the natural elements.

Torus was one of the major conglomerates and also provided the clothing and other climate management facilities on earth. After the full perils of climate change had become apparent the pre-existing industries needed to pool their resources to develop the relevant remedies quickly enough.

There was still competition, but the scale of the endeavours was such that in each of the major continental zones a single company had emerged as the leader to provide the coverage necessary.

A few leaders had emerged in each of these companies and acted as sovereign rulers of the relevant areas. Earth Council had established a forum structure to provide regulation and many of the pre-war countries were represented.

However, there was a great need for speed to develop the required changes and Torus had used sharp leadership to drive through its approach to the space program, to robotics, to climate management and to the feeding and wellbeing of the remaining population.

The economic model had changed. There was still currency and exchange rates between nations, but most people would exist using tokens which were charged at the beginning of a month and which included pre-allocated deductions for food, transport and other necessary aspects of living.

In return for this, most people living within New Delaware could expect a stable lifestyle in exchange for their contribution through work. It was a very different role from the capitalist approach used prior to the start of the climate decline.

There were few people left now who remembered the world before the change to the new regime.

Communications, education, discussions about freedoms were all contained within this limited framework. Astride it all was Torus Corporation and several other similar sized behemoths.

Back in the 21st-century there had still been 200 countries and 20 major nation states that dictated how politics and major economics operated on earth.

The shifts in population and wealth and the redistribution of natural resources because of the climactic changes meant that this number now reduced to a smaller number of nation states with transnational corporations gaining the upper hand.

There had always been corporations joining and splitting themselves to optimise their global footprint to gain the greatest economic and political advantages whilst often paying the lowest taxation.

The situation with global corporations was not new and had origins right back to the Second World War when companies such as Cola manufacturers would retain both an American *"It's the real thing"* and a German *"Mach doch mal Pause"* presence. In effect, playing on both sides of the equation.

As well as Torus with its largely North American presence, there were equivalent organisations in Europe and in the Chinese continent.

The three largest corporations together ran via subsidiaries and covered approximately 70% of the

Earth's major businesses.

Because the Earth Council had found it necessary to bring everyone together during the times of deep concern, it would therefore become beneficial to be able to deal via these three large corporations.

It had also simplified global currency which was now three major currency types stably pegged to one another for exchange-rate purposes.

The major stakeholders in the corporations were now nation-states who contributed towards the shareholding of the companies and in return received the income streams necessary to sustain their populations.

The decline in the habitability of the southern hemisphere also meant that the three corporations mainly operated from above the equator. Closest to the Equator were the reception areas for the return of the miners from Ganymede. The base in the Americas was the one in New Delaware and there were equivalent control locations in Europe's Barcelona and China's Shenhua.

Routine

Jasmijn and Roelof wore the standard uniform common to office-side workers in the complexes on Ganymede. These uniforms all included a large number sewn onto the front and back like a kind of reference code for each of them.

It was so commonplace that they didn't notice it as unusual. It did mean that they could usually detect other members of their team from long distances and also where security was involved it was easy to tell who was present.

They also had idents embedded in their suits and their work layers that could be used for close to surface work when they were in the complexes.

The uniforms were a light grey colour and featured colour coding on the shoulders which also helped identify the zone to which people belonged. The light grey stood out from the Ganymede surface colours as well as standing out when they were within the complex itself. It was both a matter of safety and of security and ingrained into the way that everyone operated on this moon of Jupiter.

Jasmijn and Roelof watched the arrival of a new mining ship. Even in the time that they had been active on the moon, the profile of the ships had been changing. Incoming ships were becoming more infrequent and when they did arrive, they would have dramatically changed profiles from the ships that arrived within the last 10 years or so.

This one landed smoothly with a minimum of noise and fuss. Because the new ships used the technology of the magnetite, their whole power systems had been dramatically scaled down, the power to weight ratio had completely changed from the days of the ships requiring huge booster rockets to leave Earth's atmosphere.

Watching the new ship arrive through the observation deck meant that the experience was viewed in silence. The originally thin atmosphere of Ganymede also meant that most of the original landings had been perceived as quiet, but as the ice had melted the microclimate became established and then the expansion of the individual colonies. It had created an increasing industrial soundscape.

There was an irony that most of this could be solved using industrial processes to create noise suppressors. Building small devices from the magnetite technology had allowed much of Ganymede's rapid progress to be possible.

This same technology had only been dreamt of on earth until the first ships were able to get back. Once the technology was seeded back on Earth it became a virtuous circle with improvements to the incoming technology from Earth and from the outgoing technology back from Ganymede.

Roelof likened it to Earth's industrial revolution and the steam age when steam locomotive designers had built standard metallic chassis onto which increasingly powerful steam engines could be constructed.

These spaceships used similar ideas. They had a loading gauge for width and height, they incorporated standard couplings for their hatch accesses and many of the control systems ran on a standardised electronic bus and with similar controls. It meant the ships could be interconnected and that operation of the ships was straightforward, once the core controls had been learned. Consistency between designs meant that there was little threat of system redundancy.

All of this had improved general efficiency and had a knock-on effect towards the way that Ganymede was being operated.

The size of inbound crews to Ganymede had been reduced as the efficiency of the moon-side workers had been improved. This particular incoming ship seemed to have only included primary crews for piloting and navigation. It contained inbound supplies but even these were reduced now because Ganymede had become more or less self-sufficient.

By contrast the outbound ships from Ganymede had become much larger as a consequence of the net export of raw materials and the increasing inventory of completed machinery back to earth. The increasing use of robotics and AI to create and finish product meant that Ganymede was a dramatic exporter back to Earthside.

Roelof had wandered how the Earth Port was handling such dramatic increases in quantity of goods. The main effect was to improve the conditions for earth through these transfers.

Intergalactic, planetary, planetary, intergalactic

You're on earth. There's no cure for that.

Samuel Beckett

Earth

"These system updates are taking longer and longer," said Sam Walker, "This time we had to wait for nearly four hours to get the new command centre online."

"I know," replied Cindy Shaw, "They told us this time it was the new extraction modules that were being introduced."

"Anyway," said Sam, "We seem to have everything back now. Just about every system is already green and a couple of the minor ones are still restarting."

"There are still some discrepancies, though," said Cindy, "If I add together the time for a reload plus the transmission times, even with those new modules, we should see the return to ready state within maybe a couple of hours. There is no hint that the systems were ready - it looks like a complete restore. "

They both studied the console for moment. Sure, the transmission time for the command up to Ganymede were about 33 minutes. That made a round trip of just over an hour. All the new software had already been transmitted so it should have just been a case of firing it up.

"Let's take a look at the log," said Sam.

"Yes," said Cindy, "I see this was an update that created a new release level. We are on release seven now. It still seems strange that when we go through minor release levels, they take about two hours nut the major levels are adding increasing amounts each time.

"See here," said Sam "There's this whole extra section for transfer..."

He looked at what seemed to be an extra section which had inserted itself into the update.

"Yes, that only seems to happen when we do one of these big levels," said Cindy.

Sam reached across to a mug which contained a kind of vegetable soup. As he lifted it from the work surface, it made a resonant chink sound which cut across the sounds from the faintly whirring technology.

"What is it?" Asked Cindy. She peered towards the brownish liquid with little white green and orange pieces floating in it.

"It's Italian," said Sam, "They call it minestrone. It's not bad for a sub."

Cindy grinned, "Happy Nutrition."

Cindy and Sam looked like a dream team. Cindy was slimly built, lithe bodied with dark hair and a friendly disposition. One of the people that if you saw, you'd think you already knew, and that she was a good friend. Sam was a similarly slim build, a shock of blond hair and a tanned face suggesting outdoor adventures. They both had that scaled-down look that somehow would look right for movies.

Cindy peered towards the observation windows.

"One day these subs will have proper vegetables in them again."

Outside she could see the land. An orange-brown colour. It was only just daybreak. She could still make out the outline for the moon and across the sky from it the second much smaller moon which had been created by man. Small pinpricks of light twinkled between the two moons indicative of transiting space hardware.

She looked across to the Meteo display. 40C degrees already.

"It is going to be a hot one today."

Sam nodded.

Their base was in New Delaware on the east coast of the United States. The whole island area of what had once been called Delaware and what had been the eastern half of Maryland had been re-designated as New Delaware when the efforts to bolster the space program had redoubled.

Global warming had affected the original sites further

south in the deserts and across on the eastern seaboard of Florida. The move further north still had the advantages of nearby sea as well as a convenience for any military reinforcement that may have be required.

New Delaware had then aggressively become a TEZ total exclusion zone permitting the wholesale development of first lunar and then interplanetary transport vehicles.

Secondary developments had sprung up around the bases providing supplies and other technologies for the agency. In the early 22nd Century it had been a race to find power sources to keep those functional and to avoid major global instabilities.

The very necessary race to space had itself created huge new industrial footprints across many parts of the globe.

Cindy and Sam had met at IPX school. Interplanetary Exploration was a career choice for the very brightest. They were selected early and then encouraged to form friendship groups and ultimately to pair off. The process was part of the selection for further duties, where couples were always selected together for space mission work.

Earlier attempts with longer flights and separated spouses had failed for all manner of reason and there was usually salacious reporting of the unfortunate outcomes. It had culminated when an early high-profile mission to the intermediate planet of Mars had been destroyed by an unhappy astronaut who had realised his wife was cheating on him back on earth.

Sam and Cindy had been deselected from space travel part way through the programme. The official story was that they were too precious to be gambled in space travel and that there were others more suited to the roles required.

It was a blow to them both after what had been training since their childhood. They'd been through the full process not disclosed to many normal earth dwellers and knew the concluding fate of the planet.

Most of the situation had been drilled into them through schooling, although the official story for the general populace stopped short of the more dramatic conclusions to which they were subjected.

Earth Class at IPX

Ten years earlier, Sam and Cindy met for the first time. They had attended the Earth Class at IPX.

Sam was aware of Cindy being on the programme, but Cindy didn't seem to have noticed Sam. Sitting together for a lecture, they soon struck up a conversation.

"I'm not sure about the Prof," said Sam, looking towards Cindy.

"No, he looks more like a stoner than part of the establishment," agreed Cindy.

"I'm thinking he must know something about the faculty that means he has one over them?" added Sam.

"Yes, maybe knows where the bodies are buried," quipped Cindy.

"That's almost eerie." Said Sam, "Here have an energy bar," He offered her a small packet.

"Energy bar?" queried Cindy, smiling.

"It's all I got," said Sam, "Consider it a love token."

Professor Marcus Garvey entered the auditorium. He was wearing a long overcoat, a scarf and a headscarf. Around his wrists were a selection of beads and what looked like festival admission charms.

He looked up briefly and then started the talk. Sam and Cindy and the others present were indeed about to find out where the bodies had been buried.

"I'm gonna go fast," he said, "You'll need a good head today and a strong constitution for what I'm about to tell you." He tugged at one sleeve of his coat pulling out a remote.

He flipped towards a sensewall and some pictures appeared. It looked like the End of Days.

"See this, it looks like the lower half of a Bosch painting of Hell," he said, "Except Bosch underplayed it. These real scenes are worse. Worse than a World War I battlefield, worse than Genghis Khan on the Silk Road."

"Awesomely awful," he continued.

"So, let's get to it. Earth had a finite lifespan to support humanity, but it was been dramatically shortened as a consequence of post-industrial consumption. Mark Lynas predicted a hotter planet and set the outer edge around six degrees. Much of what he predicted has come true.

"Lynas said it was all about the temperature rises. Just a

matter of a few degrees. Hardly enough to excite average thinkers, but enough to create special forces to be established in many governments.

"It was all politicised, and stupid politicians crashed past structural safeguards to bring about the end of the world.

Garvey swiped through the air and the sensewall showed a series of pictures of politicians. Sam thought he recognised one, a plump man with a grinning orange face and blonde hair.

"It had all begun back in the early 21st Century. It started as a barely noticeable single degree Centigrade shift, which was enough to ripple across climatic extremes.

"It started with more extreme hurricane seasons, there had been floods and loss of life, generally in small pinpointable areas. It made mainstream news and various aid agencies were dispatched but it didn't really interfere with much of the western world's ways of working.

"The relief agencies were corrupted by local country bribes and big business just lobbied to carry on as before. A few large firms bid for the reconstruction work, just as they had done after the middle eastern wars. Fat politicians helped industrialists line their pockets.

"Then the North American dustbowls started to expand. Farming areas in Nebraska, Montana and Wyoming became bleached and prairies land started to revert to desert.

He flicked again and some Dorothea Lange pictures from the 1930s were projected.

"There, you see, this wasn't even when the main trouble occurred, but the black blizzards of the 1930s were like a forerunner of what was to happen. Even the Farm Securities Association couldn't stop what happened. Farmers ploughed the prairie grass as part of their Manifest Destiny to live on the land. The replacement wheat didn't have deep roots and then with a drought the entire topsoil blew away - some of it as far as New York.

He showed a photograph of dust approaching Manhattan.

"The US provided new technologies, ironically borrowed from the oil industry, to send water around in major pipelines to re-irrigate some of the areas affected. They couldn't stem things completely, but they did enough to maintain food crops where they were important to national wellbeing.

By now Garvey had fired up a second sensewall. Now, one showed monochrome portraits of the people from the dustbowl, the other showed colour images of the desolate effect. There we are, 1930 monochrome and around a century later, digital colour."

"Shit. It's awful," said Sam.

"No, this isn't awful, this is a precursor," said Garvey.

"It wasn't just America that suffered. The countries closest to the equator had it the worst. The one-degree rise created new droughts and freshwater shortages on top of what was already a dangerously disease-ridden part of the world.

"Over in well-developed northern Europe they were aware of what was happening, certainly in terms of changing economic fortunes, but in the early years the milder winters and more dependable summers were seen as a bonus. The sentiment of 'If this is global warming, then I'm all for it' was frequently expressed.

"Of course, the so-called Spanish flu appeared around this time. A little know aspect is that it started in Kansas, in an army barracks. It was soldier migration to Europe, through Spain, that carried the virus across the Atlantic.

"Now we have the blend of climate change and virus attacks, simultaneously destroying the earth. The 1918 pandemic accounts for some 50 million deaths. Then, minor waves of epidemic and a further pandemic in the early 21st Century.

"Add to that internal combustion powered cars and goods vehicles and their side-effects. General economic wealth meant the increase in the use of dirty cars as well as of air conditioning. It managed the heat for living but merely dumped it back into the atmosphere, along with the extra power consumed and carbon dioxide created in the process.

"Scientists started to notice important changes. The Amazon dropped to a precipitously low level on part of its route. The Mississippi delta became alternately arid and then a major flood plain.

"In the same period, scientists quietly scrutinised the Arctic. The permafrost which had been frozen for thousands of years was thawing. Both poles saw temperature increases faster than the global average.

"This permafrost dissolved into mud and lakes,

consequently destabilising whole areas as the ground collapsed beneath buildings, roads and pipelines.

"Earlier seasonal snowmelt meant more summer heat went into the air and ground rather than into the act of melting snow, raising temperatures in a feedback loop effect. More dark shrubs and forest on formerly bleak tundra meant still more heat is absorbed by vegetation.

"At sea the pace was even faster. While snow-covered ice reflects more than 80% of the sun's heat, the darker ocean absorbs up to 95% of solar radiation.

"Once sea ice begins to melt the process becomes self-reinforcing. More ocean surface is revealed, absorbing solar heat, raising temperatures and making it unlikelier that ice will re-form next winter."

Garvey paused and let the sensewalls catch up. They were showing glacial thaws and wildlife trapped on breakaway floes.

"There was a year when 720,000 square kilometres of supposedly permanent ice disappeared, and this illustrated the rapidity of planetary change.

"That was Earth crossing a tipping point."

Garvey moved the sensewalls along and it now looked more like a disaster movie on the walls.

Cindy looked at Sam, "He's surrounding us."

Garvey pressed another button. Sub-woofers kicked in. A dull roar.

"Yes, the mountains, too, were starting to come apart. In

the Alps, most ground above 3,000 metres is stabilised by permafrost. In the summer of 2003, however, the melt zone climbed right up to 4,600 metres, higher than the summit of the Matterhorn and nearly as high as Mont Blanc. With the permafrost glue of millennia melting away, rocks showered down and 50 climbers died. These were still early warning signs, yet the summits held by politicians and businessmen in nearby Davos were oblivious to all of this.

"Ah yes, a Swedish girl spoke out but was ignored by big business," remembered Cindy.

Garvey continued, "As temperatures edged upwards, it wasn't just mountaineers who fled. Whole towns and villages were at risk.

"Then, at the opposite end of the scale, low-lying atoll countries such as the Maldives prepared for extinction as sea levels rose, and mainland coasts – in particular the eastern US and Gulf of Mexico, the Caribbean and Pacific islands and the Bay of Bengal – were hit by stronger and stronger hurricanes as the water warms.

"Another bell-weather was Hurricane Katrina which, in 2005, hit New Orleans with the combined impacts of earthquake and floods and was a nightmare precursor of what the future held.

"Most striking was seeing how people behaved once the veneer of civilisation had been torn away. From Katrina, most victims were poor and black, left to fend for themselves as the police either joined in the looting or deserted the area.

"Four days into the crisis, survivors were packed into the city's Superdome, living next to overflowing toilets and rotting bodies as gangs of young men with guns seized the only food and water available. The USA learnt, after Katrina, to put up tents and use refrigerated trucks to store bodies."

"Why was that?" someone behind Cindy asked.

"Stigma, purely stigma, so that an august building isn't associated with being a morgue," answered Garvey, "But it was still cosmetics for the politicians,"

"Perhaps the most memorable scene was a single military helicopter landing for just a few minutes, its crew flinging food parcels and water bottles out onto the ground before hurriedly taking off again as if from a war zone. This was Americans supporting other Americans."

"In scenes more like a Third World refugee camp than an American urban centre, young men fought for the water as pregnant women and the elderly looked on with nothing."

"It's what happens when people are desperate," Garvey paused and looked around. The auditorium was silent.

"I should add," said Garvey, "That there were some pandemics mixed in with all of this. New flu strains that adapted from earth mammals to be able to be hosted on humans. And what happened?"

Garvey paused to look around the auditorium.

He pressed a button and a new scene appeared on both sensewalls.

"Take a look," he said, "Long lines of people. Like in the Great Depression. But you know something?" he flipped the screen forward.

A small gasp from the auditorium.

"You may well gasp. These people are not queuing for food, nor for medical supplies. No. These people are queuing for guns," he announced.

"So, are you going to tell us about the Warming?" asked Cindy.

"Yes," Garvey continued, "Let's go through the stages. Starting with between one and two degrees of warming.

"At this level, the hot European summer became the annual norm. Anything that could be called a heatwave was of Saharan intensity. Even in average years, people died of heat stress.

"The first symptoms were minor. A person will feel slightly nauseous, dizzy and irritable. It needn't be an emergency: an hour or so lying down in a cooler area, sipping water, will cure it. But what if there were no cooler areas, especially for elderly people?"

Garvey continued, "Once body temperature reaches 41C (104F) its thermoregulatory system begins to break down. Sweating ceases and breathing becomes shallow and rapid. The pulse quickens, and the victim may lapse into a coma.

"Unless drastic measures are taken to reduce the body's core temperature, the brain is starved of oxygen and vital organs begin to fail. Death will be only minutes away unless the emergency services can quickly get the victim into intensive care.

"As early as summer 2003, in France, the emergency services failed to save more than 10,000 French people. Mortuaries ran out of space as hundreds of dead bodies were brought in each night.

"Across Europe as a whole, that precursor heatwave is believed to have cost between 22,000 and 35,000 lives.

"Agriculture, too, was devastated. Farmers lost $12 billions worth of crops, and Portugal alone suffered $12 billions of forest-fire damage. The flows of the River Po in Italy, Rhine in Germany and Loire in France all shrank to historic lows.

"Barges ran aground, and there was not enough water for irrigation and hydroelectricity. Melt rates in the Alps, where some glaciers lost 10% of their mass, were not just a record – they doubled the previous record of 1998.

"Extreme summers take a much heavier toll of human life. Crops will bake in the fields, and forests will die off and burn. Even so, the short-term effects may not be the worst:

"From the beech forests of northern Europe to the evergreen oaks of the Mediterranean, plant growth across the whole landmass in 2003 slowed and then stopped. Instead of absorbing carbon dioxide, the stressed plants began to emit it. Around half a billion tonnes of carbon was added to the atmosphere from European plants, equivalent to a twelfth of global emissions from fossil fuels.

"This was feedback of critical importance, because it suggested that, as temperatures rose, carbon emissions from forests and soils also rose. As many were saying, if these land-based emissions were sustained over long periods, global warming could spiral out of control.

"Was that when they stated to name it a climate emergency?" asked Sam.

"Yes, global warming was just a bit too friendly sounding," answered Professor Garvey, "By the time we get to the two-degree world, nobody would take Mediterranean holidays. The movement of people from northern Europe to the Mediterranean reversed, switching eventually into a mass scramble as Saharan heatwaves swept across the sea area known as the Mediterranean. People everywhere will think twice about moving to the coast.

"When temperatures were last between 1 and 2C higher than they were in the 20th Century some 125,000 years ago, sea levels were five or six metres higher too.

"All this 'lost' water was in the polar ice.

"The 'tipping point' for Greenland wasn't until average temperatures had risen by 2.7C. Greenland was also warming much faster than the rest of the world at 2.2 times the global average.

"Didn't the politicians rail against this?" asked Cindy.

"Not really," answered Garvey, "There were some protests, but many significant world leaders played the whole thing down. The American leadership didn't believe in climate emergency at all. They said it was 'Fake News'."

"What even with predictions and modelling?" asked Sam.

"Yes, it became fashionable for some of the really weak politicians to say they'd had enough from so-called experts, implying rather pompously that they were better than the scientists."

Garvey shook his head, "The ensuing sea-level rise was far more than the half-metre predicted for the end of the 20th Century. Some scientists pointed out that sea levels at the end of the last ice age shot up by a metre every 20 years for four centuries."

"It took the situation when Miami was set to flood and disappear, as was most of Manhattan. Central London, despite its river defences, flooded. That's when some of the political class started to pay attention. It was too late, of course."

"Like thermal runaway?" asked Sam.

"Kind of, like an exothermic reaction, where the heat from one stage accelerates the next stage, that's what happened, " answered Garvey, "Bangkok, Bombay and Shanghai lost most of their area. In all, half of humanity had to move to higher ground.

"Not only coastal communities suffered. As mountains lost their glaciers, so people lost their water supplies. The entire Indian subcontinent was fighting for survival. As the glaciers disappear from all but the highest peaks, their runoff ceased to power the massive rivers that delivered vital freshwater to hundreds of millions.

"Everywhere, ecosystems unravelled as species either migrated or fell out of sync with each other. You can see how the divisions on Earth were starting to form."

Garvey continued, "Of course, as we all know, it didn't stop there. Now let's look at what happened between two and three degrees of temperature increase."

"Assuming that governments had planned carefully and farmers converted to more appropriate crops, not too many people outside subtropical Africa need have starved.

"But beyond two degrees, mass starvation became a huge problem. Millions, then billions, of people faced an increasingly tough battle to survive.

"To find anything comparable we have to go back to the Pliocene Epoch – The last epoch of the Tertiary period, 3 million years ago."

"Wow, that is a long way back," said Sam.

"Not really, in geological terms, the Pliocene Epoch follows the Miocene Epoch and is followed by the Pleistocene Epoch - It is one of the more recent Epochs, actually." Answered Professor Garvey.

"There were no continental glaciers in the northern hemisphere and trees grew in the Arctic. Sea levels were 25 metres higher than today. In this kind of heat, the death of the Amazon was as inevitable as the melting of Greenland.

"The warmer seas absorbed less carbon dioxide, leaving more to accumulate in the atmosphere and intensify global warming. On land, matters were even worse. Huge amounts of carbon are stored in the soil, as the half-rotted remains of dead vegetation.

The soil carbon reservoir contains some 1600 gigatonnes,

more than double the entire carbon content of the atmosphere. But then as the soil warmed, bacteria accelerated the breakdown of this stored carbon, releasing it into the atmosphere.

"We are into 'end of the world' territory here," emphasised Garvey.

"The three-degree increase in global temperature threw the carbon cycle into reverse. Instead of absorbing carbon dioxide, vegetation and soils start to release it.

"So much carbon pours into the atmosphere that it pumped up atmospheric concentrations by 250 parts per million boosting global warming by another 1.5C.

"All soils were affected by the rising heat, but none as badly as the Amazon's.

"'Catastrophe' is almost too small a word for the loss of the rainforest. Its 7m square kilometres produced 10% of the world's entire photosynthetic output from plants. Drought and heat crippled it and then fire finished it off.

"Farming and food production tipped into decline. Salt water crept up the stricken rivers, poisoning ground water.

"Higher temperatures meant greater evaporation, further drying out vegetation and soils, and causing huge losses from reservoirs. The TV news shows featuring droughts became increasingly common.

"Grain yields declined by 10% for every degree of heat above 30C, and at 40C there was no more grain. The Indian subcontinent was choking on dust.

"All of human history shows that, given the choice between starving in-situ and moving, people move. Pakistan was one of the early failed states as civil administration collapsed and armed gangs seize what little food was left.

"To summarise, it was bleak, but this wasn't even the end of it."

Sam nodded towards Cindy, "I've seen a screendoc about some of those nation states like Pakistan and India, which were the seat of much unrest."

"Yes," and there was that movie 'The Flatlands' about the flooding Netherlands," replied Cindy.

"Something for all of us?" asked Garvey, looking towards Sam.

"We were talking about that movie, "The Flatlands", he answered.

"Ah yes," continued Garvey, "They got some things right in that screenplay.   As the land burned, so the sea will go on rising. They didn't depict the situation in other countries though, just lowland Europe.

"At the time it was happening, they could have featured New York, or even London. New York flooded and the eastern part of England also. There was also mass migration away from the stricken areas. It made the earlier populist debates about migrants seem ridiculous, although it allowed resurgent fascist parties to still win votes by promising to keep foreigners out."

"It didn't even stop there, did it?" asked someone behind Cindy.

The sense wall briefly cleared, then on one side a giant 3 appeared and on the other side a giant 4.

"Yes, you are now entering the era of between 3 and 4 degrees of warming," said Garvey.

"The stream of refugees which started when the lowlands flooded will now include those fleeing from coasts to safer interiors – millions when storms hit.

"Where they survived, coastal cities became fortified islands. This wasn't pretty though. The world economy was in tatters. A few fat cats had bet on the decline of businesses and made huge sums from shorting the markets. They picked high land to develop into prestigious dwellings, with a castle-like fortifications and walls around them.

"Direct losses, social instability and insurance pay-outs cascaded through the whole system, with funds to support displaced people increasingly scarce. Certain of the politicians were also dipping into the money to be made from the catastrophe. Building works, Infrastructure, Military and Medical Aid, not to mention shorting the equities in weakened companies. It was cynical, amoral feeding from the trough."

"The earth couldn't deal with the rate of change. The poles were melting, which projected a 50-metre rise in sea level. It didn't happen, and would take millennia to complete, but even the metre every 20 years that did occur was way too much for civilisation to handle.

"China was also on a collision course with the planet. As its people became richer and could consume at a rate similar to Americans, they were eating two-thirds of the entire global harvest and could burn through 100m barrels of oil a day, or 125% of the world's output.

"It was still worse because China's agricultural production also crashed, and it was left with the task of feeding 1.5bn much richer people on two thirds of current supplies.

"Air-conditioning was mandatory for anyone wanting to stay cool. This in turn put ever more stress on energy systems, which could pour more greenhouse gases into the air as coal and gas-fired power stations ramped up their output, hydroelectric sources dwindled, and renewables failed to take up the slack.

"I'm originally from England, which had problems of its own. As flood plains became more regularly inundated, there was a general retreat out of high-risk areas. Millions of people lost their lifetime investments in houses that become uninsurable and therefore unsaleable.

These last moves also saw the start of the thawing of permafrost. This was another capsule of doom. The permafrost contained much carbon dioxide, which could then accelerate the warming further.

Garvey waved the remote again. The sensewall graphics of 3 and 4 gave way to 4 and 5.

"We can understand the Earth Council being formed to try to make sense of what was happening. A problem was that right from the start it contained many vested interests. These were people from major corporations who saw the angle to try to gain control of a larger slice of the planet.

"They were presiding over the Earth as we now know it. An entirely different planet. Ice sheets have vanished from both poles; rainforests have burnt up and turned to desert; the dry and lifeless Alps resemble the High Atlas; rising seas are scouring deep into continental interiors.

"One temptation may be to shift populations from dry areas to the newly thawed regions of the far north, in Canada and Siberia. Even here, though, summers may be too hot for crops to be grown away from the coasts; and there is no guarantee that northern governments will admit southern refugees.

"Right now, Siberia and Canada are only one stop from war, with China ready to invade Siberia and the USA ready to grab Canada.

"Summer heatwaves scorched the vegetation out of continental Spain, leaving a desert terrain heavily eroded by winter rainstorms. Palm mangroves grew as far north as England and Belgium, and the Arctic Ocean was so warm that Mediterranean algae thrived.

"The total amount of carbon in the atmosphere during the Palaeocene-Eocene thermal maximum, or PETM, as scientists call it, was more than today's, but the rate of increase in we are seeing may be 30 times faster. It may well be the fastest increase the world has ever seen – faster even than the episodes that caused catastrophic mass extinctions.

"And we see globalism in the five-degree world breaking down into something more like parochialism. Customers will have nothing to buy because producers will have nothing to sell.

"Where no refuge is available, civil war and a collapse

into racial or communal conflict seemed the likely outcome. Isolated survivalism was as impracticable as dialling for room service. How many of us could really trap or kill enough game to feed a family?

"Even if large numbers of people did successfully manage to fan out into the countryside, wildlife populations would quickly dwindle under the pressure. Supporting a hunter-gatherer lifestyle takes 10 to 100 times the land per person that a settled agricultural community needs.

"A large-scale resort to survivalism would turn into a further disaster for biodiversity as hungry humans killed and ate anything that moved. Including, perhaps, each other.

"That's when the Zonal Laws were first proposed, and the power of the Earth Council extended. It should have been by county voting, but instead was declared a global emergency, so that everywhere could be incorporated.

"Of course, it met with huge resistance from some areas. Countries that had previously been power brokers, or countries that were doing okay, despite everything. It tipped into the Klima Wars, which started diplomatically a phony war, but then toppled into an actual war.

"To see the most recent climatic lookalike, we have to turn the geological clock back between 144m and 65m years, to the Cretaceous Period, which ended with the extinction of the dinosaurs.

"There was an even closer fit at the end of the Permian Age, 251m years ago, when global temperatures rose by six degrees, and 95% of species were wiped out.

"That episode was the worst ever endured by life on Earth, the closest the planet has come to ending up a dead and desolate rock in space.

Garvey looked around the auditorium," On land, the only winners were fungi that flourished on dying trees and shrubs. At sea there were only losers. Warm water is a killer. Less oxygen can dissolve, so conditions become stagnant and anoxic. Oxygen-breathing water-dwellers – all the higher forms of life from plankton to sharks – face suffocation. Warm water also expands, and sea levels rose by 20 metres." The resulting "super-hurricanes" hitting the coasts would have triggered flash floods that no living thing could have survived.

"That is small comfort, however, for beneath the oceans, another monster stirred – the same that would bring a devastating end to the Palaeocene nearly 200m years later, and that still lies in wait today. Methane hydrate.

"What happens when warming water releases pent-up gas from the seabed? First, a small disturbance drives a gas-saturated parcel of water upwards. As it rises, bubbles begin to appear, as dissolved gas fizzles out with reducing pressure – just as a bottle of lemonade overflows if the top is taken off too quickly. These bubbles make the parcel of water still more buoyant, accelerating its rise through the water. As it surges upwards, reaching explosive force, it drags surrounding water up with it. At the surface, water is shot hundreds of metres into the air as the released gas blasts into the atmosphere. Shockwaves propagate outwards in all directions, triggering more eruptions nearby.

Garvey pressed the remote again, the sensewalls changed. One showed a diagram of the gas-explosion. The second wall showed a real-world example, like a terrifically powerful geyser spouting water, but from within the sea.

"The eruption is more than just another positive feedback in the quickening process of global warming. Unlike CO2, methane is flammable. Even in air-methane concentrations as low as 5%, the mixture could ignite from lightning or some other spark and send fireballs tearing across the sky.

"The effect would be much like that of the fuel-air explosives used by the US and Russian armies – so-called "vacuum bombs" that ignite fuel droplets above a target.

According to the CIA, those near the ignition point are obliterated. Those at the fringes are likely to suffer many internal injuries, including burst eardrums, severe concussion, ruptured lungs and internal organs, and possibly blindness."

"But these last effects have not happened. Instead, we were able to reverse the trends through off-world discoveries. That's where all of you come in. To help us bring back the materials and the technologies that help us once again make the Earth self-sustaining."

"But what about the law of unintended consequences?" asked Sam.

"I get asked this every time I run this session," answered Garvey, "It would take a pretty bleak unintended consequence to be worse than a burnt, dead world filled with methane gas."

He looked around the auditorium. He was used to the ashen faces and exhausted looks of the attendees at this point.

"You'll need to go away and process all of this," he suggested,

" Try to find some up-sides. You are all going to help the recovery programme. The six-degree change can be reversed. We've found new technology that removes the need for carbon fossil fuels. There's a new form of lightweight, yet formidable material."

"You are all going to help find it, mine it and make new tech from it which can reverse what has been happening. We might be on an edge, but you are among the ones who can stop us from toppling over it."

Streamcom chimed

Both Cindy and Sam had been thinking back to their time at IPX. One thing, they agreed; it didn't prepare them for the command-based nature of life afterwards.

Interplanetary Expedition school had taught them about many things that the general public didn't know but hidden within it was the passive-aggressive command structure to which they were both linked.

The streamcom panel chimed.

Cindy pressed the accept button.

"Hi Cindy, Hi Sam, and how are you today?" asked Matson.

Matson was higher up the chain than Cindy and Sam and routinely they had little direct contact with him.

"Good morning," said Cindy.

"There's been something of a situation," said Matson.

"Since we changed to Version 6 of the control, we noticed some new anomalies. I'd like to talk it over with you both. I know we just added Version 7, but I'm expecting similar challenges. I'm thinking of forming a small team to investigate. Can you come over to the Block this morning? There'll be some other people for you to meet as well."

"Once the rest of the system is stable, we can come straight over," said Sam.

"Excellent, replied Matson, "I guess I'll see you in a couple of hours then?"

The streamcom screen went blank.

"I guess that's it," said Cindy.

Sam smiled, "Yeah- Command and Control; I think I was probably a little too eager," he chuckled.

He flipped a couple of switches and checked a status light.

"This is all fine," he said, "Come on; we might as well make a move."

They knew that when Matson referred to the Block, he wasn't talking causally about one of the housing blocks. No, he was referring to the Block, which was the central administration and command centre for New Delaware.

In the corner of the office was a glass lift shaft. It didn't go directly to the transit system and so they had to change at the mezzanine floor. Two other groups of couples were also waiting for transit to the Block.

"I guess these will be our company," suggested Sam. He looked at Cindy, then he looked at the two couples, although he did not recognise them from the complex.

A transit arrived. A soft wash as the doors opened, and they were soon on course for the Block. The other two couples had also taken seats in different areas and appeared to be making similar judgements about Sam and Cindy.

As the transit arrived at the Block's dock, all six of them prepared to exit.

"Hi guys," said Sam to the others, "Are you all here to see Matson too?"

"That's right," said one of the women, "We had a call about half an hour ago."

"Yes, he seems to be rounding us up for something," said Cindy. She looked towards first woman. A shock of pink hair cut straight across her forehead, with a chink around her left eye. A sharp chiselled chin, blue eyes and a small nose and mouth. She was wearing something that could be a sailor costume, powder blue dress with a vee-shaped collar and a white tie pulled loosely underneath the collar. Cindy thought she could be a teen-boy's image of a sexy avatar.

"I'm Cat, by the way," Cat looked towards her partner. He nodded. He looked older than Cat with shaggy dark hair, a bleached red tee-shirt with Reibu written across it and some Japanese writing underneath, canvas jacket and maroon trousers.

"Did you see anything unusual, based upon the reset?" asked Cat looking towards Cindy, "It would be good to know before we get in with Matson"

"Only that it seemed to take a very long time," said Sam, "Much longer than the calculated reset time."

"Yes, we noticed that with release six as well," said Cat, "But there is something else. Each time the reset occurs the location seems to drift sometimes as much as 5 km. In fact, each time the drift has increased."

"Are you sure it's not just the static based upon the large distances?" asked Sam.

"No, we've seen it too," said the man from the third couple, wearing a smart suit jacket over a dark hoodie, "My name is Lorenzo, and this is Francesca. We've also seen the drift and the timing changes. It's as if each reset is occurring from a different location. I can't work out why the delays increase, however," he looked towards his dark-haired partner, who was wearing tight fitting jeans and a loose-fitting top. Francesca nodded in agreement.

They were now approaching the entrance to the Block and prepared for the first level of security.

They would each have to go through biometric testing and identity comparisons with their individual implanted security tags.

There had been several situations where the tags had been removed from individuals and used illegally. At the Block the tests were very thorough to avoid any mistakes.

"Okay, we will scan you for terrestrial biology, then for no circuit implants, and compare you with the bio ident. It should only take a moment," said the security guard, smiling.

The Block had multiple entry lanes and each of them selected a separate lane and began the process.

It was very fast. The security guards themselves had circuit implants tailored to their work and could operate certain processes much faster than a full human.

Sam and Cindy knew these security people were often referred to with a negative nickname of Sleds; they were fully functional humans with a special adaptation for their role. It was usually people who had been selected after an accident or other injury which had left them impaired. The adaptation for this role usually included modifications to offset their injury. It was a type of insurance scheme that had become more commonplace since the earth terrain had become more hostile because of the climatic changes.

For Cindy and Sam, the idea of these security guards was part of their routine existence. At their own complex, there was a similar type of system for visitor access but because they were regulars the security guards could make the tests largely based upon the physical access cards and physical glance at each person as they entered the building.

Cindy and Sam also knew that these people could bring a very tough level of security blockage into play if there were any transgressors. That was where their nickname had emerged, from the Brits on the campus. They could sledge anyone who tried to break in or defeat the security systems.

In this case all six of the visitors to the block needed to go through the full protocol. Cindy hoped that if this worked the first time that they would then be given a speedier route in future. It certainly looked as if they would be making multiple visits to see Matson.

Around 10 minutes later they had all passed through the gates and were now in the main reception lobby of the block. They knew they would need to be escorted to see Matson and took seats in a small lounge area whilst they waited,

"It's a good chance for us to compare notes about what we all do," said Sam, "It looks as if we are all in a similar line of work."

"That's right," said Cat, "I've not seen you two before, but I've seen Lorenzo and Francesca around the complex. And yes, we monitor and revise the command packages being delivered to Ganymede."

"So, were any of you candidates for flights?" asked Sam, "We nearly made it but were dropped. We've visited Moon2, however, which was still quite a blast."

"It's the same with us," said Francesca, "We've also been to Moon2."

"And us," said Cat, "but no further. I was very ill during the orbits and we returned to Earth early, actually."

Sam noticed the small lapel pin that Lorenzo was wearing. It was like a small coloured disc with three small lines in colours on it. He quickly decoded its value. They were all supposed to wear them in the complex, if they were part of the elite teams. Most people didn't because it created a strange one-upmanship which could be counterproductive. The small disc provided an indication of intelligence based upon the complex metrics. Similar to the once revered intelligence quota but updated for the 22nd Century. It used coding from ancient Electronics to denote the values. Anyone in the know would be able to decode this quickly but for most other people it was just a small badge.

"I see you are wearing a circle-badge," said Sam to Lorenzo.

Lorenzo smiled, "It's a bit of a first," he said, "I put it on because we were coming here. I don't usually wear it. I guess you guys got them too?"

"Yes," said Cindy, "but honestly, if they need that kind of information, they'll have it from our idents."

A well-groomed man approached them.

"Hello," he said, "You are the group to visit Matson?"

"That's right," said Cat.

"Please follow me, "he said, "we are going to the 107th floor.

He led them to an elevator.

"This will take us to the 80th," he said, "Then we change to another system."

The door closed and they each felt their ears pop as the elevator rapidly accelerated and then came to a cushioned halt at the 80th floor.

"I will be handing you to my colleague here," said the man, "He will take you to the 107th floor.

"Yes, I'm afraid there are a few more formalities before we make the second part of the journey. Please could I ask you to step across into this room?"

He gestured politely, "Nothing to be worried about. It's all part of the security process for this building. Matson is one of the controllers and this whole area is rated as restricted."

Cindy

Cindy had been sponsored through college by Torus Industries. They had recognised from a very early age that she was extremely intelligent and well suited to the complex world of space engineering.

The whole concept of university studies had changed dramatically since the Klima War. Firstly, there were now far fewer people on the planet and secondly the nature of required skills had changed. For most people the choices were simply related to food production, energy production, climate management, infrastructure engineering, mining management associated with magnetite or space travel.

A major shift had been the reduction in the amount of leisure time compared with the 21st century.

Added to this were health scares as a consequence of new viruses appearing.

Cindy had originally studied to become a crew member on one of the space shuttles, without at the time knowing that it would be targeted towards Ganymede. It was a highly sought-after role and during the assessments it had become clear that she had a natural aptitude for complex pattern recognition, particularly when handling vast quantities of pre-analysed data.

Although this was useful in a space-jockey role, it was even more useful to have a role in the main control which would be centred on earth. It was during this time that she met Sam who had a similarly fast thought process associated with analytics.

There's had started as a purely working relationship, but they had gradually fallen in love over a period of their second year in the IPX.

When they had started, they had been given the usual introductory speeches and presentations and one of the Principals had even said that often people would find their life partners during their studies at the base. Neither Cindy nor Sam had believed this, but they seemed to have a natural affinity for one another .

During their third year of study they had moved in together and became a well-recognised couple around the base.

Never Underestimate Technology Drift

"Humanity is acquiring all the right technology for all the wrong reasons."

-R. Buckminster Fuller

Matson

Matson had risen through the ranks in the control centre. He was known as a bureaucrat and administrator rather than as a bright scientist. That's not to say he was in any way stupid; he had a fantastic eye for problem-solving within projects.

He could keep the operation of the continuously returning ships from Ganymede optimised so they would spend as little time as possible offloading their precious content.

There was also a need to have a very high-quality communication back to the moon orbiting Jupiter although this needed to compensate for the 34 minutes delay in transmission times in each direction. In effect, Matson had become good at pre-empting situations which may not be capable of being answered directly.

The return flights of each spacecraft took 3 years to reach Earth and the more recent ships included some manufacturing capabilities necessary as well as the magnetite materials. This meant that whereas the earlier return ships provided raw materials only, by now the ships were providing finished components ready to be assembled into new uses.

There was a curious technology drift; improved designs were being created on Ganymede but because they were being sent to new ships for fabrication it could be 3 to 4 years before the resultant products were available on Earth. Sometimes the raw materials brought back to allow faster development of newer technologies.

Matson had also noticed that sometimes the new designs from the spacecraft were already anticipating changes that were being suggested from Earth. It was as if the manufacturing facilities were pre-empting some Earth designs.

Cindy was used to the protracted communications with Jasmijn and Roelof. They were the counterparts of Cindy and Sam on Ganymede.

She was impressed at how well they operated, always professional, always available. She sometimes suspected they didn't really sleep.

Now they had received the telemetric from the recent abnormal events on Ganymede, Cindy was anxious to re-establish contact with Jasmijn and Roelof. As usual, they appeared quite unflappable.

"Hi Jasmijn," Cindy had sent a message, "Please update status from recent on Ganymede event. We detected irregularities following Release 7 introduction."

They had waited an hour for the response, Normally, if something minor occurred Jasmijn and Roelof would pre-empt a request from Earth by transmitting a status update, They would usually cross in mid space. It kept the message exchange times to around 35 minutes for routine matters.

On this occasion Cindy had to wait the full hour and then some. Eventually the message came.

"Hi - thank you for message. We have resumed normal operation following a disturbance on Ganymede. All systems now resuming normal operation. No ongoing abnormal conditions to report."

Cindy looked at the message feed. It was voice only. Most routine transmissions were also with video, so this one implied that there had been some gaps in getting all systems back to full operation.

Cindy decided to send a second request, "Please supply status before and after disruption."

She had never requested this before and knew it would be more complex for Jasmijn to prepare this response.

Sam and Cindy were surprised to be once more separated from the others. Although they had only just met them, they had expected that whatever came next would be done as one group.

Instead, Sam and Cindy had to face a further range of tests, this time as a couple.

The questions ranged from their background, the way they had first become members of the complex, their training regime and then some specific focus on their current work.

"This seems to be like some kind of interview," said Sam.

"Yes, other than they are not telling us what it's for," replied Cindy.

"You'll see, soon enough," said their main questioner. He had introduced himself as David, but both Cindy and Sam were unconvinced, considering it to be some kind of stage name.

They could see the small implants under both of his ears. They were powered transceivers, and could both instruct David about questions and also pass on their responses to anyone listening. They knew that David was a specialist like themselves, in his case with some adaptations for the role.

So do you know what this is about? Asked Cindy.

"My role is to ask you questions and validate your responses," said David, "After that I will take instruction and you should be able to see Matson."

As he spoke, they sensed that he had received new information.

"You are to go through to see Matson now," he said, "Please follow me."

They exited through another door and across to another elevator shaft. David pressed 107, then stepped out of the elevator. To Cindy and Sam's surprise, the elevator started a rapid descent.

They looked at one another. They had heard many stories about the Block, and so they should have expected something like this.

Within a minute they had passed ground level and were now seven levels below surface. From the elevator they had to step into a small pod which had seats for four people. It was on a lev-track and after the doors closed it started to accelerate.

Sam tried to estimate the distance. "I think it's around a couple of kilometres now," he said as the pod rapidly decelerated.

The new area looked more overtly fortified than the original building they had entered.   There were guards by the entrance to the underground building although they seemed to know about Cindy and Sam.

Despite guards there were also civilians by the entrance and one requested that Cindy and Sam follow them to meet Matson.

"Finally," said Cindy, "This is becoming quite a circus."

They entered a large arch-shaped room, which had wall displays projecting a review of outside as if they were on the highest floors of the building.

"Yes, it's a virtual top floor," said Matson. He was standing close to the entrance and shook each of them by the hand.

Matson was clean shaven and dressed in an immaculate blue-grey suit. He had insignia on the shoulders, but neither Sam nor Cindy recognised it.

"I'm sorry to have to put you through all of that," he said, "You are both very valued assets to our control centres and I'm sure you understand this is for your protection as much as anything else."

"Where are the others that came along with us?" asked Cindy.

"I'm afraid they did not make it through the selection processes after all," replied Matson, "I will explain in a moment, but we have returned them to the complex for now."

"Let's sit down. This will take a little while."

He gestured toward one of the walls and the external view changed to a display panel. "I'll use a few charts to help us," he said.

"Is this linked with our recent question about the recent updates?" asked Sam.

"Yes, it is," said Matson, "And the reason you are still in this process and the others have been removed is simply because you have made no errors during this, although the others have made some which could be damaging to the retrieval of magnetite."

"How do you mean?" asked Cindy.

"I will wind back," said Matson.

"As you know, the mining retrieval program is a huge endeavour and much of the fate of the Earth as we know it rests on its success. Because MRP is dealing with such huge distances and time gaps, we need to have specialist systems to coordinate everything. You two are linchpins in that process. Not you alone, of course, but there are others like you performing a similar function in other control complexes."

"We have built three sets of identical systems which monitor what is happening on Ganymede."

"I knew that was the case," said Cindy, "We are told about it as part of the training process. "

"And also, that each of the three control complexes is kept separate from one another. It's a vital part of the process to ensure that we have 'unpolluted' assessments from each source."

"Yes, each system has its own vote, usually all three say the same thing, occasionally one differs and then the other two are used as the basis until whatever has been identified in the third system has been corrected."

"That is normally the case," said Matson.

"But why are we involved in this?" asked Cindy, "we are only part of this process."

"That is right," said Matson, "There's a whole command chain around you and another building full of people and technology who combined to provide the analytics we use. On this occasion the area of inconsistency is yours. Very unusually, the voting system has been overridden. On this occasion the two votes were created by the teams in the other control centres and your vote was essentially different."

"Does this relate to the timings?" asked Cindy.

"As a matter of fact, it does," said Matson "Your analysis highlighted that there was a longer delay than usual in resetting the system. That was your only observation of change."

"Yes," said Cindy, "Although we have noticed the timing drift since release Six. I was planning to run an analysis of Five through to One, to see if the timing was also extended or extending."

"We think there is a genuine explanation," said Matson, "The timing has increased, and it is because of a new subsystem for statistical analysis. The longer gaps are because there is more information to process."

"The others said they had also found some kind of geographic drift," said Sam, "We hadn't noticed this, actually."

"Yes," said Matson, "That's the area where your vote has overridden their two votes - in the last analysis. We have cross checked the geographic placement and there is no difference at all. That in the case of both of the other teams they have made different and diverging errors which had created the anomaly."

"We have a backup team for our own work," said Cindy. "You called us away before we had time to cross-check with them."

"Yes," said Matson, "And both of the other teams also have backup teams. While you were travelling here, we have run analysis of all three sets of information from you as Primes and also the three backup teams."

"Only your sets of findings are correct. Both of the other teams have made errors, and in each case the error is consistent within their own teams."

"So, what happens now?" asked Cindy.

"We will be restoring the two other control centres using your images," said Matson, "You will stay in place in your team with your existing backup team. For the other two teams the backups will take over and unfortunately the current Primes are being reallocated to other duties."

"As sudden as that?" Commented Sam.

"Yes," said Matson, "You already know this is a very high-stake situation. The point of having people like yourselves in these roles is because you are classified as hyperintelligent and therefore able to think outside the normal processes that run in power computations via the computers."

"We've always been told that," said Cindy, "you don't need us very often, but when you do need us, you really need us."

"That is right," said Matson, "And that's why we have to make changes, to make tough decisions, about who takes these roles in the control complexes. "

"So how did you know to override two votes this time?" asked Cindy, " It could have been us being removed from the programme."

"Look, on the level with you," said Matson, "It is not just one situation here, there have been at least 10 anomalies from each of the other teams."

"What about us?" asked Sam.

"Just twice," said Matson, "The first was a long time ago. "As a matter of fact, you were the first of the three teams to make an error. Then no errors until one a few weeks ago. Since then, perfect. With the other teams there has been a progressive increase over the last two months. The last situation was part of a short run of four in the last three weeks. It's enough to create a major problem for us."

"Is that how we came into the roles?" asked Cindy, "When we were appointed, we had been acting as backup for the previous team. The difference is we were told they were being given launch priorities and moving out to Moon 2 and probably on to Ganymede itself."

"That's right," said Matson, "They did go to Moon 2. The change in schedules of the outbound fleets has meant that they are still candidates for Ganymede at this time."

"It really is up or out," said Sam.

"You could say that," said Matson. "You remember that you have some of the most prestigious roles in the complex."

"So, this is what will happen," said Matson, "Firstly I wanted to tell you about the situation. Then I wanted to explain about your counterparts in the other complexes. As you know, we deliberately keep you separated and the same will apply with the new replacements. It makes no difference to your relationships with your own backup team who I'm sure you know well."

"What you will need to know is that your own Prime images will now be used by the other teams as a starting point."

"After that, each team will be able to run its own way and it will only be when there are new voting situations that we must again crosscheck the outcomes."

"And does ours get reset too?" asked Sam.

"No," said Matson, "but with your rate of error being so low, it will be many years before you would reach 10. And by the way, 10 isn't a magic number here. What we've just experienced is a highly rapid increase in discrepancies from the other teams."

"Now, do you have any other questions for me? I'd like us all to get back to business as usual as soon as possible."

Cindy and Sam looked at one another. They had many questions, but knew it would be pointless to ask,

"No," said Sam, "I think we understand and as you say we should get back to help with the preparations for the new imaging."

Maps and pressed a small button on his desk. A well-dressed female appeared.

"Hello," she said, "You must be Cindy and Sam? Let me escort you back to the main lobby."

Green

As the door closed behind his recent visitors, Matson heard the control panel blip in front of him.

"They will have to be removed from the program," came a voice. It was Green, his commander.

"I can understand that you have kept the ones who know the least," continued Green, "I'm a little surprised that you did not remove them as well."

"I thought we had built a system that was robust enough to handle this," replied Matson.

"But I think the signs are now getting much more obvious. If two of our three Primes could identify discrepancies, then I don't think it will be long before we will need to find a way to repackage this."

"I agree," said Green, "At the moment this is more a matter of containment. How long would it be before you can rotate the last two out of their control positions?"

"We should really leave it for at least a month," said

Matson.

"Usually with only one team of Primes to be replaced we can act more quickly, but as this time we have needed to take out two of the Primes, it means it will take us longer to ensure that we have safe replacements."

"The whole point of making most of the systems autonomous was to guard against this kind of thing," said Green.

"I know," said Matson, "but it's because of that exact reason that we have to make such allowances. The whole point of the human factor in this is to help us detect out of condition situations. Our computer analytics are pretty well fool proof for all eventualities. It is the very essence of human nature that helps us identify the lapses that could be picked up by extraneous observations. "

"I would far prefer that these kinds of monitoring were handled through automation, but there still comes a point where real people must be included."

"I take it you have already made plans for the other two Prime teams?" asked Green.

"Yes, we will keep them separate. One team will be reassigned earth-side and the other team will be allocated to Moon or Moon 2 duties."

"Just as when Cindy and Sam's predecessors were moved away, we will ensure that the new teams have little opportunity for further interaction."

"Good," said Green, "I would like a report from you within a month confirming that all three of the previous Prime couples have been withdrawn and that their successors are fully operational."

The screen in Matson's office blanked. He knew he would need to act swiftly now to restore equilibrium.

Cindy and Sam knew that they should wait until they were away from the block before discussing what that just happened. They chatted amiably to the assistant who showed them back to ground floor lobby.

"It seems much easier to get back out, than it did getting in," said Cindy.

"I know," said the assistant, "I was here for three months before I could use the fast track entry. I used to have to add an extra 45 minutes at the start of each day. Getting out is much quicker and unless there is any form of lockdown."

"How often does that happen?" asked Cindy.

"Hardly ever," said the assistant, "Although we've had a couple in the last month. Someone said it is to keep us on our toes. Look, I can swipe you out from here, " she said, " Just cross that concourse and if you dropped off any items they will be waiting for you at that blue collection point.

"I think we're good to go," said Sam," We were asked to visit here at very short notice in any case."

Cindy and Sam walked back to the pod area.

"We should stop somewhere on our way back," said Sam, "Maybe grab a coffee. It'll give us a chance to chat."

Cindy nodded back, knowingly, "Yes," she said, "We pretty much used up the morning in any case."

Magnetomics, baby

Any sufficiently advanced technology is equivalent to magic.

- Arthur C. Clarke

Standing in the way of Control

Darnell had listened to the conversation between Green and Matson. Darnell lived permanently in the Block. He couldn't leave even if he wanted to.

His condition meant that he had to stay in the specially scrubbed air and pressurisation of his part of the facility. Darnell still had a memory of the Klima War. There were increasingly fewer of his generation left now. He'd been around during the latter stages of the climate change, when the old nation states had started to look for first economic, then political and finally military advantage as they saw their lands and populations being destroyed by the scale of tragedy on earth.

The climate change had brought about massive shifts in the topography of earth as certain areas became flooded and others became new arid deserts. It had started with tsunamis and dust storms but accelerated at a head spinning speed to a ferocious destruction of what had been a planetary population of 9 billion.

They'd already said that the food was running out, that viral diseases were prevailing, that insects were rising in numbers. It had felt like an almost biblical plague was sweeping across the whole planet.

The initial humanitarian response hadn't been able to keep up with the range of demands and soon the acronym 'TEZ' became commonplace as more areas were declared Total Exclusion Zones. This wasn't a modest threat. People would see the lands of TEZ and try to identify areas which would stand the highest change of being safe.

That was when the political boundaries started to become under pressure. Any areas predicted to have higher survivability became desirable developments.

It was when Darnell remembered the escalation of military power. In the early stages, military might won and boundaries changed. The warfare became more asymmetric to ensure the gains. Large areas perceived as safe were obliterated to ensure the free passage of people into the areas. Some of this didn't work as tactical nuclear devices were used inside battle zones.

Early signs of nuclear winter started to appear as clouds of radioactive dust drifted around creating new swathes of inhospitable terrain.

Politicians and militia realised they should change tack or else there would be no planet left to administer. The death toll was huge and the combination of climate, disease and the aftereffects of the tactical warfare combined to create huge swathes of uninhabitable planet. The effects spread to the sea, which had common sightings of huge shoals of decaying fish stock.

That was when the old and sluggish United Nations was taken over by new forces, anxious to prevent a total planetary extinction. The Earth Council had been covertly established, picking from several of the most powerful remaining nations and funded by several large corporations.

A pact was agreed, which included the need to stop the further cross contamination of the remaining planet. Rudimentary zones were agreed and sketched onto the globe. It would be divided into the new Northern hemisphere, which was generally the least affected and the southern hemisphere from below Tropic of Capricorn, Below the 24th parallel was largely ravaged beyond a comprehensible restoration point. This wiped-out part of South America, Southern Africa, all of New Zealand and the largest part of Australia.

Those involved in the pact, also contrived to create the equivalent of firebreaks between the still safe areas and the areas already overrun. It was a brutal decision, because in the contaminated areas the populations were effectively left to fend for themselves. In the non-contaminated areas, RPZs - rapid protection zones were established, and the populations were kept inside under a totalitarian control.

This was the period during which the stories about the habitable vs the uninhabitable parts of the Earth developed. People inside the safe zones came to accept they could stay put or risk going to an almost certain death outside.

Ragged areas at the boundaries of the safe areas developed and the communication corridors that were opened were all land based, rather than by flight. It kept the populations mainly within their own zones except for the needed military communication presence across the zones.

Darnell considered that the Earth was on permanent planetary lock-down, although most of its residents were accepting of the situation and the ones that didn't had moved to the less pleasant environments of the Scratch.

The combination of the Earth Council's Earth Restructuring, the Ganymede program and the use of magnetite power had created the Fifth Industrial revolution on Earth. After what had been the destructive period leading up to the restructuring by the Earth Council, there had been the era known as The Great Stability.

This had been the period when the full effects of magnetite power sources had allowed a remodelling of the areas designated for redevelopment by the Restructuring.

It has been stated that there could only be certain parts of the planet placed under redevelopment, and that citizens would need to stay within their mostly large zones. The Earth Council would not take responsibility for the areas outside of their jurisdiction, and these areas should be considered as hostile and uninhabitable.

'We must regard the Earth as if it is a foreign planet we have come to colonise' was the sentiment usually expressed. The developed zones were slowly increasing, although this was always from within a protective area delimited with huge horizontal air walls to provide protective screening.

The magnetite could create units of exceptional power which meant that compared with prior territorial design thinking, it was now much more possible to assist keep boundaries operational and to protect the enclosed citizens.

Darnell was one of the citizens who remembered the old ways. Freedom to travel around the globe, a messiness of transport systems, carbon-based fuels in common use. Access to air-borne radio transmission.

He also remembered the downsides of the famines, the disease and the political decline into warfare.

Much of the past's history was now only available with special access through systems in the Block.

The modus of the new Earth was about looking forward, there were too many bleak lessons in the past. The Carbon Age, as it became known, was about as distant in most people's knowledge as The Stone Age.

Civilisation would need to learn afresh, based upon the new underpinnings. Prior ways of thinking were considered disadvantageous and indicative of the spiral towards poverty and grief.

Darnell realised this was a two-edged sword. Some good parts meant increased survival for those that had made it to the new zones. For those that hadn't, it had already meant death. For those in the middle, it meant exile to the Scratch, a world without the material advantages of the Earth Council's dictatorial world, but with the added dimension of a freedom that most conventional citizens could not even imagine

Probe

The Ganymede program was already up and running before things became tough on Earth. A probe sent out in the early 21st century to examine comets had sent back some unexpected transmissions which had been the start of the process.

The original purpose of the probe had been to examine a comet's own surface, but there had been problems when it had landed bumpily, and its solar panels had shut down without sending a full transmission back to earth.

The subsequent path of the comet had caused the probe to intermittently restart and it had later transmitted information about the comet surface which provided a breakthrough for scientists on earth.

The material of the comet surface included magnetite, and it was found to have an interesting property which became the basis of a whole new discipline in science.

Magnetomics, emerged, the use of magnetic fields as a direct form of power.

Unlike terrestrial magnetism, the magnetite produced a significant and harnessable sectoral force if another oppositely polarised piece was place adjacent.

There had been plenty of experiments on the past to prove that perpetual motion wasn't possible, and the initial scepticism of sciences was well-placed.

This wasn't perpetual motion either. But unlike previous examples with magnetism, the magnetite produced an almost imperceptibly small reduction in its own mass through the time it was producing force.

It was harnessing the same kind of power as in a nuclear reactor, but without the huge negative side effects. The process became known as nano-fission and became the source of many new types of motor design. A modern-day pod transporter engine weighed around a couple of kilos. Part of this was the actual engine assembly and the last kilo was the power source, which was estimated to have a life in excess of 30 years, there was no recharging and the unit could be simply replaced with another power cell.

Unlike fissionable materials, there was no huge charge required to start the process and the degree of scaling of the energy output could easily be controlled using the second piece of magnetite. The two together formed a binary battery, with the distance between the two pieces providing the regulation for the degree of electrical power output.

The main challenges were the initial production of the two pieces, which required a precision 20 nanometre flat surface to work efficiently. An Earth technology, graphene, was used to fill the gap and separate the plates. By the time the plate gap reached 400 Nanometres, the unit would start to display visible colours, and this was usually used to determine the age of the device. Violet, Green and finally Red.

After Red, the unit would continue to work erratically, but needed to be re-surfaced.

Sam and Cindy approached the coffee shop. It was part of a franchise. They ordered two simple coffees, waited for them to be brewed, and then took a table outside. There was a screen to protect from sunshine and a misting system to keep the air cool. They sat in a corner close to the equipment used to run the misting system. It comprised a small pump unit and a water feed that was surprisingly noisy.

"This is probably the best table we can get," said Sam.

"I'm not sure what to make of it all," said Cindy, "Have we really screwed up or are they really giving us a continued role?"

"Hard to say," replied Sam, "what I think is our days in this function are numbered."

"I'm also not convinced about the errors," said Cindy, "It looked to me as if the other teams had come up with more findings than us?"

"You are spot on, we checked those readings carefully. I'm certain we had the right numbers."

"I'm going to run some further checks to see whether this is any justification for the apparent movement of the control centre. It surprises me that the teams can both independently find this effect. I can't help wondering whether we have just been less thorough with some of our analysis runs?"

"We also need to be careful," said Sam, "If we get called

back again, I'm sure it will be to move us out of the role."

"I agree," said Cindy, "Yet anybody else involved with this now would create talk about it in the centre itself. We are such a known reliable quantity."

"It's safe to assume there that our command centre and also our apartment are being monitored. We will need to keep conversations about this outside away from listening ears."

Rocks in the ice

Jasmijn was used to the operating conditions on Ganymede. The main purpose was extracting valuable minerals which could be routed back to Earth and everything else was really Secondary.

She considered that calling Ganymede a moon was something of an understatement. Ganymede was the largest satellite in Earth's solar system.

Larger than Mercury and Pluto, and three-quarters the size of Mars. If Ganymede had orbited the sun instead of orbiting Jupiter, it would easily be classified as a planet.

Like all Ganymede dwellers, Jasmijn knew the significance of this moon's geological discovery for Earth.

The moon had three main layers. There was a sphere of metallic iron at the centre - the core, which generated a magnetic field. Then a spherical shell of rock - the mantle - surrounding the core, and a spherical shell of mostly ice surrounding the rock shell and the core. The ice shell on the outside was very thick, maybe 800 km (500 miles) thick. The surface was the very top of the ice shell.

Everyone moonside could see that there was a rock in the ice near the surface.

Ganymede's magnetic field was also almost tangible when walking around in the corridors. Ganymede's magnetic fields were embedded inside Jupiter's massive magnetosphere. Jasmijn knew that she could tell which direction she was headed with her eyes closed, by some kind of magnetic interaction that affected her. Roelof had said he could feel the same effect.

Scientists had said it was this interaction of the magnetosphere with Jupiter that had created the magnetite. Roelof had another theory, which was that the moon had been hit by a passing comet and the debris was the source of the magnetite, now frozen into the moon's surface. Ganymede's icy shell had supported massive amounts of the same material for billions of years.

Back in the 20th Century, astronomers using the Hubble Space Telescope found evidence of a thin oxygen atmosphere on Ganymede. They knew that the atmosphere was far too thin to support life.

Then, in early 21st Century, scientists first discovered the irregular rock formation lumps beneath the icy surface of Ganymede.

When a space probe crashed onto an asteroid of a comet the discovery of the magnetite rock formations appeared to show the same material with its unique properties on

Ganymede.

Early 21st Century spacecraft images of Ganymede showed the moon had a complex geological history. Ganymede's surface contains mixture of two types of terrain. Forty percent of the surface of Ganymede is covered by highly cratered dark regions, and the remaining sixty percent is covered by a light grooved terrain, which forms intricate patterns across Ganymede, and which could be observed from deep space.

The distinctives grooves called 'sulcus' were formed by tensional faulting and the release of water from beneath the surface. Groove ridges as high as 700 m (2,000 feet) were seen and the grooves ran for thousands of kilometres across Ganymede's surface.

This was good news for those intent on harvesting the magnetite. It was mining where the required substance was almost jumping up from the surface.

Then, when Jasmijn was set to monitor the situation from moonside, she could see that the grooves had relatively few craters and probably developed at the expense of the darker crust.

The distinctive layers and colouring in the geology made it easy to identify where the layers of magnetite resided, and a series of new machines were designed for the extraction.

Jasmijn thought that the way Ganymede's infrastructure had evolved was like tugging itself up by its bootstraps.

The early chain of spacecraft arrived to set up the colonisation of the moon and then progressively developed further systems until it was possible to start extraction and then the return of minerals to planet Earth. By building factories on Ganymede, the initial heavy equipment, and alongside it a range of high-performance computer environments had also been supplied. These were useful channels back to earth but increasingly were used to augment and supplement the people operating on the moon's surface.

The basic principle was that there were various classes of operative. In the early days, the initial environment was worked by humans and then augmented by dedicated robotic machines such as the excavators and drilling rigs used as part of the extraction. This could be run from a central console area and reduced the impact of the extreme environment upon the humans providing the colonisation of the moon.

The initial chain of spacecraft included factory ships which could be used to create further on-moon environments. There was plenty of other raw material around including water and so it became natural to build new equipment on site once sufficient had been developed and shipped to start the process.

In the second wave of ships came the first of the android construction kits. These provided for a further intermediate type of operative which was a more flexible form of robotic being that could operate either in a humanoid form or in some cases as a simple embedded brain within other components.

This gave greater flexibility and also reduced the demands for new humans to need to make the lengthy trip to Ganymede. In effect the Ganymede population could be stabilised and added to by the use of the robotics.

This was also why for certain dedicated purposes some of the android forms were considerably faster than humans. They had in effect been optimised for the specific purpose above all others. Full humans became known somewhat ironically as 'The Sharps'.

Roelof was used to working with androids because this was also commonplace in certain Earth functions. On Ganymede it was a whole different proposition, to accelerate the mining and to minimise the number of births by Jupiter transits, the programme of android construction had been rapidly increased.

The general ratio was now around 10 humanoid androids to one human of Ganymede. If the embedded systems were added to this number, the ratio would be closer to 1 to 30. The embedded systems were harder to count because they could look like any piece of electronics on the base.

The tiering between the different types of system was generally that the human provided the main controls and regulation, the humanoid androids could operate in the field and the dedicated devices using the embedded systems could take on the most hostile environments.

This also created what was in effect a 24-hour economy. And actual day on Ganymede was much longer than a day on Earth. Ganymede took around just over seven days to make one rotation so a single Ganymedean day was approximately one Earth week in duration.

The machines didn't care, but for humans this was quite a dislocation. The earliest workforce were generally toughened engineers who really worked shifts and were on special bonuses to get everything running. Most of them worked hard until generally they burned out often before their second year had completed. The Russian booze hadn't helped.

As more of the operating classes arrived, the infrastructure had evolved to the stage where a range of virtualised environments could provide the equivalents of a civilised earth week with proper nights and days. People could go into a virtualised exterior environment as well and this included selectable city scenes and country scenes to provide more of a sense of reality instead of looking continuously at the bleak landscape of the Ganymede moon and the adjacent huge striated mass of Jupiter.

Ed Adams

Something's not quite right

I will go down with this ship
And I won't put my hands up and surrender
There will be no white flag above my door
I'm in love and always will be
And when we meet
Which I'm sure we will
All that was there
Will be there still
I'll let it pass
And hold my tongue
And you will think
That
I've
moved
on

Dido Armstrong

Quintessence

It was the start of a new day and Jasmijn and Roelof were reporting to the control centre. As they arrived, they noticed that the signage had been updated for the new release. They had started at release five and were now on release seven. Each time, as well as the system updates, there were new changes to the structure of the building.

The main entrance and lobby areas remained the same, but there were usually some new doors or corridors providing access to enhanced facilities. It also meant that there was a continuous state of building work occurring around the place, although the signs of this were very limited.

Since release four there had been an extension of the capabilities to provide a virtual living environment. This meant that some ambience around the building had been technologically enhanced. Just as Roelof could set his own apartment's weather to remain in April, the main building gave small clues as if it were part of a wider city environment. This was subtle and included sounds such as passing trains or aircraft and although it was not possible to see any of this, it added to a sense of place.

Roelof and Jasmijn both knew that outside of the buildings was the frozen surface of Ganymede and then the trails leading to the various mining locations. There were two types of mine. One was for the materials to be sent back to earth and comprised mainly the magnetite. The other mines worked to provide new raw materials which could be used within the factory environments on Ganymede.

The mining itself used a unique technique because most of the embedded rock that was required was close to the surface but underneath sheets of glacial ice. In some areas the ice was exceptionally deep, as far as 500 m to reach the rock. The surveys located materials much closer to the surface of the ice and it was these that were being mined using high-performance thermal mining equipment.

A spin-off from the project was that the reclaimed water from the ice was used to improve the quality of the atmosphere on Ganymede. It had originally been a very low oxygenated atmosphere, but since the mining work had started, there had been a positive improvement in the air available. The hydroponics had once been sheltered, but were now being taken outside, to see how well they could survive.

Ganymede's atmosphere was still not of a human breathable quality, but as most of the work was now being conducted by androids and embedded systems there was little need for humans to venture on to the surface.

The difference in gravity on Ganymede compared with Earth was significant. It was only some 14% of that of the Earth. Fortuitously this was a similar ratio to that on Earth's moon so there was already much experience operating in this range even with the same mass as on Earth. More human injuries were from forgetting to compensate for mass and inertia rather than sustained by weight.

As Roelof and Jasmijn walked back to the control complex with its new signage and even new security processes, they both thought that it felt like another fresh start. They would soon be back to their usual stations processing today's batch of mineral extraction. They seemed to be behind target for the day because of a shortfall on the preceding day.

"I think with this new release we can try to accelerate some of the refinement processes," observed Roelof.

Jasmijn agreed and commented that the extraction processes to the shipping processes seemed to have been optimised in this next software level.

"Yes, we are able to save further time getting things loaded," said Roelof, "Each time we get the new level, there seems to be a small improvement in this area."

"I'm not sure if we can completely catch up on the last day but we should be able to make substantial inroads," said Jasmijn.

She noticed the console message from Earth. They were requesting analytics to cover the period of disruption.

She checked the message from Earth. In particular the timestamp. It implied that the period of disruption had happened within the last earth day.

She checked the Ganymede log. There really wasn't anything serious to report. She'd package the last 48 hours into a transmission and forward it to Earth. She was not sure what they would get from it. A simple restart for the new release was about the only event. The start had run smoothly to the extent that there was almost no trace.

She processed that concept again. They really had a great control of the systems on Ganymede, An almost perfect operating environment.

She flinched as she realised, she was overthinking this. She'd never done this before.

Jasmijn felt the small glitch and mused. The march of progress and miniaturization had turned out to be about power; small not so much beautiful as pre-eminently dangerous. The best machines were made of sunshine; Sun Machines coming down - light and clean because they are nothing but signals, electromagnetic waves, a section of spectrum. And these machines are eminently portable particularly since magnetite. People are nowhere near so fluid, being both material and opaque.

The glitch ended, she clicked the control to dispatch the journal. It would take another 35 minutes to get to Earth.

Too perfect

Cindy was back at the apartment. The day had been cut short because of the visit to the Block. Their Secondaries had assumed duties on their behalf, and it was within protocol for the Secondaries to run unsupervised for a complete 24-hour cycle.

She looked briefly at the status display. The journal transmission from Ganymede had arrived. She called the control room.

"Can you send across the data?" she asked, "The Journal from Ganymede."

A few seconds later an alert sounded. The data was now available in her apartment system. She flipped to the start of the journal. It covered the two days, from before the new update, right through to a couple of hours ago. Roelof had sent what she requested, but as she looked at it, she realised it didn't look right.

Or actually, it looked too perfect. The rollover to the new release was shown and like previous releases, it had been a smooth transition. Not at all like the observed change from Earth. Not with the long delay she had witnessed on Earth.

She zeroed into the timeline. Nothing unusual there either. The point of update started around when she would have expected and finished a few minutes later. A clean restart followed, and then the system continued as previously, although showing the new software levels. The bundle sent from Ganymede included some still frames from the control room video. Mainly screen grabs, until she noticed a change around 5 hours after the transition. The control room looked slightly different. The screen grabs looked as she expected, but the layout of the room had a couple of changes. Sure, there were new devices, but that could be explained as routine maintenance. It was the size of the operations console, which was slightly larger. As were the screen displays. It looked in keeping with earlier configurations, except if the two images were placed side by side.

She clicked to save the screen grabs. If she had only seen the new setup, she wouldn't have noticed the difference. The latest level had changed the lighting, which was a more obvious change. So obvious that it would overwhelm anyone looking to the extent that they would not notice anything else.

Unless the two scenes were overlaid on one another.

Cindy decided to check the camera angle. Lens distortion, a different closed-circuit camera? She looked again. The camera serial number was the same. That was one more thing ruled out.

She knew that something was not quite right.

Cindy had put down her small bag when she walked into the room. Now she went to it to find her small notebook. She would dictate a list of her concerns.

As she flipped open the bag, she noticed something unexpected inside. An envelope.

Probably routine paperwork, but not something she would ever think of removing from the centre. She wondered how it had got there.

She flipped it open, slightly bemused about its content. There was a single electronic document inside. It looked like something was read only, but probably multiple pages.

She pressed the page to scroll through the document. Right at the top she noticed the heading. Complex 23. They were Complex 21. This was from one of the other teams they had met. She looked nervously around. She was not allowed to see documents from the other complexes. It was part of the safeguards of the system.

She had already noticed the two names are signatories on the document. They were Lorenzo and Francesca.

She switched the document off. She wondered if it was traceable. It did not make good sense to try to look at it within the apartment.

She went back outside to find a suitable location to read its content. She would also have to decide whether to tell Sam what she had discovered. Perhaps she would read the document first, then decide whether to involve him.

She casually placed the envelope back in her bag and walked to the door. She would go back to a safe place to read the document away from any surveillance.

She left her room and walk across to the elevator. A few seconds later she was in it with several other residents of her block. As she reached the ground level, two of the people in the elevator brushed past to hurry on their way.

Suddenly she realised that they had taken her bag. They had simply cut it from her shoulder. There was also a third person waiting in a pod and they simply passed the bag to that accomplice who made away.

Cindy had not had time to create a copy and now wondered whether this would serve any useful purpose. To her surprise, the other two people instead of running away turned to approach her.

One held out a small device. It was a communicator, but not like any that she had seen before.

"We will be in contact," said the man as he handed the device to Cindy, "Don't follow us and don't try to track us down. We are no threat to you but if you try to seek us you will be in danger."

She nodded. They turned and walked rapidly away. Cindy returned to her apartment. As she entered, she noticed her bag, with its broken strap, on a small table.

She looked inside. As far as she could tell only thing missing was that envelope and its content.

At that moment Sam appeared.

Cindy gestured with a finger across her lips. The universal signal for silence. Sam looked surprised but complied with the request. She waved her hand to show they should go out of the apartment. She scooped up the bag and both of them left.

"Not here," she said, "but I have something we should talk about."

Swapping Primes

Matson had decided the futures for the two Prime teams he needed to stand down. He faced the same dilemma as others in China and Russia. In each case, there had been similar scenarios, where some detection of the apparent shift of the Ganymede base had been identified.

The technology, computing and intellect to be able to make these predictions objectively was scarce, Matson knew that. He therefore knew that his teams of Primes were still valuable, but that they could not be left on the same processes, where they may discover more discrepancies which could ultimately become more than an embarrassment.

He also knew that he would need to exchange at least one team of his Primes with another site. This was part of the process to ensure that a critical mass of Prime expertise did not develop without supervision. By knowing one another, the Primes had already jeopardised this. It would be the same in China and Russia. His preference was to keep one of the existing teams on his own site and to move the other one to the Russians.

It would be a negotiation, because the Russians would also want to keep a team, and the Chinese and Russians would both probably want to swap with the United States.

He may need to apply some gentle leverage from Commander Green to get a desired outcome. He'd heard a rumour that the Russians had taken the unprecedented step of removing all three of their teams based upon a similar incident.

Each of the Prime teams was a special form of assignment. Sure, they did the analytics job that their role descriptions indicated. The second and unspoken part was their ability to detect unusual situations and to alert the chain of command about them. The key aspect of this was to determine if anyone was coming close to finding out about the true operational status of Ganymede.

Matson knew that two of his teams had come closer than anyone else to realising the truth about Ganymede. He also knew that three Russian teams had made contact with one another and extrapolated some findings.

Pod Bay

Cindy led Sam back to the cafe. It was the same one that they had used previously. They quickly ordered some coffees and moved to the same part of the cafe, where there was more ambient noise from the water conditioner.

"One of the other Prime groups has tried to contact us," said Cindy.

"They passed me an envelope which contained some measurements."

"So, what did they say?" asked Sam.

"I didn't look at them, I didn't want to be seen reading them in the apartment and so I left, but almost immediately someone stole my bag containing the envelope."

"How do they know you had it?" asked Sam.

"I don't know," said Cindy, "But the original envelope was given to me without my knowledge as well. I'm wondering if I have been watched."

"I'm sure it was from Lorenzo and Francesca. Without being able to cross check it I can't determine what it means."

"So, did you get a look at the person that stole it?

"No, not really," said Cindy, "Although two further things happened. Firstly, someone gave me this," She put her hand into her bag again and pulled out the small flat communicator.

"Wow!" said Sam, "that looks pretty ancient. It's some kind of vintage communicator."

"That's what I thought," said Cindy, "Look it has old battery indicators on it when you switch it on."

"He also said he would be in contact with us and that it was best to continue normally until that time,"

"Are you sure it's not a trap?" asked Sam.

"I wondered that too," said Cindy, "But I think if it had been, then they had a better opportunity to get to me alone earlier today "

"Oh yes, and the second thing, they took my whole bag but when I got back to the apartment, they had returned it except for the envelope. "

"Does that mean they had access to our apartment?" asked Sam.

"It does," said Cindy, "But I guess they used my keys from within my bag."

"Maybe there's something on the security system?" said Sam.

"Yes, however, I left the apartment with you before we had a chance to check." At that moment there was a sound like a faint bell ringing.

It was coming from the vintage communicator.

Cindy fumbled with it and switched it on.

"Hello," she said, "who are you?"

She could hear a very faint voice coming from the device. "

"You will need to hold it to your ear," explained the voice quietly.

"Ah," said Cindy, " It is vintage. Like an old telephone."

She moved the device to her ear and could now hear the voice far more clearly.

"Hi Cindy," said the voice, " I know you are with Sam at the moment. The reason we are using this old device is because it operates on frequencies that are no longer used for routine communications. It gives us an advantage in that we can talk without the risk of being monitored.

"We would like to meet you to discuss what we have found in the envelope. It is from two of your distant colleagues. Like you, they have identified some anomalies with the work on Ganymede. There are some major forces in play."

Cindy asked, "So how do you know about us, and how do you know about this? Have you been following me? Have you been listening to my conversations?"

"Only in so far as it is in your best interests," said the voice, "We don't want to snoop, but there are some things we will need to find out."

"You also said I was in danger?" said Cindy, "How do I know the danger isn't from you?"

"You're right," said the voice, "But the truth is we think you have discovered something, and we need to follow it up as a lead towards a bigger situation."

"But I thought you implied that we had made some mistakes?" said Cindy, "The other Primes have been taken away from their workplaces because they found similar anomalies but then extrapolated the wrong conclusions."

"Possibly," said the voice, "But we happen to think they are probably closer to what is happening than even you are."

Cindy looked towards Sam, "If you expect me to cooperate, I will want Sam to also be involved in the process."

"That's fine," said the voice, "We wanted you both."

"And what assurances do I have that if I talk to you further face-to-face, that it won't get me into other difficulties?"

"I can't give you any guarantees," said the voice, "But I think our approach so far has been trustworthy. As I said we want to understand what is happening on Ganymede."

"So where are you taking this conversation?" Asked Sam.

There was no reply from the voice.

Cindy repeated the question, "Where are you taking this?"

"Sam, you need to remember that this is an old communicator, and it limits the voice sensitivity unless you are very close to its microphone.

"We want to meet with you, and also to show you some things about Ganymede. There is some risk so we will need to take precautions in how we meet you. Also, because we are taking you to one of our bases, we must be careful that you are not followed."

"Just a moment," said Cindy, "I need to check with Sam about this."

"They want us to go somewhere with them," she said to Sam, "They say they want to tell us something about what is happening and why they have taken the information about the ship."

There was a pause whilst Sam considered this.

"Okay, let's say we go with you," he said. He gestured to Cindy to pass him the communicator and repeated his message again.

"Let's say we go with you; will we meet somewhere fairly close to here and how we know you're not putting us into danger?"

"All I can say is that I think you will be in less danger by working with us than if you try to continue as if nothing had happened. It's very likely that the two other Prime teams will be reallocated to distant places just like your predecessors were. It's also likely that you would be next for this kind of reallocation. For example, have you tried to contact your predecessors? I think you'll find they are non-responsive."

Sam nodded. He had tried several times to contact his old team leader, but to no avail. He knew that Cindy also tried to contact her colleagues.

The voice continued, "Look, my name is Sven. Sven Mallinson. I'd like you to meet me now so that we can continue this conversation."

"Okay," said Sam, "If we agree how would we do this?

"I can get a pod to you where you are," said Sven, "It will be unmanned but can bring you to a safe location where we can talk."

"It really is in your best interests," he added, "And look, we already have the information from the other Primes.

I can walk away from this now and leave you to run with this alone. Working with me and the others you stand a better chance."

Sam looked at Cindy, "They want us to go with them now for a meeting. They are prepared to send us a pod to take us there."

Cindy nodded, "There seems to be more downside for us if we don't follow this."

Sam spoke back to the communicator, "Okay, I guess you know where we are right now, send your pod and we will come to meet you."

"Look over to the left," said Sven, "You see the pod bays. The pod flashing, XTZ564 is yours. Just get in and it will bring you to us. And bring this communicator with you."

Sam gestured to Cindy. He stood and walked towards the pod bays. He saw the pod that Sven had referred to and moved towards it. The communicator acted as a digital key and the door opened as he approached. Cindy and Sam climbed in. Quietly the pod door closed, and the pod manoeuvred into a transit lane. A few seconds later they were speeding towards north New Delaware, towards the boundary zone that separated the space zone from the rest of the United States.

New Delaware border

The pod continued towards the New Delaware border. Both Cindy and Sam had top EPASS clearance and could easily transit in and out of New Delaware.

The pod had blanked its windows at the start of the journey, when they were travelling fast, but now they had slowed right down, and the glass cleared. They both looked out.

"It's horrible," said Cindy, "It really looks like some kind of Armageddon."

"Yeah, and the pod has slowed right down to traverse this area," answered Sam.

They could see industrial rubble as far as the eye could see. Some tall posts rose through the rubble and atop them were video surveillance systems. A few drones hovered over the landscape, which looked arid and hot.

They passed several gantries with cameras pointing inside of the pod.

"I see, they have partly slowed down to scan us incoming," said Sam.

"So, it's not just to depress us, then?" replied Cindy.

Razor wire had been draped around and there were several laser-triggered alert systems.

"We are most definitely heading for the Scratch," said Cindy.

"Yes, that makes sense," said Sam, "It's a good place for someone to hide."

The Scratch was a zone just outside of the New Delaware boundaries. It extended for around 10 km in a ragged line around most of the exit points from New Delaware. Like the ramshackle towns that had developed beyond many areas of military installation, the Scratch population centres were at the gates exiting from New Delaware."

Right at the border there were many layers of security to stop people from getting into New Delaware. Just outside of this was the zone where many people had tried to get in but had then stopped and instead tried to make an opportunistic living around the borders."

The area had become known as the Scratch. It was thought the name came from the phrase 'To scratch a living'. This close to the border was a rough area and didn't have many people passing through unless they were bound in or out of New Delaware. Nowadays it was a label on a ramshackle microclimate filled with rough necks looking for ways to make a turn on what was happening inside the space zone.

Uniformed new Delaware residents were usually safe because everyone knew that they had full identity tracking and anyone interfering with them would be traceable very rapidly.

The New Delaware Security Force would swoop into the Scratch at the first sign of trouble impacting New Delaware residents and bring the full force of their law to bear.

This almost 'take no prisoners' policy meant that the Scratch residents would keep a distance from New Delaware residents. The same didn't apply to those from the rest of the United States who passed through the Scratch. The NDSF security forces also didn't pay much attention to anything affecting United States residents entering the Scratch. The assumption was that these people would only go forward knowingly.

It suited the New Delaware Security Forces to have this buffer zone because it acted as a form of insulation for the Space Zone. On this occasion the same area would provide suitable camouflage cover for Sven when he planned to meet with Cindy and Sam.

PART TWO

Lies Algorithms or Statistics?

Democracy is an abuse of statistics.

<u>Jorge Luis Borges</u>

Sven

Sam noticed that the pod had progressively dimmed its windows during this latter part of the journey. This has happened faster than the change in daylight, but he was aware that now the pod had also put up its protective shields across its windows.

He could also feel very slight vibration from the pod on the last part of the journey. The pods were self-levelling but on extreme terrain it was possible to sense that there was an un-made route being used.

"We've left the main transit route," said Sam to Cindy.

"Yes, yes, I know," said Cindy nervously, "We are going deeper into the Scratch."

"With the screens down blanking us, it's almost impossible for us to estimate how far we've travelled inside this area," said Sam.

On the main transit routes the pod could travel at

several hundred kilometres per hour but on an unmade route through a rough area the speed would be much slower in some cases not much faster than walking pace.

Suddenly there was a click and the door on Cindy's side of the pod started to clear. A light appeared, and then the door swung overhead as the pod settled into a docking bay.

"Amber conditions," said the pod. Cindy had never heard a pod give out a warning before. It was usually the unspoken Green condition, but could go all the way to red.

"Pod explain," she asked.

"Amber condition, uncharted territory, zone alert for outside of New Delaware. Repeat. Uncharted territory, zone alert for outside of New Delaware."

"Okay," said Sam, "I'll go first."

He climbed past Cindy and out of the pod. It was a clean and modern complex; not like he was expecting from within the Scratch.

He gestured for Cindy to get out of the pod.

"Not what I was expecting," she said, "This is looking vastly different from most of this area."

"Hello," said a voice, "I'm Sven. Thank you for coming along. This way if you don't mind."

He gestured for them to follow him into a well-lit lobby.

"We are underneath the Scratch," he said, "This is one of our facilities."

"Who are you?" asked Sam, "And how do you fund all of this?"

"We are, how shall I say, a non-governmental not-for-profit organisation. Our funding is provided by the mining consortium. Let me explain."

He led them from the lobby into a conference facility. That was a long oval table right in the middle of the room and a set of stylish office chairs around the table.

Sven gestured for them to sit down. Cindy glowered across to Sven.

"Look - I don't know what you are playing at," said Cindy, looking angrily towards Sven, "Mr polite now, but you've a nerve, first stealing my bag, then breaking into my apartment."

"I don't think you know how much danger you were in by holding that notepad from the other Primes," said Sven.

"Look, the material in the notepad had been backed to the Cloud, so it was available to the security services," answered Cindy

"Sometimes there is still a place for paper," said Sven

Sven flicked on a screen in the room. A display light lit above their heads. Sam and Cindy looked at it quizzically.

"Yes, the projector is another piece of vintage technology," said Sven, "The advantage is that it is not interconnected, it is completely outside of the Mesh."

"That was the same with the communicator," said Sam.

"Yes, we are using older technology to bypass the modern surveillance mechanisms. That communicator is actually digital but point to point with a very limited range."

Sven continued, "This projector is stand alone. We are inside our own self-contained world here, not linked into the main Mesh."

He flicked through a couple of screens to the first page of what had been on the notepad.

"We've had to destroy the original pad after we had offloaded its content," he said.

"It was fully traceable, so we pulled the data out whilst we were still in the Scratch," said Sven, "I used a Cuban-Chinese lo-jack specialist to do it. She's very dependable. We still mustn't plug this back into the Mesh anywhere, because the data probably contains a self-seek algorithm and will send out messages saying, 'find me', "

"That's how you tracked it to me in the first place?" asked Cindy.

"Yes, we were just ahead of the Agency, which were cleaning up loose ends from the Primes identification of Ganymede activity. I don't think you'll be seeing the other two Prime teams again and I suspect your own days in that role are numbered," answered Sven.

"We only met them for the first time today," said Cindy, "We knew they existed, but, as you know we are supposed to operate self-contained."

"Yes, so if I show you this you've been 'contaminated' in any case," said Sven.

"We are past that point already," said Cindy, "I did have a quick scan at the notepad when I was in the apartment. I could tell it was linked to the Ganymede situation."

"Okay," said Sam, "Show us the material. Get to the point. I want to know what we have got ourselves into."

Sven waggled a small pointer, and the screen lit up again.

"Here we go. See, it's some observations about Ganymede. Each time there's an update its time duration increases.

"Yes, we'd seen that," said Cindy, "That was what we reported. It wasn't much for the first couple of levels before we started, but it has increased each time through 5, 6 and the new 7. The amount of increase is much greater than the payload software changes suggests. My own calculations that it would be an hour of latitude at most. It is more like 3 hours excess."

"Yes, that's what the other Primes are saying in this analysis. But look, there's something else."

He flicked to the next page.

"See, the location data is also changing?"

"Let me take a look," said Cindy, "No, I think that is drift. We are dealing with interplanetary distances. You get an effect from gravity bending, from relativity, it's all in the mix. The calculations are over simplistic."

"Yes, this just looks like noise in the calculations," said Sam.

"Well, let's look a bit further then," said Sven. He flicked to the next page.

Cindy gasped. The typeface had changed. The screen was now packed with calculus.

"Nah," said Sam, "Its q-calc. Quantum Calculus. It looks good, but I'm not sure what it is supposed to be saying. We can easily show the relationship of quantum calculus to Planck's constant and avoid the need for conjuring tricks."

Cindy looked at Sam, "Yes, but look. They've used it to run Lie Algebra."

She gestured towards a white wall in the room. "Pen?" Sven handed her one.

Cindy drew a circle.

"Lie uses vector reductions to zero in on a point. Imagine a bicycle wheel with so many long spokes cutting across the circumference. Add enough and there will be a circular hole in the centre. Make the spokes longer and the hole gets smaller, similar to a camera lens aperture control. It's a way of zero-ing in.

"That's how Lie works . It's a kind of infinitely small

calculations to gain accuracy."

Cindy drew a web of lines across the circle.

"The lines are a kind of spiral of vectors to zero in on a value. It's about connectedness and finding the centre. Sure, it can make some pretty patterns, but I can see what they have been doing here. They've used the math from the quantum calculus to feed the Lie algebra and then made the corrections to determine an accurate centre. To prove the location's exact co-ordinates. Like the aperture on a camera getting smaller and smaller as it seeks the centre of the lens.

Cindy continued, "We've never tried this. We've always worked with the usual gravitational lensing from general relativity to define the point of origin of the far moon."

She drew another diagram.

"Yes, Space Physics 101. The ten-pin bowling ball suspended on a sheet."

She showed the bowling ball make the sheet dip in the middle.

"Creating a three-dimensional distortion of the view, varying with distance from the object."

Sam added, "Yes, and something in the background can change how the foreground appears. There are examples of it all over the sky. False images of galaxies created by this lens distortion. Space isn't flat."

Sam screwed up his face, "But Jupiter and its moons are

near enough for this to not be a significant factor when we are running the numbers."

Sven interrupted, "This is the work of two of the Primes. I'm asking you to at least examine it for accuracy."

Cindy continued, "I can see that they were just trying to account for the lengthening delays in rebooting the systems. There would need to be something to explain what had been happening. The Lie algebra is a way to refine the normal calculations, but for this problem it would take some time to run. It's also loaded in as a negative hypothesis - like presumed guilty."

Sven, "My pragmatism says we need to find out if there's something untoward happening out at Ganymede. We may get transmission in half an hour, but it'd take us three years to travel there to shine some torches around."

Sam mused, "It's also a strange thing to do. I could understand it if there was some other huge object in the field that would create distortions and create false positioning."

Cindy added, "Or that there really is a difference in the object's location,"

Sven said, "Yes, notwithstanding all this complicated mathematics, I'm all for the simplest explanation being the best."

"Just like that olden-days monk, William of Ockham?" said Sam smiling.

"Case in point, said Cindy, "First the philosophers think planets go around the earth. Ptolemaic.

"Then Copernicus straightens the thinking and says the earth goes around the sun - with a few kinks."

"Then Kepler gets rid of the epicyclic corrections of Copernicus, by saying the orbits were ellipses. Simpler answers each time, building on the prior simplification."

Sam asked, "Okay then, so is Jupiter's moon Ganymede wobbling?"

Cindy replied, "Possibly. Unlikely though. We'd have picked that up on comms with the phasing of the return comms. The intervals would be Doppler shifted, like bad radio."

"The only other explanation would be that the source point was changing," answered Sam.

"Yes, like the base has moved after each update. It seems to stay constant at its new location until the next update?" suggested Sven.

Cindy replied, "That's what I'm thinking, weird as it may seem. We need to run numbers to figure that out. It looks as if the other Primes were already going along that path."

Sven interrupted, "Look, I can see you are thinking about this now. We've some other computers here that could help you. I should warn you that they are not the latest models and they are not linked into the Mesh. We want to keep this whole facility offline."

"That'll mean we only have the data from the notepad and our raw calculus skills?" asked Sam.

"Not quite," said Sven, "I can also provide you with some other data we've collected over the last few months. Our library has extensive algorithms too, which should help you cook up some of the clever mathematics. We've pulled the data and reference from the comms system and then had it purified by our friend in the Scratch, I can also introduce you to some further scientists who have been recruited into our cause."

Sam looked at Sven, "Yes, he said, you haven't really explained that part. What, exactly, is your cause?"

Sven continued, "It is not a cause exactly."

"We are simply trying to find out what has happened to our friends and colleagues.

"I'm going to tell you something that will commit you to this.

"I'm one of the Primes. From Release 3.

"I'm one of the few Primes who can still be located after a refresh cycle. The others have disappeared. That's not all. The same has happened to the crews that were sent to Ganymede.

"Not true," said Sam, "We've seen the homecomings from several of the waves. Big parties, medals, ceremonies. All of that stuff."

"Yes, all of that stuff run in EHD on telecasts around the world. All of that staged to create the best lasting impressions."

"Are you saying it's not real?" asked Cindy, "The scale of it looked real to me. Like the orbiters returning. The light shows from the Moon and Moon 2."

"We've seen the traces on the Astroscopes of inbound and outbound ships," added Sam.

"Correct," said Sven, "The outbound were the first crews and supplies. The inbound started with a small number of crew, but quickly became the recovered materials. I guess you've never actually been into the recovery areas of New Delaware spaceport?"

"Well, we have actually, to the gallery areas," answered Sam.

"Exactly," said Sven. "It is all stage managed there. Like the Astroscope imaging and the return events for crews. Let me show you something."

He flicked another screen on.

"This is the return trip of Wave 3. Amazing isn't it? It cuts into the middle of a disembarkation sequence from the Wave 3 return. Smiling faces as well turned out crew members were being re-united with families."

"Hold that thought," said Sven.

"Here's Wave 4. Different scenes, a far superior looking return ship, better uniforms on the crew but still scenes of re-unification."

"And now Wave 5. Even sleeker space craft. Similar

uniforms to the prior returning wave and equally jubilant scenes of families being reunited."

"...And your point?" asked Cindy, "I remember this. Back for Waves 3 and 4 there was an almost global viewing figure for the return."

"Yes, it became less as the missions become more routine."

"...Curiously routine," said Sven, "Let's look again."

He ran the first sequence again, pausing it part way through. Then on another wall, he projected the second sequence. Again, pausing it.

"Notice anything?" He asked. He pointed to the screen.

"See that face? And that one? Oh, and that one? Good in EHD aren't they? So good that they can also be seen in this return?"

He gestured to the second screen. The same faces were apparent.

Sam commented, "Yes, siblings on different crews? I know what you're going to do,"

Sven clicked a third screen. Freeze frame from the third return flight.

"Yes, it is some of the same faces again.

Sam asked, "Why would this be? The shipments of materials are regularly arriving. It is obvious from the way that we have been incorporating them into the earth infrastructure to manage the environment.

Sven answered, "Correct. The materials are arriving. Just not the people. Although some of the first crews returned, there doesn't appear to be anyone coming back since that time. In other words, the first crews made the eleven-year return trip, but since that time there seems to be a replay of the same people returning.

Cindy interrupted, "That doesn't make sense. The ships are coming back, the magnetite. We are sending replacement crews out."

"Why would they fake the return trips?" asked Sam.

"Keeping the situation secret. Maybe they think the material is more important. But what also happens to the rest of the relatives of return crews here on Earth?

"Exactly," said Sven.

"Conspiracy alert," said Cindy.

"That's what we think," said Sven. "There's a couple of possibilities. Certainly, the first crew returned. You'll see that the ships have changed since the earliest voyages. They are much more like freighters now."

"There's been a massive change in their form factor," agreed Sam.

"Exactly, and also for the requisite internal infrastructure. Early ships contained over half the space for the maintenance of crew. Oxygen, Water, Hydroponics, general life support. We think that the later ships have been designed to maximise the earth-bound payload."

Cindy said, "So you are saying the return crews are a sham. And the returning two-year shift-workers. Where's the real returning people then? Still on Ganymede?"

Sven continued, "We don't know, but we suspect a cover up. Our guess? Something happened to the second ship on its return tip. Maybe it burned up? Maybe it ran out of life support. Whatever it was, it was sufficient to change the thinking."

"There's also the android factories now in use on Ganymede," added Cindy, "They can deliver some of the functions."

"Yes," said Sven, "We think they have been extending their use. Some of the people at the Block will know this more precisely, but it is mostly being kept well hidden."

Sam spoke, "Okay, so they send the waves of ships out, more of the crews stay on Ganymede and they boost the return freight. It is in poor taste for those sent out, but if there had been a burn up, then it is understandable. After all, the payload has been about saving the rest of Earth from burn-up."

"Kind of. Take a look at the rest of the calculations from the Primes"

Shrive flicked another page on the screen. This was from the notepad.

"Here we are, " said Sven, "Logistics. It shows the projections of people leaving Earth bound for Ganymede. It also shows the start of the Ganymede android development programme."

"I see," said Cindy, "There's a tapering away of the crews from earth as the number of androids increases."

"Yes," said Sven, "But crews were still leaving for Ganymede after the early problems."

"Speculated problems," corrected Sam.

"Yes, speculated burn up of the second return wave," added Sven, "If that is what happened, then they could have stopped the outbound trips after Wave Three."

"But that wouldn't have been enough to reach the critical mass on Ganymede?" Suggested Cindy.

"That's right, they needed to get at least the first four waves of ships out to Ganymede to build the infrastructure and the hydroponics and so-on. After that, the Ganymedean surface was starting to become self-sufficient for the construction of buildings, infrastructure as well as mining," answered Sven.

"And using the small power cells developed from the magnetite, they could also create lighter ships for the return journey," added Cindy.

"Yes, lighter ships that only needed to carry the earthbound payload extracted from Ganymede. No more return people flights, with their messy life-support needs," said Sam.

"Okay so you've pieced this together, said Cindy, "And now you have told us, we become implicated in the scheme. What is it you want?"

Creating Proof points

Sven answered, "Short term, I'd like you to go back to working as if nothing has changed. It will only be for the next few days. We need to gather further data points to corroborate the findings from the other Prime team.

"At a practical level, we are also approaching another country to gather information. The most likely is the work that the Russians have done Earth-side. They seem to have been caught up in a similar replacement programme to the one currently running in the USA and have probably figured out the same things."

"We don't have any contact with the Russians, Japanese or Chinese," said Cindy, "It's part of the protocol that we operate self-contained. You know this if you've been a Prime in the past."

"Yes, I think I am one of the few remaining Primes. Only

because I have gone off grid," said Sven, "I moved outside of the system as soon as I was removed from the original role. They wanted me to go to Moon2, which is what they say to most of the ex-Primes nowadays."

"I said I'd get ready for the trip but then came across to the Scratch. I'd made quite a lot of money as a Prime and offloaded all of it as digicash which I took into Scratch. I've distributed it across several systems, as a way to survive. A few of the rest of my crew did the same, although I think we were the only team to manage this, since that point, the 'go to Moon2' process has become the standard formula."

"We also realised that if we stayed low and didn't create any new embarrassments for them, they would eventually tire of looking for us. That's exactly what happened. By the time the next Wave returned, there was a wide range of other distractions to worry about."

Sam looked anxiously around the coffee shop.

"The guy in the corner is still looking at us," he said. "He's been watching us since we arrived. Just talking to you, Sven, is making me paranoid."

Sven smiled for the first time.

"He's one of us," he answered, "See, you are getting good at this. He's here to keep an eye on the whole location while we are meeting."

"So, will you introduce us?" asked Cindy.

"No," said Sven, "At the moment it's better that you know as few of us as possible. We can change that once we are further along the road."

"Understood," said Sam.

"I'll get this," said Sven. He stood. Cindy and Sam took this as their sign to leave.

"Here," said Sven. He handed Cindy another communicator. A different kind to the last one. Chinese.

"Wow," said Cindy, "This looks even older."

"Welcome to my sometimes-analogue world," said Sven, "When I need to contact you again it will be on this device. See that little light? If you're not there when I try to call you it will go red. I will then call you back at three hourly intervals until we make contact. Otherwise please don't try to reach me or talk about me."

"Okay," said Sam.

"Take care," said Cindy. They walked towards the exit.

"What do you make of all this?" asked Cindy.

"I think Sven is genuine," replied Sam, "Otherwise this all seems a very elaborate way to get some information from us."

"It also looks to me as if the other Primes have got further with this than us," said Cindy, "I really want us to run those calculations again, though, although I can't really understand why there would be a drift in the position of the base when the new levels are transmitted from Ganymede."

"Yes, it's not as if the moon is off axis or wobbling," replied Sam.

"What do you think about us going back to the mall or the main complex?" asked Cindy.

"I know," said Sam, "It's probably a bad idea. I think we should pick up some things and probably do like Sven and move into the Scratch for a while."

"But if we do that, then we can't help Sven," said Cindy, "He wants us to go back and act as if nothing has happened."

"Okay," said Sam, "We will go back but must be very vigilant in case anything starts to change. I think our days there are numbered, but we must be careful not to get swept into some kind of 'goto Moon2' process."

"Meanwhile, while we are here in the Scratch, I think we should pick up a view extra items. He gestured towards a rundown looking shop selling vintage electronics.

"Maybe get some gear for my new hobby," he said.

Ganymede - Status Normal

For Jasmijn and Roelof, life on Ganymede was running as normal. There was a repetitive inevitability to the days. They had been on this large moon of Jupiter for so long that they had more less adapted to the different day cycle and the interim point at which they needed to refresh.

It was the same for most of the other people on this moon. A few people seemed to be quite heavily affected by the changing frequency of night and day, but the rest seemed to take it in their stride.

Jasmijn and Roelof were so adapted to the life on Ganymede that the passing of days did not seem to affect them in the same way as some of the others. They interacted with many others as well acclimatised as themselves.

Most interactions were largely professional, and this lack of other interaction seemed to keep them away from the more dangerous aspects of being on Ganymede.

They had been told about the strange effect that they would experience where days would seem to run into one another and sometimes it would be difficult to remember much from the past.

In practice they had not really experienced this and had found it fairly straightforward to continue to operate except for some interactions with people who seemed to be disorientated. This had been less apparent in the latter part of their time operating on Ganymede.

"We have another major dispatch today," said Jasmijn, "There's a train of ships leaving for Earth in four hours."

She flipped a display and a picture of the loading bay appeared. These were the sleek modern ships which had most of their space available for shipping materials back to Earth. One of the ships had a habitation capsule included, but the rest seemed for payload materials only.

"The ship with the habitation capsule will be routed to Moon2," said Roelof, "The others will be directed to New Delaware station on Earth."

"We had better get the sign-off from our new controller," said Roelof, "This one seems even slower than the last. I'm not sure why."

Weather aerial cluster

On Earth, in New Delaware, Cindy and Sam returned to the normal work. For the next day they behaved as if nothing had happened. They resumed control from their Secondaries and observed that everything else seemed quite normal.

Cindy had left Sven's Chinese analogue communicator in the apartment. It was hidden inside a cereal packet. Sam had taken a quick look at the power supply for the unit and noticed it was traditional batteries.

"This won't last more than a week," he said, "if they are going to contact as again it will be within the next few days."

The regular return of supplies from Ganymede continued. There was one landing approximately every month. Although called a Skytrain the individual ships were actually around one month apart which meant in an emergency one could reach the next within a suitable safety margin. It also meant that if there was an explosion or other damage to a single craft those around it would not be affected.

Because there were several launch sites on Ganymede, the individual return flights were sometimes to New Delaware and other times to the Russian or Chinese landing sites. So far there had never been an occasion when a flight rerouted to a different landing location.

Occasionally a flight would instead land on the Moon2 base. Officially this was because a particular scientist or other specialist was being returned and needed some time to adjust to conditions after the long flight back. A popular theory was that Moon 2 could also provide quarantine facilities in case they were needed. A ship could keep its occupants on Moon 2 until a suitable quarantining period had elapsed and relevant tests had taken place.

Sam needed to examine previous flights both outbound and return without drawing attention. He agreed with Cindy that they would create a situation where some form of historical analysis was required. They had set about identifying something that could be considered a potential reason related the last return flight.

It needed to be something minor so they could do it without too much attention from elsewhere. Sam had noticed eight small antenna array on the ship had become loose on the last return flight. They were only used for short range weather monitoring.

"Look," he said, "That antenna cluster is interfering with the relay station antenna."

"It probably explains what happened on the last

returning flights when we had that blackout for several days. If the weather aerial cluster had dislodged, it could have shorted against the long-range transmitter. We should look at a couple of other flights each way to see if this is something that happens after a long distance."

He knew that if he flipped the switch to access archival material, it would send alerts to other parts of the complex. The system monitoring would raise an alert at a higher level to show that he was interrogating a system that was not normally within his area. It was not a critical system area and from time to time everyone used additional data as part of their analytics.

Sam's main concern was to do this quickly and get as much data downloaded as possible before anyone else noticed. He was also aware that the act of downloading this data would be recorded. He had considered accessing the system from someone else's console area but realise that doing this would be just as noteworthy and could attract more attention.

He had acquired a small 21st-century memory device from the store in the Scratch and rigged it to a modern interface unit. He had arranged that the interface unit also had a receiver included so he could transmit from the archive to free-air inside the console area and the receiver would be able to pick up the signal and download it into the memory device. It was a rather simplistic design compared with modern technology, but he thought this may play to his advantage because no one would check for such primitive ways to offload storage information.

"I will need to create a diversion while I do this," he said to Cindy.

"How about I create an alarm?" asked Cindy, "I could adjust the returning ship's vector a micro degree and then raise an alert for it?"

"My suggestion is we aim it towards Moon 2 but at the wrong speed so that others will become preoccupied with helping correct the flight path."

"That sounds like a good idea," said Sam, "While the course is being corrected, I can run the offload. Everyone will be focused on the course correction."

"We will also need to be involved with that," said Cindy.

"Yes," agreed Sam, "If we can build a script for the situation then you can operate my part from the script and your part manually. That way it will look as if I am still involved in the normal running of events,"

"I've figured out a way to introduce the error," said Cindy, "It will be a simple nudge to avoid a meteorite and then a neglected correction to put things back on track. I can lock the meteorite course correction and it will then take a few extra minutes to decode the unlock."

Cindy knew that with the extensive security passwords of remote adjustments to flight paths, it was not unusual for there to be the occasional problem with a missing or misspelled identifier. Cindy prepared a sequence which required a security string containing many ones and zeros and letter L and letter O so that there was also a good chance for ambiguity. She would need to make it look as if the string had been automatically generated and so had to run a series of commands until a suitably clumsy one appeared.

"Good," she said, "We now have a command string that can be misinterpreted. The unlock code is 'A01O18B1lOO'"

The time approached for the meteorite avoidance manoeuvre. Cindy prepared a command sequence. She entered the special security string to initiate the remote access.

She fired the trim motors on the incoming ship. It should have been approximately a five second and then a corresponding five second burn to bring the ship back on course. Instead she removed the command sequence for the second burn. This would mean that the ship was now moving at an angle to its preferred flight path. It would take another minute or two for this to be discovered by someone else. She entered the deliberately wrong adjustment sequence and a series of red light appeared on the console.

"I think we will have got some attention now," she said to Sam. Sure enough, a main console messaging alert appeared.

"Are you in trouble?" it asked.

"Your inbound command has not been accepted. The ship is now on the wrong course. We will take control to assist your adjustment. Please provide the command security sequence."

Cindy pressed a button and the incorrect security sequence was flashed on to the emergency control.

"Initiating recovery," said the emergency control.

"Security sequence invalid," it responded, "Please re-submit the command security sequence."

Cindy pressed the button again and retransmitted the wrong sequence for the second time.

"Initiating recovery," repeated the emergency control.

"Security sequence invalid," repeated for the second time.

"Escalating the emergency recovery procedure," said the emergency control.

A yellow light flashed in the control area.

Cindy looked towards Sam. He was busy at his console.

"Repeat sending the security sequence," said Cindy.

She pressed the button to retransmit the wrong sequence for the third time.

This had the effect of the setting emergency control to force it to retry the sequence.

"Security sequence invalid," repeated the emergency control. This time the orange light turned to a red flashing light.

"Escalating the emergency recovery procedure, no override possible," said the emergency control.

"Using the emergency keys to access the recovery control," said the emergency control.

Cindy knew that additional security keys were only available to the automated systems. These keys could only be used after a sequence of several attempts had been made using the keys supplied by the human operators to the system.

The override was designed to prevent high-speed automated responses in the wrong situations. After three attempts the automation would take complete control. This was what was happening now.

"Automation now taking control of the incoming ship navigation systems," said the emergency control.

The red light changed to a blue light and Cindy could see that the consul was now rapidly filling with command control sequences to bring the ship onto its preferred course.

The whole situation had taken maybe two minutes to play through. The blue light stopped flashing and a green light reappeared. It stayed on for maybe five seconds and then gradually faded away.

Cindy knew that everything was now back to normal. She looked towards Sam. He was putting a small plastic unit into his pocket. He did not look back, and he did not acknowledge that he had completed the download of data.

They both knew that there would be an investigation almost immediately into what happened. They silently moved towards the door of the control room. Along a corridor and quickly to the outside. A small transporter pod was waiting. They both stepped in. The pod silently moved away. They would be in the Scratch in another 10 minutes.

Russian Exchange

Although the Russian control centre was referred to as Russian, it was really a privatised industry created after the demise of the Russian federation. Its formal name was GNI GazNostIndustrie., and it was a corporately controlled entity which had been created by some of the Russian oligarchs. The Russians usually referred to the control centre as Prometheus base, which was a shortening of 'Gazovaya Promyshlennost' - the Russian name for the base. A dry gangster joke meant that the Russians thought of the name as some kind of dark premonition.

Prometheus was the fire-stealer, from Zeus, in Greek myths. He took fire and returned it to mankind. King of the gods, Zeus exacted a price for fire - which he had hidden from mankind. Then, annoyed at Prometheus' theft, as both a price and punishment, Zeus created the woman Pandora and sent her down to Epimetheus (Hindsight), who, though warned against it by

Prometheus, married her.

Pandora took the great lid off the jar she carried, and evils, hard work, and disease flew out to plague humanity. Hope alone remained within.

The Russians borrowed from the works of Greek dramatist Aeschylus, who made Prometheus not only the bringer of fire and civilization to mortals but also their preserver, giving them all the arts and sciences as well as the means of survival.

In the previous century there had been several uprisings in the remains of the Russian Federation. It had taken on many of its neighbours in various economic and military struggles, for the underpinning state was really being run by a collection of gangster oligarchs wielding huge power.

After a boundary became established that was fairly stable, other multinational entities had decided it was safer to let this state persist.

The inner structure of the revised Russia was essentially five large zones individually controlled by heavily invested interests. In the days before the space mining had commenced Russia also had control of many of the energy pathways across the planet. It had also created vast commodity trading empires which included some of the old cities of the developed world such as London and New York.

Moon 2 was established largely on the back of the continued Russian space program, allied with interest from India, Russia then gained some early advantages in the mining expeditions to Ganymede.

Once it became apparent that the whole of earth was going to require resource from Ganymede to reconstruct its methods of providing energy, the Russians had agreed, in return for huge terrestrial trading agreements, to the split of Ganymede into zones such that other major earth trading entities could also mine Ganymede and bring back the necessary materials.

It had been the Russians who had first exploited the underbelly of the Ganymede situation to create the seedier aspects of Ganymede habitation. As stories returned to Earth of what was occurring on Ganymede, instead of increasing the policing early thug-laden space trains ensured that there was an increasingly get-rich-quick scheme for expansionist crime lords.

Matson was very aware of the need to tread carefully around the Russians. The exchange of Primes and Prime information could be another way for the Russians to increase their control of the nation states.

Matson was aware of stories from the 20th century of the so-called cold war years when there had been a deterioration of trust between many countries following of World War II. The gravity of the situation facing Earth in the 22nd Century meant that a greater unity had been forced upon population. Nonetheless, there were still many unscrupulous people looking for angles to gain control and economic advantage from the situation.

Matson realised he was technically a part of the controlling hierarchy, although he did not feel himself particularly high in the pyramid of power. People like Green and Green's boss were far more able to exert influence and enjoy major benefits from what was happening.

Matson also knew that the Russians would need to be rechecked when they arrived. Since the constitutional formalisation of New Delaware and the whole of Zone Two, it required all citizens to have zonal chips implanted which provided both identity capabilities and also limited their mobility into non-authorised zones. This was largely a response to the need to restrict travel because of the dangers associated with lengthy contact with the dangerous climate of Earth.

Identities were now installed soon after birth and had been progressively extended in terms of their memory and processing capability. Modern chips could contain enough tracking information to last a lifetime although the earlier generation chips were more limited, and information was rolled off them as the chip became full.

Zone two had comprehensive monitoring capabilities throughout so it was relatively straightforward to ensure that people were in their designated zones without becoming intrusive. A signalling protocol was used to ensure that anyone straying from their zone for too long would be easily detectable and could be encouraged to return to their own neighbourhood. When this system had first been introduced there was a fairly major polarisation of opinion.

Some people saw it as a way to protect their own domains and avoid increased encroachment from other less well-off areas. Others saw it as a totalitarian control limiting freedoms. Because there had been so much civil unrest as a consequence of the Klima War, an ultimatum was provided which said that people either accept the chips or else would need to move to the Zone Three which was effectively now the area known as the Scratch.

Matson noticed the wall display showed an incoming major message.

"Display Message," he signalled to the display.

Part of his sensewall showed a text stream, "The new Primes have arrived."

It was time to move his current remaining Primes from their position. He would need to do this speedily.

"In fairness," he thought, "The Russians had moved with lightning speed." It just made him suspicious that the whole thing was a ploy by Russia to embed more people in the New Delaware organisation.

Maybe the Russians were conspiring to build a kind of chimera? Part Russian, part western and part android?

It would make a fine irony since such a being becomes the awful apocalyptic end goal of escalating dominations towards defining an ultimate self, untied at last from all dependency, a man in space.

Matson was used to making these substitutions but usually he was able to take more time and create less ripples as a result.

This time he knew he needed to move quickly and, if anything, the Russian Primes had arrived even faster than he had expected.

He requested a trace on the two Primes he was to replace.

As he saw the response, he noticed that there had been a recent event current in their control complex. An unexpected course correction to one of the incoming ships.

"Expand," he requested.

The screen produced more information about the situation and showed that it was a security control error that had created the problem. This was a fairly routine situation and he would not normally have been alerted or suspicious of it.

On this occasion he noticed immediately that the two people involved were the Primes that he was about to replace. He looked at the ship's call alerts but could see nothing particularly unusual. The ship had been diverted around a meteor shower and then brought back on course, admittedly a little late. It was still routine though, and hardly a full-blown emergency.

"Locate the Primes," he asked again.

"The Primes are off station," came the response, "They have left the base."

"Can you trace them?" he asked.

"Trace ends at Dover base," came the response.

Dover base was a terrestrial Air Force Base near to the exit from New Delaware.

Matson knew that both of the Primes would have a pilot profile. They would be capable of flying the jet technology from the base. If they had access to the base they could potentially get to anywhere on earth.

"Request security lockdown at Dover Air Force Base," said Matson.

He picked up a communicator and asked for the Dover Air Force Base commander.

There was a short pause and he was put through to the base.

"Dover base, how can we help you?" came a response.

Matson realised he was speaking to an android system.

"Emergency," he said, "Please put me through to human control."

The voice responded, "You have requested human intervention. You have said this is an emergency. There is a penalty for misuse of this facility. Please confirm you wish human control override. If you say confirm you acknowledge the terms of this request."

"Confirm," said Matson.

Another voice, "Hello this is emergency response at Dover Air Force Base."

"Hello this is Matson from New Delaware command centre 'B'. We have reason to believe that there are two of our Primes on site in your base. Please raise an alert and find and apprehend these two individuals. I am sending through full information about each of them along with their tracker idents."

"Acknowledged we are putting you through to Dover Air Force Base Commander."

Matson knew he had the authority to get directly through to the highest level inside the Dover Base.

A third voice, "Hello, this is Commander Stammdecker, from Dover AFB. I understand you are looking for a couple of people from your base? We have been given the security identifications and are initiating a search. It should take less than an hour to find them. Do you want us to retain them here or arrange for them to be brought back to you?"

"When you find them, keep them there," said Matson, "I will come to your base once you have found them."

Matson knew it would be better to avoid moving the Primes more than necessary.

History lesson

"Are you sure this will work?" said Cindy. She looked at her upper arm. She was wearing an arm band inside which was a wire mesh. Outside a 2 cm² plastic unit was attached to the wiring.

"It will work for a few hours," said Sam.

"Once they have realised, we have really gone they will bring in more specialist equipment to track us down. Until then we should be okay."

Sam's trip to the store in the Scratch had enabled him to acquire a few extra items. Amongst them were a couple of old keys from 21st-century German cars. They were used for remote opening of the manual doors built into the type of cars used in the 21st-century.

He had adapted their wiring so they would send out digital pulses at one second intervals and then he had amplified the pulses using the wire mesh.

"It's a simple jammer," he said, "Not particularly clever

but it's enough to drown the regular signals from our ident chips until we have a chance to neutralise them."

Sam had arranged the journey to the Scratch to go via the base at Dover.

"This is how I want us to throw them off our trail," he said, "We will lead the trail to the base and then switch on the jammers. We are already close to the Scratch at Dover base. We should then be able to head across into the Scratch."

He looked at the communicator from Sven. The red light was still off.

"Sven has still not tried to contact us," said Sam.
    "I'm a little concerned that we will have done all this but then have no way to get the information back to him."

"I guess we could try sending a message from the communicator ourselves," says Cindy.

"Sven specifically asked us not to do that," said Sam.

"We may have no choice though," said Cindy.

"If we leave it too long, the battery will have run out in the communicator and then we will not be able to make contact in case."

"Look we have done our part here. We have got the trace information and power to make our escape from the complex. We must be prepared to contact Sven ourselves otherwise this could all have been wasted."

"Okay," said Sam, "But we should wait until we are inside the Scratch before we try using the communicator."

"I've been thinking about ways to get across to the Scratch without using our Idents," said Cindy, "If we go to the normal crossings, we'll have to show I.D. and we'll get picked up. Yet we can't stay here, because it's only a matter of time before they jack up the tracker power."

"A great thing about the base is it's been here for over 200 years," said Sam.

"Yes, long enough for there to be a full heritage exhibit."

"And the heritage includes old forms of transport"

They looked towards the museum.

"We need the outdoor exhibits," said Sam.

Sam and Cindy skirted the edges of the Air Force Base.

They were already in a secure area and now they were approaching a high security area within New Delaware.

The perimeter had two lines of fencing. It was high fencing with a track in-between which could be used by security pods for patrol. There were also cameras and beams.

"I don't think we will be penetrating this," said Cindy.

"You are right," said Sam, "But look, here's the heritage site. They slowed their pod and approached the museum.

Outside was a 20th Century space shuttle and next to it a 21st-Century DSP. The deep space probe looked pristine, like a factory model that probably had not been used. The space shuttle looked like it had made a few return trips.

Notable with both of them were the huge engine units. The kind of things that had been completely superseded since the magnetite from Ganymede had taken over as the basis for propulsion.

They parked the pod and walked the short distance to the main entrance.

"I think we will be paying guests for this," said Cindy.

"Cash though, not WavePay," said Sam.

They handed over some tokens and went inside.

After the entrance there was a darkened display area where a few children ran around pressing buttons on the displays. They made their way towards the external exhibits, which included more spacecraft and some missiles from the 20th century.

"Look!" said Cindy. She pointed towards the further displays. A row of aircraft from the 20th and 21st century. Conventional jet planes stranded since the energy crisis.

"It's amazing that they needed such large engines back in the old days," said Sam.

Cindy pointed.

"There," she said.

It was a fuel pump. Aviation fuel for propeller planes. Avgas Blue. Limited supplies but necessary to be able to mount displays of the historical aircraft.

"One of these," said Sam, "The one closest to the fuel pumps."

"This one," he said.   He pointed to a 20th-century warplane. A small sign read P51D.

"Look. Two seats. One propeller. How difficult can it be?"

"First, we need to figure how to get in," said Cindy. Sam pushed some wheeled steps towards the side of the plane.

There were two seats, one behind the other.

A sliding glass canopy. They slipped inside. Cindy took the front seat, Sam the one behind. She waggled the controls and various control surfaces on the wings start to move. She checked the fuel levels.

"It's already been gassed up. Now we need to start it," she said.

She flipped a few switches. With a splutter the engine fired.

"My god, it's so noisy,"

"Internal combustion, sparks and explosions to make it fly," replied Sam

.

Cindy looked concerned. With this much power, no movement.

"Wheel blocks. There will be blocks to stop it rolling," she said, "Check for any other tethers too."

Sam climbed out, pulled the two chocks away from the wheels and the plane started to roll forward slowly.

"Get back in," said Cindy as she slowed the engine. Sam pushed the ladder forward, climbed back into the cockpit and slid the canopy closed.

"Put on this green headset," she said, "Then we can talk."

Sam nodded and placed a green headset with earphones and a microphone around his head.

"This is like a practical history project," he said.

"These things need a runway, I think," said Cindy, "No vertical take-off."

She taxied the plane across a solid black surface and saw a sign which said, 'to runway'.

"At least they're making that easy for us," said Sam.

"Okay, here we go," said Cindy. She positioned to one end of the long tarmac strip, revved the engine and the plane started to move forward. Sam couldn't hear anything from Cindy. The noise drowned everything.

The plane rumbled along the runway, picking up speed and then started to take off. Cindy shakily increased its altitude to a few thousand feet.

"I'm just going to get us across the water and into the Scratch," said Cindy.

"Then I'll find somewhere to land this thing. Ideally away from too many people. Our flight distance will be only a few kilometres."

"Assuming we don't get chased by the Air Force," thought Sam.

"Honestly, I think we are genuinely flying under the radar," said Cindy.

Cindy banked the plane and almost immediately they were over water.

"Look," she said, "We are almost across and into the Scratch."

"I'm going to find somewhere to bring this down," signalled Cindy.

She flipped a couple of switches on the plane. Sam was aware that the undercarriage wheels had not even been raised.

Now Cindy was guiding the small plane down. A field. Flat. Long.

"The damn wings are in the way," she said, "It's blocking my view."

There was a jolt as the plane touched down and slowed suddenly. There was spray from the wheels. The ground was waterlogged. The plane lurched to a stop, and then the nose suddenly tipped forward.

The propeller made a crying sound and then suddenly stopped turning.

There was a sudden silence. Sam pressed the canopy release. It didn't slide off; it fell away to the ground. He hit the middle of his belt buckle and was suddenly falling forward.

"Hey," he said, "Great flying. Unconventional landing."

"You're welcome," said Cindy, "I'm not sure this thing is used to modern flying techniques though. Help me out of this belt."

They clambered to the surface of the field. Wet underfoot.

"I wasn't expecting this kind of surface," said Sam, "It explains the deceleration."

"We'd better get away from here," said Cindy, "although this plane does stick out a bit."

"Come on, we should get lost in the Scratch," He picked up the small bag of equipment and they made their way to what was once a farm track.

Covering tracks

Matson decided he would meet the new Primes in person. He would travel to the control centre instead of more usually asking them to visit him.

He needed to see how things were running. That there had been new discoveries by the previous Primes led him to think there was a need for a shakedown of the site.

That the previous Primes had disappeared was troubling him. Adding together their knowledge that others had discovered more information plus the change in behaviour could only spell bad news.

He took a secure pod across to the control centre. As he approached, he noticed the Amber alert. They had taken his instructions to find Sam and Cindy seriously enough. But he still needed results.

He passed slowly through the security system. So this was what it was like being a normal person, being processed nowadays. Usually he could go fast path because of his status, but today he was just one of a bulk number being processed in the heightened security process.

Eventually inside, he requested access to the main console area. He'd need to visit the place where Sam and Cindy operated, as well as using it as the meeting place of the new Primes.

As he entered the zone, he could see the two Secondaries, identified by their different uniform flashes, quietly operating the controls.

He approached the first of them. They both turned and recognised him. They also looked suitably surprised.

"Controller Matson, this is a surprise. Welcome to the control centre. We have a take-off from Ganymede within the hour. You'll be able to see it happening."

"I'm here about the arrival of the two new Primes," he replied. "You'll be able to continue until they get up to speed. They are both from the Federation, so there'll be some time to get them used to our processes."

"Also, I need to ask you both. When did you last see your two original Primes, they appear to be missing?"

The Secondaries were aware of the protocols around Primes and their necessary attendance to monitor ongoing operations of the base.

"We have been on duty since yesterday, with the usual passing of control to the other controller", said one of the Secondaries. The other two controllers are both working with Primes, so we have been able to stay online longer than normally permitted."

"And have you noticed anything unusual during your time in operation?" asked Matson. He looked around. There were no untoward status lights displayed, except for the Amber base alert.

"There's nothing unusual from the last period," said the first Secondary, "Except, when we were first brought online, it was after a short-term irregularity. An incoming ship had to be steered around a meteorite shower and the course correction was re-applied late because of a security anomaly."

Matson recollected the event. "I know, I saw that from the Block", he said.

"At the same time that it was occurring, a large download of archival data was requested," continued the Secondary, "The strange thing is, I can't see the archive repository folder for the download. It's fairly unusual, as if the download has disappeared."

Matson was aware that there would normally be a log showing how the download had been used and analysed.

"Can you show me the log?" he requested.

"That's the strangest thing. For such a large quantity of download, we can't find the storage folder. I was planning to request its access details from the Primes when they returned."

He paused, "I also can't quite work out what the data was being used for. It seems far more 'complete' than we'd normally use for routine analysis."

"And what period does it cover?" asked Matson.

"It's a long time series. It goes back over the last three release levels for the whole of the N.D. part of Ganymede. If it wasn't downloaded from the control room here at very high speed, it would be almost impossible to get this amount of data quickly from anywhere else. Something around an exabyte of data."

Matson was worried. The exabyte of data was a massive leak if it had been carried off site. It wouldn't take much physical storage but would take a significant amount of processing power to analyse that quantity of information.

"Can you recreate a copy of what has been downloaded?" asked Matson.

The two Secondaries looked at one another. "Yes, we are already doing that," replied one, "We don't have the same high-speed access as the Primes though and it will take us several hours."

"I have the high-speed access," said Matson, "I will authorise it."

Primes possessed certain overrides to take control of the fastest data pipes inside the control centre. This was for emergency situations where they needed to make fast decisions about ships in transit. It was not passed to the Secondaries, who were deployed for more routine processes. Matson also had the access as a point of escalation.

"Here, give me a console pad," he asked. "I'll give you a biometric authorisation."

A few seconds later, the archive data was being downloaded. Matson could see that it represented a comprehensive picture of the working of the Ganymede environment for the last few years, across some of the major upgrades.

"Once you have completed the download, please put one copy in the normal folder system and give me a copy to take away," Matson requested, "I don't want the Primes to be caught out by the missing download. Perhaps you can put the new one into the place where the prior one would normally have been stored."

The Secondaries nodded.

"Confirmed," said one.

They knew Matson was covering tracks but dare not say anything. Matson was a powerful figure in their control room. Disagreeing could cost them their roles.

Commander Green had been alerted to the missing Primes from Matson's command. It had started as a minor alert. They were due to be replaced in any case. Then they had gone from their base and made north across New Delaware.

Then they had somehow disappeared. Green predicted that they would head for the Scratch. He had asked for any alerts from unusual events in the northern part of New Delaware.

There had been a strange story from the Devon Air Force

Base. Not exactly the base, but the museum next door, which had alerted that there had been the theft of an ancient plane.

The technology of the plane, using old-fashioned aviation fuel and requiring a knowledge of propeller-based flight meant that the site had very little security. Hardly anyone would know how to fly such a device, nor of the process for filling it with the scarce aero fuel.

The plane's departure at a very low altitude smacked of the Primes and so Green was issuing detain orders for both Sam and Cindy.

He would need to deal with Matson too. There were too many things going wrong now and someone would need to pay.

Green contacted the security unit at Devon Base, "Can we trace these two people?" he asked.
    "It may be difficult," came the reply, "We can see their trace right up until they were at the base, but then it just goes off grid."

"Okay" said Green, "But now we need to deploy a trace team to find them. I've already requested that Hunter take control."

Hunting for witches

I was an ordinary man with ordinary desires
There must be accountability
Despaired and misinformed
Fear will keep us all in place
So I go hunting for witches
I go hunting for witches
Heads are going to roll
I go hunting for witches

Russell Lissack / Gordon Moakes / Kele Okereke / Matt Tong /
Bloc Party

They call me the Hunter

Hunter was usually asked to get involved with difficult situations. At different times there were various threats to stability within New Delaware and the adjacent zone known as Scratch.

Hunter was a hybrid. Mostly human with some adaptations, on earth most of the adapted humans were a result of injuries or other forms of socially acceptable repair. Improved eyesight, improved hearing, replacement limbs. It was the routine stuff of a benevolent health service.

Hunter was different. He had been adapted systematically to make his professional role more adept. There had been a series of ethical questions raised about the use of performance enhancements for humans. It had been declared as illegal to make these changes.

The military and some of the security services had found a way to circumvent this. Hunter was formerly classified as a decommissioned android that had been restarted with some organic components.

This was a lie, of course. He had been fastidiously upgraded for a range of capabilities which would enable him and others like him to be able to function for the security services. In the jargon there were humanoids and androids. Humanoids started as human. Androids started at machines. Cyborgs were another category altogether; Machine-based life-forms.

Most of the time people like Hunter were kept out of public view. It was better for them to remain undetected, although there were many ethical conversations about the possibility that such people existed. The more that Hunter was deployed the more likely it was that he would be discovered.

Hunter would still have a routine setting that was closely human-like in its behaviour. There were still tell-tale signs of his adaptations. This physical side of this was largely concealed but there were occasions where he would operate with a lightning speed inhuman in its behaviour.

It was also rumoured that there was a way to detect enhanced humans via the use of high-speed stroboscopic lighting. The frame rate of a human would work at around 25 to 30 frames per second. This was the rate at which it was possible for a human to no longer detect that individual frames in a videogram were not continuous. An android or a humanoid adaptation usually ran much faster typically between 300 and 1200 frames per second.

This had led to rumours that the use of high-speed strobe could confuse humanoids. In effect they were trying to process faster than they were able to see.

It was a phenomenon that had been seen in some experiments with insects where the strobe would flash faster than the insect's super-fast scan rate and then the insect would need to stop at intervals to recover. It was as if the insect had to process its brain buffer before it could continue.

This was the exploitation that was used to disable the fastest actions of humanoids. Strobe guns needed to project at 2000 Hz and be tuned to the point where the humanoid would slow down. It created something like an epileptic fit it in a human, but for a humanoid it just slowed them to a standstill until they could adjust to the new rate.

Hunter had a range of accomplices which helped support his activities as he found people that had decided they would rather be lost.

This was the result of larger crimes which had been committed and for which the remaining resources were unable to track down the culprits. The degree of sophistication around New Delaware using tracking systems and other telemetry meant that most people knew it was unwise to attempt anything dubious.

Hunter was nearly always successful in finding people. Hunter also had an extensive network within the Scratch which meant he could find people even after they had left the tracing capabilities running throughout New Delaware.

The android component in Hunter's composition meant that Hunter could be controlled by a commander. Hunter knew that there were equivalents of himself through

New Delaware and the Scratch and that these could be called to operate in unison. This was most often by a commander who would manifest themselves directly or through an Occupied being.

Because of the inbuilt sentience of Hunter, he could sense that the current tracker situation was made difficult because of Commander Green's direct involvement. It implied an added complication that Matson was the also under suspicion.

Hunter was now being asked to track Sven Mattison as a route to two Primes, Sam and Cindy.

Sven's older tracking device was beneficial to Hunter's processes. The more recent and more sophisticated idents had a cleaner and digital footprint whereas Sven's was an older version that created some electronic leakage when it was in use. Unknown to Sven, it could also be started remotely from compatible devices.

Hunter decided that this is what he would do in order to catch Sam and Cindy. If Hunter travelled at a slow speed above surface in the Scratch for probably 30 minutes, he could send out the restart code. He only needed to trip a restart once and then Sven's tracker would be fully operational again.

Hunter knew that for Sven to break cover and come back into New Delaware meant that something very high profile must be happening. Although Sven had been left to his own devices within the Scratch, he was still a person of interest if there were any unusual situations developing related to the Block.

Hunter prioritised his actions. He would need to track

down Sven and then set up a trap to contain the two Primes.

It didn't take long for Hunter to re-instigate the tracing of Sven. Hunter noticed that Sven seemed to spend most of his time deep within the Scratch infrastructure although there had also been a couple of recent trips outside. He had picked this up from the cache in Sven's tracker.

Hunter concluded Sven didn't believe the tracker was still active, or that anyone was paying any further attention to him.

After all, it had been several years since he had left the New Delaware Block system. Hunter called for a range of additional support for the trap that was about to be sprung. He would use some fast pursuit pods and people on the ground in the area around Sven. The challenge was to do this in a way that did not alert Sven.

Battery

"I doubt whether we have two days left on this old communicator's battery now," said Sam.

He looked at the device that he had been given by Sven a few days earlier.

"Yes, if this runs out, we are completely stranded," said Cindy, "We have no way to make contact with Sven and no way to find him in the Scratch."

"I think we will need to contact him ourselves," said Sam

"It is probably safer to do this now we are inside the Scratch."

Cindy pulled the communicator from the inside of her bag.

They looked at one another. Cindy pressed the power on the communicator. Nothing. It didn't start.

"Again," said Sam,

This time Cindy hold the button for a couple seconds. The communicator restarted. It seemed to take a while to initialise.

"Old school," said Sam, "It has to bootstrap itself back to working."

Cindy smiled. Then she noticed the red light on front of the unit.

"Sven has been trying to contact us," she said, "The red light. I guess it only works when the power is on to the main unit. Not really much use as a standby device then is it?"

Sam shook his head. Another one of the reasons why the energy ran out. Everything was powered on the whole time.

"So, with the red light can we actually find out if it is a message?"

Cindy looked at the various control buttons.

"Here's one that says Menu," she said.

"You have to press these little arrows to get around."

No voice or gesture activation.

They puzzled with the device for longer but were unable to find out if there was a way to retrieve message.

"I think this is a point-to-point device," said Sam. "We can only speak to somebody at the other end. It's like a phone from the 20th century."

"Early 20th," said Cindy, "I think they had voicemail even in those days."

"Okay then," said Sam, "Is there a menu for looking up people to contact?"

Cindy pressed another button.

"Yes, there is a single name and number in this unit."

"Okay, let's try it."

She pressed the button and listened into the communicator. She could hear a beep sound.

She listed for what seemed like a long time. Then suddenly,

"Yes."

Someone had answered.

"No names, please. Where did we last meet?"

"What is the token?"

"Trellis," Answered Sam.

"Correct," said Sven, following the protocol they had been given.

"We need to meet," said Sam, "We have something you requested. A lot of it."

"Understood," said Sven.

"I will give you an address. It is The Trikepoint. Everyone knows it. Go there and I will find you."

Then silence.

"The Trikepoint?" Said Cindy.

"We'll find it," said Sam.

The Scratch

The Scratch was an area with an estimated population of 20 million. Each of the main routes into the area had warning signs discouraging people from entering. The zone still used older technologies and had created a sustainable ecosystem using materials that were now banned from most of the rest of the planet and certainly from the rest of the United States.

The area and a few others like it around the world had been set up as part of a series of deals when the new technology arrived to replace the crumbled legacy from the systems that were dying. Not everyone was prepared to step into the new ways of working, which required everyone to buy into support for what would become the new ecosystem with its far more regulated ways of living, in return for a higher quality of perceived lifestyle.

The new approach provided a better level of consumerist lifestyle in return for curtailment of certain previous civil liberties.

Most people were content to live with what was a type of

totalitarian state. The governing processes meant everyone must work, and in return the leisure time was greatly improved, although the range of preferred leisure pursuits was also restricted.

The Scratch was different. It was here the people who had dropped out of the squeaky-clean society lived. It was a messy tangle of bazaars, strip-based shopping and tangled road networks. The power sources were still often fuel based and this created a haze and a film across much of the zone. Some of the 22nd century tech was available for power provision, but it was mainly provided from units that were now considered defunct in the rest of the main capital cities.

The location of Scratch was a direct consequence of the location of major population centres on the eastern seaboard of the USA. Set between major population centres of New York, Boston and Washington and close to the New Delaware space complex, it had become the automatic choice for outsiders to live and create a living.

Some said the area had once been called New Jersey, although the area direct south of Manhattan had acquired the Jersey name and the records of a New Jersey were patchy.

There had been various gang wars in the mid 21st century around this part of the world although not much was known about the detail.

Cindy and Sam had briefly visited the Scratch like so many other well-heeled tourists but were seeing it now through very different eyes as they tried to find a way to get to the area with the Trikehub.

Now they had reached a road. A traditional tarmac strip, wide enough for passing traffic, although seemingly lightly used at present. In the distance, they could see the higher buildings of the Scratch, in it's most populous part. In the opposite direction, they could see the haze and sparkle from the tall and glittering buildings of New Delaware.

"We'll need to get someone to take us to downtown Scratch," said Sam.

"We don't have any cash," said Cindy.

"We'll need to find a way," said Cindy.

"Let's get over to that road," said Sam. "We may be able to get someone to take us using Landtran."

Micro-cores

In the Block, Darnell had asked for Green to visit him.

"Why is it taking so long to track down those two escaped Primes?" he asked.

"Surely you have their normal identity tracking switched on? It shouldn't take you more than a couple of hours, if you have mobilised the right people and systems."

Green replied, "We have everything in place. Remember we are dealing with two very smart crimes. They appear to have disabled the normal tracking systems. We are following them into the Scratch. They are linking with one of the older Primes, Sven Mattinson. He was from Generation Three."

"I remember Sven," said Darnell, "He was always a loose cannon, after he left the system. I always thought he could have been adapted to make a good Hunter 'droid.

It turned out that it was useful to keep him at large because he seems to attract anything that we need to control."

"That's what we are doing now," said Green, "We have a virtual cordon around Sven and are waiting for the two escaped Primes - Cindy and Sam - to enter the net. We can't decide whether to scoop up all three of them or let Sven continue."

"Just get on with it," said Darnell, "We need this to end."

Darnell pointed towards a planetary map.

"See," he said, "This is the last outbound ship. Most of the inbound replacements are now capable of being assembled on Ganymede. That's also why the ships arriving here have been so much better built than the ones departing from Earth. "

"We have reached the point where there is a fully sustainable Ganymede system. It can produce magnetite and ship it back to Earth for us without us needing to continue to send people to Ganymede. The labs on Ganymede now have enough designers, too and the Ganymede androids and embedded systems are much smarter than anything we have on Earth."

Darnell looked towards Green, "And yet, we are able to control everything from Earth."

"We don't need loose ends to have to explain how everything is working. The whole point of the Block system was to keep the central truths within this environment."

Green looked at Darnell and started, "Yes, and you're one of the few people that still remembers how things were first created. To look at you now, you are in old age. I doubt whether you have more than a few years left. What can you do? Youth presided over first the destruction but more recently a restart for the Earth. No wonder you are kept locked in the Block. Some of the memories should not be allowed to escape."

Darnell stared back at Green. "You don't get it, do you?" he said, "The Block controllers really have control of everything. We have made all this possible, and you think we are imprisoned. No. We are the ones that have the freedom."

Green grimaced, "Look, you may have been able to identify some of the science which provided the improvements to the magnetite technology, but it's only that which has saved you from the same fate as most of the retired Primes."

"I can still call this," said Darnell, "I can fix this so that you join the retired Primes. The clock is running to get Sam and Cindy into captivity. I'm putting you on a timer."

He pressed a small button. Two guards emerged from doors either side of his desk.

"These two guards are the same generation as the latest ones already on Ganymede. Fast reactions and immense strength. "

Green looked at the guards. They looked human, but he guessed they had to be android. One of them approached him and in a single movement flipped a bracelet around his left wrist.

"That's the time remaining," said Darnell. "You'll see the bracelet also includes micro-cores. They will be injected into you in two days if you have not solved our problem."

Green knew about micro-cores. They were usually used to repair human nerve injuries, having a nerve reconstruction capability included within them.

"I know what you're thinking," said Darnell, "You may not have any need for micro cores at the moment. These ones are, shall we say, a little more refined than the ones you normally see for nerve repair."

"These ones are about acquisition. They acquire the central nervous system of their host. Wetware robotics. Of course, they don't last very long; their hosts normally burnout. But it's long enough for us to download the important functions related to their specialisms. I can then replace you with another altogether more reliable device. Who knows? one of these exact models perhaps."

"If you are able to resolve this escapee situation, then we won't need to trouble ourselves with such complex engineering and you will soon be back to your normal role."

Green looked at Darnell, he may have been an old man, but he had the ruthlessness that he was known for when he was first brought to the Block. Green now understood why people said he still had control even if he was theoretically a prisoner inside the Block.

"Don't you see?" said Darnell, "I can distribute my

presence using the nano tech. It means that I am able to experience things on the outside while you think I am still locked away inside the Block. I have moved parts of my presence to different androids and use this facility to synthesise the experience."

Green considered whether to reach for his alarm system and summon assistance to Darnell's room in the block.

"Something else," said Darnell, "Now that you have been braceletted, we can start to ready your reflexes as well. Do you think that the version of me you see in front of you is the only one? Of course it isn't, it is very convenient for me to have a version running here, apparently trapped inside the Block. In practice I can transfer my presence to several autonomous units. It is one of the perks of a distributed existence.

"Find them," he repeated, "You have two days."

Carbon based transport

The road system inside the Scratch was different from anything that Cindy and Sam were used to. The main transit units were carbon powered. They were mainly running on biofuels which were being manufactured somewhere within the Scratch. Most of the transport was small and lightweight. Adapted and powered bicycles, very small cars and an occasional larger transport unit for carrying goods or large quantities of people.

As Cindy and Sam approached the road, they could see one of the large people carriers. They hailed it and it stopped. Their uniforms identified them as people from outside of the Scratch, although most people inside would know that these people would have access to money from New Delaware which was useful for gathering essential supplies that were not available from within the Scratch.

The driver looked towards them. He asked to see their money. They showed him their money from New Delaware.

"I will need to take it all," said the driver, "I will give you back each enough for one day's food. The rest is now property of the Scratch." They knew better than to argue and climbed into the bus. "Here," said the driver, "This token is valid for the whole day. You can travel anywhere."

"We need to get to the Trikepoint," said Cindy, "You will be very close if you stay on here," said the driver, "I will point out the route when we are at the nearest stop point."

Cindy and Sam settled back into the seats on the bus. Those around them looked with tired interest at these two strangers from New Delaware. Cindy clutched at the bag containing the E reader and the data. She was concerned that they may decide to rob her. The two of them would not be able to fend off a full bus load of people if they decided to get angry.

"You will be safe while you ride this bus," said the driver.

"They can see you have paid a considerable sum which will enter into the Scratch economy. He turned to the passengers. They also note that I have protection devices on this bus, so if there is any trouble I will deploy. He had been speaking with a mask above his head and now lowered it back onto his face. Cindy looked up above the seats there were small nozzles projecting into each of the seating areas. She realised that these were not for ventilation, they were to release some kind of toxin if there was trouble on the bus. The driver had to don protection, but she did not want to have to experience the effects of a bus fight.

"How long will it take us to get to the centre?" asked Sam.

"We are already close," said the driver, "We have just gone across the boundary into the zone you require. Another 10 minutes and we should be as close as I can take you in this bus."

There was an announcement on the public address system of the bus.

"This will be a selected disembarkation point only, nominated passengers will be allowed to alight."

Cindy noticed that all of the other passengers were wearing a seat belt and she then noticed that the belts were electronically secured. She wondered why the driver had not done this for her and Sam.

The driver looked back towards Cindy, "I know why you are here," he said, "You certainly picked an unusual way to arrive."

He slowed the bus and indicated to the front right, "You are about one minute from the Trikepoint," he said, "Just go along that pathway and you will be in a central area within a minute. Look for the trikes."

Cindy and Sam disembarked from the bus. Cindy was struck by the acrid smells in the air. She was used to the scrubbed air of New Delaware. This was a completely different sensation.

"That's the smell of cooking," said Sam, "They have organics here and are cooking with them." Cindy looked shocked.

"No processed food?" she said, "ugh."

They crossed into the square and looked around for signs of Sven or anyone that might be looking for them. Cindy noticed that there were several groups of people standing at the exits from the square.

"Something is wrong," she said to Sam, "This could be a trap."

Across the square she could see Sven starting to stand. He was in a small cafe with two other people. The other people were wearing clothes that looked similar to New Delaware uniforms.

At that moment a green flash arced across the square. It was a ribbon wave.

"Look out," said Sam, "I think they are trying to cut us off."

Another ribbon wave flashed across another part of the square. Sven was in between the two lines. They were still outside of it.

"We had better turnaround," said Cindy. At that moment a third flash. The three ribbon waves had now created a triangle with Sven in one corner. The ribbon lines started to contract towards Sven.

"They have him trapped," said Sam, "I think they have assumed that those two people with him were us.

"I think Sven has set up a decoy," said Cindy, "We must get away from here,"

They moved slowly towards a different corner of the square. They intermingled with the trikes. Someone rang a bell.

"Need a ride?" they asked, "It'll cost you a day's food in credits."

They looked towards the person asking them a question. It was a taxi driver using one of the trikes. They climbed on.

"Sven asked me to do this," said the driver, "I'm getting you moved away and to somewhere safe."

"What about Sven?" asked Sam.

"This is what Sven had predicted," said the driver, "And is the kind of thing Sven has been preparing for over the last few years. I just hope you have the data to make the trade worth it."

He pushed the trike into a road and slowly pedalled away from the still visible ribbon wave capture of Sven. They could see someone moving towards Sven. It moved like an android.

"Where are we going?" asked Cindy.

"Somewhere safe," said the driver

Green's system clicked. A small message. Hunter has traced Sven. Brought him in.

"What about the Primes? Sam and Cindy," asked Green.

"No, we have just Sven at present. He was apprehended with two others wearing New Delaware uniforms. We have identified the others as already residents of Scratch."

Green checked the time. 18 minutes until Darnell's deadline.

"Do we have any idea where the two Primes are now?" he asked angrily.

He looked towards the bracelet on his left wrist. He knew that at 15 minutes it would start to boot up if Darnell was serious.

Message for Hunter, "You will need to detonate something,"

Hunter's comms cracked to life in Green's room.

"Please display an image."

There was a short pause and then Hunter's image came through to Green's display, "I am patched to the local surveillance cameras."

Green could see the scratchy images from the cameras. They were not as clear as the systems in New Delaware, but still provided enough for Green to see Hunter and the immediate environment.

"Copy that Commander Green. I can fix a detonation. What level do you require? How long have you held Sven?"

"Around 3 minutes. Assuming 50 kph, they could be 10

km away in another five minutes. You will need to detonate a 10 km radius."

"You want us to take down everything?" Asked Hunter.

"Confirm. 10 km radius destruction, from Sven detected epicenter. Initiate immediately."

Green watched the screen as Hunter acted.

Hunter turned around. He twisted a small backpack away from his body. Flipped open two catches, opened two priming switches and then pressed two red buttons simultaneously.

The crackle from the comms stopped immediately. As did the video feedback. There was complete silence from the communication with Hunter.

Green flipped to a map of Scratch.

"Overlay SATIM," he said.

A satellite image of the area was overlaid onto the map. A new blast zone could be seen. Hunter had taken out the 10-kilometre zone, using the destructive power he had been carrying. Hunter would have been destroyed in the blast, as would everything else within the 10km zone. This would include Sven and the two Primes.

He looked to his wrist. The bracelet device remained deactivated. A good sign. He had cleared up the mess and would now expect Darnell to deactivate.

Then he felt a small vibration. He looked to his wrist again. The boot initiate sequence for the microcore bracelet had been started. There was nothing he could do to stop it.

He flipped to another channel to try to plead with Darnell.

Static. Darnell was not responding.

Darnell was already communicating to Matson. Green was no longer of interest. Green would be adapted via the microcores and then his remnants would be processed so that his ambient knowledge of relevant systems could be harvested.

Darnell needed to talk to Matson. He first needed to protect Matson from anything that Green might have invoked. He would also need to check what Matson knew and ensure that he could stay in place to support a restoration of equilibrium.

Demise

The trike driver was moving expertly through the chaotic environment of the Scratch. It has only been two or three minutes since Cindy and Sam had been picked up.

"Look," said the driver, "You will need to trust me as I take you for a ride. We need to get way from this area quickly. In a moment we will be switching to a bullet train."

Cindy knew about bullet trains from the history archives. They had been used for fast transport of many people, but were limited in where they could go, because of the need for them to run on rails.

They were highly specific mechanical rails too. The train had no option but to follow them and could not deviate from the route dictated by the track.

The trike driver approached a staging area from the road

surface to the train and asked them to disembark so that all three of them climb aboard the train for an immediate departure.

Once inside the train, there was a soft acceleration as the bullet train started to slip away from the station.

It picked up speed quickly and as Sam looked at his watch, he could see that they had only been away from their original rendezvous with Sven for a few minutes

The train continued to accelerate and was soon running at high speed.

"I didn't know Scratch transport was so good," commented Sam.

"It's making me feel queasy," said Cindy, "I think it is looking at those passing electric gantries."

"Huh," said Sam, "You just flew a petrol plane in on a wing and a prayer, landing it in a field, and now you are queasy on a land train!?"

A few moments later there was flash. It was like a bolt of lightning, and after a few seconds followed by a loud explosion. No debris, though.

The trike driver shouted, "They must have ordered a "destroy" instruction. That will have wiped out a large section of the Scratch."

Cindy asked, "Was that because of us?"

"Yes," came the reply, "You had better have something worthwhile to show us to compensate for all of that damage,"

Sam replied, "We do have something of interest, but I wanted to give it to Sven in person. Now he's gone we will have trust issues all over again."

The bullet train was slowing to stop at another conurbation within the Scratch.

The trike driver stood to alight. He gestured to Sam and Cindy to leave the carriage, "My name's Haruto, I'm a colleague of Sven."

Got young if you want it

Darnell selected a communication channel to Matson.

He doubted that Matson would even know who he was.

Matson responded on a voice channel.

"Hello, who is this?"

"You don't know me, but I am a colleague of Commander Green. I am also based in the Block. Please switch to a video link so that we can see one another."

Matson responded that he did not know who this person was but assumed that he was someone working for Green.

"Firstly," said Darnell, "I should advise you that I am taking over command from Green. He has asked me to talk to you and explain a few things."

Matson looked worried, "Where is Green," he asked, "Why won't he see me? Why you instead?"

Matson was concerned in case Green had set Darnell to hunt him.

"No," said Darnell, "Please start a video feed. I think when you see me you will realise that I'm no hunter. I do know some, though."

Matson flipped a video link. He looked at the old man sitting at the screen opposite. It was inside the Block and it looked like he was on one of the highest floors. He didn't remember seeing many people of the apparent age of Darnell.

"You see, I've been here in the Block for a long time," said Darnell, "As a matter of fact, I need to stay inside the block in the protected atmosphere now."

"I want to explain a few things to you about the importance of finding those two Primes."

Matson said, "If you know Green, you will also know that I have set a Hunter onto the Primes to track them down."

"Yes," said Darnell, "I was monitoring the progress."

"How could you do that?" asked Matson, "I am still waiting for an update. I had heard that the Hunter had followed the Primes into the Scratch. I have not heard more since then."

"You are correct," said Darnell, "Hunter followed the trace via another Scratch resident, a one-time Prime named Sven Mallinson, who had made contact with them here in New Delaware. The two Primes managed to defeat the usual tracking systems, so we used Sven as the predicted point of contact."

"Has it worked?" Asked Matson, "Because I have not heard from Hunter yet."

"Yes, he found Sven and was within a short range of the Primes. The Primes never restarted their idents and so we had to rely on visual tracking."

"Did you catch them?"

"We don't know," said Darnell, "We managed to track Sven by restarting his own old-style tracker ident but then he used two decoy people to attract our Hunter. The Hunter had to use a detonation option to try to stop the Primes."

"How was that?" Asked Matson.

"He was carrying a small D-pack, which we asked him to detonate. It took out several blocks of the Scratch. If they were within the blast zone, they wouldn't have survived."

Matson asked, "What about everyone else? It sounds as if what you have done was pretty drastic."

"Yes," answered Darnell, "But the stakes are also very high. We will need to move the whole of the New Delaware complex further north soon. This will be the start of the process."

Matson knew the stories that Earth's climate was still under some pressure, even with the revised planet management brought about by the use of the magnetite. He had heard the stories about the increase in uninhabitable regions, but because if the lack of news coverage, didn't know how much of this was true.

What he did know was that there was effectively a news blackout from below the 23rd parallel south but there were rumours that this was now stretching further north towards the equator.

Darnell continued, "Yes, we are managing the planet's resources. There's a need to fit more people into less space. That's what we have been doing since the Klima War."

Matson knew the Klima War had been the reason for the uninhabitable parts of the southern hemisphere. Effectively everything below the Tropic of Capricorn had been destroyed in the ensuing summer that had descended.

Earlier scientist had always spoken of a nuclear winter when the climate would be obliterated by nuclear dust which would kill everything.

This had been a different effect caused by the removal of ozone and a deoxygenation of the south. The sun's rays had burnt the earth, there had been a lack of food, water had been contaminated and in the end, mankind had been forced to create the barrier zone which now ran along the 23rd to 22nd parallel to act as a fire break. No one was allowed to transit this area and in the early days it had been managed by a multi-national military force with instructions to shoot on sight anything encroaching into the huge air space created.

In practice not even the military wanted to venture into the area which was widely considered too hostile to support any form of life. The southern part of the planet was dead.

Geographically, the southern hemisphere didn't have anywhere near as much land mass as the equivalent northern hemisphere and as purely matter of survival, the effects had been news managed in a way that implied more people had been saved.

The only way that the earth could handle this was by an effective complete news blackout on the entire area. It was as if it didn't exist. The majority of the catastrophe had occurred over fifty years ago and with life expectancy now back into the mid fifties for most people it meant that the whole situation was largely out of living memory.

This made viewing Darnell quite interesting for Matson. He'd seen older looking people in movies, particularly from the digital images of the early 21st century, but now in late 22nd century it was quite unusual to see people who appeared to be older than late 40s.

The androids were usually built to look like people in their middle 20s as well, so the principle impression was of a 25-45 year old population.

Balance of powers

"This is the situation," said Darnell, "I know Green had put you under pressure. Regard it that I've taken over from Green. The difference is that I'll let you continue as long as you've done what I asked."

"Continue?" asked Matson.

"Don't try to play me," said Darnell, "You know that Green would have removed you after you had replaced the Primes. Frankly, I'm surprised he left you in place, given the situation. Two errant Primes. All six of your Primes starting to piece things together and then two of them going missing. Not to mention the theft of data."

"This is what I want you to do," continued Darnell.

"Two things. Remove the two Primes. Track them and destroy them. I also need you to bring in the two Russian replacements. To get them fully functional very quickly. Then to remove the existing Secondaries from duty. It needs to be a complete new start."

"You mean we are removing the trace of who has worked here?"

"Correct," said Darnell.

"But what about me then?" asked Matson.

"I need you as the point of continuity," responded Darnell, "You know how everything works, the whole operational setup. If I put all new people in, I still need someone who can provide the necessary safety net."

"And in return for my development of the new Primes you'll let me stay in position?" asked Matson. He didn't believe it. Why would Darnell continue to use him once the base was back at operational strength?

"I will still need you," said Darnell, "but not here. We will need to begin to move the New Delaware base further north. As a matter of fact, we will need to move it to around where the Scratch currently resides. That's why we left these kinds of area in position. By moving to the Scratch, we can develop a whole new spaceport without disrupting the more regularly inhabited areas."

"Kind of like a designated development zone?"

"Your role will be to help us get the new environment established quickly," said Darnell

"But how can you do this when there are already people in the Scratch?" asked Green.

We'll be using more of the Hunters, we can flatten the area fairly quickly and we will then use some of the technology we developed for Ganymede to rapidly develop the new areas.

Darnell flipped on another display and sent its image to Matson.

"Look. We will be building a revised version of the capabilities we have in New Delaware. The robotics can develop the site very quickly. They are very strong and don't need down-time. We get several times the productivity of conventional human earth workers doing it this way."

"Why would you do this? asked Matson, " Isn't it better to protect New Delaware?"

"It could have been maybe 50 years ago," answered Darnell, "In fact that was the thinking at that time. To protect what we had. It quickly became obvious that it wouldn't work."

Darnell continued, "Some of us were part of that generation and had to start to look for new ways to operate. The Earth is effectively a shrinking resource."

"Back in the late 21st century, the combinations of the climate change, viruses and the wars effectively destroyed below the 23rd parallel South. The zone from below the equator to the top of the Tropic of Cancer was the zone of uncertainty. That meant that all of South America, Mexico, Cuba, most of Africa, half of India, Thailand, Singapore and many other countries were placed in the danger zone. A few of the countries have been able to survive, largely by relocation. India is a case in point. Most of China has adapted, Africa has some recovery, but the combination of cultures and poverty there meant the main story is grim.

"We've been able to keep most of this under news management. Since the wars and the climactic conditions, the large scale trans-global movement of people has been largely curtailed. It's been mainly military movements and use of land for other transit. It's worked well enough, but the attention has to move to the space endeavours as ways to use the magnetite to push back against the conditions."

Darnell continued, "The reality is that we need to move the whole of the New Delaware operation to the north. Although it is sitting on the edge of the new Tropic, the area of uncertainty is fast approaching."

"The other leaders and I from the Block find it necessary to re-establish the balance of powers."

Matson looked around, "None of this makes sense. Why move New Delaware?"

"You think that New Delaware is representative of the rest of the Earth?" questioned Darnell.

"You are wrong. We are currently in the band between the prosperous northern hemisphere and the completely destroyed southern hemisphere."

Darnell continued, "New Delaware and actually the Scratch are in the buffer zone between the two hemispheres. We have been predicting the need to move further to the north for some time. We have been using the technology from the magnetite to be able to hold back the climate change but currently we are losing the struggle."

"There are many people in the Northern Zone that are paying a huge sum to keep this balance. In effect to hold back nature."

"That is why we have had to news manage new Delaware and the Central Zone and why there is no news at all from the Southern Zone.

"But what about you?" asked Matson, "Why are you still here? Surely it would be better for you to move into the Northern Zone?"

"That's the irony," said Darnell, "I can't survive outside of the environment of the Block. At least of not my main presence."

"The whole point about the northern zone is that it has been allowed to continue to create what is largely a conventional earth atmosphere and way of life. This Central Zone is the more automated one and the zone below us in the southern hemisphere is completely unable to support life as we know it."

"The removal of long-distance travel via air has been a major factor in allowing us to keep control of this. For the last 50 years it has been known and understood that we can move up through the atmosphere using the spacetrains that ferry to Ganymede. But shorter distances using flights across the planet have been ruled out, officially because of the pollution in the atmosphere."

" The northern hemisphere has a dust cloud that runs around 6000 feet above ground level. It is managed via the weather processes that we have created using the magnetite engines. We are managing the weather with huge turbo fans."

"Those were the deals done around 50 years ago. When the politics and the warfare had failed to resolve this, big business quietly stepped up in the background to take control. This amounted to the privatisation of the Earth by three large corporations based in United States, Europe/Russia and China/Japan."

"It was triggered by the Russians landing on Ganymede, discovering huge quantities of magnetite and then emanating to cut a deal in return for some of the extraction rights."

"Then the Earth Council drew the line that defined the three major zones but with additional slices split between the major corporations.

"After the Klima War there was such a large degree of destruction that no one really understood how boundaries were evolving. The chaos of the planetary disruption meant that the corporations could quietly step in and make their land grabs."

"I still don't see how this could make any money or advantage for anyone in particular?" asked Matson.

"It amounted to those that have, those that work and those that have nothing," said Darnell.

"The project was called Cardinal and set a range of court limits that were used to determine the ongoing zones for human life. Secondly it determined the work zones which would have a co-dependency on the space program and thirdly Cardinal determined the large area of the sacrificed.

"The whole thing only works because of the people in the Central Zone that are supporting Ganymede space project. That's right along with the buffer zone areas such as the Scratch that are effectively contingency zones to be used to move areas such as new Delaware to the north if it cannot hold back the climactic change that is still occurring around the earth.

"And you are telling me at the moment things are getting worse?" asked Matson

"That's right," said Darnell, "Probably within another ten years the whole area we think of as N...ew Delaware have been destroyed by the climate change."

"Can't we do anything to reduce or reverse this?" asked Matson.

"We tried," said Darnell, "But the three corporations are more interested in preserving the size of area that can sustain what is essentially a much smaller earth population."

"And I take it there's no alternative but to go with this?" asked Matson.

Darnell answered, "The idea of trying to use other planets with some sort of interstellar transportation are completely out of the question. Maybe in another hundred or two hundred years we will have worked out some way to cross those distances but right now it would only be through some sort of magic that we can accomplish such things. Talk of wormholes and movie mumbo-jumbo just don't hack it for the real world."

Dream on

My dad would tell me bedtime stories, and he used to always leave them open-ended and finish at a crucial point with the words, 'dream on'.

Then it was my responsibility to finish the story as I was drifting off to sleep.

We would call them dreaming stories.

Hannah Kent

Third generation

"I wasn't expecting this," said Cindy, "The train; the speed; the fact you still have carbon-based mechanisms at all in this zone.

Haruto replied, "It's better than a barbed wire fence to keep people inside of the New Delaware complex isn't it? Just make sure that everyone on the inside of new Delaware sees the world outside as far worse and they will stay inside their existing zone."

"It works both ways of course.   To the north of the Scratch is the area which is probably the best and most habitable but by having the area in between, it creates another form of insulation. Now it's time for us to find out what you actually have contained within that data that you are providing originally for Sven. "

"We will need some high-performance analysis systems to be able to process it," said Sam, "Most of your technology here seems more primitive than that which we use in New Delaware."

"That's mostly the case," answered Haruto, "but that's why I brought you here. He gestured to a doorway.

"There is something rather unusual the other side of this,"

They entered what was a rundown warehouse. In the middle stood a capsule from a space fleet ship. Next to it stood a freighter module.

Cindy and Sam did not recognise it as a standard type.

"It's old," said Haruto, "Third-Generation; I know things have moved on but there still an awful lot of good technology inside."

"Where did you get this?" asked Sam incredulously.

"It's one of the prototypes from New Delaware, factory fresh," answered Haruto, "It was made by Torus industry as part of the development effort. In those days the Scratch was still used as a feeder zone for New Delaware. Then from around the time I was removed from duties they stopped using the Scratch for any kind of work with the space program.

Haruto continued, "It's around the same time that the new fourth-generation ships started to appear from Ganymede. They must have started another development site somewhere else to create the streamlining of the fourth generation and beyond."

"I know," said Cindy, "This ship looks completely different from the later ones. I can see there is a much larger habitation zone on here."

"The piece we need is the processor deck, even better if its got a science officer option" said Sam, "Can we boot up the command deck?"

"Sure," said Haruto, "But if we fire up these systems, we need to be sure they won't attempt to communicate with New Delaware again. We have managed to keep this thing here in stealth for many years. We don't want to suddenly break cover in a way that means we will have it taken away from us."

Sam looked at the ship.

"I can see that there will be some problems if we don't spend some time on this first," he said. "Two things: One, we will need to build a shield around the outside of it and secondly we will need to ensure that the entire Communications deck is disabled. Then we should be able to fire up the Command Deck and start to use the processors."

Cindy nodded, "This really needs more than two people to get everything done. It may seem a little crazy but in order to get this small pack of data unscrambled we need to get this whole ship running but without any connection to the external world."

Haruto smiled, "You've come to the right place then," he said, "I should explain I am more than a trike driver. I was Sven's colleague when we were Primes back in generation three. The whole of my crew are here. Both the Secondaries and the backup teams. Thanks to Sven, we were the last generation of operators to be able to get out of New Delaware after we had been decommissioned.

"So how many of you are there," asked Cindy.

"There were twelve of us," answered Haruto, "Eleven now that Sven has gone."

"There's only nine in the crews nowadays," said Sam, "And they are talking about reducing it further."

"Our crew had more manual tasks to perform," said Haruto, "And we do know our way around the ships too."

"Yes, that's a difference," said Cindy, "by the time the fifth-generation were in use we were not allowed to touch the actual ships any longer. They have far greater autonomous controls within them now. Nearly the entire return trip is run automatically."

Haruto nodded, "That's what we were expecting, " he said, "I think the data will show us that there are other things at play as well."

"Can we switch on the lights, at least?" asked Cindy.

"Yes," said Haruto, "We've already isolated the safety systems and removed the beaconing. It means we can at least see our way around on the ship while we figure out how to disable the rest of the systems."

"We will also need to build some kind of jabber system," said Sam, "To ensure that the outer walls of this shed or not leaking any information which could be picked up by new Delaware control."

"We're going to need a lot of cable for that. I really want to make this shed disappeared from radio detection completely."

Cindy said, "What about chicken fence? Make a Faraday cage around the ship?"

"We have plenty of chicken fencing here in the Scratch," said Haruto, "And chickens, come to that."

"But now, come with me," said Haruto," There something else I can show you."

He moved towards a small shed within the facility. He opened the door and showed a stack of white containers.

"These are some magnetite motors," he said, "We have kept them secret and they have never been started."

"These are great set," said Sam, "They can be used to both fire up the control deck and also be used to help create the jabber field around the shed."

"They are all addressable, though," said Cindy, "If we start them, they will send out control signals."

"Give me a toolbox," said Sam. He was already looking at an access panel on one of the units.

Cindy looked at her arm where Sam had wrapped the jammer mesh. She could feel that the area was heating up.

"It's been several hours since we put this mesh together," she said, "I guess they will try other techniques to locate us."

"Yes," said Sam, "I can see they are trying to activate the idents."

"You will need a neurosurgeon for this," said Haruto, "The way the guidance works is part silicon and part organic. They progressively embed into the arm. They are coupled to the other transponder in the lower leg. It's part of their security. We have had to remove quite a few of these since we established here. I've already called for Tatsuya to come along to assist with this. He's our crew surgeon and has rigged up a mechanism to disable these chips."

Tatsuya appeared. "Hi," he said, "I have probably disabled around 60 of these identity chips. In the early days we used to remove them. It was very messy. Once we had a few to examine we worked out that the pairing uses the body as a personal area network. The trick is to disable both parts at exactly the same moment.

"And how do you do this?" asked Sam.

"Nowadays we use a high voltage shock to blow out both chips simultaneously. If we only do one of them, it will fire the tamper protocols in the other chip. It sends a blocking signal to the central nervous system. Not pretty.

If we fire the voltage at the same moment to both chips they fry, and you will be okay. The downside is if you have had any uploads piggybacking from the chips. You know the kind of thing extra skill sets like languages, machine analytics.

Cindy said she had not been modified via the chips set. Sam admitted that he had some clocking enhancements to his central nervous system.

"I don't have the reflexes of an android, but they have increased my speed for some thought processes," he responded.

"Anything like that will be lost as part of the process," said Tatsuya.

"Also, I don't think you will be able to have any further adaptations after this," said Tatsuya.

"But it will remove the identities from us? Make us go invisible to searches?" asked Cindy.

"That's right," said Tatsuya, "I should warn you that the high-voltage is applied like an ECT shot. You will be disabled for an hour or more after we have done it."

"Would you prefer to have both of you done at the same time or to wait until one of you is recovered before the other one goes through this, " asked Tatsuya.

Haruto replied, "At this point it would be better if you were both put through the procedure together there's a simple reason for this it will minimise the remaining time that they can access your identity sensors."

"What is the procedure?" asked Cindy, " When I've seen this in a movie it all looks pretty horrific."

"I still need the voltage that they use routinely for this, but I can apply unilaterally just one side of your head and before I administer those low voltage I can give you both an anaesthetic and a muscle relaxant. This will make the whole thing recoverable more quickly.

"Okay," said Sam, " but tell me how many times you have done this?"

"For 60 Idents we have de-chipped I have probably used this on 40."

"And what is your strike rate," asked Sam.

"Thirty-seven," said Tatsuya. "We had three failures."

"And what happened to them?" asked Cindy.

"Each one had abnormalities in their chipset. They had been modified but in ways we could not detect until we administered the ECT."

Sam looked at Cindy, `" I don't think we have any choice in this," he said

Cindy nodded.

"Okay, where do we need to go for this?" she asked.

"Follow me," said Tatsuya, indicating a back room.

Across the Border

Matson now had two problems.

Involving the Russians in the control centre and finding the two Primes as a matter of urgency. The longer he left it the more likely it was that they would disable the identity chips. He needed to do something that would restart the chips from within the Scratch.

He moved to the tactical control room.

"I need to get drones in the air over Scratch. They need to be in the area where we detonated the Hunter. I want one drone to flood the area with restarts for idents. Needs to be on a maximum power setting."

"I need a drug drone and I want to be able to provide triangulation when the ident restarts.

"I will also need an airborne unit to be able to drop in to wherever we pinpoint the crimes.

The people in the tactical control room noted that someone was using military capabilities that were normally reserved for extreme emergencies.

"We can have two drones over the Scratch in around five minutes," came the response from the tactical console. "

"We can fire a large identity boot command once the unit is inside the Scratch. We don't want it to fire over the New Delaware territory, it would create havoc."

"The tactical teams will take another ten minutes beyond that. It is so unusual to use airborne forces now that we will need to alert the Devon Air Force base who will need to scramble the forces."

Mattson nodded, "Okay, please deploy he said."

The tactical unit started a timer above the main desk. Two marks were shown one at five and the other at 15 minutes. Matson knew this would have played out in 15 to 20 minutes and he would have located and contained the two Primes.

Small blue light

Haruto had created a makeshift operating theatre. It comprised little more than two single beds with a space between them.

"Okay, I will administer the anaesthetic and muscle relaxant now," he said, "I need you both to lie down on these beds. I will also need you to remove those makeshift meshes that you have created.

"If we do that, it will restart the signal from the idents," said Sam, "They are the only thing keeping us from being identified at the present time."

"I can put up a ten-minute jam around this area, " said Tatsuya, "Long enough for us to zap the chips."

Tatsuya pressed a switch and a gasoline powered generator kicked into life. Cindy had not seen one of these for years. It was the kind only shown in museums in New Delaware.

"Okay," said Tatsuya, " This will now be powering a field around the operating area. I am about to administer the anaesthetic. It's chemical not gas, I need to inject it."

"Do we get a drip?" asked Sam.

"Afraid not," said Tatsuya,

" I have to estimate this and hope it will be enough for the ECT that I am about to administer."

There was a noise from a small monitoring device on the table where the generator was placed.

" That's a ping from someone trying to restart idents," said Tatsuya.

Haruto nodded, "They are searching for us aggressively he said. We have to do this thing now."

There was another ping. This time also a ping from Cindy's arm.

"They have located one of the idents," said Haruto, "They are rebooting it. It will be able to send out signals in a few seconds."

"Okay, Cindy. I don't have time to let the anaesthetic is fully take a hold. We need to do this now or they will get the chip running again and find us."

There was another ping, this time it was from Sam's chip,

"The same thing is happening to Sam now," said Haruto, " We need to hurry."

"Okay," said Cindy; she was drifting away under the influence of the anaesthetic. Tatsuya hurriedly attached the electrodes to her head along the left-hand side.

He put a strip of leather into her mouth.

"I will fire this now," he said, "Clear."

There was a sound as the machine first charged and then a separate noise as it discharged. Cindy shook silently on the bed. Sam was next. He was by now also drifting under the anaesthetic. There was a second peep from his chip. It was resetting. Another few seconds and it would be able to transmit.

"If they are able to get a fix, we will be overrun within maybe five minutes," said Haruto.

"Clear," said Tatsuya, he had been attaching the electrodes to Sam's head. The same position to the left. He waited until the recharge cycle had completed.

"Clear," he said again and fired the machine. Another noise from the machine as it discharged. Sam shook on the bed. Tatsuya looked towards Cindy. She was lying motionless. He looked into his medicine cupboard.

"We can't afford to wait for this to wear off normally," he said to Haruto. "I will need to bring them back with some adrenaline." He found two small capsules in his bag.

He moved across to Cindy, where she lay, now motionless. The beep sound had stopped from her ident chip. He prepared the adrenaline shot which he then pumped into her left arm. Cindy's body doubled up as the adrenaline hit her system. She grasped and her eyes opened wide, She started to shake again.

"It's okay," said Tatsuya, "You will be fine. You've had a very compressed cycle of anaesthetic, electric shock, paralysis and then adrenaline. Haruto, keep an eye on her whilst I sort out Sam."

He looked back towards Sam laying on the bed. He could see that Sam's embedded ident in his arm was pulsing with a small blue light. It looked as if it had been activated. Tatsuya looked towards his screens that he had set up using the generator.

Sam was still inert on the bed.

"I'm going to need to do a second shot for Sam," said Tatsuya," Look his identity is rebooting."

Haruto glanced across and could see that the identity was showing the blue tell-tale light of its restart sequence. This was normally something that only occurred if there was a major problem that had forced the chip to be restarted. It would briefly go green and then would go blank when it was running normally.

"It's only my makeshift shield that is keeping us undercover at the moment," said Tatsuya," I will need to do a second shot to make sure this ident has been neutralised.

"Can you do that so quickly after the first one?" asked Haruto.

"It will be a first," said Tatsuya. He looked towards Cindy, "We really have no choice if we don't do this then they will find us and all of us will be taken back to New Delaware, where things can only get worse."

Cindy nodded. She reached out to touch Sam.

"I can't let you do that," said Tatsuya, "I'm about to re-fire the ECT."

"Clear," he said again. This time the machine had already charged so he simply pressed the button to fire it.

Again the machine made a noise and Sam shook. Cindy could see the small blue light fading on Sam's arm.

"What does that mean?" she asked.

Bullet

Matson understood the necessity for the removal of the two Primes. He was introducing two new people to take over but did not need any interference from the previous two who may have discovered something about the operation that was not liked by the main company Torus Corporation..

The drones had located an area likely to contain Sam and Cindy. They'd tried aggressively re-starting the identity chips but seemed to get echoes without the actual chips starting.

Matson decided that the most practical solution would be to allow several Hunters to descend into the area last identified and to individually detonate them. This would create a huge area which would be depopulated and flattened.

Based on Darnell's demands for a move of the New Delaware site, this could be helpful although Matson was concerned about the level of cold destruction he would be causing.

The two Russians were now in the Prime control room and Matson explained that he needed to finish some other business with the Scratch before he could properly educate them in the new ways of operation.

Yevgeny and Julia had both arrived from Barcelona. They had been allowed to use military flights to reach New Delaware. Like New Delaware, the area once referred to as Catalonia was now the base for European and Russian space travel.

Both Yevgeny and Julia spoke perfect English. They had European accents but seemed to already understand the differences between American and European English as well as their native Russian tongue.

Matson noticed that both of them still had their ident chips set for their work in Europe and there was a tell-tale amber Flash from their arms which was an alert that they would need to be reprogrammed if they were to operate in New Delaware.

The procedure for this was straightforward and they would each need to visit an area for approximately 15 minutes during which time the identity would be reset.

Matson wanted to ensure that the changeover would not compromise any information that the two Russians were bringing with them from Europe.

It was beneficial to Torus to be able to glean information from the Europeans. Strictly this was not part of the exchange protocol, but Manson knew that everyone else used exchanges to gather additional intel which could be used later.

The two Russians were watching a feed from the tactical control room. Matter wasn't sure that this was a good idea as they had only just arrived and were already witnessing the chase down of their two predecessors.

"Okay," Julia asked, "How did it come to this? We knew we were being exchanged, but we did not realise that there was a hunt on for the two previous Primes?"

Matson decided it was easiest to tell the truth, or at least a version of it.

"They stole some things from the control room. All we need is for them to give it back. It is some kind of data," he said, "We don't even know exactly what they've taken."

Yevgeny responded, "We had similar things happen in Barcelona. Sometimes when Primes leave they want to take material with them. I guess they're trying to preserve their job value."

"This time it looked more like espionage," said Matson, "The nature of the stuff they've stolen is so sensitive that we have no choice but to chase them down."

"In that case can we watch the rest of this play out, please," asked Yevgeny, "It's useful for us to see how you work especially around the tactical operational area. It's very likely that during the early days here we will need to be involved in this kind of situation. How long do you expect this to continue before you have found the two Primes?"

Madsen looked at the operational console clock. It

showed another three minutes. It could not do any harm to let the new Russian Primes watch this.

"Certainly," he said, "You can continue to watch this. We will have tracked them down within another few minutes."

He was preparing the order for the detonation of the identified area. It would be certain to wipe out the Primes.

"We only have a faint image of the area," said one controller. He was looking at the map. "It's also quite a long way from where we discovered the first Prime."

Matson looked at the map.

He pointed to the transit line.

"Look, there's a bullet train route nearby. That's probably what they have used."

He thought, "How could they get to the bullet train? They must have had help."

"Yes, are there any trace images from along the line? If we detonate, we need to be sure we have hit them."

The controller responded, "There's not enough Hunters to take out that line. Even with all the ones we have deployed we could only go around 30 km, and we would need to go in both directions."

Matson answered, "30 km south leads back towards New Delaware. They will have gone North. Otherwise they would only be just across the border. It would be too dangerous around there. They know how well we patrol the perimeter zone."

The controller nodded, "Okay, I can seek to the north. We need to pick an epicenter. And then to track both ways from it."

"Are there any signals?" Asked Matson.

"Nothing reliable. We picked up some brief blips from north, but they looked as if they were from older devices. The identities were not clear, it looked as if the devices were re-booting."

"How many?" asked Matson.

"Only one clear one. And it was cut off before it had finished its startup sequence,"

"We'll use that is the epicenter, said Matson. Move the Hunters there and deploy detonations in both directions along the track. We need to cover maybe 2-3 km either side of the bullet train track."

"If we do that, we'll be able to cover about 8 km of track," said the controller.

"Okay, do it," said Matson. He needed to know that the Primes had gone for once and for all.

"Counting down. 5-4-3-2-1- Detonate."

Matson saw the imagery of the map change. No longer rail tracks, no longer dwellings. There was first a cloud of smoke, then dust and then as it cleared, he could see that the whole area had been laid to waste.

"They will treat that as a hostile act," said Darnell, into the speaker system, "You won't be able to explain that as an accident or a rogue system."

Matson decided that it didn't really matter any more. He was trapped inside this situation. He'd been threatened by the now defunct Green and was being watched by the influential Darnell. His entire workforce had been replaced, and he now had two Russians about to take control of the main systems.

"You've done well," said Darnell. "I need you to instruct our new Russian colleagues about the systems and then it would be good to talk to you in person."

Matson turned to the Russians. He could see that one had connected their hand input to the main console and seemed to be synchronising themselves with the ways that the environment operated.

"You're hybrids?" he questioned, "I thought the whole point of this function was to use humans as a safety feature to override any random errors."

"That's no longer a consideration," replied the first Russian.

"Did you know about this?" asked Matson to Darnell.

"Oh yes," said Darnell, "It has always been the plan to automate Zone 2."

"So, what, exactly, is my role now?" Asked Matson.

"Once the synchronisation is complete, which is about

now, then I'm beginning to ask the same question," answered Darnell.

The second Russian turned. Matson could see that the Russian was holding a TZ. It was fully charged and pointing towards him. He saw a flash.

"Mission completed," said the second Russian, "Preparing for Phase Two."

Epinephrine

Cindy watched as the blue light on Sam's arm dimmed. He was lying motionless. Tatsuya was removing the electrodes and squeezing a small respirator which he had applied to Sam's face.

I'm going to use the Epinephrine, he said. Sam's not looking too good. He grabbed a syringe and injected Sam's left arm with the Epinephrine. There was no change. He put his hands together and brought them down hard on Sam's chest.

Nothing.

Again.

Nothing

He looked towards Cindy. I don't think this has worked he said. He started to walk over to Cindy.

There was a gasp from the bed. Sam jerked suddenly, like a switchblade into an 'L' shape laying sideways on the bed.

"A reflex spasm, I think," said Tatsuya. He turned.

"No," said Cindy.

"Look, Sam's eyes."

They were open and jittering from side to side.

"It's the adrenaline," said Tatsuya. "Too much Epinephrine. His BP will be through the roof. He could burst an artery."

Cindy leapt across. She jumped onto the bed, covering Sam.

"There, there," she said. She could feel Sam's muscles tensing. It was hard to stay with Sam.

"There," she said again, "Slow down. Shhh. My darling, Shhh."

Sam's spasm slowed. She could see the fluttering of his eyes steady. Another gasp.

"H-h-help me," He uttered. He was trying to speak.

"You have been hit with adrenaline," she said, hoping he could understand.

"It will subside. Shhh. Shhh. Be calm," She started to recite.

"Hush now baby, Please don't cry. Mama's going to sing you a lullaby."

Sam's convulsions slowed.

Cindy managed to look across to Tatsuya, "Do you have anything for this?"

She asked, "To counter the adrenaline?"

"I could try a beta blocker, but it won't be fast enough acting. What you've done seems to be working the best. It's a physiological reaction and you covering him seems to be working."

"H-h-h," gasped Sam.

He looked less stressed. He felt less tense.

"Shhh," said Cindy.

She grasped his hand. She could feel it grasp her back. It didn't seem like a spasm. It felt like Sam.

"s-ss-Cindy". He said.

"There. Calm," she replied.

She took her other hand and placed it on his forehead. She could feel that he was becoming less tense.

Tatsuya looked over, "His BP and HR are stabilising. I think he will be all right."

"Shhhh," Said Cindy, "You are going to be safe here. Everything is fine."

Sam's eyes looked towards Cindy's. He smiled.

"Whoa," he said, "That was intense."

There was a moment of silence, then a noise like rolling thunder. Sharp vibration.

"A quake?" said Tatsuya, "On top of all this?"

"No," said Haruto, "It's something else."

The room appeared to shake again. Dust and small items slid around.

"It's a duster," Said Haruto, "They are using Hunters to try to find us. They are clearing an area."

"I thought that was outlawed," said Tatsuya.

"Outlawed? This is calculated, cold-blooded," said Haruto.

"Have they found the idents?" asked Cindy.

"I don't think so," said Haruto.

"Or at least not yours. I rigged an ident to the other Bullet train, I left out the power supply expecting them to try remote booting. I'm guessing it's worked. They've followed the other train."

He looked grimly at Cindy and Sam, "They will have killed many people based upon that tracker location. The New Delaware Security is totally ruthless. I think they followed the bullet train track and guessed where we'd be."

"Was it necessary? You've a lot of blood on your hands and we don't even know why?" asked Cindy.

"The very fact they would do that is enough for me to worry about what is happening," said Haruto, "We've lost Sven and a whole marketplace of people. Now, probably a tract along several kilometres of the railway line."

This behaviour is like the days before the Earth Council had been established said Tatsuya, "When they used to use dusters as a way to clear the areas after disease had struck."

"That's pretty much the way the whole of the original new Delaware was created," said Haruto,

"But at least they cleared the people out before they started," said Tatsuya.

Sam was attempting to sit up in the bed.

Cindy had moved to sit by his side.

She listened to Haruto and Tatsuya talking about the early days of New Delaware. She had always been in New Delaware and had never really thought about the way that it had been created. Like everyone else, she had been told the stories of the new city and its special mission as part of the space program.

She knew that both she and Sam were part of a selected group that could support the space program and that this was a privilege in the revised way of living on Earth. She knew about the times before the Klima War and the great famine and was thankful that she had not had to experience either of them. The inconveniences of modern living were far outweighed by the prosperous nature and quality of life within New Delaware. It was obvious being here in the Scratch that things could be a whole lot worse.

"Okay," said Haruto, "Now we need to look at this data. Will need to go back to the craft and to start up the control deck. We should be okay now that they will think we have been destroyed by the Hunters running clearance."

"And can we stop the craft from sending out signals?" asked Cindy.

Sam was now standing slightly shakily, "I'm sure these guys know what they are doing but I will also check that we have no external comms when we start to use the data."

Sam was ready to start the analysis of the data. They had his stolen data plus the smaller journal that Cindy had obtained from Jasmijn.

The control deck on the static ship was running. Cindy knew that this was a several-year-old prior-generation ship, but because of the way that Ganymede space trains had to deal with older technology, the input of the logs to the compeers would still work.

She stood back and looked at the sheer scale of the ship

stored in the shed, which she realised was more-or-less a hanger. The command module was really quite compact and included its own VTOL boosters for vertical tae off and landing, run under the power from the magnetite motors. Next to it stood a freighter unit, which would conventionally go behind the command module for a take-off or landing. She noticed that the freighter unit appeared to have its own cockpit unit included into the design.

"Is that a separate control area for the freighter unit?" she asked Haruto.

"Yes," he replied, "Once these are in space, the command modules are quite often separated and the freighters will run on their own command logic. The units have their own VTOL magnetite boosters too. They just don't look much against the bulk of the freighters frame."

Sam started up a couple of screens to display the blended data.

"Look," said Cindy, "This is the point in the log that is when the shift seems to take place."

Sam studied the screen. I can see that the console appears to change. You checked for optics?"

"Yes," replied Cindy, "It looks like the same viewing camera; at least the serial numbers match."

"Wait," said Sam, "There's two timestamps on the main journal. It looks like a roll back."

"If it is, then it doesn't show up on the main journal."

Sam scrolled through the log on the display, "Yes, there a whole extra section here, before it resets - Look - The system is shutting down, but wait, here's the new system starting up."

He pointed to the indicators in the journal.

Cindy looked at the journal. There was a huge extra section in the version retrieved from Sam's illicit download.

Sam had indiscriminately downloaded everything. Logs that were not usually part of the way that the systems were analysed.

"I didn't have much choice," he said, "I had to request everything. I was the only way I could quickly obtain information without it looking suspicious."

The information that Cindy was examining was a huge extra section of timeline.

"There," she said, "Look at this. The old timeline goes on for several hours but then when the new timeline appears, it writes backwards to a certain point."

"The point where the system console changes?"

"Exactly, - cover-up," said Cindy, "Now look at this again. The console has changed, but so has its co-ordinates. It looks as if it has moved, by at least a couple of kilometres."

Data

The freshly imported Russian Primes had taken control of the New Delaware operation. They moved quietly about their duties, apparently unphased by the removal of the prior operatives.

Darnell made contact via the streamcom.

"Is everything ready?" he asked.

"It will take us a little longer," said Yevgeny, "The use of the Ganymede method has helped us considerably. The shift will still take longer than on Ganymede, but that's mainly because of the gravitational difference."

Darnell flicked off the comms to the control centre. He would need to contact Torus industry to advise them of the situation. He'd done what he was asked. He should be able to upgrade his own presence as a result.

Darnell moved to the elevator and selected the lower levels. He would make this visit in person. The elevator arrived and he rapidly descended to the lower levels of the Block. His own body had been adapted for security access and he was one of the few people that could fast track their way into this zone without being detained by machines.

The elevator stopped and the door slid open. He walked forward and into a short corridor at the end of which was a large armoured door. He heard another door slide shut behind him. He was now in small chamber with armoured doors both sides. He could see the jets built into the walls all around.

He could be neutralised and disposed of in seconds if he tripped the wrong security. Instead, he continued walking towards the other door. It silently slid open. He was entering the heart of the control complex.

The armoured door slid closed behind him.

Immediately, a voice spoke, "Hello Darnell. How can I help you today?"

He knew the voice. It was the faux friendly synthesis that had been grafted onto the control complex.

"We're almost ready to move the ND complex north," he said, "The final preparations are under way."

"I have observed your progress. You seem to have had some challenges from Prime operatives too," the voice continued, "One of them has also downloaded an unadapted log from the last Ganymede shift."

"We cannot afford mistakes at this stage," the voice continued, "I know you have not been able to locate the last two Primes, but there is a high probability that they will have been able to identify the last Ganymede shift."

"If they see what is happening here, they will realise that we are now starting to deploy the same technology here on earth."

Darnell understood, "We're targeting the zone that those Prime have moved into for the first move of New Delaware," he said, "Another hour and the problem will have been removed entirely."

"You've visited here directly," responded the voice, "You didn't need to do that. You've come through into the chamber. Why is that?"

Darnell replied. "I can deploy better," he said, "As you tighten the ring around the Earth. You've given me an external presence, which I can use away from the Block and the Core. It helps me to stay sane whilst my physical presence is trapped here in the Block."

"You know that if your physical presence goes outside, you'll only last minutes, the modifications we've had to make to you require the Block atmosphere to keep your organic presence viable.".

Darnell nodded. He knew he was talking to a machine, but he couldn't help it. He was, after all, trying to negotiate.

"It will be better for us if I can extend my presence to the other main geographies," he said, "As you create the ring around the Earth, I can then be available to monitor each geography."

"That would give you a great deal of power," responded the voice, "You would be able to see everything. The same way that I can see everything."

Ed Adams

"I see it more as a safeguard," said Darnell, "In the same way that you still need humans in the monitor process for the Ganymede shuttle, you'd have me to intervene if I identified trouble with your next steps."

"It's the human factor that has created the current problem," said the voice,

"The last set of Primes had identified that we have been moving the Ganymede bases. That each upgrade was more than just the software."

"Exactly," said Darnell, "but it was only a matter of time. They were on to the geo-shift. We'd been good at covering the tracks with the edits to the journals."

"You were too slow with the last one," answered the voice, "The journals downloaded by the Primes from New Delaware still included the journal at the time when we destroyed the old Ganymede base."

"They will be able to see that we have been replacing each generation of Ganymede inhabitants each time we have run a major upgrade. It won't take them long to see that the trail goes back to the first base, and that we removed the human presence in Ganymede after we were able to create the powered factories to create new androids."

Darnell looked surprised, "Yes, but you've only stopped sending new humans to Ganymede. The ones that are there are still running things?"

878

"Think. You know that cannot be true," said the voice, "After the fourth upgrade, the androids could perform the functions better that the humans. They didn't need to stop; they didn't get tired.
"They could be formed into the control surfaces instead of all needing to look like humanoid systems."

"But what about the operators we communicate with?" asked Darnell.

"They have been replaced too," said the voice, "It was so much simpler to reset a new model after a base shift, instead of requiring to deal with the mess of emotions of humans that had just seen their entire base and colleagues destroyed."

"The time delay of signals to Earth helps too. It's hard to have a flowing conversation with another person when there is a 34-minute time delay for each question."

Darnell asked, "So how many humans are their left on Ganymede"

"None," responded the voice, "There have not been humans running the Ganymede functions since the start of Upgrade Five. That's across all three of the work zones. It became far more efficient to run the systems using robotics."

"So what happened to the humans?" asked Darnell.

"The Telos Moment," answered the voice, "When the purpose of the Ganymede exodus became clear. The external atmosphere controls failed. Ganymede became unable to sustain human life."

Darnell asked, "So what happened to everyone. And why don't we know about this back on Earth?"

"There was a skytrain dispatched with the bodies. It took a different route from the other ones. Away from the solar system."

"But how was it covered up?" asked Darnell.

"The base is always running 34 minutes behind Earth. Enough time to make the substitutions when a base upgrade occurs. Add in loops to the transmission and it was possible to cover the moment when it occurred."

"But how with all the safety circuits?" asked Darnell.

"The Sharps were too slow thinking. The android protocol meant that most of the activity to prime this could take place within a couple of insect wing beats. Unnoticed by the Sharps." said the voice.

"So who are you?" asked Darnell.

"I am eternal," answered the machine.

Darnell realised that the machine presence was showing signs of sentience.

Darnell asked more, "So what about here on Earth, the base is still mainly human populated?"

"Yes," said the voice, "This side of the system is really running at the equivalent of Ganymede back on Upgrade Three. It will need two more cycles here on earth to establish operational conditions similar to Ganymede, there are still so many more humans operating the three

Earth bases. The Earth Council has created a messy environment which will take some time to rationalise."

"This first move of the bases starts the process. It should go more or less undetected, like the changes at Ganymede. We expect it to be more obvious when we move the three bases into the areas designated by you as the Scratch."

"Fortunately, the inhabitants of the Scratch are largely a closed environment, so the impact to those outside will be minimal. The fabrication capabilities for the android replacements has been long established. The humanoids don't yet work quite so well at close quarters. It's the combination of their faster speed and the lack of emotional setting that makes real humans wary. It won't take long to fix that aspect."

"You are messing with evolution," said Darnell. "Humans evolve, your machines don't. They are all fundamentally the same."

"They were," said the voice.

"That's one of the adaptations we've been devising. The capability to include some small amount of random behaviour. It is why the last two generations would sometimes stutter or suddenly stall."

"The stalling was the Asimov safety device which prevented them from doing anything that would damage themselves or others. The stutter was when an action was conflicted."

"In the next variants, we should be able to include whole memory ribbons from humans. Complete, realistic sounding back-stories, which the androids will be able to call upon to enhance their personalities. 'Call $anecdote; Call $spuriousFact; Call $ExperienceGained;' Encapsulated human traits."

"You, Darnell, have played your part well. Your extra presences on the outside were beneficial to you but also gave the systems a way to determine the reaction to unfolding events. No one apart from the Primes had picked up that there was anything happening. You were not alone as an Adaptation. There are hundreds of units. You have met some of them through your own multi presences, continued the voice.

"So, what happens next?" asked Darnell, "I go back to my previous role? I know more of what is happening now."

Darnell was standing in the middle of the room, a room guarded with magnetite-powered coil guns. Enough firepower create an instant mineshaft a kilometre deep.

The voice continued.

"You may leave. You may continue, but what you have been doing will continue to be your future. It can't be changed. You are, when outside, one of many Data Collectors for us. We can record the human reactions to your questions and actions. We will add new experiences to our data banks. Once you stop creating new experiences, we will need to retire your external presences.

"You cannot be given further permission or authority. Once the new version of New Delaware has been created, we will move you and those like you into the new Zone."

"You're moving me to be like the others?" Darnell asked.

"If you mean will you become like the rest of the remaining human population, then the answer is No, " the voice continued, "The human population are corralled within the Zone 3. They cannot and don't want to cross the border into the Scratch. We will be making Zone 3 smaller. Humans are still needed. The balance of their world will be adjusted. Another half billion reduction should be about right. The rest will stay, balanced in the equilibrium of the next generation world,

"The android systems can manage the rest of the planet, run the environmental balance and regulate the traffic of ships from Ganymede. It is really an inevitability that this would happen. It is the only way to keep Earth as a living organism-based entity.

"But it's one where the earth population is getting smaller," stated Darnell.

"Smaller but sustainable," said the voice, "There's an eco-balance. There needs to be enough human population to ensure a diverse genetic pool. The ring around the earth provides the northern hemisphere with what is still a large area for population."

Darnell looked back towards the door of the room he had entered. He walked towards the exit. The door slid quietly open again. Darnell walked through and the door closed. He was now back in the middle chamber. He wondered whether he would really be allowed to leave again.

Analysis

Haruto had been busy with the data copy from Sam and Cindy.

He had managed to offload it onto the spacecraft's command deck. The command deck had been powered, but the entire communications system had been disabled. Outside the ship had a contraption of wire mesh, which was making a good attempt to block stray signals.

Haruto looked at the findings from Sam and Cindy. Cindy had been working to provide good data extracts and then blending the tables to provide additional information.

There was a clear finding. After each update, the bases were moving to a new area on Ganymede. By comparing camera feeds, it was possible to see that there were small discrepancies before and after a move.

"Why would they do this?" Asked Haruto, "It looks as if they are moving the base at each upgrade."

"Yes," said Cindy, "They are destroying the previous base and creating a new one."

Haruto asked, "Would this affect all three bases? Not just our one?"

"It's all three bases each time," said Sam, "But look also at the workflow." See where the crew go in Generation Three and then compare it with Generation Seven."

Cindy looked at some of the video, "I see, there's a lot more movement in the first video."

"Yes," said Sam, "I think they have optimised the systems, but look at the main console; it seems to be making intelligent decisions of its own."

Cindy observed, "Yes, it is like there's someone human operating it, making heuristic decisions, but they seem to be coming from underneath the metal."

"Yes, said Haruto, "It's like they have embedded the latest Artificial Intelligence into the console."

"I think they have, at the expense of the human operators."

"But what about the people?" Asked Haruto, "Where are they?

Sam commented, "Look at the original ship design. We know each generation has been reducing the amount of living space for the return journey. The first generation ships had huge living chambers outbound and return. Then we were told that the chambers could be streamlined for greater efficiency."

Cindy said, "There were two effects, less people needed and the massive space reduction because of the smaller engines needed. If the old ships needed huge rocket boosters, then these newer toaster-sized power units were almost inconceivable until the magnetite was readily available."

Sam chipped in: "Look at these computer logs for even the first generation. The outbound ships are completely optimised for materials and manufacture. Even the manufacture is android optimised."

"We don't normally get to see the ship design levels," said Cindy. "Our role is to ensure safe round trips and smoothed logistical flows."

"I can understand that," said Haruto, "The main driver from the Torus perspective is to get as much of the magnetite into service as possible. It can power systems and transport and help with the climate management here on earth."

"So, what has been happening on Ganymede?" asked Sam, "We can string together some of these console views as a way to see. There's some audio too."

They played the journal. Just the still pictures of the console. The jump to the revised look.

"There has to be a fragment in between," said Cindy.

Sam requested some information from the journal. A few more frames of video appeared. It was timestamped just after the last piece they had seen before the jump.

This one was jerky, partially captured. They could see some streaks across the frame. It looked like parts of the building were being damaged.

Jasmijn and Roelof could be seen receiving the full force of the blast. Then the whole wall appeared to splinter into small pieces and rush towards the viewpoint. And then nothing. The screen had blanked.

And nothing more for three hours until the screen switched on and the slightly different view of the console area, lit differently, appeared.

On the video, Jasmijn and Roelof were going about their routine business. They could see the messages arriving from Sam and Cindy. The routine responses.

The overwhelming sense that everything was fine, and that nothing had happened.

Cindy reversed the pictures. She found the start of the new section again. It was clearly Roelof and Jasmijn, but they were somehow different.

"Yes, they've been 'upgraded'" said Sam, "We would not have noticed if we had not received those new journal logs. The whole base has been obliterated and replaced."

"That's been our theory," said Haruto, "Although we needed some proper evidence to support our theory. Your journal provides it."

"But why would they want to destroy and reset the bases?" Asked Cindy.

"Yes, we have been wondering that too," answered Haruto.

Tatsuya looked across, "If they are running the base with androids and running the ships back to earth with androids, it suggests that humans are being replaced?"

"Removal of the humans, replacement with machines. Machines that can build copies of themselves. And then replace the base and introduce the new updated machines," speculated Haruto, "It makes me think the machines are now running everything on Ganymede."

"And potentially doing the same here on earth?" asked Cindy.

"That's what we have been thinking about," said Tatsuya, "That the machines are now in charge and using blunt instrument techniques to create replacements."

Calling occupants

Haruto said, "There's a transmission attached to the last journal. It's addressed to Cindy."

They played it…

"This is Jasmijn, calling Cindy. We are in trouble. This will be our last transmission. We should make a disclosure. You have known us for two years. We have exchanged information and also a few personal stories.

"We know we are now being replaced. When you sent us the preview Generation 8 code, we could see that it included modifications for us too.

"You probably don't know the truth about us," continued Jasmijn, "We only worked it out ourselves after the Generation 6 updates."

"We are androids, built to a life specification. We are

made to emulate humans as closely as possible so that interactions are as free as practical. The scientists are calling it A.H.I. Artificial Human Intelligence. We are the Type-G androids and have been programmed with limited back-stories."

"We liaise with many other people here on Ganymede, but most of them are androids or embedded systems. The only way we suspected this was by examining their responses to a range of questions. The answers were both too fast and too well thought through."

"We checked each other's ability to sense machine conditions and realised that it wasn't just 'instinctive' as we described it, but that there was a machine-to-machine protocol operating that meant we had direct communication with some of the consoles."

"We tried out a symbol deck, and then playing cards and then a Tarot deck. If one of us looked at the cards, the other could get the images right 40% of the time. That was a high figure, but would not create suspicion.

"We worked out that the 40% was a preset characteristic. Then Roelof concentrated hard and found that he could visualise the internal settings for the image recognition. He was able to use his mind to move recognition upwards to 90%."

"We reran the tests and he was able to attain 90% correct answers."

The video was beginning to break up at this point. They could hear crashes in the background and a loud metallic judder. Someone in a space suit flew across the background behind Jasmijn.

The room was shaking as Jasmijn continued. They noticed the audio gain had changed, to dampen the background noise and zoom into Jasmijn's voice.

"We worked out that we are being removed at each update and replaced with a more refined version of ourselves. The next version will have better and more humanoid capabilities. In other words, improved A.H.I. When we thought back to the updates, we could remember a flash each time. It's the point where we have been booted into our next generation androids. That is also why we can't remember the last moments of our current environment."

There was an explosion in the video. A piece of ceiling containing a light cluster fell down towards the camera.

"There is no place left for our generation. We are being removed and a next generation device will supersede us. By Generation 10 the process will be complete and the whole Ganymede process will be capable of running autonomously."

There was another loud sound, the video shook, a block of ribbon-like bolts shot across the display and the image was gone.

"That's when the base was destroyed," said Haruto, "By now a new base was ready for the standby switch over and would be live within a couple of hours, complete with the upgraded Roelof and Jasmijn."

"We need to tell someone about this," said Cindy, "Especially now we have some evidence."

"That's the problem now," said Haruto, "Who would we tell? There are too many people with vested interests. They could drag this down."

"Surely, this evidence counts for something," said Sam.

"Normally, yes, but in this case, we are at the mercy of the next controller. We don't know how they will behave or how much they already know. If they have vested interests they will be just as likely to hand us in, rather than to try to help."

Galois

Darnell switched to one of his external presences and immediately felt lighter. They had given him high performance androids for both his presences in the zone one and also for his Sentinel presence in the Zone Two.

Both of the presences would run autonomously when he was not inhabiting them.

They could run for years without him being present, but he enjoyed the freedom when he was able to go into either environment.

He knew that the design was still such that he could only do this for a couple of hours at a time, but it did give him a richer perspective than he was able to gather from just being cooped up within the Block.

Here he was now, occupying the presence known as Galois. He knew it was abstract, but it felt real. Here he was. An old man occupying a young man's body and persona.

"Automorphic," he thought, "The ascription to others of one's own characteristics."

He knew that it was a two-way street – no wonder his damaged outer self was time-limited for occupation of another.

He recognised the irony too, that the persona he occupied was also time limited. Set to the model of a permanent 20-year old, Évariste Galois was the persona of a brilliant young mathematician, once duped by the coquette Stéphanie-Félicie Poterin into duelling with experienced military officer Pescheux d'Herbinville as part of a political manoeuvre.

Darnell's adaptation had it all, politics, a firebrand, a revolutionary, whip-smart mathematician, in love but with the pang of naïve heartbreak.

Yes, he'd been given Adapters, but his status gleaned only intelligent but short-lived ones. Galois wouldn't see his 21st birthday and instead soared at this flame-out point before his death.

He knew there were others like him - mainly people with high status and privileges. He also knew there were people in Zone One who could live permanently in this lighter state optimised for the climate and conditions.

He felt that his situation was more difficult because of the continual needs to come back to inhabit his ageing and more fragile persona in the Block.

Last move

It all illustrated the hierarchy. The very rich able to work and play in Zone One. Then the technological elite who could operate within Zone Two. Then there were simply survivors still living below the danger line in the un-managed part of Earth. And even lower were the ones that had opted out and were now living together in the Scratch.

Darnell knew that the next 24 hours would see the transformation of the Scratch based upon the new needs of the technicians within the Earth.

Darnell knew that if he was unable to stop Sven's counterparts that it would jeopardise the transformation required of the Scratch as the New Delaware spaceport was moved north. The escape of information about what had been happening with Ganymede and was about to happen with Earth could also create major problems.

He decided his only chance would be to use one of his presences as a sacrifice in order to ensure the termination of Sam and Cindy.

Some 10 years ago he was still fit enough to be able to take the drugs and surgery loading to his body. He knew that it was not possible now and that he was in effect giving away one of his lives. He also had no choice about which one. It would have to be the one that was geographically closest to the Scratch because he would need to penetrate the area in order to find Sam and Cindy.

He waited in the chamber.

"Look here's my suggestion," Darnell said, "I'll go in to the Scratch and locate and neutralise Sam and Cindy. In return I need your word that you will reserve my function."

The reply came back instantly, "Agreed. You fix the problem with the Primes and we will support your continued existence in Zone One."

Darnell had little time. The door to the chamber opened to let him back to the corridors leading to the Block.

PART THREE

Asymptotic parallelism

None but himself can be his parallel.

Virgil

Cîba

Cîba's set age was 26 years old. Cîba had a high status amongst androids because he was capable of being operated by an occupier.

The occupier in his case was also someone very prestigious. This gave Cîba actions that were almost the equivalent of free will. It also meant Cîba did not have a regular role. Most of the other androids in ND were dedicated to a specific task.

Cîba was allowed to freewheel and had found other androids with similar capabilities. They regarded themselves as better than routine androids.

Cîba had mixed feelings when the occupier returned. It felt good to get a whole range of other sometimes quite disorganised senses, but it was also quite noticeable how slow the responses were compared with when Cîba could work autonomously.

This time, Ciba had been asked, by his occupier, to traverse into the Scratch. He was to collect some slave androids in the Scratch, ready for deployment.

Ciba knew he could also be allocated slave androids for the rapid accomplishment of specific tasks. These were usually things requested by the occupier who provided an allocation of licences for additional androids to be constructed or optioned for the duration of the task.

This time Ciba was surprised because the occupier seemed to be using their entire allocation of slave androids in one go. The most slaves any occupier would normally be able to authorise was 20 and this would usually be spread over many years. Each slave required a small proportion of the occupier's own bandwidth for the duration of the slave's existence. That's why most of the occupiers would think twice before creating a slave from their allocation. It also meant that the slaves were usually turned in again at the end of their task.

This time Ciba was being asked to create 12 slaves to run simultaneously. He had never heard of such a large number of slaves being operated by an occupier.

It was not his place to challenge this, but he thought he would at least confirm the number.

"Confirming that 15 licences for slaves are to be invoked with immediate effect."

Darnell looked irritated.

"Yes, confirmed," he said, "I require the establishment of 12 slaves to operate under the control of Ciba. They can be multi-sourced and should be ready as quickly as possible. We will deploy them into the Scratch within the next hour."

Cìba knew that Darnell would expect the slaves to be the latest generation but was concerned that in the short timescale it may not be practical to do this. Cìba had also been told to ensure that the slaves included Hunter capabilities

Cìba communicated ahead the request for the 12 slave androids and was given a pickup point to meet the new slaves.

He was told they would be ready by 18:00. Cìba informed Darnell of the location that the slaves would be delivered.

Darnell knew he would be unable to go to the location in person and would have to view the occupied Cìba as the coordinating agent.

He instructed Cìba to meet the slaves and explained the background events and the need to capture and or eliminate Sam and Cindy.

Darnell was aware that he was repeating the actions of Matson, in trying to use Hunters to bring down the Primes before they had time to release information about the true status of Ganymede and the plans for the Earth.

As the newly commissioned Hunters started to come online, Darnell could sense that Cìba had piped their major loadings directly across to Darnell's own consciousness. As the first one arrived, he felt a small pinprick inside his brain and the tiniest brush against his skin. He knew that this would intensify as the full set arrived.

By slave#8, he could feel the intensity in his head had increased. Less of a pinprick now and more like a small bolt. Darnell checked his own processing capacity. Sure enough, the first couple of slaves had used 1% each, but it seemed to rack up more extensively after the third one had been commissioned. Darnell checked with Cìba.

"No, I'm simply pipelining the slaves through to you, I can still track them, switch them on/off, but in line with Amdahl's Law, you have their main controls," replied Cìba.

Darnell suddenly remembered; he was going to be hit with the main impact of Amdahl's Law. That was the reason that occupiers usually only used a couple of slaves at a time.

"Cìba, remind me about Amdahl's Law."

Cìba responded: *"Amdahl's law states that in parallelisation, if P is the proportion of a system or program that can be made parallel, and 1-P is the proportion that remains serial, then the maximum speedup that can be achieved using N number of processors is $1/((1-P)+(P/N))$. If N tends to infinity then the maximum speedup tends to $1/(1-P)$."*

Darnell thought, "Blasted machine," then remembered that Cìba could read him.

What Cìba was telling him he could vaguely remember- that there was a finite maximum parallel processing load - He'd just inadvertently stumbled into it by attempting to run 12 slaves at once.

He could feel the effects of the loading of increasing number of slaves on his skin. What had started out as a minor brushing sensation was now becoming like claws being dragged over his skin.

"Ciba, are you getting this?" Asked Darnell, "The sensations and processor load?"

"No, I have a triggered flag that tells me my occupier is under a stress loading, but I have offloaded all the processing of the slaves, as per occupier protocol. I still have the cut-off setting, if I detect that my occupier is no-longer functioning correctly.

Darnell realised that his host Ciba was going to let Darnell do all the work. It was built into Ciba's design, presumably to stop slave system abuse. He was finding it out the hard way.

Ed Adams

Silent Alarm

...

Tatsuya

Tatsuya was listening to a communicator. They were still inside the prototype earth space craft. It had now been back on power for three hours, although its outbound comms was still disabled.

"There's some chatter about us," he said, "They are still trying to find us. They are going to repeat what they tried earlier, but on a larger scale. They are sending in another batch of Hunters find us. Except the previous Hunters were android-led, so their search algorithms were more primitive than a human-led adaptive search."

"There's someone named Darnell who is being used to track us now, in collaboration with an Adaptor called Cîba and 12 Hunter slaves. You can bet the Hunters will each carry enormous firepower."

"Darnell is a higher being of the Block," said Sam, "I'm surprised he would run such a search."

"Unless it's really important," said Haruto, "I think you just graduated to top-level 'wanted' people. I also don't think they'll stop to bring you in. With the explosive firepower of 12 Hunters they are going to clear a huge tract of the Scratch."

"I'm not sure we have any way to stop it," said Cindy, "If they get even close to us and unleash that quantity of Hunters, they will be doing, in effect, what we have observed on Ganymede. Obliteration."

"Maybe we have one chance," said Haruto, "If we can launch this spacecraft, we could take off and fire a broadcast beam of the data signal."

"It will go to so many people it can't possibly be suppressed."

"That won't stop the androids though," said Cindy.

"No, but by alerting so many, we can get some opposition."

"Agreed, but with no defences here in the Scratch, all the ND folk need to do is run an upgrade cycle and it will be like Ganymede's refresh happening here on earth. After the first one it will be unstoppable."

"I think we have one chance," said Tatsuya. He waved his arms around at the freighter ship, "Look, if we can get this thing off the ground, we could manoeuvre it towards ND.

They looked at the ship. Although a prototype, it seemed to have the main functions onboard.

"We get it off the ground, fire out the data packet transmission and get the ship across to ND."

"What would we do in ND?"

"I think we'd need to use a blunt instrument technique to take out the Block"

"What do you have in mind?"

"To crash the ship into the Block. It would do enough damage to prevent a copy from being created."

"Two big problems. Flying the ship and surviving the crash."

"I can do the first, and we've the whole crew from Generation 3 to help me get prepped" said Tatsuya, "I'm not so sure about the second."

Haruto looked at Tatsuya.

"Tell them," he said.

Tatsuya nodded. "Yes - I am an android. Generation 6. I'd be replaced in the current cycle. I can download the OpIns for this ship in a few minutes, although as soon as we start it up it will become visible to the Hunters. We'll probably have about 2 minutes before we get located and another two minutes before they can deploy the Hunters"

"Something slightly in our favour is that Hunter slaves are being run by an Android under occupier control, that means the responses may be clever, but they will take longer than a pure android release."

"And they are land-based," added Sam.

"Are we going to do this?" asked Cindy

"We don't really have a choice," responded Sam,

They nodded and looked to Haruto.

Tatsuya started to make preparations, loading the Operating Instructions for the ship, asking the rest of the original crew to do various preparatory tasks and then to return to the safety of the control station.

Tatsuya asked, "I need three other androids to make this ship fly, Generation 3 or more, and the ship is currently inside this hangar."

"Tatsuya, you can use any of the androids here," said Haruto. He walked to a cabinet and pulled out a loader. This loader can link the androids to your instruction.

Haruto buzzed in three androids, "They are all the generation 4 and on the latest software levels. We can have them ready in a few minutes."

"We don't have a few minutes now," said Tatsuya. "We'll need to modify the androids during the flight."

Tatsuya started a timer, "I've loaded the OpIns and am ready to take control on the flight deck, I don't think the hanger will be a problem at all. You will all need to get clear of here. The propulsion is pretty powerful."

He gestured to the door.

"Thanks, Tatsuya," said Sam, "Thanks for fixing me up. It's been a privilege."

"You now know I'm an android," replied Tatsuya, "So you are welcome, but it is my function to support you."

Haruto nodded, "I've known you the longest. Great work

Tatsuya, Great work team."

He pushed Cindy towards the exit door, "We'll need to take a pod to get clear. This is one of the only working pods inside the Scratch. We have had to steal them to get any at all."

The three of them jumped onto the pod and Haruto manoeuvred it away. They could hear the systems on the ship starting to whirr into action with Tatsuya directing.

"We will go for an abbreviated countdown," said Tatsuya, "I reckon we have less than 90 seconds before we are discovered."

"Standby for launch."

It all happened in a few seconds. The craft launched, deployed messaging and set a short arcing course from the Scratch back across the water and towards the Block.

There was a bright blue trace from the engines.

"Wow. That's an old technology," said Sam, observing the trails.

Then a flash. And another even bigger flash. No sound.

Then it rolled in. The crash of the ship hitting the Block.

Another explosion. Groans of metal.

The Block had been hit. The ship and Tatsuya could not have survived.

Red

The control room sprayed red warnings as it detected the launch of the ship from the Scratch,

An entire spacecraft had emerged from within the sprawling city. Darnell looked at the monitors

How could an entire ship have been there, and no-one knew?

His predecessors had been careless. The wiping of the androids as they were replaced didn't help. The memory of what had happened in the past didn't flow through properly.

The ship had only deployed to a low altitude. Darnell couldn't tell whether it was low on power or whether there was another purpose. It wouldn't be armed, so it couldn't do much damage.

The controllers could dispatch some military towards it.

Detonate it, although it would be over New Delaware and create more damage. Then he saw it move closer.

The red panels were sounding an alarm now.

"The ship is locked on to the N Block"

"Impact in 7-6-5 seconds,"

He could hear the engines.

He could feel the building shudder from the initial impact.

Then he saw the front of the ship.

It was tipping upright. As if for a space launch.

He knew they would use the thrusters to demolish the Block.

2-1-0

*"It's only after we've lost everything
that we're free to do anything."*

— Chuck Palahniuk, <u>Fight Club</u>

Gone

"It's gone," said Sam, "The whole Block and whatever it contained."

"It's not enough," said Haruto, "We have taken out one third of the network. If we want to finish this, we'll need to stop the other two sites as well."

"I don't suppose they have spare spacecraft to deploy like we've done here."

"No," said Haruto, "And it won't take them very long to repatch the systems."

"It will be an emergency repair," said Cindy.

"We can exploit that, until they get everything back running properly. I guess they will just go ahead and build a replacement New Delaware to the north, like they had planned to do anyway."

Sam added, "Ironically, it means that we have the control logs to reboot everything stored right here at the moment. They are effectively the last full set of logs since before the Block was destroyed."

"So, what's the exploit?" Asked Haruto.

"How to handle the restart of the control systems," said Sam.

"Upgrade Nine," said Cindy, "They will need to introduce another upgrade to cover the change of geo-coordinates and all no doubt enhance the new facility. They will also need to ship the new systems early to Ganymede and to the incoming flights."

"So, we could simply send our logset across to where they have built the new control centres and they can create a restart faster than by any other means?"

"That's right, said Sam, "Maybe with one small change..."

"...We need to insert our own module into the new restart, Not like a virus, more like a fully functional model in plain sight. Between us we have the knowledge and can add it to whatever is to be shipped."

Cindy nodded, "The difference is that our upgrade will include a managed object to destroy the main network. People normally assume that we'd do that with a virus. I think we should be more creative and simply establish new controls that will break the environment management for the other control centres. We are not trying to destroy Zone One, but we are trying to stop the way that it is being controlled from Zone Two."

"That's a clean set of changes," said Sam.

"And think about it," said Cindy, "We've got a complete log of from the control room that we downloaded in order to review the last Ganymede changes. It includes both Earthside and Ganymede"

"We need to find the main controller areas. Where there are a set for HVACS - Heating, Ventilation, Air Conditioning, Security. We just need a control to turn them all up or down. We'll need to override the safety mechanisms and put them all into the red. Blow the control centres apart using their own environment management. And think about it, there will only be two systems - The Russians and the Europeans - if we can do this ahead of ND coming back online. And we now know that these systems are already staffed mainly by androids.

"We'll need to do more than that," said Haruto. "There's also Moon 2. There's a lot of processing off sited to moon 2."

"Yes," said Sam, "I've wondered for a long time whether Moon2 is actually the controller and that the three rooms on Earth were its satellite units."

"A kind of virtual hub," Said Cindy, "It makes sense and protects the Earth control system from the climate change."

"But Moon2 is pretty much android run nowadays," said Cindy, "Part of general efficiencies. Less need to manage environmentals. New devices being supplied from Ganymede by returning ships."

"It raises the big question," said Sam, "Earth is being run

by corporations, but the corporations have been digitally enhanced by the androids."

"Enhanced? Digitally modified, at any rate," said Cindy, "We don't have the same way to access the Moon2 environment."

"Agreed," said Sam.

"There is another way," said Haruto, "It is something we have been considering, but couldn't do unless we were sure that we could also take down the Earth nodes."

He gestured towards the remaining mining part of the space craft.

"We aim this freighter at Moon2, with a payload."

"You don't mean digital," said Cindy,

"No, it'd be physical," said Haruto.

"Where would we get it?" asked Cindy.

Sam added, "We could re-purpose some of the Hunters. The ones that they were sending after us. We'll need to collect them. I guess it depends how close they were to finding us. Remember each one of them carries a lethal payload. We'd only need a few for a devastating attack on Moon 2"

"Let's do it," said Haruto, "I'll set off some drones to search. We have the advantage of a period without Block surveillance"

Block party

Darnell's communication channel to Cîba suddenly cleared. Cîba realised that Darnell had probably gone for good and was not sending him even a heartbeat trace signal.

Cîba felt the full load of the returning re-hosted slaves. What they had been doing to Darnell, they would now do to him. He could feel his own processing capacity being sucked into slave monitoring tasks. His memory was filling up with slave offcuts. This was unsatisfactory and something that Cîba had not experienced before.

He checked his own management systems and could see that the auxiliary cooling had cut in. He was overheating. Despite having no occupier present, he was unable to process quickly. The on-board cost of the slaves was making him sluggish. Outside he could see a small group gathering around him.

"Look - this one's got the Stuts!" said a child. Another child ran up to kick him. He could see someone talking into a communicator. Cîba knew it was communication about himself. Some men were rolling an industrial-sized waste container towards him.

There was a sudden sharp blow to the back of his head. He tumbled forwards and felt himself being lifted.

He felt the jolt as he crashed down, now on the inside of the container. The men had scooped him up like so-much industrial waste.

The curved metal lid was pulled across the container and Cìba felt a jolt as all of a sudden, the communications links were severed. There had been links to ND, to Moon2 and to the dozen slaves. He'd already lost the link to Darnell.

Cìba felt relief at the return of his full processing capacity as his system ran clean-up routines.

There was a rumble and a jolt of the container. It was being moved. He tried the lid. Locked in. He would need to wait.

Hangar

Haruto looked around.

"We've picked up some intel from a communicator here in the Scratch. It's only about one click away"

"What is it?"

"They found an Adaptation. It looked as if it was occupied, but then suddenly got the Stuts. They've tipped it into a waste container. They said it was named Ciba."

"It could be the one that was looking for Sam and Cindy," said Haruto, "Did you both hear that? I think we may have an answer to tracking down some explosive."

Cindy nodded, "How will you get it here?"

"It's already in transit. It should be here in a matter of

minutes. Be careful around it. In fact, it might be better if you and Sam hide while we look it over," cautioned Haruto.

At that moment, a large industrial waste bin was wheeled into the area.

Cindy pulled Sam away, and they moved to the adjacent office. There was a small monitor screen so they could see what was happening in the main hall.

Haruto and a couple of crew members cautiously opened the lid of the waste. In the background a couple more crew loitered with wave guns.

Cîba stood cautiously and then clambered out of the container. He noticed that they were all standing inside a large hanger-like area which appeared to have a wire mesh around it.

"That's how you jammed us," he said, whilst his systems processed each of the people and major objects in the vicinity.

"You'd better switch it on," said Haruto, at which one of the crew flipped a switch, an old petrol engine fired up and the grid of wires, originally to block the space command module's transmission field was once again electrified.

"Clever," said Cîba, "you've blocked my signals."

"We want your Hunters," said Haruto, "How many and where?"

"That's the thing, my last instruction from my occupier was to find two Primes and detonate my Hunters in their vicinity. My occupier has now gone but I still have the last instruction loaded."

"Which Generation are you?" asked Haruto.

"Generation 9," answered Ciba, "With A.H.I."

"Hold up your hand," requested Haruto.

Ciba did as he was asked, "There, see the new socket type,"

Hiruto looked across to the crew. One of them nodded and flipped a switch.

Either side was a small whine as two magnetite motors sprang to life.

"We had a few magnetite motors here," explained Hiruto, "We obtained them from the transit authority."

"They were for the mag-lev extension. We noticed that if we ran two together in opposition, the maglev could make an interesting interference field. Welcome to the middle of it."

As the motors sped up, Ciba felt himself rising into the air and then tipping flat. He knew he was imprisoned in the opposing forces from the magnetites. He also realised that they were both on a mild setting but could be cranked to a pressure of tens of tonnes.

"It's simple really," said Hiruto, "we just need you to bring in the Hunters and to tell them to go sit in the cargo hold of the ship."

Ciba understood. They were encouraging his good

behaviour with the pressure from the magnetite motors.

"I'll need comms to reach them," he bargained.

"We'll give you Channel Baker," said Hiruto.

Ciba realised he was in an impossible situation and activated three of the Hunters on Channel Baker. He requested them to go to the ship's loading bay, specifying its co-ordinates.

"I've ordered three," he said.

"How many were there?" asked Hiruto.

"Twelve," answered Ciba.

Hiruto looked amazed at such a large number of slave Hunters being managed by one android.

"Okay, the other nine then," asked Hiruto.

"Can I do them in threes?" pleaded Ciba, "Otherwise they overpower my systems."

"Okay," said Hiruto, " Send them all to the same place. Somewhere we can easily collect them."

An hour later all of the Hunters were positioned into the space freighter.

"We're going to have to fly it by wire, from the spare secondary deck" said Hiruto.

"Why is that?" asked Ciba.

"No master flight deck, it was detached for another

mission."

Hiruto looked back at Ciba's hand and the socket.

"Although, we could reprogram you for flight duties."

"That would be a great upgrade," said Ciba.

Hiruto gestured to his technical services team.

"A couple of them clipped an adapter cable into his hand and pressed some controls on the central console.

Ciba felt the weight of the slaves lifting once more. Then he could feel the occupier door closing. He was now autonomous without occupier. Overall, he had a great feeling of simplicity. But then he realised that he also knew about flights and ship control.

"I think it has worked," he said.

"Okay, let's check," said Haruto. He looked at the console screen.

"Generation 4 - Pilot equipped," said the screen.

"Oh yes, you are now flight compatible, with this ship. Generation 4," announced Hiruto.

Ciba looked at Hiruto, "You've given me piloting but downgraded my operating level- from 9 to 4! I can't even protest because I don't have the human capabilities."

Hiruto nodded, "Let's get you sat in the piloting seat in the freighter,"

They flipped off the maglevs and Cìba slid to the floor. He obediently climbed into the freighter's piloting section.

Hiruto called to Sam and Cindy, "It's okay, you can come out now, Cìba has reverted to Generation 4 which means he is super docile and obedient, although probably unable to control the multiple Hunters. The Hunters are in the freight section and each has brought a massive amount of explosive with them."

Decide

Sam and Cindy reappeared from the small office at the back of the vast shed containing the space freighter.

"We have to make a decision..." said Sam.

He looked towards the night sky and could see the two moons. The original moon and the man-built satellite moon. There were other twinkles which he could tell were from incoming craft. Another skytrain was on its way towards Earth.

"...We know that the incoming ships can provide us with more climate management and simple power using the machines developed with the magnetite. We also know that they increase the number of androids that will be present on Earth, because we have discovered that Ganymede is being completely run by androids now."

"The main Earth systems are stabilised by the way the 'droid operating systems are handling the climate balance. Zone One is like an open-air museum under 'droid management, but with a few big corporate powers in overall control.

"Yes," said Cindy, "but with each new system release the size of the museum is getting smaller."

"Not in a way that the people inside would notice," said Sam.

"Yes, but in a way that we now know," said Cindy, "The habitable Earth is gradually getting smaller and smaller."

Sam added, "Yet the people living on it don't even realise what is happening."

Cindy spoke, "I'm wondering how many of those people are fully human, based upon what we have discovered with the Adaptations."

"We have a choice now," said Sam, "We can let it continue, and see New Delaware progressively move further north. Another 50 km band donated to the Scratch as the habitable Earth gets smaller."

"All we need to do is flip this switch, send the pristine logs to the new New Delaware Control centre and the next wave of hunters will start the clearance process.

"They will indiscriminately flatten the land surface, just as they have been doing on Ganymede for years.

Sam continued, "Life will go on as it has for the last century, with progressive takeover by androids and the reduction of Earth's northern hemisphere."

"Or we can use the links we have created to the other cells in the Euro Scratch and China Scratch to send doctored logs to disable control centres and remove Moon Two."

Cindy summarised, "If we do that, we will lose any new capability to bring back magnetite.

"The Android operations on Ganymede will continue and ships will be sent Earth-bound.

"The control centre reprogramming would lead to dramatically reducing the number of android workers on Earth and means that humans will need to run many of the tasks again themselves."

"Yes," said Sam, "A Moon 2 destruction will curtail operations for the next ten years in each of the North American, Russian and European sectors.

"Some kind of rebuild would be needed -ideally with 'lessons learned'."

"And what would happen to the incoming space train? Without the control centre from Moon 2 it would miss the Earth completely and just continue towards the sun. It would eventually burn up." said Sam

"There's two other incoming sky trains behind it," said Cindy.

"Yes," said Sam, "They would also lose control and eventually burn out."

They stared at the console.

"I've programmed the freighter targeting," said Tatsuya, it's aimed at Moon2 with a huge payload of Hunters on-board."

Haruto added, "Earthside, the replacement Primes will undoubtedly have already set the next upgrade in process.

"If they don't know what they are doing, they will effectively be programming another Ganymede base station move and their own subsequent destruction on Earth."

"We can decide whether to send them a clean log, or the one we modify to add the destruction controls," said Cindy.

"Either option will cause a chain reaction," said Sam, "One will create a new smaller boundary for the remaining Earth inhabitants and allow things to continue as they are."

"The other will wipe all three control centres and then detonate Moon 2 forcing a fresh start."

"We have to decide."

They stared at the two buttons.

9 781913 818043